I0763253

TELEMACHUS

by

BILL DUNBAR

volume II

anANNAL Publishing Co.
30 Harrow Road
Stanmore, NSW 2048

ISBN: 978-0-6450592-2-9 (hardcover)
ISBN: 978-0-6450592-3-6 (ebook)

Cover design by Quick Fox Editing

Printed in Australia by IngramSpark

Credits: Front + back cover: Heritage Auctions, HA.com.

TELEMACHUS

by

BILL DUNBAR

volume II

anANNAL PUBLISHING CO.

30, Rue de Harrow, 30

SYDNEY

2020

ating Ruskin's High Middle Ages inside his own temporal boundaries for the Renaissance. I must finish this work and END. Joyce said that there is room in a man's heart for one novel only. He kept writing the same book like Proust. They both wrote auto-encyclopedias of self and place. Average life expectancy for a male born in 1882 was approximately forty-five years in the UK. Joyce died one-month shy of his sixtieth birthday. Thus, he exceeded the average mortality rate by over thirty per cent. He is right on the median in a bell curve: fifty per cent of males were dead by sixty years and fifty-per cent remained alive.

A FRENCH ARCHE-TEXT

In literature, as in all things, forces of Light and Darkness, Aristotelian levity and density, are engaged in unrelenting struggle (see epigraph 4) and we are always conscious of what Michel Foucault calls the "distant roar of battle," when *Discipline and Punish* (*DP*) finally promises cataclysm, though after the point of closure. To turn to Classical iconography, Light and Dark can be portrayed as twin robes, one of levity, the other density, entwining the Goddess Athena when she is portrayed as the anachronistic Virtue, Justice, by John Ruskin (*QA*, 25–6). As a golden robe drifts down her torso (link to EA in shower in Chapter 2), she becomes literally locked inside it by another of constricting Darkness, close upon her chest like consumption, so that it may as well be a casket encasing her, until she is left indented with its tight impress (see Chapter 10, Ana in the Lake). She becomes in this image both the emancipating Queen of the Air as well as Athena Chalinitis, Athena the Restrainer, who helped Bellerophon bridle Pegasus and is harnessed herself to necessity. This polarity within a single personage is the core precept of my next work, VAULT. Perhaps then, simple assumptions of a strict dichotomy between Light and Darkness, even when extrapolated by Levity and Burden, are merely part, perhaps the top layer, of a more complex equation. Perhaps we should also be looking behind Foucault's ominous yet non-presented, "roar," to the operations of the mouth and sound, or "noise" ("*bruits*") as Jacques Attali calls it in his *essai sur l'economie politique de la musique*. Let us look, then, not merely at strict demarcations between noise and silence, but at shifting strategies of deafness and audition which offer variations within syllogism whose promise is Utopia. For forces of Surd and Utter, they are locked in perpetual flux, interchanging and updating their roles as, first, one attempts to proclaim what suffuses it, then the other to stifle this insurgency. Or that first one may suddenly affect a defiant silence as the other tries to provoke it to Confession, precursor of Foucault's concept of Correction. Failure causes the Surd to become aphonic with rage. Then there is complete silence, if only for a moment. For then both break simultaneously into sound. Language here expires in a crumpled heap like some crumbling Babel. Let us define our terms then. (1) Polysemous Surd, from the Latin *surdus*: deaf, noiseless. Deaf to all imprecations. What Anna Funder would call a pervasive pharisaical STASI, suffocating dissent and orchestrating the deafness of the crowd to rhetoric like the tribunes in *Coriolanus* or Elias Canetti's "crowd crystals" in *Mass und Macht*, who loiter in the *agora*, which comes from the Greek, *agoreúō*, meaning "I speak in public," disparaging any elevated sentiments. (2) Utterance. Twin Definitions: (a) audible emission, and (b) unqualified commitment to struggle. Its mode is thus that of "a song sung beside," the literal meaning of the term PARODY, which derives from the Greek words, *para + ōidē*. Against Utterance, the Surd will always be a misnomer. Even its etymology is a mistranslation of the Greek word, *alogos*, meaning "irrational speechlessness," that furious dumb Erethism which travelled to English from the Arab, *jaor acamm*, or "deaf root," and manifested itself in the aphonic weeds which strangled the Utopian garden in Shelley's "The Sensitive Plant." Deleuze and Guattari repudiated all such 'arborescent culture' in *One Thousand Plateaus*. Yet "deaf root" is also a homonym of "death route": that fatal channel along which so many Romantic characters have been compelled to travel towards extinguishment. For one cannot speak of Surdity and Utterance (Aphonism and Audition) without invoking concomitant Stasis and Dromology. Stasis in this formulation acts as a kind of jubilant inertia that should really be labelled "Ec/Stasis." Dromology, on the other hand, is a psychological term coined by Paul Virilio for continuous, compelled motion. It comes from the Greek *dromaios*, meaning, "running at full speed." For deafness and audition are inextricably tied to proximity. One is self-(up)righteous; the other downground. One superordinate; the other subaltern. This one inert. The other constantly in motion. Or else both quiescent. Adjacent to each other: one endlessly intoning; the other attempting to intercede with monotonous tone. Or laid out next to each other on a raft like the sons of Clovis. One evoking; the other merely vocable. Dichotic Listening reducing any meaningful sound at this point to audible eructation. Signal Detection Theory becomes merely the determination to block out all interfering noise in this calculation. To ignore the jackhammer as it continues on your face. The jackhammer continues on your face. It has no alternative. It is negative vociferation provoked by antinomian utterance. For to position themselves in contradiction within flux is their ideal of Process. Imagery is relentlessly repeated and reworked until it forms a vast intervolved membrane like D&G's Rhizome, a prosenchymatic dome or Penelope's funeral shroud for her father-in-law, Laertes. Paul Virilio and Sylvere Lotringer note in *Pure War* that dense, interactive repetition of this kind aids internal cohesion in a writer like Livy. As Saint Paul wrote in the Second Epistle to the Corinthians: "When I therefore was thus minded, did I use lightness ... that with me there should be yea, yea and nay, nay?" (II Corinthians 1:17). Surdity and Utterance are ever-locked "yea/nay" or "nay/yea." And if it is 'yea,' it is an emphatic one. And if 'nay,' an equally resolute NO. For they will always intensify the prevailing tendency. So that when lightness is the scourge, they are utterly without ballast. Or when ponderousness, they add still more weight. They are thus either too light to have any meaning so that they float or too heavy with their own history not to collapse and sink from meaning. Either way, they move together towards an airless oblivion entwined like Swinburne's "Les Noyades" (literally, it means The Drowning). Gottfried Leibniz inserted both these means of visual and aural surveillance into his architectural intensification of the Panopticon as originally conceived by Jeremy Bentham and ultimately deployed by Foucault as an arch-metaphor. His buildings were to be constructed to enable everything to be SEEN and HEARD by means of mirrors and pipes. This was considered by Leibniz to be "the most important thing for the state, and a kind of political confessional." Instead of spies peering out of the hollowed eyes of antique portraits, an entire facility would be wired to a focal point where all data could be collected and stored for tactical utilisation. We are now very far from the Phalansteries of Charles Fourier, entering the wired fields of Richard Nixon to make the unwitting confession of our inmost impulses. This is why Jacques Derrida was misguided in *Eperons* when he discerned only a phallo visual threat to humans. For how lacking in terror is that which presents only itself to gaze! And, by contrast, how horrific is that which can prey on the imagination in blindness, pursuing it to every sanctuary! Thus, Swinburne's aristocratic lady in "Les Noyades" is first blinded as a prelude to punishment. This means that she can only hear the sentence of the court and the crowd's mockery catch the swish of the whip and its haphazard repeats, almost simultaneously with feeling them smell then endure the rough flesh of the labourer against whom she is bound listen forcibly to his close whispers experience that sublime moment in space after they are launched between the riverbank and the waters of Loire as the hubbub consumes her and, finally, sink with water filling her ears as her fellow captive weighs her dainty body down unto oblivion. But how can the Surd be 'cleared' as if from the barricades or Forum? Lund wrote in 1861: "an equation may be CLEARED OF A SURD by transposing the terms so that the surd shall form one side, and the rational quantities the other, and then raising both sides to that power which will rationalise the surd." The analogy to be drawn from this formula is that Surdity and Utterance must be isolated in opposition to each other, then built into twin towers – as if Babel was reflected in a mirror – until, finally, they overbalance and lean into one another, forming an interdependent arch. To achieve this rationalisation, material must be transposed: shifted from side to side simultaneously. They are like rock climbers locked in an unmutual embrace from which only death below or synthesis above can free them. And this must continue until they are raised to that height which will engender Epiphany. There they will merge. And it is specifically stated by Lund that it is the rationalised

Surd which will attain Hieratic clarity in these aery regions. It must be made Utter. But until that time, one side is committed to a perpetual discharge of words; the other only to ceasing it. Or while that one remains active to suppress; the other becomes inert, denying struggle, refusing to be provoked into action, which means sound, understanding that agitation only tightens its bonds (they are co-joined siblings), hastening erasure. This goads the Surd to aphonic fury. It now seeks to induce a kind of cathartic Saint Vitus Dance to delight the Demotic crowd, exhaust the capacity for rebellion and re-habituate it to mundanity. Lucius Verus orchestrated just such a purgative slaughter in *Marius the Epicurean*. Jacent palates are quickly roused by human sacrifice – the purging of a Coriolanus from Rome or Antium, for instance. Some act is required which will enable the crowd to attain communal frenzy against the STATIC POLE, which refuses to concede that the prevailing moral codes are binding (yes, this is an antinomian struggle), or to acknowledge danger, but which continues an outpouring of language girded by ascetic adherence to Truth. Confined, such a voice attains ec stasis in language. Examples include the static epiphanies of Eugenie Grandet, Lucy Snowe, Pater's anonymous female narrator in "A Prince of Court Painters" and Beckett's narrator in *The Unnamable*. In the "Journal of Henry Luxulyan," Arthur Symons wrote that, "the art in life is to sit still, and to let things come towards you, not to go after them, or even think that they are in flight" (316). This is sound advice for the totem. For its opponent is EXTANT only as an Obsessive Responsive Force (ORF). Each declaration will only increase its fury. This is the trope charted by Flaubert in "Herodias." The eponymous figure of the title, mother of Salome, is helpless to cease Iaokanann's condemnations from the cistern. His vitriol against Rome continues to pour even from the darkest place. It overwhelms her mind. She is utterly bemused by the motives for his Utterance. It seems irrational because she is only capable of the amoral, reflex jerkings of one schooled in Realpolitik. Like Coriolanus, she could inflict illimitable carnage on matter. However, each tongue that she removes from this fountain-hydra just causes more verbalising mouths to spring out of the newly opened wound. In the end, she finds a conduit, Salome, to facilitate the delivery of the silenced, severed head of John the Baptist. She is apparently triumphant. Yet this event drove Jesus Christ to wilderness Dromomania from which he emerged for his final drive to Crucifixion. This meant that Herodias had secured the ultimate Pyrrhic victory in terms of the Biblical cosmos in which this trope is placed. She became the victim of Blake's maxim that, "the cistern contains: the fountain overflows." It was Walter Pater who ultimately capped Blake's fountain later in the nineteenth century to induce a highly pressurised exploration of Being. He concluded: "on all sides we are beset by the incalculable:- walled up suddenly, as if by malign trickery, in the open field, or pushed forward senselessly, by the crowd around us, to good-fortune." This passage could pass for a manifesto of Surdity/Utterance and Stasis/

Dromology as the primary forces in a fundamental Demotic/Hieratic schism in art/life. It produces a dichotomy in which one element is vital (inside) but pressed up against an intractable barrier (outside) or moved without will towards destiny (in this case, it goes by the euphemism, 'good-fortune'). Thus, when one is anode; the other is cathode. One annunciation; the other defamation. One *anas* [from the Greek meaning 'up']; the other *ban anas*. One Bard; the other Bard-un. Art becomes the struggle between metaphorical anabas and anacondas: between the ones who wish to make Art that will cause the fishes to leave the water and climb into the trees (this is "the Greek conception of an aetherial element pervading space"), in short, the SUBLIME, and those who want to bind, constrict, crush, consume, digest and regurgitate – sapped and docile – their avowed antagonists. For the Surd seeks to prod with the electrified barb the bovine Utterer, fill its mouth with cud, govern its pasture and dam its source. And, once movement is enacted, the Surd is devoted to logistical restriction and controlled marches; the other to aw[e]ful freedom. Hieratic Utterance is either racing free of its confines, stopping, fixing itself to the ground as well as possible, and intoning. Or else it is harnessed, blinkered, pulling the Pharisaical buggy and its bloated load, racing towards no discernible finish, trying to breathe through the bit and see beyond the blinkers, goaded on by the screechings of the crowd, relying on their yelps to guide it until, like Ulysses on that raft of surd rowers, it is propelled towards fatal audition. Thus, one is imposing circularity (the track), hierarchy and Schopenhauerian order out of repetition; the other is attempting to refuse Hegelian linearity and emanate like one of Shelley's lyrics. In other words, one is centripetal; the other centrifugal (as of motion, yes, but also as of 'fugue' in terms of its meaning as 'interpenetrated sound'). One is surface; the other interstices. One shamanic; the other shambolic. Movement becomes so centripetal that the text contracts into a single room with no apparent exits. Here it can screw itself into the marble plates while evil circulates. This was the strategy implied by Shelley at the end of "The Sensitive Plant" when his subject is left paralysed and exposed to all exigencies. There is still a slim chance that it could spin on the spot incandescently until it produces a hypnotic impression of Space and Depth, underscored by a sweet humming melody to unsettle its enemy like one of Duchamp's Rotoreliefs. This is feasible. For it is also centrifugal in terms of another definition of Fugue as "amnesiac disappearance and wandering." This is a Final Outwards Movement (FOM) along the grooved channels of Virilio's numbing urban ever-in-motion (the sidewalk regrets that we had to kill them) into the extrinsic space coded by Pasolini's Oedipus, Wim Wender's wilderness dromomania in *P,T* and St Mark's Jesus Christ. For the Surd seeks to plug the Uttering mouth. To banish it to a distant perch. Or else to make it the butt of an apparent comedy. Death, farce or else rendered irrelevant by exile. These are the options. Thus, a scream but no air, only space but by no air taken. A scream by overbearing laughter taken. Or space, only extrinsic space by outer darkness taken. Link to Pepe. INSERT CONCLUSION 2 (TRIUMPHAL). "The *Odyssey* and its elder brother have withstood almost three thousand years of interpretation. *Ulysses* is only one hundred years old. But I believe it will always be studied for its rich insights into the human condition." INSERT COMPARATIVE TABLE:

TABLE 10. *ULYSSES* VS *TELEMACHUS*: OX EPISODE

	Ulysses	*Telemachus*
Subject	Birth	Death
Trope	Quest	Contra-Quest
Form	Romance	Parody
Class	Demotic	Hieratic
Science	Verisimilitude	Theory
Philosophy	Naturalism	Idealism
Slant	Humanist	Technical
Texture	Smooth	Viscous
Depth	Surface	Mire
Temporality	Present	Post
Movement	Forwards	Oscillating (flip)
Language	Lyrical	Pseudo-scientific
Technique	Compartmentalising	Prosenchymatic
Force	Centripetal	Centrifugal
Mode	Radical	Risk
Tone	Confident	Facetious
Poptones	The Beatles	The Rutles
Intent	Precision	Abstraction
Objective	Annexation of Canon	Extension of
Relationship to Plot	Intrinsic	Extrinsic
Output	Progress	Deferral
% to plot	100%	5%
Outcome	Incursion	Discursion
Next	Circe	Circe

END

7.
Circe (4–7 pm)

" ... for the theatre as we understand it today three things are necessary[1]*: actors*[2] *... an element of conflict conveyed in dialogue*[3] *and an audience emotionally involved in the action but not taking part in it."*[4]

– Phyllis Hartnoll

---

1 **SCRIBBLER** (AKA Shem the Penman): Make C7 like a Borromean knot (Lacan). Replicate the recollection of dreams in WAKING HOURS (as staccato, fragmentary, flipping like Proust/Proteus). Split stuff between script and footnotes. Make no distinction in authority of each. Try to make them both work as individual scripts – footnoted text will probably read more disconnected like *Ulysses*. One is THE REAL; the OTHER subconscious. Note that this chapter can also be read directly as presented on the page by shifting constantly between script and footnotes. This creates a third type of reading. Insert critical input to footnotes. Keep core script tight to plot. Do not simply replicate the dramatic form used by Joyce. Break up his script in Circe. Destroy continuity of dramatic form. No chronology. Itemise process as per Epigraph 3. Joyce often descends into low-life farce in Circe. Replicate. Circe vs. *Exiles* – explain why the latter failed. Invest with aleatory elements.

GYSIN: Print chapter, collect scissors, slice lines/segments, pull words at random from a hat, glue them together into a scroll (yes, like a tongue). Reference Tzara. Let Burroughs use your idea. Get expelled by Breton. Develop conspiracy theories about the art world. Live to see them ALL come true.

SCRIBBLER: The trope of C7–8 is REVELATION OF THE FALSE FATHER. That is Leer's function in the text. Use Bloom's guilt/redemption to explore my own feelings. Do not reach a positive resolution like some Restoration fluff-piece.

2 IBID: Tick. Mix real/fantasy characters. Amend naming to avoid litigation.

3 IBID: Tick. There is always a sense of foreboding in the comic interplays in C7.

4 IBID: Tick. Everybody is performing in this chapter. There is no true interaction. This mimics the Bard. See Harold Bloom, Footnote 74.

[INSERT PROLOGUE[5] *Blind Basil Kiernan slumped in a vinyl armchair by the gaming*

---

5 **MEILLON:** The Shakespeare Hotel rose out of the pavement like a giant maw.

MELVILLE: Like a whale?

POLONIUS: Aye. Very like a whale.

BURTON: The silhouette of its liver brick peak protruded like a hatchet above King Street.

MEILLON: Its windows glowed like Medusa's jaundiced buzz-eyes.

MELVILLE: Ahab watched from the cockpit as it inhaled.

[*Jangling of bells*]

MILKMAID/ELIJAH: See mist. See dark figures. Hear prophecies of death. [*His final words gurgle out of blood-loosened lips*] Fedallah!

SCRIBBLER: Joyce opens Circe with the voices of Dublin prostitutes yielding to a Guignol's band of idiots and urchins.

MEILLON: Insert quotidian scene setting.

BURTON: Note symbolism.

MEILLON: A vagrant wrapped tight like Athena in a filthy butcher's apron enters Brennan Automotive Services.

BURTON: A deafmuteimbecile w/goggleyes saintvituspasming.

MRS BRENNAN: If you don't want petrol, a drink, sweets or smokes then fuck off.

KIERNAN: [*Leaning forwards*] Cigarette?

BELLA: I gave 'em up for Jesus.

LEER: He warns awe kinder sack orifices, doughknee?

SCRIBBLER: The use of Strine predicts The Citizen in C10.

BELLA: It's conceptual.

LEER: Like sin?

BELLA: Like lots of things.

YOUNG MASTER SHEM: I offered them all the prize of a crab apple for answering my riddle.

OLDER SHEM: Old fruit in a can is best.

YOUNG MASTER SHEM: "When is a fox digging in a holly bush, not a man," I asked?

SCRIBBLER: They would have known the answer if they'd just read *Ulysses*. Just ask Kelly from the Blooms & Barnacles blog. Neither JJ, SD or HCM wrote it. It was a nonsense riddle, common in Britain at the time. Foxes actually dig up their dead. They don't bury them. The cock is associated with guilt. Eleven is a death number. The students were just reading Milton's "Lycidas," an elegy with 11 stanzas. The only change that SD made was to change the solution from MOTHER to grandmother. This was a deflecting device. He reburied his ma. But she kept coming back, like when Stephen perceives maternal love in Sargent's hair soon after. This was a typical gadget of Joyce.

machines in his smutty white suit rolling a Craven "A" between freckled fingers until the last tendons of tobacco had been worked inside the semi-transparent lingerie of a damp Tally-Ho. He spat a lank ginger tassel out of a sunk eye-socket. A distracted smile played upon his face. He pursed thin pink lips as he recalled some slight sycophancy towards a giant of a man (AKA a very large dramatist), causing his imagination to spool down Darling Street spankingly in a fresh Carmen Ghia back in the Nineteen-Seventies when all the bright-cheeked Turks in new cowboy boots brandished contracts from Wilde & Woolley and ate cold pork pies with Hot English Mustard and soothed their throats with schooners of Flag Ale from the sunny front deck of the London Hotel. A smoker's yellow smile fissured through. He drew back, sucktinna and exhaled indeterminately. His grey eyelids batted. He surveyed the assembled dignitaries.[6] *Tenured fags flustered in orbit.*[7] *He allowed exaggerated white lashes to touch. Shift to present tense. A barmaid is wiping down the service area with quicksilver slashes. Grey-gazing Able Goldstein's green moccasins bustle over the carmine carpet of the banquet hall bearing an aluminium tray with four inverted and stacked middy glasses, one jug of Resch's draught beer, a large bag of salted crisps (unopened), a quiver, one carafe of house red and two wine glasses.*[8] *A gold molar twinkles amongst his false teeth. Medical Dick + Medical Davy are ploughing through sacramental hand-steadiers prior to nightshift.*[9] *A television projector reels black and white documentary film footage.*]

ANNOUNCER

On the nineteenth of February 1942, war came to the Australian mainland with the first devastating surprise attack on Darwin.[10] [*FX: Droning airplanes. Bombs falling*]

YOUNG MASTER SHEM: All THIRTEEN respondents offered deft logic. Some even wrote out formulae. But still I rendered unto myself the prize. What can I say? I was hungering!

6 SCRIBBLER: Keep writers and academics separated. Proust believed that the artist must also be a critic. But he didn't go far enough in laying bare the hermeneutics and symbology infesting his text.

7 **BURTON:** C7 is aligned to the inverted moral values, cynicism and intrigue of Restoration audiences. Also, Volume 7 of Proust. Thus, it is a link with VAULT in the future.

8 SCRIBBLER: Note contents as symbols. Intellectual vessels. Some overturned.

9 IBID: Nightshift = Holles Street = also Nighttown.

10 IBID: This is the first of a sequence of historical inserts in C7. Chronological facet.

ANNOUNCER: This event precipitated a historic shift from Britain to the United States.

SCRIBBLER: List Australia's modern political struggles in a cultural and economic context in this chapter.

A formation of two hundred Japanese bombers made their dreadful approach across clear skies. And, as the bombs were falling, the town sirens finally sounded. [*FX: Belated sirens. Portentous tone*] Much too late for many.[11]

NARRATOR

Joyce uses personification and anthropomorphism throughout this episode.

ULAN

[*Speaking in discrete linguistic units. In tongues*] He produced Circe in the spirit of the Georgian playhouse. It was his decisive struggle with Shakespeare. Joyce was a Regency dramatist at heart. Bloom's dream/trial represents Joyce's resolution of Lear's madness in pathos, not death. His reconciliation with Molly at closure is a *clinamen* of the death of Hamlet Senior. Shakespeare operated in the magic hiatus of dynamic and ferocious Elizabethan crowds.

[*A bartender in tight leather trousers and a fishnet singlet rises onto a high stool to manually change channels on the television by clicking a large silver dial. West Indians pace bowlers hammer their own batsmen in the training nets*]

M.D. COSTELLO

[*Animated*] First Test is always played in Brisbane. Been played there since 1928. Bradman's debut, for fucks sake![12] But not this time. Oh no! Our boys are going to get sent into bat tomorrow on the fastest pitch in world cricket[13] against the greatest pace bowling

---

This was Joyce's basic social formula for Ireland in *Ulysses*.

11 **ANNOUNCER:** Australia was the most advanced social democracy in the world at Federation. It was already a nation. British leaders feared this influence back home. The Gallipoli myth was a reactionary backlash to recast Australia as a societal LACK needing definition through Britain and war.

EXAMINATION PAPER: Examine this statement in the context of modern Australian history since 1939.

SCRIBBLER: Link to Gallipoli as Iliad > MacArthur as Odysseus > Australia as a member of Odysseus' crew (the US alliance). Ithaca was a small state in the larger corpus of Attica like Australia in the context of Empire. Disclose Britain as a false parent.

12 **MEILLON:** The man later revered as The Don scored 18 and 1. He was demoted to 12th man for the Second Test.

13 **ANNOUNCER:** The WACA in Perth.

SCRIBBLER: This is a motif for maladministration. LINK bowling with bombing. Also, invasion threats. Parody (reductive).

attack in history[14] on Day One of a new test series.[15] It's nuts!

M.D. LYNCH

Fromelles Part Two, mate.[16]

M.D. COSTELLO

Most lopsided match-up since 1975.[17]

JABBER LADIESMAN

When Chang shot his fit in the roll.[18]

MILKMAID

A modern arena tragedy. See Patroclus and Hector. See Achilles hobbling from the battlefield. See coma. See death.

ARISTOPHONES

Mocking gulls assailed him.

HOMER

But they would not touch the solitary drunk lying washed up on the beach.

DON CANE

I met Richie on holidays at Bantayan Island. [*Romantically*][19] I was feeding the carp

---

14 **ANNOUNCER:** Holding, Garner, Marshall and Walsh came together for the first time in Perth.

15 IBID: Australia vs. West Indies, 1984–85. It precipitated a dominance that was to last 10 years.

BURTON: Like Troy.

ODYSSEUS: Like my voyage.

16 **SCRIBBLER:** Note: inappropriate analogies between war and sport is a feature of Australian culture.

17 **ANNOUNCER:** The New South Wales Rugby League Grand Final. Final result. Easts 38, St George 0. The Roosters will hold the J.J. Giltinan Shield for the next year.

18 IBID: Insert allusion to Dick's bloody big prick (needle) and Davy's bucket of gravy (sperm). Joyce cites this ballad in Circe. Composer: Oliver St John Gogarty, c.1903. Also, link to Willy.

19 A fabricated reminiscence. Search 'feeding carp' elsewhere in TMAC for the source of this image.

when the weeds parted for a moment and her squat form came into view. [20]

MOTHER BLOT

[*Kicking her prostrate husband*] Take up your crutch and walk.

~~**20** [*TV Comedian 1 enters grocer's shop wearing a tweed jacket and pork pie hat. He approaches the counter. TV Comedian 2 is dressed in women's clothing*]~~

~~**TV COMEDIAN 2 (SHOPKEEPER):** Hello, Mister Beckett. Who are you today?~~

~~**TV COMEDIAN 1:** Skeezy Sammy, Ma'am.~~

~~**SHOPKEEPER:** Who give you that name, son?~~

~~**BECKETT:** [*Wistfully*] Old Shamrock.~~

~~**SHOPKEEPER:** Well at least it's an advance on Scoffynosey.~~

~~**BECKETT:** I'm not so sure of that. I'll get him back one day by renaming him Hamm, Pozzo the Blind and Krapp. [*Brighter*] I'm going on holidays, Mrs Brennan.~~

~~**SHOPKEEPER:** Very nice, dear. What would you like?~~

~~**BECKETT:** [*Extracting a prescription from his coat*] Two balloons of warm porridge, a pound of tripe and a yoga mat please.~~

~~**SHOPKEEPER:** So where would you be taking those comestibles, Mister B?~~

~~**BECKETT:** On my honeymoon. [*Modest canned laughter*] My travel agents told me to pack for an interminable journey made up of hiatuses.~~

~~**SHOPKEEPER:** And who would they be?~~

~~**BECKETT:** Messrs. Berkeley, Descartes and Langlands upon Trinity Square. They said I would need all these ingredients because I can only make love to my wife by analogue.~~

~~**SHOPKEEPER:** And where are you taking your bonny new bride?~~

~~**BECKETT:** [*Extracting itinerary*] We're going to Casa del Solipsism. [*Canned groans, laughter and scattered applause*] They say you can perceive the sand, but never actually feel it.~~

~~**SHOPKEEPER:** At least your soles won't get burnt, love.~~

~~[*Cut to famous philosophers in front row of set. They groan, smile and applaud. Ionesco laughs outright. Breton remains po-faced taking notes with chalk on a stone tablet.*]~~

BURTON: Samuel Beckett took dictation from Joyce on a number of occasions during the drafting of *F(W)ake*. He inadvertently contributed the phrase, "come in," on page 208 ("queemswellth of coocome in their combs") when he literally transcribed Joyce's command to a visitor who knocked on the door to enter. This is a famous anecdote, perhaps apocryphal, cited in Richard Ellmann's biography of Joyce on page 649. He also contributed the essay, "Dantay [paws] ... Burno. Veeco [parse] Joyz" to the collection of marketing puff-pieces known as *A Symposium - Xagmination Round His Incamination of Work in Progress* (1929).

DRAMATIC FORM

Blot raises himself from the canvas groggily as the referee's counts SIX.

BLOT

[*Slumping*] I can't. Me tendons' bung. I think they cuttem.

M.D.'S

[*In unison. Banging empty vessels on the bench.*] Change the blooming channel!

[*The barman obliges. Footage of Graham Langlands hobbling in back play. The camera zooms onto his footwear*][21]

WHITE BOOTS[22]

[*In unison*] Don't blame us! It was still only five-nil at half time!

M.D. COSTELLO

They'll roll us for a hundred tomorrow.

M.D. LYNCH

Correct. [*Exclamatory*] Beecawsehgotnorunsinem![23] [*He drains dregs of ale from his tankard*] I mean Henry Lawson's batting eight. Ahead of Neilson, O'Dowd and Praed. He's a glorified number nine at best.[24]

---

21 SCRIBBLER: Joyce consistently makes this type of artificial transition in the novel. A comment on a given subject (in this case, the 1975 Grand Final) will be succeeded by an apparently arbitrary, chance corollary (footage of the game being seen on the television screen).

22 IBID: Personification is a key device in Circe. It can be linked to the work of Freud on dreams.

ANNOUNCER: Langlands' calamitous performance in the 1975 Grand Final has become infamous in rugby league circles. Rumours abound as to its cause. White football boots, which he was wearing for the first time as part of a new sponsorship deal instead of the traditional black galoshes, were held accountable by both fans and media. Later, it was revealed that a misplaced painkilling injection in his leg had nobbled the champion FB.

SCRIBBLER: Note correspondences with 1969 Melbourne Cup favourite, Big Philou (see later in C7). Also, heroin use by Willy and Tom.

23 IBID: The weakness of the top order meant runs from the tail-enders were imperative if Australia was to remain competitive in the forthcoming series. This passage is symbolic of Australia's economic condition in 1984.

24 IBID: Always connect apparently irrelevant, coincidental narrative comments to the largest symbolic

NAMELESS RETIRED MILITARY FIGURE[25]

We only had a few ack-acks and some Hudson bombers that got strafed on the runway.[26]

NARRATOR

He said gesturing at the screen.

MILDLING

[*Entering the pub. Sagely. In error*] Like Sergei Lermontov with a duelling pistol.

CHOC WHEATON

Shot in the dark.

DON CANE

I gave one to your plump white ewe out in the black paddock.

CHOC WHEATON

Outside the perimeter wire.

CHAUCER

Ful fetisly ydight with herbes swoote.[27]

DON CANE

They burrowed up to our positions through the jungle and threw themselves in human waves onto the wire.

HELEN

We turned our faces.

---

issues in the novel. See next line for template.

25 IBID: In Circe, characters from Bloom's memory suddenly appear in Bella's brothel.

26 **S.DOG:** I am stuck on a tarmac in Shenzhen waiting for clearance crammed into economy class. I can hardly even read my laptop screen on the fold-down table let alone type freely. I just watched the Johnny Cash biopic while I ate jufan. I wish Tom had seen this movie. It contained five useful messages: there's a lot of time to waste over the course of a single life; sometimes the most creative periods are the most uninspiring personal ones; there are OK times even as you go down; the mundane details in life can carry you along for decades; and you can bail out for a while and still make a big comeback (see Lacan "F").

27 **A/P ROGERS:** This line can be translated as "Very elegantly strewn with sweet-smelling herbs."

DON CANE

Hoping Penny wouldn't appear at the flyscreen door.[28]

HELEN

Hoping she would.

DON CANE

[*Urgently*] Because it made me harder.

HELEN

It made him hotter.[29]

DON CANE

I heard her call my name.[30]

PENELOPE CANE

[*Heavily pregnant*] Are you out there, Donny?

[*A kettle whistles*][31]

DON CANE

[*Ejaculating*] I'm done!

COLERIDGE

"A mighty fountain momentarily forced."[32]

---

28 SCRIBBLER: C7 should disclose new information or facts insinuated in earlier chapters. Also, reposition emotional meaning and deepen characterisation through reveries and dreams. In this instance, we perceive Penelope Hallem as a lonely, vulnerable figure.

29 SCRIBBLER: See Joyce and Nora for analogue.

30 IBID: Reference "White Light, White Heat" (1968). Read the full lyric to attain the significance of this quote. Note – Don Cane could NEVER have known this song due to cultural, temporal and spatial disconnects. Thus, it is imposed from the writer's cosmos onto characterisation like something in Proust.

31 NARRATOR: A sequence of male orgasm images and metaphors follows.

STEPHEN: Professor Swift says that one man 'd'amour' will beat ten men in armour.

~~**32 TV COMEDIAN 1:** [*Irish accent. Dressed as a priest*] As the priest said to the nun. Uga uga ugh [*Canned laughter*]~~

STEPHEN DEDALUS

Ad deam qui laetificat juventutem meam.[33]

MILKMAID

"A scream in Lilith's church."[34]

[*Penny turns to the dim interior of the palace. The doorway is vacant. A drape twists at the threshold. A tin whistle expires*]

DON CANE

I thought I pulled out in time.

HELEN:

[*Heavily pregnant*] NO YOU DIDN'T.

CAPRI

Drip-drip-drip like Uranus' ballsack.

MACRITIS

Or Mussolini's head.

MILDLING

Zeus leaking Athena.

~~**TV COMEDIAN 2:** (Fat balding male in a full nun's habit) Our milkman came every evening at the back door. Always left a fresh dab of cream on the top of mum's pail.~~

~~**ULAN:** Link to Don and Helen.~~

~~**TV COMEDIAN 1:** Sometimes he drove 'round the block so he could come twice.~~

~~**TV COMEDIAN 2:** Did he always enter via the rear driveway?~~

~~**TV COMEDIAN 1:** (Nudging her ribs) Ah-ah-ah!~~

33 **SCRIBBLER:** Stephen Dedalus makes this drunken toast to "the goddess who gladdens my youth." It is adapted from the Latin Tridentine Mass. There are multiple links here with Telemachus.

34 **MILKMAID:** See Troy, a temple, Cassandra, her extraction, a rape, her apparently perverse grin when she learns her fate as Agamemnon's concubine, Athena's rage against this desecration.

NEWS READER

A miraculous escape for a construction worker in America today. He was impaled in an industrial accident by a steel rebar, which shot through his body and exited through his open mouth. He was rushed to hospital where doctors performed a ten-hour operation to save him.

M.D. LYNCH

[*Speaking at a press conference*] The angle of entry and exit is what saved him. [*Cut to x-ray*] The spina bifida missed his heart and other vital organs then proceeded up his throat and out his maw like Botticelli's Chloris. It's incredible he's alive, let alone upright.

NEWS READER:

[*Over heroic music from 1940s newsreel*] Doctors are amazed that, despite the severity of his injuries, young Master Chaim is already up-and-about on his new set of stainless steel crutches.

LEON DANIEL

[*Riding a motorised wheelchair onstage*] Here! A gift for you, son. One fit for Lord Byron.[35]

CHOC WHEATON

[*With clipboard. Pen poised*] Kill Ratio?

DON CANE

One dead son. Two living.[36]

LEON DANIEL

Unholy Trinities.[37]

STEPHEN DEDALUS

Elizabeth, Chaim and HIV.

MULLIGAN

Three stumps with the bails off like Peter Abelard.

---

35 **SCRIBBLER:** More dead kids. More false gestures. More limps.

36 IBID: A calculation of sons.

37 IBID: Insert list of hat-tricks. Restate Joyce on numerology. See later for further threesomes.

CAPRI

Father, me and Tom.

JOYCE

Earwicker, Shem and Shaun.

TOM HALLEM

Les, me and my real father.

PENELOPE HALLEM

Me, Les and Dick of Dick Stone meats.

JOYCE

Bloom, Stephen and Simon Dedalus.

NARRATOR

John Joyce, James Joyce and any one of your choice out of Stanislaus, George, Nora, Lucia or William Shakespeare.

JOYCE

Molly, Bloom and Blazes Boylan.

GOLDSTEIN

Professor Krafter and her twin Alex's.

ROSIE PROBERT

[*Wistfully. Folding washing*] A Pope and a hope.[38]

KRAFTER

Poor dead Jimmy.[39]

38 IBID: Note pun on surnames.

39 IBID: James McAuley.

RICHIE

Pieta.[40]

ELIZABETH ARCHER

You lived a day and a night then died, Chaim.[41]

LEON DANIEL

Once only, with one hand, your mother, in farewell, touched you.

DON CANE

Nobody's fault but mine ... and General Westmoreland and Robert McNamara, Harold Holt and good ole L-B-J.

CHOC

Nape, Purple Grape and sweet hot Orange Crush.[42]

HALLEM

Elizabeth, Leon and I.

BARBOUR

Gertrude, Claudius and young Hamlet.

ILKS

Hamlet's status is uncertain. The death of his father has reduced him to the level of a blood supplicant. He lacks legitimacy.

STEPHEN DEDALUS

The character of Hamlet is Shakespeare recalling his youth with Anne Hathaway.

O

Joyce made Stephen obsessed with Hamlet. It was the cold case which could make

---

40 **EXAMINATION PAPER:** The poem's title links the death of Christ to the subject of infant mortality. Compare and contrast.

41 **DON (YOUNG ERIC):** My bounty stretched like a skinned-rabbit on the spina bifida slab.

42 **SCRIBBLER:** Slang term for Agent Orange.

him famous if he could only crack it. It had never been solved.

ILKS

Unlike Ibsen.

[*Don starts the car radio*]

JAMES CARR

[*Singing*] Hiding in shadows ... where we don't belong ...[43]

ULAN

"Circe" is the most musical episode in *Ulysses*. It is full of lyrics from popular tunes and operas – often ironically employed – to indicate that Joyce wanted music to work like a film soundtrack for his novel.

[*FX: David McComb in the role of Tom Hallem sits at a table in London and writes 'Consider the Lilies of the Fields' on the spine of a piece of paper which he folds and places inside a cassette case*][44]

JOYCE

London's Burning – Follow me up to Carlow – Shule Aroon – Un Poco Il Cuore (I am Don Giovanni, Manny Others as Zerlina) – Love's Old Sweet Song – Garryowen – Jim Bludso hold her nozzle – La Cigale – Dignam's Dead and Gone Below. [*In a fine tenor voice*] "... He knocked the old woman who stole from his Punch."

PATER

All art aspires to the condition of music.[45]

BARBOUR

Joyce called his technique in Circe "hallucination."[46]

43 IBID: Quote from the 1960s soul ballad, "Dark End of the Street," by James Carr. It is the musical emblem for Don and Helen. The use of songs to explain relationships and advance plotlines was a key Joycean device.

44 **NARRATOR:** See Matthew 6:28. Also, Homer Smith in the movie with this name.

45 **SCRIBBLER:** This was a key slogan for nineteenth-century aesthetics.

46 IBID: Circe traces Bloom's psychic journey through Nighttown to emotional resolution. Joyce sequenced

ULAN

It is a moot point with critics whether he was alluding to George Berkeley.

ULAN

In the *Odyssey*, Circe casts a spell over Odysseus' crew turning them into pigs. He is protected by chewing on Moly.

O

This episode is inundated with porcine references. Joyce is clearly playing with the capacity of symbols to withstand over-utilisation. He gorges on them.[47]

PERSIAN JONES

If you want to dispose of a human body, the best way is to feed it to pigs.

O

The connection with the Circe episode is that unleashed sexuality turns human beings into swine.

[*Billy Capri enters the Shakespeare Hotel. He circumnavigates the bar. Professor Milkmaid is sunk in a deep lounge picking at wounds on his paperback hand. He reaches out to his younger self-image.*]

MILKMAID[48]

William, sit down with me a while.

---

his hallucinations and dreams to achieve closure. This purged Bloom so he could take on the role of father figure for SD.

47 ULAN: First, Bloom appears as an Irish peasant, leading a pig, begging to be allowed to return home. This pig-imagery continues with Zoe telling Bloom she is from "Hog's Norton, where the pigs plays the organs" (15.1983). Zoe then seduces Bloom, who is turned into a pig-like brute. He follows her with a "lifted head, sniffing" (15.2039–40).

SCRIBBLER: INSERT OTHER REFERENCES.

48 IBID: This naming is a pun on Mother Grogan in Chapter I of *Ulysses*. Later, he transforms into Mím. Short form and acronymical naming was prominent in *F(W)ake*. In Norse mythology, Mím is renowned for knowledge and wisdom. He was beheaded during the Æsir-Vanir War. Odin subsequently carried Mím's head in a bag, extracting it for data, secrets and counsel as required. Both Milkmaid and Capri are outsiders in Faculty. Professor Milkmaid symbolises another of Billy's various substitute fathers, who help him avoid the fate of TH.

CAPRI

[*He sits*] You're alone, Professor.

NARRATOR

"Adrian is buying a round of drinks," Milkmaid said pointing at the congested bar.

SCRIBBLER

This device inserts NOW into the chronology of events set down in the opening stage directions.

CAPRI

He'll be a while yet.

MILKMAID

[*Amused*] Yes. Big crowd here tonight to celebrate your success.[49] I enjoyed your paper. It wilfully eschewed ... [*long pause*] compliance.[50]

CAPRI

Like your lectures.

MILKMAID

They're just greasepaint etudes, Billy.[51]

CAPRI

You were a leading critic once.

MILKMAID

That was 20 years ago.

NARRATOR

What happened, asked Billy Capri mildly.

---

49 IBID: This is a jape. The actual reason was Melbourne Cup celebrations.

50 IBID: It was hard to find the right word here.

51 IBID: See previous footnote.

MILKMAID

I was sidelined by The Leavisites. I had a family to support like Shanghai Dog. I barely hung onto my job.

CITIZEN

Anderson's elves. Occam's razor gang. Knife fights with Matthew Arnold down The Push.

CAPRI

Why did you stop writing?

MILKMAID

[*Holding Capri's face with gaze*] I've never stopped writing, son.[52]

NARRATOR

The text pivots at this moment from a forlorn silence (two seconds in real time) to a sudden eructation.[53]

[*A man in a tweed jacket climbs onto the bar. Insert internal monologue: "poetry once possessed a communal, frequently oral and performative dimension in Australia that has now largely disappeared." A chestnut strand wipes the piece of paper he is reviewing. He blows it away and clears his throat. Scattered applause.*][54]

MULLIGAN

Some say that I'm a great big fucking 'furter
I prefer Antipodean Goethe
I'm six foot eight so I'm no runt
Just a cliché-addled, sanctimonious cunt

---

52 IBID: Note self-reference.

NARRATOR: Proust appeared like a salonnard to acquaintances in Paris but all the time he was working in secret on his epic novel, which charts social change across all classes in the Belle Époque period in France up to the aftermath of the Great War.

53 **SPRUIKER:** Last Card Louie says, "THIS IS THE BIGGEST SHOW IN KINGS CROSS! Fourteen Lovely Girls. One Big Continuous Show. Roll up, roll up!"

54 **SCRIBBLER:** ASAL conducted a literary parody competition at each annual conference dinner.

With symbols as big as my big flat feet
Bestriding the macrobiotic shops on Darling Street
In a giant kaftan like the Dalai Lama
Making pencil notes for a topical new drama.
I take the bogus ideology of hippie-flips in Balmain
And grind them through my lobotomised left-wing brain
Then I intellectually wank while holding forth
That gob I call The Club; this one Travelling North.
Nothing against Malouf and his libretto
But he should set it in an urban, koori ghetto
With sensitive young social workers
And wise elders seeing truth despite trachoma's
Tugging on the Meth to stop the pain
Of bruvvas selling smack down Redfern lanes.
But poor Dave's obsessed with Greek homo-aesthetics
I tell him, "mayte, write about diabetics.
No one's ever taken up their plight.
It's a sure-fire hit, all you got to do is write."
As for me, well, I'll just go on working.
After all, to me, it's just like ... jerking.

[*Cheers. Calls for encore. Capri and Milkmaid shift attention to the Bloomsbury Set*]

CAPRI

Everybody's in good cheer.

MILKMAID

[*Bitterly*] The Australia Council grants were announced today. They're all celebrating.

CAPRI

Who got one?

MILKMAID

Adam Aitken for poetry. Jennifer Maiden. All the tyros over there. The senior fellowships went to the usual suspects: Drewe, Foster, Hall, Hospital, Koch, Tranter.

JABBER

[*Loudly*] My new book will be called *Life is Such-a*.[55] The hero is a guy called Nosey Tom. He walked into an Evinrude outboard motor when he was a kid. Left a gaping hole in his face. This enables him to snort massive quantities of speed. Calls it his "blowhole." He goes blind fixing smack behind his eyeball.

ULAN

Oedipus with a stick injury.

O

[*Disdainfully*] More slapstick splatter.

FLIGHT-FALCONHURST

I'm writing an erotic diary called *Peeps*.

LABIAMEISTER

My work-in-progress is provisionally titled, *Twin Tailles of Eurydice La Change, Seventeenth-Century Hermaphrodite*.

MACRITIS

My last novel was praised as a powerful indictment of the capitalist system by *Socialist Worker*. My new work takes on the CIA coup against the Whitlam Government ... head-on.

MILKMAID

[*Internal monologue*] Unpublished works. Rejected essays. My opus. *Prometheus Rebound*. A trope of disillusionment. To be published privately by my executor after my death. After spending some time on earth amongst the human race, the Titan implores Jupiter to chain him back up on the rock.

[*Jabber rises from his stool. Shanghai Dog and Xiao Fang enter Time Passage Bar on Caojiayan Lu. Two expatriates are watching a business show on a small TV perched upon the spirits shelf. A waitress in a white plastic boob tube, white plastic mini-skirt and white plastic*

55 IBID: This title inverts the title of Joseph Furphy's great novel, which were allegedly Ned Kelly's last words. See C8 for further details.

thigh-high boots leans against the filthy bar. She is wearing a green sash advertising HEINEKEN. A heater presses warm air at her feet. She is playing on a smartphone.]

NEWS PRESENTER

In Washington DC, the IMF has forecast a sustained global recession. This announcement comes on the back of today's dramatic cuts in interest rates in all OECD economies.[56]

BARFLY 1

Another pint of Paulaner, Elvis. Same for Uncle Roy.

NARRATOR

The Chinese barman collects two tankards and begins to tap loose draft.

SHANGHAI DOG

[*Gesturing at screen*] Looks bad, fellas.

BARFLY 1

I just got told to pack up the family and head home to the States.

[*He forces dregs down his throat and slams down the glass. An email notification purrs. SD takes a Blackberry handset from a black pouch on his belt. He scrolls the wheel and clicks*]

INBOX/OPEN

Merrill's gone. NAB wobbly. Shinhan still OK. But won't lead. Need co-investors. Need new cornerstones. Chinese options?

REPORTER

Carnage at Bourses all over the world today, Mishal.

[*Shanghai Dog commences typing.*]

56 **EXAMINATION PAPER:** *Ulysses* and *TMAC* both use drastic economic conditions and social breakdown as the background for their plots. Joyce's deconstruction of style and form mimics this subject matter. Explore.

FINGERS

[*Typing*] I'll try Ping An. Also, China Life. BTW BOC A/C under 300. Please t/fer Q3 funds.

[Xiao Fang touches his arm]

XIAO FANG

What's wrong?

SHANGHAI DOG

[*Shrugging*] Just work stuff.

[*Three sonar blips announce the arrival of a new email. Shanghai Dog reads the screen*]

SCREEN

No more funds until we raise fresh capital.

[*Tom Hallem enters the bar from King Street. A man rushes towards him.*][57]

LEER

Tommy! Come over here, lad. Give me a cuddle. Let me buy you a drink. Grandpater! Off yer arse, you old goose. Get the yung fella a beer. Here. Take my mug.

GRANDPATER

Hey?

LEER

[*Leaning through beer slops. Dropping twenty-dollar note on table. Loudly*] GO GET YUN TOBBY ERA SCUBA RESCHS![58]

---

57 **SCRIBBLER:** Leer is suddenly introduced into the novel at this point as a character. Describe his physical appearance.

58 **SHANGHAI DOG:** [*In Chinese*] Pint of Heineken please. What do you want?

XIAO FANG: Bu yao yingliao.

SHANGHAI DOG: Not even Perrier?

XIAO FANG: [*Blowing out her cheeks*] Rang wo tai pang.

MILKMAID

Keatzes charr-med cup.

[*Coins taplap the laminated table. A dog reaches towards a discarded take-away wrapper in the trough. Leer lifts his bar stool emphatically*]

LEER

Empty!! Owta that, you grub!
[*He slaps dog*]

ELLMANN

James Joyce had two phobias – dogs ... and thunder.[59]

JAMES JOYCE

[*Contentedly*] Corpse of a bloated dog.[60] [*Smiling*] Splendid!

[*He pushes his walking stick at the Citizen's red setter*][61]

SHANGHAI DOG: [*Incredulous*] Fat?

WAITRESS: She is correct. The bubbles make you fat.

STAGE DIRECTION: [*Puts palms on belly. Pushes out cheeks as if bloated*]

XIAO FANG: Like frog.

WAITRESS: Yes. We don't want to look like Western women.

XIAO FANG: Dui. Kan qi lai li.

STAGE DIRECTION: [*She makes the shape of a pear around her rump*]

WAITRESS: Yes. Especially after childbirth.

STAGE DIRECTION: [*The bartender slams a pint of beer on the bar*]

BARTENDER: Thirty-eight Renminbi, Mister Billy.

SCRIBBLER: Search numerology.

BLOOM: I'll pay for his drink. Also, that handbag. Let me slip a few hundred kuai into your wallet as well. That should help pay the hostess at the KTV later.

59 STAGE DIRECTION: [*The great author leans on the northern railing of Rathausbrucke watching the swift spring tide of alpine waters flow south towards Zurichsee. The corpse of a bloated dog passes beneath him.*]

60 SCRIBBLER: See C1. Arbitrary location. Substitute Trieste. Any of Joyce's nine homes there will suffice. They were all within a five-minute walk of Via San Nicolo. This image portrays Joyce as a metonymy of Sir Lancelot. The walking stick is a polearm. Hat as helmet. No horse. Link to Cervantes.

61 IBID: The Citizen's dog is named after a champion Irish Red Setter, which was a household name in

GARRYOWEN

Jumpstickatchstickruncango!

[*The dog grabs the tip of Joyce's cane. It turns into a stick of dynamite*][62]

JIM

Watch out, he's making for the fire!

[*The group of prospectors abandon the campsite*]

ANDY

He's chasing us!

JIM

Thinks it's a bluddy game!

[*Jim dives down an abandoned shaft. Andy jumps behind a log. The dog rushes past them. Empty chases it hard and grabs the other end of the stick of dynamite. The dogs wrestle. It explodes*]

JAMES JOYCE

[*Gleefully*] Like Tchaikovsky!

[*Odysseus enters disguised as a beggar. Argos sniffs his foot and dies. The corpses of Argos, Empty and Garryowen are dragged from the stage by a retinue of INSERT.*[63] *Canned laughter*]

[*Satisfied*] It's equal to the climax of *King Lear*.

[*He raises a glass of white wine and toasts his father's portrait*]

Ireland at the end of the nineteenth century. Simon Dedalus, John Joyce and their cronies would have all smoked Spillane's Garryowen Flake, a pipe tobacco named after James Giltrap's famed canine.

62 IBID: Note allusions to Henry Lawson's sketch, "The Loaded Dog."

63 IBID: Choice of slaves, hobbits, dwarves, comedians, council workers.

RUDOLPH VIRAG

[*Seated at a desk. A vial of monkshood beside the ink well.*] Son, please care of dear Athos.[64]

BUSINESS REPORTER

In New York, the Dow Jones plummeted 4.6 percent, nearly matching Wednesday's 480-point slide.[65]

[Shanghai Dog continues typing]

COMPOSE EMAIL

Will try Clearwater. Also, CKI + Nanfung in HK. What about SING? Not GIC or Temasek. Any family offices? [*Hits 'Send'*]

---

64 IBID: He consumes the poison vial. Leopold Bloom is the son of an immigrant Jewish father from Szombathely, Hungary, who committed suicide in the Queen's Hotel, Central Ennis. See Chapter 10 for more details.

65 SHANGHAI DOG: *Xia zha nong.*

TRANSLATOR: This means "thank you" in Shanghai dialect.

STAGE DIRECTIONS: [*He gives RMB100 to the bartender*]

WAITRESS: You speak Shanghainese?

SHANGHAI DOG: *Yi dian dian.*

TRANSLATOR: This means, "a little," in Mandarin.

WAITRESS: [*Disdainful*] I don't speak it. I come from Jiangsu province. I hate Shanghai people.

XIAO FANG: [*Nodding*] They are all arrogant.

WAITRESS: They talk too fast. And hiss.

XIAO FANG: Like snakes.

WAITRESS: Three years now I am living in Shanghai. Still, I don't understand Shanghai people.

XIAO FANG: *Dui. Tamen gang xi huan wei guo ren bi Zhong guo ren.*

TRANSLATOR: This means, "Correct. They prefer foreign people to Chinese people."

WAITRESS: When all the Shanghai people have relocated to Pudong, they are going to cut it off the mainland and float across the sea so they can join Taiwan.

XIAO FANG: [*Shocked laughter*] Don't say that! It is very bad thinking!

STAGE DIRECTIONS: [Another customer *arrives. The waitress exits. Xiao FANG takes out her iPhone and begins texting intently*]

BUSINESS REPORTER

Toyota has slashed its annual profit forecast, Mishal.

PRESENTER

Shares were down another 10 per cent today ahead of an earnings announcement.

BUSINESS REPORTER

The market is now expecting job cuts in the tens of thousands right across the car sector.

TSUTOMU YAMADA

This is a real shock, Mishal. I don't think anyone expected such a large correction.

MILKMAID

I've been reworking the same text for twenty years.

DAVID WILLIAMSON

I could have written ... twenty plays in that time.

PETER CAREY

Four novels.

JAMES JOYCE

Finnegans Wake.

THE CRADLE

Have you got a mental condition?

[*O rises onto the bar. She leans back to read from a scrap of foolscap paper*]

O

Tom Keneally, you've got no rivals
But I can't understand your titles.
Why can't you be more like Franz Kafka,
And name your books for existential factors?
All that stuff about larks, heroes, paracletes and Aurora's
victim

For books about the harshness of nature and the convict
system
Or the demise of ordinary but nonetheless heroic guys
Like Erzberger, who worked on the Treaty of Versailles.
Sometimes you remind me of Patrick White
With his penchant for o'er-strained poetic flight
And partiality to sensationalised plots
Which test the patience of your avid Lord and Lady
Read-a-Lots.
Jimmie Blacksmith with his bifurcated ethics
Was a better subject than Joan of Arc's hysterics
While Marshall Tito's heroic partisans
Seem just like a Baltic spin-off from The Sullivans'.
But at least, dear Tom, your pretensions are confined
To the cover, the Manly Sea Eagles[66] and the spine.[67]

[*She bows. Crowd whoops. Jabber lays his gear on a toilet lid. The Cradle has been suspended beneath. He boots.*]

MISHAL HUSAIN

Banks worldwide have taken seven hundred billion dollars in write-downs and losses since the start of 2007, according to data compiled by Bloomberg.

[*Grandpater places glasses on the table with a shaky grip.*]

LEER

Gubb on yer, Grabpater. Here you go, Tom.

[*Billy Capri observes Tom Hallem across the bar. Suddenly, he rips off Milkmaid's head*[68] *and strides towards his brother. Rumbold plunges his hand into the gaping belly of the whale and extracts a head clotted with coiled entrails.*]

---

66 **SCRIBBLER:** This is a reference to the Manly Warringah rugby league team.

67 IBID: This pun references both the spine of a book jacket and key positions in rugby league. Numbers 1, 6, 7 and 9 are known as the spine. Langlands wore number 1.

68 **NARRATOR:** In Viking cultures, he is known as Asgard. In others, "Hag" or "Mím."

RUMBOLD

God Save the King!

NARRATOR

He cried. Meanwhile, Billy Capri reached his brother.

[*Holding Mím's mouth against Tom's ear*]

CAPRI

Listen, brother!

MÍM/MILKMAID

See your blood father falling to earth. See wooden cow. Elizabeth will sire your only child. But you will never provide a roof for your daughter. You kill a friend and die alone. On your back. Wild at heart like blind Oedipus.

LEON

[*Wearing a dentist's outfit. He rips away a white sheet to unveil his latest invention*] Look, I built this fine beast for you, my darling. It possesses a cunning flap for anonymous intercourse.

[*Elizabeth enters the machine. Her bare backside emerges. Absalom kisses it. Poseidon fucks her. She retires with her husband's aid. He is dressed as Joseph. Her belly distends. She enters labour. Albert assists her into the stirrups.*][69]

ALBERT THE GOOD

Just hang onto these straps.

ELIZABETH

For God's sake, give me an epidural!

CIRCE

[*Taking vial from purse*] Drink!

69 **ULAN:** The Victorian scientific impulse has gone horribly wrong in this passage.

[*Elizabeth swallows the potion. She gives birth to Minotaur*][70]

AUCTIONEER

This champion foal was bred at Widden Stud. Sired by Cane out of Pasiphae. Examine the fine lines of her transformation. A perfect segue. Renaissance construct. Consigned to the Inglis Sales Yard. Bidding starts at twenty ducats.

TOM

[*Waving a big cigar*] It's a ... it's a ... girl!

CAPRI

Entelechy!

MIM/MILKMAID

The male line ends.

PLAYER QUEEN

None weds the second but who killed the first.

ELIZABETH

Weedafirstingkillthesecondeurs.

MÍM/MILKMAID

Inverted pervert. Infamy of Blasphemy. Aegisthus was made from rape. Christened the "male goat."[71] Killer of Atreus. With Clytemnestra, killer of Agamemnon. Cousin kills cousin. Orestes killing his mother. Murdering Aegisthus' son. Mating with his enemy's daughter. Bit off his own finger.

ELIZABETH, LEON

[*As Chorus*] After his sperm we got.

MÍM/MILKMAID

---

70 SCRIBBLER: This is all relevant to the Circe episode of the *Odyssey*.

71 IBID: There have been many references to Billy Capri as goat-like since C4. The word 'Capra' means goat in Latin. Joyce used a similar sequence of porcine terms in Circe.

The queen lay with a prize bull.

ELIZABETH, LEON

[*As Chorus*] We shall name him Minos.

[*A pagan ceremony ensues. Tom achieves orgasm*]

MÍM/MILKMAID

The bull has been milked.

TOM, BILLY

[*As a Chorus*] You must decide which child is at the head and which at the tail.[72]

DON CANE

[*Pontificating*] All are equal in my sight.[73]

MÍM/MILKMAID

Two heads, two tails—

JOYCE

Entelechy of entelechies.

MÍM/MILKMAID

The son must repeat the journey of the father.

TOM HALLEM

Head of a bull, tail of a bull, body of a man.

WEASEL BOB

Yung mulebludd.

MÍM/MILKMAID

---

72 IBID: Link to Bloom and Molly in bed.

73 IBID: Compare with Gloucester, K. Lear.

From his forehead arise mosaic horns. [*Rolling his eyes dramatically*]

HALLEM

[*Stabbing Mím/Milkmaid with a commando knife*] Death, fiend!

MÍM/MILKMAID

[*Dying*] Ah! Brutus comes with a warm wet blade.

CASSIUS

Rome holds your name in high regard, sire.

CASCA

And fears Caesar's ambition.

CASSIUS

He would make himself King.[74]

---

74 **SCRIBBLER:** [*In Blank Verse*] By rights, *Julius Caesar* should have been the tragedy of Brutus. Up to the assassination of Caesar, Brutus is the principal character. His cogitations resemble Hamlet's angst. Antony's eulogy in Act 3, Scene 2 steals the play. From that point, it becomes a basic revenge drama. It is as if Shakespeare was diverted by the power of his own monologue and changed the entire focus of the plot. Brutus is reduced to a mere target. His language drops a key. He even becomes aphonic at some points like Caius Martius Coriolanus. Shakespeare could be playing with convention with this flip in plotline. Or he might have just failed to sustain tragic structuration.

ILKS: Shakespeare is said to have produced a play of action – not reflection – in *Coriolanus*. It is often called a 'busy play.' Yet *Coriolanus* is, in fact, the most stagnant of plays. There is no moral or intellectual progression. No movement towards amelioration. It ends where it began. Nothing has been clarified. It is a circuit. The principal change is that Coriolanus has died. Only the operations of language itself seem to have been exemplified by this drama. It is Rome as the site of linguistic flux which is paramount.

HAROLD BLOOM: No character in Shakespeare listens. Not even the minor ones. They are all too busy giving soliloquys.

ILKS: Like Tom Hallem, death has already claimed Martius by the time he is forced to step forward in the Forum and make the confession of what he is. No stable definition of him is possible. He must remain forever an enigma. He is a Protean character of temporary masks and poses: a man of action who performs no acts during play-time; highly sophisticated yet credulous; sensitive yet not to flattery; a gull of love. He is ineffectual even in death.

O: Dialectic is Coriolanus' natural mode. He has the will to alter the natural world but only with language. He claims to have 'fled from words' yet he relentlessly updates, revises and examines his own monologues until they produce grotesque parodies of their original sentiments. Metaphor is piled upon metamorphosis until no thing is left untransfered, untransformed. First, animals. Lions become hares; foxes, geese. Then natural phenomena are inverted: "coal of fire" is seen on ice; hailstones in the sun. Human metaphors of illness and

BRUTUS

Why should his name be sounded more than mine?[75]

EDGAR

Mine is as fair.

CONSPIRATORS

[*Stabbing Caesar multiple times with used syringes*] Let us all share the same blood with Caesar.[76]

TOM HALLEM

Carve him as a dish. [*Showing syringe to Billy Capri*] And you, brother?

CAPRI

Hold fast.[77]

---

depravity follow. He goes beneath the ocean to conjure oxymoronic "fins of lead" then flies into the sky to flap against an oak tree like an ineffectual bird. The will to utterance is paramount. Its cause, secondary. Content is always subservient to style.

MILDLING: He was the first Spasmodic poet!

GOLDSTEIN: A Byronic hero.

BARBOUR: Like Pechorin, his acts of bravery always seem TOO desperate ... as if he was motivated by a subliminal craving for self-destruction.

BILLY CAPRI: Tom was always looking for the wild crowd.

PENELOPE HALLEM: Right from an early age. The first thing he did was pull himself upright on the fence to squash a bug. He was always covered in bruises from his early efforts to walk. People used to look at me as if I'd beaten him.

75 **SCRIBBLER:** Link Brutus on naming to illegitimacy. See naming in C6.

76 **NARRATOR:** Sharing heroin from a dirty needle was common practice up to 1985. Many participants were infected with Hepatitis and/or HIV/AIDS as a result. The first recorded case of HIV/AIDS in Australia was in Sydney in October 1982. The first Australian death from AIDS occurred in Melbourne in July 1983. The Bobby Goldsmith Foundation was founded in 1984. It was named in honour of one of Australia's early AIDS victims, who was a successful Gay Olympian. The Foundation had its origins in a network of friends who cared for Bobby Goldsmith, allowing him to live independently until his death in June 1984. In 1985, Eve van Grafhorst was ostracised at school on the NSW Central Coast after contracting HIV/AIDS from infected blood during a transfusion. Her family moved to New Zealand where she died at the age of 11. NSW didn't have an AIDS Council until 1985.

77 **ILKS:** *Coriolanus* is another parody of Tragedy. Its climax is rushed. Aufidius is no Fortinbras, no Malcolm, not even an Antony. The play ends with him mouthing inappropriate platitudes in a parody of denouement.

[Barman changes channel. Slow-motion replay of a photo-finish]

ANNOUNCER

Master jockey Roy Higgins[78] had already won the Cup on Light Fingers and Red Handed in consecutive years. He might have made it three in a row but his mount – short-priced favourite Big Philou – was scratched at the barrier.

LEER

Doped by the bookies.

GRANDPATER

Hit him up with Danthron.[79]

LEER

They would have taken a bath on the Cups Double.[80]

GRANDPATER

Nobbled eight horses that day.

SHAUN

Left nothing to chance.

LEER

Rain Lover won by a long-neck.

GRANDPATER

Mick Robins never found a horse that good again.

---

78 **A BANNER:** *[Rolling text across base of TV screen]* Superstar filly Samantha Miss wins the VRC Oaks to end Melbourne Cup week.

79 **LYNCH:** A powerful laxative. Note syringe link. Also, crime and corruption.

MEILLON: Premier Askin's nickname amongst SP bookies in the 1960s was 'crime' because crime doesn't pay. He was notorious for welching on lost bets.

BURTON: This term was a derogatory reference to Welshmen.

80 **ANNOUNCER:** The Caulfield Cup over 2,400 metres and the Melbourne Cup over 3,200 metres.

BRUCE MCAVENEY

For many punters, he became the Steve Bradbury of racing.

BARBOUR

Sensations replace time in Joyce's teleology.

MILDLING

Mulligan was a true dandy.

STEPHEN DEDALUS

At the House of AEIOU.[81]

GOLDSTEIN

He wore yellow kid gloves like Young Bob Browning.

MILDLING

Also, a dark cloak with a blue velvet collar.

BARBOUR

He hymself as sweete as is the roote of lycorys or any cetewale.[82]

GOLDSTEIN

Browning's submissiveness in matters of the heart is redolent of Leopold Bloote.

MILDING

Not weaned properly.

GOLDSTEIN

Both Joyce and Browning tried to represent the slow and minute progress of life.

BARBOUR

They both erected narrative monuments that seemed calculated to outwit the ingenuity

---

81 RICHARD ELLMANN: This is a clever pun on Joyce's five-quid debt to the writer George William Russell, who wrote under the pseudonym AE.

82 SCRIBBLER: See Chaucer, The Miller's Tale (l.3206–7).

and perseverance of even the most acute reader.

GOLDSTEIN

A hyper-extension of both Romanticism and Realism.

MILDING

Hieratic poeticisms in highly-erratic prosceniums.

FLIGHT-FALCONHURST

Slogans from men's magazines.

O

Leopold Bloom paying out the brothel mistress for a smashed chandelier.

CAPRI

He who desires but acts not, breeds pestilence.

JAMES JOYCE

Unheavenly body. Obscene matter. A fool's cap.[83] Shem the penman.[84]

LEOPOLD BLOOM

No love is true but that from far beneath.[85]

CAPRI

Chidley's code compresses a system of significations into a series of acronyms. His writing is metaphorical not literal. A metonymy of its own signification. A crumpled shirt is seen as a source of synecdoche. Part for the whole. Furrowing of the brow becomes corrugation. It is evidence of self-abuse and moral abasement.[86]

---

83 IBID: Pun on cuckold and paper size. Link to *F(W)ake*.

84 IBID: Phallic naming. In C7 of *F(W)ake*, the dominant brother, Shaun, mocks the weaker sibling, Shem, with a list of traits from Joyce's own life and personality such as blindness, fear of thunderstorms and exile from Ireland. Shem's defence invokes the power of literature to express the human condition.

85 IBID: This is a self-deprecating, polysemous pun on Bloom's buttock worship. Also, his Masoch-like tendency to erotic servitude.

86 IBID: In 'An Encounter,' Joyce's subject desired "real adventures." However, he is waylaid by Chidley on his mini-quest towards the Pigeon House by a masturbating stranger. This causes paralysis because the seed

O

He corrugates the system.

GOLDSTEIN

What did Samuel Beckett say about *Sordello* at the end of *Malone Dies?*

MILDLING

That Sordello had backed his way into the title like Lawrence of Arabia.

BARBOUR

Perched on the footpath with an ivory cane in his Eton suit wearing glass slippers holding Stephen's ash plant while he puked in the gutter.

JAMES JOYCE

A nose in the street.

STEPHEN DEDALUS

Down on my kneecaps prostrate before an altar with my ashrod erect.

JAMES JOYCE

His shadow lay over the rocks.

STEPHEN DEDALUS

[*Purging last contents of his stomach*] Bile and flecks of breakfast in the mode of Cassiopeia.

TOM HALLEM

The green and the gold.

ELIZABETH

Spissfields.

NARRATOR

Mucid wattle.

---

is not used for procreation. Chidley was, in many regards, a refracted Methodist preacher.

ELIZABETH

An emblem of Australia.

ROD MARSH

Under the Southern Cross, I stand.

HENRY LAWSON

Fling out the flag of the Southern Cross![87]

NARRATOR

"Think of it as a memento," said Elizabeth rising. A handkerchief floated to the floorboards.

HENRY LAWSON

Beg not of England the right to preserve ourselves![88]

MÍM/MILKMAID

A dead man's head shifting slightly on the slab.

GUSTAVE FLAUBERT

A rush of black liquid.

JAMES JOYCE

Green rill of bile.

[*Elizabeth in labour*]

M.D. COSTELLO

Her waters have burst.

M.D. LYNCH

Breach delivery, Sister.

---

87 ANNOUNCER: The title refers to the Eureka Flag flown at the Eureka Rebellion in Ballarat, Victoria in 1854.

88 NARRATOR: Lawson's overt racism in the poem is often glossed over.

MÍM/MILKMAID

Arse-first like Saint Peter.

LEON

[Emaciated with AIDS. Placing a hand under his testicles] Kol Nidre!

M.D. LYNCH

[*Presenting a minotaur to the mother*] Twins!

NURSE

[*Tearing a chiton into rags*] Apply them to the wound quickly.

DEIANIRA

Yes, Sister. [*She hands some strips to the attendants including Tom Hallem*] Take some.

TOM HALLEM

You're still hot from the stage lights.

ANA LAFEI

Yes.

TOM HALLEM

Swab your brow.

[*He hands a rag to Ana. She mops her forehead, cheeks and neck*][89]

---

89 **SCRIBBLER:** This is a reference to the shirt of Nessus, which was given to Deianira by the dying centaur. It had been doused in the venom of the Lernaean Hydra, which Heracles used on his arrow tips to kill Nessus. Deianira gave it to Heracles to wear in the mistaken belief it would ensure his faithfulness. He was consumed by burning poison. To extinguish the pain, he built his own funeral pyre and threw himself onto it. In this instance, it is used as a symbol of Tom Hallem poisoning Ana Lafei with a speedball made out of a combination of Willy's heroin and Elizabeth's cocaine, which both possess excessive purity. The lair of the Hydra was the Lake of Lerna in the Argolid, which was a subterranean entrance to the Underworld. It is a direct correspondence with the abandoned St James rail tunnel where Ana will die. After the fix kicks in, she is left thrashing on the ground like Proteus. References to her musical performance create a link with Tom's mother. Insert reference to various Nick Cave victims. He sings "Box for Black Paul" as his encore. This appropriation clearly refers to the future of Tom Hallem (whose death also comes after the 'main show' of the novel).

GERTRUDE

[*Wiping Hamlet's death mask*] Don't hate me, son.

NARRATOR

Insert other fatal mothers.[90]

TOM HALLEM

Could a son hate a mother?

NARRATOR

He asks himself.

DON CANE

My boys!

NARRATOR

Says Don Cane opening his arms for two invisible children to enter.[91]

LEER

A pot of good double beer, Tom. Drink, and fear not![92]

[*Leer fills their glasses from a jug*]

GRANDPATER

Where'd yer get all the cash, Kenneth?

LEER

Randwick trifecta, Gran'pater.[93]

---

90 ILKS: Examples in Classical literature include Niobe, Jocasta, Clytemnestra, Althaea, Medea and Agave who inadvertently tore her own son to pieces.

91 SCRIBBLER: In his reverie, he sees a pair of bronzed twins with golden locks like Greg Wheaton rushing towards him.

92 IBID: Incursion of the false father shifts narrative back towards the plot. Note juxtaposition with Don Cane.

93 LEER: My father was a deeply religious man. Especially when he was out of luck at the pokies.

SHAUN: Bit of a gambler then?

LEER: [*Incredulous*] Bit of a gambler?! Bit of a gambler?! They'd bet on the intervals between the trucks passing in my family. Bet on the length of your toes.

GRANDPATER

How much?

LEER

A full brick.

GRANDPATER

Numbers?[94]

LEER

Seven, four and three in descending order.

GRANDPATER

Not me own lucky ones.

XIAO FANG

How many houses do you own in Australia, Billy?

SHANGHAI DOG

[*Counting on fingers*] One in Sydney.

JACK LANG

A modest brick bungalow.[95]

STAGE DIRECTION: [*Cut to Stratosphere Casino, Las Vegas*]

TEXAS MILIONAIRE: [*Staring across the roulette table*] I'm worth 60 million bucks.

THE BIG FELLA: [*Extracting a silver dollar from his pocket. Laconically*] Toss you for it.

MAX PRESNELL: Packer's most famous attack on bookmakers came during the Autumn Carnival in 1987. He punted $8 million on young speedster Christmas Tree to win the Golden Slipper. It finished fourth. Next, he backed boom three-year-old Myocard for $7 million to win the Sydney Cup at odds of 4/7 ON. It came second; ironically, to a Packer-owned gelding, Major Drive. He was known to remark ruefully that anyone who suggested Sydney races were fixed need only look at that result.

94 **SCRIBBLER:** This is another allusion to Joyce's obsession with numerology.

95 **THE BULLETIN:** (A breeze flicks pages until a cartoon is reached) The Auburn Plute.

SHANGHAI DOG

There's my investment property on the Gold Coast.

BLOOM

Stay at my place tonight.

STEPHEN

No, thanks. I'm going home.

SHANGHAI DOG

And the farm at Bulahdelah.

THE BULLETIN

He counted his fortune by the total number of water closets in his possession.

SHANGHAI DOG

That's ten in total.

MULLIGAN

Give me your key, Kinch.

BLOOM

[*Incredulously*] You're g'ack to your father's place?

STEPHEN

Yes.

BLOOM

[*Patting his shoulder. Wistfully*] You're a good lad really.[96]

[Exeunt Stephen Dedalus. Waitress returns to table]

XIAO FANG

Tell me about your castle, Billy.

---

96 SCRIBBLER: A memory of Rudy, of what he might have become, infests our hero.

SHANGHAI DOG

I can do better than that. I'll show you a picture. [*He scrolls to the Pictures Folder of his Blackberry*] You can see the Sydney Harbour Bridge and the Opera House from the piazza.[97] [*He passes the phone*]

XIAO FANG

[*Laughing, Shocked*] Is that it? But it looks so old! I think a new apartment is much better.

WAITRESS

[*Grabbing handset*] Let me see. [*Chuckling*] Ah! It looks like an old farmhouse.

XIAO FANG

[*Excitedly*] Yes. It looks like my grandfather's farmhouse in Anhui!

SHANGHAI DOG

[*Disgruntled*] That house is worth thirty million kuai.

WAITRESS

That old dump?

XIAO FANG

How much does a new apartment cost in Sydney?

SHANGHAI DOG

Five million.

XIAO FANG

You could sell that old farmhouse and buy six apartments.

WAITRESS

Yes. An apartment on the twentieth level of a new building in Pudong is beautiful.

SHANGHAI DOG

It's got ... charm.

---

97 IBID: Also Fort Denison, the last Martello Tower.

WAITRESS

Charm?! Charm means old dump. Only foreigners like "charm." I wish they would pull down all the charming old buildings in Shanghai and build some tall towers for people. Get rid of all the dirty buildings and alleys. Make the roads wider.

XIAO FANG

Those old buildings remind us of bad times.

WAITRESS

Yes. They depict our century of national humiliation.

TV NARRATOR

The magnificent avenues and villas of the French Concession are now seen as emblems of Foreign Imperialism by the Shanghai City Government.

DOCTOR GU

It all started with your Opium War. The British East India Company forced Chinese people to buy drugs. They got everyone addicted.

[*A street-walker enters the hotel. She tugs on the arm of Jabber's denim jacket*]

CUNTY

Can we go home to bed yet?

JABBER

[*Adjusting his bianzi*] No way. Here. Chug on a pipe, Candy. Chill out. You can go back out later.

DOCTOR GU

The British devils were losing all their silver buying Chinese tea. So, they stole our tea plants. Stuck them up their god-frocks. Smuggled them to India.

MAX WEBER

You wouldn't have the city of Shanghai without British initiative.[98]

---

98 HUANGPU PARK SIGN: Chinese and Dogs Not Admitted.

JAMES JOYCE

Tell me why you think I ought to change the conditions that gave Ireland and me a shape and a destiny?[99]

DOCTOR GU

[*Turning off English language television*] How can you say that? Is that what you told the Aboriginals? Chinese people built Shanghai. Chinese people did all the work. They did all the work inside the buildings as well. You just took the profits. That money was rightfully ours. We would have still built places like Shanghai without you. Look at Shenzhen.

WAITRESS

[*Picking up Billy's tankard*] Would you like another beer ... nongmin tongshi?[100]

SHANGHAI DOG

[*Irritably*] No, thank you.

WAITRESS

You probably like brown wine best.[101]

[*The waitress turns on her heel breezily. Xiao FANG is scanning her phone. Shanghai Dog checks his handset. The television screen plays an advertisement*]

ANNOUNCER: In addition to the derogatory meanings of being called a dog across all cultures, this association had extra potency for Chinese. Han Chinese used the 'dog' radical when describing minorities.

TRANSLATOR: Zou gou.

ANNOUNCER: Now, the tables were turned. Associates of 'foreign devils'—

TRANSLATOR: —Wei guo er mo—

ANNOUNCER: —Were referred to as 'running dogs.'

99 **LUKE GARDINER:** Nelson's Pillar marked the end of an era – of a civilisation – and the culmination of the great period of eighteenth-century Dublin. It was all downhill to Belfast from there.

100 **TRANSLATOR:** *Nongmin* means peasant in Mandarin.

101 **SCRIBBLER:** Peasants brew their own spirits from rice. Many Shanghainese drink brown wine, which is the same strength as sherry but sour.

TRANSLATOR: *Suan.*

SCRIBBLER: Beer is considered a luxury.

BLOOM

[*Holding up a cardboard packet to the screen*] Conversation trouble? Try one of my fast-acting tropes. [*He inserts a golden lozenge into Billy's mouth*] Sweets are for the sweet!

XIAO FANG

My moon cake is full of jelly.[102]

BLOOM

Anytime is the right time for Waddington's sponge!

[*1920s Chinese model in a red qi pao raises an ivory opium pipe to the camera. A Filipino bar band commences sound-check. They start to play "Cocaine" by JJ Cale. Shanghai Dog and Xiao Fang leave the bar*]

HALLEM

Can you fix me up?

LEER

Let's go into my office.

[*Tom follows Leer to the bathroom. Leer stands at the urinal with a smoke in his mouth. He drops his zipper*]

BENNETT'S DISEMBODIED FINGERS

[*Wagging*] You can't stand up here. It's reserved for clergy.

LEER

[*To Tom*] Just ignore them. [*To Fingers*] You don't have any status in here. You don't even constitute a full set.

BENNETT'S DISEMBODIED FINGERS

But I'm a war hero.

---

102 IBID: See B. Smith (sugar, bowl et cetera).

LEER

Rubbish. They fell off.

PRIVATE COMPTON

He doesn't half want a thick ear, the blighter.

PRIVATE CARR

[*To Cissy*] Was he insulting the U.J. whilst we was piddling, Ma'am?

[*Leer tidies his clothing and beckons Hallem into a cubicle. He locks the door and raises the toilet lid to dispose of the cigarette butt. Excrement is suspended on a matrix of toilet paper*][103]

NARRATOR

How do you even do that, asked Tom incredulously.

INVESTIGATIVE JOURNALIST

The Cradle was the unique faecal calling card of an anonymous individual in hotel washrooms across inner Sydney during the New Wave era.

POE

Who painted it nobody knows.

W. Y. TINDALL

[*Closing the lid violently. To an approaching Policeman*] Officer! My wife's bird is under that hat. Can you watch it while I get a cage?

JOYCE

Hey Shitbreeches, are you doing the hat-trick?[104]

---

103 IBID: Symbol of writing as scat (acts). Penelope at her (B)loom. Dropping Bloomers.

104 IBID: A riddle cited by Joyce in which an Irish criminal covers a turd on the pavement with his hat and tricks a policeman into watching it while he escapes. At a metaphorical level, Ireland represents the turd for Joyce. Generally, a 'hat trick' refers to the achievement of a feat three times in succession in sport. Also, the Blessed Trinity. Cited by Stephen in his exchange with Old Gummy Granny.

LEER

The third one is always called “the charm.”

JASON

A golden fleece.

ATHENA

A gold cap.

ULAN

There are numerous descriptions of hats in *Ulysses*.

BLOOM’S CHAPEAU

The style of headwear chosen by a man is a mark of character.

BELLA

A hat is a condom that men pull down over their brains.

BERKELEY

Fashioned from the finest immaterial.

LEER

Clamping cockjaws!

BLOOM’S CHAPEAU

It will always betray the true personality of its owner.

ULAN

Bloom wore a black bowler. Boylan had a light straw boater in contrast.

ILKS

[*Gravely*] There is symbolism in this comparison.

BANTAM LYONS

Bloom’s got a hot tip for the Gold Cup.

ULAN

He was a dark horse like Throwaway.

BOYLAN

I was the front runner against Molly's front. I was beaten by a short half-head.[105] [*He stands at the threshold of 8 Eccles Street. The door opens. He enters. It closes. No occupant is seen. Cut to inside shot of hall. He propels his boater across the room and it lands over a moose antler*] But not before I hanged my hat on Bloom's cuckold horn.

STAGE DIRECTION

A card falls from a leather headband and lands on the floor.

ULAN

Both Joyce and Homer left their texts hanging at closure as if they were planning blockbuster sequels.

[Leer shuts the lid. He flushes the cistern. He opens the lid. The Cradle remains]

LEER

Impressive—

NARRATOR

he says.

HALLEM

Even if we had a stick, it would just create a different kind of problem.

[*Leer closes the lid again. He flushes the toilet again. He opens the lid. The cradle is still present. Leer closes the lid and sits down*]

LEER

[*Laconically*] Must be a sign. Now what do you want?

HALLEM

A score for a friend.

105 IBID: This is a pun on Bloom's size and intellectual prowess.

LEER

Cool. I'm loaded. Got a new supplier at Cabra. But make sure you cut it down. It's hot stuff.[106]

HALLEM

Great. How much?

LEER

Twenty for you.

HALLEM

Can I take it on credit?

LEER

Sure. But I ain't got the product here. You'll have to come back to my place.

HALLEM

How far?

LEER

Down the hill. Fifteen-minute walk.

HALLEM

Fine. When can we leave?

LEER

Now.

[They leave the washroom. A female enters stage right. She moves towards Leer with conviction]

106 IBID: In C10, Tom Hallem does not cut down the smack due to his awkward circumstances in the bathroom at Frenchs. This carelessness precipitates Ana's overdose. Therefore, he bears moral responsibility for her death in terms of tragic emplotment, which necessitates his own death in turn to resolve the plot.

LEER

Ah! If it ain't Sweet Alison![107]

ALISON

[*Slaps his ear*] You said you was coming at four.

LEER

Can only plead damnable pisstness, my love. Come. Sit down on my lap. Let me rub your adorable globes.[108]

ALISON

I'm staying right here, thank you. Get me a Bourbon and Coke.

[*Leer exits to the bar. Tom Hallem grasps his lemman harde by the haunchebones to rage and pleye as hir housbande is away at Osenebar. Thomas seys he'll spille*[109] *withouten. Alison responds with lickerous [e]ye. They cement a bond. Leer returns with a tray of drinks, catches his back foot on frayed carpet and stumbles. Liquid floods the bench*]

ALISON

Yew've spilled it all over me!

TOM HALLEM

A flood! A flood!

[*Leer plants a wet kiss on her cheek*]

LEER

Against her lips I bob and on her withered dewlap pour my ale. Sit down, dear.

107 IBID: See Chaucer, "The Miller's Tale." Joyce got full marks for an essay on "The Good Parson" in Padua (1912). He considered Chaucer's writing to be "as precise and as slick as a Frenchman."

108 IBID: Chaucer parodies the medieval blazon in "The Miller's Tale." This literary device compares a woman's body parts to other objects, such as eyes that glisten like stars. By contrast, Chaucer's analogies for Alisoun are all quite base. Her body is presented as a weasel. She is also depicted as a helpless mouse, a colt and a young chicken. Alisoun is the only character in Chaucer's tale who remains unpunished. She is destined to commit adultery against her older husband. She is thus a prototype for Molly Bloom.

109 IBID: Die.

ALISON

Look at my boob-tube!

LEER

I can't stop looking, believe me. I'll suck on it if you wish.

NEWS READER

The Australian dollar traded weaker today on the back of worse economic news.

LEER

We should never have floated the currency.

GRANDPATER

It was pound for pound before Britain left the Gold Standard.

ALISON

Call themselves Labor. They're worse than bloody Thatcher.

BLOT

Worse than Scullin.

PAUL KEATING

Lang was the only one that stood up to them.[110] He was a hero to working people.[111]

JACK LANG

Lackeys of Niemeyer all.

---

110 NEWSCASTER: *Business Review Weekly* has released the first list of Australia's richest people. The BRW Top 200 has Rupert Murdoch tied in first place with the Fairfax family.

ALISON: The Herald advertising section is called a river of gold.

NEWSCASTER: Kerry Packer is in third place with 250 million dollars followed by the Ingham brothers. The Chicken Kings have a combined fortune in excess of 200 million dollars.

BELLA: He's a regular.

111 JACK LANG: I will introduce a widow's pension and a worker's compensation act.

TV DOCUMENTARY

Australia has never had a violent revolution like America or Russia.[112]

STAN WELLES

The further you move to the Left, the deeper the snout goes down in the trough.

ALISON

Moneygrubber's pushing them.

GRANDPATER

Branded with a hot coulter.[113]

NARRATOR

Nicholas races around the room fanning his burning hind.

JOHN THE CARPENTER

Cut loose the vessels!

BLOT

Is that my signal?

MOTHER BLOT

No, Blot. Not yet.

[*Jack Lang stands on a soapbox in the Domain in the robes of Hamlet Senior*]

JACK LANG

I will reinstate the jobs of the victims of the Great Strike and restore the 44 hour working week.[114]

---

112 CHRIS MASTERS: When Allan Bond purchased QTQ-9 in Brisbane, he immediately settled an outstanding defamation case with Queensland Premier, Joh Bjelke-Petersen, for $400,000.

ALAN BOND: Sir Joh left no doubt in my mind that he expected the matter to be resolved in his favour if we were going to continue doing business in Queensland.

113 SCRIBBLER: This is Absolon's revenge against Alisoun.

114 NEWSCASTER: The cut-off for inclusion was $10 million, which is equal to the total amount of wealth

KEATING[115]

The Big Fella was our political Ned Kelly.

JOHN JOYCE

Your very own Parnell.

JACK LANG

This depression is the work of bankers and industrialists.

MENZIES

It would be better for Australia to die of starvation than repudiate British debts.[116]

HAINES

[*Holding a saucer*] The problem lies with the Australian character. [*Turning to an old scullery maid. Presenting his tea cup. Loudly*] Ba mhaith liom bainne.[117]

MOTHER GROGAN

[*To Haines*] Are you some kind of wog?[118]

---

of 357 ordinary Australians.

JOHN CURTIN: (To the assembled press after emerging from a private meeting with General McArthur in August 1942) After this war is finished, we will ensure the Capitalist wolf will not be able to feed on the lambs in the factories and workshops as it has done for the last fifty years in this country.

115 SCRIBBLER: Hamlet in this trope.

116 MENZIES: I did but see her, stirrups high.

CITIZEN: English lickspittle.

SCRIBBLER: The ballad quoted by Menzies was composed by Thomas Ford in 1608.

ALBERT THE GOOD: The squawking infant was plucked from his mother's sky-turned womb.

TRANSLATOR: Mutters Himmel verwandelte Gebärmutter.

117 IBID: I would like a glass of milk, Mother Grogan.

118 GRAN[DP]ATER: Téigh trasna ort féin. Cross over yourself.

CITIZEN: Díul mó bhad. Suck my boat.

GRAN[DP]ATER: Feisigh do thoin fein! Fuck your own arse.

GEOFFREY BLAINEY: Australia's religious tolerance is epitomised by its Prime Ministers. There have been four Anglicans, six Presbyterians, four Catholics, two Methodists, one Baptist, a Unitarian, one Spiritualist and

BLOOM

[*Speaking in tongues*][119] Aleph Beth Ghimel Daleth Hagadah Tephilim Kosher Yom Kippur Hanukah Roschaschana Beni Brith Mitzvah Mazzoth Askenazim Meshuggah Talith.[120]

MOLLY BLOOM

Where'd you learn that? Off a soap label?

JAMES JOYCE

It's an ancient charm.

BLOOM

[*Opening a large paper bag of confectionery for the assembled characters*] Here. Suck on this ju-jube. It'll fix you.

JAMES JOYCE

[*Taking a selection of sweets*] Dog red, Davitt orange and snot green jellies.

GRANDPATER

We should have learned Ireland's harsh lesson.[121]

JACK LANG

The same capitalists who wasted our sons at Fromelles now demand "bank blood."

---

four who professed no religion at all.

CITIZEN: [*Disgustedly*] Not a Fenian amongst them.

[*He throws a Molotov cocktail then runs from the scene*]

119 SCRIBBLER: Hungarian, Yiddish. There are more than two hundred references to Judaism in *Ulysses*. Jewish tropes are arguably more important than Classical ones in the novel.

120 TRANSLATOR (Morton P Levitt): "This idiosyncratic combination—of letters of the alphabet, religious holidays and practices, fraternal orders, dietary customs and cultural groupings, pejorative slang, misspellings and mispronunciations—seems all of the Yiddishkeit that Bloom has managed to retain in his life among the Gentiles. It is, in his own word, just a bit crazy (*meshuggah*)."

121 SCRIBBLER: Integrate Irish and Australian-Irish historical figures. Revitalise Irish links with Australian culture. Reject all British tropes. Destroy masonry.

PADRAIG PEARSE

You'll get nowhere negotiating with the English. You need to apply Physical Force.[122]

NED KELLY

[*Dictating to Joe Byrne*][123] All of true blood, bone and beauty that was not murdered on their own soil, or had fled to America or other countries, were doomed to Port Macquarie, Toongabbie, Norfolk Island and Emu Plains, and in those places of tyranny and condemnation, many a blooming Irishman, rather than subdue to Saxon yoke, was flogged to death and bravely died in servile chains, true to the shamrock and a credit to Paddy's Land.

MANNIX

It is less than a decade since Australian Catholics stood fast while their brothers in Ireland were crushed by the British army.

DAVITT

Tear up the New Departure!

PARNELL

Two Land Bills defeated. Constitutional means have failed.

NED KELLY

Fitzpatrick will cause greater slaughter to the Union Jack than Saint Patrick did to the snakes and toads of Ireland.

YEATS

Learn your own language. Start a mass movement. Establish a national press. Rediscover Ossian poetry. I believe your name should be O'Malley.

DR JOHNSON

Gaelic is the rude speech of a barbarous people.

---

122 IBID: A working knowledge of Irish politics is essential to understanding Ulysses.

123 MAX BROWN: This letter was drafted some time before the Kelly Gang's raid on Jerilderie in February 1879.

DONALD HORNE

Australians are anonymous, featureless, nothing-men.

A.A. PHILLIPS

Cultural cringe is a disease of the Australian mind.

A.D. HOPE

Without songs, architecture, history.

JOSEPH FURPHY

Know me hereafter as Seosamh Ó Foirbhilhe.

MILKMAID

Our Laurence Sterne in Shepparton.

A.A. PHILLIPS

Confronted by Furphy, Australians grow uncertain. We fail to comprehend the original structure of his great novel.[124]

NED KELLY

What would England do if America declared war, as it is all Irishmen that has got command of her armies. Even her beef tasters are Irish.

JOHCU[125]

We feel therefore in view of services the A.I.F. have rendered in the Middle East that we have every right to expect them to be returned as soon as possible to the defence of Australia.

ROOSEVELT

The fall of Burma would place Australia in extreme peril.

---

124 SCRIBBLER: Insert self-reference. I had a good story, I knew it, but I had to take risks to try to get to the next level.

125 CITIZEN: John Curtin was a jailbird, a drunk, a coward and a lapsed Catholic. But, for all that, he was still a loyal Irishman.

CHURCHILL

India is under threat. The Australian convoy will be diverted to Burma. I will inform the Australian Prime Minister.

JOHCU

In view of superior Japanese sea and air power it is a matter of some doubt as to whether this division can even be landed in Burma.

STEPHEN DEDALUS

[*Nervous, friendly, pulling himself from the gutter, his mouth bleeding*] I understand your point-of-view. You die for your country. I die for your cuntery. Let my country die too.

BRITISH GOVERNOR, BURMA

The Australians would have died in useless defence at Rangoon.

PRIVATE CARR

I'll wring the neck of any fucker says a word against my king.

BLOOM

We fought for you in South Africa. Irish missile troops. Royal Dublin Fusiliers. Honoured by your monarch. Does that count for nothing?

CHURCHILL

While I was breaking out of a Boer prison camp, Curtin was making anti-war diatribes in Melbourne.

NED KELLY

Would they fight her for the sake of the colour they dare not wear (GREEN) and to reinstate it and raise old Erins isle once more from the tyrannism of the English yoke, which has kept it in poverty and starvation and caused them to wear the enemy's coat (RED/WHITE)?

JOHCU

[*Radio broadcast*] Without any inhibitions of any kind, I make it quite clear that Australia looks to America, free of any pangs as to our traditional links or kinship with the United Kingdom.

CHURCHILL

Melodrama by design.

ROOSEVELT

Smacks of panic.

CHURCHILL

Mummery even.

BOB HAWKE

[*Cut to television*] We have eliminated much of the confrontation and bitterness that was tearing Australia apart just 20 months ago.

ALISON

He is presiding over the death of the trade union movement.[126]

BLOT

Kelty is selling-out historic worker's rights.

MOTHER BLOT

Hawke was their creation.

BARBOUR

Frankenstein's monster.

ALISON

Enough of his calumny. I'm going to the loo.

[*Bloom follows her expectantly. He is transformed into a female*]

MÍM/MILKMAID

[*Seated on a three-legged stool*] Deformitisation. Spina bifida births. Heracles' brood as beastly murk. Ophelia face-down in swampaste. Desdemona's moist pillowspit. Young

---

126 JIM MIDDLETON: In 2008, union membership dropped beneath 20% of the workforce. Back in the 1980s, it was over 40 per cent.

Edward betrothed to a foetus. Rough wooing.

FOOTMAN

Prince William Duke of Gloucester.[127]

DR MOREAU

How does he fair on Hakim's triad?

FRANKENSTEIN

Poorly. We must pierce the head and draw off fluid.

M.D. COSTELLO

An acute case of Hydrocephalus.

[*A helicopter passes overhead*]

BELLA

Flim-flum-flum-flum-flum-flum-flum.[128]

CHOC

[*Excitedly*] Incoming!

DON CANE

Must be a dust-off up.

M.D. LYNCH

[*A buzzer reverberates in his white medical coat. He speaks earnestly*] Emergency ward.

M.D. COSTELLO

Another crashpara?

---

127 NARRATOR: Edward the Seventh appears in an archway holding a slops bucket, according to Joyce. A roar of acclamation greets him.

128 SCRIBBLER: Seven times like Rachel.

DON CANE

[*Completing forms*] North-west of Quang Ngai. Half an hour into flight. A loud bang rocked the fuselage. The helicopter started auto-rotating. We hit the ground hard. It was a dry paddy about the size of a football field. There was a village surrounded by tall bamboo about 500 metres off. We knew it was a Viet Minh stronghold. Shots snapped over our heads. Two columns of troops rushed towards us. I had a pistol but I was still out of range. Choc ripped a machine gun out of its socket on the Huey and let rip. The first burst took out the grass roof of the temple. I held it down with my body while Choc directed fire on the enemy. Hot grease spattered our skin. The noise was deafening.

RICHIE

Did you kill men?

DON CANE

Probably eight or ten that day alone.

RICHIE

[*Taking hold of his palms*] But they seem so harmless.

DON CANE

[*Laughing*] What did you expect? Claws?

RICHIE

[*Stroking them*] Harsher skin. A chill touch. [*She looks at him*] And later?

ODYSSEUS

I fought in Troy for ten years. You couldn't help but kill men. We did it at close range and long range. We directed artillery right on top of us. Called in air support. Laid mines. It was war.

JAMES JOYCE

I've put enough booby traps in *Ulysses* to keep academics busy for 3,000 years.

NARRATOR

By what faculty am I able to transmit these facts and figures?[129]

MÍM/MILKMAID

Strange power of prophecy.

JAMES JOYCE

Narrative invention.

CHURCHILL

Enigma machine.

TELEVISION SET

Cut transmission.

SHANGHAI DOG

There must be a guy in Beijing who hears the words "unrest in China" and pulls a great big bloody plug out of the wall.

EXIT THE DARK TOWER

LEER

[*Suddenly*] I'm sick of this shit. I'm off. [*To Hallem*] You coming?

HALLEM

What about Alison?

LEER

She can find her own way home.

HALLEM

I've got an exhibition opening later tonight.

129 IBID: When Dante went to the Underworld, he took Virgil on a leash to explain its mysteries.

LEER

When?

HALLEM

Seven o'clock.

LEER

Plenty of time. Do you want that fix for your girlfriend or not? Come on. We'll have some fun on the way. Don't worry. It's all on my tab.

[*Leer and Hallem depart the Shakespeare Hotel. Dinnertime carcrawl. Unctuous art deco signage of the Marlborough Hotel. Beta House ahead like a squat brick pillbox. Hallem dimly perceives an old couple huddled against the breeze down a dunny cart lane. A stooped male comes to a halt. A female figure shuffles beside him. Shanghai Dog and Xiao Fang leave Time Passage Bar. They enter Xing Guo Lu. The trees have been pruned bare. Everything is grey. They proceed alongside the high brick wall of the Radisson Hotel. Shanghai Dog pulls Xiao FANG under his arm. A passing pedestrian hisses softly*]

SHANGHAI DOG

Did you hear that?

XIAO FANG

Yes.

SHANGHAI DOG

What did she say?

XIAO FANG

It doesn't matter.

SHANGHAI DOG

Does it bother you?

[*They approach the compound. Two guards are talking to local residents at the gate. Xiao Fang lets go of Billy's arm. The guards greet him. Her gaze remains fixed on the ground. They proceed onto the grounds*]

XIAO FANG

It would be better to arrive in the car park in a taxi.

SHANGHAI DOG

Why?

XIAO FANG

They hate me. I'm a xiaojie.

SHANGHAI DOG

Forget them. Let's get inside.

XIAO FANG

You don't understand.

A VISION OF THE THRONE OF GOD AND OF THE LAMB

[*Leer scampers across King Street between stubborn vehicles. He lunges into a shop. Hallem leans against a light pole. He looks into Beta House. His former apartment space is dim. Light leaks from the upmost floors. The garage door has buckled. A temporary barricade has been erected over an exposed section. Leer returns with fresh cigarettes. Missus Brennan appears at the door and waves. They proceed between horizontal bars of a steel-piping fence. Hallem steps aside a headless bird crunched flat against laneway asphalt. Its grey feathers are scattered in a bloody plume. A lone cat is huddled against a telegraph pole in a soft round lump. Its head rears sleepily and drops back into fine warm fur. Leer pushes a swollen wooden gate. They enter a backyard. Both sides of its broken concrete path are smattered with debris. A cement staircase leads to a red door illuminated by a single red light. They rise. Leer knocks. It opens. They pass along a corridor lit by spirit lamps. The back of a female wearing veils evaporates before them. Their bodies cast discordant rainbows on the plush velvet wallpaper.*]

NARRATOR

Mabbot Street is the entrance to Nighttown. Stephen and Lynch stagger in drunk.[130] They are mocked by locals. Bloom follows obediescently. Events and characters stimulate his guilt.[131] The text becomes the scene of visions. Bloom speaks with a street worker, Zoe Higgins, who knows Stephen's location. She stimulates scenes of an imaginary legal triumph.[132] Bloom becomes an exemplar of the "new womanly man," gives birth, and is denounced as a charlatan and whore in this episode. He finds Stephen in the music room of the bordello carousing. He thinks about past lovers. In a discussion on theology, Stephen metamorphoses into a Cardinal. Bella Cohen appears. She and Bloom reverse gender. Ritual sado-masochistic humiliations ensue. Stephen, in his drunkenness, tries to settle the bill. Bloom ensures he isn't cheated. The ghost of Stephen's mother appears. He breaks a chandelier, and they end up thrown onto the street. A fight with some English soldiers leaves Stephen prone on the pavement. The police appear. Corny Kelleher and Bloom smooth things over. Bloom persists in trying to take Stephen home. He gazes at the unconscious Stephen and experiences a vision of his dead son Rudy.[133] END

WILL THE CIRC(L)E BE UNBROKEN?

[*A spotlight smashes the floor. A human form enters. Its identity is concealed by two enormous Japanese fans. Brilliant sequins tap sensual flecks of Morse on the hem of an evening gown*]

THE FANS

Say the password and you shall see our treasures, Aladdin.[134]

---

130 IBID: Circle back to the maw image at start of chapter.

131 **EDGAR:** Keep thy foot out of brothels.

132 **SCRIBBLER:** In his fantasy, Bloom is arrested for public nuisance. He stands trial in a Surrealist court that resembles the high farce of "Toad of Toad Hall." His identity constantly changes as characters from his past and personifications of his perverse desires appear to give evidence against him.

133 IBID: Reciprocal feelings of paternity from Stephen Dedalus to Bloom are NEVER made clear.

134 IBID: An hour is not just an hour, according to Proust. It is a lamp or vase filled with perfumes, sounds, designs and climates. The sections of this chapter have been drafted and timed to consume exactly one hour each of real time. When Marcel comments to Jupien in *DTP* that he feels like he has just witnessed a scene from the *Arabian Nights*, Jupien replies that he cannot furnish a full set of forty thieves for Marcel's pleasure but he can collect ten vagabonds almost immediately. Marcel just needs to check that the light in Jupien's window is illuminated. That is his signal; a kind of 'open sesame.'

LEER

[*Aggressively*] I must find out what's behind the veil.

FAN

[*Withdrawing*] Not yet – soon – but no – wait. Patience, dear.

LEER

[*Pulling the fans open*] You!

MEILLON

Ftt-fit-fitt-fatt-fa-fa-FATHER!

BELLA

My word! I'm all of a mucksweat.

[*Her eyes rest on Leer*]

LEER

Look!

[*He discloses a wad of bank notes. Coins cascade to the floor*]

THE FAN

[*Flirting*] Married, I see.

BLOOM, SHANGHAI DOG, LEER

No. Not Yet. Yes. No longer. Partly ...

LEER

[*Cowed*] Exuberant female. Enormously I desire your services. I am exhausted, abandoned, no more young, mashing syntax and grammar,[135] inserting blandishments, also making insipid pig metaphors and blunt references to my hat and umbrella as phallic icons, which is all hubris, I am consumed with insecurities, lastly remembering my father and sons.

135 IBID: Links TMAC with Joyce's Circe. This is the literary equivalent of the subsequent sexual act of Leer and Tom.

BELLA

One hundred for an hour. Extra fifty for Greek.

LEER

We'll have the works!

[*Leer extracts three hundred dollars and hands it to the brothel manager*]

BELLA

You had some luck today.

LEER

Miracle in Melbourne, they call it. A Black Knight tupped your white Chagemar.[136]

BELLA

What did it pay?

LEER

Enough, Psychopomps. Enough.

BLOOM

[*Reaching for the cash*] Let me count it out for you. I will save it. Let me store it here in my pocket with a cake of lemon-scented soap for Molly.[137]

BELLA

After you, gentleman. [*Taking Hallem by the elbow*] I've got new girls and boys.[138]

[*Bella and Tom proceed along the passage together. Leer wanders behind them. He peels a silver strip of gum and commences chewing. Shanghai Dog and Xiao Fang proceed into his apartment. A bank of LEDs illuminates his lounge room madly. Xiao Fang kisses him aggressively*]

---

136 IBID: Both horses were geldings.

137 IBID: In *Ulysses*, Bloom intervenes to protect Stephen's salary.

138 IBID: The evil nature of Mabbott Street is reinforced by the repeated offer of sex with a virgin to passing males by Last Card Louie.

XIAO FANG

Have you forgotten me yet?

SHANGHAI DOG

No.

[*He looks at their bodies in a mirror. She pulls back a fan from her face to reveal Judy*]

XIAO FANG

Make love with me.

SHANGHAI DOG

[*Withdrawing*] Not like this.

XIAO FANG

Yes, like this.

SHANGHAI DOG

I can't.

XIAO FANG

Then you don't really want me anymore.[139]

COURTING RITUALS IN THE TIME OF QUEEN ELIZABETH

[*Leer and Hallem are escorted to the dock. Three prostitutes are slumped across a dirty velvet sofa. An incense burner on the mantelpiece produces the scent of heliotrope and citron. They rise on black stilettos adjusting loose lingerie*]

LEER

Good evening ladies.

---

139 NARRATOR: She says, turning towards the door.

BELLA

Do you remember Baron de Charlus, girls?

CANDY, SOLANGE, BIDDY THE CLAP

Yes. Greetings, my Lord!

LEER

This is my cousin Keith, ladies. Keith, this is Miss Candy. Mistress Clap. And Miss Solange.

[*They pull Tom Hallem onto the settee*]

BELLA

I'll get some drinks.

[*She draws Leer aside*]

CANDY

[*To Tom Hallem*] Did you see his eye? He looked upon you to lust after you.

SOLANGE

O, Kinch, thou art in peril.

BIDDY THE CLAP

Get thee a breechpad.

[*Cut to Bella and Leer*]

OF MATTERS DIONYSIAN

BELLA

What's your pleasure?

LEER

Threesome.

BELLA

For yourself?

LEER

No. One girl, me and the lad.

BELLA

No boys?

LEER

Not tonight. I've got him.[140]

BELLA

Suit yourself. Price is the same. [*She raises her voice*] Excuse me, gentlemen. Ladies, a word.

[*She draws the women together and opens her fans*]

BELLA

Who's up for a three-way?

NARRATOR

Not I, said Solange. She exits. Biddy indicates weariness.

CANDY

Depends.

[*She runs her fingers through peroxide hair. Some brittle ends snap adhering to her fingers. She shakes them to the floor awkwardly*]

BELLA

[*Gesturing at Leer*] Well, we both know he's tiny.

---

140 NARRATOR: He gestures with his thumb.

SCRIBBLER: Marcel noted that all the young men selected by Charlus looked like Morel.

CANDY

But what about his mate?

BELLA

Doesn't look like a monster.

CANDY

I'll do it for a ton.

BELLA

Thanks love.

[*Bella grasps Peroxide Girl's forearm. She feels a trail of old scars and scabs. They return. Bella whispers to Leer. He nods. All rise.*]

ODE TO A NIGHTINGALE

[*They walk down a long hall. Bella opens the door to Room Seven. They enter*][141]

LEER

[*To Tom*] Your turn. Hop up on the operating table.

THE CISTERN CONTAINS

LEER

Lie down on your back. [*To Candy*] You ride.

[*Candy takes a blast of amyl nitrate from a hazel vial then straddles Tom Hallem. Leer gets up on the bench. He penetrates as well*]

---

141 **NARRATOR:** The room contains rudimentary furniture and fittings indicating that it is meant to represent a doctor's surgery. They all undress. The prostitute handles the men. She performs oral sex. Leer makes eye-contact with Tom. She is instructed to lie down on the examination table. Leer engages in perfunctory intercourse. Tom Hallem stands alongside the bench. She handles his erection harshly. It induces an involuntary memory of having his penis jerked unevenly by XXXXX behind the garage at Burwood. This makes him hard. He licks at the roof of his mouth. His throat feels dry suddenly.

CANDY

Slow down.

[*She gasps. Leer ignores her*][142]

LEER

[*Looking straight down on Tom Hallem's face*] Can you feel me?

TOM

[*Gulping*] Yes.[143]

---

142 IBID: Both men are highly aroused.

143 SCRIBBLER: Joyce blurs content in Circe. This was one of his rare concessions to the risk of censorship. This passage contains a sequence of analogies with Bloom. Bella leads Tom to a stockade. Three Nubians appear. They shackle him roughly. Bella slowly turns the handle of a winch. Hallem rises on birthing stirrups. His torso is split. He is prone. She straps an enormous black dildo over a black latex body suit and approaches Tom.

BELLA: No gag.

COMPTON: Make a bleeding butcher's shop of the bugger's arsehole.

NARRATOR: Tom turns his head away. In another part of the dungeon, a young Moroccan is standing in front of the so-called 'man in chains' revolving a nail-studded whip with increasing velocity. The proprietor whispers salaciously to the supplicant.

JUPIEN: He's a milkman but he's also one of the most dangerous thugs in Belleville. He had several convictions for theft and burglary. He's been in a punishment battalion Africa. He murdered an African on the beach. He even killed his own parade sergeant.

MAJOR TWEEDY: [*Gruffly*] Up and anatem! Mahar shalal hashbaz.

[*Bella thrusts the bienfaiteur into Tom's mouth. Bile pours out of his nostrils. An attendant flays his thighs. Another attaches jump cables to his nipples. The third applies a vice to his scrotum. Suddenly, he recognises them as the Attic youths at the start of C2*]

NARRATOR: "Look at me," Bella demands softly. Tom does. With terror in his eyes, he sees Leer. He presses into Tom and lowers his head towards Tom's mouth.

PRIVATE CARR: [*Advances at Stephen*] How would it be, governor, if I was to bash in your jawbone?

BLOOM: [*Plucking Stephen's sleeve vigorously*] Come now. That carman is waiting. Let's scarpaflow.

STEPHEN: [*Turns*] Eh? [*He disembogues himself*] Why should I not speak to any human being who walks upright upon this stage?

BELLA: [*Unzipping the suit to reveal a thick body*] Do you like what you see?

HALLEM: Yes.

BELLA: Gaze on my gut.

THE FOUNTAIN OVERFLOWS

LEER

[*Grunting*] Together.

[*Leer presses Candy harder. She squeezes Tom's nipples. Leer ejaculates loudly. Tom makes no sound. Leer withdraws rapidly. He rips off the condom. A long ribbon of sperm laces Tom's thigh. Cunty dismounts. Tom Hallem rolls into a foetal position*]

LANCE HORNER

Missy lay on her side burning and murmuring with pride.

[*Cut to a car passing under the gateway to the Westside Motel in Ashfield. It parks in front of the rooms. A woman emerges. She walks towards a ground floor door which is slightly ajar*]

PENELOPE HALLEM

Sorry I'm late.

DICK STONE

[*Propped against the bedhead. Naked. Legs splayed*] No problem.

PENELOPE HALLEM

I've been playing catch-up at work all day after I took my son home.

DICK

How is he?

BOOT: Your tongue, slave.

OTHER BOOT (WHITE): Lick it clean, Pig.

BELLA: Taste.

[*She transforms into Elizabeth Archer. He is dressed as Severin*]

HALLEM: I am your servant.

JOYCE: [*Composing a letter in a café while he drinks a glass of wine*] I wish you would smack me or flog me even, Nora. Not in play, dear, in earnest and on my naked flesh. I wish you were strong, strong, dear, and had a big full proud bosom and big fat thighs. I would love to be whipped by you, Nora love. This is a transcription from ACTUAL correspondence.

PENELOPE HALLEM

Useless as ever.

TELEMACHUS

What chance did I have?

DICK STONE

How was the function?

PENELOPE HALLEM

I got a couple of fresh leads.

MENELAUS

A coward is always eager to sleep in a brave man's bed.

TELEMACHUS

The goods of my father's house were being consumed by the suitors. Our palace was full of enemies. The farmlands ruined.

SERVIUS

It was said that Penelope copulated with all one-hundred-and-eight suitors then gave birth to the great God Pan.

NARRATOR

In *Time Regained*, the participants in Charlus' orgy conduct a casual, good-natured post-mortem. This prolongs the sexual fantasies of the victims. It also enables the boys to earn extra fees.

BELLA

Stay.

TOM

I'm cold.

BELLA

Put this on.

[*Bella gives him the bloodstained gown of Hydra. It tightens over his shoulders, tearing his skin away and exposing bare bones*]

LEER

Time to leave.

BELLA

[*Romantically*] It doesn't have to end like this.

LEER

How do you want it to end?

ELIZABETH

Logically.

BELLA

Profitably.

ELIZABETH

Yes. Both!

MÍM/MILKMAID

The hero can't control the myth.

BARBOUR

That is the logic of all Classical tropes.

LEER

[*Drunkenly. Hugging Bella*] Let's part as friends.

[*Tom Hallem rolls onto his back and stares at a pallid light bulb dangling from the ceiling. Leer staggers towards the door. A child skips gaily down the hallway of a stark Modernist apartment. She vaults over the prone form of HH-1970. Sandals click on polished concrete as she regains her lope. Tom Hallem reaches towards the aquarium wall. He presses his mouth against the glass to yell a single two-syllable word. The girl approaches the tank inquisitively, presses her own lips against the glass then withdraws, turns and runs away*]

BLOOM

[*Bringing his mouth near an unmoving face*] Rudy!

LEON DANIEL

Chaim!

DON CANE

Robert!

TOM HALLEM

Father! [*Despairing*] A name you call.

JAMES JOYCE

My father was an original fellow with a grand wit and voice who gifted to me an ineffable quality which is really the source of what talent I have.[144]

STANISLAUS JOYCE

I was always perplexed by Jim's loyalty.

A LETTER

[*In Joyce's hand-writing*] "I feel that a poor heart which was true and faithful to me is no more."

[*T.S. Eliot lays down the paper on his desk, removes his spectacles, wipes his eyes and winces*]

STANISLAUS JOYCE

Justice towards the characters of his own creation became an artistic principle of my brother.

LEOPOLD BLOOM

Wore out his wife, now sings.

---

144 SCRIBBLER: See C6 & C10 for further analysis of father-son relations re-Joyce.

STANLISLAUS JOYCE

He made a vague attempt to strangle our mother.

JOHN JOYCE

Her grave is over there, Jack.

JAMES JOYCE

Mary Dedalus fixes her son with bluecircircled eyesockettes and opens a toothless mouth to utter a silent word.[145]

MARY DEDALUS

I am dead.

STANISLAUS JOYCE

Pappie has been drunk the last three days. I am sick of it, sick of it.

DILLY DEDALUS

Give it up, father.

NARRATOR

Circe ends in a parody of knightly combat.[146]

ULAN

The quarrel with the British soldiers, Carr and Compton, is the low point of Circe. Stephen's erudition seems utterly pretentious in this exchange.

JAMES JOYCE

[*Writing in margin of galley proof*] REPRISE IDIOTS, CHILDREN, PISSING

145 NARRATOR: We are never told the identity of this word. It was probably "son" or "pray." Her maiden name was May Goulding. Everyone knelt around her deathbed reciting the *Liliata* except Stephen. Go back to Meillon, C2. In *PAYM*, she was an active agent. She died in the gap between novels. By *Ulysses*, she is a moth decomposing into dry fibres against religion's stark electric globe. Stephen refers to her melodramatically as "lemur," which means 'spirit of the dead.' He asks who promulgated this 'trick'? There is a clear reference with gender inversion to Hamlet in this apparition.

146 IBID: Loop back to ballad competition earlier in C7.

WHORES, BROKEN-DOWN DRUNKS, MORE SURREAL FIGURES.[147]

[*A flash of smoke. They are gone. Tom Hallem has been deposited on King Street. Leer is kneeling on his haunches*]

CONSTABLE RAFTOS

[*To Tom Hallem*] Your mate there looks a little skew-whiff.

HALLEM

He had a big win on the Cup, officer. He's had a few too many ales. Doesn't know what he's saying. Complete wanker when he's drunk, actually. I'll take him home. I know his family. Very well-respected around town. [148]

---

147 STAGE DIRECTION: [*Ken Leer hobbles down King Street on an artificial leg. Don Cane's skull appears in the window of the Milton Hotel. It sits neatly inside the reflection of Tom Hallem's distorted head. The bar is populated by sailors. Leer slumps to the pavement*]

~~**TV COMEDIAN 2:** [*Popular Irish host of BBC comedy series. He is dressed as a barmaid. A cigarette dangles from the corner of his mouth. A plaster bust of Shakespeare is fastened to the shoulder of his Elizabethan cloak, which reaches down to his gyrdlestead. He starts giggling a he speaks*] It's so nice to have the Old Watering Hole full of seamen again.~~

~~**TV COMEDIAN 1:** [*Dropping out of character*] Who wrote this rubbish?~~

~~**TV COMEDIAN 2:** [*Also dropping out of character*] You did. In fact, you said it was a comic masterpiece.~~

~~**TV COMEDIAN 1:** Well, it looked good as text. Was it cleared by the Vatican?~~

~~[*Canned laughter*]~~

~~**TV COMEDIAN 2:** Yes.~~

~~**TV COMEDIAN 1:** How long does this scene go on?~~

~~**TV COMEDIAN 2:** Oh, about 8 inches ... [*Canned laughter*] as the priest said to the nun! [*Delirious canned laughter with scattered applause at this trademark punchline. He drops out of character again. Male voice*] I got you that time. [*Spontaneous audience laughter. Both actors break up. Hiatus. They resume role. Affecting a female voice*] Oh Father O'Fartagan! You're a live one to be sure.~~

~~**TV COMEDIAN 1:** [*Breaking wind*] Ooops! [*Canned laughter. He breaks wind again*]~~

~~**TV COMEDIAN 2:** Father! Manners!~~

~~**TV COMEDIAN 1:** Well, you know the story, Sister Cuntworthy. Fartagan by name. Fart again by nature! [*Canned groans. Some laughter. Mild applause*]~~

148 GOLDSTEIN: This is another example of Joyce's use of misunderstanding or mishearing as a plot device. The British soldiers believe that Stephen has threatened to assassinate King Edward the Seventh. This technique has already been used in the famous Throwaway scene between Lyons and Bloom.

CONSTABLE RAFTOS

I don't give a fuck who he is.

PRIVATE COMPTON

Stick one in his knackers, Jemmy.

CONSTABLE RAFTOS

Can't be assed. [*To Tom*] You pick him up and get him home.

HALLEM

I will, sir. Come on, Ernie. [*Raising Leer*]

BLOOM

[*To Stephen*] Come home with me, lad. You'll get into trouble out here on your own.[149]

---

149 ULAN: We have now reached the climactic point in *Ulysses* when Leopold Bloom offers to take Stephen Dedalus back to his home. It takes place in the midst of a wide-ranging hallucinatory narrative involving BIDDY THE CLAP, VIRAGO, THE BAWD, A ROUGH, THE CITIZEN, CROPPY BOY, RUMBOLD (DEMON BARBER) & EDWARD THE EIGHTH. This is a typical example of Joyce hiding a climax in irrelevant content.

MCCREEDY: He sucks you in with the first episodes. It's fairly mediocre story-telling up to Chapter 6. After that, it's almost unreadable.

O: It is still a work of art.

BARBOUR: Much of it highly polished.

MILDLING: Yet it feels like a first draft.

SCHRIBBLER: INSERT QUOTE FROM YEATS.

JOHN B. YEATS: I think every work of art should survive after all the labour bestowed on it and survive as a sketch. To the last it must be something struck off at a first heat.

ILKS: You can see the writer constantly processing his critical knowledge throughout the work.

HAHAHA! DAMN STRAIGHT! :)

JESS: [*Typing at a keyboard*] Now that the corrected text is locked into In-Design you must delete one word for every word you add.

O: [*Older*] With Proust and Joyce, it is more satisfying to read **about** their books than to read the books themselves.

BARD-UN: Once a work-in-progress is finished, it becomes a true FORM. Then you think about it differently. You no longer fret over individual sentences. You talk about it in TOTAL terms.

EMILIO FERRER: This book was inevitable. It was inevitable that one day someone would show that the true point of interest in the *Odyssey* is not the actions of the father but the trauma of the abandoned son. And it was inevitable you would be the one to write it.

[*Leer and Hallem hurry along King Street*]

NARRATOR

The use of dramatic form in the "Circe" episode can be explained in part by Joyce's humanism. He always wanted to render HUMAN BEINGS sympathetically through proximity to speech as a material record. This gave average lives power. Drama is the best mode for this task. It creates a reality TV show. But there are some things you can't depict in a play such as Molly's physicality in Ithaca, which would have reduced any script to slapstick. It appears that Joyce had already written parts of Circe separate to the rest of *Ulysses* by 1916. He wrote *Exiles* just before commencing the novel. He continued trying to become a popular dramatist up to the time when *Ulysses* made him famous. The entrance to

---

O: It reflects the switch in postmodern psychiatry to examining the impact of the absent father.

JAMES HERZOG: Call it 'Father-hunger.'

JUNG: *Senex and puer aeternus.*

BARD-UN: The son must transcend the journey of the father.

FREUD: In the case of Schreber, the Rat-Man, we find ourselves once again on the familiar ground of the father-complex.

LACAN: Le nom du père, le non du père, les non-dupes errant.

O: Lacan parodies the Trinity. The name of the father represents GOD. The 'NO' of the father is our damnation for sin, which was countervailed by Jesus.

BARBOUR: The *Odyssey* is one of the rare occasions in literary history when minor characters get to step forward.

RANAJIT GUHA: We can only reconstruct subaltern consciousness from the administrative records of the colonial master class.

BARBOUR: The *Iliad* represented the last stand of masculine group 'heroics.' The *Odyssey* shows the repercussions of war on the last hero.

O: The *Odyssey* was the first psychological drama. Telemachus is its subject. Odysseus is a simpleton in comparison.

BARBOUR: Penelope shows him up using the tool of dream interpretation. This was Freud's template. He has become a monomaniac.

MILKMAID: Hamlet is a paralysed version of Telemachus.

BARBOUR: Because his father did not fully return. Only an apparition. He had no certainty.

ULAN: The other difference in Shakespeare is his mother married one of the suitors. That really fucked with his head.

BARD-UN: This must all be handled inside footnotes. It cannot be allowed to penetrate the pages of the REAL.

Nighttown evokes the slice-of-life sets of *Dubliners*. Its fantastic style owes much to Joyce's exposure to Dadaism in Zurich and his Agon with Freud. Bloom is made to lie down on Joyce's couch and dream. Joyce always fancied himself as an actor. He could have played the part of his own hero or the psychoanalyst or both. The stage enthralled him. I am the same with radio-plays. He was always a popular partner in charades at the Sheehy household where he excelled at dumbshow. He played Captain Hawtree in Margaret Sheehy's production of *Caste*. Then there was Ibsen. Henrik Ibsen was Joyce's first and most sustained literary passion. He read the plays in text form initially, beginning with the *Master Builder* in William Archer's translation for Heinemann in 1898. Stanislaus refers to it as a slim yellow volume that his brother stayed-up all night re-reading. His first prominent review was "Ibsen's New Drama." He was only eighteen years old when he wrote it. It was published in the prestigious *Fortnightly Review*. He began a correspondence with the famous playwright, who was then aged seventy. His brother notes that Joyce found in Ibsen what he subsequently cultivated in his own work: WONDERFUL CALM, STAYING ABOVE THE FRAY, NO CONFLICTING VOICES, FINE PITY FOR MEN and DEEP SYMPATHY WITH LIFE'S CROSS-PURPOSES. Of course, Joyce was particularly influenced by Ibsen's replacement of epic heroes with 'average lives.'[150] His brother wrote that "no writer in

---

150 BARBOUR: Nineteenth century writers hid their sources well. They veiled energeia inside entelechy. Look at the way Pater appropriated Ruskin. Not so much as a single reference. Later, Wilde did the same thing to Pater. The "golden book" of Marius became Dorian Gray's sickly "yellow book."

GOLDSTEIN: Wilde's genius here was degraded colouration. Gold is reduced to yellow with all its symbolic associations with jaundice, adultery, jealousy, melancholy, degradation, death and decay.

ULAN: Wilde debased Pater. Joyce removed the aesthetic element.

MÍM/MILKMAID: [*See disembodied head*] When Cain ate Abel, SHAUN consumed his share.

BARBOUR: [*Plucking at her heart and lifting her right forearm*] To dream of Abel is a favourable omen. It indicates you are rising in the world not falling.

ILKS: Wilde leaves me cold. His texts are too mechanical.

MILDLING: They often seem to be just a pretext for a sequence of set-pieces highlighting his epigrammatic wit.

GOLDSTEIN: They always approach perfection of form.

O: Yes. There is very little dilation in Wilde's texts. Certainly, less than you find in Pater, Joyce, Proust or even Beckett. And just look at the variety of his forms. Only a genius could be successful in such diverse genres: a novel, short stories, plays, melodramas, essays, farces, children's fairy tales, Poe-like fables, lectures and finally the great prison ballad. His trademark is the seamless execution of familiar, sometimes hackneyed forms. And then there are his Poe-like twists. Just look at the way Dorian Gray turns from an aesthetic novel into a gruesome thriller that ends up as a morality tale.

GOLDSTEIN: Wilde was a master of forms. Joyce was a master of forms within one text.

English since Sterne has exploited the minute, unpromising material of his immediate experience so thoroughly" (52). Joyce also liked the way that action in Ibsen's dramas remained subdued, with the plot slowly disclosing 'some great ideal conflict' as the Nolan said. [INSERT FOOTNOTE]. These factors were crystallised in his lecture, "Drama and Life," at University College Dublin in 1900. Like most of his generation, Joyce was a theatre addict. He travelled to London to watch Duse in D'Annunzio's *La Gioconda* and *La Citee Morta*. INSERT MORE in FOOTNOTE. He loved the flow of movement and voice on the stage, uninterrupted by footnotes and qualifications. He could never be bothered 'drawing' characters like most novelists. They were immediately defined visually when put on stage. The appearance of a play could be changed in every new production, giving the director and players the kind of sweeping creative freedom of interpretation that fiction denied. It is therefore ironic that Joyce's fiction resisted this liberty for its readers by virtue of its intense and obscure Gaelicism, intellectual inserts and parochial settings. It would be impossible for any of Joyce's works to be transferred to, say, a nameless totalitarian state in Eastern Europe as with Shakespeare's historical dramas. *Ulysses* can only exist in one place. Inversely, Joyce was able to imbue fiction with features that he was never able to bring to DRAMA. *Exiles* is his major dramatic legacy. Like Swinburne's aborted novel, *Lesbia Brandon*,[151] it accelerates and expands Joyce's principle interests and style[152] until it produces a distortion of the true machine.[153] *Exiles* is set in Dublin in 1912. It is based on "The Dead" in *Dubliners*. This lodges it firmly in the mainstream of Joyce's oeuvre. Joyce described the play as "three cat and mouse acts." It is less than that. John MacNicholas wrote, "it is generally agreed, perhaps especially among Joyceans, that *Exiles* is a bad play, opaque to both reader and viewer." It is really the turgid public confession of Joyce's mania for sexual jealousy. This mood overflowed in letters to his wife. Some critics think that *Exiles* is the failure that Joyce had to write in order to commit himself to fiction once and for all. The language is stilted. The characters

---

151 BARBOUR: Swinburne did not apply himself to fiction. The fragments of what is known as *Lesbia Brandon* were written in the first phase of his literary career in the 1860s around the time of *Blake*, *Atalanta in Calydon* and *Poems and Ballads – First Series*. Although his correspondence in the mid to late 1870s indicates that Swinburne was very interested in completing *Lesbia Brandon* (and frustrated by Watts-Dunton's failure to return missing portions of the manuscript), the novel remained incomplete. Its fragments were never definitively ordered by Swinburne. Indeed, it was never even titled by Swinburne, being given its title by either Wise or Gosse.

152 O: Swinburne was searching for a way to infuse prose with poetics in *Lesbia Brandon* and *Love's Cross-Currents*. His style, however, was confined by its direct transference of poetic devices. He made no attempt to master the mechanics of prose. In *Ulysses*, Joyce found the right formula.

153 SCRIBBLER: See C4. In an inadvertent correspondence (and irony), Swinburne also attempted to introduce elements of flagellation and incest like Joyce. It was left to Proust to incontrovertibly depict this element in Baron de Charlus.

contrived. He learned what didn't work in dramatic writing which he then corrected in Circe.[154] Critics list the following reasons for the let-down of *Exiles*: Joyce just couldn't write in any received form; he didn't create enough distance from Ibsen;[155] he was too autobiographical; the script was stiffly reasoned and lacked spark; it was a hiatus between *PAYM* and *Ulysses* where Joyce let his hair down.[156] The plot revolves around the ordeals of Richard Rowan, an emerging author. He has moved back to Dublin from Rome with his common law wife Bertha. They pretty much represent Joyce and Nora. In this regard, Joyce probably wanted the play to act as a direct message to his wife as she sat bored in the audience.[157] They are joined on stage by Robert Hand and Beatrice Justice.[158] Both men are former lovers of Beatrice. Plot development revolves around the renewed intimacy of Hand and Bertha. This stimulates Richard's desire for pain and degradation.[159] He actively seeks to be betrayed. He refuses to provide counsel or opinions when his wife confesses to Robert's advances. He wants a liaison to happen "secretly, meanly and craftily." He encourages Bertha to keep an assignation. This is an active version of Bloom's passive delight in contemplating Molly's adultery with Boylan. Robert also tells Bertha that her husband wants to be betrayed as it will 'liberate' him into a state of perpetual doubt once and for all[160] and disqualify him from false adherence to social conventions forever.[161] Joyce's character naming is not subtle. The men's first names are virtually

---

154 **MÍM/MILKMAID:** The lessons of *Exiles* resonate throughout the dialogue in *Ulysses*.

155 **BARBOUR:** Joyce does differ from Ibsen in a key theme. Core Ibsen themes include dishonest actions, guilt, secrets and torture by conscience. Any image of lightness is a prospective symbol; craving freedom from these drags. Joyce begins *Exiles* where Ibsen stopped. Richard Rowan is determined to avoid any action which may cause him to feel liability in the future. As such, he tries to OPEN THE SCRIPT to candour. He acts like a libertarian. But his real agenda is to use his knowledge of events to torture himself in a different way like Severin, Swann or Marcel.

156 **GOLDSTEIN:** This is contradicted by its tone, which is tendentious.

157 **BARBOUR:** There was no certainty that Nora would even attend a production of the play given her contempt for Joyce's profession.

158 **MILDLING:** It is not known if the romantic union of Hand and Justice was a conscious comic allusion to masturbation by Joyce.

159 **GOLDERG:** Likewise, Joyce subsequently encouraged Presiozo to flatter Nora in Trieste. This became one of the spurs for the plot of *Exiles*.

160 **O:** Joyce did not endure the same Promethean angst as his main character. He visited his last true friend, John F. Byrne, at Seven Eccles Street before he left Dublin. Byrne reassured him that it was a "blasted plot" by Cosgrove to break him. He trusted Byrne so much that he gave Bloom his house to live in.

161 **GOLDSTEIN:** Joyce exchanged violent notes with Nora in Trieste after he became convinced of her betrayal with Cosgrove.

interchangeable, like some satirical Wildevice. Beatrice was Dante's great romantic obsession. Bertha is a plod. Her name was associated with abnormally large weaponry in Joyce's time. Unlike Hedda Gabler, she has no skill in intrigue. There is no vital force within.[162] She is "like a sea mist." She becomes a predictable female romance figure bifurcated by dominant men.[163] Beatrice's surname, Justice, was the same as Joyce's cherished cousin, Elizabeth, who died in 1912. In Celtic mythology, the Rowan tree is known as the Tree of Life and symbolises courage, wisdom and protection.[164] Robert Hand is a prototype for Mulligan. Joyce draws on both Oliver St. John Gogarty and Vincent Cosgrave for characterisation.[165] Power, influence and argument are used to try to extract sexual favours. But the outcome is left unclear.[166] The play is static. It has a dianoetic structure. Richard's dilemma is whether to accept an appointment as a university lecturer in languages and stay in Ireland ... or return to an unknown future on the Continent. It is not resolved at closure. He and his wife are left stranded and immobilised by events.[167] *Exiles* is less emphatic than any of Joyce's fiction. What it does do is draw attention to Joyce's own life-choice, which had been to escape from Ireland in 1904. In this regard, the play is an act of self-justification. Joyce was not a famous writer at the time of writing *Exiles*.[168] He could have ended-up as a middle-ranked author of the Edwardian era. *Exiles* dramatises his insecurity.[169] In fact, it contains far more self-serving epic afflatus than any play by Ibsen or any other work by Joyce. He may have been enduring retrospective doubts about spurning a solid career in

---

162 ULAN: Rowan feels like he has turned his wife into a literary character. There is no humanity left in her – or between them. She is a cold statue that he observes. Joyce did not make the same mistake in *Ulysses*. He made an autonomous female character out of Molly Bloom, one who has the last word.

163 O: Richard and Robert are considered halves of a whole (Joyce) by some critics.

164 ILKS: It is hard to believe that a writer as acute as Joyce would select this family name without interrogating its origin and meaning.

165 BARBOUR: Both men bore Joyce malice. They had read his crude characterisation of them in *Stephen Hero*. Joyce saw "Gogarty's fat back" spying on him when he got off the boat in Kingstown. They hunted him down. They offered him drugs. Joyce resisted. Finally, Cosgrave claimed that he had been seeing Nora in Ringsend and down along the banks of the Dodder during her courtship with Joyce.

166 ILKS: It is left unclear whether coitus occurred with Robert and Bertha in the gap between Acts 2 and 3. This trailing anxiety is in fact the perfect emotional state for Richard. It also suited Joyce. Nora never confirmed or denied liaisons with Cosgrave. This excited Joyce's passion and triggered his latent masochist tendencies which received full characterisation in Leopold Bloom.

167 BARBOUR: Or 'non-events.'

168 GOLDSTEIN: Publication of *Ulysses* was still 7 years away.

169 MILDLING: A letter from Stanislaus confirmed Cosgrave's treachery. This spurred intense guilt in Joyce.

Dublin at this time, given the hardship of life in Trieste during wartime.[170] *Exiles* was rejected by numerous companies in England, Ireland and America including The Abbey Theatre.[171] This forced publication. It got bad reviews as a script. It was finally produced at Munich in 1919.[172] A brief second production was mounted in London in 1926. The first significant staging was directed by Harold Pinter at the Mermaid Theatre, London in 1970. The best that can be said for *Exiles* is that its plot craved to live life in some kind of awkward freedom like the chorus of a Leonard Cohen song.

SUPERVISOR

How is Circe better than *Exiles*?

NARRATOR

Circe is successful because it inverts the style and structure of *Exiles*.

SUPERVISOR

How do they differ?

NARRATOR

One is all reason, overtly autobiographical and tight. Yet it ends in abeyance. The other is loose, free and associative. Yet it ends with hope. One contains blunt, ponderous symbols. The other is informed by symbolism from psychoanalytical readings. One is confined. The other freewheeling. They both challenge moral customs. *Exiles* does it in a bourgeois setting where there is individual choice about sexuality.[173] Circe resides in a slum where sexual usufruction represents the only option. Edna O'Brien has listed relevant images from Joyce's notes about Nora, sexuality and women which found their place in *Exiles*. The same kind of fragments were not collected for Molly Bloom.[174]

---

170 ULAN: Rowan's proposed appointment was a realistic outcome for Joyce had he remained in Ireland.

171 O: Joyce wanted to cast his future patron, Edith Rockefeller McCormick, in the part of Bertha. Her qualifications seem to have been her wardrobe, jewellery and the financial benefit that might have accrued to Joyce.

172 MILDLING: The only review caused the production to be closed. Joyce made a famous retort: "did they want a steeplechase?" This was better than any line in *Exiles*.

173 GOLDSTEIN: Some critics even discern homosexual desire.

174 BARBOUR: Joyce is already working through the significance of a dead mother in *Exiles*. Richard Rowan contrasts the dead body of his mother with the live body of his wife in Act One. He also raises the same religious defiance that tortured Stephen Dedalus: "Do you think I do not pity her cold blighted love for me? I fought against her spirit while she lived to the bitter end. It fights against me still."

SUPERVISOR

Explain the function of the Circe episode in *Ulysses*.

NARRATOR

Bloom and Stephen share this episode. It is their point of convergence in the novel like Telemachus and Odysseus at the swineherd's farm. Joyce acts as Circe. The text is his bestiary. The past comes forward. Use of Hallucination as a theatricalising device. There have been many excellent expositions of Bloom's hallucinations,[175] madness, Fall, guilt and redemption in Circe.[176] However, they are generally too pious. They miss the fact that Bloom's 'falls' are generally petty and trivial. They are the average falls of an average person, which should elicit low levels of guilt and restitution. The principle narrative objective in Circe is to show that Bloom suffers an exaggerated sense of blame[177] as well as to mock the Catholic Church's hyperbolic judgments about sin and the Fall. To be clear, Joyce was an atheist and church-hater. He did not suffer any residual pangs of self-reproach as a result of his religious upbringing.[178] He was committed to freedom of thought and action. He lived this creed himself. He was a true Libertarian. It makes no sense for him to simply transfer Catholic notions of guilt to his leading character without any critique or alternative vision that mocks and even cancels religion. It is pretty clear that Joyce deliberately over-dramatised Bloom's angst in Circe as part of an extended parody. The long sequence of symbolic citations of his Fall are inconsequential and strained. Joyce uses numerology bluntly. The mathematical speed of a falling object is 32 feet per second. The number 32 recurs five times in Circe. Bloom falls upstairs and is saved by Zoe. This flip in religious spatial projection is a comic reference to the prospect of Bloom's accidental entry into heaven-as-whorehouse. Indeed, Bloom trips harmlessly throughout the novel in a physical parallel to his ethical lapses. He also carries a scar on his wrist close to Christ's stigmata. This is such a ponderous analogy that it could only be seen as sardonic narratorial judgment by Joyce on his character's crucifixion complex. Finally, the supposed moral deprivation and salvation of Stephen in Nighttown is really just another bourgeois affectation. All Bloom really does is stop Stephen losing the rest of his salary in a brothel

---

175 **O:** Hugh Kenner's ratio is 10 per cent real events and 90 per cent hallucinations.

176 **SCRIBBLER:** See Eunice Rojas, "Madness as Redemption in 'Circe'" (2010).

177 **ULAN:** Maybe this is due to his exposure to Christianity, although Bloom is not even a real Catholic.

178 **GOLDSTEIN:** This is made very clear by his brother in *My Brother's Keeper*.

then getting beaten up by the filth.[179] This does not mean that Bloom's redemption at the end of Circe is not authentic. Joyce creates really HIGH VALUE moral and emotional power via a sequence of blood images. Bloom's true sense of personal responsibility doesn't come from obviating everyday sins relating to sexuality. It comes from an opening-out and transcendence of repressed duties. This bursts forth at the end of Circe in the image of his dead son Rudy, memories of his father and a renewed need for tenderness with his wife. This is a HEROIC denouement at the end of a long sequence of trivialities. Joyce is saying that all Bloom's foibles are irrelevant. It is his spiritual tone that is ESSENTIAL. In evaluating Circe as a vehicle for Bloom's fall and redemption, critics often point to Joyce's statement in *PAYM* that the artist needed to drop into sin to develop the necessary skills for true creativity. This is clichéd drivel that self-justifies bad behaviour. Anyway, Bloom is NOT AN ARTIST. He is an average guy feeling bad on this day about the past, probably because he went to a funeral, had a lot on his plate and feels exhausted at midnight. Other critics argue that Bloom has ALREADY fallen.[180] This is a bit rich. It's not as if Bloom killed anyone. He didn't have a REAL FALL. He isn't POST-LAPSARIAN. He doesn't resemble a tragic hero.[181] This misreading of Circe is exacerbated by the presumption that Stephen Dedalus becomes a substitute son for Bloom, acting as the agent for cosmic harmonisation between Bloom and Rudy. As noted, an alternative interpretation of the exit of Stephen Dedalus from the novel is based on the premise that he returns to the home of his biological father that night. This is MUCH MORE CONGRUOUS with Bloom's reconciliation with Rudy at the end of Circe than Stephen becoming a surrogate son. The telepathy and fusion between Bloom and Stephen in Circe is all based on ALIGNMENT. NOT CONFLUENCE. Bloom as father WANTS Stephen as son to be reconciled with his TRUE father, no matter how flawed. Bloom wants to be reconciled with his REAL SON, not find a substitute in Stephen Dedalus. Other people's kids never smell right. This ethical consistency creates the potential for true closure of *Ulysses*, which is Bloom being able to emotionally reconnect with his wife. He can only do this by REALLY OWNING THE FATE OF RUDY. Rudy Bloom is the grandson of Rudolf Virag. They share the same chosen name. Likewise, SD is the son of SD. They

179 **BARBOUR:** A brothel visit is a fairly mundane literary device in Victorian literature, as Wilde showed in *Dorian Gray*.

180 **SCRIBBLER:** See Tolomeo (301).

181 IBID: Telemachus contains two figures who could qualify for this status – Tom Hallem and Ana Lafei. However, the narrative technique resists/repels this mode of emplotment. There is ZERO EXPOSITION of narrative events which could induce a structure or tone of TRAGEDY. This is no place for sentiment.

share initials and family name. Sticking SD into Rudy would only make a blasphemy of reconciliation, especially as Bloom has already conjured an adulterous vision of Stephen with his wife. Continuing this trope suggests that the ultimate blasphemy for Bloom-as-Severin is creating fertile ground for incest. That is definitely not Joyce's intention. He has used Circe to purge Bloom of this type of BDSM fantasy. Bloom is purified at the end of Circe. Human values displace aesthetic purposes at last. The omniscient narrator entwines the sub-conscious realms of Bloom/Stephen. No new content is provided. There is hyperbolic reprise. Pivotal events get blurred by a seer's tongue. Metafecundity of style is offered. Unwinding reality. A clock starts going backwards towards Jung. Now Joyce must come out from behind the harlequin masks of his myriad characters to make a full disclosure of his own presence. Extreme metaphors mirror the exigencies of this extreme technical quest. Bloom suddenly displays knowledge of Stephen's reading (*Nebrakada*!). There are Circean transformations. Their min(e)d data becomes interchangeable.[182] It is made clear to the reader that all characters have sprung from the imagination of James Augustine Aloysius Joyce. Bloom and Stephen share the same vision of Shakespeare by narratorial telepathy. Stephen said Mr WS saw his birth star just after he had finished fucking Anne Hathaway in a field. Don on Helen. Hamlet's father wafts over battlements. Silhouette of Bob Capri taking out the garbage as seen from a child's bed. Severin/Bloom. Gerty clomping onto the stage in a leg brace. A bawd offers a virgin for sex. Stephen/ Lynch fade into black. But they are not far. Bloom wanders behind them. Billy Capri is surrounded by peers yet he cannot make spiritual contact. This is an emblem of his isolation. It is time for him to depart Australia like Joyce in 1904. Kickstart his own Telemachiad. He tries to visualise his birth-father. Bloom encounters his deceased father and mother in a dream. My father is dead to all intents and purposes. My mother comes back as Bella the brothel keeper. Costume change. Soap symbol of Molly. She is whore and angel. Standard dichotomy. Insert list of past female conquests. Bloom's first trial. Dublin Don Juan in the Dock! S&M fancies. Kingpin Leop. Policy platform of mild prosperity. Attack on sexual abnormalities from the pullypit. Hidden rind. Bloom transforms into a woman who gives birth to eight babies like a bloated sow. Mister WS as a commercial traveller. Bloom and Stephen are flipsides of the same coin. The spinner launches his kip. Stephen sees Shakespeare-as-person in all his characters. Metempsychosis. Stephen's artistic father is not Leobard Ploom. Bloom's trinity is thus: father's suicide; son's death; wife's adultery. Haines' Black Panther equals God. Barry Kiernan wearing Rudy's unseeing

182 IBID: This occurs periodically in C7; for example, the spoken allusion to White Boots is followed by television coverage of the GF. INSERT OTHER EXAMPLES.

eyes like some cauterised Yeats. Fergus lives in a painless palace. Bring him back across Lethe. Bella Cohen waits on the bank vault. Invert gender. Become Bello the sex tyrant acting tough like Jupiter. Bloom watches over the whorehouse. His masochism relieved. As a sex slave he is auctioned. Taunted as Molly's cuck. Signs his own death warrant. Mourned by passing Jews. You've got to die to get resurrected. This fulfils his Jesus trope. Enter Nymph. Poulahouca waterfall. Wanking in a forest. Molly needed sex after watching dogs fuck. Don is not spraying his seed efficiently. Bloom breaks the spell with a potato. Circe/Bella charm. An Irish vegement. Blowback on Zoe's thigh like hot Hephaestus. Athena's airish ligament. Prostitutes and lovers dance to their favourite songs. Poor pretty girls just out to make money for their families back home in Anhui. Shanghai Dog talking to a girl from Heilongjiang in a Qing theme-room. Debased Shakespearean references. Green eyes. Pigging out on the Bard. ALISOUN: "Oh not another porcine reference!" Bloom almost watched Boylan fuck once. Second-best bed. Strawberry pillcase. Propensity for the word DOG. Adulterated Shakespeare wearing reindeer horns. E-I-E-I-a-gogo. Beardless youth and cuckolded man both see the Bard in their own way. Holding a mirror up to Nature is weird. Barry Capri watched Don Cane and Helen McFadden go at it like beasts in the back paddock at Campsie. Don in the form of a steer mounted a milky white box. Watch yourself in a ceiling mirror. Salome in gold bikini standing in the fish tank on Huaihai Lu. Dances of death. Full of quick steps. Stephen's mother beastly dead. Countess Cathleen. A whore fucked in Kelp. Stephen smashing a chandelier. Glass everywhere. Beta House nocturne. Samson's Darkness. Failing masonic tools. Time's last fling. Precursor of renewal. Bloom's wallet. Couple of British Privates. Call them Tennyson and Ed. Bloom sort of saves Stephen. Hound chasing a fox. Lame pet. Explosive stick. Tortoise and hare trope. Joyce's Jew was called Hunter in real life. Irony piled on irony. Joyce needed saving himself in Dublin, Trieste, France and Switzerland. Stephen in the shape of a foetus passed out in muck. Suddenly stretching stiff like a waking baby. His exposed spine leaked lymph-flecked blood. Tom Hallem stirs. His eyelids part. A whitewashed ceiling looms over his groggy gaze announcing entrance into the awakened realm. Rats scurry below. The last dramatic cue in Circe is the father seeing dead Rudy Bloom as an adult dandy with a slight Jesus slant. My father had a living child but chose to not inspire that vision. Onec upno tiem (n)ever (n)ever.

8.
Eumaeus (7 pm)

PREPARATORY TO ANYTHING ELSE[183]

SHANGHAI DOG

[*Sitting on the edge of a low king size bed overlooking Hunan Lu. The road surface is blown with dust. Thick power lines cut the street. A tall brick fence opposite protects the grounds of the Radisson Xing Guo Hotel*] Evening. Open window. Port city. Late autumn breeze. Recycling man passes on his bicycle cart. They are finally wheeling the horse into the compound. His stretched and burned face, scratched with irregular bristles and moles, is typical of Anhui people. You cannot hide peasant origins. They can't be blanched or softened. In the sweat of thy face shalt thou earn thy bread until you return to earth. Rags hang off his torso all the way down to dirty white sandals. A cow bell has been taped to the handle bar. He bangs it with an iron tube. An old megaphone strapped to the back of his seat releases a recorded loop: kongtiao diannao dianshi bing gui. Air Conditioners – Computers – Televisions – Fridges. Scooters surge and ebb. Occasional cars. Always horns. Interregnum.

---

183 SCRIBBLER: The Eumaeus episode concerns the return of Odysseus to Ithaca. It is the beginning of Chapter III of *Ulysses*. Now Bloom is himself again, as Cibber said of Rich. He has recovered from the hallucinations of Circe. Bloom and Stephen are alone at last. They take sustenance in a cabman's shelter. An old seaman tells apocryphal tales. They proceed towards Bloom's home. Always revert to the following themes – family, homecoming, imposters, deception. Insert idioms. Detach emotions through convolution. Employ Euphuism (see Lyly). This style involves extended verbiage; self-contradiction; narrative redundancy; recycled language; misplaced phrases; puns, clichés, errors and inconsistencies; rhetorical questions. Blend techniques from different episodes. Selective use of Strine. Also misspelling and misnaming. Mix first person (direct but limited to single POV), multiple first person (broader) and third person narrative (boundless POV). Disrupt chronology (XF/SD, TH). Note that Eumaeus in *Ulysses* is set after midnight. Here, it is still early evening. Make Shanghai Dog prominent in this episode. He represents Odysseus back on Ithaca. Judy = Circe. Xiao Fang (Su) is Calypso. Bring out the sadness in this equation. Allusions to Narcissus reflect the basic self-possession of all characters in Eumaeus in both *Ulysses* and the *Odyssey*. They interact productively – and may even become closer in spirit – but there are no true emotional connections. In fact, all revelations make them more self-focused. This annotation represents a segue with C7. It is the last footnote.

Two too-loud female voices pass on the footpath beneath. Irish washerwomen discussing ALP's letter. I can see their greasy black crowns. Large flakes of dandruff are working free from viscous follicles. They are speaking the local dialect. It has a bitter sibilance compared to Mandarin. Chinese people are always having public disputes. Crowds gather quickly. Sometimes a policeman intervenes; making himself a target for both sides. It is nerve-wracking listening to external dialogue within the hollow horse. Before you can interpret language, you assume it's a debate about whether to torch the contrivance. Plane trees line the streets shedding their rich summer growth. It is November Six. Harsh pruning commenced yesterday. Piles of branches fill the parking lanes along both sides of Xing Guo Lu. Gardeners feed them into chippers throughout the night. All that remains are smooth stumps. The withdrawal of this natural screen discloses the peeling *art deco* facades of the old French Concession. You can see past stainless-steel security grids into char-seared, simple kitchens. Bare lounge rooms are lit by harsh fluorescent lights. Xiao Fang is huddled under my duvet on her smooth soft belly. She's sleeping. And safe. Soon I must leave her. One muscular leg is exposed. It makes me harden somewhat. I put on a sweat shirt from the fake product market. It is branded "DETROT: MOROTCITY." I walk to the local C Store to buy smokes. Nobody notices my exit. The security guard at my compound is asleep in his booth at the front gate. Old couples are doing *tai chi* in the corner park. Time files. Some widows congregate in a cluster with long gymnast ribbons. The last time Liu Shao Qi and Wang Gang Mei held hands was on the stage of Beijing Workers Stadium just before they were beaten unconscious by Red Guards. It was done by people like these ones but in another life, bewitched by specters. This is what the Gods do to humans. They are wearing a mix of gym gear and traditional costume. Children play on intricate paths dissecting neat garden beds. Loud muzak is distorted by a cheap ghetto blaster. Some old men are loitering around exercise equipment in silk pajamas smoking Chungwha cigarettes. I recognise the plum aroma. Hunan Lu is always alive. The locals start pacing the street in pre-dawn haze. Some walk backwards swiftly. It's an acquired talent. They still buy xiao long bao or fried bread for breakfast on Wulumuqi Lu. It is one of the last strips like old Shanghai with snack stalls, a wet market, live butcheries and noodle bars spilling over the footpath under frosted globes hung off sloping bamboo poles. The children are rushing to extra classes before school. Shiny red bandanas loop their necks. Migrant maids drag them quickly. They can't loiter like Western kids. A new song commences. The love-lost wail of an er hu is drowned by vocal commands. Guanyin is intoned repetitively. She's big in these parts. Putuoshan is only four hours south by boat. Thirty years ago, they would have been chanting, "The East is Red." Today, the goddess of compassion is supporting aerobics routines for retired cadres. Everybody in this precinct has some connection to the Shanghai Government. City headquarters is just across Huaihai Xilu. Jiang Zemin owns a lane house on Wukang Lu. It's got a makeshift ventilation duct that spews hot air over the top of a high electrified fence onto passing pedestrians. This is a metaphor for Troy. There must be one hell of a bomb shelter down there. A retinue of guards stand watch at a bolted gate. This whole area is gridded with tunnels. They've converted one cluster in a carpark behind Chunky Party Party KTV into a gay bar. Lovers make milk runs down dark plastered alcoves. Murphy leans on the bar, waxed and gleaming. The number 16 is tattooed above his cleft left nipple. He claims it was mangled by a gunshot, a knife attack, even botched cancer surgery sometimes. Les Hallem strokes the arc of his hind. Cars drift through scooter traffic. Critics have argued that Joyce's choice of sixteen is a reference to the position of the Eumaeus episode in *Ulysses* or the date of *Ulysses* (__ June). Don Gifford has claimed it is slang for homosexuality. He cites obscure allusions in Eumaeus to support his theory. Murphy is a natural liar and lair. He lifts a white singlet to display three tattoos – an anchor, 16 and a man he calls Antonio. The anchor represents sailors, who are historically associated with homosexuality. Antonio was a Greek, the term used by Mulligan to tag Bloom as gay earlier in the novel. Yet, perhaps the most vital point from a textual perspective is that THERE ARE NO FEMALE CHARACTERS IN EUMAEUS. Women like Molly Bloom, Katherine O'Shea and the anonymous streetwalker are all held outside the narrative. They are defined by the opinions of men. Each is subject to sexist attack. Photographs of naked women are passed around the gang. This is evidence of the fact that James Joyce sees a world without women as the equivalent of lost sailors at sea turning to sodomy. Their society becomes false and crude. The public toilet block on Gaoyou Lu is besieged by vacant taxis. Drivers stand in packs while they wait for the next fare. One recognises my face and waves. His peers mock him. He says I am a good fare repeatedly. A girl is studying her profile in the long aquarium glass of a catering supplies showroom. Bogus Italianate muses decorate its staircase columns. The Goddess of War and God of Speed are guarding the showroom of a diversified semi-conductor business. Park music evaporates. Shanghai streets blend old residential zones with modern commercial buildings, states the realty brochure. There is no urban continuity. Historic lanes are separated by neo-classical offices. Faux marble arches are crowned with gold eagles. I am longing to feel Xiao Fang's back against my gut. Her body is pigmented like weather-beaten brass. Murphy follows a plump crossdresser. His lazy gut is veined by cheap lingerie. Su suffers intense contractions during orgasm. It has an elliptical quality. Murphy catches his fingers in torn tights as he lifts aside a black silk thong. I can't spill my seed now. I need it to satisfy Doctor Gu tonight, thought Billy.

INSERT ENDS

Don Cane rested in the hire car. He had time to kill. He turned on the cabin light. It cast a buttery beam. Speck in darkness. He extracted a spiral notebook from his shirt pocket and opened it from the rear. It was headed: "**Sydney**". He took up a pen to make amendments.

1. Penelope ~~Cane~~ Hallem – ~~16 First Avenue Campsie~~ 25 Weldon Street, Burwood
2. Helen ~~McFadden~~ Capri – ~~20 First Avenue Campsie~~ 16 First Avenue Campsie
3. Bob Hensley (RSL mate of a mate of Choc) – 46 Weldon Street, Burwood.

He took a Gregory's Street Directory from the shallow glove box. There was only one Weldon Street in Greater Sydney. It means 'hill near a spring' in Old English. You smash down Parramatta Road. Take a broad left onto the Hume Highway. Pass through Ashfield shopping centre. The first thing to note is Western Suburbs Hospital on your left about two miles past the high street. Count three streets. Turn right at the next. Penelope lives about 100 years downhill. It was a dull, soggy evening like that time in Phu Bia when I drove straight through an ambush. Unsprung. They expected a whole platoon. Sometimes you get inklings. Most of the time it's just fear. You retrofit intuition. It's a survival mechanism to help you go back out. The best tactic is routine. Consult Athene. Get into the same filthy camouflage gear. Never wash. Blacken your face. Try to leave no trace of yourself in the jungle. It's better to become a vegetarian then you don't stink like meat. Never chew gum. Smell is the first sign for Charlie of foreign presence. Your pace should never slacken or hustle. Like Telemachus, always take a different route back to base. Dodge Poseidon. This is a model for Shanghai Dog in this chapter. There are consequences if you don't follow normal precautions. Charlie feinted towards Dong Phu at Nhan Hoa. A raw US adviser sucked the whole company down the road. THE TRAP SHUT. Fifty soldiers were slaughtered in two minutes. We never did find that guy's carcass. Agamemnon went straight to his bath when he got home. Cassandra was wailing from the vestibule. Argos stank like a slaughter-house. She foresaw carcasses rotting in the yard. Village square post-incursion. Charcoaled chooks and kittens. Bamboo ablaze. One marine took his anger out on the body of an older boy. Couldn't happen at Saigon, they said. Then came Tet. I saw a thousand corpses laid out in the main square of Nam Hoa. Femurs with femurs. Skulls with skulls. A Buddhist shrine lined with plastic body bags. Thick incense smouldering in a forty-four-gallon drum. Judy raised joss-stick stalks high above her serpentine face as she prayed at Lingyin Temple. Clytemnestra wrapped Agamemnon in a cumbrous robe. The hotel manager unlocked our room during the night so assassins could kill us in bed. She threw lumpen fishing net over her husband and swiped him thrice with a double headed axe.

His bloodspray was dulcet like rain on a liefer seed, she said. Revenge for bringing Iphigenia into her house. A swift coup. No different to Minh, Tran and Khanh taking down the Ngo Dinh brothers. Conein used Lodge to play *Realpolitik*. The Ambassador was totally out of his depth against Vietnamese court intrigues, concluded Vann bitterly. Diem and Nhu were both shot point-blank in the back of the head then their corpses were sprayed with bullets and stabbed with knives. Cassandra walked consciously into a trap. Apollo spat in her mouth. She knew the script. Task Force Oregon. Son Thang. 101st Airborne. Tiger Force rapes. Ajax the Lesser pulled her off a statue of Athene. Odysseus was going to have him stoned. An internal investigation cleared all senior officers and NCOs. Agamemnon's testimony swayed the assembly. A bunch of lies got his hands on Cassandra. No US solider was ever prosecuted. Word of the nigger Robinson against a gang of whites. Bummer's fifteen hundred gook body count. Shoot some old farmers, pile them together then blow the bodies apart with grenades. Allows you to claim a multiple of three or four on the Kill Ratio. Wet sticky body parts clung to both sides of my fatigues. I put on all my clothes against the cold of death and lay down. Su entered the bedroom. She laid an overnight bag on the ironing board and stared through the pall. I pretended to doze. It was soothing to watch her disrobe without sensing observation. I could see the dark imprint of homemade inks on her body. She had been thoroughly marked by the Kunming gang. I gave way in the bunk. Our backs simmered from touch and I slept. Les lolled in his arm chair in front of the TV. I'll just insert another Proladome, mused Tom Hallem. It gives me the temporary flavour of well-being. The morphine blooms in my bowels like a Moreton Bay fig. Insert a sequence of stick metaphors relating to heroin addiction. Don't just follow Joyce down the path of stylistic routine. That is the operative word in this chapter. A car crash victim is choppered into Cabrini. They cut out the pieces of the corpse still wanting to pump. The fateful call comes. Willy drives me to hospital in my smashed-up Honda. No time now for niceties. I am hauled into the compound. Substitute "theatre." They position me on the slab (sub. "operating table."). My pale belly blares at the morning sun. Change to "surgery lights." They reduce my eyes to runny glue (soon, they will seal shut forever). The surgeon slides the scalpel through my flesh. They've opened me up. I'm raw and bleeding. They pin back the wet inner veils. It's time to saw right through my rib cage. The valve retractor is manipulated into place then churned until taut. More tears in my gaping. They install a sternum spreader to keep the low road open. Beckett should have grown sick of this image-sequence by now. But he always wants his characters to re-experience torture on some other remote by-way. It's his mealy-mouthed version of a SUBLIME. My mind and my body are laid out next to each other like the sons of Clovis. Abraham raises a pearl-handled dagger. The sound of slop unravelling in tin light. Flies harangue me. Beige machines data-flicker. Sun grinding across finger-marked panes. I yawn at its ebbing in the west. In with the good organ, out with the bad. They bound me back together with wire. I went "tock." They fixed my body, but they couldn't fix my mind. SHIFT TENSE & TIME CONTINUOUSLY. I examine the worn faces of the hungry crowd around the bonfire (AKA junkies huddled in front of my television set). Go back to bed, someone said. ______ [INSERT DEITY] plucks out my eyeballs and leaves them face-to-face opposite my ... my ... 'soul.' I watch it twitch to a halt in the ever-deepening gloom. And FEEL myself watching ME also. Insert explanatory graphic. The horror of Joyce's predicament is enhanced by Birmingham's clinical prose. A summary of his narrative is as follows: Dr. Sidler felt the retinal arteries throbbing against the wall of JJ's eye; Joyce was always conscious during surgery; he was medicated with atropine and cocaine; Blepharostats prised his eyes apart; the surgeon held the eyeball with fixation forceps; Joyce's eye had to watch the blade come; Birmingham adds the bayonet as a simile, associating JJ with WW1 soldiers; the cornea resisted momentarily before the blade sliced the surface and slid into the anterior chamber; exudate gushed into and out of the incision; the nurse took the forceps and turned the author's eye downwards; Sidler used iris forceps to enter the chamber and pull the top edge of the iris out through the incision; Birmingham uses another simile of a tissue being pulled out of a box to elucidate this facet; Sidler took the iris scissors and cut away a triangular piece of the iris and pushed the severed edge back inside with a spatula. Joyce confines his dream sequences to Circe. There's a paper and pencil somewhere on the floor. But I'm in too much pain and too high now to bother recording this image. For a while I deny my dealer, as Saint Peter did Christ. Likewise, Stephen Dedalus is equivocal about his paternity when Murphy asks if he is related to Simon Dedalus. But I could never reject Willy for long (those baleful globes!). Soon a request for succour comes brimming out of my lips in bloody bile like birth to the romantic soundtrack of a one-day cricket international. God (SMACK) heals the incisions (belatedly) until just my mindset is left trapped inside this bone sarcophagus. Rachel entered the Family Court holding her governess' palm. She did not recognise me as her father. The man she called DAD was an emaciated figure she wasn't allowed to touch. I studied her face for signs of flesh-identity. Willy refreshes the canula. I am not like Proust. All my pasts have collapsed under the pressure of reverie. I hardly even notice the aircon, shaking hard, like bits inside a broken light-bulb, as it is cranks-up for another performance (of Tarrilup Bridge), until the sudden easy breeze. February is hot in Melbourne. Not worse than Perth. Just different bad. Something's gone wrong with the TV eyes in my head. Iggy's lyric is monosyllabic except for the title image. I call a name. Is anybody out there? I can't lie alone in this black box forever. Say THE WORD weakly. Insert various death scenes from literature. A plucky British infantryman blinded by mustard gas, all shot up and tangled in Turkish wire calls for his mother, fiancée or the baby he has never seen. He joined a snowball march when his wife was eight months pregnant. P. J. Harvey sings Battleship

Hill like it's some kind of place. Let Nelson finish his apocryphal slot then shove him overboard and insert the next victim into the recording booth. Shakespeare used death-talks all the time to resolve his insipid dramas. Everyone is always raging or apologising as stab wounds or poison grip their guts. This was a formal convention of theatre to the end of the nineteenth century. Shakespeare could have produced plot innovation if any one of the following characters (or multiples thereof) had survived denouement: Hamlet, Claudius, Laertes, Gertrude, Ophelia, Duncan, Banquo, Macduff's lot, Macbeth, Lady Macbeth, Othello, Desdemona, Coriolanus, Romeo, Juliet, Cordelia, her sisters, their husbands/lovers, Richard's miscellaneous victims or most of the cast of *Titus Andronicus*. Shakespeare also employed ghosts with alacrity just like Seneca. The appearance of Banquo-as-apparition is a failure. It was the dramatic equivalent of a montage. Brutus' proleptic dream of dead Caesar is a genuine novelty. The utility to plot-ambiguity of Hamlet Senior was his major technical achievement. It created a monster hit. My mother's funeral took the full forty-five minutes. My father's service was all over in thirty. Racine condensed all the fluff using a geometric formula. It enabled him to balance his plays perfectly. He didn't end up with misshapen wordfests dragging their intestines across the stage. Macbeth has got one death scene too many. Duncan's murder is necessary. But we don't need the Macduff slaughter. Joyce avoided this type of verbal contrivance. Death is largely absent from High Modernism. It lost piquancy. There was too much bloodshed in real life. Art needed the hyper-accelerated splatter of Tarantino after the Vietnam War to reinstate death as a valid narrative device. He converted it into a fact of life. This had social consequences. Scribbler writes, "I am frightened, said Tom," on my behalf. It's a kind gesture, kind-of-guilt-laden, but heartfelt nonetheless. Nobody knows if death is a conscious experience. I have read that a bullet in the head will kill you long before your brain has registered the event, let alone generated pain. Some theorists associate death with the Sublime. Maybe I'll reach that point of false solace. Pater did in text. I'll hold up my thumb if I am still able to communicate. Billy swept down the staircase to the public phone in the foyer. Stan peered out of the caretaker's flat. A government official put down his headphones and went to the water dispenser to refill his tea canister. Cassandra picked up the phone. She says I always end up dead. But I will never abandon my daughter. No one is listening.

ORTHODOX SAMARITAN FASHION

Leer leans against Beta House. He gestures at the door with his thumb. I need a crap, he said. Can you get me inside? "I don't have a key," replied Tom Hallem. "I took all my stuff home this morning."

"Home?" asked Leer pointedly.

The odour of the sty arose from his person. Why did you leave your father's house? asks Leopold Bloom near the start of Eumaeus. To seek misfortune, Stephen Dedalus jokes back. This is exactly what Hallem will find in Nighttown. Bloom replies tactfully. He is careful to display a cloying respect for Simon Dedalus. It probably annoys Stephen. For he was nothing if not honest about his father. Eventually, Bloom asks, "where does he live at present" (540). This is the crux of his whole line of inquiry. He has already noted Mulligan and Haines trying to give Stephen the slip. He dislikes Mulligan. He is too goddam brutal. Stephen never answers him. He has no interest in confiding in Bloom. He is too busy reconstructing a memorial image of his mother. Also, drinking diluted cocoa in another rented kitchen with his sister, Dilly. Sardonically, he calls it, "his family hearth." The cat seems to eat best consuming scraps under the table. Mary's absence is the cause of their domestic debasement. His father has lost all will to maintain appearances. SURFIN' BIRD COMMENCES. Leer careers down Georgina Street into Chronos' sick black wings. "I thought you needed the bathroom," said Tom Hallem volubly. INSERT ALLUSIONS TO PULP FICTION. Tarantino is a master of reworking clichés through careful deployment of ungainly human traits. Tom Hallem turned on a dime, grasping his back. Persian Jones crossed the mouth of Georgina Street. Two henchmen followed (call them Vincent and Jules). We could hang out with them all day. One will die; the other gets religion. This is another redundant trope applied obliquely by the auteur. There are almost no original components in Tarantino; only the arrangement of non-complementary parts into artificial rules and false logic. His movie proceeds without acceleration. Time is chunked and reordered. The sloppy hitmen do average things like eat muffins in a diner. The ethics of foot massage and miracles provide esoteric lines of inquiry. They become like modern-day philosophers. This creates a natural empathy in the viewer. Victims are consequently reduced in status. We acquiesce to life on their terms. We laugh at the execution of human beings. This creates shock value in a controlled filmic experiment. Tarantino is Stanley Milgram for cinema. Society itself calibrates the dial. The Eumaeus episode begins after a street struggle. In *Pulp Fiction*, there would have been multiple deaths. But Leer had no interest in combat. He was more concerned with conflict avoidance. Tarantino has a similar interest in the limits of diplomacy, which he explores on multiple occasions (Butch/Marsellus, Jules/victims/Ringo et al). Joyce's Euphuism in Eumaeus continuously impedes the reader's ability to get a clear picture of what's going on. The narrator adopts a verbose, often enervated style. He sounds similar to Bloom but it is probably not Bloom himself acting as narrator. Possibly, he represents language-without-art. This episode is sometimes described as the most conventional in *Ulysses*. Perhaps Joyce used a straightforward style – albeit convoluted – so that the reader could easily grasp the significant events in the plot, as it represents the climax of the novel in structural terms relating to Homer. The same tactic was used in Ithaca with the Q&A structure. Maybe, the narrator is the author impersonating Bloom. That would be consistent with the plot in this episode, which contains numerous imposters. It would also be consistent with Homer's storyline when Odysseus returns to Ithaca. He proceeds to the swineherd's hut in disguise to gather intelligence because he fears the same fate as Agamemnon. The Yanks were never good at that stuff. They always paid informants upfront. It meant the source felt obliged to manufacture content like some novelist. Language submerges all the characters and storyline in Eumaeus. Errors and banality abound. Tired characters = tiring style. *Ulysses* can be seen as a STYLISTIC life-cycle in five parts: Telemachus – youthful verve; Calypso – maturity; Eumaeus –decay; Ithaca – technical writing; Penelope – future (language in dreams). In Eumaeus, Joyce connects the Telemachiad (Stephen in C1) with Calypso (Bloom at the start of C2). He told Stuart Gilbert that Telemachus was "narrative (young)" while Eumaeus was "narrative (old)." He replaces Mulligan's dominance of Stephen with the mentorship of Bloom. Mulligan represents artful chatter; Bloom careful discourse. He provides sound advice on the perils of drinking, prostitution and association with bad company. This is in stark contrast with Mulligan and Lynch (Judas). All characters struggle for identity and expression in Eumaeus against the overpowering alliance of received language, Dublin's economic privation and Ireland's suffocating moral load. It could be said that Joyce sacrifices the art of *Ulysses* in this episode, subjecting it to the stultifying influence of conventional literary practice to set the baseline for his creative leap in the last episodes. Both Eumaeus and Sirens explore the relation of the individual to society and how language functions to enslave and/or liberate the speaker. Sirens introduces a new style of writing beyond the mandate of *Ulysses*, pointing the way to *Finnegan's Wake*. Eumaeus does the opposite. It reverts to platitudes. *F. Wake* was the synthesis of a struggle in which language and narrative are subjected to unyielding deconstruction, linguistic distortion, pulp neologisms, feints, lies, truisms, global re-mythologising, and formal innovation (see Attridge). This doesn't make it a more successful text. It was just the inevitable place to go next. It proceeded beyond the borders of the known world like Odysseus venturing out again to find a landlocked place at the end of the *Odyssey*. There was never a more land-locked text than *F. Wake*. Both LB and SD struggle to make meaningful contact through language as they traipse the empty streets late at night. Bloom is drained and nagging. Stephen is drunk and dazed. They can only communicate with covert glances and bodily mannerisms. It is the spontaneous act of singing by Stephen that brings them together. This reflects the anthropological theory that song is the most basic effective form of communication. The power of Stephen's voice (a metaphor for Joyce's own skills) arouses Bloom's admiration as well as opportunism. He contemplates coupling Stephen with Molly. It becomes a sexual metaphor powered by Bloom's submissive and voyeuristic tendencies. In direct contrast to Stephen, Bloom has just been disclosed as possessing a tin ear when he whistles a tune at the beginning of the episode. This narrative mix explains why Bloom suddenly shows Stephen a revealing picture of Molly.

BLOM

[*Internal monologue*] I could pair them up. Pitch them as a duo. Sell lurid postcards. She might even come to the attention of the Prince of Wales. [*Reaching into his wallet to extract a photograph*] Here, son. Have a gander at my wife. Does she please you? Would you like to come back to my home for a ... duet?

STEFAN DE DAHLIAS

[*Gazing at Molly's cleavage*] Mother!

SPIKEY OLAN

Bloom is no better than some Nighttown madam in this exchange.

BARBOUR

The other factor driving Bloom's search for a gimmick is the grind of Dublin life.

MILKMAID

All Ireland was held in thrall by English suitors.

THE TALE OF ALCINOUS' GUEST BY JOHN LYLY

CHANDLER

They say a cat always lands on its feet. So does a man wearing cement shoes.

SCRIBBLER

In Eumaeus, Leopold Bloom takes on the role of lecturer to try to correct or redress the bad habits of Stephen Dedalus. Here, everything is reversed. Bloom is full of good advice and practical measures. By contrast, Leer is trying to lead Tom Hallem down a depraved path with wild conduct and unbelievable promises. Tom baulks at such an extreme option. He wants to retain control of his circumstances and future, whereas Stephen Dedalus is throwing everything away in disgust. Stephen offers a destitute acquaintance, Corley, his job and gives him a half-crown. Bloom is dismayed by Stephen's abandon. He doesn't have the requisite insight to analyse this type of behaviour. It all operates on a different psychological plane to him. This is a key reason why Stephen could never accept Bloom as a substitute father. Likewise, Tom Hallem must ultimately reject Arthur Leer. The risks are too perilous. SHIFT. Our protagonists hastened across slimy slick ficus bulbs, paying much attention to alliteration and other sound patterns, rapidly descending, as if skiing over the surface of a freshly-urned sky, conversing hastily, phrases of unequal length appearing successively, thus mimicking the erratic steps which tumbled out of their discrepant forms, heavy with antitheses and antipathies but a syntax nonetheless, shaking both anatomies, which were confluent also in TERROR, albeit mismatched in density, grating-out anecdotes of such poor wit as they possessed, key verbal elements increasingly unbalanced, a discord unballasting their intimacy which they sought to redress by recapitulating times distant and shared as well as mutual acts still more topical and fresh, such as those enjoyed at a summer residence in Upper Mecklenburgh Street in the company of a cast which included, according to the deposition of Master S.B. Mulligan, two gonorrheal ladies, known by the sobriquets 'Fresh Nelly' and 'Rosalie, the coalquay whore,' with whom they constructed a coupling of style and matter so artificial and affected that it recalled the literary technique *Euphuism*, which takes its name from the romance, Euphues, derived from the Greek for 'graceful, witty,' of John Lyly in the last quarter of the sixteenth century, was reduced to Mannerism and subsequently restored by Walter Pater, the greatest theoretical thinker in English linguistics before Joyce, 300 years later in *Marius the Epicurean*. Leer withdrew a subaltern guise as they edged from danger. Tall tales of adventure, homecoming, imposture, deception and death became characteristic of his mendicant utterance. In *Ulysses*, Murphy is presented as a sub for Odysseus. He has just landed in Ireland after decades of travel. In the *Odyssey*, Odysseus tells an erroneous story of being a Cretan warrior who was taken as a slave to Ithaca, where he escaped in rags. Murphy offers the audience a lacklustre account of his own legendary voyages which, in sequence, elucidate: (1) the barbarous practice of cannibalism; (2) the circumstances and routine of various knife attacks of his observation; and (3) the experience of observing expert marksman, Simon Dedalus, shoot two eggs off two bottles over his shoulder left-handed at a distance of fifty feet at Hengler's circus, Stockholm, Sweden. There are 3 references to the Grande Cirque in *Ulysses*. The others are: (1) Calypso – trapeze act allusion; and (2) Ithaca – the creepy experience of a clown entering the audience to proclaim that Bloom was his lost father ('papa'). Murphy's image of Other-SD has been interrogated by critics with inconsistent results. The action is clearly a reference to the archery contest on Ithaca. But, of course, the actor is a different Simon Dedalus. The bullets are usually seen as sperm with the eggs as ova. However, the eggs are blown apart. This could be seen as an allusion to homosexuality. Left-handedness has also been linked to queerness (see Canadian scientists, UT, 2000). The eggs could also represent a pair of exploding testicles, effecting castration. The art of Eumaeus is navigation. The organ ascribed by Joyce is nerves. Derek Attridge writes explicitly that the narrative in Eumaeus is always "looking over its shoulder." There are clear parallels with TMAC, albeit inverted on occasion as per the following examples: (i) Tom Hallem (SD) is the character who holds his nerve as the pair avoid Persian Jones whilst (ii) Leer (LB/ODY) is devoted to further indulgence. The following notes have been transcribed from their conversation relating to Leer's ontology, according to the Pitman system. At this critical juncture in their expedition, Leer asserted, *non ignara mali miseris succurrere disco*, as the great Roman poet would have it: (A) he had lived life to the fullest in the various positions granted to him by an ambiguous Creator. He immediately reinforced this statement with incremental repetition to the effect that: (B) he had lived life fully, under vicarious guises, fulfilling the purpose imposed upon him by an omniscient God. This train of thought yielded a corollary in the form of a query regarding the apparent disconnect between (A) and (B) in relation to human volition. For, Leer reasoned, how could he presume to have lived independent of constraints given the severe and controlling hand of such a deity? This deduction was succeeded by a series of deprecating remarks in which the subject queried whether he had: (i) revelled in what could actually be defined with some accuracy as monotony; (ii) fostered self-delusions as to his actual status; (iii) over-rated (see Levi-Strauss) the concomitant value of his experiences. Finally, he posed a precise rhetorical question: "am I floating around in lymph like some hairy foetus, huddled into a ball to conceal my shrivelled genitals?" He turned to Tom Hallem, who had no vital rejoinder, let alone sop, tears welling in his offended eye, and grasped the loose black denim on his companion's wilting shoulder like Stephen Dedalus steadying himself against Leopold Bloom, symbolically the act of a child as it rises to take its first steps, which is a clear image of paternity in *Ulysses*, part of his education by Bloom, which extends to instruction on how query not disclaim, and to acknowledge ignorance and vulnerability, traits which do not come naturally to the arrogant youth, all the while dictating as proof of his value to human amelioration a chronological list of relevant functions over the course of his lifetime: (1) employee, slag factory, weekdays; (2) Sharpie (AKA Town Terror), nights and Sabbath; (3) husband, of dutiful bride; (4) father (see sons); (5) entrepreneur; and, in the near future, (6) he concluded by announcing that [JERKING], "they said they'd installed a bomb in my heart and if I told anyone they'd blow me up ... and also Mother. Blahblahblah. They're in complete control. I'll do anything they say." He swung violently around a telegraph pole at this moment, revolving round'n'down like a finely calibrated drill bit. His body pitched. Splinters inundated his palms. Leer's speechifying induces a Beckett-like impression of humanity possessing ZERO freedom of choice or realistic opportunity to alter or modify the random or deistically devised course of events in life, rather resembling that plasticine creature of Promethean abstraction who was fashioned to bend and blow in the breeze of existence like a fresh reed yet not snap, which would have been its fate if it had been subject to more brittle composition, thereby in fact illustrating the benefits of fluidity in the human condition. These were precisely the virtues ascribed to Odysseus, which won the day at Troy. Leer then answered his own question in the affirmative to the effect that periodically he had indeed indulged in self-aggrandisement or at least expended his energy in alchemical production. At this point, a revelation occurred as to the meaning of the Legend of the Brazen Head, its supreme ironical qualities of nomenclature as a public house in Dublin being noted by the author, wherein the devil endows a mouthpiece with the power of prophecy to entice unfortunate friars to spellbound observation, by which means they miss the decisive moment of UTTERANCE, at which point it goes silent thus it spoke then it broke. All versions of this legend end thus. Analogies to Odin's Mim (see C7) should be noted. The upshot of this deduction was that perhaps Leer had been premature in his assessment of relative levels of sentient autonomy and that he was now able to perceive the glass as proverbially half-empty rather than nominally half-full and thus bobbing mid-range like the axiomatic cork. This is considered a hallmark of Late Western Capitalism in its Post-Theocratic stage. Materialism has supplanted ethics. Some ascribe this collective slough to the associated rise of science. This is a valid theorem. Leer confessed openly that he suspected a tendency in himself to accept this hypothesis in order to shield himself from the consequences of spilling his metaphoric legacy on a symbolical mattress as per infamous Onan. Suddenly, he asked aloud of Hallem, as if of Kant, as if he was some sceptic of the school of Saint Augustine, "so what is good then ... what evil," all the while conceding that he had been bedevilled by this dichotomy ... but not really. Finally, he moaned: "this must have been how the apes started. Everything becomes part of some causal sequence. You charge the turd running down your legs with meaning." Tom Hallem demurred. Their association was more in the nature of non-verbal handstands and shared experience than gushes of empathy, which was an appropriate correspondent to the interaction of Leopold Bloom and Stephen Dedalus post-Nighttown when they listed tastes and opinions on opera, poetry and politics, the principal distinguishing feature being that the enthusiasm of the younger man for rapid amelioration had been tempered in the elder by faith in incremental progress. Nonetheless, Bloom was sensitive not to disturb SD's ardour, and not in a patronising way, being alive to the risk that puncturing an under-developed afflatus at such a sensitive juncture might sow the seeds of what the Germans call "world sorrow," the French term "Existentialism" and theoretician's "Nihilism," or in its practical manifestation "Anarchism." Such violence both LB/SD abhorred. It was prevalent in the epoch during which Joyce composed his *opus*, no event being more illustrative than the assassination of Archduke Fuckface by G. Princep, which became the catalyst for the Great War. Rather, the mentor herein acted in the mould of Machiavelli's archer who, in seeing that the object appeared too far distant, and knowing the inadequate force of his fully stressed device, raised it to a much higher mark allowing gravity and draught to assist the arrow's passage to its intended mark, which was finally struck with less fervent force yet still with sufficient penetrative power to cause a decisive puncture. Some would conjecture that such a lukewarm and diluted philosophy of gradual betterment as proposed by Leopold Bloom would incite the scorn of historical revolutionary figures in the period before and after the composition of *Ulysses*. However, analysis of relevant tracts discloses that time's passage necessarily plays a pivotal role in tying off the thick-flowing vein of custom and inducing public opinion towards conversion in matters of reform, culminating in the eventual deshabille as it were of the worn vestiges of Empire and immolation of those frayed and musty robes which HH-1970 perpetually wears upon his stunted personage. In such an arrangement, one can only expect Euphuism to pursue cumbersome, discursive metaphors; for example, the representation of the body politic as a husband who spills his seed on barren earth through vigorous semaphore rather than inject his life-milk into the designated empirical receptacle, which may or may not have been polluted by his brother, as in the ambiguous instance of Catherine of Aragon, wherein an ostensibly dutiful wife, due to vagaries of papal dispensation, came to represent a mere hand-me-down object bearing the sweat stains and scratches of an elder, nay better, sibling, now sadly departed, passed away and passed on, thus ensuring her own disposal. The cross-currents, knots and ambiguity of correspondences between these historical figures and both Penelope Hallem and Helen Capri were duly interrogated in all earnestness by this author. Tom Hallem, in contrast, focused on his own predicament, as modified by unforeseen events which had unfolded today, whereby his now-disclosed younger sibling, although evincing a mere four months delay in succession, yet still represented a whoreson as per the precepts laid down by the Duke of Gloucester in his proposition on social mores at the high watermark of the Elizabethan age. In addition, Tom was pre-occupied with the meaning of his father's sudden reappearance in Sydney after a period approximate to Odysseus' absence from Ithaca. This conundrum had not stopped him discharging the obligations of erection but not coition with Candy, courtesy of a masculine ability to block out spiritual matters during the discharge of corporeal obligations. On the other side of the equation, emotions were running high as his semi-sibling came to terms with a new and wholly different set of familial relations, in which his heretofore 'father' had been relegated to the status of a mere guardian of the prize due to the lack of injection of relevant genes and chromosomes via spermatozoon into his mother's uterus, which redefined him as a direct contestant in the spectacle of the repatriation of Donald John Cane [INSERT BIRTH CERITIFICATE] rather than a supportive yet, ultimately, detached bystander as in the analogy of a full English breakfast where the pig is said to be 'committed' while the chicken is merely an 'interested spectator.' Alone in his apartment, amongst discarded possessions and packaging materials that bore the proof of a dissembling residence, Master William Capri reviewed psychic bygones for tell-tale signs of deception from his mother and her consort. They now appeared in the roles of scheming Gertrude and usurpatory Claudius respectively rather than say Polybus/Merope, Philemon/Baucis, Simon and Mary Dedalus or John and Mary Joyce. As a scholar, he observed from a scan of literary referents and historical precedents that there were very few stable, continuous family structures across time. Here we should acknowledge Count Tolstoy's dictum. It was all too much for the neophyte on the eve of his relocation to Great Britain, where he intended to continue his studies, Laertes-like, although it had no impact on physical logistics, which had been calculated well in advance to match the university calendar and seasonal fluctuations in airfares, and which were now merely a matter of due process, but rather bore on the emotive angle. Euphuism is employed in this section with the same intent as Joyce using the catechism style to deny the reader any sentimental triggers. W. Capri did indeed resent the belated revelation by his erstwhile 'parents' while conceding, in moments of reflection, that they had limited alternatives to full and frank disclosure given the prevailing circumstances. The principal alternative in his estimation would have been transferring him to the airport post-haste in ignorance of the facts. This scenario was predicated on the assumption that Donald John Cane intended to reveal himself to the assembly ASAP and that he would either undertake the Capri confrontation first or have sufficient time to discharge both disclosures. There was no evidentiary basis for this supposition. Paranoia rather ruled the faculties of the participants in this at present one-sided drama, or shadow play in its colloquial sense. It should also be acknowledged that Don Cane was not aware of his younger son's prospective travel so it would have no bearing on his strategy. At this point, the subject became re-agitated like a washing machine resuming turbulent function after a pre-set hiatus of deep soakage. He steadied himself against my shoulder as we proceeded towards Wilson Street with its broken prospect of Macdonaldtown Railway Station. Suddenly, car headlights – pale, strong and faintly loitering – flamed from darkness. Cruising they was. A torch shone on the face of a lone pedestrian at the corner of Pine Street. Hallem felt cold air pass over his skin. It was like the precedent breeze of a train before it bursts out of a railway tunnel. Three silhouettes punctuated the dim cabin. I grabbed Leer by the shirt sleeve and pulled him along Burren Street. Our bodies were partially hidden under a low Camphor Laurel. My goal: to get out of their sight-line ASAP. To keep Medea off the Colchians. For they is bad dope. We dashed past a row of worker's cottages. A bald brick rail buttress shaded our forms. Argent fluorescence announced the station entrance. Sanctuary. We passed the ticket booth turned right and climbed the stairs to the platform lickety-spit. At the summit, Sydney's flat sandhills spread south towards port cranes. A lone aircraft lowered itself from the sky. Empty trains sped lightly down express tracks. SH/SH, they said. Hallem turned to Leer. "COME ON," I said. Leer's mouth moved. SCH/SCH/SCH. An iron drain caused Leer to trip. Hallem held him upright. We spun west towards a parapet. Keep your head down. We descended onto the tracks and hid behind a brick maintenance shed. Hallem grab a length of lead pipe lying next to the crushed stone ballast of the track bed. Kubrick's monkey. Slightly too long to use as a bludgeon. Need swinging space. But a weapon nevertheless. Rest. Suck. Pause. Hold. Listen. Sound. It ebbed. Crawl over tracks to a rusted fence overlooking the street. Limited angle. No sign of vehicle. A train slowly approached swinging into a late curve next to the signal gantry. Grinding to a halt, it disgorged a few passengers. Let them pass then tailgate. Descend. Odysseus skulked into the palace in rags telling people any old shit that came into his head. Isolating the traitors. In studied silence. The enamel passageway gleamed like pale mica. We reached the threshold. I scanned the road. No sign of trouble. We set off south down Burren Street. INSERT ROUTE-MAP (Newtown > Alexandria). It would only be a few metres until we were safe in paperbark trees and parked cars as the road tightened into a dead end.

INSERT MODERNIST DEVICE

What related imagery did Leer and Hallem envision which was symptomatic of their respective backgrounds?

To Leer and Hallem flowed a subcutaneous image of City Rail diagrams conveniently positioned on the walls of passenger railway stations and carriages. To Hallem, it depicted the suburban rail network (or "Sydney System") of the Sydney metropolitan area (or "Sydney Region"). Leer, by contrast, focused on the rail system of the State of New South Wales. To Hallem came a sequence of stations along the Main Western Line: Macdonaldtown Nighttown Stanmore Petersham Lewisham Summer Hill Ashfield Croydon Burwood Strathfield then all stations to Bankstown via Regents Park. To Leer, the Main Western Line was the flinch of Countrylink Services stopping at Parramatta Blacktown and Penrith then all stations to Katoomba and Lithgow change at Lithgow for Bathurst Blayney Orange

Molong Manildra and Parkes change at Parkes for Condobolin set-down only at Euabalong West Ivanhoe Darnick and Menindee train terminates at Broken Hill. The Silver City Comet was the first diesel-powered, air-conditioned train in the British Empire. It commenced operations in 1937. There was a famous train trip of Broken Hill families to hear Tom Mann expound socialism across the border at Cockburn, South Australia in 1909. Leer alighted three stops before Broken Hill.

Link to *Ulysses*.

Murphy-the-sailor's tales in Eumaeus remind Bloom of his own unrealised travel dreams. He has taken a safe option in life. This is part of the reason for Molly's boredom. By contrast, the reader is already aware that Stephen Dedalus – as a proxy for Joyce – will eschew security for the life of an expatriate in Europe.

Name another literary icon who utilised sequences in rail timetables.

Marcel Proust.

How does Proust fit into *Telemachus*?

He doesn't. TMAC sits alongside him. He provides a technical and autobiographical model for the next volume, *Vault*, which deals with my mother through the lens of Jeanne Proust. The title exploits the opposite effects of this word. For my mother was sealed shut as a person, yet floated freely through space via music. These works will form a triptych, *One Million Words Like Proust*. The final volume, *Binary Nights* (*1111101011 Nights*), tells the story of a postgender family, based on the legendary figure of Sc(he/her)azade. Gertrude Stein is its technical pillar. Man, woman and family – that is the subject matter of *+1m Words*.

Describe quotidian events.

Hallem reviewed Burren Street warily. A taxi squealed in the Albert Street chicane. Its strong headlights blinded him. Both men turned involuntarily towards an abandoned gasometer scaffold. Set in prairie grass on a ruined concrete base. The tank had been dismantled and removed from site. They continued towards Erskineville Road. The footpath thinned. Hallem fell into line behind Leer, who paused against a wire gate. He tested the padlock. It would not yield. They would have to expose themselves to detection crossing the rail overpass. The Rose of Australia Hotel lay somewhere ahead. In Eumaeus, Bloom takes Stephen a short distance from the brothel at 82 Tyrone Street Lower to a primitive transport workers' shelter beneath the elevated double track on Nighttown's treacherous south border, where steam-powered freight trains painstakingly pass all night up and down Montgomery Street making for the port. Ireland had been a comparatively advanced manufacturing country in 1800 when full union with Britain was imposed. By 1904, Dublin was outdone by Belfast with its modern shipyards and factories producing fine Irish linen. It had been stripped of industrial capacity and suffered the largest mass emigration in modern history. The only factories left in Dublin by Joyce's time were the Guinness brewery and Jacob's biscuit factory. Cheap raw materials such as timber and marble and, of course, agricultural produce like potatoes and livestock were exported straight to Britain. Up to 2,000 prostitutes worked the streets of Monto. Amiens Street Station nearby disgorged country girls desperate for work. They made their keep streetwalking around the military barracks at Aldborough House. If they went mad, they ended up in a crowded cell in Magdalen Asylum. Discharged patients huddled outside its walls with nowhere else to go. Joyce captures this carnivalesque blend of madness, sex, filth and privation at the start of Circe where the thick floral odour of over-perfumed petticoats scraped against unwashed loins and sweat. Today, it's all been renamed. Montgomery Street is called Foley Street. Tyrone Street, Railway Street. Mabbot Street itself has been ironically renamed James Joyce Street. You can even traverse Joyce's Walk north-south directly towards the Talbot Street overpass.

What emotions did The Rose of Australia Hotel elicit for the companions?

To Leer: the thrill of a blues harp driving grunge boogie. Straw hat over thinning pate. Heavy beards matted with tobacco stains. Faded blue jeans and Victory steel-capped work boots. Eureka flag crucified across the back of the stage. Irish barmaids serving icy schooners. Change for the cigarette machine please. Controlling the pool table for six or seven games with Big Vic. The glow on a Sunday session as the sun sinks under rain. There's still time for two more schooners if you're fast. Eight o'clock closing time. Stagger down Union Street six pack under each arm your girlfriend's tit squashed under nicotine digits. Movie of the Week. Appetite at 10 pm. Pizza shop's still open. Fanciful lust about midnight, settle for a grip in the sack then restless dreams, nocturnal piss and Monday's grubby work slate. To Hallem: dope-dealers in ragged flairs. Struggle for service at the bottle shop when all you want is a pair of warm VB long necks. One elbow resting on a sodden bar towel seeping through your shirt-sleeve. Raise an intemperate arm to attract attention when all they're interested in is fossils falling out of Harley t-shirts. Their bulbous guts obscure Marlboro belt buckles. Put on the wobbly boot and get totally maggoted. Chance of a thrashing if you're not dutiful. Beer plus that half-bottle of McWilliam's port in the pantry will do the job. All these images are symbols, ending with the invocation to return to technical writing under the 2-FWD, 1-BACK influence of booze.

OF THE POSTMODERN

What devices from episodes other than Eumaeus are employed in this chapter?

1. Ironic/comic headings (Aeolus). This started in the previous chapter.
2. Q&A format (Ithaca).
3. Recurrent paternal and birth imagery (Oxen of the Sun).

Why?

1. To demonstrate that this is not just a simulation of *Ulysses*.
2. To disclose Joyce's own methodology, which made wilful use of the Homeric template.
3. To reassert the postmodern element.
4. To create stylistic continuity between the previous chapter, Circe, and the next chapter, Ithaca.

Outline the plot of this episode in *The Odyssey*.

In Book 13, Odysseus returns to Ithaca. He considers the risk of suffering Agamemnon's fate if he goes straight home announcing his identity. He consults with Athena. She gives him news of his beleaguered household and Telemachus' voyage. This arouses conflicting emotions. Athena disguises him as an old beggar and counsels him to seek out the hut of the swineherd Eumaeus. Eumaeus receives Odysseus with hospitality in Book 14. Book 15 is divided between Telemachus, who avoids an ambush set by the suitors as he returns to Ithaca, and Odysseus, who receives news of the situation on Ithaca. In Book 16, Telemachus arrives at Eumaeus' hut. Odysseus interrogates his son. Telemachus answers thoughtfully. He sends Eumaeus on a secret mission to Penelope. Father and son are left alone. Athena enters. She transforms Odysseus with her golden wand. Odysseus reveals himself. Father and son are reunited. They start planning to recapture their home.

Consider Eumaeus from the POV of Telemachus.

Telemachus visits Eumaeus as soon as he gets off the boat from Sparta as directed by Athene. Eumaeus is overjoyed to see him return safely. He enters the hut. An old beggar from Crete is present. Telemachus expresses embarrassment at his inability to offer *Xenia*. The drifter expresses empathy with Telemachus' plight. He asks pointed questions. Telemachus answers frankly. They discuss the role of brothers. Telemachus notes that Zeus has made his house a place of single sons only. He provides some insight into Penelope's plight. Eumaeus is asked to go and advise Penelope of his homecoming. Telemachus rejects Eumaeus' suggestion of a side journey to advise his grandfather, Laertes. That can happen later. Exit Eumaeus. Enter Athene. Behold Odysseus. Telemachus is awed by the transformation. Initially, he demurs. Odysseus persists. A kiss. A tear. His artful tongue sways his son. They embrace. More tears. A story. Odysseus is impatient. He has come to the hut to consult on how to slaughter their enemies. They are two men only. But they have Athene and Zeus behind them. Odysseus instructs Telemachus to hide a cache of weapons around the palace. A herald announces his return to Penelope. The suitors are upset. They discuss next steps. Penelope appears before them and upbraids Antinous. He replies stridently. It is the start of his death monologue. Eumaeus returns to the hut. Athena transforms Odysseus into an old beggar once more. Odysseus, Telemachus and Eumaeus eat a meal then sleep.

NARCISSUS OVER THE POND

Explain above headline.
Joyce looking at Homer seeing himself.

Is Joyce observing Homer or gazing into it himself?
Leave that sentence as a solecism. A: Shakespeare's bust.

Compare "Ulysses" with its Homeric model.
Ulysses is a metonymy of heroic tropology, which condenses the epic scale to quotidian margins and reduces the action from high to low mimetic. An apparently simple structure conceals deep formal and stylistic licenses with its source. Like the *Odyssey*, the text of *Ulysses* occupies a short time span. It is the fruit of substantial gestation. Joyce does not appropriate the *Odyssey* directly. Rather, he exploits its prestige by using segments to act as a proxy for teleology and narrative resolution. He alters the Homeric order. *Ulysses* is imbued with complex Classical referents, which sustain its power and inform additional layers of meaning. The Homeric association evokes links with the fantastic elements of Classical literature, enabling Joyce to lighten his narrative and pointing the way towards Magic Realism. This festive tone is consistent with the operations of a drinking spree, which is the basic plot. *Ulysses* is a text about a world ruled by arbitrary death and conflict, like the *Odyssey*. It relies on the fullness of Homer's narrative to provide architectonic power that its confined, quotidian structure could not sustain. In other words, it exploits correspondences with the *Odyssey* to insinuate meaning. However, the *Odyssey* as such is only selectively employed. Instead, tangential associations are promoted. Characterisation is fluid even relative to Joyce's immediate needs. Molly acts as Calypso to Bloom's Odysseus when she is first introduced only to be re-characterised as Penelope at the end of the novel. This use of updated or shifting characterisation is justified

by Stephen Dedalus during his discourse on Hamlet when he talks of how the artist must weave and unweave his image (194) to energise Shelley's 'fading coal' of the imagination. It is a distinctly Shelleyan form of literary relativity. Without the authority of the *Odyssey*, both Joyce's structure and characterisations would seem unbalanced – even insubstantial. The novel is a pastiche of a homeward voyage. Each episode in *Ulysses* ends with everything "up in the air." It is only the Homeric template which implies fixity. For example, we do not know what happens to Stephen Dedalus after he leaves Bloom's residence on Eccles Street on the night of the novel – only what happened in real time to his alter ego, James Joyce. Information is introduced without context only to be clarified later in the text. Joyce lays grid across grid so that narrative segments intersect and time stalls. The progress of Earl and Lady Dudley on the vice-regal residence is used to summarise and clarify narrative actions up to this point. It provides a snapshot of characters already introduced – or about to be introduced – into the novel including Simon Dedalus Rev Love Lenehan McCoy Gerty MacDowell John Wyse Nolan Mulligan Haines Dilly Dedalus John Henry Menton Blazes Boylan Master Patrick Dignam (son of the deceased) the blind stripling. Such innovations may seem clumsy to contemporary readers. *Ulysses* can be likened to the first cart: its discs are a clumsy approximation to circularity, true, but it still represents a revolution in terms of speed and distance of motion.

What of Homer's 24 divisions?

Not utilised by Joyce. He employed 18 units. This is characteristic of his selective use of the *Odyssey*.

What is shared in the numerology of both works?

Eumaeus is book/episode 16 of each work. This is the only time that Joyce is numerologically aligned with Homer. Elsewhere, he toys with the *Odyssey's* plot and chronology.

How could one update Joyce's structure?

Scatter his order. Re-impose Homeric order upon. Blend into a new system. Dissolve at will, according to plot needs. Select a symbolic number for each chapter.

How has Joyce's literary strategy been updated by later trends in literature?

Ulysses represented a type of closure like the end of the Classical epoch after the *Odyssey*. Joyce himself could not produce a coherent successor. *F(W)ake* was an exercise in literary extremis. A ty(r/p)e puncture. Postmodern fiction took-up self-conscious appropriation of master narratives. It became valid to extend the text BEYOND the term of the model (e.g. *Sargasso Sea*). Characterisation could also be altered. Today, many novels rework the life of a character, usually for ideological purposes. Magic fiction was introduced by South American writers and taken up by European novelists complete with plot deficiencies, a lazy approach to symbolism and a keen eye on brand-positioning. Its formal naming ludicrously but cunningly annexed the term 'realism' to create an oxymoron at its core, thereby disqualifying criticism from both ends. Its flights of fancy in a demotic setting simulate the worst elements of medieval fantasies. They 'cop out' of life. The Big Novel has also made a comeback as if Trollope was immortal.

Examine the word count of *Ulysses* against relevant samples.

Table 10 contains the word counts of twenty-three famous works of literature in no

TABLE 11. WORD COUNTS OF FAMOUS LITERATURE (EDITION NOT SPECIFIED)

1.	*Ulysses*	265,222
2.	*Middlemarch*	320,264
3.	*Le Temps Perdu*	1,267,069
4.	*Poor Fellow My Country*	852,000
5.	*War and Peace*	587,287
6.	*Midnight's Children*	208,773
7.	*The Brothers Karamazov*	364,153
8.	*1984*	88,942
9.	*Finnegans Wake*	204,960
10.	*The Sun Also Rises*	67,707
11.	*Term of His Natural Life*	81,740
12.	*Bleak House*	360,947
13.	*Pere Goriot*	87,846
14.	*Sentimental Education*	133,255
15.	*Portrait of the Artist*	117,120
16.	*Dubliners*	23,055
17.	*Paradise Lost*	80,055
18.	*King Lear*	26,145
19.	*Hamlet*	30,066
20.	*The Bible*	783,137
21.	*Voss*	141,520
22.	*The Iliad*	84,419
23.	*The Odyssey*	119,368

formal order. A representative sample of Australian literature is included. Series are not included (except The Bible). Some works have been counted in translation. There are word count variations according to edition, despite the availability of modern computing. Nonetheless the data yield enough quantitative evidence to produce a series of conclusions and recommendations.

The table indicates:

- Total count is 6,295,050 words
- Arithmetic mean is 273,698 words
- *Ulysses* has a total of 265,222 words. It is the work closest to the Mean. This places it seventh on the list by volume. Surprisingly, it is 30% longer than *Finnegans Wake* (see analysis below).
- The longest work is by Proust followed by Herbert.
- Drama provides the shortest works for the reason of time-limited performance.

According to Wikipedia, the typical word count of a modern novel is 80,000 words. This precludes DIY vanity publishing. Most agents and editors will consider a first novel with a word count under 100,000 words. It is worth contemplating whether other art mediums enable the same level of intervention as book publishing. For example, does an art dealer directly alter the image on a canvas? Sociologists claim that the contemporary reader cannot sustain the necessary concentration for long works. However, the Harry Potter series had a total word count of +1 million words in 7 volumes. By comparison, Shakespeare wrote 835,000 words in 37 plays. Word count does not consider the impact of textual complexity – in particular, style, but also, to a lesser extent, plot, on reading time. Readinglength.com calculates that the average reader will spend 17 hours and 40 minutes reading *Ulysses* (Shine Classics) at 250 WPM (words per minute). This is the same speed as conventional narratives such as *Middlemarch*, *Pere Goriot* and *Bleak House*. Such works would be consumed at a faster speed than *Ulysses*. A more extreme example is *Finnegans Wake* which contains a multi-layered plot, remythologises Western cosmos, fractures characterisation, creates endless neologisms, cites 60 different languages and is supported by a "multifractal structure" only recently discovered by mathematicians using heat mapping. Philip K. Dick wrote: "I'm going to prove that *Finnegans Wake* is an information pool, based on computer memory systems that didn't exist until centuries after Joyce's era. He was plugged into an alien consciousness from which he derived the inspiration for his entire corpus." INSERT WEB CITATION. Daily production count varies. Hemingway was said to produce 500 words per day. Ballard claimed 1,000 words per day, even with a hangover. This is the equivalent of one A4 page of single-spaced, ten-point text in Calibri font. Joyce said in a letter to Miss Weaver that he spent almost 20,000 hours writing *Ulysses* (*Ellmann*, 510). This is 833 days across a seven-year or 2,555-day period. It thus represents ~32% of Joyce's total time from 1914 to 1920. In "*Ulysses* by Numbers," Eric Bulson analyses the compositional practice of Joyce, particularly in response to publication requirements. Bulson concludes that "even after serialisation stopped, Joyce was still writing by the numbers" (26). He always wrote in 6,000-word instalments, as suggested by Pound. This is what Bulson calls "the serial logic of length" (6). His analytical approach produces some interesting insights. The complex Circe episode, for example, was designed to fit into eight instalments of *The Little Review*. "We can indeed count" words, concludes Bulson, and therefore "the counting must go on" (4).

What is the word count of this work as at this point in C8?
Approximately 240,000 words.

Prospective word count?
+300,000 words.

Objective?
To defeat Joyce in terms of volume in a game of "ignore the pattern, just feel the width of the material, sir" variety (as noted in C6).

Insert more valiant goals.
To recalibrate Joyce for the digital era and click(bait) culture. To match Joyce in presenting the city as a complex data set. To write *Joyce for Dummies*. To differentiate Homer in this task. To help. To submit for public inspection the full corpus of my miscellaneous writings over three decades, using the postmodern novel format. To write something substantial in this genre because I haven't read anything truly satisfying to date. To rewrite *In Memoriam* for David McComb. To register my historic sins in code as a means of expiation (see Foucault).

What conscious swerves have been executed?
To avoid competing with Joyce on style. That was one of his strong suits. His innovations in Modernism can never be repeated. We are all "styled-out" in terms of shock value. Vico was wrong. There can never be a Second Beatles. I wanted to write clearly and directly like Samuel Beckett in the fictive passages and densely and academically in the literary critical mode. To deploy Joyce's own styles in each episode only as necessary for disclosure of the unpresentable

became my limit. Otherwise, it felt unnatural to ape Joyce's signature styles. I didn't like it. I didn't know when to stop. Portmanteau words and puns verging on the incomprehensible emanated out of my cosmos like thorns (See pp. 17, 467).

What challenges to Joyce were accepted?

To deploy Lyotard's definition of the postmodern and engage directly with Joyce on form. This was his other great strong suit. To be more adventurous than Beckett in terms of form. He was left with a very limited palette in the aftermath of Joyce and WWII. I felt that a genuinely new path in literature was possible using this tactic.

What is the main point of academic interest?

Can a writer act as his own best critic, that is, the central conundrum of this volume?

Compare the composition and publication of *Ulysses* with this work.

Joyce was already a prominent writer when *Ulysses* first started to appear in non-sequential instalments in *The Little Review*. There was strident feedback for the author to consider. Each episode was subsequently amended by Joyce before final publication. This process has been exquisitely chronicled by Kevin Birmingham. In contrast, TMAC has been produced in isolation by a nonentity. It has been drafted and refined without any publication of extracts. There is no support network for the writer. It will be a DIY publication under the AnAnnal banner.

Why did you decide to bifurcate the Telemachus figure?

1) To create a different structure to Homer and Joyce.
2) To set down makers of originality.

I wanted to make human exchanges more complex than a simple father/son dyad because I believe that the POV of the son figure is more problematic than Joyce espoused. He was extremely secure in his lineage, which he reflected in Stephen Dedalus. I set out to find a biological quandary/quotient which reflected the mess of human relations. I wanted these young men to be friends but more than friends. I wanted them to be reclassified as brothers but not really be brothers. I wanted their relationship to be tested by forces beyond their control. Tom Hallam had lots of friends. I wasn't his best friend but he was certainly mine. He was my Arthur Hallam. I was his Horatio. In Eumaeus, we reach the frontline of the father/son dynamic in the dramatic reunion of Odysseus and Telemachus. Joyce eases the reader to the same point by stealth. One is epic, the other cursory. It is all so uncomplicated. Shanghai Dog reflected that this unbound period had never been resolved.

Atmosphere of this episode?
Blithe (i.e. postmodern).

Give an example of this strategy in practice anywhere in your work.
The appropriation of the form and style of Circe as a template for Chapter Seven.

Stylistic Similarities?
Loose association with the archetype. Use of dramatic form. Arbitrary incursions of dream. Discursion. Accumulation and juxtaposition of fragments. Incongruous elements. Fantasy figures. Unrealistic interaction of disconnected characters. Some dead.

Differences?
Absence of Lynch. Copulation of father and son inside same female consecutively. This is a symbol of degraded paternity (false father figure or FFF).

Genealogy of this prosaics?
Signposted but not acknowledged appropriation of form, style and content was the currency of Hieratic literature in Victorian England. Just as Pater wilfully subsumed Ruskin without citation so Wilde, in turn, playfully and silently subsumed Pater.

Joyce's precursors (receding)?
Wilde > Pater > Swinburne > Shelley.

List Joyce's influences in the Circe episode.
The whore-mistress, Bella, is a Swinburnean giantess stripped of Classical dayglow. Her descent onto Bloom's face alludes to G.M. Hopkins' Sonnet 69 ("Lord, You Squat and the Sky Your Cunt-lips Bury Me"). Bloom's concomitant outlook (or up-look) recalls Baudelaire: "we must get down on our hands and knees like dogs, roll over on our backs and lick the cunt of Mary Magdalene" (1864). This motif was taken up by Georges Bataille for the climax of *Story of the Eye*. Rossetti is infamous for digging up his wife's corpse and fucking her skull through the eye socket. Samuel Beckett incorporated the adjective 'loving' into ironic images [ie. loving licks of his toad-skinned scrotum (*Trilogy* 345)]. Note also general influence of Jacobean dramatists, Ibsen and Dada (Swiss subdivision).

Compare attitudes to sex of Bloom and Stephen.
An obsession with sex is firmly part of Bloom's universe, along with Molly, Boylan and

a host of older characters. Stephen Dedalus is generally uninterested in carnal matters. For example, when Bloom sermonises about disease-ridden prostitutes in Eumaeus in a "DO/SAY NOT DO/DO" moment, Stephen immediately lifts the conversation to a cosmological plane. Bloom is completely lost at this level. This is another instance of his inapplicability as a father figure. His hypocrisy regarding prostitution should also be noted in this instance.

Of Bella and the Marquis de Sade?

Circe alludes to Sade, Sacher-Masoch and Victorian pornography's contempt for Roman Catholic clerical immorality and, of course, women. An example is the anonymous novel, *Autobiography of a Flea*, which chronicles the observations of a louse secreted in the *mons veneris* of a voluptuous virgin named Bella. She is surprised by a priest named Ambrose during her first sexual act then subjected to an orgy with local clergy in a parody of absolution. This is structured according to a strict hierarchy in which each successive cleric escalates in rank and phallic dimensions until the sacrilegious denouement: "'Let us F**k,' piously ejaculated the Superior ... 'Amen,' chanted Ambrose." The novel offers a sequence of immoral activities including: (1) instruction of virgins in *ars erotica*; (2) schemes to ensnare new recruits through incestuous sexual substitution (echo of Chaucer, *Measure for Measure* et al.); (3) plot resolution in establishment of conventual brothel. It inflates sexual usufruction to absurdity so that clerical miscreance is its final intelligence and misogyny its latent affirmation.

How could the Circe episode be modified for a contemporary audience?

Joyce's parody of pornographic flagellation could be updated with explicit sex and violence. Add drugs and guns. INSERT gangsters. Soundtrack by N. Cave. Also, we could explore gender fluidity from the perspective of family power relations. NOTE – this work is already more explicit in rendering sexual practice.

Exemplify the influence of Swinburne on Joyce.

Joyce shared Swinburne's interest in affronting conventional morality with blasphemous and/or pornographic matter via elevated style in idealised settings. This was also comic antinomianism. For example, Swinburne used romance language and an elaborate formal apparatus to explore necrophilia in "The Leper." Likewise, Joyce has Bloom conjecture whether the statues of Greek goddesses were granted anuses. Both writers sought to hide the highly-charged sexual content of their works in a mandible style; thereby deflecting contemporary outrage and censorship. Swinburne employed classical characters and medieval language. Joyce employed a range of surrealist devices and Modernist High Style.

SHE WESSHE HER GOODLY BODY BARE

How does Joyce tread yet efface the path of Swinburne?

Joyce heals the disjuncture in Swinburne where attention to poetics (style and form) requires reversion to remote historical matter. *Ulysses* deploys Modernist High Style in a demotic setting. This means it is a formal and thematic advance on *A Portrait of the Artist as a Young Man*, which was still tied to esoteric conceptions of art, as evidenced by its numerous Latin quotations, dense philosophical and aesthetic discourses and fragments of poetry and songs. Incidentally, these were all strategies utilised by Swinburne in his aborted novels.

Project Swinburne's influence onto Joyce through literary third parties (1870–1900)?

Swinburne's early poetry must be considered in the wider context of the nineteenth century ethical debate over the future of religion and the validity of existing moral codes in the wake of Darwin's Theory of Evolution. Swinburne propelled himself into this vacuum through the virulence and carnal range of his subject matter. No blasphemy seemed beyond his capacity to poeticise with consummate style using the full range of forms. He perceived the potential intellectual and moral freedom to be attained by expanding into this void and challenging conventional morality and aesthetics. His poetry did not offer a philosophical system. It simply demolished social mores. Swinburne galvanised a generation of readers against the moralising, utilitarian strictures of demotic aesthetics and provided a platform for later writers as diverse as Pater, Moore and Wilde. Each exploited quite specific facets of Swinburne's poetics and persona: Pater as the austere Heraclitan/Epicurean; Moore, the Francophile dilettante; and Wilde, the arch-appropriating celebrity.

Remove Swinburne's influence to its origin (1790–1821)?

The influence of Percy Bysshe Shelley on Swinburne has been widely examined. It was also acknowledged by Swinburne through numerous references in his own poetry, critical writings and correspondence. Direct references, allusions, appropriations and correspondences litter his works. An obvious example is the epigraph to "A New Year's Message," which comes from Shelley's "To Emilia Viviani." In another vein, the late poem, "In the Bay," is an elaborate allegory in which the evening star acts as a symbol of Shelley and his death. "The Eve of the Revolution" appropriates the emotional power of "Ode to the West Wind" with Swinburne working Shelley's anthemic political rhetoric into his own refrain, "I set the trumpet to my lips and blow." (See "light the lamp," Appendix A) Similarly, "Prelude" and the Epilogue to *Songs Before Sunrise* are deeply indebted to "Ode to Liberty." From a biographical point of view, Swinburne was clearly immersed in Shelley in the late 1850s. He presented a paper on Robert Browning's monograph, "Shelley," to his reading group, Old Mortality, soon after its publication in 1858. Swinburne was particularly taken by personal correspondences with Shelley such as aristocratic birth, schooling at Eton and the achievement in being "sent down" from Oxford.

How does Joyce influence Samuel Beckett?

Beckett was forced to literary extremes to sidestep the Joycean impasse. One could argue that he paralysed his prosaic before Joyce in the same way as his characters, creating a perfect alignment of form and meta-form. The body of Beckett's texts are always positioned so close to the end of their apparent tropes that there is hardly any narrative movement available and closure always seems imminent. Joyce is like a cathedral spire at sundown casting an increasingly elongated shadow that pierces the heart of Beckett as supplicant.

What is the link between *Ulysses* and *Under Milkwood*?

Under Milkwood is *Ulysses* as a radio play. Both are set on a single day. Both are comic. Poetical. Humanist. Captain Cat combines James Joyce with Odysseus (a blind old sailor). Thomas adds dreaming thereby extending his scope BEYOND *Ulysses* towards *F(W)ake*.

List divergences.

Bucolic location. Brevity. Style.

Where do you acknowledge this correspondence?

At the start of Chapter 2.

FROM PHOETUS TO ORFAN

"But it would be better," opined Leer, as they crossed the railway overpass, "if we turned backwards ... backwards in Time, which is ironic, because it is only by going forwards again, beyond this point at which we are now stationed, that we will reach the close (SEE VICO). But where do you begin such a story? A story of violence, capture and conviction. A story of romance, redemption and the soul. Born I have been, but how, when, where ... these things escape me. I do not remember Mother or Mother's sack, bursting for me as she struggled down the track one morning when it was already thirty seven degrees at dawn and the mini bus swaggered away from her like some indolent tight holed virgin pumping Indian Red dusting powder in her wake, its aroma stunk all around her plump burdened undercarriage. Mother missed the bus to work. And dropped me that day. But I don't remember. I really don't remember. Nor have I tried. Was it even she who bore me, as the saying goes? It seems pointless to me to disturb yourself with reminiscences. I am told that it was she. This book tells me. There are certificates. It's even written in code on the bus advertisements. I saw it through the slits in the back of the paddy wagon that time. There was a picture of a mother and her baby. Baby giggling. Mother towelling. The word "Dickie!" And diesel grime. Ah, Mother! Once at her mammaries, now she's hardly memories. I can't recall her at all now even though it was only a few moments ago that she, her baby, and the brand name Dickie! were close to my soul. She has disappeared very quickly, leaving only the CODE. Because it's my identification with her as Mother that's important to Dickie! Yes, that's all they want off you these days, apparently. Just the right of impregnation – with an image – in your dome. I can't help feeling grateful to them somehow for only wanting me to identify with Dickie! and buy. [EXHAUSTED] It's a crude game. [GATHERING BREATHE. LOUD] I was conceived off the end of a meathook personally ... conceived in Slam mammon on an overcast afternoon ... so that I was already struggling against slime from the very beginning. Oh, they spit you out and cut away the umbilical cord, true, but only to replace it with a tourniquet or veil, which they stitch into your stomach, leaving you with blood oozing from your navel. [WISTFUL] How I yearn to regather that first flash of consciousness when I pusht through the sodden underwood, pungent sap leaked all around me and my half-whittled form peeped out of the cunt.

Link Leer's testimony of birth to *Ulysses*.

Above txt all SYMBOLIC. Refers to Joyce's obsession with motherlode. Apocryphal tales of Eumaeus episode. Link back to subject matter of C6 (Oxen). Banal nature of advertising [DICKIE]. Typical of his strategy to make symbolic what was mundane even awkward. Link to Bloom's profession. Also, Joyce's infancy before his father's behaviour and economic fortunes began to bear down on Mary Joyce. The death of George Joyce clubbed her down incontrovertibly.

ARROWS WOOD SMAIR HOSE WHEAT

Leer and Hallem reached the Housing Commission complex alongside Erskineville Park. Leer walked into a stand of sleek, spotted gum trees. His body went slack suddenly. He bent and vomited in a rose bed. I inclined against nobbled bark. The street was deserted. Apartments abandoned. No light. They planned an expedition to western NSW as they rode. This westerly directional pattern is commonly known as the Course of Empire. When the Pope carved up the maritime world between Spain and Portugal in the Treaty of Tordesillas at the end of the 15th century, he designated that the Portuguese held everything to the east and the Spanish all things west. Refer to the list of rail stations contemplated by Leer earlier in this chapter as a template for initial discussions on the route and timetable for their road trip. He favoured a direct route through Dubbo, Nyngan and Wilcannia to Broken Hill. This would be the base for striking north to Mungo and east to Menindee. Hallem expressed supplementary interest in a diversionary circuit from Dubbo to Gilgandra, Coonabarabran, Narrabri (Mount Kaputar), Walgett, Brewarrina, Bourke then down the Darling River to BH. TBH he would have been happier going through Tamworth rather than Dubbo. This would have enabled them to take in Gunnedah.

A MECHANICAL, MOVABLE TYPE

Shanghai Dog bought Xiao Fang some treats from C Store. She liked xiangchang impaled on bamboo sticks. They gushed chili oil when the thick casing was punctured. The cashier deposited them in a greaseproof bag. I also bought two hard-boiled eggs dyed in vinegar water and a can of Wang Lao Ji. The vendor at the news stand held up a copy of *China Daily*. S. Dog waved it away. He passed the Sichuanese restaurant. They made traditional hot dishes. There are five basic food styles in China. Like everything, there's a code: suan, tian, ku, la, xian. We have already observed the use of 'suan' meaning sour with reference to Shanghai brown wine in C7. Shanghai-style food was sweet. TIAN. Also, too oily. TAI DUO YOU. A rusty aperture in a tall cast iron gate opened. Gilles Bourdieu popped onto the pavement and pulled the door shut. Its lock rattled in the stiff frame. The Trojans were stunned. He was wearing broad grey shorts. His slender brown legs planted themselves in hi-tech, fluorescent green walking shoes. A yellow windbreaker was zipped to his throat.

"Off to the gym?" asked Shanghai Dog.

"Yes. I'm climbing Mount Damavand next month. I need to get in some serious training. Will you join me?"

"Can't. I got Su back at my place."

"OK buddy," he said with a grin. "Give her a big mouthful of that sausage for me."

He pulled at the bottom of the bag so it sagged warm grease.

"Hey, you got to come to Archie's tonight. I'm seeing a Chinese supplier. I'd like you to meet him. We've got a great deal."

"What is it?"

"We want to import high-quality printing presses from the States. These machines cost three million dollars. They are used for glossy magazines like *Vogue*. The manufacturer in the States has surplus stock because of all the GFC bankruptcies. We can buy them in their crates for one-third of that price including delivery to the docks at Shanghai. We can on-sell them in China for two million dollars each. That means we make one million bucks per machine. Plus, I will get a technical fee for assembly. Plus, a long-term maintenance contract. My business in Kunshan will supply all the parts. All we need is seed capital."

"How long is the loan period?"

"Depends on Chinese customs. I think six months MAX."

"That could cost one hundred and fifty thousand dollars in interest at the moment. People are paying thirty per cent for cash on the grey market. Can you get pre-commitments?"

"Sure."

"Maybe we can juggle the capital requirement. It would be good to get a deposit of say ten percent to cover our holding costs. That's only one hundred grand. Once we've done the first transaction, we can recycle our profits as we scale up."

"That means we can cut out the seed investor after the first deal."

"Correct. I can talk to Doctor Gu. But she'll want security."

"She can have security over the press."

"She'll want dirt."

"I've got the factory. It's worth fifty million kuai."

"So, registered capital is fifty?"

"Not exactly."

"So what's the actual equity level?"

"About ten."

"That could still work. Who did the valuation?"

"Some local firm."

"Do you hold title?"

"Standard fifty-year lease. Expires in 2057."

"I'll be dead by then. Land size?"

"Twenty Mu. Good position. One day it will be rezoned residential. Then it will be worth megabucks."

"We can pitch that package. I'll send you an email with a blank spreadsheet. Just plug the key inputs into the table. Then Jay can build a model."

"Will I see you tonight?"

"I'll try. But I'm committed to Doctor Gu."

"We'll get to Archie's around ten."

"I'll text."

They reached the intersection with Hunan Lu, hugged and separated. The paper holding Xiao Fang's sausages had virtually liquefied. Shanghai Dog hopped to avoid some red purls and settled the remnants of the bag in his palm. A one-third stake in that deal would total one million bucks by say the fourth transaction. Get-out-of-jail money. Print-set censors didn't examine Blake's poems. Six Acts of 1819 suppressed liberal thought for a generation. The Australian government banned *Ulysses* before it was finished. A young lady reading *The Little Review* managed to interpret the masturbation scene in Nausicaa. That in itself was the work of a disordered mind, quipped Joyce. The Feds hunted the first edition down on the docks. Roth's piracy escaped pulping. Charlie Soong started in Shanghai selling counterfeit textbooks and noodles. Joyce did small print-runs of *Finnegan's Wake* in key countries to generate copyright protection. I must not marry Doctor Gu, thought Shanghai Dog. I need to find a way out of this trap. Get home. I'm going to call the kids. He took out a battered Blackberry. China Mobile hadn't suspended his account yet. Should be OK until the fourteenth. Landlord has locked us out of the Beijing office. At least I don't have to pay that bill now. Drip feed the landlady. She wouldn't get 20,000 kuai per month in the current market anyway. Plus she's got the bond. I could use that money to pay out the Shanghai team. The telephone rang-out to O's answering machine. Odysseus post-Phaeacia. O's recorded accent. "I'm not available at the moment," she said. "Please leave a message and I'll get back to you." It was dinner time in Sydney. Maybe the kids had swimming lessons at North Sydney. I maxed-out my AMEX last month to pay school fees. I've got to play hardball with G. Nothing personal. Maybe squeeze another hundred playing both sides. Shanghai Dog reached his compound. He hailed the bao an who buzzed the entrance to his building. Xiao Fang would be lying on bed still dozing. He reached the bedroom. She had pulled the sheet over her lower torso. He put the snacks on the floor, undressed, slipped into bed and held her soft crotch sadly.

AN OBJECTIVE ACCOUNT OF OUR HEROES BY BOZ

A red cabriolet crossed Erskineville Station overpass. The driver looked north towards the city skyline then back at the footbridge. Copious whiskers extended the full length of his Cambrian jawline to the collar of his sky-blue work shirt. His colourless eyes stood in bold relief against unshaven cheeks. This was what the ancients would term "a triumph of artificial workmanship." He was trawling Swanston Street for fares. It was a deader than usual Tuesday night. He noted Bloom and Stephen locked in intense interchange. He slowed. Their tete-a-tete concerned sirens, enemies of reason, personal history, usurpers. Suddenly, Leer lurched right into the bushes. Moses Boses Bouwsers and Boz. The Inimitable. Goldsmith speaking through his nose during a bout of Common Cold. Our parish. Scenes from daily life. Curious Characters. Made-up tales. This is the range of literature. The taxi flashed its spotlight at them. Joyce used third person observation of Bloom and Stephen in this episode to flash an objective bulb on them. This is what they looked like to the outside world. Hallem waved him away politely. A resident of the Housing Commission estate had taken the normal precaution of muting the television set before she pulled back a single slat on the venetian blinds to discover the source of that noise. One bloke was leaning against a tree beyond her lounge room window dropping a load. His mate was standing some way off. She could smell the sick through the caked dust on the flyscreen. She lowered the wooden window.

HE SOWED THE SEEDS OF HIS OWN CHEMISE

LEER

[*Returning from scrub*] Did I ever tell you about my wife? [*Extracting a crumpled photograph*] Look at this picture.

HALLEM

Nice.

LEER

[*Bloom nudges Stephen*] Any man would want a piece of that action. But you wouldn't want to end up like old Jock Ross.

HALLEM

[*Asking the question posed by every reader*] Who?

LEER

[*Grins. Not answering the question*] He's a sad man now. [*Pointing into darkness*] Let's cut across the playing fields.

What reflections did Leer's photograph induce in Hallem?

1. Family history.
2. A portrait of family males by Harold F. Sykes, Broken Hill, 14/12/1913. An unknown relative's hand had written their names and ages on the back: Harry 33, William 37, John 40, John Tonner Kelly 68. All the boys left town and never went back like Odysseus' deckhands. One of those men got shot in the buttock in France. His mother joked that he was running away from the enemy. The genealogical records showed that this soldier was wounded multiple times, gassed and suffered repeated bouts of dysentery until his death shortly before the Armistice. He returned to the front each time after rehabilitation. Never let the truth get in the way of a funny story, observed Hallem.
3. His brother.

Of Billy's paternity?

His birth certificate was kept in a plastic sheaf at the bottom of his mother's dresser. He had found it searching her drawers for no reason when he was young. There was a cipher on the birth certificate in the column marked FATHER. He was too young to comprehend it.

Later?

No matter how much it was subsequently explained, how many excuses were made, how much adult experience he brought to the situation – and how much generosity – even if his brain had been injected with Coleridge's esemplastic power, Billy would never be able to rationalise this situation.

Classical analogue?

He was trapped inside this information like young Theseus. Or like the Minotaur.

Why did JJ select the name, Dedalus?

For himself. To take-over the Classical myth and reshape it to his own ends. Because one day he will build the maze (*Ulysses*). It was a name he selected way back in the time of *Stephen Hero* (1903–05, published 1944). He dropped the letter 'E' when he used it in *PAYM*. Stephen working his way through the significance of naming was one of the driving forces in that novel. It became an emblem of his struggle for self-awareness. Identity = language. It sets his character apart from the entire population of Dublin. *Thom's Directory* never contained such a name. Stephen looks Irish. But he is marked out as a freak from the moment you hear his name. This makes him the other side of the coin to Bloom with his replacement name. SAME COIN AS BLOOM BUT. Stephen is NEVER Icarus. He is destined to become Daedalus. His own father (see Proteus). The first artist. Cunning artificer. A great inventor. Only he can escape from his own labyrinth. That's called Art. It becomes hard to tell which came first: the freakish name or the freak. Joyce sketches the following core characteristics in Stephen: latent genius, misplaced self-confidence, bluster, miscalculations, craving inclusion but isolated from his peers because of temperament, partial learning from errors, incisive analysis of what motivates other people, appropriation of what he needs, lack of product to justify his sense of self-worth at this point in life but, nonetheless, gathering up the material for greatness and therefore engaged on an unrelenting drive towards fulfilment (link last point back to this work).

Examine nomenclature in Eumaeus.

Names are unstable, except Dedalus. This is ironic given that it is the least Irish name in *Ulysses*. Joyce uses naming to reflect the personal instability of characters, a fact of life prior to the twentieth century. Children were passed between relatives and amongst the community (see W.J. Chidley, *Confessions*). Sometimes, they were sold during famines. Occasionally, they were exchanged to be murdered and eaten during the Great Leap Forward. Slaves were given functional titles. Nicknames became surnames. People took on new identities. Chairman Mao considered replacing all names with numbers during the Cultural Revolution. Murphy has many nicknames in Eumaeus. Both M and Skin use pseudonyms. Bloom is misnamed BOOM in the newspaper. His family name is Virag. Parnell changed his name to "De Wet" to escape Ireland. We have already seen how Ho Chi Minh had numerous names over his career. Simon Dedalus shares his name with a famous circus marksman on posters around Dublin. There is the mysterious Antonio the Greek. Also, the Man in the (Brown) Raincoat. People trapeze aliases. Surnames were originally based on family occupations like Shake/spear, Black/smith and Iron/monger. Bloom's anagrams in youth included Ellpodbomool and Old Ollebo MP. False or equivocal naming in Eumaeus also reflects the fact that the source of Odysseus' name is ambiguous. It is rendered in diverse forms on ancient vase inscriptions, including Olyseus, Olysseus, Olyteus, Olytteus, Oulixes and Oulixeus. In Latin, he was called Ulixes or, less correctly, Ulysses. Ironically, this last corruption has become his definitive nomenclature and the title of Joye's book. Beekes believes that the name has a pre-Greek origin from Etruscan (Uthuze) or even Minoan (Oduze) civilisation. This would place it as far back as 1800 BC, almost 1000 years before Homer. It has been suggested by Beddell (1968) that Odysseus was an amalgam of two separate mythical characters, thereby producing his uncanny personality (Capri + Hallem = Narrator). The etymology of the name is unknown. Ancient writers linked it to the following Greek verbs: *odussomai*, "to hate"; *oduromai*, "to lament, bewail"; and *ollumi*, "to perish, to be lost." His criminal grandfather, Autolycus, is said to have given the baby this name as a testament to his perpetual irritation with people (*odoussomai*). All these names work for Odysseus. Odysseus was a good hater (just ask the suitors and serving girls). He continuously lamented his troubles to gain sympathy with women. He may also be considered lost at the end of the *Odyssey* when he is required to leave Ithaca to start an unspecified new journey.

FORSAKEN GARDEN

There was a construction site on Ashmore Street. Leer opened a gap in the temporary fence. Hallem followed. SD thought of Ibsen. An open roof. A D9 Caterpillar rested askew on a broad soggy mound of earth. Baird's Bobcats. Ponderous mass. Leer mounted the wide metal track then slid into the cockpit. Strapping-on wax wings. He frolicked at the controls. Nothing deader than a dead machine. Richie took a posy to her baby's grave. North Cemetery bubbling under sun. Always eighty-eight degrees. She kneeled in damp Manila Grass. Her infant in the pram was distracted by a bright red wooden horse.

"What are you up to," said a steady voice from darkness.

Both men turned. A policeman approached.

"I asked you a question."

"Nothing, sir," answered Leer.

"I guess you always wanted to be a bulldozer driver when you grew up."

"Yes, sir."

"Well you grew up to be a fucking dope."

Leer remained silent. Hallem looked down.

"You're trespassing," concluded the Policeman waving his hand at Hallem. "But I can't be fucked with the paperwork. So, I am going to turn around and go back to my vehicle. And you two clowns are going to exit this site. If you are still here after I drive around the block, I am going to take you back to the shop, knock you about a bit in the cells, get a search warrant, go back to your place and tear it apart. We might find some interesting stuff, I reckon. OK?"

"Yes, sir," said Leer.

"Have a great night, fellas."

The policeman went back through the fence. Private Carr was convinced not to kick Stephen in the crotch. Leer scrambled from the bulldozer. Hallem took his arm to steady his decline. Bloom led Stephen from the scene with the aid of Corny Kellaher. A wagon door shut. Ignition. Receding lights.

"How far is your place," asked Hallem.

"One block," Leer replied.

"Let's get there fast."

IN NATURE'S UNAMBITIOUS UNDERWOOD

Belmont Street had been blocked in the middle to create two cul-de-sacs, separated by an elevated lawn. This is where Leer's house was located. It is neither the home of Eumaeus or Bloom in this chapter. It shifts negatively against both these places, ultimately providing no refuge for Tom Hallem. Odysseus spends three whole books at Eumaeus' compound. It became his strategic hub. The *Odyssey* is split between Ithaca-without-Odysseus and Odysseus-at-home. They receive 12 books each from Homer. This perfect balance was not something that interested Joyce. *Ulysses* is primarily concerned with the first half of the *Odyssey*. In fact, perverting conventional publication requirements was one of his objectives. Chapter II covers almost 70% of total text, whereas Chapter III is only 25%. The ratio in this work is similar. The final 3.5 chapters (8–11 + Appendices) are approximately 30% (170/360/530). "Good spot," Leer said. "No risk of drive-by shootings." He pushed the front gate. It sagged as it opened, grating against the concrete path. "Do as I do," he said, stepping over a low trip wire. A floodlight triggered as he hit the front step. These are all metaphors for the reading experience. Leer admired the entrance. "This door looks completely average," he said. "But it's extremely difficult to break down because it's reinforced on the inside." He jiggled a Chinese bell that hung off the door handle. "Another simple precaution," he said. One could see the narrative thread with Shanghai Dog in this vein. He turned to the ground floor window. "Never open the curtains. Never clean the glass. Let it get dirty. Then nobody can see inside. But, look, there's a small crack." He pointed to some loose woodwork. "Just enough for me to see out." This image inverts the Lyotard epigraph. It puts Leer into the orthodox narrational camp. His thinking is dominated by the desire to create a sheer façade, behind which he can hide, occasionally peeping out like the Wizard of Oz. He pulled a key chain from his pocket. "Single deadlock. Extra locks just arouse suspicion." He opened the door marginally and slipped inside. "Wait here," he said, entering the hall. "Got to disarm the alarm system." The door closed but did not lock. This is all about the reader. "Come in," said Leer's disembodied voice. "It's OK now." This whole elaborate apparatus responds to the overt threats against the author's life by Barthes. Hallem pushed the door ajar. It was dark within. This is the space that literary criticism tries to inhabit. Homer describes the swineherd's hut with unusual detail. In fact, it is anything but a shack. It possessed a high-walled courtyard. Dead-ground had been cleared to create good vantage. There was a Herisson to divert attackers. He had built the main pen against the internal wall with stones he had quarried himself. Wild pear grew in vines over them. There were twelve sties holding fifty brood sows each. Hogs were kept outside the enclosure. Their numbers had been reduced by 360 in total by the suitors. Eumaeus sent a fattened hog to them each day. This is a clear metaphor for the situation of Odysseus and his tiny band of men, which really comprised only Telemachus and Eumaeus himself. It also tells us the suitors had been in residence for almost a full year. Leer opened a security gate bolted into the brickwork at the end of the hall. "If they get inside, they can only go this far." He had set up a killing-field between the main gate and the Bailey. "I got the same set-up out back. The centre is my safe room." Joyce was proud of the booby-traps that he inserted throughout *Ulysses*. He flicked a light switch in the lounge room then waited for Hallem to pass. Telemachus stood in the doorway in homespun raiment, white strip-light flooding his face. He was self-conscious before his father at what the palace had become. A stale, dry hulk. A portable television on an upturned brown milk crate balanced in the corner. A VHS player was perched on top. A string of black aerial wire passed up the wall to a loose picture hook, where it split like proboscises. Two green fabric armchairs leaked brittle foam. Leer locked the gate behind them.

"See. We're as safe as two bugs in a rug now," he said. "Beer?"

Leer unlocked the rear gate and entered the kitchen. Hallem followed mutely. Bloom arranges food and coffee for Stephen at the cabman's shelter. Later, there is cocoa at his home. Leer's intentions are anything but sobriety for Tom Hallem. He is turning on a show. He opened the refrigerator and took out two lukewarm cans of VB. A tide of ice washed over the freezer tray like a thick white tongue. Hallem analysed the sparse, mouldering cabinet. His eyes passed over rancid milk cartons, bread, sugar and condiments to six bags of dopeheads stacked on the middle shelf, wrapped tightly in brown masking tape.

"Part of my stash," Leer said.

He opened the vegetable crisper to reveal a brick of fifty-dollar notes.

"And bank," he added.

"You're not making much of an effort to hide them. They're an easy score."

"Ah!" exclaimed Leer. "That's exactly what the average crim would think. He'd take this low-hanging fruit and leave. That's my strategy. There's a lot more to this set-up than meets the eye."

"Why are you showing me?" asked Tom Hallem.

"Because one day it will be all yours," laughed Leer. "Come on."

They ascended the staircase. Eumaeus is a generous HOST, giving bread and wine to Odysseus and slaughtering hogs for later meals. Joyce reduces the lavishness to a "socalled roll," but the sentiment is the same.

"I removed all the carpet so I can hear every footstep. There are two bedrooms upstairs. I got them fitted out like there's two residents. It's bad if they think you're alone. The lights are set on timers. I change the setting every night. They're always looking for patterns. You know, LOOPS."

Leer pointed at a mattress on the floor.

"You're welcome to stay."

"Thanks. But I just moved my stuff home."

"Offer's there," replied Leer walking into the front bedroom. "I mean you came to see me tonight because you need a place to stay," said his distant, now disembodied, voice. "So ask." The narrator (E.Norton) looked flummoxed. He made his trademark scoffing noise. "Cut the foreplay and just ask," Derdun said boldly. Hallem still did not reply. He kept moving, examining the trail for risks. Three pitchers of beer and you still can't ask, laughed DERDEN. Drug-addled, drunk, fucked-out and exhausted, Stephen Dedalus did not ask for help from anyone even though his condition was desperate by the time Bloom intervened. This is quite unlike the narrator in *Fight Club*. He called DR.DUN on a pay phone. He initiated contact with himself. I too am all these characters. Even more than just the Norton/Pitt dichotomy. There is TH, BC, SD, the narrator, DC, LEER, LD, SH and elements of all the female characters. Leer's room was furnished with a double bed mattress on the floor pressed against a common terrace wall (south facing); a single brown sleeping bag was shitting all over it; there was a small bed lamp bent hard so light was severely muted; a high pile of books imperfectly ordered; a shallow field of clothes, some clean, some worn; and a long rectangular mirror leant at an acute angle off the northern wall. The room avoided both the privation of the derelict squat in *Fight Club* and the enamel soft-shadows of *Trainspotting*.

"You like war," said Hallem picking up the top book.

"Yea. Macarthur was a great man. Manchester could really write. His descriptions of the jungle are incredible. The rest is mainly Vietnam stuff."

"Did you fight over there."

"Yes, I did."

He handed the narrator a propaganda book from the late Sixties. The first image was a line of girls riding water buffalos through a field. The tail of an American fighter plane protruded from the rice crop. Next, a beautiful young man with his mouth torn open. He had thick eyebrows and a wide flat nose with massive nostrils. His shirt was sodden with drying blood. The caption read: "This man, though tortured, refused to speak. He was shot by the ARVN." Hallem turned the page. Two American soldiers stood over an old woman and a child in a saturated paddy. The girl was naked with her left hand covering her vagina. Hallem replaced the book.

"My father was in Vietnam," he said.

"Yeh. The cripple."

"No. That's my step-dad. I'm talking about my biological father."

"What did he do," asked Leer.

"I don't know. I've never met him."

"Do you know when he was there?"

"Just after I was born, I think."

"Probably First Corps. There were advisers. I was down south in Phuoc Tuy with the other Nashos."

"He hooked up with the Yanks. I thought he was dead for a long time. He's just got back today. They told me this morning. He's been living in Manila."

"Why was he hiding?"

"He got my aunt pregnant."

"So, Billy is your brother?"

"Yea."

"I can dig that."

"It was wrong."

"What?"

"Immoral."

"Are you serious?" Leer scoffed and proceeded down the stairs. "Come on. I got something special to show you."

Leer took Tom Hallem to a broom closet under the staircase. He pulled up a small square of carpet, which had been secured with staples along a thin stake. The floorboards had been cut at the cross beams, bound together, replaced and hinged to make a trap-door. Leer opened the hatch. "Look," he said. Hallem went to the ledge. It was pitch black down the hole. "Pass me that torch," Leer said, pointing to the wall. Hallem collected a black Maglite hanging off a nail and passed it to him. Light glowed. Leer descended the ladder. After a few seconds, a bright light ignited. "Come on down," he whispered. "But make sure you close the hatch." Hallem shut himself in the cubicle as he descended the ladder. A large cellar replicated the dimensions of the lounge room directly above. Like Guy Carrell in Poe's great tale, Leer had built an elaborate vault for himself. It was equipped with several safeguards, although not in case of premature burial. Quite the contrary. There was a long work bench along the side wall. Poison elixir bubbled in a lab beaker. NEEDS MORE JOYCE SCIENCE SHELLEY A portable picnic table was pushed against the clay foundations. There was a crypt off the main chamber. Leer disappeared. Hallem followed. Leer held a safety light on a thick orange extension cable.

"Look," he said proudly.

Hallem peered at a bench of VHS machines. Two deep bookshelves packed with video cassettes stood behind it.

"I can run my whole operation down here. There are two hundred videos on those shelves. It's not soft stuff either. People pay good dollar for that stuff. Come back to the lab."

Hallem followed Leer back to the cellar. Leer opened a bar fridge.

"This is my pantry. I got enough supplies to last for days."

A slab of beer had been cut in half and stuffed into the cavity. Two blocks of brown heroin were jammed in the door. Maybe 500 grams each. Probably 80% pure. Cut it down to street purity and you could multiply the value twenty times.

A RECORD OF INTERVIEW

"I deal drugs. Sell videos. A few hand-guns. Nothing major. Don't want undue attention. It's a diversified business model. I'm always looking for new hands if you're interested, young Tom. You don't often meet a well-credentialled lad. You've got great networks. Ones I haven't been able to tap. You can make good money. In time, I could cut you into the business as a full partner. Anyway, enough of my bullshit. Just think about it. Get back to me. The offer stands until revoked. Let's go back upstairs."

They ascended the ladder. Leer carefully concealed all traces of the cellar, went over to the small portable television and pulled the start knob.

"Now let's get blasted," he said.

"Cool," replied Tom Hallem.

"You don't mind sharing, I hope?" Leer asked, holding up a syringe. This is a corrupt equivalent to Bloom returning Stephen's ashplant, which Joyce uses as a symbol for the Cross. This act at the start of Eumaeus creates the impression that Bloom is a restorative Christ figure to Stephen-as-representing-humanity. Stephen himself recognises this correspondence when Bloom relates his earlier confrontation with The Citizen. Ironically, this is the tallest tale in the entire episode and the only one which can be verified by the reader.

"Of course not," Hallem replied hastily.

Leer watched him keenly. He cultivated an air of indolence, even dimwittedness at times, which concealed sharp analytical faculties of a decidedly not-Samaritan variety. In short, he used EQ as a predator might. He recognised the vanity and pretensions of his youthful companion, coddled by a protective mother and the blandishments of an expensive school. These inputs were very different to his own misfortunes and thus it was difficult, nay impossible at times, not to reach a tipping-point of resentment that induced the desire for revenge against the entire class system through an act of violence against this individual representative thereof. Fortunately, Tom Hallem did not act with the same affectations as his Joycean foil but rather presented himself with deference and reserve like well-appointed Telemachus. There was no assumed air of unwarranted insouciance exhibited in his personality. These younger males shared a personal flaw caused by the following issues: (1) lack of a father; (2) a remote mother; (3) unfortunate family circumstances; (4) perpetual threat of disinheritance (5) temporary or perceived risk of vagrancy (6) attack by external enemies either literally, spiritually and/or aesthetically (7) a general tenor of permanent siege. Tom Hallem eyed his companion warily. Leer's cheeks were pitted like worn rubber, hiding tight eyes. Don't flinch, he demanded of himself under their ready gaze. He reviewed Leer's vita. (A) This guy carried baloopies through Customs for Terry Clark back in the day. (B) He's a drug-addled vet. (C) He's got you locked inside his safe house. (D) There are weapons everywhere. He could take you down at any moment like Kathy Bates. Tom Hallem resolved to just focus on the Score. That'll mellow them both out. Then get Ana's fix and leave Circe's cave. Risk the pig-shots. Get HIV. Lot of hype about sharps in the news lately. Another infection every sixteen minutes. Proud Antonio with his tattoos maggoting in a grave. Plato compared homophobia to idea-hate. The Wall has gone dead since AIDS. A fog had descended over Darlinghurst. The nightclubs have just got louder and faster. Sacred Band of Thebes. They're calling it The Ace in the States. Sharing pixie-sticks is the fastest form of transmission. Faster than anal. In July, the Albion Street Clinic reported 20% of all tests had returned POSITIVE. Leer turned the dial on the television. *Prisoner* starts in 30 minutes, he said. He pulled a small side table in front of him. It was getting late. They started watching *A-Team*. Martial drum roll. Leer lifted an old cigar box off the floor and opened it. Neat bundles of smack were strapped together with rubber bands. Ten bags each bale. Probably half a gram total. Maybe thirty parcels in the box. There was also a small mound of powder in a loose bag and a pile of unmarked currency. Leer extracted his gear. It wasn't a special kit like Willy. He took no pride in his tools. They were just functional objects. He loaded the gun and rolled up the sleeve of his flannelette shirt. He was badly bugged. He tied off. Some problem finding a vein. Mister T. was driving a convertible along a low-grade light industrial strip in outer LA. Hallem turned to starboard. "If he's flyin' then we's dyin'," chimed Bosco. George Peppard took a vial labelled Novocain from his desert jacket. He slapped B.A. on the shoulder with a laugh. A cotton wool bud sterilised the driver's skin. Finally, Leer got himself pricked. The blood backtracked into the vial. He let half the solution rush into his body, extracted the tip and turned towards Hallem. I let him hit me up. Hannibal popped the needle into Bosco's neck. He found a vein easily. I wretched. The rush started. It took less than a minute for the drug to make B.A. stumble. He got one punch at Hannibal before collapse. The television volume dipped. The slam was DOA. One hundred times better than the best rush from popping a handful of eighty milligram tabs. Then the nod. Hallem slumped in an armchair. Leer was already gone. A warm blanket of spit rolled down his face. Broken bust of William Shakespeare staring down. A long scar ran askew across the Bard's forehead. One thick bar of super glue held in his whole brain. I turned to the television screen. Green and blue bars. MTV. An alabaster-cheeked girl in a loose carmine gown receded up a lush green hillside. England's pleasant landing. One day Bloom plans to take Molly on tour. She turned showing lips too large too red but shiny not real like blood.

OF THE ROMANTIC VICE & ITS VISIONS

"We need music," said Leer. He stumbled on his knees to a turntable and pulled open its clear plastic flap. The needle dropped about halfway through *White Light*. It didn't make any difference where it started. This song was basically ALL DRONE. "Sounds are impostures like names," says Stephen Dedalus in Eumaeus as language is used to propagate lies and fabrications, undermining human trade. A lamp cut suddenly. Shadows weakened on the Laminex table so that its pale pink marble pattern assumed a deep, almost reverent hue. The television screen went dead. "Shit," said Leer bent over like a beggar fiddling with a power board uselessly. Only music hovered now in the can-hardly-see-through. He smoothed out as "The Gift" started. Like Joyce in Eumaeus, Reed makes heavy use of clichés to give his climax genuine (shock) value. Unusually, he distances himself from the narrative voice, substituting Cale as vocalist. This song is all about the moment of a single sound effect. Only Spector had explored the impact of sudden noise in pop music, albeit as BANG, not reverberation, like Odysseus' arrows, although it was a standard device in classical music (Wagner, Mahler, 1812, Odetta). A green shawl draped over a gilded lampshade made Leer appear dead like dead

Cadmus. Everybody is bugged by the time Bloom and Stephen sit down in that makeshift shed. Both Leer and Hallem started speaking, not listening, trying to outdo each other in match-making utterance (see C6). Hallem turned his life in Campsie into a street-smart gang epic. Leer (Max Cady, Bobby Peru) preferred to inflate his intellectual credentials like Leopold Bloom. Hallem came off like some lame *West Side Story* Jet; Leer as pompous as Ayn Rand, this job or Saville's Oedipus. But it kept both men conscious, at least periodically, against the otherwise overwhelming coma of drugs. Waldo Jeffers too lay wide awake, tossing and turning under his tight pleated quilt protector. This opening image of confinement will perfectly balance his demise at the end of the song. Insert allusions to graphic film sequences (mainly French, Scorsese, David Lynch). Joyce was an early adopter of cinema. His commercial efforts in Dublin are chronicled by Ellmann (INSERT PAGE NO). Film is an important adjunct to Joyce. He wrote each scene with obsessive detail like a film-maker composing the elements of a set. We must recalibrate Joyce for film then prepare his evolution to the digital era. Everything in Joyce has meaning. There are no sloppy props. Everything must be described. Everything is rendered in a visualizable form like a scene by Kubrick, Tarkovsky, Fellini or Kurosawa. Joyce invented product placement. The reader needs to become a CONTINUITY SUPERVISOR to make an imaginary motion picture of *Ulysses*. *Trainspotting* employs filmic archetypes via Sick Boy. But it is really just offering a tenuous connection with the Scottish actor, Sean Connery, in the role of James Bond. This is an isolated trope. It's only tangible output for the plot is the shooting-in-the-park scene. It doesn't trigger any sustained meaning in the movie. Powerful imagery is lost in the rush of *Trainspotting*. It is, indeed, like a trainspotter witnessing a fast steam train from a rail overpass. Important statements like Renton's monologue on Scotland as a vassal of Britain – and his relocation to London as a nihilistic act of cultural assimilation – are lost. You can go anywhere in the mail these days, thought Waldo Jaffers. Tom Hallem came back from a short trip into the beauteous forms of Leer's cigarette plumes, as beguiling as Chandler's gallery of slender women, thin straps rising out of ivory censers like silver sea ribbons CUT Marsha tightened the silk belt on her Japanese robe CUT Leer chewed down hard on a miracle filter CUT Black insects shook in the sulphurous air SHIFT I kicked back CUT Helen of Troy came down (maple curls of a spiral staircase) her languorous gaze sliced my eyeballs (Bunuel + Dali = a cow, a jumpcut) tears streamed down my face (Cocteau) in this blind stupor I was taken by the succubus in dreams (*La Jetee*) her kisses gashed my mouth (Bunuel again) I gulped at her swirling river (Shelley, Noyades, *Cape Fear*, *Sunset Boulevard*, Ophelia, Poseidon) All that is not Helen is nothingness (*W. Heights*, *B. Velvet*, *Vertigo*, *Dracula*) And the Helen that I see is but an apparition (*The Shining*) Sheila ran a long nail through grey masking tape (*B. Swan*) gilding stuck to her fingers (Flaubert, L. Macbeth, W. Asaji) Waldo managed to secure himself inside the crate with a wire mechanism (Odysseus,

Houdini) the post office had agreed to pick him up at three (oh honey don't be late) he'd marked the package FRAGILE (Tom Hallem, Stephen Dedalus) insert another cataleptic fit (Poe, Dickens, Dumas, even Zola) he curled up on foam cushioning (Reed's great fetal image) both girls tried fruitlessly to lift the flap (Pandora) Sheila's father kept a collection of tools in the basement (Hephaestus) Eucleia came back upstairs with a large sheet metal cutter (Von Triers) Sheila (Eupheme) sank to her knees like some satanic priest at a virgin sacrifice in a low budget British horror film (Hammer) grasped the cutter by both handles (Faure's "Requiem" started), took a deep breath, raised it above her head and plunged the long blade right through the middle of the package, through the masking tape, through the cardboard, through the cushioning and (THUD) right through the center of Waldo Jeffers head. Which split slightly. Little arcs of brown blood pulsed gently in the morning sun. Reed ends at this point. Willy the Pimp rolled me on my stomach on the cool damp carpet (Death of Ana) and stuck a girder through the base of my spine (syringe symbol) until it speared out my mouth (AKA Birth of Language). He wrenched me in half after that (see Plato). The gravedigger stopped whistling and beckoned Carrell. I am screwed into the earth like some fast-fallen rocket (SALO). Albeit askew (Tatlin). Yet fixed in place like an inanimate object nonetheless (A. Symons). Life is like a screw turned deeper and deeper into hardwood. You apply more and more pressure until the thread frays and it becomes unworkable. Until you can no longer move. Try to extract yourself. A pun. Chopper blades. Ftt-ftt-ftt-ftt-ftt-ftt-father. Hot extraction. Pleiku 68. This series of images all relate to Tom's fear of Leer's dungeon (see *In Black Box*). Marsha and Sheila were able to extract Waldo's carcass before the cardboard yielded to soft pulp. Like "The Gift," Poe's "Buried Alive" is an extended metaphor for the impact of DRUG ADDICTION. *Trainspotting* is laudable for its depiction of the scientific approach taken by professional addicts to meeting narcotic needs. Willy the Pimp and Slope evince the same pride-in-occupation of Renton as they describe experimental methodology (Daedalus) and scope of exploration (Odysseus). Carrell's wife delivered an ultimatum. Get off the Junk or else. He destroyed the vault (lab). He changed inputs (methadone). Slowly, he became more amenable under the care of a registered psychoanalyst. Eventually, Doctor Moreau suggested that I open my father's coffin as a final form of closure. What oxymoronic irony in that choice of words! Poe does not describe the subsequent sight which caused a decisive seizure in Guy Carrell. Let it only be known that he is declared dead. He lies in state for a number of days. He is buried. He opens his eyes. A scream but by no air taken ensues. Paradoxically, it is only the intervention of graverobbers that saves him. We can manipulate this scene into an arch metaphor for this work. At the end, Carrell returns home to seek revenge like Odysseus ... but this time against his own family. What is *Ulysses* in the end but an outsider text? Joyce aimed to settle all his scores in Dublin. It was his personal attack on the local literati (suitors) of his youth. I too have come back to Sydney. Neither of us produced much work of consequence as young men in these locations on the days on which these novels are set. A few lyrics. Some scraps of critical prose. Infrequent fictive sketches. Short book reviews. [END] "Lady Godiva" started. Leer pushed the needle to the centre of the turntable. A growl of agony sounded then silence. The arm lifted like a crane, returned to its starting perch, dropped onto its roost and CLICKED OFF. I reached for a glass of water with the same stiff mechanism. *Trainspotting* is too slick, too cynical, too irresponsible in the final analysis. Under the rules of tragedy, Renton should die for bringing on the infection of Tommy. Without his death, the dramatic cosmos is left a poorer place at closure. Boyle is an innovative film-maker, producing some of the most powerful sequences of magic realism ever projected onto the silver screen (worst toilet in Scotland, liquid draw, cold turkey delusions). But *Trainspotting* is ultimately an MTV clip promoting drug use via subliminal marketing techniques. It's like Tyler Durdun splicing single frames of pornography into family films. Nobody knows they saw it but they did. I admire its brilliance with a sense of shame. *Trainspotting* is like a Monkees movie. It showcases the whacky lifestyle and humorous opinions of bandmates sealed together in an Edinburgh funhouse. Warhol never treated drug abuse so blithely. T-SPOT does with film what VU did with music thirty years earlier. It is too sheer, too ebullient. It never SLOWS DOWN. In fact, it is a SPEED movie, not a SMACK movie. It should have been set in the 1960s with Mods. Everything is hyper-accelerated. Baudrillard would have sanctioned this velocity. It should have made history disappear, according to his theorem. However, *Trainspotting* is chained to the self-loathing of Colonialism. This is its strongest plot arc. But everything is camouflaged and neutralised by haste. Like *Pulp Fiction*, *Trainspotting* as a narrative contains almost no technical novelty. Welch, however, is a premium stylist. The plot deploys only received, familiar tropes. It is really just a hackneyed coming-of-age tale. The monologues that bookend the movie represent the most specious writing in the whole novel, veiled by the heart-pumping brilliance of Iggy Pop's song, "Lust for Life." It is just a list of clichés, flipped with hate at both ends. This should give the movie a sense of stasis like *F(W)ake*. But everybody is shagged by this stage. The storyline relies on a sequence of sentimental tropes to give the proponents (Welch, Boyle) ethical cover. The dead baby, bathetic infection of Tommy and Renton's miscellaneous betrayals enable Welch to leave a gingerbread trail of moral markers as a sop to social norms. They are more Renton than Renton in that case. Joyce would NEVER have written with such reductive feeling. His enterprise to disclose the tender mote in the human condition has never been more important than it is for the VIEWER NOW. Likewise, Tarantino deployed the miracle of Jules' survival and Butch Coolidge's decision to spare his nemesis in the pawn shop to give his work fake ethics. Perversion of standard tropes at speed in these movies suspends moral capability in the viewer. Time is cancelled. There are no gaps for reflection. This is in keeping with conventional sales techniques. Fast music gives false charm to degrading scenes, inducing a disconnect between image and tone. Even bad songs are perfectly-p(l)aced. PF is a sequence of three-minute music videos. Anybody who has ever been young and hated the system will immediately grasp the fact that these movies are product placement campaigns for heroin. It is easy in reflection for the analyst to accumulate a list of scenes which showcase the perils of drug abuse. Yet we NEVER FEEL this critique in the moment of audience. We are distracted by FASHION. The design element of *Trainspotting* is exemplified by the hovels inhabited by its junkies. These sets are realistically constructed. They look like filthy squats bereft of basic furniture with punctured walls and collapsed ceilings. But they never seem uncomfortable to the viewer. They feel like boutique hotel suites specifically designed for addicts. Everybody in *Trainspotting* is beautiful like Burt Bacharach's song. Ewan McGregor glows in the lead role. Johnny Lee Miller turns on the charm as an erudite Billy Idol. Begbie's bouffant is sharper than his blade. His comical moustache acts as a clever trap to lure the viewer into complacency. He is CARTOON BAD. We are always meant to take the side of evil and violence in *Trainspotting*. Everything else is uncool. All Begbie's scenes are banal stereotypes. He is never called to account for violence. At the end, we farewell him trashing a hotel room like some Hibernian Keith Moon. The American tourist attack is the most unfortunate scene in the movie. Violence is always played for laughs. The arrest of Renton and Spud exploits car chase dynamics to make crime appear like comic slapstick. Yes, this is an inversion of good–bad. Yes, Renton's leering face over the bonnet of a car is one of the most amusing scenes in modern cinema. But there is no fullness to the craft. It is a thirty-second TV commercial. We never see the consequences of action. We are not exposed to the experience of incarceration. Similarly, we never see Tommy's decline with AIDS, only his farewell scene at the funeral, which ends with overt smiles of forgiveness and resolution with Renton. Everybody in straight society remains obliging. Hospital staff act professionally. Judges apply the system fairly. A taxi driver takes Renton to Emergency after his OD. This taxi would NEVER have stopped in REAL LIFE. The respectable people that Joyce turned into his heroes in *Ulysses* are mocked as dolts and gulls (see Renton's parents, Gail's family, Spud's mum). The benign dealer, known as Mother Superior, neutralises the Manichean evil inherent in the narcotics supply chain. This character is perhaps the most misleading element in a plot loaded with lies. In REAL LIFE, he would have dumped Renton in an alley. Just like W-the-P when he escapes over the back fence after Tom's OD later in this work. *Fight Club* shares this moral equivalising. It says, please excuse me for exploding some bombs. Like PF, it is OK to be a thug if you're cool. *Fight Club* loops like *Trainspotting* and *Pulp Fiction*. Start and end merge to de-time form like *F(W)ake*. These are all basically BUDDY MOVIES (between Jules and Vince, The Narrator and Tyler, Renton and

Sick Boy). FC contains the same elements of cliché and the same hackneyed tropes as its stable mates (they are all sprinters not stayers). It is filed down flat with the same flaws. Yet, it remains perhaps the best movie of the twenty-first century (as at 2016). *Fight Club* is a sophisticated heist movie like *Ocean's Eleven*. It starts with a ticking time-bomb like a conventional thriller. The plot constantly outguesses its leading character. It is self-aware of its function as film (see the projector scene). *Fight Club* is a homemade invention. Its list of useful contraptions includes, but is not limited to: Project Mayhem, IKEA, illness support groups, Robert Paulsen, single-serve friends, car-recall economics, various conspiracy theories (oxygen, napalm, soap, vibrating suitcases), my dad setting up paternity franchises, famous people I would like to fight (Hemingway, Shatner, Lincoln, Gandhi). Tyler and I just gave it a name, started a fight and lost. Palahniuk is endlessly inventive with stock themes. He has a radical game plan to execute, unlike Welsh or Tarantino. His purpose is no less than the radical destruction of capitalist consumerism. He is no less ambitious in this regard than Joyce, who wanted to heal Ireland with words. *Fight Club* leads by example. It contains all the chilling elements of white male supremacism. It shows us how anarchist cults can form and spread until they reach a point of ignition and achieve critical mass. Pitt/Norton calls it evolution. It is a template. It would be labelled an Instruction Manual under their terminology. It can be put together with just an Allen Key (product included in box). *Fight Club* moves fast to convert clichés into new stuff yet at the same time it remythologises the human project by hitting reverse. It is a car crash in both directions. Palahniuk goes back to a glorious past where medieval knights clashed in hand-to-hand combat then he goes back even further to reinstate full classical topology. The oldest myths and tropes are reborn, coming to life in the present time like Pater's reanimated Dionysius in "Denys L'Auxerrois" (this was another model derived from Poe). *Fight Club* relentlessly intensifies extant tropes. It piles influence upon correspondence until no part of the film is non-referred. The multi-faceted car crash trope fuses James Dean ("chicken") with J.G. Ballard then adds new meaning through the Narrator's job. Finally, he perceives its underlying causation. This is the lightbulb moment that dictates the end of the film. Icarus has dodged death. The only question is what will our hero MAKE of redemption. He works out that he must destroy Daedalus-as-self. It should be an act of expiation but, in fact, it is just another act of self-mutilation. This revelation is much more satisfying than Jules' miracle in PF or Renton's moment of clarity (which really occurs because of the dictates of conventional movie length rather than plot. In other words, *Trainspotting* could have gone on indefinitely or ended a bit earlier). The Narrator starts to fight against everything he created in an appropriated Frankenstein trope. Self-inflicted violence is his greatest invention. It is the equivalent of junkiedom. The gun's in my hand, he says. Of course, it is also a syringe. Also, a detonator. A penis as well. In death, there is a name:

it is Robert Paulsen. In non-death, the Narrator loses a name: Tyler Droy. *Fight Club* manages dual identity (schizophrenia, multiple identity) without either confirming or denying its presence until closure. It manages to forestall the audience reaching this conclusion due to relentless novelty. But it repeats the errors of *Trainspotting* in closing-out its plot, albeit due to different design flaws in the fuselage. *Trainspotting* reinforces its innate cynicism when Renton decides to partake in our nihilism like Winston Smith. Similarly, *Fight Club* reverts to a beautiful image of sunset and resurrected love via a series of explosions. This may as well have been the opening fireworks of "Love American Style." The weakest element of *Fight Club* is female characterisation. It is another misogyny flick like both TS and PF. Marla Singer is a remnant of the kind of stale narrative that Palahniuk would otherwise depose. She is an avant-garde cliché: hot, Gothic, cynical, neurotic, sharp, suicidal, street smart, combative. This is all one big YAWN because, ultimately, she is just another pawn. Her path in the film follows standard filmic patterns for women. This is the worst insult we can give Palahniuk. She starts out as a hate object (but it is clearly a love thing). The Narrator can never abuse her enough. She becomes a proxy for his need to express misogyny. She is Ophelia to the author's Hamlet. She cannot release herself from the Narrator because of his intellect, humour and sexual prowess. She keeps coming back for more. Palahniuk injects some derivatives of gender norms, such as gross eating habits. He deploys a stock "suicide-call" motif to kickstart her re-insertion into the narrative. Eventually, our hero acknowledges his feelings. For he is always the ACTIVE AGENT. It is a plotline as old as medieval romance. Classical heroines didn't act like that. They had guts like Cassandra. Or kept tactical control like Penelope. Or separated their emotions from sex like Helen at Troy. Marla is none of these things. She becomes a ragdoll female lead in a conventional Hollywood drama. The hero gives her an apparent mode of escape like Keanu Reeves in *SPEED*. Of course, it fails. She ends up tied in ropes and brought back to the scene of the crime by evil henchmen. Palahniuk is writing *Austin Powers 2* by this point. His script is dictated by focus groups and executives. Each of these moviemakers fail to create a single effective female protagonist. For this reason, their works must remain forever marginalised as great art. They are all linked to redundant patriarchy. Women never have power in their films. Even Uma Thurman is ultimately just a passive junkie rescued by John Travolta (as Sir Lancelot with an adrenaline shot). Joyce by contrast created Molly Bloom. He rejected violence. And mob mentality. I want to be like him. That's the message of this analysis. Also, to be wilfully discursive like Proust. To insert apparently irrelevant matter into the plot. To be repetitive. And to loop back to reprise apparently completed arguments. Defying conventional narrative. Yet suggesting some kind of deeper symbolic meaning. Marla Singer is a facile romantic interest whose sole technical purpose is to provide Palahniuk's Narrator with a path to salvation. Palahniuk is far too sentimental about this ... 'Narrator.' He is a spoiled son. He doesn't even need to kill himself at the end like a normal tragic hero. He just wanders off. Some might see this device as KENOSIS against outdated modes but Palahniuk is really just giving the viewer A HAPPY ENDING. This AVOIDANCE necessitates a torturous plot manoeuvre. He has just blown up eleven skyscrapers ... but no one gets killed so it's all OK. He ducks liability. This reduces Palahniuk to snatches of ironic monologue to end the movie. Polemics are also the worst elements of *Fight Club*. We already know how modern male characters feel. It is received baggage. We know they didn't have enough wars to fight in recent times. We know they feel like God's unwanted children. We know they are drowning in useless products. We know they feel emasculated. It's a stock line of right-wing apologists. It justifies terrorism against the State. We never really get to explore the dehumanisation of Tyler's robot army (the space monkeys). We accept cruelty against individuals. It excuses their ultimate form. We laugh at acts of vandalism and intimidation. Like Tarantino and Boyle, gang action becomes normalised. They are like automatons forged by Hephaestus. Tyler's Brown Shirts are the latest trend in fascism. It will all end in hate. There are no consequences in FC. There is no balancing element. *Fight Club* is yet another symbolic rejection of the COMMONWEAL. It is part of the erosion of the social compact in western society. It epitomises everything that James Joyce loathed.

IF THIS IS HEAVEN, I'M BAILING OUT!

"What about Ana's treat?" asked Tom Hallem.
"Got the dosh?" replied Leer.
"I was hoping for some credit. I'll pay you back in a couple of days."
"Unusual for a guy like you to be broke. You've always got plenty of money."
"I'm waiting on an advance from my agent."
"What?"
"She pays me as I paint."
"What ... cash in hand <u>before</u> delivery?"
"Yes."
"Is there good coin in your caper?" asked Leer gently.
"For the top blokes."
"Give me some names."
"READ is highly collectible."
"What would his work fetch?"
"Fifty for a major piece."

"And you exhibit with blokes like that?"

"Yes."

"Where is the showroom?"

"Paddington."

"Should have guessed. What's its name?"

"E.A Times," answered Tom.

"What?"

"The initials are the name of the owner. Also, a pun on the French term, *Epreuves d'Artiste*, which means artist's proof. Times is also a pun. On epochs and multiplication."

"What wankery. Where is it exactly?"

"Macdonald Street."

"Number?"

"Sixteen."

"Interesting," said Leer. "I might pop over some time."

Suddenly, he sat up. Hallem let his head loll wearily (follow use of "loll" in this chapter).

"Let me show you my new toy," he said.

Leer got up quickly and climbed the staircase. Hallem took the chance to steal some cash. Ignore the smack. Too blatant. He'd just had a blast anyway. He could give Willy's treat to Ana. He grabbed a few bank notes and stuffed them in his coat pocket. Leer's footsteps clacked. Victim in reverse of his own system. He returned brandishing a cut-off crossbow.

"Isn't she a beaut? A conventional bow would be too big for this space. But I can cock this baby in 2 seconds. It shoots 370 feet per second. This room is 18 feet on the diagonal. That means I can hit a target in point o-two of a second. Imagine the force! It would pass straight through your face. Here."

He thrust it at Hallem. Who held out hands. Leer placed it in his hold like a baby. Hallem observed it disconnectedly.

"I don't think you're getting into the spirit of the hunt," said Leer. "Maybe you'll get more excited if I put on a show."

Leer took back the bow from his companion and positioned himself on the staircase. Hallem pivoted his chair to observe the demonstration. He was bound like Prometheus or James Bond.

"Imagine this scenario. Persian sends some bikers to break into my place. They split up and take the front door and back door simultaneously. I am upstairs in bed. They lose a couple of blokes to my booby traps straight off. I don't want to use a firearm because it will alert them to my position. Instead, I wait silently here on the stairs. They disclose their positions with torch beams. I raise my crossbow. WHAM (Leer shoots an arrow through the security door bars. It THWACKERAYS into the kitchen wall). Dead. His mate is too stunned to move. I reload. (Leer cocked a new arrow). Second shot. THWACKWAY. Two down. I slip into the lounge room. Biker with a mash hammer. Biker with a bar. THWACK. THWAM. (Arrows lodge in the wall). A torch beam strangles the dark room. Persian catches sight of the crossbow with my cold eyes over the sights. THWACK. Right between the eyes."

Leer grinned. Hallem jumped up.

"I got to go man," he said in a voice like John Jacob Niles.

"Cool it," replied Leer. "It's just a demo."

Tom Hallem turned circles on the spot shaking his head. He dropped to his knees. Begging. Bile came lightly in spasms. He shook the bars madly. He began whimpering. Suddenly, Leer pushed him hard against the GRILL.

"Calm down, dickhead."

"I got to go," Tom Hallem pleaded. "Right now, please."

"That's fine. You can go."

Leer let Hallem's body droop in his grip then smashed it against the bars again.

"But just remember, Tom. Never cross me."

Hallem rattled the cage. A groan came low from some unnamed place underneath his throat. He could not produce tears. Leer released him.

"You'll need the key," he said.

Hallem shook his head in affirmation deferring gaze.

Leer released the locks.

"Remember what I said," he told Tom.

Hallem raced down the corridor, opened the front door abruptly and entered the street. It was hot wet and vacant. He pined for the sight of a common citizen putting out garbage or walking a dog. A woman in particular. But there was nobody present. He accelerated down Belmont Street. No sudden arrowhead cored his brain. He turned back one last time to make sure he wasn't being pursued by that buckminsterfull grin. Don't retrace your steps. Stay on Mitchell Road. Comfort of passing traffic. Telemachus returning from Pylos. Avoid the suitor's fleet. Odysseus starting home. Sneaking under Poseidon's guard. Hamlet working his way through clues outside the main narrative. Unsure if he was sane or crazy. Maybe seek right of asylum in Gothenburg. Hire double-agents. He felt the screwed-up bundle of notes. Maybe a bad move. Hide out on the other side of town. Never come back to Newtown. Stephen Dedalus really wanted to escape the creepy old guy who followed him from the hospital to the pub then all the way through the red-light district to a brothel. Name of Bloom. Knows my father.

Probably a swinger. Showed me nude shots of his wife. Tea-bagger. Obvious BOTTOM. Re Bloom/SD, the narrator of Eumaeus concludes, "Though they didn't see eye to eye in everything, a certain analogy there somehow was, as if both their minds were travelling, so to speak, in the one train of thought." This is a polite bow, in both senses of the word. Joyce hardly ever wrote such an equivocal sentence. We never get a sense of spiritual alignment in this chapter. There is always underlying tension and latent violence from Leer. The two men are drawn to each other, yet this flame contains revulsion as well. They eat each other's cream on an empty stomach. To revert to the testimony of a Bard: Music brought them together and music tore them apart. Tom Hallem hated the music, more than Leer himself, whose attractions he acknowledged as allied to a susceptibility to undesirable males, perverse sexual desires and risk.

A NOSTALGIC SUBLIME

Judy worked as a waitress in the top floor bar of a five-star hotel near People's Square, where middle-aged Western guys went to pick up migrant girls and rich Shanghai wives went to get sex. Her name tag said JUDY but her actual name was Zhu Di. It was a lucky linguistic match. She didn't want a Western name. It was just a work thing on her name tag that stopped foreigners calling her ZOO DIE. She knew what that meant literally. DONGWU YUAN SI. It had no logic practically speaking, unless you committed suicide by jumping into a tiger cage. This is a metaphor for our relationship really. I never knew her last name. This made it impossible to trace her when we split. She just blocked her cell phone. Everybody had an agenda at the JW Bar. We all used aliases. Nobody expected a straight story. Judy didn't give a fuck. For a few weeks, I watched her stride around the room with the solid assurance of a schoolmistress. She wasn't beautiful in either a Chinese or Western sense. She had broad calves, a lean trunk and almost no cleavage. A lot of Chinese girls get this type of muscular body shape from riding bicycles. Her eyes were set across a broad flat bridge. You could hear a fast, cold river flowing behind them but never gain a glimpse of its churn. Her nostrils started low and spread flat. She had a wide mouth with truly sensuous lips. This was S.Dog's abiding memory, long after physical contact had passed into legend. Judy always looked like she ran the palace, even though she was only a serving girl. Penelope was shocked when Eurycleia said they'd strung-up all the best domestic staff while she was stoned in bed. There was a degree of hatred in how scores were settled on Ithaca, not just by Odysseus himself. The whole society had been degraded by the Occupation. Odysseus gave free rein to his acolytes from the old days. His violence gave them a mandate to violence as well. There was no evidence that these girls had done anything wrong. They weren't necessarily collaborators.

They just got on the wrong side of the WIN. In Classical myths, sex is a zero-sum game for women. They either succumb or die. If they submit, there's generally payback later. They are passed from victor to victor, growing used to rape. Even queens just make tactical selections about the perpetrator of sexual assault. It's different for goddesses of course; but not always. Joyce is singular in literature for avoiding patriarchal defaults. I used to find a quiet spot down the end of the bar near the bartender. He liked to chat, but I could never make out his words under ice-cubes jangling inside a Boston Shaker. This is a metaphor for all enclosure in this chapter (see Poe), deafness/audition, cross-cultural exchange, rattling language, shaking the canon, general human barriers to comprehension as well as a reference to Mallarme's dice throw, Tom/Leer and by extension Stephen/Bloom. INSERT OTHER PLOT REFERRALS. Judy watched me mutely. At the start, we exchanged basic pleasantries in Mandarin while she waited to collect drinks. She didn't want to talk much. She looked around the bar restlessly. I was just another foreign guy who presumed that all staff were occasional prostitutes. I started to go back every couple of nights. Always alone. Never consecutive. Eventually, we started to converse more freely. She was a product of Deng's delayed implementation of *Gei Ge Kai Fang* in Shanghai. Her family had been relocated to a new apartment complex in Pudong in the late-Nineties. She had a basic high school education. She never had the cash, connections or grades to get to college. It made her disinterested in school. She started to work in local restaurants at age fourteen. She learned English watching movies on satellite TV. Slowly, she moved up the chain. She married her first boyfriend when she was twenty-one. He worked as a loan officer in a regional bank. They should have had a baby inside two years. She stalled. She never explained why. It was kind of obvious. He got sent to Suzhou. He met another woman. Judy was still processing their divorce three years later. Her situation was bad on one hand. She was now in her late twenties. No kid. This was over-the-hill by Chinese standards. But the low female-to-male ratio meant she would easily find a new husband. Zhu Di had a rough laugh which displayed a straight set of discoloured teeth. She smoked too many cigarettes. She never ate much. This was normal. Chinese women don't take on much fluid either. They say it makes them feel bloated but they really mean it helps them look thin. She had a very physical sense of humour. She'd poke me in the cheek with her chopstick when I got distracted. Punch my arm hard. This was how she expressed LOVE. I knew this behavior well. It reminded me of Australian men in my childhood. Judy had a crater about the size of a one-cent coin between the bridge of her nose and her right eyebrow. It was the legacy of an abscess a few years back. She got really sick straight after her divorce. It was the kind of facial imperfection that really turned off Chinese guys. They wanted CUTE. Zhu Di used to sit up all night after work watching TV then go to bed at dawn. We'd sit in City Extra watching CCTV5 sports channel while I ate a hamburger and she picked at my fries. She like this women's pool competition. It was Thai. Judy was a hustler-with-a-cue in her own right. She must have worked in a sports bar sometime. She wouldn't say much about her past. I wasn't big on pasts either. We pretended that I wasn't married. I never talked about my kids. It was hard to start dating. Zhu Di only got one day off work each month. In May, she had to go to her parent's home. In June, she was busy. I finally scored a date in July. It was hot and humid. We met at Starbucks. She brought a friend. He disappeared after a while. I took her to dinner at an Italian restaurant. Later, we went to a JAZZ club on Fuxing Lu where she could get free drinks off friends behind the bar. We had seats in the VIP section right on top of the band. My apartment was nearby. She came back to watch Chinese soap operas. I made tea. She curled up in a ball on the long white sofa. We made love at dawn. It wasn't great. But we stuck at it. I set her up as my mistress in a small apartment in Hongkou. It was a hardcore local district. You didn't hear Putonghua on the street. I paid the bills. She wanted to keep her job. I respected that decision. She never harassed me for gifts. I should have read all these matters as SIGNS. But I interpreted them as it suited me. We used to eat breakfast together at the Coffee Bean on Shaanxi Lu near the Jade Buddha Temple. I hated their coffee. But it was her kind of place. She had a VIP card. Sometimes local people stared. But they never abused us. Zhu Di wouldn't have tolerated it. We could have gone on like this for years. But she was impatient to have a child. So she hooked up with Johnny.

THE HIGHEST FORM OF CAPITALISM by V. Illich

Tom Hallem's mood shifted to greed as fear receded. He had taken to sea at dusk in a beautiful pea-green boat. He was curious to ascertain how much cash he'd purloined from his erstwhile companion. He extracted the wad of notes and uncrumpled Lawson's profile on some ten-dollar bills. Gulgong inked. "Time's Bakery," the awning sign read. Vulcan beating an alarm clock on a cake tin. Fertilising sparks. Arms for Aeneas. Ocresia turning over the ashes with a stick. Elizabeth Archer burned her index finger with a match-head whilst discussing the muscular art of Luca Giordano. Leopold Bloom tries to marshal the every-diminishing financial resources of Stephen Dedalus over the course of Eumaeus. The young man seemed determined to squander his entire salary on a single night. Lawson ended up begging for booze money down Circular Quay. He never got a government stipend. But they gave him a State funeral. That's how we treat great artists in Australia. Chris Brennan was the same. A hollowed-out drunk. Q: It's hard to believe an Australian wrote such a work? A: It took me twice as long because we're so retarded. Adam Lindsay Gordon is the only Australian writer with a bust in Poet's Corner at Westminster Abbey, just down the row from Tennyson (see Chapter 3). The

Duke of York unveiled it 64 years after his death in 1934. He bought a box of cartridges with his last monies. Next morning, he rose early, walked into the tea-tree scrub, and shot himself. Joseph Furphy sweltering all summer in his brother's foundry at Shepparton. Tom Hallem expiring wet and desperate in bed. He wrote his novel late into the night on a simple, home-made table in the beaten-earth kitchen. Hung a fob watch off battered iron tongs in the family hearth. Lawson's fading coal memory. A Trojan Horse on Mayne Street. Jim and Bertha. William and Tom. Locked in a box at Starvinghurst Gaol. Hallem turned over the currency. Derelict poet to convict draughtsman. A reverse chronology. He studied Francis Greenway's voluptuous face. Maggotfield architect. Forger of some repute. Perfect for Chapter Eight. Macquarie's Speer. Saint James needle-stick finery. Hyperdermic barracks. Same end. Also died destitute. Beggar's eulogy. Time baked them both to a brittle crust. Unmarked grave at Maitland. Hallem quickened his pace. Leer was someone who was doomed at about the same level that a fly is doomed ... doomed to see too much with his gigantic eyes ... too much for his simple brain to handle. I should betray him to Persian Jones and get him out of the way for good. Empty out his safe-room, buy a ute and drive to Queensland with Justin. He crossed Mitchell Road quickly so he could get onto the back side of Erskineville Oval. Cross Harry Noble Reserve. Gasfitter since 1908. Short-term MP. Died 1949. Joyce reconstructed Dublin 1904 from maps and guides. He made inquiries of friends. St Mary's Church. Our Lady of Perpetual Succour. Byzantine icon painted by Saint Luke on the dinner table at Nazareth. Public school where my mother went. She fought her way home every day down back alleys to her mother's corner shop in Ferndale Street. Blood on the door step one morning. Hauling in milk crates (see Chapter 3). Malnourished trees covered his vanity all the way back to Burren Street and safe. He paused on the railway bridge to catch breath. Stephen leaning on a telegraph pole. He looked down the line. Dung sky o'er acrid flaps. Day's carcass dismembered by sudden dark circulation. It was still much earlier than Joyce's timeline in Eumaeus. The night had but begun! He glassed air. Almond-tanged vomit. Rich wormbeer. A passenger train swished under his feet. Dense rumbles. Half-distant scream of 707 engines in steady descent. Thick black plumage. He turned east where the shining rail tracks split into the arse-end of unkempt terraces and factories all their pest-eaten illegal extensions collapsing into night through sagging smokestacks. Old brickworks held together by rows of iron rings. High-rise housing commission blocks in Waterloo ever-bright. Insert lyric by Alexander Smith. Still o'er him rose those melancholy stars! (l.5). It was a horizon that could have been concocted by Claude Lorrain: sky dominating the picture; dark ground beneath; unwieldy figures framed by nature and ruins; cool shadows of damp stones and trees; faint hills staining the phlegmatic background; none of Poussin's talent for closing off space. Lorrain's work was always composed of two intersecting cylinders in which light was stored: one horizontal shaft from the viewer's eyes to the horizon (usually over water); the other, a vertical shaft of sunlight down the front of the painting through a hole in the forest's canopy onto foreground earth. Tom Hallem was crosst by new streetlight (west) by truck headlight (south) and, in turn, he impresst his own silhouette upon the earth. His shadow faded with the waning day like Marsyas' torso just after the last lash of Apollo's beams (prolonging his death throes). The pelt of the famed piper was left suspended in the public square at Celanae until it became an indistinguishable part of the landscape. Only fresh eyes noticed its remnants flapping in the breeze that floated lightly down the banks of the winding Maeander, that river which, legend has it, created language over its course to the Aegean Sea, near Priene. It grew cold too soon. As with Claude, it was either dawn or dusk but mainly dusk. Only the sun's last lukewarm spray stalled verging night. Hallem's limbs went all numb. I am LATE, he thought. Elizabeth will kill me. He loitered looking for a cab. The last carriage of a commuter train passed beneath. Ref. *Trainspotting*. A blue guard light bit. Resonant clatter like an electric fan murmuring ever-softer until it ceased to be heard. Hallem walked up the last stretch of Erskineville Road. Procession of Christ into Sydney. Harsh biro marks shining on sheets of glossy butcher's paper. Materials as subject. Hanging a screen off tacks. Go right down Wilson Street. Look down the vestibule. Dry mouth. Uncomfortable gulps. So deep his epiglottis trembled. Messaien-low organ. Stiff and exposed was the front of his throat. Raw passion passing through clerical lips. Slop of the River Acheron. Up to the ankles of loose-fitting garments. Most loathsome are spurned. Chase a banner. Obdurate gadflies. Receding chambers in which man cowers and dreams. BABEL. Massive breath-strokes of disconnected language. Ginsberg's air of Dylan. Collage factory. Corner of Brown Street. A single dry leaf blew against his trousers. Goethe's *urpflanze*. All nature it encased. New layers locked into place all the time like Bloom's Tessera. Altering the significance of every text. Deepen the membrane until reality is blurred. Opaque glass. Space gets closer then. Books are like tiles. Leather-bound spines resting around concave page leaves. Spina bifida babies. Prosenchyma. An unmarked grave in Woronora Cemetery. Communal pits. Leather coverts. Turn down Brown Lane. Full circuit. Snorting a line of Jack Brabham. The journey back is always completely different. The vertebrae of a cement staircase rose straight to a single red light. Hallem passed a par-open gate. A tabby slumbered under the back of a van. Corpse of a pigeon now flatter, less liquid, part of the road. Hallem past a concrete slab surmounted by steel-piping parapets. He turned into the taxi bays. Purple sky void. Reflection in a mirror of the word POOL. Go back to the starting-point as ever. Four Italian taxi drivers were huddled around a packing crate playing poker. Spin the Kip. Always EWAN. Spin again.

"Anybody working?" inquired Tom Hallem.

"Depends where you're going,' said The Supervisor not looking up from his hand.

A wad of thick bristle rose like a plume over his forehead, receding on both sides to bare skull. Suddenly he looked straight at Hallem. A matted beard descended from his chin. A sky-blue synthetic shirt spread over the top of his belt. A girdle foul with grease. Masonic master. He scraped a metal spanner as if dragging a paw.

"Change of shift you see," added another player.

A smile played on his speakeasy lips (C1). Psychopomp. A helpful beast with a guiding lamp in its jaws. Sweet Beulah. He looked back at his cards and shook his head then laid the hand fanned-out and face-down on the makeshift table. His hair was parted straight down the crown like a hatchet clout. It hung in slick ruins. His cheeks puffed slightly as if his hunched posture impeded satisfactory breathing. A small cleft softened his otherwise bulbous chin.

"Ireland perfected the art of itinerance," he continued. "That's why we're all so-at-ease Down Under."

"It wasn't such a doddle at the Battle of Castle Hill," replied Grogan. "When Johnson tricked Cunningham into parley and they cut our compatriots down."

A squeeze box started. The narrator sucked on a fresh cornpipe. A swagman approached the narrator's hearth on his hands and knees. "Ah! (moralised the pipe)," writes Joseph Furphy in *Such is Life*, twenty years before inanimate objects were given voice in Circe. A long, convoluted description of a German meerschaum follows. *SisL* is still the greatest technical achievement in Australian literature, one of the great novels of English literature and certainly a precursor to *Ulysses* in terms of its form, style, narrative perspective and use of emplotment for comic effect. It is a downtrodden Irishman's sardonic tale of the vicissitudes and ironies of existence in the harsh environment of the Australian Bush. Furphy is an Irish family name, O'Foirbhilhe, meaning "descendant of the perfect one" in Gaelic. The clan originated in County Tyrone, smack-dab in the centre of Ireland. His father emigrated to New South Wales in 1840 and he was born in 1843. The only books in the family home were the Bible and Shakespeare. He was reciting passages by heart at the age of seven. They formed the backbone of his Prosenchymer. This passage about the anthropomorphic pipe contains Furphy's great postmodern moment of self-reference:

"'What's your name?' he demanded, as I placed my foot in the stirrup.

"'Collins,'" the narrator replied.

Tom Collins was the pen name of Joseph Furphy (adopted 1892). It is an Australian slang term for an imaginary foe who slanders men in public (See Crowe, ASD, 1895 cited in Barnes, *The Order of Things*, 1990). SISL is the ultimate shaggy-dog tale. It is indubitably what Barthes would call a Writerly Text. Its antinomian subject matter is veiled – like Nosey Alf's face – by Euphuism like Swinburne's poetics and Joyce's Modernism. Homosexuality, gender fluidity, cross-dressing, theft and murder abound behind the narrator's misperceptions and confusion. Phonetic speech by German, Scottish, Irish, Chinese and First Country characters stalls the text, while also offering an insight into Australian multiculturalism in the late nineteenth century. Furphy proceeds down intellectual channels discursively like a precursor of Proust. False naming, deliberate narratorial errors, mistaken identities and patent untruths predate similar innovations in Eumaeus. Some chapters constitute individual essays in their own right. Tom Collins = Leer. They act as outgoing marionettes of their respective authors. Like the narrator in *ALRDTP*, Tom Collins acknowledges the fluid modes he adopts to suit different audiences. He is totally self-aware of his role as a FRONT and ACTOR. The title mimics Ned Kelly's famous last words before being hanged. *Such is Life* is a great novel, the greatest (yet) written in Australia, because it is still the only one to try to make technical inroads into the canon. "The plan of the book is not like any other that I know of," Furphy wrote to A.G. Stephens. It reflects, and gains strength from, the cosmic ambitions of the Federation period. What Furphy called the "loosely federated" structure of *SISL* matches the constitutional output of Becoming Australia in 1901. Like Joyce, Furphy is not just a technical writer setting out to achieve literary goals. He offers acute portraits of daily life in the Australian bush amongst the low classes. Shearers and swagman roam the dry, unyielding countryside living hand-to-mouth in a bucolic Monto redolent of Browning's wasted landscape in "Childe Roland." They share food, fire, smokes, money, stories and jokes. Occasionally, they come across liquor. They steal from each other without compunction and forgive each other with alacrity because they KNOW that existence in the Bush is a Darwinian contest in which opportunism (Mallarme's kip) and collective action determine survival or death. There is an aleatory connection between Furphy's novel and his family name. A 'furphy' in Australian slang refers to an improbable story claimed to be factual by the teller. It comes from the name emblazoned on the side of water carts designed and constructed by J. (John) Furphy & Sons of Shepparton, Victoria. These cast-iron tanks were first manufactured in the 1880s for water storage on farms. John Furphy was the novelist's brother. The author worked in the foundry most of his adult life. Furphy-branded carts were later used extensively by the Australian Army in the Great War, especially in the Middle East and at Gallipoli. They became a popular meeting place for Diggers to exchange gossip. A rumour became known as 'furphy' as a result. Loop back to Tom Collins. *S'Life* is itself a FURPHY (like Joyce's Eumaeus) although the author was long dead by the time it was coined (he died in 1912). Its origin had nothing to do with Joseph Furphy. It is a pure coincidence; an example of what Freud termed the Uncanny [*Das Unheimliche*].

"Such is Life," added Slick Ruins perfunctorily.

"Now there was another great Irish upstart," replied Grogan adamantly.

"His father, Red, was a Tipperary pig thief," retorted Small Cleft with a Galway snarl. Intimidation is central to social interplay amongst the underclasses in Connacht. The upper classes sound like Peter O'Toole. Originally, the Joyce family came from this county. His wife, Nora Barnacle, was born in a Galway workhouse. It is the site of Joyce's great story, "The Dead". It is also the place where underage Millie Blom is studying pornography on the date of *Ulysses*. She is the proposed recipient of Alec Bannon's prophylactic in Oxen. Jabber Ladiesman inverts Furphy's title in Chapter Seven. However, this pun is really the end of Ladiesman's adventures in inter-textuality. The remainder of the novel is standard drug-slapstick as his anecdotes about addict sub-culture from *Cunty* are laboriously reprised. As with its predecessor, the novel finally resolves itself in equivocal moralising with woman-as-victim. This places it in the same category as the films, TS, PF and FC. To re-claim Australia's Celtic spirit must be part of any negotiation with James Joyce.

"There's a crude type of oppression lingering under that fair dinkum charade," replied Grogan. "The Orangemen and Masons always kept us dowen. The first political prisoners were transported as convicts after the 1798 rebellion. We were not permitted to practice our religion until 1820. We were blamed for the conscription vote in 1917. Why, Catholics couldn't even get jobs in a department store."

"It's a better shop today," said the Supervisor.

"Better than the alternative," added Psychopomp.

"True. Our Irish foundlings preferred the luxury of British cellars to starvation back home," added Grogan, "where they were penned in darkness by John Bull's window tax eight to a bed, head to toe like Molly and Leopold Bloom back in Dublin, one blanket covering their shame. No human being deserves to live in such squalor."

"We can thank Mister Engels for that," replied the Helpful Beast. "His factory in Levenshulme was a bloody gob of shamrock spittle on Manchester's black bed linen."

"He left a beautiful account of life in Irish New Town," added Grogan caustically.

"Yes," replied Chin. "He loved to promenade with sweet Mary Burns along the banks of the Irk down St George's Road, where there was an Irish pub she favoured."

"Harp or Lion, as the old song goes."

"Pick a shamrock from the ruins or a rose from an English garden."

Suddenly, a ballad sprang hard from Grogan's cracked lower lip: Only think of Hugh O'Neill / Thundering down in furious style, / To assail, with lead and steel, / The rapists from our SISTER isle!

"Aodh Mór Ó Néill," nodded the Supervisor. "He led Ireland in the Nine Years War."

"They all fled," exclaimed Stephen Joyce goading his sub-continental compatriots.

"To carry on the struggle in Spain," replied Grogan vehemently. "They embarked at midnight on Lough Swilly. Driven by Atlantic gales. Ah, who would be an Irishman at sea? They took shelter on the Seine like Beckett and Joyce."

In the cabman's humpy in Monto, Bloom recounts his confrontation with The Citizen to Stephen. They discuss the Phoenix Park assassinations and Parnell. Bloom rejects The Citizen's violent nationalism, again disclosing Christ-like tendencies. But he becomes better than Christ or pagan gods to Stephen. He is mortal, fallible and tempted to bad ways, yet always tries to transcend base tendencies. This makes him greater than the immortals, like one of Shelley's fatal heroes. Stephen acknowledges this trait, which Joyce sees as essential to greatness. It is not enough to be well-educated and verbose like Mulligan or well-connected and polite like Russell. Joyce requires art to become a moral enterprise. Bloom is the vinculum for that ascent by Stephen. It was Bloom's presence in Circe that enabled the reflection of Shakespeare's face to appear over Stephen's head. Bloom is the intermediary to get Stephen to extract the literary DNA from Shakespeare as his REAL father. He isn't really interested in his biological one. His value has been played out. Stephen is quite prepared to disown Simon Dedalus, as he did in Scylla and does again here in Eumaeus. Eventually, however, Stephen gets bored with Bloom's goody-two-shoes verbosity. He is anxious to move on. He needs to get the future rolling. He doesn't believe that Ireland can be changed, except by his own heroic art. He says as much to Bloom. He needs to start right away if he is to make it happen. He needs to keep all these great new thoughts in his head. He doesn't want his brain cluttered with more of Bloom's information so he shifts the conversation with an abrupt command to Bloom to "change the subject." Well, that got the whole crew started.

"On my first night back in Carrigloe," said Murphy drily joining the conversation, "like Flaubert at Cairo, in dirty overcast weather, we boarded the S.S. Nil, a steam packet of 250 horsepower, which rolled like a drunken man as it made but little headway across Cork harbour. The city flickered and ceased under levin. Rain slid down the decks like snakes, perforating the ocean top. The fish sank deeper into mire until they were only buffeted by a slight swell from the hull above. My nametag read Odysseus Pseudangelos as per the Linati schedule, which literally means FALSE ANGEL in Greek, just as Murphy means "sea warrior" in Gaelic. What with my gnarled appearance and outlandish yarns, Joyce made me appear more like a real Odysseus back on Ithaca than his putative hero, Leoplod Loomb. That was my only significance to the novel. I came and went as a false double. I possessed no stench of brine about my person but rather the odour of a prison cell. This was what alerted Bloom, with his keen olfactory sensibility, to suspicions as to my authenticity. He had a great taste for perfume. Leer was my equivalent some ways back. It became clear from my landlubber anecdotes that I had no experience of seafaring. It was all tall stories garnisheed off books. In fact, I was terrified of the sea and could not swim.

Once, I was rescued off the beach by a young dandy with seaweed hair called MALACHAN. I crossed myself in the storm on that old ferry. It seemed to suck in our vessel alive and consume its iron hull. I thought it was Fatal Woman! But I was still alive at the dock after this sixteen-minute epic, although swamped in gum. I had only my carpet bag and a harpoon. Like Ishmael, I scoured the sunken streets for food and shelter in Absolute Darkness. Ah was one very hungry and wet young mewt by now! The sky was godless mud, fireflights tingled through barbed-wire walls, Homer's sea spewed food-flecked refuse in my face, Original Sin burdened me, I seemed to be someone else (Satan), from some other time (the Fall), and some other text (*Paradise Lost*) and the only sound left in the world was a few coppers that I rattled nervously in my pocket on my dromological wobble against. I passed up the Necropolis Hotel on Bachelor's-Walk-and-Brine and settled on the St. Outer Inn for lodgings. My host, P. Coffin, offered me a double room with Bung. While he processed my papers, I studied a print of the Norwich School tacked up in the foyer. It was a landscape by Cotman in the style of Jacob van Ruisdael prior to his switch to rice-paste and pigment in 1831. The gloom and dust layers, which seemed to have been fastened onto the surface in the manner of Duchamp's sieves in The Large Glass, I later learned by fly spray, completely doused the sun. It had become an image one step beyond Dutch Nihilism. Involuntarily, I thought of Sebastian van Storck brooding on some soft polder, his Hamlet-face gripped with torpor. This is further evidence of my campus pedantry and lack of real-world experience. When Coffin returned, I told him to clean the surface at once. He grinned. And told me it epitomised Old Dublin. Then he took me to my hovel. And left me. I put on all my clothes against the cold and lay down. After a while, my room-mate entered prefaced by a kerosene lamp. He laid it on the ironing board and stared through the pall without noticing me. Then he started to undress. I could see the dark imprint of inks on his body. He had been thoroughly marked by the Designer with the phrase, "thou shalt not (illegible)." The tail of this proscription had been hopelessly blurred by blunt needles. Thus, he was pockmarked but with effacement. I gave way in the bunk for him. Our backs simmered from touch and I slept. And dreamed of a metal girder inserted under the base of my spine and thrust up through my body until it protruded out my mouth. I would have asked somebody to tie a red rag around it and walk in front of me ringing a cowbell except that I was utterly unable to articulate language. I grabbed it with both hands but I didn't know whether to push or pull. This is where Chaplin would have come in handy with his slapstick guile. I was left clasping it like an icon. So, what could I do when the sun came up next morning but get up, sun coming up my arse, dawn sicking on me with gold, and shave. I borrowed Bung's cut-throat razor. It was brighter than a blaze as I held it against my cheek and gazed into the mica-wafer mirror at my face (link to Buck

Mulligan). Like Mahood in Beckett's *Unnamable*, I used to worry about waking up one day with my two retinae facing each other because of the crumpling effect of what Chidley called "corrugation". I was thus reassured to see them pointing only slightly askew from straight-at-the-mark as usual. They watched with the vigilance of two shiny rocks stuffed into the sockets of old Oedipus as my gormless features were scythed off the map until a single asymmetrical 'I' stared back at me: ah was Cyclops! The floor teemed with vermin and louse. Felt one crawl across my soul. An enamel mask was fitted onto my face. My other eye was just left bobbing in the lukewarm basin-water, looking up, as if for God, at the sombre prospect of that "enormous dice blinking a mournful eye," that Huysmans describes in an image by Odilon Redon.

Skin the Goat Fitzharris now took up the taille with vigour. He was the most infamous man in Dublin, famed for his role as the Invincibles' driver; the unusual manner of his arrest by Inspector Mellon; his long term of imprisonment which caused considerable public dismay; and his unannounced return to his brother's home in Mullingar after sixteen years hard labour.

"It was a tempestuous winter's night when the Dunbar arrived off Sydney Heads," he commenced. "Heavy rain obscured the sandstone cliffs at the entrance to Port Jackson. Captain Green on deck misjudged the ship's position. On the run into port, he thought they were approaching North Head. When the shout came, 'breakers ahead,' Green ordered 'hard-a-port.' The Dunbar crashed straight into South Head. It heaved broadside in the swell and broke up immediately. Waves sank the lifeboats."

"That's a FAR DISTANT TALE, Jim, what you could have only learned off," said Corley. "It must be one and fifty years back by now. You were never there, old son. I mean, you could move that event twenty years forward or backwards like Cavendish's murder and nobody would know the difference. Now, I myself personally was lying low on furlough in Hobart on the fateful day in 1975 when the Derwent Bridge collapsed."

"Taking a break at Risdon, no doubt," taunted Joyce.

"That was a terrible omen for Whitlam," added Skin G. "Nature always turns against Titans shortly before their fall. Look what happened to Mao in 1976."

The protests started in January with his obvious disrespect to the memory of Zhou Enlai. This unleashed a surge of popular feeling. The same thing happened after the death of Hu Yaobang in 1989. But Deng learned his lessons well. He cut Zhao Ziyang down and put him under house arrest. This was the same method that Jiang Jieshi had employed on the Young Marshall after the botched Xian coup in 1936. At Tangshan, earthquakes and aftershocks on 28 July collapsed the central districts of the city shortly before the Chairman finally died in Beijing. Everything crumbled dry and stiff like a Hiroshima groanbox. In all,

250,000 people died. It was the worst natural disaster of the twentieth century. The first time S. Dog went into a room on the twentieth floor of the Jin Jiang Hotel on Xin Xiang Road, he pulled back the thick night curtains to reveal dominoes of cheap apartment buildings stretching all the way to a steel plant thence to a field of inflected cranes where the horizon dissolved in a smear of yellow pollution.

"*Wollongong* took out two central pylons," Corley continued ignoring the young eye-tie. "It was left swirling on the Derwent in impotent circles like Giambattista Vico with its cargo of silver phosphate spilling into the drink."

"That's ADJACENCY," scoffed Grogan. "You probably watched it on TV. You might as well have been back on the mainland. Now, I had DIRECT EXPERIENCE of shipwreck. I was a crewman on *Voyager* when she got split in twain by the flagship, *Melbourne*. I woke up in agony on a stretcher in C Hangar at Albatross."

He raised his work shirt to show the other drivers the sagging scar left by a molten burn. Tom noted a turtle tattooed on the back of one hand and a ship's anchor adoring his forearm. Two swallows faced each other across the soft flesh above his pectoral muscles indicating ten thousand nautical miles of sailing.

"One hundred and twenty-one souls went down," continued SGF sagely adjusting the Vellum parchment over his crumpled kneecaps. He was a broken man by 1904, working as a night watchman for the Dublin Corporation; which may be where a young James Joyce encountered him. "Only James Johnston survived. A cabin boy of tender years. He never spoke of that awful night. It remains the worst maritime disaster in Australian history."

"Her captain was dumb as the dopey Yanks what sank *Maru*."

"Now they're selling-off the grand old girl for scrap."

"Not before time. *Melbourne* was jinxed."

"Yes. She was laid down in Forty-three, then the War ended. She sat offshore like a prison hulk for more than a decade. Finally, she was commissioned in 1955. That's what let all the bogies get into her."

"Largest vessel ever built at Sunderland. Duncan Dunbar paid thirty thousand quid."

Hull and frames of British oak. It bore the British Lion on its figurehead. A three-masted clipper. In Proteus, Joyce combines imagery of such a ship with thoughts of death to induce a self-proclaimed moment of artistic epiphany for Stephen Dedalus, which he hurriedly transcribes on a torn corner of the envelope containing Garrett Deasy's letter. In fact, this scrap of lyric is just another hackneyed piece of sub-Swinburnean poetics: "On swift sail flaming / Through storm and south / He comes, pale vampire / Mouth to my mouth." *Ulysses* is ultimately a self-conscious story of arrested artistic development like the movie *Fight Club*. This image later links Stephen to the ambiguous figure of D.G. Murphy, who tells his audience in Eumaeus that he reached Dublin on board that very ship. "We come up this morning eleven o'clock," he says, on that "threemaster Rosevean from Bridgewater with bricks." This is a clear allusion to Odysseus returning to Ithaca. But it also places Murphy on a domestic boat as a local traveller rather than as an international voyager like Homer's hero. Joyce returns to sea-faring and waterflow throughout *Ulysses*. This is natural for an island dweller. It is another reason why the selection of the *Odyssey* was apt as a governing trope for the novel. Ithaca was a minor island nation like Ireland. Yet both were self-sufficient. Historically, Ireland was big enough to sustain the development of the society, economy and culture of the Gaelic race. They had no need of overseas adventures. There was enough mystery and haunted climes on its craggy shores and foggy, damp meadows to invent a full panoply of myths, gods and heroes. Then the English came with their restless eye in the twelfth century. The sea was converted into an escape hatch for Irish youth. Joyce recognised this reality from an early age. In THE ENCOUNTER, the protagonist knows that good things, "do not happen to people who remain at home: they must be sought abroad." But, like Des Esseintes abandoning his plan to go to London after enjoying British fare in Paris while he waits for a train, the leading character evinces a very confined response to this insight. He merely crosses the Liffey on a ferry with a friend and wanders on the opposite side of the river for a while. They are exposed to intimidating individuals in a debased landscape and quickly return to the known-confines of the city. Joyce was a minute diarist of human life like Pepys but it is the aspect of the market-place he knows, not the ocean. His characters are always near the shore observing the sea from without suspiciously. There is hardly any reference to the reality of life on board a ship in his work. This is actually *tranche de vie* fidelity by Joyce. He was an exponent of WHAT HE ACTUALLY SAW rather than a fantasist. Yet Joyce must still negotiate the disconnect between Homer's brackish sub-plots and his own fixity-on-land to complete *Ulysses*. For the *Odyssey* is indubitably a sea-set tale. Its action is best understood by sailors. They are only too familiar with the changeableness of Neptune's realm and vagaries of maritime life. Joyce turned the psychological dimensions of Conrad's sea-stories to homeland purposes. His characters find their own version of the Congo at night in their own city, which becomes a strange foreign place of danger, risk, thrills and slaughter. Aside from Odysseus, mythical sailors mentioned in *Ulysses* include Sinbad, the Ancient Mariner, Robinson Crusoe and the Flying Dutchman. All these figures represent a single dominant trope which is also applicable to D.G. Murphy – that of the isolated sailor in exile striving against nature to return home. Every reader knows this trope. Its conclusion is always return to a homeland that is not the same place envisaged in memory. This is what Don Cane is enduring on this day. The sailor can no longer relate to, enjoy or reintegrate into life at home. The trope always ends with bitter death or relaunch on new adventures. *Ulysses* utilises many conventional symbols and motifs relating to water and travel but its sea journeys are always prospective trips, deferred excursions, derided caprices or idealised fables. It remains as rooted to the earth as Shelley's PLANT. The single sea journey of significance in the novel is retrospective. This is the case of Stephen Dedalus returning by ship to Dublin-as-Hades for his mother's death throes. As a result of this experience, the sea becomes inextricably entwined with imminent death for Stephen. The appearance of ships in Joyce's work is usually linked to existential torpor. In *PAYM*, Stephen sees a feverish vision of a ship carrying the corpse of Parnell back from England over "long dark waves rising and falling." At the start of *Ulysses*, he is urged by Mulligan to admire the sea. He goes up to the viewing platform of the Martello Tower and observes a "mailboat clearing the harbourmouth of Kingstown." This is a clear image of transferral in which the boat represents his waning hopes of fleeing Dublin. Mail becomes an extended symbol for his writing and art. Mulligan looks at the same scene and sees "our moghty mawther." It is a place he embraces with glee. He subsequently dives full forty feet to reach its waters and swim within wild rocky tides. It is the scene of his famous rescue of a drowning man – the exact opposite of what he does for Stephen Dedalus on land. Like Mulligan, Joyce was an excellent swimmer whereas Stephen is a self-confessed hydrophobe. This has political implications. The Imperialist Haines, of course, shares a highly positive vision of the oceans. The British Empire, after all, is "the sea's ruler." It controls the movement of trade and people globally. Ninety-eight per cent of Irish exports went straight across the Irish Sea.

"I went through school with Ben Lexcen," interjected Raper, who had been silent up to this point. "Now there was a man who knew all about boats."

"Benny's mind games spooked the Yanks."

"They've never been good at the soft stuff."

"Yairs. They're better suited to BIG BANGS."

"His real name was Bob Miller," said Corley explicating the words slowly. "I knew him when he raced skiffs."

Rumors of Dutch masterminds confounded the American camp. Winged keels encased in canvas veils. Wax wings. It all came down to the final race. More officers died in the air than soldiering in no man's land. The horizontal foil has aerodynamic benefits over a conventional shoal. Better resistance. Better downward lift. Decrease in draft. Higher aspect ratio.

"Benny was putting wings on eighteen footers back in 1959," said Corley. "He used them on *Taipan*. *Venom* had a winged centerboard."

"The *Dunbar's* anchor rests at St Stephens's Cemetery just over the way," continued Goat pointing north-west across King Street.

"He changed his name when he went to work for Bond," Corely concluded sagely.

They all nodded. Eumaeus is full of impostors. Cut-throats. Criminals in disguise. Fugitives on the run. West of Custom House. East end of King Street. A conventional style for an untrustworthy text. The neon throb of Salona's Talking Tables stalled suddenly. Everything went red. Town Hall clock struck so many times that Hallem lost count. There is a basic disjuncture in Eumaeus between the candor of Bloom and Stephen and the misrepresentations and untruths of all secondary characters. The reader must see them as the only truthful ones, or else the chapter descends into ignominy.

Why did Bob Miller choose the surname Lexcen?
It was the least popular name in the *Reader's Digest* mailing list.

Why is the anchor of the *Dunbar* in St Stephens's cemetery?
Goat took up his pipe. Newtown was home to the main Sydney cemetery in the 1850s. It lay just beyond the city boundary stone. The land was originally owned by Captain Bligh. He named it Camperdown after the famous sea battle in which he distinguished himself. It was registered as an Anglican General Cemetery but took all denominations. Saint Stephens is home to Bathsheba Ghost. She was the Matron of Sydney Hospital. Sometimes, she is still seen sitting on William Ebbett's grave in a brown frock coat. On moonless nights, a soldier views the stars with a telescope near the grave of Major Mitchell. Hannah Watson's lover died on the *Dunbar*. She was wife of the Sydney Harbour Master. Later, her husband poisoned her out of spite. She emerges in the form of a grey lady and slowly drifts to her beau's veined, marble bed. It lies near Miss Haversham's headstone. Dickens based his character on Eliza Donnithorne. Her home was called Cambridge Hall. It was back down King Street a short hop nor-nor-east, pointed out Grogan. The Art Metal Workshop of James Castle & Sons now stands on the site. She was jilted on her wedding day and refused to discard her wedding gown nor have breakfast cleared from the table. It mouldered into dust and decay. She kept the front door of her mansion open until the day of her death. Penelope as a Currency Lass. Dickens' son lived in Newtown in the 1850s. He had a room above a milliner's shop where he wrote puff-pieces under the pseudonym DRUD. You can read about him in *Household Words*. His code name was Compeyson. Abel Magwitch worked for him as a forger. They were well-known Sydney convicts. Magwitch got fourteen years transportation. Compeyson seven. The cemetery closed in 1868. Bad air was rising from the communal pits, upsetting the local population. They buried the paupers in piles. Left mass graves open until each hole was filled then covered the corpses with a few inches of clay. Reverend Kemp was known as the pastor of sixteen thousand souls because of this practice. His ghost still haunts the cemetery. Stephen Joyce abdicated his hand face-down,

got up and walked towards the cab bay. Tom Hallem was leaning on a pole. Australia is also an island of land-lovers, he thought. Once, everyone landed at port. Now they just fly over the sea like my father.

"Where are you going?" Stephen asked.

"Darlinghurst," Hallem stated.

"It's on my way home. Just wait while I fill up the tank."

Tom walked to a red pay phone in the service station. He rang his mother. Long wait. Finally, a man's voice. "Hi. Is mum home? OK. No message. Just wanted to chat. Bye." He tried Bob Hensley. No answer. Maybe the old man sleeps. Suddenly, sharp headlights cut his gaze. The passenger's side window dropped automatically.

"Get in," said Joyce.

Rework the regal cavalcade in W.Rocks to Eumaeus (insert prolepsis).

The route selected by Stephen Joyce was as follows: proceed 1.7 kilometres along King Street > turn right at Cleveland Street > proceed 1.8 kilometres > turn left into Crown Street, Surry Hills > continue on Crown Street for 1.6 kilometres until you reach Oxford Street, Darlinghurst. You have now reached your destination. Insert the following characters crossing route but not in this order (sort according to poetics): Persian Jones admonishing a drug mule under the awning of the Native Rose Hotel on Cleveland Street; Blot pushing his shopping trolley down City Road against the prevailing storm; his wife drifting down a path towards Victoria Park swimming pool; D. Flight-Falconhurst pulling Jabber Ladiesman across King Street at the Queens Street traffic lights on course to her front first floor bedroom in an attached terrace on Forbes Street; Ana Lafei walking through Prince Alfred Park with her guitar towards the Musician's Club on Chambers Street (Tom's taxi passes the perimeter of this park, creating a symbol of their fated disconnection); trains crackling beneath the rail overpass; Francine Hackett waiting for a break in the traffic to cross Cleveland Street (she has just left her bedsit on Baptist Street); Leon Daniel driving a black BMW up Oxford Street as the taxi waits at the Crown Street intersection; entry into Darlinghurst down the steep dip next to Royal Court then turning into Burton Street then taking the second right into Palmer Street and parking opposite Riverina Flats at number two-sixty-five.

GIMME SHELTER

Billy Capri stood at his kitchen sink doing dishes. He looked out a tall window. Another wave of cars passed swiftly beneath him on Crown Street. A taxi turned into Burton Street below. He left his apartment and walked to the hardwood staircase. The red pay phone in the foyer was available. He descended a single flight of stairs. Do not disturb Stan the Caretaker, he thought. He rang home. No answer. He went back upstairs. Climb a tower. Lock yourself inside. Swallow the key. Don't answer the doorbell. Only allow entrance to what you can see through the security hole. He sat on his bed overlooking Darlinghurst as it flattened into Woolloomooloo Bay. The spur-tips of the Opera House lifted above RBG. Odysseus' ship was entering harbour. Sacred to the old god Phorcys. He came to the far side of Ithaca, where he would not be seen by informants through olive trees. What the Eora saw. Cook's handkerchief. Warrawarrawa. You're all dead. Ghost ships. Vaults of Utzon's maze. The cave where Odysseus offered due sacrifice. Rising slopes like the smooth slopes of Neriton unfolding into a rich forest. Soon he would be gone from Sydney. To England. Odysseus also came from a remote island. Get inside the walls of Bloomsbury in a fucking great cape. Hide the facts under a purple chiffon dress. Disguises fit nicely into the Eumaeus episode. Meet Derek Attridge. Recently appointed at Strathclyde. Make up some stories. Fantasies of travel like Robert Louis Stevenson. Tusitala. A house is also a teller of tales. Tom going to Europe. Don coming home. Odysseus incoming. Telemachus outgoing. Shanghai Dog both. Nobody fits into a trope neatly. We are all and none of the above as well as the narrative to be disclosed. Letter of Invitation from Professor Krafter. Another surrogate. It would be easier to connect if he was still at Southampton. Never mind. Chance to visit Glasgow. We can talk Joyce and sport. READ some South African literature. Start with Olive Schreiner. Learn the names of leading figures in the Apartheid debate. A poignant allusion to Strijdom should impress. Mix in references to places like Bophuthatswana and Transkei. Work on my pronunciation. Both homelands. Vals nations. Passports. A sham. Might explain his interest in Joyce. Try to meet some black students. Maybe get an ANC badge @ Camden Markets. Too much? Billy went back downstairs. He telephoned again. Barry Capri answered.

"Hi."

"Hi, Pup. How're you doing?"

"I'm OK. Where have you been?"

"Your mother went to see Penelope. I closed-up shop."

"Has he made contact yet?"

"No. Nobody knows what's happening. I know it's bad timing. Another 24 hours and you'd have been gone."

"Would you have told me the truth today if he hadn't come back?"

"No."

"When would you have told me?"

"We never had a plan."

PAUSE.

"Is Vanessa with you?" asked his father finally.

"No. She went home. I think she's coming back later."

"Are you going to wait for her."

"No. I think it's better if we're apart tonight."

"Would you like me to come get you?"

"That'd be nice."

"I can help you pack. Give me one hour."

"OK, Barry. Bye."

Billy hung up the telephone and went back to his apartment. He was not able to say the word FATHER. Maybe he should add 'yet.' Maybe not. He didn't know the answer. Everything felt stiff suddenly. He picked up the *Aeneid* and opened Book Two. It was the last book left in his apartment. Everything else had been packed into boxes. The story of the Trojan Horse does not appear in the *Iliad*, which ends with Hector's funeral. In the *Odyssey*, it is only mentioned in the third song of Demodocus at the palace of Alcinous in Book 9. Odysseus never explains his method of defeating the Trojans. All he says is, "I left Troy and made for home." This left a gap for Virgil. This was always the way with Classical literature. They reworked the same myths and legends to their own ends. We've been on a novelty drive since ... the Enlightenment, he guessed. Billy wondered how Joyce perceived the Trojan Horse trope in structuring *Ulysses*. If the entry of Bloom to his marital bed represented the return to Ithaca then Molly's monologue in Chapter III may hold the seeds of a Trojan Horse episode. This would enable Joyce to write BEYOND the end of Homer's narrative, giving him hegemony over his precursor (H) and creating a linkage with his successor (V). Thus, Joyce would position himself inside the core Classical dyad: Hellas][Dublin][Rome. HomerJoyceVirgil. Hell as Dublin, so roam. Now he can even reverse temporal notions of influence (see Harold Bloom). This is what Stephen Dedalus wanted to do with Shakespeare. To become his own father. Billy went on to speculate on Joyce titling his novel after the Roman god rather than the Greek. The Romans had a very different perspective on Odysseus. Virgil labelled him *dirus Ulixes*, *pellacis* and *fandi factor*. Billy wrote a note on the topic on the back of an envelope from the Electricity Commission then dozed. **NARRATOR**: The driver manoeuvred his taxi into a strait beyond the bowsers. Tom entered the cabin. They set off. The taxi sped down City Road. Hunger gnawed at Hallem. He was strapped in his seatbelt like plumbed Odysseus to the mast hot ears upbraided with Sirensound. Deep in a lop-sided dream. Meals recalled through shrivelled cellophane. Sitting with Les in front of the television waiting for Penelope to return home. Curried sausages lolling cold on a tray like severed cocks. Not father. Not son. Despite all those years in the same house. Taking his name. So what. All names are unstable. Murphy and Skin-the-Goat use pseudonyms. Murphy has different nicknames. Bloom is misnamed BOOM in the newspaper (see page 605). AEIOU is George Russell. Olive Schreiner was Ralph Iron (after Emerson). Add a letter to the end of any name changes it completely. Races morph new identities. Jews lived in Ireland disguised as Catholics. Everybody in Vietnam changed their family name to NGUYEN when the Ho Dynasty collapsed in 1407. Indigenous people were told to be Greeks in the Sixties. Hungarian migrants took names like Wright off Sydney street signs. Parnell transformed into the mysterious Dutchman, Jean De Wet. Ho used many fake names to avoid detection. Escape acts. Houdini. Simon Dedalus' namesake was a carney marksman. Antonio the Greek. Rose is a name. Smellidiom. Odysseus always used different labels. Leopold Bloom also. I'll be home as soon as I can, Penelope told Les from a noisy phone booth in the city. He leveraged himself into a dining chair and picked up rusty tongs. "I learned to make this dish on a one cube burner. Jungle banquet, we called it. Must have made Charlie drool. He always attacked at chowtime." Achy Les (advertise pun). Fatal flaw in his foot. Bits of shrapnel commuting through his hip. Arrow stuck in bone. A long shot out of the blue struck his gilded heel. He expired plodding towards the shore. Bloody venom slithering into sand clumps on Cheviot Beach. Poison tips. Harold Holt striding into outflowing surf in flippers. Lone yachtsman passing from port. Leering Neptune. Careless love look how you carried me down. Faked his death to elope with Marjorie Gillespie. It was suicide by water. Zara had named a gentleman as co-respondent. It was all about to hit the news. Water is linked to volatility, instability and madness in *Ulysses*. Irrationality is feminine to Joyce. Women are seen as material like water, as opposed to the ethereal spiritual and intellectual tone of men. In this vein, he told S. Gilbert that Molly "is a manifestation of Nature herself, the antithesis of art." Thus, Sirens become enemies of man's reason. Mina Purefoy is called the "goddess of unreason." Her fertility and the womb are associated with water. Bloom experiences the bath as "a womb of warmth." He comes out of it like a baby in a blasphemy of birth (like Leer) that is then juxtaposed with death corpse of Dignam's funeral. He must cross the four rivers of Hades to reach the cemetery. The Styx, Acheron, Cocytus, and Pyriphlegethon become the four Dublin rivers, the Dodder, the Royal and Grand Canals, and the Liffey. Water is always associated with mutability by Bloom. It becomes a form of FATAL WOMAN. This is a highly cliched association, which Joyce uses to display Bloom's cosmic and intellectual limitations. He compares time to "holding water in your hand," says that "life is a stream" and later, "always passing, the stream of life." There is little doubt that Joyce was personally aligned with this thinking. He includes many minor allusions that reinforce this position such as the drowned man dying off Maiden's Rock. Woman-as-water extends to gender patterns for Bloom. He says women are "as easy to stop as the sea." It is the same for Stephen

Dedalus. In fact, gender prejudice is one of their chief correspondences. They have little intellectual complementarity. This is quite different to the *Odyssey* in which women and female gods are active agents with a full aesthetic and intellectual kit. Stephen Dedalus sees women on the beach in Proteus as inhabiting their core element: "Tides, myriadislanded, within her, blood not mine, oinopa ponton, a winedark sea." There is a clear link to (fear of) menstrual flow. Judy always stepped left foot first over the thick floor-beam that marked the entrance to the Mahavira Hall when she was menstruating. She bought incense and prayed silently over the steaming brass urns. I observed the Shakyamuni Buddha. It had been freshly painted for the Olympics in August. Its head-dress was Powder Blue. Gold leaf embellished the edges and folds of the Buddha's robe as well as the lotus blossom on which he prayed. He taught a middle way like "Socialism with Chinese Characteristics." Deng conceived this tactic on the walking trail to the Xinjian County Tractor Factory. Gautama. Not everyone can get rich at the same time, he said. Judy told me once that she would have just gone straight to the hospital and had a termination if she got pregnant. Tidal imagery is extended to association with the moon. This is a dominant yet hackneyed motif in the ill-advised Ithaca episode. It pairs Stephen and Bloom with men like W.J. Chidley and his perverted symbolism. The corollary of water and death is the act of drowning. Drowning is often mentioned in *Ulysses*. Stephen is always thinking about it, especially in association with his mother. By extension, this suggests that she drowned in the confines of her own gender. His sister Dilly, product of her womb, will share the same fate of a "salt green death." Yet drowning also brings peace. Both Stephen and Bloom note that it is considered a relatively pleasant form of death. Stephen also notes its transformative impact on the body in the image of the drowned man's eyes turning "saltblue." It becomes an emblem of resurrection, which Joyce liked to associate with his novel, Ireland and himself-as-Jesus. Derrida called suicide ("S") a gift to death. As if Hades needed more tribute. He was already known as the Rich One by his peers. Current affairs investigation into events. Another *coup d'état* was brewing in the corridors of power when Holt went home that Xmas. Things would have been different if he hadn't drowned, said Les emphatically gaping a spoonful of mashed potato. We got Gorton because McEwan wouldn't cop McMahon, he hissed at the television greedily. I was in Saigon anyway. It didn't matter to me. Intense conversations in the change rooms at Manuka squash courts. Sporting a fresh black eye in the chamber. He told the press, I got hit with a squash ball. An arrangement had been reached at Beppi's in 1966. Penelope sired three colts with ten different men. Pan was the birth-product of all the suitors. Their daughter was actually the only biological son of Harold Holt. Gay-beat in Kingston was where they met to seal the deal, so to speak. Blazes Boylan was leading a double life. Les passed me the bowl. Coleslaw on his palms. Christmas suicides on the rise, according to a new report commissioned by the AMA. Rock-black writhing sea. White foam spinning around his head. Bubbles of diminishing return. Reaching for the surface with a wrinkled fist without vim. Full water tank in his gut. Furphy brand. Foetus in brine. Downword sinking apace. Secret love letters. Names spelled backwards as codes. Broken palindromes. Message in a mirror. Trying to impress Nausicaa with goofy-foot moves in Poseidon's odious surf. Odysseus would have been 45 years old by the time he returned to Ithaca. Ripe age by Classical standards. Seen all corners of the known world. Quick death at the hands of a stolen Claymore like Bobby Horne better than a slow death at home by stealth. Blind rage raging at my hampered body. You could see it in their stares after a few shots. Disconnected Titans. We left mum's portion in jelly on the dining room table then Les hobbled-up Shaftesbury Road to the RSL. I went to bed. He was still absent when I heard the door lock crack. Lemonscent. My mother entered my room. Smell of fresh motel soap. I can't go back there, thought Tom Hallem leaning back in the taxi seat. But I can't begrudge her, muttered Oedipus. Bloom like John Joyce still supported Parnell even after the scandal with Kitty O'Shea. He visits the "dead king's" grave in Hades. Menelaus and Helen were ultimately reunited. There are conflicting accounts about what happened with Penelope and Odysseus. Hard to press. Marriage is like different hemispheres. Water going down the sink the wrong way. No air. Only water. Then water by darkness overtaken. Body washed ashore. Place yourself at the mercy of Poseidon. The city skyline became apparent as they passed along the edge of Prince Alfred Park.

"First time I saw really tall buildings was here in Sydney," said Joyce. "The tallest structures in Ireland are church steeples."

"You're kidding."

"It's true. The Church of Saint Augustine is 250 feet high. There used to be Nelson's Needle back in my father's day. In the end, they had to blast that bastard down. The tallest modern building in Dublin would be Liberty Hall. It was built in the 1960s on the site of the rebel stronghold in the Easter Rising. It was called James Connolly's fortress in 1916. The rebellion started on its very steps. It was the last redoubt. The British levelled it with an artillery barrage."

ODYSSEUS DISCLOSED

Billy was awakened by the buzzer. He got up groggily and went downstairs. The caretaker's door opened a crack. Billy jerked in acknowledgment. It closed. Enter Barry. He handed Billy a paper bag.

"Sandwiches," he said. "I was worried you hadn't eaten."

"I got take-away in Newtown."

"They'll keep," he babbled. "Hammondjeez. Nice toasted. I'll eat them tomorrow for lunch. After you're gone. I'm parked on Liverpool Street. What have you got left to move?"

"Just some bookshelf parts and a few boxes. I've broken it up. I'm leaving the rest of the furniture and kitchen stuff."

"Why did she go home?" he asked.

"I wanted some time alone."

"But it's your last night in Australia."

"I know."

He patted his son on the shoulder. They climbed the staircase together. Flat Ten was sparse. Billy turned on a lamp. Khaki-board boxes were stacked around the walls like quarried sandstone. Bronze bars cunningly stowed. Ship it all off to Alexandria because they're burning everything in Rome. Fahrenheit 451. Bob sat on a blacksmith's stool. A carved wooden screen above the kitchen doorway was hung with novelty lights. On this day, both Tom and Billy have been de-homed.

"We can strap the beams to the roof rack," he said. "Probably fit four boxes across the back seat. The rest in the tray. You don't need those bricks. I got heaps behind the garage at home."

"OK," REPLIED HIS SON. "Look there's no rush. Let me buy you a beer after we finish packing."

POEMS (1913)

Shanghai Dog left Xiao Fang lying flat on her belly. Billy Capri pulled on an elastic strap and stretched the exposed hook until it caught under the roof-rack. The bookshelf beams were compressed into a solid rectangle. The car undulated. Its suspension groaned. He let go. Everything relaxed into place.

"How about that beer?" asked Barry. This image can be seen as the flipside of Leer and Tom sharing a drink earlier in the chapter.

"Let's try the Lord Roberts," his son replied.

They walked down Crown Street picking up speed on its precipitous slope. It flattened-out near Bar Reggio. They passed a sentry box with stones, brazier et cetera where the municipal ranger was wrapped in the arms of D.B. Murphy dreaming of automated systems. There was still some life along Stanley Street. John Hughes and Bruce Currie were discussing *Crust* outside Bill & Tony. Julie Cunningham walked towards the Palmer Lane squats with her three-legged dog, Sparrow. She had been scripting *Double X*. These works represent the tail-end of the avant-garde epoch. Billy nodded acknowledgment. The Lord Roberts was vacant, damp and threadbare. Likewise, Joyce's style in Eumaeus is utterly stale after 40 pages, just as his catechism structure in Ithaca ultimately failed as ART (increase font size). These chapters become a matter of "seeing-it-through" to closure, regardless of critics who claim that Eumaeus was a cunning ruse intended to mirror the characters' own tiredness. In fact, Joyce's Euphuism has shown no sign of flagging in this episode. It remains as disciplined at page 533 as when Chapter III was launched. He rigidly executes yet another of the panoply of styles which make up *Ulysses*. This was an act of hardcore will which cut against any comfort in reading. But that was Joyce's whole purpose. He took the scattered components of Modernism picked up on his personal journey around the European diaspora from Ireland (subjugated colony) to Paris (wild republic), Trieste (bordertown of a dying Central Empire) and Zurich (Dada) and fused them into a cyborg like Hephaestus. This exercise had already been started in the visual arts (see Duchamp), but literature had lagged up to this point. *The Large Glass* and *Ulysses* were finished almost simultaneously. They both parodied confidence in the power of technological progress. Joyce, in fact, started *Ulysses* as Europe itself cancelled out this delusion with the First World War. *Ulysses* is the tombstone of Enlightenment shibboleths. It also became the Joan of Arc of Modernism. Joyce rejected gunpowder, its diplomacy, Malthus, workhouse hypocrites, secrecy codes, social etiquette and good form (in both its custom and literary senses). "Let's walk on," said Barry Capri. "I need somewhere with a touch of life about it." The men turned into Lower Riley Street. "We'll go to The Bells," replied his son. "Some cold air off the harbour will freshen us both up." Watters Gallery sat black across Stanley Lane. Mike Brown's exhibition had just closed. A Hamilton-like sample still hung in the feature window, teetering on plagiarism. Billy compared this work unfavourably with Tom Hallem's nervy pleasure signs. It was also the home of James Gleeson's psychoscapes. Perhaps the greatest art produced in Australia since S. Nolan. Matta meets Bosch. Seafood machinery (see MD, TLG above). They passed an unmarked warehouse where Billy used to work for a gangland pirate breaking-up boxes of pornographic magazines and videos (see Leer), sex toys (including the Bona Constrictor in C5), bondage outfits and novelty prophylactics for distribution across the LOVSTUFF chain of adult stores. This was the type of low-life venue that disseminated *Ulysses* for many decades while it was banned (see *The Most Dangerous Book*). Joyce would have enjoyed the irony of his work being hidden from plain view like *Sweats of Sin*, although his desire for fame and profit would have tempered his glee. *Ulysses* was banned in Australia in 1929–1937 then 1941–1968. The full list of prohibited books was not made public by Customs until 1958. They wouldn't even give Curtin a copy when he was PM. An archive of 793 boxes of proscribed items was finally discovered by Nicolle Moore, author of *The Censor's Library*, seven levels underground in a government book repository in WS in 2005. Cast iron toilet-pipes jutted out the back of Jazz Age apartment blocks. Some wept rusty bracelets. Two drunks were urinating hard in penumbra against a backcloth of rock posters in Yurong Lane. Joyce uses elaborate, almost technical language to describe this scene in Ithaca, harking back to the Euphuism of Eumaeus. It is his own ironic blasphemy against father-son bonding. L. Bloom (Archer House – RED) was capable of the highest arc of trajectory amongst 210 students competing in the senior school. This is almost the only time that Bloom is held up by Joyce as a champion in the whole of *Ulysses*. Otherwise, he remains mediocre, unscored. The companions turned from each other to allow safe passage to earth for the timely jets that were now evacuating their distended bladders of ale. It would be worthwhile tracking the use of single words like "distended" and say "evacuat(e-/-ed/-ing)" through the course of this work with NAVIGATION function (this is a linguistic equivalent of sea-faring). We can check to see if the author has embedded any strings of meaning or symbolism out of word re-utilisation across different plot zones. There may also be instances of antonymy and juxtaposition. This approach employs digital technology to treat individual words with the same intensity as motifs. "Lamp" could be another useful term to audit in this fashion. It appears over fifty times over the course of this work, culminating in its recurrence as part of a primary – albeit sardonic – statement of HOPE in the invocation to "Light the lamp!" in Appendix A. At this moment, one individual male rocked back gazing up the sheer wall-face. There was no sky, stars or moon here. All the astronomical terminology employed by Joyce in Ithaca to displace emotion was negated (this is about to be challenged by Bob Capri's candid sentiments below). Just carmine clouds swirling orange vapors around buttered lamps. Our heroes reached William Street. This journey exhibits a rough correspondence with the progress of Bloom and Stephen after they leave the taxi shelter. We are trying to reach a tentative moment where the father–son bond is revealed as resilient despite the shock of its biological cancellation at 1pm today, a mere nine hours previous in text-time. They waited for a hiatus in what was really sporadic traffic flow to cross to the elevated median strip. Barry Capri turned to look at Billy, whose face was dark against the brilliant backing of an advertising halo for Coke, which evinced the famous white wave symbol across a brilliant red flag [HEX COLOR: #F40000; RGB: (244,0,9) CMYK: (4,100,95,0)].

"I was thinking we might not see you tonight."

"Why?"

"Well, it's all a bit much really."

His mouth tightened. Words trailed. Cars crossed them both ways; behind and afore. Billy contemplated his father against Hyde Park's dark woodland. Barry's gaze, by contrast, rested askew, seemingly fixed on a sequence of illuminated signs lining the north face of William Street.

"Why did you marry mum?" asked Billy frankly.

Bob looked away as he spoke.

"She was in trouble. She needed help. It was my big opportunity."

"Did you love her?"

"Oh yes," he said producing a blind grin. "But I was a shy bloke. I didn't have lots of girls like Don. I wouldn't have had a chance with someone like her under normal circumstances."

"So, everyone knew the whole time except me. And Tom."

"Not everyone. Just close family. Penelope forgave your mother pretty fast. She was big like that. She wanted you boys to be like ... brothers. It was easy when you were both small. Then she married Les and moved. That made it even easier."

They crossed William Street. Classical literature is filled with stories of separated brothers and heroes who did not know their true ancestry. This is especially true where a god was involved. It was a trope handed all the way down to the creators of Jesus. Joyce doesn't explore this aspect in *Ulysses*, although it is pertinent to analysis of the Odysseus myth. I guess you could argue that Joyce has Stephen Dedalus father-shopping in Eumaeus. But he has solid bloodlines (see C5, E1: B. Turk). Many scholars have propounded theories about Odysseus' genealogy. We know that he was short, hairy and dark unlike typical Greek champions. I think of him as a nuggety chap, maybe a light middleweight fighter (147–150 pounds weight range) or a tough rugby league second row forward who punched above his weight through ball-skills and superior tackling technique like Steve Folkes. This division has produced countless champions and crowd favourites since its formation by the Austrian Boxing Federation in 1962 including Nino Benvenuti, Manny Pacquiao, Roy Jones Junior, Sugar Ray Leonard, Thomas Hearns, Roberto Durán, Oscar De La Hoya, and Floyd Mayweather Jr. We don't know much for certain about Odysseus' heredity. It is a messy bloodline, as reflected in the characters in this work. According to Pseudo-Apollodorus, his supposed paternal grandfather – or perhaps step-grandfather – was Arcesius, who was the son of either the god Zeus or the Aeolian hunter, Cephalus, whose name means "head (of a great family)" in Ancient Greek. Cephalus had a tempestuous and ill-starred marriage with Procris, the daughter of Erechtheus, king of Athens. He was kidnapped by the goddess Eos for eight years and became her reluctant lover in a precursor of Odysseus' own 'bonded' relationships with Circe and Calypso. Eventually, he returned to Procris but their relationship was beset by jealousy and shame. He inadvertently impaled her on a javelin when she pursued him to the forest in the mistaken belief that he was going to see a new lover. Hyginus argues that Arcesius was the son of Cephalus and Procris. But this is disputed by most other accounts. One legend argues that Cephalus remarried Clymene, a daughter of Minyas, and that Arcesius was their son. Eustathius and scholia to the *Iliad* attest that Arcesius was actually a grandson of

Cephalus via Cillus or Celeus. Aristotle even claims in his lost work, *The State of the Ithacians*, that Cephalus was told by an oracle to copulate with the first female animal he encountered and mated with a she-bear, which turned into a woman who then bore Arcesius. There is a lot of animal-fucking in the Classics but its infamy has been exacerbated by the prevalence of scenes depicting bestiality in Renaissance art. Ovid, Eustathius and scholiasts claim that Zeus was the father of Arcesius, through a woman called Euryodeia. There is no further information about her in any Classical text. Things become much clearer after this point. Zeus mandated that Arcesius' line would only produce only-sons. Arecesius' son was thus Laertes, whose only son was Odysseus, whose son was Telemachus. We know nothing of Telemachus' children, although the tales of his marital status have been documented in Chapter One. The maternal line of Ithaca's rulers is more interesting. Arcesius' wife was Chalcomedusa, whose name means chalcos ("copper") and medousa ("guardian"). She was probably a protector of Bronze Age technology. The story of Odysseus' magical helmet, stolen by his maternal grandfather, Autolycus, probably enters the myth through this family talent for metallurgy. He was the son of the god of logistics and propaganda, Hermes, and Chione, the beautiful daughter of either the warrior Daedalion or the god, Boreas, of north wind fame. She was drugged and raped by Hermes and ultimately killed by Artemis. Such is life for women in the Classics. The guile of Odysseus comes from his maternal line. His father, Laertes, was a nondescript king, who retired to a hovel on the far side of Ithaca leaving Penelope to her fate with the suitors. His pusillanimous behaviour has not received due analysis in classical literature. He reminds me of my own father. It is hard to reconcile this weak figure with Odysseus, given the direct link between human character and DNA in the Classical cosmos. This has led to claims that Sisyphus was Odysseus' father and even that Laertes purchased the baby from Sisyphus. Such paternity would strengthen the cunning gene in Odysseus. Sisyphus was renowned for his tactical deceit of the Gods to avoid death. Laertes' wife was Anticlea, daughter of Autylocus. She was Odysseus' mother. Her name means "without fame." Her grandfather was Hermes, the trickster god. Aeschylus' lost tragedy, *The Judgment of Arms*, recounts her seduction by Sisyphus when he goes to retrieve some cattle stolen by her no-good dad (see C3 for allusions also Polk-Salad Annie). Odysseus actually meets Anticlea in Hades in Book XI of the *Odyssey*. There is little emotion in this reunion, reflecting Chapter Three of this work as well as Penelope's barriers to intimacy with Telemachus. Odysseus is visiting Hades to see Tiresias when he encounters Anticlea. At first, he has no interest in seeing his mother or visiting local tourist attractions. He is all business like the eponymous father in Cat Steven's famous story song of 1970. Finally, he schedules a meeting with his mother after work. At this exchange, he whines about his misfortunes constantly. She tells him that she died of grief during his protracted absence. He milks her for information about the state of things on Ithaca. This is useful IP for our hero. Joyce creates a clear correspondence to the condition of Mary Dedalus in *Ulysses* in Anticlea's maternal heartbreak and death as well as the burgeoning angst and guilt of her son. In the end, Odysseus tries to cuddle his mother three times before he leaves hell. This is impossible because she is a ghost. His arms pass right through her incorporeal aura. This is a metaphor for many mother-son relationships.

"Billy," said Bob Capri stopping on the footpath outside the Boulevard Hotel. "I want to say something. I've been proud to be your father. To be honest, I never wanted you to know the truth. I wanted to keep being that man. I know it was weak. But I'm only human."

In *Ulysses*, LB starts to see SD as a full person at this point. Not merely Simon Dedalus' son. Stephen for his part notes Bloom's unmusical rejoinder. It is a significant symbol of Bloom's impossibility in filling the role of Stephen's father. Simon Dedalus is a fine singer. Like father, like son.

"What a fuck up," Bob added laughing incredulously.

"A tall tale but true," replied Billy Capri with resignation. They turned down Bourke Street together. It was a straight run now to water. Woolloomooloo dropped to a broad shore-plate. History pressed out of its close-built chambers and gusts. You could feel it rising like time against a slow floodmarker. Homer's sea gasped last rites (Poem 10). Our host, Chris Brennan, was lingering alone at the dock drunk on waterdust. Dirty old townscape. A ghastly shore (Poem 5). Men poured though sewage looking for scraps. Ophelia's face was bobbing through a rusty carapace of brine. Fat and strange-eyed urchins scraped at thick waste. Mirror of mutant waterlife welling always welling in tide unstilled tide. A regretful guest crept past a smoldering gin palace (Poem 4). Tremulous in wake. Just another pack-dog crawling like a broken lizard amongst meaningless stone masts. Billy and Barry Capri paused on the verge of The Bells Hotel to wipe their soles. Yellow gas was burning in the street lamps. Sclerotic walls. Dead temples. Just then, Cassandra got pulled down Temple Lane by her flaming mane. No one can help her down there. They'll force strong spirit down her throat. Apply the razor. Skulk off when it's done. Day taken at the throat by Achilles and stuffed full of uncreated mud. Dawn will never really follow. Upturned Nature all matt. Bells of the colonial fleet quired. Liquid crystal. Sweet silence. Stasis. A sublime instance. Incantatious. Dead ships of the line. *Voyager*. *Dunbar*. The second *Sydney*. It was tricked by *Kormoran's* subterfuge. Burnett took her recklessly close. The Germans brought all their guns to bear. Six hundred and forty-five sailors drowned. It was the largest Allied warship lost with all hands in World War Two. Those wrecks have never been found, said Murphy. A murmur passed from Captain Cat. His crew were pressing through the slate halls of the massive outer deep of his mind. Odysseus' crews all gone under. He alone reaches shore. A single grey destroyer was moored at Garden Island. Barry

Capri entered the main bar suspiciously. Bright light caught his sharp profile. Regulars studied him from the bar suspiciously. Athene drew near in the likeness of a barmaid. She waved a sparking tea towel. They clung to their stools in supplication. A dog knows its master. Billy examined his father from beneath. His fallow beard, dark cheeks glistening with sea-sweat and drizzle, burnished, wrought of bronze. His massive chest-cage, laden with age, burst against the confinement of his grey overalls.

"You've certainly got them marked," said Billy.

"Kind with kind," answered Barry Capri as he pulled a black stool at the bar in front of the draught taps.

HERE IN THIS UNLOVELY STREET

"Burton Street please," said Tom Hallem. "Just past the Boundary Street flyover."

"You mean Macdonald Street then."

"You're the expert."

The meter started ticking in haste. My drunk patter commenced. The taxi driver was an implacable hearhole of receipt. Eventually, he started reminiscing about his boat passage to Sydney through Suez, Colombo, Singapore, Hong Kong like a bloodystiffturdthrewintestines. The Telemachiad took place over a period of one year. Those months felt like daggersinthebackof Caesar to his mother yet she never betrayed her emotions. I struggle against Joycess' st.yell like a surfer thrashing in a sharkbag. Lightless shopfonts rented no revealment: frosted pub glass showered nonternal: curving steepscrapes plined the route: tenses change gears all the time in a replica of manual transmission sequences during this fare: I imitate Joyce's method for a few necessary lines: we are moving to the end of Eumaeus: the Blots proceed on their implacable journey to Appendix A: past corrugated sheds of tin dance troupes: the driver ignored the ferris-wheel fun of Cleveland Street and slammed straight down the guts at the twin illloominated bawlbells of Grace Brothers (symbol of Tom/I): the Australia Hotel's front bar spills print workers: John Fairfax & Sons gone blackned: Tooths brewery stage right: putrid wort is leveraged inside back-lane terraces: tumberling Chip-and-ale alleys: Central clocktower registers Nine sixteen. We proceed under low-bred arches: residual travellers in bus shelters loitered or, homeless, leant on roughcut Yellowstone sipping goons. The taxi rose up Wentworth Avenue. Hallem rested tired eyes on Hyde Park. Dellit's Agora. They swerved in a giant arc onto Liverpool Street stymying a stream of pedestrians in front of the Burdekin Hotel. Someone swore at them. They freewheeled down Liverpool Street. Red lights bleated in wiry white curtains along a row of cheap terraces. Madames offered their rind. Shemale street walkers scattered along Darlinghurst Road. The taxi reached the shattered lego of Saint Vincent's Hospital. Tom Hallem called halt. "I want to clear my head," he said. Time to get into character. He spondulicks had. He extracted Leer's ill-gotten notes. Sponc. A nixer. Redistribution of wealth. This motif inverts Bloom's retention of the bulk of Stephen's salary. The younger man is a thief, albeit extracting tribute from a false father. Dublin like Sydney had experienced the dead hand of British oppression. Payback was long overdue. It had been the fifth largest city in Europe in Georgian times. By 1904, there was virtually monopoly trade with Britain. The first visit of the Famine Queen to Ireland for thirty-seven years was to drum up fodder for the Boer fight. Joyce was inevitably close to the battle for Irish independence by virtue of his family connections. "Ivy Day in the Committee Room" is set on the anniversary of Parnell's death. The dinner scene in *PAYM* clearly discloses Joyce's political allegiance. His friend, George Clancy – Michael Davin in *PAYM* – was arrested in 1916 during the composition of *Ulysses*. He went on to become Mayor of Limerick but was murdered by Black and Tans in 1921. Joyce desperately wanted to do justice to his friends and family with his great work. He felt that art lived in the vanguard of rebellion and reform, like a Constructivist or Suprematist artist in Russia. *Ulysses* should always be seen as a tract. This work doesn't have the same graphic sweep. Australia is a mild nation. Yet it embarked on its best series of economic and social reforms since Federation in 1984. Characters are negotiating the revitalisation of a redundant economy over the course of the day. Joyce dealt more extensively with the reality of Dublin's economy in *PAYM* compared to *Ulysses*. The opening scene of Chapter Five is a brilliant depiction of life in a failing household as Stephen eats the dregs of breakfast, sorts through pawn tickets and is bathed by his mother. This strain is tempered in *Ulysses* by the fact that the text is confined to a single day when Stephen is flush with a full month's salary. We can't register the full extent of his profligacy. He will descend quickly back into poverty, denying any aid to his sisters. In addition, Leopold Bloom is a solid provider who maintains a middle-class household with all its accoutrements and pretensions, albeit with piecemeal and heavily competed work. Many young characters are living on the Dole in TMAC. Jobs are scarce. Ana has a temporary position cleaning railway carriages. Low-level drug-dealing is common. Professionals are doing well. The art market is buoyant. Gambling on the Melbourne Cup reached record levels in 1984. Yet there are cracks in the machine. Elizabeth is over-leveraged. Penelope Hallem is trying to attract new clients. She has been threatened with redundancy from Besley's Stationery if the downturn persists. She is cultivating a wealthy local businessman, Dick Stone. Stan Welles is trying to pull off a big deal with foreign investors to prop-up WIG. His sons act as poles. One lives on welfare hand-outs from a family trust. The other displays all the signs of stress from trying to hold a family business together. He is unpredictable, bombastic, coarse and cruel. He uses money as a tool. This is not just a function of resentment at his illegitimacy. Shakespeare was more complex in his characterisations. In *King Lear*, the central struggle between the brothers is physical, economic and political. The tragedy assesses the merits of inherited wealth against the self-made man. Only if the nobility gets real-life experience, implies Shakespeare, can they take their place as national leaders. That is the message of Edgar's odyssey. He must be tempered by a FALL and remake himself from the flattest conceivable base. By contrast, Edmond is ultimately undone by his over-indulgence in intrigue. He gets stuck in a power/sex bubble and consumed. Joyce was determined to NEVER let his work lose its political edge. He would never have been satisfied with esoteric greatness like Proust. *Ulysses* was a revolutionary work in all senses. I can never compete with that. Just showcase the abandon of Sydney's cultural elite in Chapter Nine. Tom told the driver to keep the change from ten. They parted on good terms. He commenced crossing the overpass. This is a simple symbol. A Rubicon moment. Tom passes back to the business side of art. This puts him squarely in the same camp as Edmund Welles. He is jettisoning friends and family. The tightrope walker falls alone. This is quite different to the status of Stephen Dedalus when he leaves *Ulysses*. Talking with Bloom is seen by critics as a breakthrough for Stephen in both his development as a person and career. He witnesses Bloom's no-strings empathy. He is impressed by the apparent commitment to decency and candour of the older man. Bloom is careful and attentive, in contrast to most characters in *Ulysses* who misunderstand, goad, abuse or dismiss Stephen. Of course, Bloom is leading a double-life. He is an adulterer and cheat. But as far as this story goes, Stephen's search on this day is, for this day at least, laid to rest. Regardless of whether he later capitalises on this new personal connection (something left ambiguous at the end of Ithaca), this is the moment to which the text has been building. The noise of Dublin all day finally gives way to silence. As they leave the cabman's shelter, Stephen allows himself to lean on Bloom as they walk toward his home. The climax of Joyce's great epic is simply a moment of humane attentiveness, the basic kindness which will save us all. Thus, Stephen Dedalus leaves *Ulysses* on a note of hope. "Und alle Schiffe brucken," he chimes at the end-point of Eumaeus in mangled German, altering Jeep's refrain in *Dulcia*, "das Shiff in Ungluck bringt." This is a polysemous linguistic pun by Joyce, predicting the intensified melding of languages in *F(W)ake*. Gifford notes that, literally, Stephen sings: 'and all ships are bridged.' But he really means ALL SHIPS BRIDGE. Clearly, this is a positive metaphor for the eventual making of human connections. Its direct source comes from the phrase, 'Schiffebrucken uber den Hellespont,' in the German translation of Herodotus, referring to Xerxes construction of floating bridges between the Dardanelles (Troy) and Thrace in 480 BC. It brings together the two methods for humans to negotiate water: by transport upon and by dry passage over. Ships like the *Rosevean* in C3 pass underneath bridges (unless they hit a pylon and become 'bridged' as per Corley's tale earlier in C8). The command centres of ships are also known as bridges. The phrase thus contains both direct reference as well as indirect resonance to the maritime themes of the Odysseus myth. It closes the emotional loop for Stephen Dedalus, who talked about piers as "disappointed bridges" in C1. At the end of his appearance in the novel then, Stephen is able to move from an isolated image and pun about a pier to a sincere, euphoric affirmation of the communality of a bridge. The significance of an apparently oblique joke all the way back at the start of the novel is now revealed at the end. Stephen is no longer "disappointed." He has moved from feeling like a jetty to "becoming" as a conduit. Joyce must have been delighted to recall *Dulcia* as he wrote *Ulysses*. You really need to read all four verses of Jeep's lyric but Don Gifford has translated the key section thus: "From the Sirens' craftiness / Poets make poems / That they with their loveliness / Have drawn many men into the sea / For their song resounds so sweetly, / That the sailors fall asleep, / The ship is brought into misfortune, / And all becomes evil." This passage clearly alludes to the Sirens episode. It is the perfect musical accompaniment to the Odysseus myth in terms of Joyce's own theories of art. He becomes the Baudelaire of Modernism. This is the last time that Joyce has a formal character quotation in *Ulysses*. From this point, he uses Q&A in Ithaca and Molly's internal monologue in Penelope. Thus, the last SPOKEN WORD utterance in *Ulysses* is the plural form of BRIDGES in German ... sung.

REFLECTIONS IN A STILL POOL | LOOP

How does the Eumaeus episode end in the "Odyssey"?

Tom Hallem walks towards EA Times. Elizabeth is waiting at the threshold. Odysseus reveals himself to Telemachus in Book Sixteen. Eumaeus leaves the compound. Athena draws Odysseus outside. She touches him with a wand. He receives an instant makeover. His son perceives him to be a god. But Odysseus answers: "I am not a god ... I am your own father, the very man for whose sake you have grieved long and borne much and suffered the violence of men." This is the most moving moment in Classical literature. As the last of the great texts about the last hero, it can be seen as the climax of the entire Classical enterprise. The Gods now subside. The chilling time-clock of human mutability steps into the spotlight. Joyce never attempted to compete with the pathos of this exchange in *Ulysses*. He just let Stephen go.

And *Ulysses*?

It is impossible to put the interaction between Bloom and Dedalus into the same category. Leopold Bloom assumes a much more equivocal role as a father-figure. There is no revelation in *Ulysses*. Joyce is considered by most critics to have insinuated Bloom into the role of Odysseus. I would argue that Bloom is semi-assessed for this role and rejected by Stephen Dedalus in a straight shoot-out with his genetic father. Bloom is mild, measured and intellectually constrained. He cannot sing or drink. Stephen has no way to respect Bloom. He hardly even knows the man. He is just a slight acquaintance of his father. Stephen mocks Bloom's utopian vision of Ireland. There is nothing he finds more galling than political naivety. It is even worse than bad art. By contrast, Simon Dedalus – like John Joyce – was an extreme character with a pungent wit and virile mind who exhibited a clown's loneliness and a drunk's lack of shame. Stephen – like James Joyce – identified strongly with his father. He must have found Bloom lame in comparison. For all his sins, Simon Dedalus will always remain Stephen's father. James Joyce carried his father's portrait across Europe loyally almost as a talisman. There is no doubt about paternity as there is with me, Odysseus and even Telemachus. For better and worse, but mainly worse, he is his son's role model. They are both self-obsessed figures squandering funds, borrowing freely, getting drunk, abusive, abused, comical, the butt of jokes and always desperate to please. They seek out any stage where they can cast off their inhibitions and go crazy. They act like fools for the entertainment of cynical boon companions. They soak up jibes that come their way timorously. They crave human attachment. But it can never be achieved due to their fundamental self-hate. They reject family. They have no true friends. They are cultural insiders who have become outsiders by will. Bloom is actually much closer to being an insider in Dublin by the end of *Ulysses*. He has conducted daily life effectively. He has interacted with integrity with other people. He has provided munificence and comfort. He is largely selfless. He is flawed in a different way. A secret sinner. A furtive type. An EVERYMAN across the full range of human traits. Simon and Stephen Dedalus by contrast see themselves as anything but 'everymen.' They want to be larger than life. They are wide open and always on display. Indeed, their paths around Dublin are remarkably similar. Stephen's Telemachiad is recognised as a core part of the plot of *Ulysses* but there is a SHADOW journey undertaken by his father further around Dublin on that day which remains largely undisclosed. He is always adjacent to his son at all times in the plot. Occasionally, he bobs to the surface. But he never comes into focus. Simon Dedalus is the ghost of Odysseus on Ithaca. He is Hamlet's father lurking on the parapets. At the end of the novel, Stephen Dedalus walks away from Bloom to go find the swineherd's hut. This will be his father's latest rented house in the relentless downwards spiral of his family. Eumaeus is the lowest of the low. That is where the real re-union of father and son in *Ulysses* will finally take place.

9.
Ithaca (Penelope)

These days, Ulysses may seem more eccentric than epoch changing, and it can be difficult to see how Joyce's novel (how any novel, perhaps) could have been revolutionary

– **Kevin Birmingham (224)**

Place Ithaca

Ithaca [now this episode will have to end with "I"] is not a place. It's an Ideal (Archetype – ROMANCE). Joyce's favourite episode. His "ugly duckling." Pride of Daedalus in a technical achievement. Cherished like Vulcan's ember. Or Shelley's fading coal. A storehouse of facts. A perfect lie. The real ending. The last bit he finished, long after Penelope was scored. Flawless in memory. Like Penelope herself to her husband.

Outline the plan for this chapter

To fuse the Ithaca and Penelope episodes. To make the same purposive misuse of Joyce as he did of Homer. To highlight the calculated nature of Joyce's practice. As an exemplar. To conflate two climactic episodes in *Ulysses* into a single chapter (thus showing I have the power at my desk to reduce them in scale). To create an embarkation pier for Gibraltar (post-*Ulysses*). Ithaca tells the story of rimming the cosmos. Penelope inserts the narrative straight into the flesh like a syringe.

Method?

Deconstruct the catechism [Q&A] format of Ithaca. Cut-up its temporal flow. Insert apparently random events in disorder. It may all become clear over text-time. Note cinematic precedents in Welles (*F for Fake*, *OSW*). Insert diary format to complete journey of forms (*Ulysses* is an odyssey of styles). Intensify the sandstream consciousness of the Penelope episode. She must remain in brackets compared to the concrete form of Ithaca.

Her role is examined from Question 30 onwards (employ false numeration). Convert Molly Bloom's monologue into a weft of voices, like the choir of serving girls strung-up by Telemachus after the slaughter of the suitors. This chapter is ALL MEN then ALL WOMEN. They can't intersect. This is a symbol of Joyce's stark gender division. Press towards the style of *F(W)ake* (loop back to C6). *Other Side of the Wind* (*OSW*) is a kind of acronym for ORSON W. Make unreadable. Dodge death just like Sisyphus. TO KILL THE AUTHOR, YOU MUST READ THE BOOK.

List the three greatest artistic figures of the twentieth century
MD, JJ, OW.

What did they have in common?
Unbolted form.

What was your first exposure to Welles?

As a judge on the *Gong Show*. It seemed perfectly normal to an Australian teenager in the late Seventies for a legendary film maker to work on a popular TV series. I knew nothing about his back story until I read the biography by Barbara Leaming. I thought Chuck Barris was the really famous guy on that show, what with his bumbling persona and exaggerated applause. I feel like I never saw Chuck's eyes. The Unknown Comic remains a creation of comic genius. He reversed Barris' mannerisms, resembling a paper bag Ned Kelly. Barris wrote a moving biography of his daughter, who died of a drug overdose. She is a model for (Morg)ANA LAFEI. Barris claimed to have been an assassin for the CIA in the 1960s in his book, *Confessions of a Dangerous Mind*. This turned out to be a fake. There is an odd symmetry with Welles in this subject. Perhaps Barris was inspired by *F for Fake*. Synonyms for fakery include deceit and cunning, which are qualities associated with Odysseus and his forebears.

What was the lesson from Leaming's book?

That Welles did whatever it took to keep making movies. This demonstrated a High Romantic commitment to pursuit of a goal regardless of exigencies (see "Alastor," which means "demon of solitude" in GK). He worked as a writer, director, producer, impresario and actor across multiple fields including movies, theatre, radio, journalism, advertising and even politics. He was considered as a running mate for Roosevelt in 1944. He usually acted the part of himself. Only Shakespearean roles and his own works had the aesthetic majesty to dislocate him into an alternative characterisation.

Rework Joyce's use of water as an arch symbol in Ithaca to Sydney topography

Joyce tracks the journey of water in Dublin from the reservoir to Bloom's tap. It is a symbol for the flow of life etcetera. This connects to images of the Liffey. Sandstone is a complementary metaphor for Sydney.

Correct Joyce's shortcomings in Ithaca

Joyce's weakness in using water as a life-symbol is that he only treats it lyrically. He should have recognised the commercial value of natural resources (see Polanski, *Chinatown*). This oversight has been corrected in TMAC (See C5).

Compare their properties as narrative symbols

Sandstone moves slowly under the surface. Water moves fast usually upon. One is almost eternal, the other vitally ephemeral. One has cosmic scope beyond the range of human existence, the other is fast and unpredictable like life.

Apply this element to our heroes

(1) Tom Hallem moves imperceptibly on the surface almost not at all. He has no depth. Other people's actions dictate his status. There is no apparent flow.

(2) **How is Billy's life like sandstone?**
Unlike. Overall, he is methodical even stoical. An aberration occurs in the period directly after this novel. Insert diary entries from West Berlin.

Compare with Stephen Dedalus

No formal intervention by an older male as per LB assists Tom. Billy gets rescued from a predicament by the intervention of the gods (see also 'decent burgher' in C1).

Where are they both going?

Back to Australia. For Tom, this is a humiliating backdown (AKA Stephen Dedalus). For Billy, it is a homecoming (AKA Telemachus).

Outline the scale of Sydney Basin Hawkesbury Sandstone (known as "Yellowblock")

Sandstone escarpments surround Sydney on all sides. They form the spatial boundary of the city. The bed is six kilometres deep. Currents have leached most of the minerals from the sandstone leaving a very poor quality rock with insipid soil. Ironically, the infirmity of its loam has nurtured a highly distinctive selection of flora and thus fauna.

What is the structure of Yellowblock?

Yellowblock is composed of very pure silica grains with a small amount of the iron mineral siderite bound within a clay matrix. It oxidises into a watercolorist's hue known as BUFF. This tone has become the distinguishing visual swipe of public buildings and walls in Sydney.

Explain its relationship to water (and thus "*Telemachus/Ulysses*")

Yellowblock is a highly porous stone which acts like a giant filter. Its distinguishing ripple marks disclose the flow of an ancient river that carried streams of sand grains over 1,000 kilometres from rocks formed 700 million years ago in the vicinity of Broken Hill to the coast, where they were laid down in a 200 m thick bed. Channels carved out grooves. Sand banks around Sydney display characteristic cross-bedding.

Where does Tom Hallem awake in West Berlin after a shock?

I face the workerday dawn on my back in a sandpit underneath a flying-fox noose in a local playground by The Wall. Two-thirds of a bottle of Pernod is wedged upright in the sand. No cap. Must have got it at the duty-free U-Bahn. A Mercedes hood ornament is lying flat on the sand with a wire hook thrusting out of its oiled brass base. My suit is full of silt. LINK TO SANDSTONE. Must have gone harvesting with Peter Johnson last night. He makes belts out of them to sell at the markets. I can't remember anything at all. Tom Hallem remembers about as much of last night as Stephen Dedalus would the next day in *Ulysses*. There is no indication as to what time of day SD slept after his riotous night. At noon, Francine was supposed to leave for the clinic so I went home to help pack her stuff. They were already gone. I got the U-bahn to Merringdamm. That's where I saw them together. Like the Owl and the Pussycat, waiting for a pea green train in the other direction to Charlottenburg. Bill's satchel slung over her shoulder. It must be full of private items. Intimate things. Plus, mandatory stuff on the photocopied list from the clinic including medical purchases that might be necessary after the procedure. They stood awkwardly, like any device in a holding pattern. A train smasht out of a neat tunnel and flashed in front of them. They'd have to change lines at Wannsee, near the Brucke Museum. I watcht them disappear into the crowd in the front carriage. Siren. Doors shut. Train slowly grating to life. Billy went to the Post Restante after he dropped Francine at the clinic. He backfilled his diary for the first time in weeks. It was a series of cursory entries regathering what he could. INSERT EPISTOLARY FORMAT. Note use of manifold forms (aping Joyce). Tock another box off. He got a letter from his father. It described Don's re-entry to Sydney. I didn't recognise him, Bob said. Using the full text of letters is a step too far.

Describe the utilisation of Yellowblock by European settlers

The first European convicts hewed sandstone from surface outcrops to build simple homes. They tunneled to create the Argyle Cut in the Rocks, which linked Miller's Point with the town. Yellowblock was dumped into mangrove swamps at the head of the Tank Stream to establish the dock that eventually became known as Circular Quay.

What was the major source of local supply?

Fifty quarries operated in the fringe suburb of Pyrmont throughout the nineteenth century. They were the principal source of Yellowblock. Saunders' Quarry supplied the sandstone to build the University of Sydney. Other quarries later opened in Botany, Randwick, Paddington and Waverley. Steam drilling was introduced in 1880.

Categorise local quarries by reference to their nicknames

Saunders' three quarries in Pyrmont were known as Paradise, Purgatory and Hellhole. They were named by the Scottish quarrymen who worked them in the 1850s. These names related to the degree of difficulty in working the stone. The best stone was self-evidently located in Paradise. It was a soft rock that was easy to carve and weathered to a warm primrose hue. The Paradise quarry was located near the intersection of present-day Jones Street and Distillery Drive. It left a distinctive escarpment which is now heritage-listed. The site of Purgatory Quarry was Crown Road, Ultimo near Pyrmont Bridge Road. It produced a hard stone with a grey streak that was prone to crack. Hellhole Quarry was situated in Jones Street near Fig Street, overlooking the modern Wentworth Park racetrack. It was named because of its depth and the fact that it filled with water during storms. Jones Street was once an unbroken two-kilometre thoroughfare from Broadway to Jones Bay. This continuity has now been disrupted by urban development, principally elevated cross-roads.

What landmark workplace conditions were negotiated by Pyrmont sandstone workers?

Their trade union was the first in the world to win the eight-hour day in 1855.

Why were they able to achieve this concession?

Quarrymen who worked with sandstone were highly skilled and exercised significant leverage over government and private enterprise due to the preferred construction of major buildings in Sydney with Yellowblock. There was no alternative pool of stonemasons (i.e. scabs) due to Sydney's great distance from England, some seventeen thousand kilometres. In the 1850s, this voyage still took over eighty days by steamship. This was a reduction of some thirty days since the First Fleet arrived under sail. Demand for Yellowblock surged during the Australian gold rush. Millions of cubic feet of Sydney Basin Hawkesbury Sandstone were excavated on Cockatoo Island to build the Fitzroy Graving Dock, Australia's first dry dock. It was used on the seawall at Circular Quay. Rock-cuts were used for underground grain storage. From the 1870s, building sites in Sydney had up to 300 masons working each day. There were more masons in Sydney at that time than the whole of Europe combined. In 1928, it was estimated that total production of dressed sandstone from Pyrmont was more than half a million cubic yards (460,000 cubic metres).

What diseases did quarrymen suffer?

Stonecutters were subject to a range of lung diseases including bronchitis, pneumonia and stonemason's phthisis, which was suspected to be a form of TB.

List major public buildings featuring Sydney Basin Hawkesbury Sandstone

Sydney Town Hall, Queen Victoria Building, St Andrews Cathedral, St Mary's Cathedral, The Great Synagogue, The Mint, Hyde Park Barracks, Sydney Hospital, University of Sydney (main quadrangle), Central Railway Station, Sydney GPO, Conservatorium of Music, NSW Governor's Residence, Sydney Observatory, Art Gallery of NSW, State Library, Australian Museum, NSW Treasury, Department of Education, Department of Lands, Sydney Technical College (see lizard statues), Darlinghurst Law Courts, Custom's House, Strand Arcade. Ten statues of famous explorers in the Lands Department building on Bent Street. Early sandstone buildings that have been demolished included Vickery's Warehouse, Pitt Street; Robert C. Swan & Company warehouse, Pitt Street; Mason Bros stores, Spring Street; Harrison Jones & Devlin warehouse, Macquarie Place; Mutual Life building, George Street; and The Union Club, Bligh Street. Turn all of the above into hyperlinks.

Are these buildings all cited in *Telemachus*?

Yes.

Examine the history of remediating heritage sandstone assets in Sydney

Urban encroachment covered the quarries of Pyrmont in the early years of the Twentieth Century. This blocked access to the traditional source of Yellowblock. The natural deterioration of sandstone from exposure to Sydney's warm, humid climate necessitated major remediation works in the 1990s. Good quality sandstone from the Debden and Pine's Creek Quarries on the Central Coast was rejected due to unsatisfactory colour-matching. A flirtation with Queensland Capricorn Custom Buff was terminated for the same reason (see Swann). In 1985, the NSW Department of Public Works and Services negotiated an access agreement with the property developers of a new apartment complex on McCaffery's Hill, enabling the government to extract sandstone for the remediation of Sydney's heritage buildings. The financial details of this contract remain commercial-in-confidence. Quarrying re-commenced in Pyrmont for the first time in over 50 years. In all, 4,500 cubic metres were extracted. The availability of a large quantity of Yellowblock led to the development of a major heritage conservation and rehabilitation program by the NSW Government.

What was the outcome?

Colour-matching results were disappointing. The mismatched stone is now considered by some critics to have defaced historic architecture.

Why did new Yellowblock cuttings not match the hue of original stone?

See Swann, "Sydney Yellowblock – Is Its Revival a Blessing or a Curse?" *Discovering Stone: Issue 13*. The critical factor misjudged in stockpiling McCaffrey's sandstone was its incapacity to retain oxidising potential when exposed to the atmosphere for long periods of time prior to processing.

Explain the oxidisation process of Yellowblock

When freshly quarried, Yellowblock has a pale grey-white colour. As moisture (or 'quarry-sap') within the stone moves to the surface, trace elements such as iron, silica and calcium are deposited (at 1–3 mm depth) in the form of iron hydroxide/oxide, silica and calcite. Their oxidisation on reaction with the atmosphere leads to a yellowing of the surface through staining of the intergranular clays within the stone. The presence of siderite within the stone also contributes significantly to yellowing on exposure to the atmosphere. Within a short period of time after quarrying (2–8 weeks), the stone has developed its characteristic colour. If the surface colouration is removed, yellowing will not occur again in lower layers. In short, Yellowblock oxidises once and once only. This is a potent metaphor for lots of stuff, which will be over-egged in the rest of this work. Whilst McCaffrey's quarry blocks yellowed beautifully on their external faces in stockpile, they retained little or no ability to oxidise further when eventually sawn and processed by masons for matching with extant walls. This rendered the entire program useless and a waste of taxpayer's dollars, according to the Opposition.

Measure the strength of Yellowblock

Yellowblock's compressive strength has been measured at 2.57 tons per square inch or 39.9 megapascals (MPa). Some tests put its compressive strength as high as 70 MPa.

The crushing strength of ashlar masonry and lintels averages 4,600 pounds per square inch (31.7 Mpa).

What botanical process triggered by Yellowblock results in a distinctive Australian odour?

Yellowblock is the geological foundation for the aroma of Australia's signature eucalypt trees, due to its paltry nutritional value. When nutrients are scarce, plants cannot afford to lose valuable leaves to herbivores so they release toxins that make their foliage distasteful as food. The resultant eucalypt toxin is recognised as the characteristic smell of the Australian Bush. Note Murray Bail analogue.

Illustrate the significance of smell to human beings

It is the last sense to expire before death. The stench of the battlefield always precedes sight (but not noise). The act of falling in love is largely governed by odour (although initial attraction is a visual phenomenon for men). When I opened the front door of our house after we got back from Shanghai, it smelled like an antique chamber and cabbage. In the now famous T-shirt experiment, it was shown that women preferred the smell of men who have immune systems most different to their own. Olfaction in women is generally better than men. It peaks during ovulation. This may explain why peri-ovulatory women tend to exhibit an increase in sexual activity. Occasionally, my husband brings home a native pig from Quezon City. It lives in our room for a few days. I have to watch the baby. The neighbour's complain. But when he slaughters the animal and barbeques the carcass, everybody in the street queues to buy pork belly. Body odour is rarely in evidence in China. Don Cane's body was pungent. It glowed with sweat. Odorant molecules pass into odour receptors. Billy smelt like Xinjiang lamb the first time he came to the sauna. I made him take off his dressing gown and pushed him into the shower cubicle. First (*Xian*), I made lavender soap froth over his chest until it dried like a crust. Then (*rang hou*), I took the shower head and blasted his body until it was all gone. Lastly (*zui hou*), I performed sex. It started to feel different when he came back the third time. Men's scent gets stronger as they thicken with age. Stock characters in the *Commedia dell'Arte* wore longnose masks to symbolise phallic endowment, a tradition that lingers in the figures of Punch and Cyrano De Bergerac (see Fliess). Jungian psychology connects odours and sex. Freud believed that suppressing odours was necessary for the maintenance and expansion of civilisation. Ambrose E. Welles liked a clean female body, superbly bathed and lightly perfumed. He was a prude by his own account. He farted – the other side of the wind – when he unleashed his libido. This was the direct product of Oya. Welles always considered overt sex scenes to be a lazy stunt that reduced the power of narrative. Madame Rochas was Joan Crawford's favourite perfume. The area of the brain that processes smell is part of the limbic system, or sex box. A female moth can release a pheromone that attracts males as far as one mile distant. During sex, we start breathing like dogs. Nasal engorgement causes less air to go directly to the lungs. More pheromones reach the olfactory epithelium. Smell attractors are not universal. Women shave their bodies in Chinese culture because smell and sight are considered unpleasant. Yet Continental European cultures highly prize this odour. A study of 31 males in Chicago assessed the impact on penile engorgement of 30 odours (Hirsh and Gruss, http://www.aanos.org/jrl_an_article.htm).

How do Bloom and Stephen interact in "Ithaca"?

SD is not interested in LB's politics. Bloom is not interested in SD's aesthetic reveries. When Stephen is quiet, Bloom presumes he is composing a lyric in his head. He thinks of poetry like advertising slogans. Stephen will not wash. Bloom is clean and carries a fresh cake of soap in his pocket. This revives a motif from Chapter One. Unlike Mulligan, Bloom gives a positive interpretation to Stephen's hydrophobia. He sees it as ascetic disinterest in bourgeois pretensions to propriety. This is another cliched image of the Artist. It is for these kinds of thoughts that Stephen ultimately rejects Bloom as just another ridiculous Homais. He is insensitive, even crude, in return, especially as he grows more contemptuous of Bloom's intellectual scope. Stephen sings a song about a Jew's daughter who murders a child. It is hard to believe this is not a provocation. Bloom ignores it. This doesn't make Stephen feel more respect. In fact, it hardens his disdain. Stephen often appears to be goading Bloom behind the pretense of drunkenness. Soon, Joyce creates a false dialectic with Bloom as the 'scientific' one and Stephen 'artistic'. Bloom is, of course, pseudo-scientific. He is a crank. He reflects naïve interest in the random inventions and follies of his day. This raises the option that Stephen is being similarly characterised by Joyce as a bogus intellectual. This type of self-mockery of his younger self is not unknown to Joyce. Nonetheless, they find common ground eventually. Joyce emphasises this stance with a Spoonerism: "Stoom and Blephen." If he had used surnames, it would have been insidious: "Doom and Bledalus." They go outside to piss in Bloom's garden. This becomes another caustic motif for Bloom's condition. Tom Hallem did a dump in The Collector's swimming pool at a NYE party 1983–84. This explains some of the lingering hostility towards him in the restaurant scene in Chapter Ten. Joyce unloads a lot of star names, facts and astronomical history on the reader before he gets to the end of the Ithaca episode. He links central male characters to their birth constellations to reinforce existing plot facets (see Table).

Table 12. Celestial alignment – Male characters and constellations in *Ulysses*

Character	Constellation	Naming Tale	Correspondences to *Ulysses*
BLOOM	Corona Borealis	Dionysus gave a crown of Venus to Ariadne after she was abandoned by Theseus. They married. Dionysus flung it into the heavens in joy to commemorate their union.	• A nova appeared in this constellation in the year of Bloom's birth (1866). • Seduction and abandonment (Boylan as Theseus). • Bloom's residual joy at (re)securing Molly as his wife. • Happy ending fantasy.
SD	Andromeda	A girl is chained to a rock by her father to atone for her mother's bragging. She is rescued by Perseus. They marry. After her death, Athene places Andromeda in the sky next to her husband and mother.	• A nova appeared in this constellation in 1885, soon after Stephen's birth. • Dysfunctional parents. • SD is chained to his family. LB helps to unchain him (Perseus). • Proximity to mother in eternity. Ostracised father.
RUDY	Auriga	Also known as Ericthonius. Chthonic son of Hephaestus and Athene (see also Gaia). Product of sperm spilled on Athene's thigh during rape. Wiped off with wool. Put in a box. Conception followed. He became King of Athens. Invented four-horse chariot. Zeus made him into a constellation.	• The nova T. Aurigae was discovered in 1892, just before Rudy's birth. • Lameness is symbolic of Rudy's frailty. • The name equates to "grave" in Greek and thus reminds us of Rudy's demise. • Spoiling of seed (AKA infant mortality – see Don Cane). • The box as coffin. • Bloom muses on his son's lost potential due to death (he could have been a king). • Glory of the Gods.

Explain the Classical Source of Gemini

Castor and Pollux, the twins of Gemini, were Greek heroes. They were the sons of Leda and Zeus-in-the-guise-of-a-swan. This union resulted in the production of two eggs containing: (1) Helen of Troy and Pollux (immortal twin) and (2) Castor and Clytemnestra (offspring of Tyndareus). Castor (horseman) and Pollux (boxer) were inseparable comrades. They accompanied the Argonauts. They calmed the seas during tempests. They are still present in the form of St Elmo's Fire. This is one of the 13 constellations of the Zodiac.

Correspondences to "Ulysses"?

LB = Castor; SD = Pollux. This is an ironic, provisional association. Bloom is only a horseman in that he is directing Stephen like a taxi driver. Stephen is an intellectual pugilist. C&P represent the northern tips of Gemini and thus the heads of a co-joined celestial representation. SD&LB are by no means attached similarly.

How long does Stephen Dedalus remain in the text?

He is present for approximately the first half of Ithaca.

How does Stephen exit the novel?

Stephen Dedalus leaves Bloom's home. He is left wandering into the ice-cube sharp brittle streets of Dublin a solitary figure gone null. He has become a wanderer like the stars at which he stared with Bloom. He is returning to the house of his true father, Simon Dedalus.

Insert equivalent to Bloom in W. Berlin

At last, I confront the Samaritan turning from the steel urinal with soft hands over a breathing zipper. He has a slender, blonde face. His keen clear eyes are glazed by a surface of glass in steel-rimmed spectacles. Hiding ingenuousness maybe. Wise in place. A small grin pumps bright-teeth.

"Thanks, Michel."

"You're lucky I'm a medical student."

Zeppy returns with Becks. I take it with a nod. He exits.

"Want some beer?" I ask.

"Sure.

"You go first. It's going to taste pretty bad after touching my lips."

Bloom smiles and tips back the bottle. The silver foil around its peak shines then glows. Froth gathers on the up-ended surface.

"You were talking outside about 'artisanal' painting before, Billy. What do you mean?"

"I mean art that betrays labour. All great art must possess an artisanal quality."

"Like Brueghel?"

"Yairs."

"A lot of detail then?"

"Not just that. Duchamp's work possessed this tone as well. LHOOQ was just two strokes of paint on a cheap print but it contains a whole canon inside it."

"Like Kiefer for us Germans?"

"Yes, sir, like Anselm-fucking-Kiefer!" [DRINKS] "You've got to make work that's dense ... like a novel. You need to hold the viewer's gaze."

Mallarme said that everything in the world exists in order to end up in a book. In this work, we see literature, art and music competing with life to make satisfactory meaning out of experience. It is the writer who survives to recount the tale of Tom Hallem.

"And you need a gimmick, of course. It's the whole working-class thing these days. You know: Jackson Pollock in mechanics overalls and red flannelette shirts, unshaven."

"What's your gimmick?"

"I'm no one," said Billy waving his hand. "I don't need one."

"What about your brother?"

"He's got style. And erudition. And a great big fucking bug up his arse about life."

"[Grins] Like Nick Cave?"

"[Snarling] Yes sir like fucking-Nick-Cave. He's been working with the same wet glare, that kind of streaky thickness, a texture of inhabiting an inexplicable station, not really acute within it, but a citizen of it nonetheless, not an interloper, creating out-of-tune elements at the selvedge of the frame, co-opting the tunefulness of other – what Ginsberg would call – Bards, like Rowland S. Howard, to persuade a recognisable work to come forth, with a comprehensible melody, in a received format, which is then re-distorted by other collaborators, people who are otherwise beyond conventional methods, like Blixa Bargeld, so that each story is comprehensible yet not quite right, not real like Realism, not moral like a parable, but not wrong either, rather possessing a psychic truth, through a chronicle of sudden and inexplicable acts, instructive like fable, but in reverse, by opposed rendition, making a parallel world in which characters speak poetically, not prosaically, like in vaudeville or mummery, with a shared bank of recurring images, regardless of ostensible place, be it Alabama or Nhill, which are wholly irrelevant to our own epoch, which deliberately contradict our fixation with pressing political issues like the Cold War or feminism, and thereby impress an other-obsession, an alternative cosmos, a bad place where evil is omnipresent, but not a dystopia really, a reconstruction of those Classical sites in Homer or Sophocles where the Gods bring down unjust terms on mortals and make mortals damage themselves and each other for THRILLS. That is what these two artists share. I don't know why they both come from Australia. It's Ultima Thule.

Explain Thule

Thule refers to an actual island that Classical mariners knew well – beyond the north-western tip of Britain – maybe Greenland – or Auden's Iceland. It's our galactic edge, Michel. The reason we're going to inherit SPACE. Every single Australian is coded with that DNA. Even if they've come from another place. We're all like Bowie in *The Man Who Fell to Earth*.

Only Australians can understand that movie. Its complacency in creature comforts. Its relentless recourse to anaesthetics. It's brittle coating of success. It's anguish. Only Australians can understand a planet without water. Only we can really understand drought. It's inside our heads. All Nick Cave's characters are like that. All his landscapes are Australia. All his songs. He'd really like Tom's stuff."

"Why don't you show him your brother's work? He lives right here in Berlin. He hangs out at Irizico."

"Why should I go to him? Tom's more famous. He's been hung in Paris. His agent wants to show him in New York. Nick Cave should come to him!"

"You are very proud of your brother."

"You bet, I am. He's great. Let me buy you a drink. Wait. I'm broke. But it's still my birthday. Can you shout me another beer?"

Note Billy is drunk. This device enables the narrator to put forth preposterous ideas without ownership. Part of a loosening of style in the final chapters. An aversion to revision. What Kerouac said. The CLOUD is a prison. Don't upload your spontaneous thoughts there. This passage corresponds to the state of SD at the end of *Ulysses*. He is still quite inebriated. His ego has been pumped. He is obviously superior intellectually to Bloom. He humours the older man. It enables him to sustain this sensation. Billy is kinder than SD. He took more time to get to the point where he had no time left to waste. He was diverted by the need to live life to the fullest. SD leaves the novel full of fresh momentum to become a writer like Marcel at the end of *Le Temps Retrouve*. This is precisely the course that James Joyce himself followed after 1904.

Moving from stars, itemise Joyce's moon/woman correspondences in "Ithaca"

1. Night power
2. Engaging a circle of admirers (satellites)
3. Incandescence
4. Predictability + reliability
5. Artificial yet non-changing appearance (especially to the mind/gaze of others)
6. Evasiveness under interrogation
7. Power over estuarine motions
8. Capacity to induce love, terror, embarrassment, splendour by association with, madness, vandalism
9. Enigmatic features (see Penelope)
10. Awe-like gazing at a sublime landscape
11. Tranquillity

12. Various portents (positive & negative)
13. Dynamic in effect as per luminescence, movement, manifestation
14. Beauty upon entrance into the midst of
15. Desire upon separation from
16. Chthonic endurance.

Relate the quantum above to Joyce's obsession with numerology

Sixteen is a numeral of cosmic significance in Ithaca. It is considered a kinetic number for introspective people setting out on a spiritual path. This is directly relevant to Stephen Dedalus at the end of *Ulysses*. Sixteen is one of four numbers associated with karmic debt. In a birth date, it indicates that the owner is dealing with issues from past lives. Joyce lets his interest in matching numbers run wild in this episode. Everything is dates, costs, values. Sixteen sucking stones are selected by Molloy in *The Unnameable*. This is a direct allusion to *Ulysses* as well as a sentimental tribute to the foibles of Beckett's mentor. *The Unnameable* is Beckett's version of the future of Stephen Dedalus. The tower is the sixteenth trump in a Tarot deck. It was a noteworthy number in popular culture after WW2 due to its association with teenage sexuality (i.e. Sweet Little Sixteen, You're Sixteen, Only Sixteen, *et al*). Later, it became the legal age of consent. Joyce's karmic number is 23/5. Twenty-three represents the Royal Star of the Lion. It promises success, help from superiors and protection from high places. The life of James Joyce as well as the history of the sponsorship and publication of *Ulysses* bear this out. People with five in their number have natural charm. They are innately courteous. It is associated with love of movement and travel. It is also linked to earth-magic. People of Five have a natural desire to believe in fairies, elves, magic and mystery. Again, all these qualities are relevant to Joyce. Almost all the people who helped him were women. They have a natural attraction to this karmic number. JJ always used telepathy. LB guesses Gerty is about to menstruate. She guesses he is a cuckold. These are both baseless biases that just happen to be correct.

Detail events of Billy's twenty-third birthday party

Billy overdosed at X'n'Pop last night. We found him slumpt on the steel bog with bile packing his nostrils, chin presst on chestplate, shiny drool threading its way down hisslap. I was brought back to some semblance of life (albeit grudgingly) by an angel mounted on the uneasy walls of the dim cubicle like some stone gargoyle. Leopold Bloom eased himself onto the concrete floor, pulled back my head by the mop, opened my eyelids with cool slender fingers and shone a lighter in my face. When they slipped shut again, he slapped me hard once across the fates. Out of the conch came comfort's familiar sounds: agitated voices; the latch cracking (I had given up on existence itself rather than face this complex operation only a few minutes earlier); running water in nearby basin; ripped paper towels; shoes slipping through my waste; hands warming my underarms; my fraille body lifted up to shone shellpearl; head dropping to gaze at my new winklepickers all covered in muck; waterfall feedback; the rush of life; someone in German clucking "cut him some speed, it will help"; gritty grey paper towel on my nose; they said BLOW; I blew; my feeble snort a disgrace to Kleenex; polyps of fleische suckt back; sudden aerate; spit; my head pushed along the laminex plank; five mark note shoved up my nostril; SNORT, they said; I did; grains flush; my eyeballs pop; congealed ball of amphetamine in my throat a little (w)retch but wasted-not-not-want; I've got a stomach of steel; clamp my teeth and pop upright grinding my mandibles like wet chalk: I am ALIVE ergo VITAL! In the delicate mirror green smiles were released. You alright, William? "Yes." Thanks, Zeppy. [Blown windy nose] Sorry. It must happen to any one of us. "Could," I corrected him. Yar. Whatever you said. This is exactly the type of junk scene that I complained about in C1. Pocket I rummage in unseamly dirt-crispened depths for change. Nix. I so self-righteous back then. I thought I'd ever stoop this low. But what with all bad inputs. Think you could get me a beer? Of course. It's your birthday. Jus. Cold bristles cross my shudderblades. This was the outermost location on my journey.

What is the role of Penelope in the *Odyssey*?

Homer cannot separate the plot from Penelope. She imbues Ithaca. It is her domain (DNS). Her name combines the Greek words *pene* for "weft" and *ops* meaning "face." This suggests inscrutability of mannerism. She is the antithesis of a character like Arachne. She is not coarse or boastful. She doesn't antagonise the Gods. She is careful to manage relations with the suitors. She makes a series of strategic withdrawals to buy time like Chiang Kai Shek. She allows the suitors' abuse of *Xenia* to evolve unchecked so they are ripe for retribution, hopefully by Odysseus if he returns. Her only ostensible narrative act is to weave a funeral shroud for her father-in-law, which she then unravels every night. It becomes symbolic of her marriage and life.

How does Joyce deploy this plot device?

The "webbing" technique in *Ulysses* is conceived from this trope. Molly's reveries are woven from crossover-stitch tendrils into a continuous narrative by incremental repetition. Language becomes dense like textile. It can be represented as Borromean rings. Her monologue plugs into earlier events in the novel and recasts their meaning. She casts a retrospective lens over other characters' opinions challenging superficial gender representations.

(30) Insert Shakespeare reference
[equivalent: Ophelia's daisy chains].

Compare Penelope and Molly using water imagery

Penelope is designed for drought; Molly for refreshment. A still pool versus a swollen creek. A full reservoir against the vital force of the Liffey. Both women endure long periods of absence. For Penelope, it is actual. For Molly, it is sensual. Both test their husbands – Penelope literally and Molly by computation. They measure them practically against alternative suitors. It is said that Penelope exemplifies female fidelity whereas Molly is an adulteress. But sex with Boylan is just Molly's way of forcing herself to pass judgment on Bloom. Both characters practice deception. Molly offers insights into her personality in her monologue. We get no insight into Penelope's thinking. O switched on the light in Billy's apartment and walked into the empty kitchen. A gang of American cockroaches scattered off the sideboard and down the scratched brass drain. She placed a tall can of fumigant on the floor. I will let it off when I leave, she thought. This scene reworks an image in Ithaca. She started to open the cupboards so that the gas could infiltrate every recess. The shelves were gritted with dry mouse pellets. She decided to buy some traps. Elizabeth Archer checked her watch. Tom Hallem was late. Never mind. It gave her more time to prepare herself. Heartburn consumed her throat, sucking the moisture from her chest. She rubbed her belly roughly.

Apply this task to sandstone

Sandstone occurs when the earth's crust BREATHES in and out, filling with sediment. It is extremely old. Over 300 million years by some calculations. It moved extremely slowly towards the coast by virtue of subterranean forces of nature. Today, it is smashed by the ocean repeatedly, causing erosion. This is a metaphor for the relationship of this work to Joyce (water).

How is Penelope represented in spatial terms?

Like all estimable women in Classical literature, she is fixed at the centre of a field of centripetal forces. They hold her body in place. She is able to direct them in play across her face. But she cannot find physical freedom, even inside her own bed chamber. There are numerous traitors amongst her serving women. She cannot leave the palace. Her allies know of her struggles only by secondary transmission. Stress has made her pallid and gaunt. This is an inwards spatial projection. She presents a very different image to her cousin, Helen, who is apparently blooming back in Sparta. Helen moves freely over the city airing opinions, even overriding her husband, in contravention of Classical convention. Penelope's dreams oscillate between visions of revenge and utter supplication. Pan was born from one such dream, according to the Ancients.

Link to this work

There are four major female characters who suffer spatial indignity. Elizabeth Archer is contained by financial woes. Her husband's illness further constrains her. She must remain focused on conception. This is another inward act. She is piling all her resources into a mound to withstand the future. She wants to burrow inside (see Winnie). Penelope Hallem must stay fixed in place to sustain her crumbling family. Her partner is a Fallen Laertes figure. She has precarious employment in sales like Leopold Bloom. Her son appears to be spiraling towards dissipation (AKA Stephen Dedalus). She has always been restricted by convention. She married according to schedule. This is what you did back then. The rest of the plan went awry. She had to bounce off the inside of the system as a non-conforming female in the 1960s. She endured the innuendo of being divorced and a single mother. It was all too much. She remarried and moved across town. She never got the chance to progress freely. Her life has been a slow, dry movement down an underground channel gouged by someone else (Don Cane). Helen Capri is checked by the past. She cannot find peace after all this time even in her bed and dreams, let alone aspire to the freedom she imagined as a teenager. One mistake has dictated the course of her life. Ana Lafei Pepese (ALP) represents a younger prototype of these women. But she will never reach maturity. Her mistake is fatal. She is stuck in a dead-end job and a bad relationship. Her association with Tom Hallem will kill her. The concert is her swansong. She goes down the tunnel and along the Lake towards death.

Compare the trials of Penelope and Odysseus

Penelope endures her own siege in the *Odyssey* (mirroring that of Troy) transcending attack (the suitors act as a metonymy of the Greek heroes) and employing her own stratagems (weaving and unpicking the shroud) to position her chosen vessel for victory. Odysseus is placed inside the horse in Troy then placed inside his own palace in disguise as another type of subterfuge by Penelope.

How does Odysseus love Penelope best?

In absence. As an ideal. Not necessarily in actuality.

And her?

The same. Certainly, however, it is better to have him back than endure the suitors another day. The best option is for him to get rid of the suitors then leave. This goal is accomplished by Penelope.

Gauge Penelope against Odysseus in a battle of wits

Penelope is more than a match for her husband. She is impassive like Odysseus. She never relaxes her guard. She exhibits no flaws. Yet she is also operating in metaphorical contradiction to him. They are like masters countering each other's favourite moves on a 3D chess board. In fact, Penelope operates more analytically than her husband in their opening encounter as her construction of the goose dream demonstrates.

Compare Penelope and the Trojans in terms of Odysseus' stratagems?

Penelope proves to be superior in judgment to the Trojans, who are gulled into complaisance by Sinon's tale and destroyed.

Are dreams used as a vehicle for truth or deceit by Homer?

There are five significant dreams in his epics:

1. Agamemnon – Troy will fall if attacked immediately (Zeus)
2. Achilles – spirit of dead Patroclus pleading
3. Penelope – reassurance (Athene)
4. Nausicaa – marriage/consummation (Athene)
5. Penelope – eagle killing geese.

Dreams 1 and 4 are deceitful. Item 1 sets off a ludicrous chain reaction. Item 4 initiates events resulting in the destruction of Phaeacian civilisation for assisting Odysseus (inverting the ethics of *xenia*). Dream 2 provides truth in the form of a prophecy of Achilles' death. Dream 3 provides succor but not truth. Item 5 is a cunning tale offering divergent channels – one truth of feelings, the other of error.

Why are the gates of our dreams made of ivory and horn?

This is a play on words in Greek: κέρας, horn, and κραίνω, fulfil, as opposed to ἐλέφας, ivory, and ἐλεφαίρομαι, deceive (see Arthur T. Murray). True dreams pass through gates of horn (2 & maybe 3); false dreams through ivory (1 & 4).

What act preceded Penelope recounting her dream in Book 19 of the *Odyssey*?

She withdrew behind the curtain so that Eurycleia could wash Odysseus' feet.

Why did Penelope select this act at this specific time?

She selected this moment because she knew it would expose his scar. She trusted that the old nurse would be surprised and make a telling utterance.

What did Penelope overhear?

She heard the gasp of Eurycleia when the old nurse saw the scar. She heard the undertones of Odysseus' threats against the nurse. This would have confirmed his identity. But his aggression would have chastened Penelope. It was imbued with a ruthlessness that was not apparent in him prior to the war. She thus resolved to test Odysseus with her dream. This would provide more data.

Examine the different levels of meaning, interpretation and truth in Penelope's dream

A leading analyst, Dr Kelly Bulkeley, has coined the term, "post-critical hermeneutics of dreaming," for a technique of oneiric interpretation based on Penelope's dream. In Book 19, Penelope describes a dream to Odysseus-as-beggar in which an eagle swoops down on her flock of twenty pet geese and snaps their necks in turn, killing them. It then perches on the roof and exclaims in a human voice that it is her husband who has just put her lovers to death. Significantly, she notes that the geese are still alive grazing at their trough after she wakes (like the suitors in the palace). Odysseus interprets the dream as a simple prophecy of his revenge. Penelope would certainly understand this self-serving interpretation. A woman of her intellect would not need Odysseus to explain such a dream. Such a construal is obvious. In fact, Odysseus has made a lax, facile reading of the dream, which undersells Penelope's intellectual capabilities and misreads her emotional locus. This is a bad sign. Penelope actually wants to work out whether her husband's principal goal is revenge against the suitors or their reunion. Odysseus' answer – and the haste of his reply – tells Penelope a lot about his mindset, especially his remark that "twist it however you like, / Your dream can only mean one thing." This is a 'closing down' of analytics – a withdrawal from productive interaction – that must have shocked her. For Odysseus was renowned for his inventive mind. She can now see that he comprehends the situation on Ithaca solely through the prism of personal honour. He does not retain any sensitivity or empathy that incorporates her experience. He cannot perceive how she has developed and changed over the last 20 years of utter self-reliance. She is now as wily as Odysseus. In fact, she consistently displays superior cunning to her husband. For Penelope has NOT RECOUNTED A DREAM AT ALL. She has posed a strategic conundrum to test Odysseus. The twenty geese in her dream correspond to the twenty years of Odysseus' absence. It's true meaning is that he has slaughtered TIME. He fails the test, despite the fact that it contains obvious inconsistencies to assist him (for example, he knows that there are 108 – not 20 – suitors) and that he possesses information from multiple sources of how Penelope has trenchantly and skillfully resisted the suitors.

How is the 'dream' designed to work on Odysseus' emotions?

The dream is complex. It is a trap. And goad. Penelope uses her dream to inflame Odysseus. His artless interpretation turns it into a spur. It suggests that the gods are supporting him. Yet it is also a gibe at his smug security in her fidelity. For Penelope has said of the geese that she "loved them all." To him, this means that she has 'loved' the suitors literally. In fact, it means that she loves even her lost years.

What would have happened if Odysseus interpreted the dream correctly?

It could have deflated him, leading to failure and death. Perhaps it is providential that he did not analyse the dream accurately.

How does Penelope react to the performance of Odysseus in the 'dream' test?

Penelope must have been extremely worried after Odysseus' performance that he would rush the timing of his revenge. He was clearly not functioning with his typical cognitive prowess. He was thinking in haste, ignoring strategic dimensions. He betrayed panic. This would have left Penelope contemplating the risk of his failure and her subsequent sacrifice to one of the suitors. This was the catalyst for her decision to bring on the challenge with a test where the odds would be stacked in Odysseus' favour. She announces that she will marry the man who can string Odysseus' bow. Penelope knew that the suitors were young men, untested in battle and weakened by their indolence and recent revelry, whereas Odysseus had been hardened by his arduous voyage. If no one succeeded, she at least bought more time.

Examine Homer's use of the motifs in Penelope's dream elsewhere in the *Odyssey*?

The other reference to geese and eagles occurs in Book 15, when Telemachus is leaving Sparta to return to Ithaca. An eagle carrying a tame goose in its talons swoops down in front of Menelaus, Helen, Telemachus and Peisistratus to display its prey then flies off. Peisistratus asks Menelaus for his interpretation. Helen interjects to say it is an omen that Odysseus is poised to sweep home and exact revenge on the suitors. As she is not an oracle, she says that the gods must have flashed this thought into her mind. Her interpretation is entirely plausible – and ultimately correct – but it is not the only possible interpretation, especially at this crucial stage in the text, when the reader is seeing Odysseus continuously thwarted in his efforts to return to Ithaca. Certainly, Odysseus can be seen as a noble bird and the suitors as domestic geese. Yet the eagle has not killed the goose. Bulkeley believes that we should only interpret dreams from what is ACTUALLY depicted and not project any extramural meaning. Employing this theory, the reader should conclude analysis at the flight of the eagle and not project the implied/assumed death of the goose. A plausible counter-analysis is that the event represents a successful suitor (Eagle) departing Odysseus' palace (represented as Menelaus' palace) to return home with Penelope (Goose) as his bride (Whiteness) after triumphantly displaying his prize to assembled noble families (represented by Menelaus, Nestor, Odysseus). In this regard, the event could be seen as a re-run of the Iliadic plot in which Paris (Eagle) takes Helen (Goose) from Sparta (Sparta) to Troy (Lair). It could even be seen as an invocation to Telemachus to act as an eagle himself by collecting his mother (Goose) and escaping Ithaca (Lair).

What did Helen's intervention show Classical readers?

Helen's interjection was improper. She was hasty to give her opinion just like Odysseus in Book 19 (unlike Menelaus and later Penelope). She interrupts her husband. This symbolises lack of respect for male authority. The contrasting behaviour of Homer's cousins, Helen and Penelope, is patent. Its meaning for women is clear. Penelope carefully recounts her 'dream' to Odysseus-in-disguise. She asks the male beggar for an interpretation and awaits his full reading before speaking. She remains composed and respectful. This uses restrictions of female propriety tactically.

What was Penelope's final word to Odysseus?

Her invocation to Odysseus enabled Penelope to return to a meditative state. For Penelope must put all distractions to one side. She must remain in focus. She needs to be quite still in order to continue work. She cannot abandon her post. She must continue weaving. It is the salvation of Ithaca: her inertia (another correspondence with the protracted battle for Troy). She must internalise her existence so she can shut out the suitors, just like Molly Bloom must internalise radical speech. They cannot be allowed to inhabit space – at least any space they would desire. This totemising centralises Ithaca into her person. For Ithaca without Penelope is as impossible to imagine as Aeaea without Circe, or Ogygia without Calypso. Ithaca has gone on for a long time without Odysseus. It has even survived without Telemachus or Laertes. But not without Penelope. She is the essential *enacting presence*.

What happens to women in motion?

By contrast, women in motion like Dido and Helen are inevitably fatal to themselves, their lovers and nations. This is a rule that defies personal attributes (Archetype–TRAGEDY).

I wanted to put ALL MY FEMALE CHARACTERS IN MOTION. It was Olive Schreiner's great rebuke to c19 readers with the characterisation of Lyndall in *Story of an African Farm*. She demonstrated that Victorian culture was no different in its treatment of women to the pagan world. Women needed to be present but fixed. Those places without women are isolated and belated like Eumaeus' hut or the farm of widower Laertes. Fecund, yes, in an agricultural sense but lacking women, family and therefore human spirit, like Waldo's farm after Lyndall has gone. Joyce employs the same sense of woman/place in *Ulysses* (Archetype – IRONY; sub-category – ROMANCE). That much is clear at the end of Ithaca when LB slips into bed beside his wife as man/ghost. While Molly is designed to be a 'real' woman – not some feminine icon – she shares the same powers, drives and flaws as goddesses like Aphrodite, Hera and Athene. Elizabeth Archer took Stan Welles into her office and closed the door. Her husband watched them through a wall of glass panels. She leant against an architect's board which was used to display prints to clients. Leon examined her face. Her mouth became swollen and dark with feeling. Her lips retracted around a broad smile. Molly is deliberately slack. She and Boylan make no effort to disguise their adultery: his betting tickets are arrayed on the kitchen table; the sitting room furniture has been re-arranged so they could sit side-by-side at the piano; his outline is branded on the mattress where LB comes to lie. Penelope Hallem sat on the edge of the bed pulling on her shoes. Dick Stone dried his plump, naked torso. She rose and closed the bathroom door then went to the bedside table and picked up the telephone. Xiao Fang pursed her lips as Shanghai Dog shut the apartment door. A great wave of absence struck her. Alone without a key in a stranger's home. She girded her loins. She would hold on. Judy had finished her shift at Glamour Bar. The metro slid under the river deep into Pudong. She needed to collect Xiao Nong from Johnny's mother. It was cramped in their two-bedroom apartment. Her daughter's name meant "small whisper." She was not given an English name. I am sick of all that foreign crap, she said to her husband when he suggested the name Joyce. Molly is greater in spirit and scope than any male character in *Ulysses*. She represents Joyce's major advance on Homer. He continues the narrative of *Ulysses* after the Homeric ending by adding her monologue. This is the moment when Bloom and his wife are shown to be best matched – in spiritual reverie – and therefore truly united (this is also an example of metempsychosis as the consciousness of the departing Bloom imbues Molly).

How have Feminist critics approached Molly Bloom's monologue?

Conflicted. This episode was considered a major event in literary history at the time of publication. This contributed to its banning. It dealt candidly with women's issues such as beauty, love, marriage, motherhood, sex, fidelity and adultery. It introduced previously taboo subjects like female orgasm, labour, birth and menstruation. It constructed a complex and nuanced female consciousness without resorting to stereotypes of sentimentality or malice. Molly assessed her options and the variables and made informed decisions about her best interests. Some feminists viewed the episode as patriarchy continuing to define female experience. This is fair enough. It shifted the discourse to another battleground. The whole Ithaca episode takes place in bed. Female confinement was a common plot element in Victorian literature. Joyce used it in an extraordinary manner like Walter Pater's Virgilia. But that work is still oriented towards MEN. The first thing Bloom notices is the impression of Boylan's body. He gets into bed in a fetal position. Molly becomes his mother.

Briefly address rumours surrounding Joyce's personal motivation for the content of Molly's internal monologue?

Molly was based to some extent on Nora Joyce. He suspected adultery when he was courting her. His erstwhile friend, Cosgrave, a competitor for Nora's affections in 1904, lied outright on this matter in 1909. Joyce was jealous, reproachful, passionate and vulnerable in subsequent correspondence. John Francis Byrne assuaged him in this crisis.

What was Joyce's objective?

Joyce was projecting himself into Hades. Bloom's resignation at bed time represents Joyce's best effort to neutralise his own masculine jealousy. He acknowledges responsibility for lack of sexual intimacy. Molly reconciles the fact of adultery with ongoing feelings of love, affection and desire for her husband. At its highest level, it symbolises the Spiritual versus the Physical. Molly is not a serial adulterer. Bloom is not acting like a cuckold. Likewise, Penelope and Les Hallem are not typical. Their estrangement is due to physical incapacity. Barry Capri is characteristic. He is sentimental about his wife but has at least one long-term lover. Shanghai Dog exhibits hypocrisy.

Compare Molly's sexual profiling by men with fact?

Molly is represented as a powerfully sexual woman with a bountiful figure, voluptuous skin and sensual face. This image is confirmed by various characters over the course of 16 June 1904. While she appears to be highly sexualised, in fact, she has endured a long period of sexual abstinence with grace. Molly has not had sexual consummation with Bloom since the death of Rudy more than ten years ago. *Ulysses* is set on the day of her first adultery.

And Bloom?

Bloom, by contrast, has had sex with countless mistresses and prostitutes. He is obsessed with sex. He is a compulsive philanderer (verbal and written formats). Yet he is not a lustful figure. He offers no coarse external commentary, unlike other male characters. Sex becomes almost mundane in his musings. He is vulnerable to risk-taking behaviour like the act of masturbation in public as he observes Gerty McDowell. He is impotent with his wife. His fantasies adhere to the Sacher-Masoch strand. The double penetration scene in C7 is the physical realisation of Bloom's reverie in Circe. He fancies seeing his wife with other men, including young Stephen. These symptoms can be consolidated into a general diagnosis of Compulsive Sexual Behaviour Disorder (CSBD), which has recently been ratified for inclusion in the International Classification of Diseases (ICD-11). The causes of CSBD in Bloom cannot be isolated to the death of his son. A broader range of sources of trauma should be investigated going back to childhood, including the early death of his mother (causing fear of abandonment) and social ostracisation (anti-Semitism). This created a deep sense of otherness. You should look for signs of repressed sexual abuse and check medical records for physical abnormalities, especially at puberty (e.g. girls with excessive facial and body hair, boys growing puffy nipples and breast tissue). The suicide of his father is not relevant due to his age. The ruling personality sign of CSBD is insecurity. Acts of promiscuity classified under CSBD[BD] help the patient temporarily compensate for under-developed self-worth, low self-esteem and self-loathing. The flipside of CSBD is Narcissism. Patients with CSBD often evidence disinhibited behaviour through drunkenness and drug abuse. Stephen Dedalus cannot be diagnosed with CSBD based on his actions in *Ulysses*. What can appear as arrogance is genuine self-belief. It is not compensatory bravado. His substance abuse is a direct product of guilt about his actions during the death throes of his mother. He does not exhibit other symptoms of CSBD. James Joyce split the full suite of his own CSBD attributes between Stephen and Bloom. Male characters in this work can be assessed against a diagnostic framework for CSBD in ICD-11 with the following results (see Table 12):

TABLE 13. ICD-11 CLASSIFICATION OF MALE CHARACTERS IN *TELEMACHUS*

Male	Indicators	Diagnosis
Don Cane	Early death of father. Succession of step-fathers. Mother leaves Australia. Raised by grandparents. Sexual congress within family and flight. Multiple simultaneous partners historically. Insistent flirtation on day under analysis (predatory).	CSBD confirmed
Ambrose E. Welles	N/A (long-term adultery with single person only). He had been called a genius since the age of two. He was reciting Dale Carnegie at twelve. There may have been suppressed homosexuality in his work.	Businessman
Tom Hallem	Absent father. Remote mother. Dysfunction of step-father relationship. Dysregulated behaviour. Compulsion for sexual contact (gender non-specific). Service complex (lack of self-worth). Inability to connect emotionally with potential sources of genuine affection.	CSBD confirmed
Barry Capri	N/A (long-term adultery with single person only).	Compensatory
Leer	Use of sex as power/hate device.	Psychopathy
Shanghai Dog	Multiple simultaneous partners. Regular use of prostitutes. Voyeurism (visits gay bar with Murphy). Inability to connect emotionally.	CSBD confirmed
Leon Daniel	Sexual promiscuity and hypersexuality (non-binary)	Repression of sex identity in youth leading to over-compensation (historic misfortune of infection with HIV/AIDS)
Billy Capri	N/A (single partner as at this date)	Normal, however, the trauma of today's events cannot be underestimated.

NOTE – Q&A style here is designed to displace personal associations with the writer.

What is resolution for L. and M. Bloom?
Continuation. To go on together. Not alone.

When and where?
In thought. Unstated. In bed. Pre-dawn. Like Odysseus and Penelope. Arse about. Head-to-toe. Synchronous.

Next steps?
No confrontation. Will to be transmitted in modified behaviour. Perhaps commencement of awkward intimacy. Maybe proceeding to fumbling sexual encounters. Hopefully deepening with time. Regular setbacks.

What has science discovered that would assist sexual bonding?
The male tongue carries testosterone so the act of kissing increases female arousal. The male brain is hard-wired to repeat orgasm with the same partner. This does not apply if the wire is broken (e.g. adultery, prostitution, etc.).

Insert alignment with *Telemachus*
Penelope Hallem listened to her unanswered call home until the line clotted. She visualised Les Hallam stuck on the toilet unable to move swiftly. She would try again in a few minutes. Helen Capri focused on the impact of a youthful indiscretion on the course of a good life. She weighed the positive experience of maternity against its causation. She acknowledged her shared history with Barry. There was no gain in any sudden revelation of knowledge about his affair. Using the same measure, Ana reached a different conclusion about Matt Supplejack. Shanghai Dog moved across Shanghai like a snake.

Compare Molly's monologue with other characters
It is more sustained than anything by Bloom or Stephen (even the Shakespeare theory). She speaks in thematic cycles inching by increment towards conclusion propelling the turbines of Joyce's gigantic word machine. Revise to employ Joyce's favoured water imagery (sub. 'mill').

(60) Examine Joyce's style in Penelope
Joyce uses only 8 'sentences' [linguistic units] in the episode. They are demarked by

spacing not punctuation. There are only 2 punctuation marks in forty-five pages – one of which closes the text (Sentence 8). The other occurs after the word "ashpit" (Sentence 4), although it is omitted from the Penguin Modern Classics edition. The linguistic units in Penelope are delineated by conventional paragraph markers – each 'sentence' beginning on a new line with a slight indentation.

Analyse the significance of the sentence/paragraph markers in Penelope
The episode begins and ends with the word YES. A breakdown follows:

Table 14. Linguistic units in Penelope – Beginnings and ends

	(A) Beginning of unit	(B) End of unit
1.	YES	THEY
2.	THEY'RE all so different Boylan talking about the shape of my foot	I'm sure you WERE
3.	YES I think he made them a bit firmer	O Lord I cant (sic) wait till MONDAY
4.	FRSE(x8)FRON(x4)G train	Bottom of the ASHPIT
5.	MULVEYS was the first	One more SONG
6.	THAT was a relief	O how the waters come down at LAHORE
7.	WHO knows is there anything the matter with my insides	THOUGH
8.	NO that's no way for him has he no manners	YES

The sentence-breaks above generally relate to sexual activity (LB, HBB, SD, Mulvey) and gender issues (coitus, voyeurism, marriage proposals, menstrual cycle).

Compare subject matter either side of each unit

Table 15. Linguistic units in Penelope – Subject matter

1.	(1A) Bloom asks for breakfast in bed	(1B) Hanging a woman for murder
2.	(2A) Boylan is a foot fetishist	(2B) Molly's breasts are ogled
3.	(3A) Her breasts are sucked hard by LB (foreplay) – note use of "Yes"	(3B) Discussion of frequency of coitus with Boylan – 7 occasions (Thursday to Sunday)

4.	(4A) Strength of train whistles/engines (sexual metaphor)	(4B) Of female redundancy with age
5.	(5A) Marriage proposals beginning with Mulvey	(5B) Boylan associated with SONG – phrase also refers to "pianissimo"
6.	(6A) Act of coitus as a RELIEF (succeeded by flatulence)	(6B) "Waters," which symbolises flood > tempest > orgasm > urination etc
7.	(7A) Possible pregnancy followed by countdown of menstrual cycle	(7B) On SD singing, becoming her lover, writing for her and becoming famous
8.	(8A) Boylan's lack of manners. Note – "No" to Boylan here contrasts with "YES" to LB at closure. Also revises preliminary "YES" to Boylan earlier in episode.	(8B) Yes to Bloom. Note – use of "YES" at beginning and end of episode creates a textual LooP enclosing her reverie. Joyce repeated and updated this device in Finnegan's Wake.

Molly prevaricates but ultimately accedes to another rendez-vous with Hugh Boylan at the same time as she contemplates reconciling with her husband. This is sound tactics.

Examine the role of breakfast

There is acute symbolism in Bloom's demand for breakfast in bed. It shows him trying to break the bad habits in his marriage. Molly understands that this statement of apparent mastery is in fact another request to be controlled but differently. Chinese women never eat breakfast. It is a weight-control tactic. Tondo starts chirripping at 5 am. My husband lights up a Marlboro. I dump our baby with my cousin. We wend our way to Herbosa Street. I am mopping floors at a private hospital. My hair is still wet. It helps me stay cool. We walk up to a jeepney at the front of the pack. It can drop my husband at the warehouse. Barry and I usually drive together to work. I run the shop. He works the pit. We still have driveway service. People like a personal touch. Petrol is worth nothing to the business. I wear a bright apron. It keeps the rainbow purls and fumes off my clothes. Les is still in bed when I rise. It takes him a long time to get moving. I make him black coffee and go. He doesn't like to be made a fuss of. Billy didn't ask for the red rope again. He could see I was not comfortable. Breakfast in bed I just don't like, thought O. Crumbs in the sheets are like splinters. I prefer to sit in the kitchen at the table with milk coffee and toast. I like one piece of toast sweet and one savoury. I read the newspaper. Billy knows how to prepare breakfast. It makes him look at me differently. He sidles up behind me to stroke my hair. It is a primal comfort. I don't have to speak. He squeezes my neck gently. That's nice. I can keep reading. He needs the idea of home. I like to roam. He does need to wander periodically. It mitigates his angst. But he is like a cat. He knows his way back.

Compare the use of keys in relation to ingress

Both male characters have lost possession of house keys. Stephen by consent. Bloom by inattention. It is a straightforward symbol of phallic emasculation. LB took comfort in the fact that he gained entry to his home without a key (incertitude of the void). The contrast with Stephen Dedalus is noted. "He must wander who has no key," concluded the prophet. There are perfunctory references to keys throughout *Telemachus*.

Explain the narrative benefits of the Catechism format in Ithaca?

The Q&A device (309 in total) promotes an objective authoritative voice in *Ulysses*. It references religion and science and suggests a search for Truth. Modernist technical-speak abounds. This detaches emotion from the text. There is a windfall of information. It takes a full systems approach: physics of Bloom falling, engineering of Dublin waterworks, inventory of LB's kitchen, bookshelf contents, profit-making schemes, ameliorative activities, indignities of the day and contents of table drawers (x3), daily budget. This device tightens – and further elucidates – JJ's representation of memories, fantasies and abstract ideas in earlier chapters (e.g. Dignam funeral; LB's list of female admirers). It should be noted, however, that this episode does have a mechanised tone. It is a clever idea executed expertly. However, it does make for strained reading (note resemblance to this work).

What is the model for this device?

It has been accepted that Joyce's utilisation of the Q&A format was parodic. The essay, "The Nature of James Joyce's Parody in 'Ithaca,'" *Modern Language Review* 64 (1969) by R.A. Copland and G.W. Turner, proposed that the source was a popular elementary textbook titled *Historical and Miscellaneous Questions for the Use of Young People, with a Selection of British and General Biography, &c., &c.*, by Richmal Mangnall. This work was republished with over 100 editions in the nineteenth century. Joyce made three references to *Aristotle's Masterpiece (ArMa)* in *Ulysses* as well as recording thoughts on it in his notes (see *Joyce's* Ulysses *Notesheets in the British Museum*). The singularity of Joyce's model was disputed by Sheon-Joo Chin (1996). Chin cites *Tristram Shandy* as an alternative model. He also references *ArMa*. He notes that the format of Ithaca resembles *ArMa* more than Mangnall with questions and answers being visually distinctive rather than integrated into the line of text. Finally, the comic tone of *ArMa* is redolent of Ithaca.

Explain the history of "ArMa"?

Its full title was *Aristotle's Masterpiece: Displaying the Secrets of Nature in the Generation of Man*. It was also known as *The Works of Aristotle, the Famous Philosopher*. It was a sex manual and midwifery book popular in England up to the 19th century. It was first published in 1684. It became the world's most widely circulated guide to childbirth and sex. It claimed to be the work of the famous Hellenic philosopher. This was a hoax. As a consequence, the author is now described as a Pseudo-Aristotle. *ArMa* mixed classical medical writings and 17th-century midwifery treatises with popular folklore. It described sexual anatomy and reproduction as then understood. The tone of writing varied from reverent to bawdy. Banned in Britain until the 1960s, it had a long and clandestine career as a quasi-pornographic book. Grubby copies were produced in back-street print shops, sold in rubber-goods stores and Holywell Street, and passed from hand to hand until they disintegrated. Billy Capri worked in such a warehouse in 1983. It was the type of work that Leopold Bloom would have purchased from 'beneath the canvas flap' at a riverside bookstall. Many young boys got their first knowledge of sex from *ArMa*. It was also sometimes given to women about to get married by their mothers. Penelope and Helen got nothing. It has been cited by Evelyn Waugh and Anthony Burgess. The sexological writings of Havelock Ellis are more in the vein on *ArMa* than continental theorists like Jung and Freud.

Compare and contrast with *Ulysses*

ArMa juxtaposes images of sexual practices, foetuses, child birth & female bodily functions with examples of mutants and legendary freaks. It debases femaleness by historical citation. The Penelope episode contains an unprejudiced account of female bodily functions and sexuality. Joyce was an activist in employing such antinomian imagery. He always presented the human form positively, regardless of function. Proust undertook the same campaign in his depiction of Charlus, albeit he couched homosexuality in negative terms. There is, however, much pathos in the famous BDSM scene in LTP. Both writers were Naturalists in the true sense of the term. Sometimes Zhu Di came along on my business trips. ~~She didn't have a passport so she couldn't travel overseas. It was hard to get a visa anyway, according to my agent. The government liked Chinese people to travel in tour groups.~~ I took her to Xiamen once. It was her first trip on a plane. She tried to act cool but I knew she was nervous by the way she kept pulling herself upright in her seat. After a while, she gazed out the window intently at the clouds, thick and fattened below us, yielding gently to silver scarves of jetstream followed by patches of coastline dun-green and grey. INSERT DESCRIPTION OF VIEW FROM AIR, MOZAMBIQUE DEAL. In aeroplanes, clouds are too close to see all the whorling shapes that make up stories. For that, you need to be a child lying on its back on tough grass in a paddock. See Point 2 (Below) re-Sublime. Also, Maralinga cloud. Also, use Navigation Tool to analyse the 17 uses of the word 'cloud' as a thread of symbols in TMAC. ~~Cut all embellishment from the subsequent passage.~~ We went to Hangzhou to visit Ling Yin Temple. Judy liked to go there during *Zhong Qiu Jie* to pray. We fucked hard on the first night in a suite overlooking Xi Hu. I took her over the desk while she watched the laser show above the lake ~~like the start of Love American Style~~. We only left our room ~~briefly~~ to eat dinner downstairs in the Shangri-La buffet. She ate a lot more food than usual. Odd stuff that she didn't normally eat. We slept like shift workers waking each other to fuck aimlessly. Later, I worked out that she must have just started seeing Johnny and this was a kind of farewell tour. In the morning, we went to Starbucks for breakfast in a small shopping mall along the waterfront. She ate like a horse. First, she had glazed donuts with café latte then a Danish pastry with a bowl of hot chocolate. When we had finished, Judy asked to go back to the hotel. I waited in the lobby looking at a souvenir shop. I picked some gifts for my kids and had them sent to our room. Zhu Di had changed into blue jeans, a long-sleeved blouse and a cardigan with a thick neck when she returned. I got the concierge to hail a taxi. We got in the back seat together. It was a long drive around the lake. The road was cut into the side of a hill. There was a long traffic jam near the temple gates. That was OK. After all, it was Golden Week. I started dozing. Suddenly Zhu Di took my hand.

"I got bad news," she said.

A shudder went through my body. She never had any news at all. She was always totally neutral. She slipped automatically into Mandarin trying to explain. I can't remember her exact words but she said something like, 'dui bu qi, Bi Li, dan shi wo ...' then I lost comprehension for a moment ~~as if we were driving at night in a sports car that had just entered a brightly lit tunnel~~. She used words like 'shiqing,' 'jingqi' and 'qian de.' I don't know what you mean, Judy, I replied. I tried to get clarification but my word order became tangled. I reverted to an English syntax. Ni de dou zi bu hao song wanfan zuotian ma, I asked first. I meant to say, zuotian wanfan rang ni de dou zi bu hao ma? I repeated my sentence correctly.

"Yes, my stomach is bad," she said. "But not from food. I am *liu xue*."

"What?"

I was perplexed.

"Are you going to study abroad?" I asked.

"No. Not *liuxuesheng*. I mean, woman's pain. From eggs."

"Do you mean morning sickness?" I blurted.

She nodded. My head started spinning. I gripped her hand. It went floppy like a typical Chinese sick person. She never acted like that. I put my arm around her. She nestled into my shoulder. She could hear his heart beating fast. I pressed my palm on his soft breast. The Narrator came back to this passage many times. Sometimes he updated it. Changed the tense. Added new information that clarified the Protagonist's reaction. These were usually manufactured extras which he subsequently erased. He deleted the whole incident for three years only bringing it back in the last weeks before publication to act as a prolepsis to Molly's menses in C9. We sat in silence while the taxi squeezed past tour buses and shunted pedestrians off the road. The same bunch of lao bai xing kept catching and passing us repetitively when we got stalled in traffic. They glared at the driver. Then they saw me. So, they glared at the wai guo ren instead. Then they saw Judy. So, they came to the window to glare at her. Eventually, we all arrived at the palace gates simultaneously. They looked excited when I emerged from the vehicle. Maybe they had never seen a foreigner before. This was not unusual back then. I also attracted attention because I was 1.88 m tall, hirsute, unshaven, with wavy chestnut hair. I paid the driver and said bu yong zhao le. It means "no need to look for (the change)." I can't stand getting back a palm full of shrapnel. They repeated my words appreciatively. An old man gave me thumbs-up. I waved back. He showed a broken fence of nicotine-stained teeth. We walked towards the temple gates at the south wall. Judy was slow to press into the long incline. I bought our tickets while she sat on a stone fence doubled-over holding her belly. Eventually, she struggled to her feet. We entered the temple complex. The crowd diminished as people went towards their favourite place. We circumnavigated a low Spirit Wall that blocked evil ghosts. They can only travel straight. A lot of apartment blocks in China possess holes so spirits can pass through the building without visiting. Judy saw a toilet block and went straight inside. She was gone a long time. I considered my circumstances. I was still married. I had three kids back in Australia. I didn't want more children. But I had to do the right thing. I couldn't stop a Chinese woman having a baby. As a single woman, she might go to the hospital for a 12-week check-up and end up locked in the termination ward. I started to focus on finance. I would have to get a divorce. My wife could have the family home in Mosman. I would take the holiday house at Whale Beach. I could sell that and generate enough cash to buy a studio apartment in Cremorne as well as a decent 2-bedroom flat in Gubei. That was a good place to raise children. The streets were wide and new. There was a big Carrefour. Foreign schools. Good doctors and dentists. The international hospital was out that way. It probably had a birth clinic. I didn't want to live near her parents in Pudong. But then again grandparents are primary carers in China. Maybe our child could live with them. Lots of Chinese people did that. It would make life a lot easier. I actually felt quite buoyant when Judy returned. Perhaps I also loved her.

"Do you want to go back to the hotel?" I asked.

I clasped her arm squeezing the sinews and smiled.

"No. I am OK now," she said brightly holding up a wad of bloody tissues.

"What happened?" I asked.

She made a chopping motion and grinned. She had heavy, carved teeth set slightly apart which gave her a carnivorous zeal.

"Did you just have a miscarriage?" I asked.

"What?"

"Did you lose our baby?"

I pointed at her belly.

"What baby?"

"Our baby."

I pointed at the tissues.

"No baby, Billy," she said laughing. "Every month the same. But this time a little bit early. I am sorry but we can't have any more sex this holiday."

"That was your bad news?"

"Yes."

I took the tissues, crumpled them in my fist and inserted them into a public garbage bin. It was crested with fresh spittle. Some Chinese guys were standing in a pack smoking Mongolian cigarettes. They smiled. I nodded. I went back to Zhu Di. We walked uphill to the temple. She put her left foot first over the wooden beam that marked the entrance to the Mahavira Hall. It was a ritual for menstruating women to go left first. She bought a bouquet of incense sticks and prayed; waving them over smoking urns. I observed the Shakyamuni Buddha. It had been freshly painted. Probably for the forthcoming Olympic Games. Its head-dress was royal-blue. Gold leaf embellished the edges and folds of the Buddha's robe as well as the lotus blossom on which he sat. He taught a middle way like Socialism with Chinese Characteristics. Milk and rice pudding. Sitting under a Bodhi tree. Deng's walking trail to and from the Xinjian County Tractor Factory. Gautama. Not everyone can get rich at once, he said. Princelings went first. Children of the elite. Later, Judy said she would have just had an abortion if she got pregnant. Much later, I realised this scene was a bit like Boylan and Molly in that Zhu Di was going back to her own people via Johnny.

Itemise the outlook of various human cultures towards menstruation with citations where relevant

— Sacred, powerful, celebrated
— Increased psychic capacity
— Ability to heal the sick
— Power to destroy enemies (Cherokees)

— Herbicidal powers in regard to young lettuces (toxic rot)
— Scares off hailstorms, whirlwinds, lightning (Pliny the Elder)
— Walking naked through a field at this time causes noxious bugs to drop off ears of corn (Pliny the Elder)
— Dangerous to male power
— Magic fluid (African charms: used to both to purify/destroy)
— Punishment of Eve
— Unclean (Leviticus 15:19–30)
— Unable to visit sacred shines, climb consecrated mountains or take devotions etcetera (Mongols, Leviticus, Orthodox, Hindu, Buddhism, Shinto)
— Probable influence on taboo on female clergy
— Intercourse is banned or discouraged during (Koran, Judaism)
— Transformation of fluid into snakes/insects then moon goddess (Mayan)
— Requiring spiritual cleansing – niddah/mikvah (Judaism): see also Ghusl (Islam): Hindu
— Untouchable: isolated: separated (see *Dakkini*, Kerala architecture): requirement for use of discrete eating implements: barred from pooja room: no singing: no tailoring (Hindu)
— Deceitful because it is concealed by women (Sumba)
— Cause of sexually transmitted disease (Sumba)
— Respect ["women should not be pestered"] (Islam)
— God-given process necessary for human life thus to be treated without prejudice
— Can visit gurdwara, pray and undertake Seva (Sikh)
— Horror
— Deflection (taken off-screen)
— A blue liquid (Western advertising)
— 59% of American women have expressed interest in not menstruating (non-contraceptive product under development).

Outline Classical processes for minimising the inconvenience of menstrual flow

- Egypt – use of softened papyrus as tampons
- Greece – lint was wrapped around a small peg
- Rome – pads made of soft wool
- Other – moss, grass and animal skins employed.

Insert timeline of modern product development

Table 16. A timeline of menstruation products

1839	Goodyear invents vulcanised rubber enabling manufacture of condoms, intrauterine devices, douching syringes and the diaphragm ("womb well" brand).
1850s	Patenting of catamenial sacks and bandages; receptacles from springs, wires, buttons, flaps, elastic straps, valves and girdles.
1873	Cornstock Act – pornography and conception-related products/texts banned in the US. Term "feminine hygiene" coined to rebrand sanitary products.
1896	Lister's Towels (Johnson and Johnson) – first commercial sanitary pads released. Named after pioneer in sterile surgery. Commercial failure.
1900–	Use of homemade pads from cotton wadding used for baby diapers (known as "bird's eyes").
1911	Midol goes on sale. Becomes popular for menstrual pain relief.
1914–18	WWI nurses start to use cellulose bandages (developed for wounded soldiers) due to superior absorption properties compared to cotton.
1920s	Kotex and Modess released. Disposable pads proliferate. Closed-crotched underwear enables belt and pad to be held in place comfortably.
1930s	First re-usable menstrual cap patented by Lenoa Chambers. Commercial failure.
1931	Tampon with applicator and tampon compression machine patented by Dr Earle Haas. Gertrude Tendrich acquired patent for $32,000.
1933	Tampax founded by Tendrich using Haas patents (still in use today). First Tampax made at home on sewing machine.
1950s	Pursettes introduced – small non-applicator tampons with a lubricated tip in a discrete case.
1959	Menstrual Caps reintroduced by Tassette. Again, a commercial failure.
1969	Stayfree minipads with adhesive strips go on sale. The end of belts, clips and safety pins.
1971	Menstrual extraction promoted (Rothman and Downer) with women joining self-help groups to extract menses including fertilised eggs. Over 20,000 procedures performed.
1972	TV advertising ban on female hygiene products is lifted.
1975	Rely tampons released. Later withdrawn by Proctor and Gamble due to links to Toxic Shock Syndrome.
1985	Courteney Cox uses the word "period" for the first time in an American TV commercial.
1987	The Keeper released. Another reusable menstrual cap. Commercially semi-successful.
1990s	Super Minipad tucked horizontally between labial folds is developed. Commercial failure.
2003	US FDA approved release of continuous birth control pill suppressing periods indefinitely (4 per year). Studies on long term safety for adolescents not yet published.
2007	US FDA approves Lybrel – first birth control pill to eliminate periods. Menstrual cramps and vaginal bleeding still experienced by users.

Insert text on Francine's abortion (West Berlin, September 1985).

"I'm pregnant," she said.

"But you said you were infertile," replied Tom Hallem.

"I got fat."

"How pregnant?"

"Eight weeks."

"Is that why you've been sick?"

"Yes."

"What are you going to do?"

"Have a termination."

"How?"

"It's legal in West Germany."

"How much does it cost?"

"I don't know."

"Can you get some money off your mother?"

"Yes."

"I've got some money coming soon from a show in Brisbane. I can give you some."

Frances lit an HB and rolled the match around the ashtray until its head turned into grit among the stale butts. A ribbon of smoke rose. Tom was finishing a fast, black ballpoint drawing on a sheet of A3 paper. He was too poor to buy art products. The EA Times exhibition in Paris was a dud. I did some work on Ken Unsworth's installation at the Biennale for pin-money, he told me when I got to Berlin.

"You don't have to," she said.

"I want to."

"But I don't want you to."

"Why?"

"Look, I've been seeing Billy. It's probably his—"

"What?"

"Well, I never got pregnant off you but as soon as we started—"

"That's a nice way out of a jam, Frances. I mean, being pregnant. It makes it really easy to announce that you've been fucking Billy."

"I guess it is convenient, if you choose to look at it like it."

"That's exactly how I choose to look at it. Because it could still be mine. We've still been fucking."

"Yes, we have."

"So, it could still be my ... responsibility."

"It's not your responsibility. I don't want you to have any responsibility towards me, Tom. I can't trust you. Billy accepts his share of responsibility. He's solid. I trust him."

"He's totally fucked-up, Frances. I mean, look at him. He's either drunk, stoned or hungover. He hasn't even got a job. He's living off hand-outs from his parents."

"He's emotionally stable."

"That's a bit rich coming from you. You know what I've just been through with Elizabeth. You know what it means to me. Now, you've done exactly the same thing. But maybe I'm not seeing things clearly. Let me try to get it straight. It's not like you're just fucking anyone. You're fucking my own brother. But what I don't understand – what I really don't understand – is how he could possibly get involved with you. He ought to hate you."

"Maybe he hates you."

"Did he tell you that? Asked Tom Hallem fiercely.

"Ask him."

"I'm not going to ask him. I'm not going to say anything at all to him. I don't even want to be here. I need some space."

"Go and see your girl then."

"Who?"

"The German."

"What do you care? It's not like I'm fucking your sister or something."

So I walkt out the Spanish doors onto the grimy landing in front of our apartment and was given damp air like illuminating gas. It looked like the walls hadn't been cleaned since the Russians came. A waterfall of relief smashed over me. I skippt down the ancient staircase. Hate and euphoria grippt my senses. The clinging sheets of a Berlin summer evening full of eastern plant particulates had turned the sky into a Joe Turner slideshow. I decided to stop at Ambrosia for a drink before I went to see Sylvana. We were never close again after that day.

Align with the work of Orson Welles

Every one of his movies starts with a death (C1). They are all about two friends who betray each other (Tom/Billy). TMAC is indebted to the kaleidoscopic anti-form and unfinished brutality of *Other Side of the Wind* as well as the buoyant trickery of *F for Fake* [*F(W)ake*], which in turn owed so much back to Joyce.

Compare the style and form of the Ithaca and Penelope episodes

Ithaca: impersonal, dialectical, rigid order, confident, scientific/factual (pretence only), elemental, universal themes. Penelope: human, personal, internal, dense, minimal punctuation, revisionist (corrects errors of fact in "Ithaca"), bodily, quotidian. Joyce makes the reader endure the emotional deadzone of Ithaca to heighten the power of Penelope. This is an act of genius.

Insert example of the use of catechism in the plot of *Ulysses*
Bloom made Molly recite a catechism of potential lovers for his erotic satisfaction.

Compare Bloom's homecoming with that of Odysseus
His pseudo-son (SD) rejects his hearth to wander off alone into the night despite no fixed abode. The suitor (Boylan) has exited safely and arranged his next assignation. His home and bed disclose the fact that his wife has committed adultery. He sleeps upside-down in the foetal position. Odysseus is a beggar who sleeps on the floor of the palace. But he has connected with his son and the suitors are doomed.

List critical reception of "Penelope" in terms of historical periodicity
1920s – Obscenity. 1930–40s – Earth Mother (AKA Goddess). 1950–60s – Amoral Whore [Moll: 1604]. 1970s – Product of Time/Place (gender/history/Marxist theory). 1980s – Feminist (victim of Joyce's patriarchal assumptions). 1990s – *ecriture feminine* (Cixous, Kristeva). Note – Critics of each successive generation have claimed factual insight into Joyce's TRUE intentions that previous analyses failed to identify.

How did Joyce's canonisation as a Modernist genius affect critical perspectives?
Ironically. Pre-genius [1920–40s]: critics were reticent to attack Molly lest collateral damage was done to Joyce's reputation (see Deming's "Odyssey of the sewer"). Post-genius [1950-onwards]: unrestrained belligerence.

Compare Molly with Gaia
Critics idealised Molly as a latter day Gea-Tellus to defend Joyce against accusations of immorality. This also reduced the threat of the sexualised female. Joyce invoked the comparison himself at the end of Ithaca when Molly was presented "cumbersome with seed" in the languid repose of Gea. She possesses x-ray vision, can mimic animals and is also a good literary critic.

Classical Female Referents?
Penelope, Juno, Medb & Morrigan from *Tain Bo Cuailgne* ("Oxen Raid of Cooley").

Molly's literary successor?
Anna Livia Plurabelle (ALP). She represents the 'riverrun' symbol [see I.8 contra

III.3], whose procession opens and closes *F(W)ake* just as Molly Bloom's "Yes" opens and closes Penelope. The reader does not learn much about either character through the course of the text; just snippets of prejudice from third parties. Molly gets to unleash a verbal stream after the Homeric superstructure has been played out. See also Beckett's Molloy/ Moran as heir.

Graph Molly's Exchange/Value System
— Woman: given
— Sex: for trade
— Bloom: soft touch (broken watch penury no coitus unclear relations)
— Boylan: debtor (trip to Belfast gift linen/kimono, etc.).
— In summary, Molly gives physical gifts. In return, she expects bounty.

Insert table with key critical conclusions about Molly Bloom

TABLE 17. MOLLY BLOOM – LITERARY CONCLUSIONS DRAWN AND ASPERSIONS CAST

Bugden	"fruitful mother earth... (her) obscenities of thought... good mothers would warn their sons to have nothing to do with her"
Tindall	"absence of mind... essential being of everywoman ... fundamental and symbolic as her cat"
Gilbert	"the voice of nature herself" & "faithful too – in her fashion" see 389 & 395
Levin	"(her) animal placidity.... teaming... compliant... ripe..."
Blackmur	"necessary to any culture but not at its foundation; she is rather the basic building material: the problem that first and last must be controlled... ploughed, penetrated, seeded like the earth"
Huddlestone	"the vilest whore in all literature"
Leslie	"a very horrible dissection of a very horrible woman's thought"
Unkledes	"Mister Joyce has done the entire nation of England an immense service by accurately depicting the diseased psyche of a whore. Molly is a typical slut of the kind that he would have regularly encountered in Catholic France directly after the War. It should be compulsory reading for all British schoolboys"
Tindall	"the center of natural life"
Joyce	"perfectly sane full amoral fertilisable untrustworthy engaging shrewd limited prudent indifferent Weib. Ich bin der [sic] Fleisch der stets bejaht" (Letters, 1.170)

Richardson	"bitch ... the product of inflamed not healthy nerve ends ... Howling like a bitch in heat ... her destruction will inevitably include Bloom and Stephen" (184)
O'Brien	"she is at heart a thirty-shilling whore"
Morse	"the centre of paralysis ... she is a dirty joke. No one regards her as anything but a whore"
Adams	"a slut ... a frightening venture into the unconsciousness of evil"
Kenner	"Molly's 'Yes' is the 'Yes' of consent that kills the soul ... (with) authority over the animal kingdom of the dead"
Henke	"fluid and feminine, deracinated and polymorphic ... but the contours of her monologue are fearfully phallomorphic, determined by the pervasive presence of a male register of desire"
Bachelard	Boylan more length and girth (Space) / Bloom more voluminous quantity of semen (Water)
Henderson	"the male authorial fist"
Herr	"She is not having a period at all. In fact she is a man"
Derrida	"the beautiful plant, the herb or *pharmakon*"

This interpretation enables Derrida to detach Molly from a single characterisation and let her float freely over the surface of the text like Shelley's interpenetrative dew. First, she is a sensitive plant. Next, a magic herb like Moly. Finally, he describes her as *Pharmakon* – sorceress of ritualistic sacrifice. Derrida first employed this term in *Plato's Pharmacy* when he wanted to tear open all his options. *Pharmakos* was polysemous in Ancient Greek. Its meaning flipped in Plato's dialogues according to his tendencies towards the act of writing. It means both remedy and poison; love potion (*'philtre'*) and medicine; charm and recipe (*Phaedrus*); substance and spell; artificial colour and true paint. In *Phaedo*, Socrates uses hemlock as a purgative; employing *logos* to disclose *eidos* itself. In *Phaedrus*, it becomes both things. Teuth presents writing as a type of a recipe or food that will enhance and enshrine the memory of King Thamus. In reply, the King rebukes Teuth saying that writing is a poison that will destroy his memory. To write an external supplement to internal memory that modifies memory itself; that is the effect of *pharmakos*. The *pharmakon* is thus the space between opponents. Derrida notes that this term becomes so over-determined in Plato's writing that it is like the concept of Signification itself. Actually, Plato never uses the word *pharmakos* directly, preferring to keep it outside his discourse as an oppressive atmos [Plato also chose to shield himself behind Socrates]. It looms through and inside related word-products. It becomes a trace element as well as a trademark. Molly Bloom is seen by Derrida as coiled and coded throughout *Ulysses* until she comes to the fore twisting and spitting like a live wire. She acts as a tool for Boylan for pure physical release. Her proximity to him places Molly within the field of a power that can annihilate her. She is also harmful: a BAD trip. She erases *character* in a certain type of male. She is an anthropomorphising presence – metonymised in a foot; representing bounty; synaesthesised in the fragrance of sweat-stained lingerie. She is associated with a popular brand of poison. Yet she is also presented as the opposite of death. In linguistic terms, she is the *anaphora* which creates anaphoric reactions for other characters and motifs in the text. She inhabits the instant/locus of the flipping point from centrifugal to centripetal force. She is Charybdis. Also Aeolus. She is Styx with Charon accelerated to light speed. She acts as the space/stage where the discrepancies between reader/character (*pharmakoi*) and author (*pharmakon*) are represented and resolved. In this role, she does not select the type of victim (slave, criminal, cripple, child, virgin); the type of drug to be used (*pharmakeia*); the form of sacrifice (burning, stoning, caning, beating with fists, rope torture, piercing with arrows or knives *inter alia*); or even comprehend the reasons why it is all taking place (famine, plague, earthquake, invasion, unnatural practices don't matter). She is the atmosphere of violence and purgation – the ceremony upon which the crisis is played out. She becomes *clou*. A musical hall diva. The star-turn. An actor reprising the monologue which sealed her scandalous reputation. Primed by Boylan all afternoon. Observed by a crowd of chaps as she wades into the ocean. A midnight matinee starring Eleanor Duse.

Why did Joyce abandon drama despite his intense admiration for Ibsen?

See C7. Joyce was driven from drama by the structural, thematic and moral limitations of English theatre in the late nineteenth century (Herr 69). Instead, he turned to prose that was dramatic in tone and form. His characters speak like pantomime figures projecting their voices from stage. Ironically, he made it possible for drama to re-emerge as an innovative form via Samuel Beckett.

Examine Penelope as a precursor to Beckett's prose

Beckett used this episode as a template for *Trilogy*, denuded of Joyce's humanism and the plethora of places, names, devices, neologisms and verbiage that gave energy to *Ulysses*. Joyce's huge life canvas (think Ensor, Brueghel or Bosch) was reduced to minimal allusions and references, reductive content, dense narrative flow, apparent asides, comic motes and isolated characters trapped in space that was both extrinsic and intrinsic at the same time (like Bacon or Duchamp). He is not interested in causality. Beckett thus became Joyce's Antistrophe. If Joyce is like a dead spider then Beckett is the fly caught in his web ... surviving but hardly 'living' ... buzzing persistently ... waning into staccato Morse but never going dead on the other end of the line. *O les faux beaux jours!*

How does Molly characterise her husband?

Leopold Bloom is presented by his wife as a Protean impersonator, imbecile, sex addict, blowhard and fraud.

Compare with Don Cane

Lieutenant Colonel Cane served in the AATTV, Special Forces, Strategic Hamlets program, WHAM, VIS, MATs, Operation Phoenix, Accelerated Pacification Campaign and Vietnamisation. He even did tour time in the National Field Police in 1974. His personal life displayed 60% of the qualities listed in the above classification of Bloom. However, he remains an elusive figure. He resembles John Paul Vann (see *Bright Shining Lie*).

How does Joyce represent menstruation?

Joyce's makes numerous puns on women's periods {INSERT COLON}. Bloodloss. Eggloss. Bloodeggloess. Blogloss. Eggreggrious. Egglessloss. Leggloss. Earthtung. Linguistically, Joyce does away with periods altogether {:;., :;.,- ;.,-:,-:;} inducing textual smooths. He is likely to have been mindful of this irony. A bloody flow is necessary so that Molly can speak freely. Again, this would be a conscious device by Joyce.

Recapitulate the central elements of Molly's monologue

Ba Gua. Wu Gua. A stage. Molly's disembodied voice in darkness. A woman always visualised by others makes herself Visible with words. She is never fully 'seen' in the whole course of *Ulysses*. All we see of her body is a hand reaching out the window to throw coins; recollections of her body by various male characters; and her husband contemplating her somnolent form motionless and face-down with her arse on display like a Pierre Bonnard nude. Immediately objectified. She interrogates Bloom. Catechism within catechism. She speaks from her bed, gazing at the ceiling, proclaiming herself a "wronged woman" like Lucrece. Her monologue passes through a sequence of hackneyed stage sets from Romantic tradition – a picnic at Sugarloaf Mountain; ignoring Bloom as he conceals compromising correspondence under a slab of blotting paper; rifling through the chamber maid's room; walking between her husband and her future lover armthruarum down Sackville Street; warbling "May Moon"; swinging off Nelson's pillar {they blew the fucker up finally, who could have guessed they would erect a statue of Anna Livia in its place}; placed in her boudoir before the obdurate eye of Don's upstanding member at first she was bashful till she got used to the rolling sea then up down the little petlet hops he came 3 or 4 times the last time inside. Boylan is aroused by the sight of Helen's foot in the DBC tea room. Rising from bed, her night garments flutter in the early summer breeze.

Chronological scenes of her early life follow in a limited edition of 12 colour prints by renowned illustrator Kate Greenaway:

1. Thunderbolts in Gibraltar
2. By the Moorish wall
3. Promenading with a handsome British officer
4. Passionately entangled with a young man overlooking Howth
5. Aborting Bloom's first proposal (because he chose the wrong stage set – she was rolling potato cakes in the kitchen at the time)
6. Giggling with Josie uncontrollably
7. Accepting Prince Leopold's second proposal (Yairs ...)
8. At her bath on a fine morning
9. In a costume pink and white as he passed to the door whistling the four note chorus by Jeffers turning the brim of his hat in his fingers
10. Self-cast as the "Wife of Bath"
11. Out by Donnycarney where the bats swing from tree to tree sweet were the words she said
12. Destitute wife leaning out of the upper casement in common Eccles Street ... she eloped with that Liverdublian Jew and became a music hall performer now everybody disrespects her despite being an officer's daughter I have only just begun to bump, bump, bump, just a little bit with a respected impresario after years of career-stalling abstinence.

What moral shibboleths are applied to Molly and critiqued by Joyce?

Victorian obsession with conjugal issues. Popularity of *Measure for Measure*. A dull play. Even ordinary women are capable of adultery with an officer, cad or gardener. Brain fevers. Vapours. Scarli's wife. Step forward and make your confession. Of making Semen Dedalus swoon. Admiring Boylan's prowess. Recollecting Bloom fondly as a flaccid Christopher Sly. A backwards chronicler of romantic adventures. Once engaged to the eldest son of Don Miguel de la Flora. Courted by brave Mulvey latterly dead in the Khurd Kabul Pass with a bullet hole popped through his khaki breast pocket and his testicles stuffed in his lipless mouth. Gardner kissing her goodbye on a canal lock and praising her hue. An Oriental slut. Dressed as a nun in Bloom's pornographic tableau. An idealised nude. Print of a marble sculpture. Subject to a proposal at Howth's Head. In Old Madrid, two glancing eyes a lattice hid ... two eyes as darkly bright as love's own star-summer wind murmuring happily but softer its breath was the kiss she gave.

Why did Joyce choose Gibraltar for Molly's childhood?

Classical and modern analogues. Dante's Ulysses had to navigate the Pillars of Hercules to pass the point between the known world and extrinsic waters. The Pillars are generally considered to have been located at Gibraltar. Likewise, Gibraltar represented a site of British Imperialism against which Irish colonial subjugation could be set. It was a key naval base that enabled Britain to control the entrance to the Mediterranean Sea. Its ability to sustain this small outpost in hostile enemy territory displayed Britain's naval hegemony over Europe – in particular Spain and France. Gibraltar also acted as a centre of British military life. It was a staging post for armies travelling between England and its African, Indian and Asian colonies. Gibraltar was also a racial melting pot where British soldiers and administrators interacted with Spaniards, Africans, Moors, Jews, Arabs, Maltese, Italians, Greeks, Persians and even Russians. Molly represented a specific female identity molded by these colonial, military, ethnic, religious, linguistic and gender inputs.

When does the reader find out that Molly was raised in Gibraltar?

As she hears thunder and feels mnemonic fear (see Vico on the *Giganti*; also the Bible). INSERT REF to post-Lapsarian thunderclap in the opening of *F.Wake* (p.1):

Bababadalgharaghtakamminarronnkonnbronntonnerronntuonnthunntrovarrhouna wnskawntoohoohoordenenthurnuk (101 letters)

Modern Gibraltar?

West Berlin 1985. Shanghai 2008.

Explain

Wild places on the edge pivoting on the cusp between old and new.

(92) Link these places to *Telemachus*

A destination where Tom Hallem and Billy Capri are reunited (see C1). Home of Shanghai Dog (expatriate).

Chronicle Billy's passage to West Berlin

I bailed out of Oxford after 6 months and went down to London for a while. The band-house in Queens Park was the ground floor of a typical two-up, two-down attached terrace. It had a large front bedroom partitioned to accommodate three people on single bunks plus a smaller bedroom for REDACTED. I split the main characters here like Joyce across different facets of myself. Between the bedrooms and the back half of the house was a secondary corridor leading to a side-path. I squashed a piece of foam into this gap and used piles of books to make a shield against traffic flow along the hall. My bedhead was Tex Perkins' apparently empty black suitcase. I opened it once but I will not reveal its contents. This would be the type of list-making that Leopold Bloom relished. REDACTED slept on a beige sofa that lined the back wall of the living room. This meant he had to stay up until the alcohol ran out each night. Despite his moderate appearance, he was well-suited to this task. I quickly got a job as an usher at the Rank Odeon Cinema on Kensington High Street. The manager told me to go to the staff room where George would fit me out with my kit. DESCRIBE RASTA. Other employees on my shift were a sour Mancunian and a jovial Scot. I was provided with a neon blue uniform with richly embroidered gold epaulettes, brass buttons and gold braid around my cuffs. A peaked blue hat made me look like some psychedelic chauffeur. It was fortunate that patrons were rare as each cinema was allocated one usher only, who had to control four entrances. I felt like Odysseus aiming up in some existential play. This theatre specialised in dud movies. Maybe it was a tax dodge. Everyone was dealing drugs. *The Falcon and the Snowman*, *Mean Season*, *Carmen* and *Cotton Club* screened in daily rotation. This is pure fact, not symbolic stuff. I was quickly confronted by the mathematical hopelessness of earning seventy pounds and needing one hundred pounds to survive in London. Besides, it meant working 43 hours per week. I decided to join Tom in Berlin after reading an interview with Nick Cave in the NME. I departed on 12 July 1985. He was staying with Francine on the floor of a painter's studio in Schoenberg. I got a bunk at a hostel in Kreuzberg until they moved into a room in the squats and the studio floor became vacant. He had been unsettled since Ana's death. He didn't know yet about the birth of Rachel. That happened in mid-August. Marion Hackett told him when she arrived. Francine was pregnant by then. End Ithaca now, writes I.

What maritime term is relevant to Tom's situation?

Becalmed. Odysseus on first approach to Ithaca in Book Four. Scope of his situation still crystallising. Final trial yet to come. Hamlet at start of Act 3. In Berlin, he will encounter the Lotus-eaters, Cyclops and Aeolus in that order.

Compare with Billy

Adrift. But still on some kind of course.

In symbolic terms, why are their entrances into Berlin from Paris and London, respectively?

Tom has gone to the historic centre of Modernism in the visual arts. Billy has gone to the historic heart of the English language. Both are disillusioned by this experience. They try to find new models in W. Berlin (Billy = N. Cave, Tom = Kirchner). Neither provide an immediate breakthrough. Tom eventually gives up art. Billy sustains his core belief that writing represents the utmost human endeavour. But he has a very long voyage ahead (30 years – much longer than Odysseus' absence).

Describe Billy in Berlin

Debased Telemachiad. Itineracy equivalent to Stephen Dedalus in Dublin.

Summarise Hallem's outlook

No essential change since C3. Still reactive. If Earth was a human head, he was being pumped from the farthest place back at Time, sailing against history and Empire. This isn't necessarily a trope that ends heroically. See Oedipus, Heracles, Australia et al.

How is the diary format used in literature?

The diary is by necessity presented as autobiographical and intensely personal. It is seen as an intimate journal. A dialogue with self in progressive, chronological form. Diaries can act like a montage to rush narrative forward (see TEAM AMERICA). They operate like an e-pistol. Diaries are always associated with candour, truth, confessions. It was the favoured mode of Saint Paul. They inject a more realistic representation of life into any text, compared to omniscient or third-person narration. Diaries are highly vulnerable to faking due to human gullibility around this axiom. Rousseau's *Confessions* put sex into the diary format as a stock subject. This was wish-fulfilment by a disgusting old man. Logbooks of fucking have been the bane of readers ever since. Mediocre writers fall back on diary entries when they lack requisite narrative skills. Often, diaries chronicle periods of drug abuse. This is always a preface to transcendence. Diaries are associated with place. This is why Pepys is considered the greatest diarist. He became EYES on London. Too much sperm has been spilled in diaries. Baudelaire said the greatest literary adventure of all time would be a diary in which the writer left no facet of humanness, no incident however petty unrecorded. It would include itches, imaginary pains, fake mannerisms, the utter banality of existence and the intellectual limits of its subject, outstripping even Leopold Bloom's relentless plod. Diaries are vulnerable to false narration. Diary entries can easily be undercut by jumbling chronology, mixing entries between different first-person characters and different POVs, making outrageous claims, lies.

Diaries often form part of an epistolary novel, in combination with letters, newspaper clippings, radio broadcasts and, more recently, internet data. Fantasy elements are levied regularly. Tick off another form of literature inserted into this work. One which Joyce did not use in *Ulysses*. He got it out of his system in *PAYM*. MAKE A PLACELESS DIARY. This would denude the form of the geographical and cultural substratum that sprouts meaning. Diaries are not really about people. They are about SPACE. The geometry between the eye, pen and paper make a critical triangle or Trinity. Diaries are always written at desks. No diary should be read as a true list of events as they occur over time [i.e. sequenced FACT] without considering narrative intent. Each diary entry in a writerly text must be imbued with symbolism directly relevant to plot, according to Barthes.

How does the author impose a diary format on the reader?

Via an instruction manual with the injunction: "PLACE OVER EYES FOR THREE-DIMENSIONAL VIEWING."

How is authenticity eroded in diaries?

Sins of omission. Obvious malfunctions. Wilful fabrications. Bloom does not include the cost of the brothel visit in his daily budget at the end of Ithaca, for instance. SEE *GO ASK ALICE*. This was a fake diary written by a religious fanatic to slap down drug use. It is the model for the life times & death of Ana Lafei Pepese.

Why is the diary section inserted into C9, not C10?

C10 returns the narrative to events on the night in question – 6 November 1984 – including the gripping reunion of father, wife and son. It is already written. Like Joyce, I am writing Ithaca after Penelope is finished. Homer took the reader back in time in Book 6 of the *Odyssey* to recapitulate events to date. I am going ahead in 'time.' Proust did that through occasional comments secreted into the textual flow. It conditioned the reader to future plot developments. It removed suspense from the work, refocusing attention on his aesthetic theorising. It is termed Prolepsis.

Insert headings for extracts from Berlin diaries, prior to commencement of Penelope

1. ENTER TOM & FRANCES (PARIS > W. BERLIN)
2. ANGELA'S STUDIO
3. BILLY'S ARRIVAL (LONDON > W. BERLIN)
4. EAST BERLIN
5. BILLY'S 23RD BIRTHDAY PARTY

6. SOLMSTRASSE
7. FRANCINE'S TERMINATION
8. BILLY'S EXIT
9. TEMPORARY RE-UNION WITH F.H.

Link to Homer/Joyce (Telemachiad)

1. N/A. Mulligan & Haines. Telemachus enters Sparta.
2. Nausicaa. Martello Tower. Polyphemus' cave (squatters as Cyclops'). Dido.
3. Enter SD.
4. Alcinous' palace. False sanctuary. Doomed.
5. Circe episode in *Ulysses*.
6. Aeaea. Ostensible friends as swine.
7. Calypso. Sibling betrayal. Telemachus/Telegonus. Inverse of Holles Street.
8. Telemachus leaves Pylos (Odysseus leaves Phaeacia).
9. Gibraltar.

List difficulties associated with this game of correspondences

There are insufficient female equivalents in Joyce. Homer, however, has multiple relevant females. There should be no direct transfer of tropology anyway as both foundation models are now being actively deconstructed.

Insert select diary entries (ref. pastiche)

July 9, 1985: London. Awake, pack, keep myself together. I call mother reverse charges [SYD 9 pm]. Bob answers phone. They have become strangers over the last nine months. McComb comes over. We have tea in Queens Park [DESCRIBE]. I put my suitcase in the taxi. Hysterical. We have travelled so far but not together to the same place. He goes back to Pylos. I go on alone. The bus fills. Dinner at ferry terminal. Boat leaves 11.30 pm. Ten-hour crossing. I watch movies in the Kino Haus feeling seasick: *Performance*, *Tin Drum*, *The Mirror*, *F for Fake*, *Other Side of the Wind*. Each of these films has direct relevance to the plot of this work.

Wed, July 10. Told to meet bus at Deck D, Door 5. Miss bus in bowels. Scour terminal. Find it at exit gates. Almost stranded at Zeebrugge (like Patroclus). Amsterdam 9.30 am. Reach Checkpoint ALPHA at Helmstedt about 2.30 pm. Wait in the car park queue for over an hour. Finally enter the high concrete walls that seal the channel to West Berlin. Stop once at a communist roadhouse so they can fleece us of hard currency for vodka. It takes 3 hours in total to go thru DDR. Billy arrives at 7 pm. Gunter helps organise a hotel [Gotland] in Kreuzberg. His friends drive us there. 60 DM per night. Walk around neighbourhood near Wall [SEE POSTCARD]. Drank vodka in our room.

Thurs, July 11. U-Bahn at Gorlitzer Bnf to Bahnhof Zoo. Get maps and walk to Technical University. Ask random student to translate apartment ads on noticeboard. She happens to be a painter from New Zealand. Later, bump into her again at supermarket. Get her address. Walk to Tiergarden. Look at disappointing Middendorf exhibition (7 paintings, 2 gouaches).

Friday, July 12. Exit Gotland. Student hostel, Meisingerstrasse 10. Taxi costs 16DM. Beds cost 24 DM. Went and did some shopping. Angela offers her studio floor in emergency. Nollenhorf Platz to buy Nick Cave tickets (DEMODOCUS 1). Walk to National Gallerie to see Kirchner's "Potsdamer Platz." I don't want to get suckered into Friedrich's use of light. Or his techniscope sense of space. It's novel for Europeans but we've seen too much of both these sublimating symbols in Australia. Billy and Frances wander off to look at Dix and Hoch. Kollwitz' "Mother with Dead Son" makes a huge impression on us all. None of the German museums has Kiefer. Bizarre. Got to go to Stedelijk in A'dam then. Return to hotel. Get drunk on Wisbier. Walk across car roofs and bonnets. A little late for gig (Metropol). Down back of auditorium. Work our way up front outside fake columns. Post-*Eternity* set. End on Mutiny. Meet English guy, German girl and Jill from Scotland. Francine leaves. Billy soon after.

Sat, 13 July 1985. Artillery blasts when I am standing in the shower. Just my luck, I think, to arrive on the morning the Cold War ends and WWIII starts. Turns out to be Russian planes timing their run to break the sound barrier over West Berlin. Market at Reuter Haus. Walk to Technical University. Almost make it to George Gross Platz. Home listening to BBC World Service: Live Aid Day. This work is a historical arte/fact like *ALRDTP*.

Mon, 15 July 1985. Move to Angela's squat at Eisenacherstrasse 103 with our stuff in stolen shopping trolleys. Staying in her studio with a South African refugee named Winston. We roll up our mattresses each morning and need to stay out until nightfall. I sit in Tiergarten and read the newspaper. US helicopters fly circuits over the park using statues as MARKERS. This is a symbol of occupation. Also confines of plot. Walk along Wall. Climb an observation tower. East German guard motions me to back off (see Pte. Carr).

Tues, 16 Jul. Take Billy to East Berlin first time. Easy passage through Customs.

Frances gets taken into a side-room, searched and asked questions. Walk up Unter den Linden to the Pergamom Museum over canals (see photographs). Looking for our beloved slum areas. Stop at a supermarket in Rosa Luxembourg Strasse. It is full of one brand of each commodity (1 x pickles, wurst, cheese). Coins are made of shit-metal. Fight with Frances. Billy says he'll go and calm her down. Last I see of them that day. Go to Alexanderplatz. Catch tram out of city. High-rise apartment blocks with little evidence of life. Visit a statue of Lenin in Leninplatz. Back to Alexanderplatz. I buy a wide-brimmed felt hat, Czech oil pastels, and some East German flags at the main department store. Half a litre of beer costs 1.15EDM. Walk to Brandenberg Gate. Pass monument to victory over fascism. At 10 pm, I return to W. Berlin. Walk to nightclub area and drink. Wasted 136DMs talking to my mother.

Thurs, 18 July. MY BIRTHDAY. Spent PM in Grunewald Forest overlooking the lake drinking beer. Lost Tom and Frances. Mechanical sex on a bed of soft needles in a channel of tall pines deep in the woods. At 4 pm, we all went to Die Brucke Museum and bought Kirchner postcards. Dinner at Trinity. Frances gives Billy a copy of the *Odyssee* in German. He's never read Homer, he says. Inside, she has marked a significant passage with a posy of small blue flowers. Fine old time drinking and playing pool. Billy poured wine in my ear then overdosed on the toilet. Vision of Michael Deekeling hopping over the cubicle wall to rescue him. Angela disappears. Tom too. Walk home singing feedtime songs. F.

Link to Stephen/Bloom
Angela + Michael = Bloom. She gives shelter to Tom (Calypso, Nausicaa). He rescues Billy.

What does the symbol "F" mean?
Fuck.

Tues, 23 July. Michael leaves. Angela to follow next weekend.

Wed, 24 Jul. Come home to find Angela in tears over hostility of housemates towards us. Bastards waited until Michael was gone. We've got until end of summer vacation to get out. All go to Ex and Pop. Play pool and drink. Come home at 3. F again.

Thurs, 25 July. Go to Steinstucken exclave with Justin and Tim. Billy stays home. S-Bahn Wannsee (end of line) then long walk down forest tracks to B.Beyer-Strasse. Typical tree-lined German avenue. Over 1 km length. Wall both sides. Death strip beyond. Inside island, inside island. W. Berlin. Russian dolls. Note irony of naming. Gunter said turn north at the power box on the dog leg. Pass under rail bridge. End up on Teltowerstrasse. Weird Wall-made dead end. Thick woodlands. You can get right up against the Wall here. Climbed a tree. Took pictures of university. No guards. Go back to Zoo. Billy and Francine meet us at Rowena's (fantastic bar overgrown with foliage in bombed-out building).

Sat, 27 July. Move into A & M's room for 3 weeks. East Berlin. Assemble at Wittenberg Platz fountain. U-Bahn to Hallesches Tor. Walk to Checkpoint Charlie. Smuggle cash in shoes (20 DMs = 100 EDMs). Buy lunch on Unter den Linden. Huhn mit pommes frites. Rubber skin like Blixa's pants. Shitmetal utensils. End up ripping off the casing and eating stringy dry muscle with our hands. OXEN-LIKE. Buy art products on Chausee Allee. Tram to Schonhauser. Walk to Alexanderplatz. Drink beer all afternoon with two East Germans. Billy and Frances go walkabout. Meet at 6 on bridge near Otto Nagel Haus. Go to Fernsehturm (= Nelson's column). Revolving restaurant (LINK C5, S-E1). Massive menu. But they only have mushroom soup and the blue cocktail available. WE just drink. View West Berlin from afar. There are many vantage points in the East from which to view capitalism. Spit plum seeds off the observatory deck. Walk through Linden, drink coffee and go back to passport control. Drink at Swing and Metropol. Frances gets really drunk. We fight. Smashed window. I sleep in the foyer.

Sun, 28 July. Get up and go straight to Parchimer Allee. Billy doesn't want to come. Lunch in backyard. Go to Britz via Friedrichstrasse Interflug. Buy 2 bottles of cheap Pernod. Evade West German Customs. Drink with Tim and Pete in various parks. Pete teaches me how to rip Mercedes symbols out of car hoods. F. Next thing I know I wake up in the sandpit next to our squat with a bottle of Pernod. Can't find lid. Can't remember anything at all. Get inside. Go to bed.

INSERT NOTE – Excised entries for the next 3 weeks as they yielded no fresh data. The patterns of 28 July are largely repeated. This period represents the profligacy of the suitors in the *Odyssey*. Also, Dublin 16 June 1904 on a loop. Sometimes, the chronic alcohol abuse inherent in daily life is lost in the sheer scale of *Ulysses*. It is meant to depict a TYPICAL day in Dublin. The novel is set on a Thursday. So it does not represent a weekend spree. Stephen just happens to be the one with cash to spend on the day in question.

List correspondences between individual daily entries and Homer/Joyce as relevant

9 Jul: Leaving Peisistratus. Note – Stephen Dedalus has NO TRUE FRIENDS in

Ulysses. 10 Jul: Scylla & Charybdis. Also suitors trap. 11 Jul: Nausicaa (A. Dwyer, NZ). 12 Jul: Hades (dead art objects). 13 Jul: Siege of Troy – various (squat, W. Berlin). See also next entry. 15 Jul: Odysseus as beggar. 16 Jul: East Berlin = Penelope (she cannot conceive of freedom). 18 Jul: Aeaea. Bella Cohen's brothel. Molly/Boylan (F). Achilles, Agamemnon and Briseis. East of Eden (Timshel). 24 Jul: Cyclops. 25 Jul: Inside the horse. 27 Jul: Alcinous' palace. 28 Jul: Bow contest. Bloom/Dedalus pissing. 15 Aug: Frances tells Billy she's missed her period by 2 weeks. This isn't a crisis yet. Her menstrual cycle is erratic due to bulimia. 19–26 Aug: various failed Martello's. Odysseus wandering unable to find a safe harbour. 19 Aug – 1 Sep: Billy trying to nest. 26 Aug: A. Naboul = L. Bloom. Solmsstrasse = Eccles Street. 26 Aug: Odysseus/Penelope spend a single, last night together after the shock and excitement of the violence that day. 29 Aug: Enter Goneril. 31 Aug: Enter Martello. Stephen is trapped inside the horse with Mulligan and Haines in the first chapter of *Ulysses*. 9 Sep: Tom makes a last effort to create a home and work. 11 Sep: confession (see Foucalt). 9 Jul – 1 Oct: Billy's Telemachiad. Tom as Alastor. We see different aspects of the possible future of Stephen Dedalus after the end of the novel in the characterisation of the half-brothers.

Mon, 19 Aug. Billy and Francine looked at an apartment at 9 am. Sucks.

Fri, 23 Aug. Billy and Frances find out about a warehouse in Steglitz: sounds too good to be true! Go tomorrow. Walk over to Yorckstrasse, Monumentenstrasse, etc. Ring Mother. Money problems. Call EA. Justin, Tim, me go to Japan Imbiss about 9 pm then KOB. Don't bother seeing band. Drink beer outside. Home to watch Francine's Super-8's of our European adventures.

Sat 24 Aug. Go to Steglitz but it's too far out and not ready until 6 September. Help Uta move into her new flat. Broke. Borrow 100 DM from Tim and go to Kreuzberg 61. Drink, talk, catch late U-Bahn, drink coffee at Metropol. Avoid F.

Sun 25 August. Angela and Michel return tomorrow. We sleep in their bed one last time.

Mon 26 Aug. Steglitz in morning. Pack up Angela and Michel's room. Move things outside. Studio for next couple of nights. Billy on couch. Only hope is Dave moving out of Zeppi's flat. No money. Go to see Tim at Britz. He packs us off to Hermannplatz into Zeppi's squalor. Meet Angela and Michel at Kleistpark. On walk home, we are cornered by a Turkish guy with a knife. I tell Frances to run in English. I go the other way. It confuses the guy. We run for our lives. Make love in the studio for the first time in weeks.

Tues, 27 Aug. Final look at Zweite Hund and there it is! Solmsstrasse, 2 bedroom flat for 3 months for 1500 DM per month. Francine contacts A. Naboul, who gives us 15 mins to get over. Clinch the deal. Contact Tim at Bergmannstrasse with news. Go to Anfall. Meet Dave and Zeppy. Ring Tim again, who invites us over for dinner. Arrive at 6.30 pm. Go back to Anfall for more beers. Arrange to meet Zeppy. U-bahn to Eisenacherstrasse. A metaphor for Odysseus' wanderings. Sneak down to Werner's bedroom to sleep.

Wed, 28 Aug. Collect combined finances of Frances and Justin for bond: $A1200. Exchange rate now 2:1. Was 4:1 when I left Sydney. Meet A. Naboul at 2 pm. He says, "call me Arkadin." Sign contract then go out to celebrate. I buy a powder blue suit at Gneisenauestrasse. Visit cemetery. I finally read the Steinbeck novel Francine gave me for my birthday in May. Move onto Anfall. Meet Tom and F. Very drunk.

Thurs, 29 Aug. Finish E of E. Fucking saga. Eat chicken, rice, salad and beer at Japan Imbiss. Marion Hackett arrives at 11 pm, Zoologischer Garten. She can't wait to tell Tom about Elizabeth's baby. Wow. Tom and I go out drinking. He's OK. He said Marion's installation FALL was really quite good. I expressed surprise after what he wrote about their first encounter. He said, it just goes to show. In fact, her talent was to NOT execute her conceptual framework correctly. In this regard, the text mimics Marcel Proust's *ALRDTP*, in which the Narrator's initial aesthetic verdicts are incessantly updated, overturned or superseded (see La Berma, Bergotte, Venteuil, Elstor, Bloch, Octave et cetera). Home late. Sleep in Barbara's room.

Fri, 30 Aug. Francine sick (7.5 weeks). Ring Arkadin. 11 am: collect key from Mrs. Naboul. Go to Aldi Markt, buy a poppyseed strudel and drink coffee. Walk to Schiesse record store on Mockernstrasse. Buy 3 Johns ("Death of a European"). Back to Eisenacher. Help Angela and Michel cook dinner. Taxi to Solmsstrasse. Tom turns up at 9.30 pm. We go see Peter and Dave at Anfall. Arrange to meet Angela and Michel at Irizico's at 11.30 pm. U-Bahn to Yorckstrasse. See Mick Harvey and Anita Lane. Walk home.

Sat 31 Aug. Solmsstrasse. Buy caffeine implements: filter, coffee, milk, sugar. Hang East German flag off balcony (asked to remove it within 30 minutes ... comply). Take medicine. Go to Eisenacher. Buy frites at Kreuzbergstrasse and eat them in cemetery at Yorckstrasse. Tom buys couch (Odysseus' bed). Get shopping trolleys to cart luggage. Drink beer, go for dinner on Gneiseneaustrasse (Lebanese). Sleep in front room for first time on A. Naboul's mattress.

Sun, 1 Sep. Frances is sick again. Walk to market via Anhalter Bahnhof and Wall. Buy household items: cutlery, plates, pots, bed sheets, toothpaste.

Mon, 9 Sept. Bump into Cushla on Martin Luther Strasse. Exhibition by 65 Australians including Mike Parr and Ken Unsworth. Parr's installation is a chair at an angle in a dark room with charcoal on the floor, grey light and a single drawing covering one wall. Unsworth offers a group of small fans with flying material suspended from the ceiling. Marion has rebuilt FALL. Tom is right. It's OK. Go to Pollock's art shop. Buy 111 DM's worth of Brera Oils (12 tubes and one huge Rowney Georgian White). I don't know why. I'm not working. Also buy double-bed sheet, pillow slips, bottle opener. Make spaghetti with eggplant, mushrooms, tuna and steamed vegies. We go to Ambrosia's and get very drunk. Sylvana. Tom goes off with some German girl. F: 9 weeks. Second time missed. We must tell Tom. Fight. I lie down on the cold ground and refuse to move until she leaves. Entreaties of passers-by. Eventually, a local resident gives me some black coffee and money to get home.

Thurs, 12 Sep. Long walk alone uphill from Bergmanstrasse to Willibald-Alexei Strasse. Sylvana's flat. She talks to her friend in German on the phone while I tongue-fuck her. Angela and Michel come over for dinner. No sign of Tom. Leave to drink at Ambrosia. Drink at Schlemeels.

AUTHOR'S NOTE – there is a gap of almost two weeks from this point in which the diary is blank. Tom Hallem may have visited Dresden during this period (see below).

Tues, 24 Sep. Francine's termination (11 weeks).

Thurs, 26 Sep. Frances sick. Pill working. Hang around flat. Tom ignores us. Sylvana comes over. We could hear them in the next room. Marion comes home. She has sold a new series called EUROPEAN to the Berlinische Galerie. It's a photographic sequence of READ standing stark naked in the middle of a clear summer's day on a bald sandstone ledge overlooking Jamison Valley. He looks so tiny and vulnerable. His pale torso has no hair. It blares at the sun. His skin is starting to burn. Corkscrew mop falling onto his shoulders, matched by long locks of apricot hair coiling around his shrunken penis. He is standing awkwardly, almost like a soldier at attention. His knees are locked. His arms rest by his sides somewhat stiffly. Marion says these images strip the power of technology from European men. They show us impotent and exposed in the Australian bush. Juxtaposed with Read, she has collected a sequence of early Colonial drawings of First Nations warriors. Their painted bodies gleam and shimmer.

Tues, 1 Oct. Exit Berlin. London. Going home.

Explain the symbolism of these last entries

Marion arrives in Europe and enjoys immediate success, whereas Tom has flatlined. She has a new product, tailored to the global market's perceptions about European settlement in Australia. She is not just reselling FALL. Billy Capri is to return home. His position on arrival will be similar to those images of Read. Francine's termination contrasts directly with the birth of Rachel in temporal terms.

Chronicle Billy Capri's activities during the period when Frances Hackett was disclosing her pregnancy to Tom Hallem

Walk down Potsdamerstrasser through Allied Powers Building to Grunewaldstrasse. Buy *Perverted by Language* by The Fall. Note irony of title. Weather clearing (first time in weeks: always overcast or night). Catch U-Bahn at Kleistpark to Karl-Marx Strasse, eat Turkish kebab, go back to Solmsstrasse. Tom gone. Don't remember dinner.

Which sister in *Lear* does Marion Hackett resemble?

Gonerill. She is the creative catalyst. In comparison, Regan has no genuine ideas of her own. She likes to work out methods to increase the intensity of pain inflicted on her victims by other characters rather than commit the actions which cause that pain herself (see Stalin).

What other correspondences to the sisters in *Lear* could a superficial analysis yield?

Elizabeth = Goneril. Marion = Regan. Frances = Cordelia. In fact, Ana = youngest sister.

When did Billy and Frances' affair end?

No formal separation. Billy decided to leave as soon as possible after the termination.

Calculate the emotions of the half-brothers towards W. Berlin in retrospect?

Mixed. See C5, 13. Insert poetical descriptions.

What was the reaction to Tom Hallem's work in Paris? Trace flow-on impact

Polite sycophancy. Absence of Elizabeth noted. Reverse charges call to Sydney (drunk). Funds for fakes will come with Marion, she said. I can't risk a wire transfer. I went onto West Berlin with Francine. No contact from Elizabeth. Limited access to my daughter was granted after lengthy court action upon my return to Australia. Tom Hallem remained despondent about this rerun of his own experience of paternity. Also, add the situation with Billy/F. He accepted the impact of his own behaviour. His main grudge was separation from the Hackett fortune. He joked to Billy at the time that "no friend has ever made a greater sacrifice than you just made for me." Orson Welles also felt betrayed by people all his life. His movies often involve two friends separated by deceit. Their relationship was never close again, although Tom solicited money from his brother during his last months in Melbourne.

Insert examples of Tom's hubris

Tom Hallem derided Julian Schnabel at a civic reception in Paris while the famous American painter sucked on a fat cigar. "You're entrenched in your era. And it's over," he said. He loathed Schnabel's Hemingway pose. Yeats quoted James Joyce thus on their first meeting: "presently he got up to go, and, as he was going out, he said, 'I am twenty. How old are you?' I told him ... He said with a sigh, 'I thought as much. I have met you too late. You are too old'." To be helped, he meant.

Describe Hallem's visit to Dresden

Like Durer visiting Bosch's village, I made no inquiries after Kirchener's various residences between 1906 and 1911, nor visited his training institution (Königliche Technische Hochschule), nor viewed Konigstrasse, nor asked the dotards playing dice in the town square for a few lines of oral history about their childhood before WW1. Their defunct mumblings were of no interest to me, who was making Today's Sound.

What is significant about Kirchner to Hallem?

"Self-portrait as a Soldier" (Berlin, 1915). Its amputated hand is a symbol of Hallem's subsequent blockage. Kirchner wrote in 1906, "Everyone who reproduces, directly and without illusion, whatever he senses the urge to create, belongs to us." This was an ideal of speed-in-realism to which Hallem adhered. Also, Joyce. However, Tom's brother was prone to manic adjustments. None of Kirchner's paintings set in Dresden are located in Dresden today. They were scattered after the Nazis assumed power. Likewise, Tom Hallem (substitute Sydney and Elizabeth, respectively). He relocated to Switzerland in 1917 to kick pill addiction. There is a museum in Davos housing his later works. There is no evidence that Kirchner met Joyce or they knew of each other's art. They are still perhaps the most famous artists to die in Switzerland, along with Meret Oppenheim, Giacometti and Paul Klee.

Kirchner committed suicide in 1938, aged fifty-eight. He shot himself in the right temple. We know that he was right-handed due to "Self-Portrait as Soldier" in which he symbolically amputated his painting hand. He had battled mental health issues for at least 40 years but it was the political situation in Germany that tipped him over the edge (see also V. Woolf). Famous writers who died in Switzerland include Nabokov, Borges, Canetti, Hermann Hesse, Graham Greene, Thomas Mann, Erasmus, and Alistair Maclean. Many stars of the Hollywood silver screen passed peacefully in this neutral realm beginning with the silent era siren, Paulette Godard. Later thespians buried in its moist alpine graves include Charles Chaplin, James Mason, Peter Ustinov, David Niven, Audrey Hepburn and Richard Burton. Many wealthy individuals settled in Switzerland for tax purposes after WWII. If these actors had been available to Joyce in 1917, *Exiles* may have enjoyed a successful production. INSERT CAST LIST FOR *ULYSSES* (David Niven as Bloom, Peter Ustinov as Simon Dedalus, Richard Burton as Stephen et cetera).

Outline Tom's work schedule in Europe?

Occasional oil pastels executed on hotel beds and floors. Seldom use of a desk but when available accepted gratefully. Like Giacometti, I worked small. But I had well and truly stopped by the time we reached Berlin except for some drawings of Frances. She was an exceptional subject. She changed form so many times that in the end I hardly trusted signifiers as a breed. LINK TO PROTEUS.

What information did Hallem receive from Australia during his absence?

Short, formal letters from his mother. Professional correspondence from EA Times Gallery including cheques from official sales. A postcard from Willy (Aug 1985) created out of a B&W photograph of hotels on William Street, Sydney, sealed under bubble wrap. It read: "Dear Bully. Things are crap. It's a fucking ordeal to carry on. I could tell you a million things but why bother. Hope you are enjoying the same fantasm in that funny familiar forgotten feeling: Europe. Give my love to the inmates. See you in October. Lovey love from Mandurah, WA." In the event, Willy did not arrive in Berlin until early 1986, after completing a short prison term. Billy Capri did not write to Tom Hallem after his arrival back in Sydney (in October 1985).

What of Frances … was she 'of' or 'through' the surface as a personality type?

Chimera on the wind not drill-like Oread. Flaming like spewm out of the mouth of Zeus and therefore incapable of heuristic burrowing.

Compare with Rita Hayworth

Barbara Leaming's intimate biography of the famed auteur contains many poignant remarks by Welles about his second wife. There were "terrible, terrible nights," he said, "when she'd fly into rages, break all the furniture and drive suicidally into the Hollywood Hills." This evidence of destructive behavior was affirmed many years later by her daughter with Prince Aly Khan, Princess Yasmin Aga Khan. "I just saw this lovely girl destroying herself," Welles concluded. He couldn't stand feeling like a failure in their marriage. "I admire Yasmin so much," were his final words on the subject. *Citizen Kane* became a mil(l/e) stone around his neck. Rita Hayworth was later recognised as the first high-profile victim of Alzheimer's disease. Conversely, Frances Hackett achieved equilibrium in the 1990s as the release of funds from a family trust enabled her to purchase a waterfront home in Sydney and start a successful business in the events sector. Her sister became a famous figure in the Australian art world.

In general, how did Tom Hallem feel about his relationship with Frances, upon reflection?

He was inured to its upheavals. Like Joyce, he believed that uproar was essential to creativity. Fighting is still a form of epiphany, albeit debased. Returning to normalcy after violence is the equivalent of sensory exhalation after the sublime. Tom even seemed to crave punishment sometimes, especially after hearing about Ana's death and Elizabeth's baby. This propensity became more marked as his aesthetic ingenuity waned.

Insert SUBLIME (adj.) moments

1. One afternoon, Frances beat Tom around the head continuously in a hotel room in Paris (third arrondissement). Finally, there was a knock on the door. Hallem went to open it. In that split second, Frances scuttled under the table so that she appeared like a victim to the concierge and male guests in the doorway. They flung Tom downstairs and onto the pavement. His bag followed. In the instant after their boots ceased contact with his body, he experienced a rush of intense feeling at his utter solitude, meagre possessions, the myriad of people who had passed over this granite gutter in history and the fact it was spring and he was an Australian in Paris.
2. On a visit to Grunewald, lying flat on his back with limbs spread-eagled, and weighted into the autumnal earth by foulest circumstance, Tom Hallem gazed into the sky, recalling the frothing clouds that formed exotic dragons and giants in childhood, then flipped onto his belly on soft pine needles, tasting nature, dirt

acting like braille for his mouth, before rising up onto his elbows and arching his back like the subject of Kirchner's "Liegender Akt vor Spiegel" (1909). Doris Grosse is smoking an opium pipe in Kirchner's image, which owed much to Velasquez, Goya, Manet, et al. Pierre Bonnard produced a similar composition, SIESTA (1900), now housed in the NGV. Its provenance commences with acquisition by the celebrated art dealer, Ambroise Vollard, after which the painting entered the collection of Gertrude and Leo Stein (1905–07), before being exchanged back to Vollard for a work by Renoir. Vollard subsequently sold it to Sir Kenneth Clark, where it was housed in his Surrey estate from 1914 to 1943. LINK TO CRITIQUE OF ART DEALERS & EXPERTS IN "F FOR FAKE." ALSO NOTE 'NO-SIGNATURE' CHARTRES. His household was the model for D.H. Lawrence's Reid family in *Lady Chatterley's Lover*. After Reid's premature death, the painting ended up at the Lefevre Gallery, London, where it was purchased by the Felton Bequest in 1949. There is no evidence that Kirchner saw Bonnard's version, which is one of the superlative erotic images of modern art. The German artist in contrast depicts a misshapen, humpy female in gross streaks of green and orange paint delineated by bright blue borders. Only in the reflection of a large rectangular mirror positioned strategically above the bed is the sensuality of Bonnard's representation reprised.

Describe the end of their relationship

Frances and Tom reunited after Billy left West Berlin. Willy arrived in February 1986. He went to Amsterdam with Tom in spring. It was a good place to be a junky. He stayed in Europe until the early 1990s. Tom went back to Sydney. Eventually, they reunited in Melbourne. This is a good location for a drug addict due to: topography (flat); broad suburban aspect; orderly street grid; low cost of living (compared to Sydney); profusion of high-grade brown heroin from Asia; cultural pre-eminence; and comparatively liberal government policies.

Where was Hallem one year after the events described in this work?

Domiciled in Amsterdam without painting or shelter, scavenging money for hard drugs. When winter started, he got his mother to wire some money and came home.

Outline Billy's route home?

London – Sydney, early October 1985.

Outline Tom's travels?

Berlin – Amsterdam – London – Sydney. Relocated to Melbourne 1992. Dead 1998.

Forms of employment?

Hallem was a taxi driver in Sydney. He cleaned offices. He worked as a kitchenhand at Fingers Gourmet to Go! in Martin Place rail station. In Melbourne, he got a job driving a fork-lift in an import-export warehouse on Gipps Street, Collingwood. He did low-level drug dealing out of the Park Hotel, Abbotsford, to supplement his meagre income. He lived in nearby Vere Street. Bob Dylan spanned the entire geography of the USA in a bold straight line between the Great North-West and a fishing boat outside Delacroix Island, Louisiana, in Verse 2 of "Tangled Up in Blue." In fact, his first-person narrator ends up offshore in Black Bay overshooting the mainland in a clear symbol of his personal trajectory towards suspension in time, loss of chronology and professed intent to get back from the Gulf, like Odysseus returning from Troy. In Australia, Dylan's song would have spanned the desert from Perth to Sydney.

Five years later?

Tom was still working multiple jobs in Melbourne to save money for legal fees in his custody battle with Elizabeth.

Outline the temporal history of *F for Fake*

Welles struggled to get this film made. It adhered to NO KNOWN FILMIC MODE. He made commercials for Paul Masson wine and appeared on television variety shows to raise funds. It turned out to be his last completed project. It took him three years to get a limited release in the USA. Nobody was interested in a treatise which exposed the raw spine of its creator to the audience. It wasn't even a usable length being too long for television and too short for a main feature. This was a deliberate act. Welles himself had moved on by 1973. He was trying to get a new generation of Hollywood directors to help him make *Other Side of the Wind*. They idolised him. His triumphs, trials and evisceration at the hands of the old-time studios only increased his outlaw chic. But they were never real outsiders. They were all quite happy to revert to situation comedies as required. They could never produce work with the profound sense of self-abasement that Orson Welles put on screen in *F for Fake*. They could never have spoken so directly into a camera lens to the audience. They could never present themselves dethroned. Lear was the clear model for Welles in *F for Fake*. He always believed in the innate curiosity of the average onlooker. He never produced work aimed at the lowest common denominator. Orson Welles managed to make *F for Fake* into a unique anti-product, operating on numerous levels of truth and falseness, authenticity and affectation, cliché and pathos, story and auto-story, self-reference and observation, magic and mundanity, austerity and flamboyance, art and sex. But in the end, it was all about HATE. Welles detested both himself and the American film industry. It was his bête noir. He turned his actual body into a reflection of that ... that ... thing. Insert fragments from horror movies. Welles spliced together routine documentary footage, historical film stock, apparently irrelevant artefacts and sublime imagery into a bloated parody and self-parody. He employed ground-breaking editing techniques of piled jump cuts to create a breathless sense of abandonment to speed. Only in the dark central space of a screen for a very confined period was such an output possible. This could never been done in text. SHIFT (SUDDEN).

Analyse Molly's monologue in accordance with the eight-sentence structure of Penelope

Bloom asks for breakfast in bed before going to sleep (Sentence 1). He has not made this request for twenty years. It spurs Molly's memory. Because making breakfast is his job. The reader has already witnessed his detailed attention to Molly's petit déjeuner, as he calls it, at the beginning of Chapter Two. He makes a nice breakfast. I stay warm under the sheets. That's the deal. First, he brings tea. Then food. I like his deportment. He makes a good servant. Boylan would only hold open the door for a lady to get a fistful of her arse. Poldy doesn't even want my meat and potaters. It's been years since we fucked. But I can tell he got some tonight from the smell of cheap lemon-water on his collar, although it could just be a recurrence of his hand-washing ritual. He gets anxious like that. When Billy comes home late, I know if he has been to a brothel. He is freshly showered. His hair is damp. He doesn't smell of beer. Sometimes he goes straight to sleep on the sofa. Or he comes to bed wired. His breath is loose. I hope he hasn't brought back the clap not that it matters we haven't done it for years not even orthodox Samaritan style he's only behaving like most middle-aged men yes it would be an irony I know straight after I've finally done the beast with Sir Longercock but that's life. I am looking forward to fucking with Hugh again (Sentence 3). I am not sure if my husband would be angry or intrigued or both, probably both, he has wanted to prostitute me as a high-class whore for discerning gentlemen for some time always full of money-making schemes it is all his invention I have been a dutiful wife cooped up in this flat while he wanked on my toes, kissed my buttocks, spanked them, disseminated pornographic literature for my enjoyment and edification, sucked on my nipples, used my breast milk to flavour his tea, posed me semi-naked for French postcards, got his eyes down other ladies' garments compulsively (oh excuse me Mrs Purefoy! you've got a mote of dust down your cleavage please allow me the honour of removing it with my lick) and conducted scabrous little affairs while I was out singing. I mean it's not as if I'm another Wife of Bath with five husbands dead and the latest one choking. I kept my dignity while he went mouthing-off all over Dublin. Hugh knows how to handle himself in bed. He's a man of action. He dropped twenty pounds today on the Gold Cup. Not that we have much in common. I am better matched with my husband. Poldy was a beautiful young man. End of Sentence 1. A list of my previous relationships is contained in Sentence 2 (see also Sentence 5 for details of Mulvey). There is an unclosed reference to my mother's identity. Bloom's incredulity is remarked upon. He is flawed as a narrative figure. The watch he gave Molly doesn't work. This is a polysemous metaphor invoking: his hapless acts of generosity; ill-conceived struggles with technology; parsimoniousness; failed attempts to impose temporal regularity on Molly; the periodicity of marriage; Molly's function as a static female as well as her resilience (the watch does not "go" and neither does Molly). I wish he would quit that peripatetic sales job and get something steady in a shop (Penelope/Odysseus allusion). He should also forget all those crazy campaigns for social amelioration (Sentence 3). It might even keep him clear of tramps. "Sparrowfart" was her nickname (See Sentence 5). Molly broke wind as she enunciated the second syllable. Mind-word then deed. That's a type of Metempsychosis. From text to act. Puncturing a veil. I was born in Gibraltar. My mother is apparently dead. Her name was Lunita Laredo. A Jewish apparition. This is a secret I kept from Bloom. That she, me and Milly are the real Jews not him with his bog Christian mother. Another of Joyce's games. He knew that Semitism is a matrilineal set-up. Bloom's mother was the Irish Protestant Ellen Higgins. Her father brought Molly back to Dublin as an adolescent. But she never really mentions him. It's a surprise given his dominance of her childhood. She believes that her daughter will probably remember her as a listless presence. She complains about only getting a postcard from Milly whereas Poldy got a whole letter (Sentence 4). He is an unsound witness. A train rattles past (Sentences 4 > 5). It becomes a streaming mind symbol for cock-thrust > lust > heat > old Gibraltar. Molly remembers her bodice in bud. Also posting letters to herself full of blank scraps of paper. Such a rich, sad and poignant image of isolation and anxiety by Joyce. The opposite of writing. She stutters over the word "precipitancy." This is a device used regularly by the author to symbolise both her educational aspirations and limitations. It also suggests that association with the autodidactic Bloom has broadened her intellectual horizons. You can link it back to the frustrated cravings for knowledge of the Dedalus sisters in Wandering Rocks. I don't know if I will ever make it off this commode what with all the water and blood trickling from my spouts in what do they call them "purls" (Sentence 5) another egg gone their getting tired and poorly made but it's inconvenient for Hugh after all his rigorous planning to meet me Monday down the Ashpit more cash down the drain from his perspective I assume he won't want blood all over his pecker but who knows men are strange creatures he might be overjoyed (Poldy would have liked a look down there for sure) maybe all that intercourse today induced it prematurely he ploughed me four or five times in the muck yes I came precipitately and often who would have thought it I didn't cum at all until I was 22 and that was thanks to dear old Poley we were lying together on the floor in S. Hills with the sun setting across my west window pane as he found the groove with his fingertip and tried and tried until I just gave up it was all too much today the mattress sucked me in until I was glued by the rump so I just let my legs wand open Poldy would have been down on his hands and knees having a good old gander he is the kind of man who always seems to have tweezers handy but he has a delicate touch unlike Boylan it could have been any old slag by the last shot he represents the Physical whereas Poldy is Wit like when he quoted verse and batted his pretty long eyelashes at me like a Spanish beauty (Sentence 7) I could have strapped on a porcelain cock and plundered him with hermeneutical force a 'body' being a metonymy for my lack (Sentence 3) of course it's an item of beauty and a joy forever tra-la-la imagine if I gave young Dedalus a blowjob look up with spunk across my cheeks apostrophising his organ he could drop a cambric kerchief across my eyes like a belly dancer's veil "*sono a posto mi amore*" I tell him wiping the embossed sleeve of my apricot faille morning jacket as I rise to leave the boudoir "*analizaran beber algo mi copioso el fluido seminal*" he replies tenderly it's a pet name I call him *Don Pana* I am Poldy's companion but no longer his flame I am desperate to change this dynamic like Penelope at her loom wishing for a primal YES weaving Leopold's dark locks into a funeral shroud to lay over my face as he lies in our bed resting his dainty feet against my cheek like Rossetti flowers on Dublin's hillside shining under sun glare (my glare) 16 years back he asked and I said YES concisely the whole world knows that now because Joyce turned it into the most famous climax in Modernism passing seed cake from my tongue onto his lips like a mother bird it is my GREATEST memory I don't want to lie here waiting for Billy to come back from Pudong I know he will go straight to Hongkou when he sees I am gone my cell phone will ignite with the picture of a puppy and a song by Rain I will ignore it down the dark disjointed path along the Moorish wall [MULVEY] I know what he will say that they just drank champagne together there was no fun Gu was bleeding I am amazed at his audacity he is very different to a Chinese person we speak readily of errors we fabricate confessions we learn how to calibrate our disclosures but Billy never blinks just LIES I can't be angry with him about it I look my husband right in the eyes and accept his vow while I squeeze my baby's arms how do I end this sentence his flesh gives me strength. I told the priest I still love Donny but he is tired of my contrition. The weary tone of his voice betrays his resignation. We both understand I will keep coming back for absolution. I mean it's not like we've fucked. It's just my love. He instructs me to attend Mass and pray the Stations of the Cross. He gave me a plastic bottle of Holy Water to wash with. I let my husband lie on top. They can hear our mating ritual through the iron partitions. It starts with my hand then my mouth. I encourage him to go quickly. I want another baby fast. Johnny and I have already got our allocated child under the one child policy. I could have had all the babies I wanted with Billy. He would have given me a foreign passport as well but I told him I did not love him this was not a fact but it needed to be said so I did it. He put his head in my lap. I let him touch my raw belly. I was already pregnant, I think. He put his hands under my clothes on the floor. The carpet burned my shoulders. I let him make me cum. But I would not make love. The last time I saw Donny I went back to his house in Pandacan. It was close to his office. The army made it hard to get there after Ninoy's execution to protect the Caltex depot. But they wouldn't stop a woman-so-heavy-with-child. I passed into the blockade like a spectre moving through the stone wall of a ghost city. I entered the compound. His maid sneered. I deserve ridicule. I was not nice to her when I had power. Donny was always the same with all people whatever their terms. We drank coffee. I did not want to go back to Tondo. But I could not stay. I took a little money. Just enough to cover the first few weeks after my son's birth. I made him promise to watch over my child if I died. Then I left. It was hot and wet. He kept paying the rent on my apartment in Hongkou. He left letters in bad pinyin under the door. Johnny would sit on the bed and read them aloud. They made him gleeful. I can understand why. Chinese people endured a century of humiliation at the hands of foreign demons. Billy should have offered more concessions when he still had power. That is the classical code in China. Now I have all the power it is no time for trading. But I don't want to gloat. You should never drag a wounded animal through the courtyard. The place gets infested with bad spirits. It attracts predators. Penelope's suitors remain undead. They circle the walls howling. Someone has to drive them off or they will find a way inside eventually. It's always up to me, thought Penelope. I had to cut Billy fast so I got pregnant. It all happened in one month while he was back in Sydney. I could never leave Shanghai. Billy arrives at my room. He hands me the latest bank statement for my sister's account in Hong Kong. It is a good sum. We stand next to a sculpture of a giant horse in my gallery. The facts spill out of my mouth like loaded dice. I tell Stan all about Leon's illness. He listens. It is an askew moment. Finally, he took a cheque book out of his jacket. He placed it on the table. I watched him fill out the value in words. He etched numbers in the RH box, applied a hasty signature, tore the perforation and drew himself up to his full height. His mouth hovered over my eyes. Once, he was taller. Now, he is stooped. "I can't help Leon," he said. "This is all I can do." I drew the leaf from his grip. Not even our fingers touched. I would have liked to take hold of his palm and run my fingertips across the back of his blotched hand. There was sadness in his gaze but it was not about money he had plenty of that no it was time passing it hit him dully and irrevocably like a cold stat. He walked out of my office while I stood dumbly. I will never confront Les with the facts. I don't need to hurt him. I will see Dick next Monday. He should bring me a small gift. A bronze tripod. Something discreet. *Xenia*. A silver mixing bowl with a gold-plated rim. He'll probably grab a meat pack out of the cold room as he hastens from the shop. He wants me to leave Les. I don't know why. I just need to hold him at bay until he gets bored. We passed the point of fidelity way back. Claymore blew off too much tackle. I didn't care. There was never a shortage of men. Our love feels bigger since Leon got diagnosed. We both know I need a child. We are working in tandem. In an ideal world everyone would assume it's his baby. We are unscrupulous. I hold onto Barry with a frozen grip. I will be a pillar like Gertrude. Les protected me. He never slipped. I will never know what Barry thought. Maybe he had misgivings. I recited the whole tale like a mantra. I even knew where to insert pauses. Effective lies are all about a steadfast voice, watery eyes and some sleight of hand ability. Odysseus had Sinon rehearse his story before he was sent to Troy. He interrogated him. Bullied him. They will try to trick you, he said. Some people will never believe you. You just need to engender enough doubt to distract them. They tortured the VC kid in front of headlights. Hooked him up to a lie detector. Truth serum on his nuts. "What if you don't come," asked Sinon. "We will be there," replied Odysseus coldly. That one inch of wood may as well be a wall. The Trojans are testing its guts. They tap tap tap seeking a dull sound that shows it isn't hollow. Finally, it is wrenched into Athene's temple (WHAT IRONY). Laocoon makes his futile thrust (TRAGEDY). Cassandra starts wailing (TRAGEDY). Billy Capri has gone home with his father (SITCOM). Tom Hallem is wandering the streets of Darlinghurst alone (ROMANCE QUEST). He fled Leer's house like Aeneas absconding from Troy. Priam has been decapitated. He was left to rot on the shore like Pompey's carcass. Head wrenched off its shoulders. Hungry dogs sniffing his trunk. Another nameless corpse unburied. He needs interment so that Charon can bear him to the other side. Just 20 ships escaped at the start of the *Aeneid*. Shanghai Dog sat in the taxi. It reached the Wangpu tunnel. It will emerge in Pudong facing the towers of the financial district in Lujiazui. He told me about Doctor Gu when he was a customer at the shop. She gets him deals. He puts money into a private account. She books a room at the top of the Pudong Hyatt. They drink French champagne. Sometimes they have sex. I am glad to send him sore to her. She will poison him one day. When I miss Donny, I look at my baby's face. I am glad to be rid of pain. No more stillbirths. My husband is a good man. We don't have money. But we are a real family. My son is my cousin's son's half-brother, mused Helen. Note cognitio parody in *Major Barbara*. I took a risk when I left the spa. The money was not so good with Billy. My mother complains. I am sending less home. I said that the old company in Qingpu went broke. Now I work for an Australian business. The salary is lower but there is stuff I can steal and sell. So I will send even more money home soon. I told Billy I needed some cash for my father's cancer treatment. He understood my strategy. Elizabeth looked at Leon. His cough was worse. He ran his teeth over large white blemishes on his tongue. Billy changed the subject. He gave no formal answer. That was very Chinese of him. I withdrew. I don't know if I want to hold out. He only comes back to Sydney in the school holidays. We never touch. He sleeps in the study. He claims it's the time difference. I don't know how much time I've got before he makes the decision for me. We are all waiting on Don's next move. Lucky Sinbad. Seven times wrecked. Seven times rewarded. The timing is tricky. I've got to get rid of Tom as soon as I'm pregnant. Leon could be dead in a year. I met Donny on a pedestrian bridge over Quezon Boulevard in 1978. He was taking pictures of the traffic on Recto Underpass. It just made me laugh to think that a man would take photographs in that place. He smiled back. Took me by the arm. Now I know he was following someone. Did he grasp me like a friend to distract his prey? We went for a walk in Paco Park. We couldn't go on dates. I worked at a night club. Shanghai Dog sat at the bar until I finished then he would go down to the ground level and wait outside the staff entrance in the car park while I changed out of my uniform. Donny didn't like to go down to Ermita because he might be recognised. I know he snuck down to Club21. But he never went to places like the Kangaroo Bar. He avoided my boss. Dennis had 50 cops on the payroll. Donny called them Ticks. I danced in the ring at Dennis' club. Telemachus tightened the wires. Our throats locked. Air was insisted. None came. Truncated birdsong. It was a better job than working as a P40 streetwalker in the hot boxes off M.H. de Pilar. I make ice candy after work. We swap it for barbeque. The rest we sell to neighbours. I make 1 peso per bag. It doesn't sound like much. But Tondo has 65,000 residents per square kilometre. Donny got us an apartment in Sampaloc when I left. But we couldn't afford to stay there. So we moved here. Billy is going overseas in two days. I've got to get sorted. You can't argue with facts. I was more useless than my brothers. I took food from their bowls. My mother wanted to transfer my burden. When I turned eighteen, she took me to a farm beyond the industrial limits of Daqing. It was a bare house surrounded by bare fields. I was strong, she said. She pointed at my legs. "Good open; good closed," she said. The old farmer looked at his marble kitchen floor the whole time. He made no face. His daughter did the talking. She would not pay dowry. I should be free. My mother got angry. She stormed off. I was left standing in front of their television set. A Japanese war series was playing. The daughter waved me away clocking the pavement on high heels. It all stopped when I started sending back money from Shanghai. I went to Manila to help my mother. She got 1 peso for each rice seedling. My father left when I was a kid. I had three brothers with two step-fathers. They all left as well. I became a bar girl. I sent money home. Sometimes I had sex for USD if the sailor was nice. I will surprise them when I come back with Billy. Shanghai Dog will pay a dowry of 88,888 kuai. It's the luckiest amount. My mother will give back 50 per cent if she is satisfied with him. If she does not like him, she will only give 10 per cent back. That is Chinese tradition. She will want to keep as much money as possible. So, I suspect she will not like Billy very much at the start. Penelope was a single mother ostensibly. I would like to meet Elizabeth, she said. This was many years later after Tom died. I was also a single mother. I understand her instincts. I would like to meet my granddaughter as well. Tom was an only child. She's the last one left in our line. I would like to tell Rachel all about her father. He was such a talented man. I closed my eyes and our daughter's adulterated face appears like a tortured rag. Eyes seared open. Frangible. I laid her out in a simple white frock and placed a pretty lace bonnet over her head. It hid her broken form. I stroked sweaty ribbons of black hair from her swollen scalp. A smooth yellow river rock. The priest came. I held her. She struggled. But she was baptised before death. The priest blessed her unfinished body. Arms awkwardly hacked. Wings of a fallen angel. Not clean like Achilles or Hector. No palms to touch or to feel. Her toes scratched at my forearm. She had no air. I wanted to blow life back in her mouth. But I knew that I could not. Donny had seen too much slaughter. He was all closed up. It was the last time we tried to have children. We decided to divorce. We got sick of looking at each other so miserable across the kitchen table. We only shared pain now. She had just eleven days of life. Also Robert Richards, aged three years. Susan Richards, aged two days. Together again. Bloom could not contemplate intercourse with Molly for over ten years (27 November 1893 – 14 May 1904) after the death of Rudy. Beatrice was absent for precisely this period. Penelope waited almost 20 years. Donny is superior to my husband. But my husband is OK. He works. I accept the ghetto. It has always been his home. He hasn't walked in the jungle. I don't like external surroundings. They have no meaning. Only my son counts. And church. Penelope never connected with Telemachus. Never had a good word to say about him. She observed his progress with complete detachment. She held him at a safe distance always. She couldn't solace him. It would have made him a target. She was solely focused on the survival of the State. Tom had to find his own path. She didn't have time. In a keepsake box, she kept the shrivelled apple found in his pocket at Gallipoli. That was another battle near Troy. The phone was still unanswered. Dringdring. Penelope sat unstitching the day's work in her bed chamber late into the night mulling over her son's fate trying not to interfere nor overtly push him closer/away but rather guide him by abeyance in the direction of exiles like Eumaeus and Laertes. Les wasn't a strong presence. But he wasn't absent either. Like shade-cloth. He enabled us to live in piety. In the end, I took Johnny. He's a porter in a four-star hotel at Hongqiao. I am almost thirty. I need a child. I should go back to Shanghai and confront my husband.

There's always a risk in love voyages. My grandmother travelled from the UK to Sydney to get divorced in 1928. She decided to stay here. She came back to get me. Left her fiancée. Uncle John. My grandfather had another child with his mistress while she was travelling back and forth on boats. Leon accepts Tom as the best vessel. He got access to the medical records. Fraught line. But no madness. Johnny wanted to marry my cousin at first. She held him at bay. I never thought about him as an option until I could not wait for Billy any longer. My mother was restless. If Don asks to see his son, I will say YES. I can't deny him. I want him to see Billy. I am proud. I don't want him to meet Tom, her cousin answered. He doesn't deserve it. I can't stop him, of course. But I can make it difficult for him. Every day, I make progress. Every night, I unstitch it all in restless unrestful sleep. Our bed is uncomfortable. I keep moving it around the chamber. It's too big and heavy and too tall like it's still growing. Barry says I'm crazy. That bed base is Penelope's last challenge. Another way to goad Odysseus. She always resets the bar. Les and I lie in bed together not touching. I put a line of pillows down the middle. He turns his wounded hind to the stars. Bill huddles into my back and puts his arm over my trunk. Sometimes he slips it under my nightgown. We doze. Narrative events are always an anti-climax. Our forms weld together. Les whimpers. Darkness is the worst time during war, he said. The enemy always comes on moonless nights. Les groans at a ghost. I lean over the mound of cushions and grasp his shoulder firmly. It stills him. This is a metaphor for time not healing. Donny and I always slept face to face then he left I was alone and heavy with Tom who came forth swaddled on his back I always kept him in my bed as a baby then he got his own bedroom then eventually there was Les. Most time with Les in the end. I took his surname. Chairman Mao wanted to get rid of all lao bai xin. Give everyone a number. I pick up the receiver to ring home again. Girls in China get simple names like SMALL (Xiao). FANG means fragrant. Daedalus means 'cunning worker' in Greek. INSERT ACROSTIC. Nothing is known of him prior to his appearance in the *Iliad*. He designed Ariadne's dancing ground. Penelope knits with a ball of Ariadne's string. My cousin was at the flicks with the other preggos. My parents slept. Don motioned me softly. I went through the back fence. He was waiting in the alcove. He led me to their bedroom. It was unlit like a robber's cave. Sin/bad the sailor. Her impress still marked the worn mattress. I could never regret bearing his child. Barry does his best. But he isn't the one. Like Menelaus to Helen. I would have had children with Bob. But we could not. Billy leaned over one side of the bed and I leaned over the other. His copy of *Ulysses* went bouncing onto the floor spine-upwards pages fanning bookmark disgorged. His course notes spilled over my shoulder bag. Tampons dropped out of my purse. Some nights it feels like a giant limb is growing out of that bed into my spine. I could start spitting vines like Botticelli's Chloris. Don walked towards the corner of the yard in his thongs. He opened his fly. Urine hit dry kikuyu grass. It spat and swirled. LB and SD observe a shooting star while they piss. LB a longer stream; SD higher. Correspondence by variance. This was Joyce's special trick. Don was still firm when he returned. He stood tall. He kneeled between my legs, examined my loins (I froze) and lowered his chest. My breasts parted. The heroines of both the *Odyssey* & *Ulysses* endure long periods of celibacy. He interrogated my body from a prone position. His orgasm was weak, dry and fast. But it made him less separate. Billy took me on Saturday night. I told him about my period in the taxi on the way to Lingyin Temple. He thought I was pregnant. What a sad joke. Molly has just started bleeding in the interval between Boylan's exit and Bloom's return. Both men have merits. Molly walked between them on the street singing a happy song like someone from a Hollywood musical maybe Debbie Reynolds in *SintheR*. We walked to the Xujiahui di tie zhan in silence. Johnny loitered behind. We said goodbye. Billy kissed me on the cheek toppling. I continued down the escalator. Johnny followed. We joined hands forever. I left Billy standing on the street. We were always happy. But I had to break it off. We had no future. Barry secured one leg to the floor with an L-bracket. Bloody great builder's spike, he said. He was one of Bernie Hall's boys sparring with professionals like Sharkey Ramon down the fag end of First Avenue near the Cook's River. Stripped down to his shirt wog-brown and strong. Broken beak. Orson Welles always wore prosthetic noses. Odd surname. A famous island, he said. As if his name was Fiji or something. His family came to Australia between the wars. Contadini, he said. It's a cruise line, I think. Mussolini put a stop to all that. Barry was half Australian. Australian born. What's in an Irishman? Insert Shane McGowan's teeth into the gob of Jonathan Swift. "With a Higgins for his Mam / And a Hegarty gran / you could hardly ever say he weren't Irish." Accordion flourish. Pint slops. Jew to Irish. Irish Jews. Gaebrew. Heblic. My own children are the same mix. O'Connell and Shalom on their maternal side. The latter means 'peace' in Hebrew. Bloom's got more conversions in him than Tony Ward. LB is always defined externally. From Without. Dedalus and Bloom are parallax. Coal lighters careering in circles down the murderous wires where the Jialing Jiang and Chang Jiang merge. *Wollongong* crashed into the Derwent Bridge. SD is brilliant yet dissipated. LB is solid but limited in intellectual scope. Both live in a state of discontent. Stephen has knowledge but not satisfaction. Bloom achieves survival but not grace. They are separated in four respects, according to Bloom in Ithaca – name, age, race, creed. Joyce does not investigate the long-term sustainability of their father-son proxy. It is difficult to avoid the conclusion that they would have fallen out quickly if they tried to progress their surrogate union. Butting-heads like Les and Tom. I am going to leave Matt, thought Ana. Helen made one break with convention. It wasn't a real accident. Donny was worth it. I can see that in retrospect. I am a rebel in my quiet way. I paid the price gladly. It's like Melbourne Cup day really. Everybody makes a big fuss. They run the race. Then it's never mentioned again. LB is a quiet man, mildly persecuted. He is a type of female character. The spiritual cosmos in *Ulysses* revolves around his presence. Without him, there is no narrative drive. Most critics point to his acts as evidence of Joyce's rationalisation of Odysseus to the level of everyday life. But in many respects Bloom is more like Penelope. His wife could be said to display masculine traits such as venality, callousness and pride. In the end, I just wanted Donny to go. I could cope. Dido pretty much runs her own race by the time Aeneas hits Carthage. I had a mixed business opposite the local school. I kept boarders. There was space for Tom's pram behind the counter. I just wanted to wash my hands of the whole fiasco with a bar of lemon-fresh Palmolive soap. I could never purge myself completely. Forget. Or forgive. I feared blanking my own spirit. But I keep it suppressed. You'll see all kinds of things in my compartments. Unused subway platforms loaded with files. A lake that is home to a three-metre eel, according to Scottish legend. Saint James Bell mounted in mid-air simulating the sound of Big Ben. GONG. A telegraphic cable passage runs from the GPO to Newtown. First real graveyard in Sydney. Fragments of the headstone of Elizabeth Steel. Bankstown bunker. Hyrieus' treasure chamber. The Qi Emperor's tomb at Xian is only now being exhumed in all its majesty. Dedalus' labyrinth. Parola Tondo winds alongside the river. You got to move on foot by tweaks through the traffic. It's like a Rubic's Cube. Horns gust. Turn off Herbosa Street. There is an abandoned rail line running right down the centre of the street gathering long puddles where the tracks have been stolen for fuel. Manila's purview. You walk down a side alley weaving through clusters of motor-trikes and pedicabs. Kids play football across your path. Garbage is piled on small abandoned yards guarded by sick dogs. Old men extract nails from timber to get coins. A couple more turns of the maze and Smokey Mountain disappears. You need a guide now. The road keeps narrowing. The hutongs in Beijing got tighter with age. Concrete blocks have been slapped together to make square hovels. They prop-up weaker wooden shacks on all sides. But all these buildings are just the carapace of the real ghetto. It is a tin-capped warren that shoots in all directions like a rhizome. It is always wet-hot in here. Cooking makes it more humid. Nobody is wearing much clothes. All the young girls are pregnant. Everybody has a moist bronze glow except the children. Strokes of slippery filth cover their flesh. The rooms are composed of layers of scraps; heaped. Flip-flops work better than shoes. Our place is down the back of a kind of hall. There are ten rooms in total. Plywood screens give us some privacy. A tall man like Donny would be able to see over the crown of our screen. Prison of a Minotaur. Child of the wooden cow. Pasiphae's hole. Bloom lowered himself into the gutter under the front stairs clumsily, checked under his garments for wounds, forced open the flimsy basement door, dropped inside, lit a candle, removed his boots and went up to the entrance to get Stephen.

Go down Leer's eight step ladder to the maw. Master's chamber. Damp seeped through its rough cheek. Tank Stream trickling across gutters of arched sewer pipes dirtied and choked to dead pools. She lit a candle. Voices in the corridor. Glowing Yellowblock vault. Dates from the Triassic period. You can use road headers with certainty across the entire Cumberland Plain. LB went to the sink to fill a battered kettle. Tap water started its journey from Roundwood Reservoir. Bloom extolled the properties of water: its egalitarianism in seeking gravitational equilibrium; its dominance over human form; its buoyancy beneath sea level; its Protean faculties; its utility as a transport artery. Link to Sydney sandstone. It comes all the way from Broken Hill. Time never gets in its way. You can make buildings out of it. Grind it down for spoil. Use it as construction sand. It is a fine product mixed with cement and water. What choked Juanita. Caliban's rage. It was all over in a split second. Take her to the foundation cut. Heracles' tasks. Make sure the pour takes place before dawn. Financial exchange with the BLF. Morbid slaughter. Hera's doppelganger. A contested field. Odysseus gone wild in the palace. ARVN screeching like cockatoos as they pump Charles' corpse. Waste of good bullets in a man long dead. Makes them feels tough but. Mind always beat form in Joyce. Bloom escapes the Cyclops. He outlasts Boylan. Eventually he evokes uncanny tenderness in Molly. I waited in the recess of Tom's studio beside the low mattress examining a stack of his art school works. A series of black biro heads. Here was the bedrock of his paintings. A sure draftsman. Hippolyte. Unbridled mare. Nemea. Isabel Archer. Brokenin. She chose to be gulled. I was always on the lookout for impostors after Don. He conditioned my thinking. It was hard for a woman back in those days. I called Leon from the payphone. I've got to keep hacking away at the heads. Stan knocked the tip off one of his gold antlers. Met him in the Strand Hotel. Chunky new bracelet on white cotton bed sheets in tattered sunset. *Vitamultin*. He leant across the bed in a navy robe. Lame in his net. I didn't want to escape his generosity. A monthly remittance to my personal account. Occasional trips to the Continent. Rendez-vous in Spain. Awful thunderbolts. Hercules smashing through Atlas Telemon. Erytheia. Celestial spheres bulging over his shoulders. Two eggs no hankie. I'll fetch the apples. Take them back to Eurystheus. Just hold them while I adjust my shoulder pads. *Nec Plus Ultra*. Dante said that Odysseus soon tired of Ithaca. He raised a fleet to venture beyond the Pillars seeking knowledge of the unknown depths but died in a whirlwind at the mountain of Purgatory (*Inferno* 26). Sixty degrees in winter. Hackney carriage. Buying old prints at Beanland Malin. Bristol Hotel. Faded Empire. Just fitted hot water pipes. Twin beds. Sunken mattress. Weight right. Stan wanted to move up The Rock. We slept with the balcony doors open framed by thick vines. Standing against the rails under a canvas awning as a ferry passed Tarifa Lighthouse. Crossing the Strait. Molly hears a jagged steam trumpet and farts. When she was a girl, railways circumnavigated the island. Rubber love letters of Lieutenant Mulvey. Alec Bannon boasting in Burke's pub that he could have had Milly Bloom in Westmeath last week but for no prophylactic. Yes (F.). He plans to buy some condoms during his visit to Dublin. You can't get them out Mullingar way. It's a Taig jack-full of mogs and boggers. They don't like Jackeens. She is only fifteen on the date of the narrative. Bannon suddenly realises that the man standing nearby is her father. Drop a spear on my foot. My period never came. Soon I got morning sickness. I would have done anything to escape. Chiron taking the place of Prometheus. Driven pregnant into dead winter. I felt like hiding in a pot. Barry told me to forget all about it. The world only existed outside our gates. Now Don has put his horse back in the compound. Hit the repeat button. Sydney's Athenian glow. I dumped my body in surf. Tamarama's deep-cut swell pulled me this way then that treading water a rip dragging you south towards Bronte. 1972. Last trip to the stables. Clean out my cash deposit box. Get the gallery in shape. My assistant needs to touch up the whitewash. Go get catalogues from the printer. Pick up a floral bouquet. Catering will be delivered at 5PM. I will brief the critics at six. Bronze beaks. Need to hand-feed them eye fillet. Toxic reviews discouraged. Eat poison dung. The band starts at six-thirty. Hephaestus' rattle. They're coming to set up their instruments at four. Seven members. Geryon's cattle. Don whistled merrily as he strode down the corridor in his BVDs. LB slapped Molly's behind. She laughed but was angry. He opened the back door and ushered me out. He was gone next day. I gave him my girdle lightly. Common labour by night. Hera. A few weeks later, he sent me a note with a Kings Cross postmark. Hiding like Eurystheus in a jar. He was flying to Vietnam tomorrow. Argo. He is still stuck in Hades like overbearing Pirithous. Yellowblock's fire resistance is superior to hard stone like granite. It has withstood temperatures approaching 800 degrees before being plunged into cold water. Pour a bucket over Vulcan's hearth. Steaming shroud. Useful contrivance. Juno chucked Vulcan over the edge of Olympus. Atmospheric pressure of 19 tons. Joyce was obsessed with the rate of a falling object. Thirty-two feet per second. The mutant fell for a day and a night before his body crashed in a swamp. Smashed-up leg like Oedipus. It means Swellfoot in Greek. Snatched from the aquacitial floor by Calypso. Raised by monkeys. Exhibited the communicative patterns of apes. See Burroughs. A fetish for earlobes. Pearl-fondling. Jane Porter. Lawrence and Austen. *The Sexiest Primate*. Directed by Desmond Morris. *Tactile pleasures until now unseen by regular cinema-goers!* Lord Byron limping along the shore. SHIFT TENSE He found an ember in an abandoned fisherman's fire on the beach. Shut it up in a clamshell, he did. Blew iron, gold and silver flakes off its surface. Wendy and Hazel stripping sequins off their rumps under stag lights. Vulcan's slaves. Prometheus at a campfire playing with clay. Enter Neddy with baseball bat. Smash all their icons. Dennis told Donny he would have him executed by a bent cop. But nobody could touch Donny. He was too tight with the crowd at Subic Bay. Helped them get Speed into the Philippines on a glass-bottomed boat. I scored off the bass player in The Gag. I was involved in group sex on occasions. The men shout from the shore: "What-ho! she bumps!" If to one, why not to all? See Adams. Birth of Pan off all my suitors. Donny got me sick in Manila. He could have just left. But he brought penicillin and took me home. Marcos was in his prime. London abortions. A quack knocking you out with Bennies. I was never going to lose Billy that way. We all got Chlamydia. IUD perforations. De-string the bow. I don't know what would have happened without Barry. There weren't places that teenage girls could hide in Sydney in those days. They used to lock us up in Catholic institutions. Work them long hours all summer over boiling coppers hoping they'd abort. They were forced to sign adoption papers straight after birth. There were even stories of girls tied to beds and drugged who never saw their babies the nuns came padding insolently down the hall they said it would be easier that way then the footsteps receding first the carpet in my brother's room then parquetry then boots on a concrete stairwell. Bloom heard the double reverberation of retreating feet (SD) kicking up dirt. Nobody is answering the phone. My son isn't home. Les isn't home. I am not home. What kind of 'home' is it anyway? I am calling every 20 minutes from the motel room. I am not going back to an empty house. I will go back as soon as someone answers. I don't want to be there alone. Not tonight. Molly heard him from bed. She dreamed of his young body. Whisper quotes from Sade in his ear. Sin/bad, the Lay/saw. Tom makes love like he's smashing himself on rocks. It's hard on an ageing frame. I am sore tonight. Insert Masters and Johnson data. Ten thousand cycles. Three hundred thousand eggheads are produced in the female. Six hundred periods until what is technically known in the trade as 'Senility.' I met Billy on Huaihai Zhong Lu. There were sixty girls in the basement each night. We went to the fishbowl in groups of six. The managers mixed different heights, skin tones and shapes. There are six different styles of vagina. I am a butterfly. It is the most coveted. He was my first white client. So much hair made me giggle. This is the 10th day of my cycle. He left me lying on my back with my knees wedged between the garage and the paling fence. Feeble late dew. I lay there gasping for a few seconds. Suffocating. I wanted it done. Entwined in Choko vines and turning from the stars. I felt him pull out urgently. I the host. SD and LB are part of the constellation Gemini. Hung with nightfruit to double-dark obscurity. A thick sticky load slipped down my thigh in a gob. He wiped it off with a crumpled handkerchief. And stood. "Everything's fine," he said. His arm moved as a weak antumbra discarding the crumpled rag. I've got nothing to apologise for. My husband cheated. I was pregnant. My cousin was a foolish girl. It was a bad time. I'm not going to fall back into Donny's trap. I never liked him much anyway. You can't say he was a volatile man because that implies lack of control. He was a solider. Yet he also had a reckless streak. How else could he get into such a mess with Helen. Perhaps it was hubris. He thought nothing could touch him back then. I know he killed coldly. I know he excelled in terms of self-will. I always have one big orgasm then stop. I like to clean-up quickly. Get back to my book. Go to sleep if I can. Otherwise I get up and work. Sometimes it's too intense and I just can't cum. My body is excruciated by touch. It used to make Bill angry. He got better later on. Now I suspect it's just apathy. That's sad. We have shared LIFE together. But the tenderness left. Like Molly and Bloom, we need to hang on and hope it comes back. Once upon a time, everyone got married forever. There was no such thing as divorce. Married couples had whole decades where they didn't get along. They just waited it out like snipers. Eventually, another cycle would come. That's what Vico tells us. It's the philosophical structure accepted by Joyce. Why did he pick that one? I don't know. Maybe he was just a typical Renaissance thinker. Maybe he wanted another great epoch for Ireland to come. Water makes cycles. Sandstone is a one-way slot. Nobody dies in *Ulysses*. Tomorrow never comes. You can churn on the spot without even thinking temporally. But this work is all about progression. Contrast water on sandstone. LOOPOND.

Contrast Bloom and Stephen at closure

There is psychic alignment with Stephen's dream of meeting an Eastern man (Bloom) bearing a melon (crude sexual reference to Molly) through a street of harlots (Nighttown). But their night's actually close in counterpoint. Bloom ends the day as a sexual predator. He is reassured about his self-worth by the illicit letter from Martha as well as what he interprets as highly sexualised encounters with Mrs. Breen, Nurse Callan and Gerty. His marriage to Molly cannot achieve true reconciliation while he finds value in this behaviour. But Bloom has started a journey. He really gets HOME when he kisses Molly's rump at bedtime. It enables him to sleep. Stephen is still awake at this point. Sleep would give him no solace. His nightmare about his mother as a haggard corpse in C1 is the opposite of Bloom's image of fullness here. Likewise, Stephen sees history as a nightmare whereas Bloom's past with Molly induces feelings of tenderness. This resolves the events in the novel positively. The physical facts of daily life can now cede to the realm of the Spiritual. The stage is set for the reconciliation of human desires in Penelope. This is also the apogee of Joyce's technical journey in *Ulysses*. He has made it through all the different styles and tropes in literature to reach something truly original.

What is the meaning of the last three questions?

"With, when and where" correspond to Bloom's basic questions of Molly regarding adultery with HB.

Explain "with?" and "when?"?

Bloom's dream is a childlike recapitulation of variations on the name of the heroic sailor, Sinbad, from BINARY NIGHTS [1,111,101,001 Nights], reworking it in his mind with an infantile joy in language. Sinbad joins other adventurers that Bloom has cited that day including Rip Van Winkle, Enoch Arden and the Wandering Jew. Like Joyce/Bloom, Anonymous/Sinbad was another channel for elements of Homer to be disseminated. The *Odyssey* was translated into Arabic shortly after 800 AD and many of its stories were reused such as the Cyclops (see Voyage 3). Sinbad appeared in *Binary Nights* relatively late (say c18). Bloom's identification with Sinbad becomes a substitute for knowledge of Homer, whom we gather Bloom has never read. Bloom is able to regress from the stark reality of Molly's adultery to a boy's world of tall tales and wild fables, aligned with Joyce's own governing myth for the novel. Some names like Tinbad and Whinbad correspond to a Christmas pantomime produced in Dublin in 1892, which Joyce attended as an eight-year-old child. Perhaps it is also a crew list. Maybe each name corresponds to a character that Bloom has come across that day. They might also relate to different occupations that Bloom has practiced over his lifetime. All this is conjecture. At first, Bloom pairs first letters to make new names out of occupations (i.e. Jinbad the Jailer). These occupations are real (tailor, jailer, whaler). As this technique becomes exhausted, he creates new words for extant trades (nailer/handyman, bailer/farmer-crewman-policeman, mailer/postman). First letters are still paired. Alliteration is still the paramount driver of composition. Finally, the text drifts into rhyming nonsense (e.g. Linbad the Yailer). There appears to be NO PATTERN to the selection of lead consonants: T, J, W, N, F, B, P, M, H, R, D/K, V/Q, L/Y. The cataloguing mania of *Ulysses* is breaking down. The catechism device starts to elicit absurd responses like a computer printer gone wrong. Words seem compelled to utterance without thought, as if the text is now lodged in Foucault's confessional. This is a clear segue to the conglomerative neologisms of *F(W)ake*, which was already absorbing Joyce's thinking as he neared the end of his Modernist classic. Bloom's last character name, Finbad the Failer, definitely alludes to the next work. Bloom's mind is undergoing the journey towards sleep through the last light dreams of consciousness. Some critics argue thus that this is just a simple throwaway with very little meaning. How little such pedagogues know of their ostensible subject! Given Joyce's extreme care with language and interest in the significance of dreams (including Freud), his commitment to making each sound and syllable inscribed on the page resonate with pure and total meaning, in fact MAXIMUM VARIABLES OF CONNOTATION, as in the finest lyric poetry, it is likely that this passage took a VERY LONG TIME TO CONSTRUCT. It is doubtful that Joyce just threw it off like automatic writing. He would never have ended his masterpiece of characterisation of Leopold Bloom thus. He loved pranks, but not this much. It was a highly deliberat(iv)e passage. Bloom's bedtime litany is a parody of the religious catechism that underpins Ithaca. It has also been interpreted as a slide from the mental volition of waking to the involuntary rubbish of sleep. This discourages any projection of dense meaning as per Barthes' Writerly Text. Bloom's thought patterns still reflect the limitations of his character as revealed over the course of 6 November 1904. He is an average man off-centre, possessing enough outsiderness to countenance radical options but ultimately still constrained by a need for conformity. He is more Sinbad the Porter than S-the-S. He aspires to wordsmithery but possesses only secondary linguistic tools like nursery rhymes and pantomime dumbdowns of classical tropes. He lacks the deep content of sustained scholarship that produces genius. He is a quasi-intellectual as his exchange with Stephen Dedalus so amply revealed. Yes, he is the portal to *F(W)ake* but that place of dream-pissery and poseurtry gives to each human the centrifugal sweep and prosenchymer of symbols, tangles and neologisms of a **GOD**. I have no further insight to offer the reader. The question, 'when,' too stumps the literatist. I have trawled the hermanyouticklе catalogue for a satisfactory explanation for this bizarre thirty-five-word riposte. Sinbad, that Asiatic Odysseus, comes to the fore again. Perhaps he is a link to Molly's exotic childhood in Gibraltar. We know that the "dark bed" = Bloom's resting place although it also alludes to the ocean floor, where drowned sailors rest. Joyce then shifts to a linguistic unit describing a "square round an egg." This represents Molly (egg = female fertility symbol) lying in a square bed (like Penelope laid down in Odysseus' olive framed cot). It reprises the imagery of "the quadrature of the circle" cited earlier in Ithaca. This is a direct reference to Dante, who uses a mathematical simile, "like the geometer who fully applies himself / to square the circle," to characterise the last moment of consciousness before Incarnation. Dante rejects logic at this climactic moment, giving way in abandon to "the Love moving the sun." The square also refers to a framing device. It is a picture gone inside-out so that the image fits the perimeter of the circle. Here, we have Joyce definitively aligning his work with Dante post-catharsis in resolution – a clear sign that Joyce considered *Ulysses* 'complete' before the start of Penelope. The "Roc's auk's egg" alludes to Bloom's obsession with easy money but also danger. It is a typical fantasy of escape like a lottery ticket. It helps Bloom get to sleep contentedly at night. Likewise, Tom and Billy use alcohol to erase consciousness. In Sinbad 2, a roc transports him to the valley of diamonds where he steals a massive gem. But in S5, his crew break open a roc's egg for food bringing down devastation upon themselves, another allusion to the Oxen of the Sun incident. Again, this shows that Bloom is aligned with the thinking of the *Odyssey* and thus *Ulysses* but via a secondary source within his limited knowledge base. The reference to an 'auk' remains a mystery. An auk is a smaller, diving bird. It may be an image designed to create a Russian doll effect with eggs. Its migratory pattern across the Atlantic may appeal to Bloom's fantasies of travel and escape. It descends into the sea, a clear contrast to Bloom's repressed landishness. For the sea is always associated with adventure, while land is a continental grind. Joyce now starts to re-run this stream of words in reverse like a palindrome, beginning with the word BED. This is the operative trigger. The sequence of l-units merges into a final, internally balanced and dialectical image at once human and material, personal and immortal, ultimately even religious: Darkinbad the Brightdayler. Like Othello, Sin/bad becomes Darkinbad here. It is a portmanteau word for Boylan-inside-Molly. Against nullity, however, comes the forgiveness of Brightdayler. Dawn will come after sleep. This is a reference to some kind of Jesus. Darkinbad brings light. Adultery has forced Bloom to make a decision. It is a positive one because Bloom is forever an optimist. The resolution of this dialectic is the final synthetic DOT of Ithaca. Critics are split about the end of Ithaca. Some see it as an anti-climax. Others as bigger than the characters. It becomes about language itself. The stilted efforts of Bloom and Stephen to communicate in written Hebrew and Gaelic respectively have already signposted their desire for affiliation, basic disconnect and ultimately the pre-eminence of words. Bloom feels somewhat dejected at the end, suspecting he will be forgotten by Stephen. In fact, this is probably a reasonable conclusion on a basic physical level. Stephen may not remember much about the night given his high level of inebriation. In any case, Joyce's deconstruction of language, of sequence, of conclusion is a failure by any measure.

Examine the symbol at the end of Ithaca

Joyce wanted the very last question in *Ulysses* – WHERE? – to be followed by a large dot or magnified period. He wrote to the French printer thus. When the mark wasn't big enough, he asked for "un point bien visible" and, later reiterated that he wanted, "Ce point doit être plus visible." Ultimately, he got satisfactory dimensions for the first edition. Subsequent editions have repeatedly changed the scale of the dot or deleted it altogether. There is no doubt that this was an elaborate joke. But Joyce often undercut his use of technical forms in this way to reduce the risk of appearing pretentious. There is equally no question that Joyce was also deploying these marks to annex all the prestige of philosophical and mathematical logic to his fictive cause. Gifford (12) argued that *Ulysses* was a gigantic syllogism and that the dot represented QED. This has been a controversial remark. QED stands for *quod erat demonstrandum* ("that which was to be demonstrated") in Latin. It is a bulbous notation placed at the end of mathematical proofs to mark conclusion. But it wasn't introduced until 1950 by Paul Halmos. He claimed to have appropriated the idea from popular magazine articles, where it was a pure design feature known as a TOMBSTONE.

Chronology thus renders this QED tit-bit of Gifford impossible. There are many times in *Ulysses* when the formal structures of logic are cited. There are repeated references to syllogistic features – such as Kinos and O, felix culpa – as well as the use of 'punkt,' the German equivalent of QED, in Stephen's Modernist poem of Shakespeare's will. Gilbert's scheme claims that Aeolus was syllogistic. Which mentions it was the guiding form of that episode. There are numerous orientation maps supporting *Ulysses* both internally like W. Rocks and externally as with Linati's schema. There is a school amongst Homeric critics who believe that the *Odyssey* ended with reconciliation of the married couple in bed (23.296) and that subsequent chapters were bolted-onto the text later. In this interpretation, Joyce acknowledges the real ending of the *Odyssey* before adding his own appendix. Some just perceive it as a simple black hole, even a representation of a vagina. Perhaps it is akin to L. Carroll's rabbit hole in *AinW*. Maybe Bloom is dropping into a netherland. Perhaps the reader is being presented with a place to jump. At least one critic has argued that Bloom dies at the end of Ithaca. The dot represents his last breath. But this is not the end of him. In Penelope, an act of metempsychosis occurs in which Bloom and Molly are fused. Anybody familiar with Joyce's attraction to mysticism would consider it feasible that this theory at least forms PART of Joyce's thinking. He always employed manifold meanings, false leads and dead ends.

How does Joyce definitively break with the *Odyssey*?

Odysseus' homecoming is not sustained by Homer. Joyce leaves Bloom asleep in bed at Eccles Street.

Compare the *Odyssey* and *Ulysses* at closure

Joyce's Penelope episode takes place after Bloom and Molly are reunited at the end of Ithaca. They trade words. Cursory details of the day. Enough to transition the narrative to Molly and stimulate her reverie. They turn away from each other ostensibly to rest. It is an ambiguous denouement. This is quite different to the extended exchange of stories between Odysseus and Penelope after their reunification. The reunited couple lie face-to-face until dawn smiling with pride as they recount tales of cunning stratagems and survival. Joyce leaves Bloom and Molly in exactly the opposite pose, head-to-toe, flipped yet together, passaging entropy. Joyce then goes backwards in time outside place to Molly's reverie of youth. Conversely, the narrative events in the *Odyssey* continue long after the scene in the bed chamber. Homer goes forward to the next day. In fact, the *Odyssey* now assumes the quotidian structure of *Ulysses*. Odysseus and Telemachus travel to Laertes' farm to prepare for a final confrontation with the families of the suitors. Reconciliation on Ithaca follows.

As the final act of the *Odyssey*, it can be seen as a process of resolution. In Classical terminology, as for Shakespeare, stabilising the social order rated well above romance. We like to believe in both eternal love and never-ending hegemony nowadays. The *Odyssey* contains only temporary reunion. It is just another stage. But absolute conclusion will never be seen. That is a sacred termination which must occur beyond the reductive rules of narrative. Not that this means Homer was averse to severance. The *Odyssey* is all about ENDS and LASTS. It sits on a cusp. It presents the belated homecoming of an ageing hero to a fading place in a cosmic tradition that has run out of steam. Its ambience of imminent termination is a progressive revelation of redundancy. For all the myriad texts that succeeded the *Odyssey* – appropriating Homer's characters, symbols, style and events – it is ironic that the first great book is all about the expiration of its own genre. Everything afterwards is belated. We know that Odysseus went on. We just don't know what really happened or even how he died. His future adventures are only insinuated. They will happen in new places across new oceans going west into oblivion / not on a well-known sea going east with a bunch of mates visiting familiar destinations en route to landfall at Troy. Joyce's selection of Gibraltar as the scene of Molly's girlhood is symbolic in that it is precisely the other end of the Classical map to Troy. It makes PLACE head-to-toe between Homer and Joyce like the Blooms. Gibraltar also represents the "last place" – just as Odysseus was the "last hero" – where the mythical Pillars of Hercules pinioned the watery border of the known world. Beyond lay that extrinsic space into which Odysseus must sail after the end of the *Odyssey* to appease Poseidon. It might seem like the perfect hiding place. But it is a never-never. Donny kept spiralling until he found landfall in Manila. S.Dog went back to Hongkou every day. Billy went home. Tom was centrifugal. Virgil tried to kill off Odysseus. Dante also (*Inferno*, Book 26). Dante has Ulysses taunt Virgil with how he continued exploring to gain knowledge of the Unknown. Joyce, Dante, Virgil – in fact, all subsequent readers – have known that the heroes did not really die at the end of the Classical epoch. They were reprised, reconfigured and renamed throughout time drawing fresh impetus from new add-ons, Protean morphs, mergers and circumscriptions. They got dug up like Pater's Denys L'Auxerrois or Heine's Exiles. They were turned to Christian forms. Odysseus had to go somewhere where they'd never seen the sea. That's inland from Perth on NE setting. *Ulysses* ends at this point. Bloom must still commence his final voyage towards reconciliation with Molly. Who is Bloom appeasing? Does Molly equal Poseidon? Or is Bloom perhaps struggling with himself in a diffident manner trying to dredge up some anguish out of Molly's affair with Boylan. But how important is a fuck in itself? Molly has no regrets about copulating with Boylan repeatedly in their marital bed. After all, he presents her with a handsome fruit basket. The reader has seen him staring down the blouse of the shop assistant. But Molly wouldn't care.

She isn't possessive. Now if Poldy had been caught in a similar posture it would be a different matter entirely. Isn't that really 'love' then? Feeling enough pride to be damaged by indiscretions no matter how bland. The aegis of Athene was suspended over the palace. It emboldened Odysseus. Telemachus waited within. I, his wife, also. I suspected his presence. Soon we would be reunited. Everything else was minor. My eyes looked up from the redundant loom. Athene's majesty shone into my casement through the vine branches, projecting an anamorphic stamp of Medusa's scarified face across the marble floor of our bedroom all the way to the thick-coiled olive trunk of our marriage bed. O symbol of Athene shine upon this symbol of Ithaca! Prophetic image: a smashed skull. Holbein's Ambassadors. INSERT ELIZABETH. The beggar smashed Irus to the floor with one fell blow and propped his body in the doorway. Then he sat amongst the suitors partaking of the capran paunch and loaves. He warned Amphinomus. He was the mildest of the suitors. The son of Nisos of Megara rose and wandered about the room dejectedly. But he did not exit. It was Telemachus who finally slew him. Ironically, it was Amphinomus who stopped the other suitors murdering Telemachus twice. I passed him as I entered the room. He caught my unwashed eye – red inside hollow cheekbones – and resumed his soft seat. Athene had endowed my form to the astonishment of the suitors. Their passion rose. I lambasted Telemachus as a matter of course. I solicited gifts. We removed more jewelry to my apartment. NARRATOR: I did not return. I could only hear the revelry coming from the dining hall. Later, the serving-maids arrived. They had been sent away by the vagrant. Even Melantho came chastened. Women in this chapter crowd the exit of the text. They escape like refugees. It was at this point in Book 18 (p.250) that Ctesippus of Same mocked the authority of Telemachus by hurling a gnawed cow's foot at Odysseus. The batsman rocked back to evade a steepling bouncer from the fiery Thiakian. This act kickstarted the endgame of the *Odyssey*. Notably, it is Telemachus who makes the FIRST THREAT, not Odysseus. He threatens Ctesippis. This signals his advent to power over his homeland. Antinous curses their failure not to murder Telemachus at Asteris. Athena beguiles them. They start to laugh hysterically. Tears overflow their eyes. Food goes foul. Theoclymenus forecasts doom. The walls become dank with blood. Ghosts invade the halls. An eclipse douses the sun. Brown mist hovers over the scene. Primordeal Erebus coats the whole scene with dearth. The audience tenses. Thoughts turned to utter desolation. Theoclymenus is the last one to leave. The doors are bolted from outside. The suitors cannot arm the tense bow. Everything is strung as tight as an Aeschylean tragedy. There is no more reverting to a chorus for plotlines. The beggar fires. A target splits. The contest concludes in confusion. Odysseus seizes the stage. This is a metaphor for all kinds of performance. He scattered arrows from his quiver like so much straw. This is the same technique he used against the Trojans. Pick and fire. Poisoned arrows of Philoctetes. Napalm barbs. A rotten foot stomping hard. The mob baulked. Antinous brought the gold cup towards his lips. Stephen's rage against mean-hearted Mulligan. Willy's sharps. Link back to Leer's lounge room (C8). The first arrow shot out of his neck like a bolt. His body stumbled into the sideboard. Air, words, wine and blood spurted from his wounds against the whitewashed wall. Blowhard Eurymachus deprived of all his fine rhetoric by a swift stroke to the chest. It tore between his ribs and opened his liver. He is the equivalent of Hugh Boylan. His mockingbird song could never match my husband. The wood in LB's desk let out a crack. Kill count rising. Athena made Penelope sleep through it all. I walked to the entrance and lit a cigarette. The gallery was packed with revellers. A whorl of sophistication. My assistant was plying Stanley Welles with champagne in front of a group work called Exquisite Corpse. Tom Hallem had drawn a flayed arm running off Matt Supplejack's Head of Ana. Stan was listening to a diatribe from Meaghan Morris. His flute began tilting. Wine topped the brim. He straightened alert suddenly. I looked downhill. Tom Hallem was crossing the Burton Street overpass. Bright light on pale concrete. Background, St Vincent's Hospital. He was about to start the slow ascent up Macdonald Street. I looked away. A shooting star descended over Kings Cross (north). Just a mote made bright briefly. Humanspeckinhistory. LB and SD finished pissing in the backyard. One accepting, the other rejecting this phenomenon as a symbol. Torchlight illuminated the underground station box. Don rolled off Helen McFadden leaving her broad belly exposed. Starscreen pinned onto the sea-top around an overloaded fishing boat. Startrail suddenly gone. Ephemerality as in Ibsen. SD disappeared into darkness in its wake. So many different metaphors crowd this simple act. Joyce probably intended Stephen to pass into the future ambiguously. His exchange with Bloom had served its purpose. He was going to find his father's latest rental. This was an unstated but defining disjuncture when set against Odysseus reclaiming his palace. There wasn't much time left in Dublin. Joyce had already met Nora Barnacle on this date: 16 June 1904. They left in October. Tom Hallem mounted the steps. His back crunched. I recognised his swollen gait. He was trying to relieve pressure on his right hip. He got closer. He looked up. Our eyes met. He smiled. It is a hard task to betray him. I look awry. Stan's cheque is pressed against my breast plate. Safer harbour. The baby will be born before Tom gets back from Paris. If he comes back at all. He might get a show and stay. I have organised a great set of introductions including Daniel Templon, Lavignes-Bastille and Studio Cannaviello in Milan. I want my son to have a more fortunate life. I am already putting money away for his education. I might go overseas to work as a maid. He can live with my mother back on the island. There are many jobs in Singapore. They give you a small room outside the apartment next to the fire stairs. There is no air conditioning. You cook, clean and get the kids from school. Sunday is a holiday.

It is not so different to Tondo really. We all start at church. Sacred Heart on Tank Road is supposed to be good. Some women baby-sit to make extra money. Others clean. The rest go to Orchard Road. They eat cheap food in the cellar of Far East Plaza. It's a magnet for Western men. Don left me pregnant to bursting and my poor cousin in the first trimester. She was seventeen. He would have gone to jail if my uncle had his way. Helen confronted her son's gaze. He was sitting at the dining table. Barry was making tea. LB made cocoa in a similar situation. O went to the refrigerator. Inside, there was a fresh casserole in a ceramic dish covered with foil. There was a card on top. It was Billy's hand-writing. "I made stew," it said. "Please return the dish to mum." Tom observed Elizabeth's profile in the sharp spotlight highlighting the gallery nameplate. Heracles catches a glimpse of Hera before she fled. *Eminence grise*. I took another swig of Tequila. Jupiter fell. Prometheus descended. Tom is like Milton's Satan. He is still notable in decline. An American friend cycling down Jiangning Road near the Jade Buddha Temple saw Billy embracing a Chinese girl. He must have thought it was safe on the north side of Shanghai. His secret bedpost. I didn't confront him. I just made my own plans. I had used up my sabbatical. The kids hated China. It was an easy decision to make. I had to move on. Donny didn't have the ability to make children. He started to talk about Sydney as if it was still a real place. Not some abandoned palace overgrown with vines. A deserted courtyard. Best cattle all consumed. Fields fallow. Odysseus waned in his allegiance to Calypso over time. First it was great. Then it was OK. There were always the kids to consider. Two boys – Nausithous and Nausinous. But, in the end, it was time to go home. In summary, I went out with Billy. He went overseas. I took over the lease on his apartment. We lost touch. I went to Oxford. He was long gone by the time I got there. Nobody recalled him. I came back and got a post at a regional university. He was hanging around Sydney. We saw each other sometimes. He got a government job. He was the world's best clerk. We got back together. Tom died. We got married. Promotions came quickly. He chased wealth. His logic was sound. If he made a lot of money then he could stop and write. He had a lot of crazy schemes to get rich quick like Leopold Bloom. We went overseas. He was always hustling. But he never quite closed that big deal. He hated this existence. I accepted his latent rage. It was the price he extracted for having a family. They use the word "estranged" to describe our current state. It's a polite term like "job seeker." I don't know if Billy can ever come back to Sydney and settle down again. He might disappear in the end like his father. I just go on like one of those Victorian heroines by Hardy or James who accepts cold penury. We know that Joyce liked to dredge up the vain prospect of reunion at the end of his novels by reaffirming the basic congruence of his mawkish characters. In that he was somewhat influenced by Pater. Ever the optimist. I guess he couldn't liberate his country without the yin/yang mattress layout of Molly and Bloom at closure like

Ulster and Eire sleeping late until the bells pealed eleven and the riddle of Stephen's mother wafted past their drawn casement into Howth's litmus sky over peat-blue sea, blotchy green scales peeling off the sandstone bark of the island stretching couchant west to the eastpoint stack of its Martello full-stop like Ithaca-in-a-bottle it was first named for the goddess Eria then the Vikings misnamed it Ey which the locals rebadged with a wink as a pun three-masted memories bearing the cracked looking-glass lens of James Joyce that Galylic Oedipus poisoned with arsenic in his earhole and tripping on wild phosphorous sparklers back in time from kismetkate Hollyhead to Dublins-past past Trieste-Zurich-Paris to the swampy, slate VD pupil of Ireland's Fucking Eye INSERT BIG 'O' HOLE FONT SIZE

72

10.
Gibraltar

"And that is where the old tales come to an end, for Odysseus was really the last of the heroes. There were no stories about Telemachus or his children ..."

– **Unknown**

Riverrunonyellabrickspissspeckswornndownendrainedouterbrokenilsilverslewsendsludunder Wiljalicountryon Birrahgnooloosfluddleechingterramotesseverndunderendedmillingearsbrake thrule Barkindji Barindji Wiradjuri Dharug and Eora lendsies all-the-LBJ twowars the lennylowerlands of the coast-is-clear wear Flip's Pieredmount-Sexcolony broek against Parsific seeklifts in supple rinds of corroded stone hewn into locks and scarbrous foundnations by Sinney's convict re-fuse.

Why commence Gibraltar with a stylistic reference to *F(W)ake*?

Because we have now passed the endpoint of *Ulysses*. The Classical period has closed. This is the last (male) novel. The last (white) one. See epigraph.

What is the significance of the date on which this work is set?

We have selected a single day when everything changed. The first cog shifted in a huge industrial clock. It was not recognised at the time. But with the benefit of hindsight, it is indisputable that the world was different after this date (insert proof list of cultural, demographic, gender and economic factors).

How is time used?

Not arbitrarily. Like Snakes and Ladders (link to Mallarme's dice-roll & Proust). To turn back and churn the smooth temporal flow of text as symbolised by the River Liffey. As AC against Joyce's DC. Like a transformer functioning with manual calibration (25–60 HZ) between Berlin and Shanghai, the brothers, their father, other characters, Homer and Joyce, Joyce and Virgil (look ahead), him and Proust, Joyce's time period and TMAC, Sydney 1984 and NOW.

Compare indigenous notions of time with Western thinking.

TIME is a long non-unit for First Nations people, not the sizzling shot-fuse "nuk!" (INSERT SOUNDBITE) of our ontology.

Relate time to motion by natural elements in both works.

Water has fast passage, stone extremely slow. One is linear, the other of evolution. Indigenous mythology has a much more sophisticated understanding of the TRUE EXTENT OF TIME. This is mimicked by Yellowblock's seepage towards Sydney Cove. It is ironic that Western science should laud its discovery of earth's antiquity when it was already embedded in the creation myths of most first peoples.

How do you characterise this work?
As DIY. As an Indi 45.

Would this work stand on its own merits as a plot?
Yes. It's a ripping yarn.

Compare Homer with conventional fiction.

There'll always be a place for stories. They tell the tale of human civilisation. But Homer was also a supreme technician. Each image, every plot element was fully integrated into a myth and brimming with symbolism and meaning. There was no wastage.

Was *Ulysses* meant to be bright reading?

Only for readers interested in technical marvels. Its plot is insubstantial stripped of Joyce's pyrotechnics. But that was really its point: to present a demotic storyline in hieratic style. It became synonymous with greatness-as-impermeability. Its legacy has haunted the written word. All subsequent texts have been conditioned by it. Even Joyce himself was held in its thrall [see *F(W)ake*].

What was Joyce's media strategy?

Ulysses was designed to attract mainstream print coverage with its gimmicks and graphic content, even if it remained largely unread by the general public. There is a strong argument that Joyce produced increasingly salacious text as each new episode published in *The Little Review* was attacked, banned and confiscated. Bob Capri cut the headlights, laboured onto the driveway slab and came to a halt. A ship docked. Two men left the car with a sports bag in each hand and walked back to the footpath. The street was deserted. Bob stopped to drag an empty garbage bin off the verge; scraping it over worn concrete (see C3). A blank land but safe. *Mons Calpe*. Canto 26. Odysseus in utmost hell. They proceeded through a cyclone-wire gate. Bob waited until his son (insert inverted commas now) had passed and shut a border on the outside world. The stark alley resonated under their soles. Barry pressed a finger against thin lips gesturing at the lodger's unlit transom. Billy nodded. Tranh was a foul sleeper. They opened a tall mesh postern. A black dog emerged from her kennel. "Down Empty," Bob growled. She circled then submitted. He patted her pink gut. Kitchen lamps still glowed. Billy looked through the casement. Dishes and pans were stacked on a freckled concrete bench. A bucket in the sink collected grey water. Habits of thrift. Never know when the Spanish will turn off the taps. Bloom dropped through the hatch down the front of 7 Eccles Street. Helen was seated at the dining table unstitching a Fair Isle Vest. She'd miscalculated a row of its complex pattern. Shadows roused her. Bob bundled Billy up the steps. They entered the laundry. Helen locked the door behind them. She touched her son on both arms and lingered, not able to hug. Shanghai Dog exited a taxi at Jiangsu Lu. He was about to assume the plot mantle of Odysseus. The Telemachiad is a cold cracked ember, black as death. It may be years until he found his way back. And then what? He was carrying a shopping bag containing a bottle of Henschke Hill of Grace (1992), a 250-gram jar of Manuka Honey (UMF 18+), some duty-free French perfume in a box (Flower by Kenzo) and a Hermes Kelly 32 cm handbag, etoupe brown, togo leather (2006 – certified). He hoped it constituted sufficient *xenia*. He entered Starbucks and asked the waitress for a double-shot espresso and a glass of warm water. I must marry Doctor Gu, he thought. He only held one trump card: the gift of progeny. A foreign trophy. Why Circe loved Odysseus. What made Calypso hold him from home. He doused the coffee in sugar satchels and popped a teardrop-shaped Cialis. Sweet syrup slipped towards the rim. He extracted a fake Mont Blanc pen from his coat and ground a SWOT box into a recycled serviette.

Table 18. Shanghai Dog's SWOT analysis – Remarriage

STRENGTHS	**WEAKNESSES**
Stay in China Comfort Status as the father	Loveless Sperm bank Lose contact with kids (Sydney)
OPPORTUNITIES	**THREATS**
Business (*guanxi*) No need to work anymore Political connections	Disposable Government (fubai)

Shanghai Dog weighted each square in turn. S = 35 per cent. W25. O30. T10. He had built this kind of matrix many times for M&As. Most of the items in STRENGTHS and OPPORTUNITIES corresponded to Tom Hallem's status in West Berlin if Frances had not terminated her pregnancy. There was a much lower risk rating on WEAKNESSES and THREATS. This was predicated on a neutral reaction by his wife. It should have toughened his decision-making process (S & W represent internal assessments). But Shanghai Dog felt utterly conflicted like Leopold Bloom. Extrinsic like Stephen Dedalus

(O & T deal with external factors). Marriage to Gu would probably rank AMBER in a traffic-light system. He only needed a few cursory mitigation strategies to turn it GREEN in the post-treatment column. Gu's money should smooth over the cracks. Residual risk of this project was thus LOW. He tried to suppress any moral sentiment. To sacrifice virtue to convenience, as Doctor Johnson complained. To commit an uncon(scion)able act. Show forged papers. Fakes. Misaligned motives. Link to Gerty MacDowell. Mother. My own first cousin did me betray. Shredded Ginger thrusting out her straits. Bold Elizabeth passing through Sydney Heads. Between which oars glide. Judy. He accepted her exit with Johnny now. He was a younger man. A local. I lied. It was only fair she lied back. Put a bullet in an old horse. Polyphemus was a rejected lover. He wooed the sea nymph, Galateia, with song. Insert rousing chorus of "Croppy Boy" led by Simon Dedalus at the Ormond Hotel. Bloom's outsider status is affirmed in this scene. He cannot participate in their drunk sentimental karaoke. His wife is a singer. But he remains mute. It is a critical component of their yin-yang. This traditional Irish ballad recounts the tale of a young rebel who visits church on his way to battle. A cloaked figure hears his confession. He assumes it is a priest. In fact, it is a British soldier who has taken refuge in Catholic skin. He reveals himself and arrests the insurgent, who is subsequently executed This is an apt metaphor for all Anglo-Irish exchanges. It is the perfect song selection by Joyce. It turns an apparently minor moment in the novel involving the debased Simon Dedalus into a secret climax working on multiple levels. Link to Stephen's encounter with Private Carr (reductive parody). For there are always more counterfeit personas that can be manufactured. Always more messages in *Ulysses* about the risk of disclosure. Bloom would have turned this lyric to his own circumstances. That truth-telling leads to death. Candour is the enemy of man. Bloom is lucky. Molly doesn't pry into his affairs. She has the opposite temperament to her husband. O never reads my text messages. She isn't suspicious by nature. She accepts Billy as he is. When Polyphemus discovered Galateia with Acis, he crushed the boy with a rock. This is symbolised by The Citizen's projectile in C2. Polyphemus is represented in a sympathetic light by Theocritus. The reaction of the other cyclopes to his injury demonstrates what happens when commonweal is debased. Mao destroyed the social compact in China. Graft has dominated since Gei Ge Kai Feng. For one bare Guinea, he sold my life. Cancel out bad with good; death with life etcetera. I have to scratch so many times on the left so many times on the right making sure that everything is done in multiples of three (Trinity). Isosceles triangles. Tom/Billy/Don. Billy Bob Helen. Helen Penelope Don. JUDY and O. Me. She gave me every chance. Maybe it was just bad timing. An unlucky air-shot killed Achilles. Loss of an eye to a glass shard. *Mingnian*, I told her. NEXT YEAR. *Ruo guo wo de gong zuo hai hao*. IF WORK IS STILL OK. *Yi hou wo de tai tai likai Zhong Guo*. Another qualification. *Rang hou women shang liang ... bao bei*. THEN WE CAN DISCUSS ... (pause) BABIES. My Mandarin got worse as I prevaricated. *Zuihou women xuyao qian*. We would need money. Plenty of that stuff wrapped-up in a five-pound note. A nursery-rhyme my mother read. Large format edition. Comfort lost long ago. Now I am master of my own ship, thought Shanghai Dog. Note Joyce's three-master at the end of Chapter One. *Xian* > *rang hou* > *zuihou*. First > then > lastly. Logical progression. *Zhong wen you luo ji*. No endpoint but. Never say anything final. Lam chopping at his palm. Add *keneng*. It means MAYBE. Not yes, neither no. Customised equivocation. Contrast this epistemological approach with *Ulysses*. Molly's famous YES at closure. The *Odyssey* ends on affirmation after the appearance of AEGIS. Even Beckett concludes with the invocation: GO ON. Athene's goatskin shield. The heroic individual was dominant all the way to Modernism. WE NEED TO LEARN TO LET THE WORLD CONTINUE WITHOUT US. Pater's Dionysus what disappeared come back and got slaughtered. "OK Billy," Zhu Di said. That was all. When I went home at Christmas, she got pregnant. No time for niceties. Damp Shanghai afternoons so cold and clammy. She barred our apartment door. Some whispering was heard inside the compound. Insert mundane transactions to preserve dignity. I will pay the rent and electricity until the end of the lease term, I said. Leave the bond. Inferred chivalry. Scouring the bars on Hengshan Lu for a sub. Indignant texts from the fish bowl at the Shanghai Hotel. They moved back to Pudong to escape my ... ministrations. Judy blocked my number. I borrowed Xiao Fang's cell phone. Johnny took the hand set off his wife and yelled down the line in good English. CUT. It was the last time we spoke. Her daughter is six months old now. Dawn extends rosin claws. Odysseus gazing overboard into sea brine bubbling with silky scales. Just out of reach. Dashed visions of homecoming. Aeolus' gusts. Find a safe place fast. Even a sequel on Aeaea. Too much time has passed. An empty sack. Richie's baby. IR8. Chaim. Death of Astyanax. Swollen woodsalt. Fuck a gem-like flame into being. Old mongrel pushing a pram through Mandarine City. That is what I am NOT going to become, thought Billy. As if Faust could marry Juliet. Or Bloom and Gerty. Odysseus reclining on a tree-anchor back on Ithaca. Sisyphus shining his rock. Contingent harmony. Hephaestus' chains. To go on NOT passively. To NEVER be reconciled. ALWAYS PURSUING. TAKING RISKS. That is Odysseus' GEIST. He represents an ideal of masculinity placed in an everyman setting by James Joyce. Shanghai Dog unfolded a leaden FAX sheet and scanned the shattered print. It was a list of refrigerant gases from Gansu Brilliant Industry Products in Lanzhou City. All mumbo-jumbo to me. He took out his Blackberry handset. Battery half-dead. Cockweight in his palm. He typed the first gas on the list into the search engine. R11. Slow bar shunting. So, this was life after the GFC. Like Rome in 1000 AD. No institutions left standing. Classical period DONE. Live by your wits trading. Belated like Odysseus. Washwake. Last Exit.

Tralala. Aeneas sets off from the blazing ruins of Troy. Everything is reductive. Wires stripped bare. Only a charred skeleton left of the true machine. "Do you know *The Odyssey*?" asked Paul Javal. "Yes," replied his wife (B. Bardot). "It's that story about the guy who's always travelling." Shanghai Dog swallowed the scratched screen. The barista was reheating milk distractedly. It bubbled into steam on its journey towards atmos. The television displayed footage of an open truck hanging off an elevated overpass spilling freon cylinders onto a local road below. Exposed steel rods bent like broken mantis limbs. A concrete slab turned on its side like a dead animal. *China Daily* has denied any fatalities. The Blackberry started downloading results. "Some scaling models back at the Wayward Machine," it read. A term outside the bounds of any Chinese search engine. A kind of extrinsic space. Gibraltar's portal breached. Unknown waters. Coal lighters spiralling down the Yangtze where it meets the Jialing tributary in Chongqing. Spaceships tumbling through OUTER space like buttons rotating in bath water. Container ships ploughing into the South China Sea. Turn off JavaScript. Insert Disclaimer. Les Hallem shifted his busted-up torso in front of the late news. Billy picked up his father's log. A cluster of invoices were fastened with a rusted bulldog clip. He lifted a Post-It Note. TO BE FILED, it said. Years sliding. Soft ebb. Bob's greasy smudge on the top corner. His watermark. Family business since 1959. Laertes' acres were well-fenced. Take the Douglas Street dog-leg. Tack hard-port. A curved cream awning opened an opal vault over Stanmore village. Mechanical Repairs, it read. Transmission Services. Insert correspondences with the production, publication and dissemination of *Ulysses* as well as this work. Pale slabs gleaming all summer. Isaac's stomach on display. Texta "X" marks the spot. Abraham raised his blade. Soft asphalt. Bob breathing the air of his own earth down the back of the dark workshop. Dead-end of a cave. Cracking open the studs on his grey overalls when Helen called "time." Five o'clock sharp each day. Mucid wind hit his pileous chest. I jumped on his back when he wasn't looking. He let me hang off his neck. Smell of Valvoline in his hair. Wiping those great big mitts in a frayed bath towel as he walked towards the lubricant bay. Steal from the world slightly. R11 reduces the temperature of any object it contacts during evaporation. Like Shelley's chrome dew-balls. Ice circling unseen in random sprays like some ghost ship being buffeted offshore. Banned in most countries. Start by rebranding the product. Maybe call it ... *Ice Mist*. Falsify the ingredients on the customs declaration. False labelling. Hire a local sales team. Sell direct to major building managers. Don't try retail. There are a few blokes I know in West Asia and Africa who could move this stuff. Shanghai Dog folded the FAX again, put it into his pocket and left the cafe. He proceeded to the subway aperture. It's hot enough there not to fuss over ethics. All about price point. Commuters pressed against a DVD salesman settled on a milk crate. He smiled upwards at Billy. Huang se dian ying, he asked. Shi kuai! Billy shook his head. Jintian buyong, he replied. Cialis kicking in. Bob Capri brought his son a wide tumbler of cool water with thick ice cubes.

"Your last night in Sydney," he said. "Better get some rest."

"Yea. I'm feeling pretty flat," replied Billy.

"Fair enough," Bob said.

He could equally have chosen the depersonalised axiom, 'She'll be right.' Echo of Stan Parker's prose. Son of a blacksmith and an educated lady. Came back from the War to a lifetime of dour labour. Don Cane could never have countenanced an existence so mild. His sons neither. Billy needed a BIG LIFE. Fifty years added up in Stan's mind to a single numeral. Answer to all sums, he said. ONE. White's flop at embodying climax in a single word. Joyce's YAIRS in Strine. Tongue-swell. Mandible cud. Thin-lips like silicon tracings. God target sum mawlassies intern meow, may, seared Lauder. Protean utterance. A secret code like Shanghainese. Hit Linespace Carriage Return Lever. Cog-loadings of an enigma machine. Hints hurt Somme hairy. Bee Lee gouter gorf ter Ing Lane term oiler, seared Blob. Tom Harem gnaw veer gunner glow Bee-tart How's air-knee maw. Shank Hide Og kneadster fog eggnishner flute fur catch. Lizard breath wans turbo cum peg leant. Anal Laugh Eh ice duned art thick climb axe blob fizz chapped her. Donk Aim's mercurial business dealings in Manila attracted the attention of ASIO. Translate the following phrase into Strine: he always got a helping hand off his American mates. His fingerprints were all over it. Bob Capri displayed discoloured palms.

"I need to wash up," he said.

He left the dead hearth. Dark green velveteens. Curious soft-quenched waning. Transitory like Mellors. Arising off a base station. Provisional status. Anybody could get commissioned in the Great Slwarter. All you needed was survivor's luck. Like Lawrence. He pincered the gap between Nineteenth-Century Prose and Modernism. A winning formula of post-war torpor, class conflict and sex. He was Henry James Rated AO. Havelock Ellis would have writ such muck if he could. *Kangaroo* was still the best attempt at a political novel in Australia until *P W/out G*. Lawrence's characterisation of Connie Chatterley removes any ambiguity from the Elizabeth Archer trope. Iago-green Merle. Link to portrait of Lady Peasoup (C5).

"What are you going to do about Don," Billy asked his mother.

"Nothing," Helen answered with an idle tongue.

"Do you hate him?"

"No," she replied. "It was all for the best really."

Her hand touched mine. Dead for a ducat.

"Do you hate me?" she asked back.

"No," I replied.

"I think it's time for bed. We've got to get you to the airport early."

My mother held fast. I also. Maybe out of shock. No frippery. Gibraltar is always an exit. See also Thrace. Find endpoints. Under Aldebaran. Look deep south. Low on horizon-rise piercing the flank. Odysseus must still make good with Poseidon at the end of the *Odyssey*. Billy Capri slipped down the hall to his bedroom and closed the door. The lock clicked shut. He opened his backpack and took out a black paperback. He laid it down on a bedside table. Light the lamp. Bookmark C3. He removed all his clothing. Isaiah naked and barefoot as a peeled mandarin. Re-Adamated. Throw off the figleaf and grab Flavian's mitt. Sew and unsew. Job One. Bathsheba. Odysseus on Scheria. He took a pencil stub from his desk, slipped it behind his ear and propped himself against the varnished bedhead. Shanghai Dog descended into the subway. Streams of people seeking surface moved against him. Mao swimming *Chang Jiang*. Wastewater grottos. The station concourse was wide, bright and white. Billy purchased a three kuai ticket. Boylan's gift. Import–export. Price of admission. A deal made under duress. Our deadline. Size of my belly. Matt's stare. He swiped the ticket and skipped down the short staircase to the platform. Banks of fluorescent lights and electric advertising scrolls heightened its grids of marble tiles and shining steel fascias. Next train to Longyang Road was three minutes. A supermodel on the cover of *Chinese Vogue* clicked into frame. He took an iPod from his jacket and swished the dial to Playlists. It landed on "Shanghai Roadkill." He depressed the dial. The Stooges "Down on the Street" commenced. Locomotive drill. Iggy grunted then growled. The train sped fast before him. Chinese faces shone as it slowed. The doors opened. Overflow. He wrestled the crowd around the hatch to gain ingress then pressed his index finger against the ceiling for traction. The gazing commenced. Yet Shanghai Dog felt invisible like Odysseus. He was utterly concealed by cultural dialectics. The train started. A couple were playing "Anti-Japan War Online" on golden consoles. Their fingers moved with disjunctive speed. P. J. Harvey started. "Look out ahead," she sang. An LCD screen broadcast CCTV1. Cut to footage of Chen Yun-Lin's visit to Taiwan. Highest level meeting since 1949. Chen and You Ma were exchanging gifts for the media. Chen presented Ma with a horse painting. *Ma* means "horse" in Mandarin. In return, Ma gave Chen a priceless piece of porcelain. This was an ambiguous gesture. The KMT took boatloads of relics when they shipped off the mainland in 1949. Now there was talk of a Panda swap. That passed for diplomatic progress. "This world's crazy," the chanteuse continued. The news broadcast switched to China's stimulus package. It would be released in a couple of days. The Chinese government never put an exact date on major announcements. But the newsreaders were already gloating. He was tired of poses everywhere. Don Cane rolled his eyes at Yankee prowess. "I wanna go to a different land."

Should have arrived in Shanghai back in the Nineties. They were desperate for FDI back then. "Know Your Product" started. He had to marry Doctor Gu. Her English name was MELANIE. His penis began to swell involuntarily. Supply-side narcotics. Quantitative easing. He would reach her suite in 30 minutes. He could fuck her with detachment. Maybe he couldn't cum. But that was OK. She only noticed her own SHOCK, as Lawrence termed it. Joyce's style in this episode discloses the mechanics of closed systems; in this instance of Writing and Empire. Shanghai Dog butted the window. A face peered. Benjamin's *Arcade*. Beckett's Plan B. Joyce chronicles the harsh conditions prevailing in Imperial Dublin in "Lotus Eaters." Bloom is proceeding to the funeral of Patrick Dignam. It is modelled on the service for Matthew Kane, who drowned in Dublin Bay in July 1904. He is Joyce's Elpenor. Death has left his family bereft. We are shown images of their NO FUTURE by the author on route. It is executed with Naturalism. Bloom sees a boy smoking a cigarette butt as he hauls a heavy bucket of offal. A girl scarred with eczema undoes his idealised image of female beauty. Bath heat belatedly sweated out of Bob's body. Doctor Gu was sitting at the vanity unit rubbing thick cream into her face. A beggar disfigured with burns sat in a tortured heap outside the Shangrila Hotel. A smashed-up child staggered into his path with her palms held out for alms. The old man swung at the girl with a stick to drive her off. A war veteran in a ragged PLA uniform was propped on rotten crutches at the entrance to Baker & Spice cafe. A fat woman in a floral dress leant on the entrance to a fashion house watching frightened lovers cling. They huddled under shopfront awnings waiting for a bus. The train passed directly underneath Nanjing Lu. Shanghai Dog's throat was starting to swell. Bob Capri steadied himself against the plastic towel rack. The profile of his ageing pelt shone under heat lamps. Odysseus biding his time. A hard coat hard-won worn and dimpled. Get Polyphemus drunk. Blind it with yer wooden stake. Suitor families were milling outside the palace gates. There was always a heavy crowd at Lujiazui. We should fuck them up once and for all with a torpedo, says Flett. Telemachus began a slow ascent behind a screen of vines that his grandfather had planted to cool the wall of the west bedroom against the full summer sun on Paliki. War-ran-jain-ora. It was getting late. He looked down to the ground. Faithless serving-girls were still strung-up in full view of the household. Blood coarsened their tunics disclosing the outline of slender trunks. A blackbird sang in an adjacent grove. Its last note now mimicked their dying pitch. Thin men of Haddam circulated below. Telemachus was well-hidden. In the old days, he used to spy on his mother naked at her bath from this vantage point before launching himself into her parlour brandishing a xiphos, crafted by Laertes from fine Hickory selected by Karya, the famous Hamadryad of walnut orchards. The servants were always taken by surprise except old Eurycleia. She had become inured to such pranks as Odysseus' nurse. You're still young, scoffed Claudius. Sprinkle cool patience on thy flames, added Laby Fry. He's actually done well to date given his age and breeding, said Merlin. Note link to restaurant scene later in C10. Time gets unhinged in this chapter. Complete reverse search of MERLIN using Navigation Tool. It constitutes an exact chronological retraction. Note elegance of "B. Button" concept. This is where Joyce differed from Proust. He was scrupulous like a Swiss watchmaker. What is your will Unk, asked Edmund flourishing his cape? Insert more dialogue from the screenplay, *Toto Against Hercules*. This B-Grade success was the accidental literary triumph of Godard's failing flunk. Link to this work. Today, Telemachus had been freshly-tested in battle. He still wore the lifeblood of the suitors caked on his bronzed, serpentine forearms. Their carcasses had been piled against an interior wall beneath a deep portico to slow the stench. Their rotting flesh would eventually announce their demise to the city. Vassals were washing blood off the tables, floor and walls of the dining room before meeting their own fate. Again, link to forthcoming restaurant scene. Hamlet's father had been a tyrant. It is implicit in the sense of relief at court after he is killed. Claudius was a calm-bringer. A good administrator like Tennyson's Telemachus in "Ulysses." Too slick and cunning for his step-son but. Claudius + Hamlet Senior equalled one complete human. Killing Polonius, the alter-ego of his father, was Hamlet's only decisive act in the whole play. It also constituted his FIRST ERROR. He would have been better off prevaricating some. He wrapped the body in a rug and lugged the guts into the next room. Everybody's wearing nightgowns – Gu, Bob, Gertrude, Penelope, even Odysseus. All the characters in Shakespeare's play are abominations. Telemachus suppressed a sullen after-gasp, guiltily at first then quizzically, wondering at the source of the ferocity which had consumed him during the slaughter of his enemies. A blackbird choked on its opening note. Telemachus craved the peace of familiar inflections. Lingering. Waning. Betoning again. Not even Molly Bloom could fertilise this colony. Not that she was much of a breeder. Henry would have added her to the beheaded list. Tom Hallem could not look at Matt S without SICK. Merlin opened his trousers. He took Tom's arm and guided it towards his elaborately wired cock still unfull. A cool wind from the Ionian Sea was refreshing Paliki. Odysseus had constructed his palace to maximise the benefits of its sheltered location on the underside of a peak. It also optimised lines-of-sight to the horizon, disclosing any enemy vessels when they were still well upwind. Hold hard, Merlin demanded. Not now, said Tom batting off his hand. Yes, urged Molly. Not here Patroclus. We should be forever testing new places, Eromenos. Never acquiescing in orthodoxy. Kinaidos I am not. You will be cast out of the Sacred Band, spat Merlin like Lady Verdurin. He barred the door. Cockswell under grey folds of slackbelly. Furdecked. Tom watched him unmoved. Bald head flecked like a dog-belly. He jerked fast. Ruthless. Hating. Swann delivering a spray of cattleyas to Odette. Gilbert Osmond getting the job done with his wife.

He pressed an index finger into his elastic prostate. Sperm spat. A single thread grasped Tom's lower leg. Scrawny purl. He let it rest on his trousers. Symbol of Hephaestus. Merlin withdrew his penis from sight making careful folds. The breeze muffled Telemachus' movements through the upper branches. The blackbird spired. (IV) He nestled in proximity. Seven Lamps. Pen and ink sketches by John Ruskin. Lamp One: Sacrifice. The last lamp: Obedience. The ultimate nexus of Ruskin's flames was Hector arriving at the battlefield outside Troy. Achilles brandished his new shield. An Australian Flag by Jasper Johns. Odysseus Leaving Ogygia. Fox on Aeaea by Juan Davila. The Martyrdom of Whitlam by Andrea Mantegna. Gough would have wanted to go the full Grunewald, Comrade. Suddenly, the bird emerged from its ambuscade and crossed to-and-fro like a finely calibrated pendulum before Telemachus' eyes. He could not determine if it was a god or an omen. The river whirred swiftly. It whirled in the autumn breeze. Telemachus rebalanced his body. He intended to bide his time in this bower until his parents were asleep then slide back to earth. He feared his father's fast blade. Odysseus would have considered every rustle in the undergrowth to be the potential entrance of a new assassin. The vines acted like a sling. Aeolus was stirring. Occasional gusts cleansed the palace grounds. The television reported that Tangcao Expressway had been closed. Traffic was being rerouted down G205 to Caofeidian. The blackbird landed on a cedar-limb. Telemachus pressed his cheek against the warm stone wall, just beyond the ken of his parent's bed. He could make out lax conversation. It was afternoon all evening. His father recounted his passage home from Troy. Short form poems a pennyeach. His mother replied with Ode on Solitude. Unlamented let me die. Like Troy, she had lived by stealth under siege for years. Billy Capri slid on his stomach along the shag pile carpet until he reached his parent's door. Weak light as if from an olive lamp washed under the crack. He rested his cheek near a ribbed aluminium plate. Waiting for cannibals. Media pack. Grab onto the underbelly of Australian landscape traditions. Hang on for grim life as you struggle against. Hawke kept his eye injury secret throughout the election campaign. It occurred when he was hit in the face batting for the Parliamentarians in the annual cricket match against the Press in July. A man in a black suit left the disabled toilet cubicle. Fuller averted his gaze. Small tastes of radioactive waste floated in his soup. Perhaps he would be eliminated in a car crash. Nobody would find his fly-blown body for days down a remote embankment.

"We need to get Billy to the airport soon as possible tomorrow," said Barry to his wife.

"We've got to clear the air first."

"But what if Don comes?"

"He'll go straight to Penelope."

"What if he don't."

"I know him. Now put out the bed lamp. Let's get some rest."[1]

Helen Capri turned aside. Her husband slid into her spine and put a tamed arm over her trunk. They always began the night thus. Later he would turn so that they pressed back to back like Plato's first humans. Billy waited until there was tranquillity throughout the household and withdrew to his room. He got into bed and took up his book to search for the famous story of the Trojan Horse. This tale does not appear in the *Iliad*, which ends with Hector's funeral, or the *Odyssey*, which begins with the Telemachiad. It is Virgil's special construct. Homer's Odysseus himself never explains his method of defeating the Trojans. All he says is: "I left Troy and made for home." Billy wondered how Joyce perceived the Trojan Horse trope in composing *Ulysses*. It was inconceivable that he did not ponder the opportunities left by the gaps between the *Iliad* and the *Odyssey* ... as well as those presented by placing his text between the *Odyssey* and the *Aeneid*. If the entry of Bloom into bed represented Odysseus re-entering his own bed on Ithaca then Molly's monologue is the seed of its aftermath – GIBRALTAR. It is the crossing point between the known and unknown: a symbol of humanity's irrepressible thirst for NEWNESS. It enabled Joyce to write BEYOND the end of Homer's narrative giving him hegemony over his Hellenic precursor and alluding to a bond with his Roman successor, Virgil. Joyce was thus able to reposition himself – in fact, squeeze – into the crux of the GREAT Classical dyad. Homer–JOYCE–Virgil. You can almost see the road sign. It enabled him to revise – even rescind – temporal notions of literary influence (see H. Bloom). Titling his novel after the Roman figure, Ulysses, rather than the Greek one, Odysseus, reinforced the sense that Joyce was straddling giants to create his own 'space-for-ego.' He stood with a footsole planted on each head/land like the Colossus of Rhodes while subsequent literature sailed under his patched trouser crotch. Nora laid down her darning to excoriate her husband. Telemachus was startled from reverie by his father's voice suddenly coming rich and deep from the gloom. "Come Telemachus," he said. "Now you have heard my tale. You have also heard your mother's story. Sit with us for a while on this bed which I assembled out of an olive trunk, and in which the Gods in their mercy and wisdom granted us the good fortune to create you." The young man crawled through the casement. Bloom watched Stephen at the door. He is still a boy at heart, thought Bloom, who has never received the gifts due to an eldest son. Peri. No point of comparison. Odysseus pushed a glowing bowl at Telemachus. "Here," he said, "taste the last of the Ambrosia that the goddess Athene in her bounty has left us. Then go to the cellar and take any of the serving girls you choose. They will go with you gladly." A Spa and Sauna is located in the basement of the Shanghai Hotel. Boys lead

1 See Appendix A (Odysseus & Penelope if they had stayed together).

you to the locker room where you undress. Some mock, others admire, my hirsute form. They provide a frayed towel and escort you to the shower area. You must clean your body well. Government officials recline in steaming tubs. Mao liked to dine on fine food. He also loved dancing. He enjoyed the company of young ladies. They dress you in cheap summer pyjamas like a child. Jiang Qing idolised Hollywood movies, especially musicals. She was an actress herself, after all. You are escorted to a private room which plays pirates of Japanese pornography. She watched them in a home theatre with her cronies. She kept a wardrobe of elaborate qi pao. Eventually, you are escorted to the fishbowl. Mao was always constipated. His doctor purchased a Western lavatory. They used to stop his special train and set this ceramic toilet in the rice fields where he would squat pondering the scenery for hours. The girls enter the box. Sunset spread across the farm flats behind Wushao Expressway. *Da Hong Pao* was brewing in the meeting room alongside the banquet table. They take a mouthful of Fujian tea and warm your cock. Doctor Gu was encrusted in four red robes. Telemachus consumed the sacred floss. It had been blown with Athene's sibilant breath. He examined the raised-relief of the Goddess etched into the nest of the bowl. Chidley high on grapes. Coleridge tugging on his pipe. Schlickeysen's fruit diet. Live an Elysian life and your star will start floating. Telemachus left his parents in bed. His body cast an elongated glow down the corridors. Like Shelley's heroes, he erased all impression as he went. No guard challenged him. He drifted towards the basement. Pies with his devil's fingers innem, as Ruskin wrote (see C6). Unholy sweat. She hooked the red rope into her ankles and rotated over his loins. Big as a house he was. Shanghai Dog groped at his trousers pressing and rubbing the corrugated zip. Tom Hallem strained to recall the cab ride. The driver had turned up the radio shaking him free from a drunk stupor. Stephen had been dreaming of Eastern potentates, Joseph the Talking Horse and his dead mother again. Ghost in a dream like Hamlet's father. Jafar to King Haroun. This is a good example of Joyce's use of metempsychosis between Stephen and Bloom. He fucked the Caliph's sister and lost his head to a curved sword. Cut a wet watermelon. Hold it up to your face. The word 'dream' is used seventeen times in Nausicaa, largely during the internal monologue of Gerty MacDowell. She sees Bloom's fantasies for what they really are: lame romance fancies. Likewise, Tom Hallem still invades my visionary realm, albeit with a loss of fact over time; not to mention gaps, misremembrances, impossible intrusions and plain misnomers. Dreams go by contraries, interjected Florry. Tom in his own oneiric catalogue witnessed Ana's wasted mane spreading across the fizzy black lemonade of Serpentine Avenue like a sodden carpet. A loose brown dress clung to her frame. Blued feet clapped the slummy sand. No longer to trudge. His hand moved under the cotton seam until it encountered an askew needle. He turned her over in shock only to see Willy's creamfruit face. Ace of Spades climbing the staircase to Bella's place of business. There is no odour in dreams. The smell of a bedroom can affect the content of dreams however. This conclusion was supported by a study of 3,372 dream reports by Zadra, Nielsen and Donderi (1998). Thus, Stephen Dedalus could not have experienced the smell of wax and rosewood – except from observing live candles and dead flowers in cut glass vases – in his dreams, let alone delineated the stench of wet ashes. Go abroad and love a foreign lady, said Zoe reading Tom Hallem's inky palm. See Sylvana. Wilhelm Meister was an ineffectual dreamer who came to grief against hard facts. Bloom would never face that trauma. He kept dreams in dreams-place and lived by cold realism. Chapters 3 and 15 chronicle three dreams linked to the figure of Haroun al Raschid, who was the audience for many of the most famous stories in *1,001 Nights*. They all turn into nightmares of history. Joyce uses this historic figure and his theocratic interface with Leopold Bloom to explore the hypocrisy and failures of nationalism, ethnic cleansing, Colonialism and Zionism. For Joyce, the persecution and aspirations of the Jews were directly applicable to Ireland. Like Aboriginal genocide. Every country hides its shame. That's why nations are a tragedy. Whereas individuals are just babble. Simon Dedalus' version of Croppy Boy is the Siren's song in episode 11 of *Ulysses*. Its lyrics describe brutal betrayal. Joyce presents it as a call to violence by a bunch of useless drunks. Bloom's breaks wind as he leaves the pub in their honour. "I like this song," said the driver. Hallam nodded meaninglessly. "But that singer," he laughed. "He does like his idioms." Bloom remains a pacifist at heart. Yet he is constantly trapped between identities. In Circe, he invokes the war record of his father-in-law to defend his patriotism. This occurs again when he is saving Stephen from the British soldiers. Later, he buys a snack of pork meat from Dick Stone Butchers then feeds it to a starving dog after guilt at consuming unclean food assails him. This is an acute political symbol by Joyce. *Why did you leave Ireland [asked Tom Hallem]?* "Ubi panis, ibi patria," replied Joyce. "It's the migrant's creed." *Q: I'll tell you a joke if you like. A: Go right ahead. Q: Riddle me this. How does an Irishman get a university degree?* The Australian shook his head. "You catch a ferry to Stockholm, throw a brick through a shop window and get put in a Swedish gaol." Hallem snorted and grinned. Michael Collins at Frongoch Prison. Physical Force Republicans. Criminal scholars. Wolfe Tone. Young Ireland. Fenian dynamite. Sent to the Tower. Millais' Two Princes. Harrow Road cache.

"Will you ever go back?"

"No. But I return each night."

Michael Davitt Green Yeats Joyce. Bobby Sands who died on a hunger strike in Maze. Bernadette Devlin shot seven times on her own doorstep. Spirit too strong to yield. Eight hundred years of British sponsored bloodsled. Tread softly for you tread on my dreams. Graveswarm and sweet. *Fianna Fail* and *Fianna Gael* banjaxed the State. The Troubles caused another wave of mass emigration in the 1970s.

"Parnell said that Ireland could not spare a single son. But we've been leaving in droves for three centuries. Tans stole our providence."

Inselaffe. Farang. Angmor Lang. POHMs.

"I know a lot of Irish boys," replied the passenger. "I grew up amongst Devlins and Mullany's in Campsie."

"O'Dobhailein and O'Maoldhomhnaigh. Grandsons of the Unlucky and servants of the Catholic Church. The poles of our heritage. Australian has always been a proxy for the Irish nation."

Chisholm's Popish plot. Morgan hanging off a gibbet. Second Vinegar Hill. Two thousand strong the Rum Corps came. True to the shamrock, we were flogged to death or bravely died in chains. Therry's chalice. Certificates of Freedom. Mary Kelly's lash. Rich emancipists. Fenian convicts. O'Reilly's escape from Bunbury on the sloop, Gazelle. *Clan na Gael*. Breslin's deception. Six wild geese snatched by the whaleboat Catalpa while the English garrison watched the Perth regatta. Donegal Relief Fund. Derryveagh evictions. British landlords withdrew the right to graze. Three hundred armed constables were sent with a Jury Warrant to collect 3,000 pounds for alleged stock losses. Forty-seven families evicted. Cruel John Adair. Two hundred police demolished their homes. Half the children were still of tender age. Swift's sweetmeats. Five shiploads brought to Sydney. Loyal Orange. O'Farrell's mad pot-shot at Bunny Prince Alf. They hanged the loony at D'hurst gaol. Polding's seven thousand sacraments. Patrick Francis Moran buried in Saint Mary's crypt. Les Darcy bent double with Daniel Mannix. Easter Uprising. I.N.A. Sinn Fein police. Fig-leaf Empire. The problem lies with the Australian character. Give London bank-blood. Irish beef tasters. *Ba mhaith liom bainne*. Celtic wogwords. Gaelic is a rude tongue. Learn your own language. They gave us our national songs and epics. Rediscover Ossian. *Seosamh Ó Foirbhilhe*. Genial climes of a minor literature. Australia is the Irish idyll. Honest Joe Cahill leaning on a palm tree column outside Saint Brigid's, Marrickville. Vietnamese Vigil each Saturday night these days. Diem's cronies. Latest gag of refugees. *Thanh Le Tai 6g toi*. Illawarra *Pho Ga*. I married Bob with my pale belly blaring under a plain cream dress at the nave(l) of Saint Mel's staring all the way down Evaline Street to the stagnant sludge of Cooks River.

"Is that why you came here?"

"Nah. It was a process of pure elimination. I wanted to get ... far, faraway," he said concluding the discussion with a bellicose wave of his wrist and a breathless sigh.

The taxi careened down Crown Street nin'ty to the dozen. PUNKS + POOFTAS YEH HUP, announced a painted hoarding. The alliance between alternative music and gay culture in the 1980s turned Darlinghurst into the most humane economy in Australia. YOU ARE

NOW ENTERING PINK ZONE. Worker's terraces crunched together with wire. A third of all families lived in one room in Dublin in the time of James Joyce. Fetishism of place. See Proust, Ruskin, JJ, Sydney. Never multiple locations just a kaleidoscope screwing down on one place. Joyce only leaves Dublin to invoke Paris as its antithesis. See Berlin > Sydney. Also, Shanghai = Sydney. Write a book about Sydney w/out describing SHB or SOH. XI NI DA QIAO. XI NI GE JU YUAN. We passed the demolished Women's Hospital site. Sydney's Holles Street. Birthplace for one-child Penelope and only-child Helen. A wild sea breeze, coming off Baird's stonecutting works, sweeping off Botany Bay towards Newtown, in Talbot Place from George's Dock, east of Loopline Bridge and Monto, always made Stephen think of Ibsen, always recalled Elizabeth Archer. Joyce went back to the great Norwegian dramatist whenever it came time for female characterisation. SEE GHOSTS. The setting of an impossible quandary like some Hellenic paradox. *Ulysses* was a simple tale by comparison. The Wangels in LADY OF THE SEA provided the model for the Bloom marriage as well as Blazes Boylan. Ellida chooses her husband over a belatedly returning lover, a sailor, when he finally grants her freedom of choice. [**LOTUS EATERS**] Elizabeth Archer withdrew behind the thick walls of her brownstone gallery. The patrons were herded inside. Tom Hallem followed like a pin yielding to flesh. Bright floodlights suckered powdered moths. Their nutmeg wings spotted freshly whitewashed walls. Industrial melanism. The crowd shifted in spurts. Tom forced his way into the ruck. Make your way upstream, unthinkingly. Apply the antmound method of characterisation evident in *Ulysses*, as well as its earlier models like *B. House* and *M. March*, to this chapter. Use references to books and paintings like they too were players. READ was play-acting for SLUT HAROLDE and MERLIN in his posh Bowral accent like some pious Peter Carey slumming down Phoenix Park. THE COLLECTOR giggled and rubbed his head. Not a single hair ever rested in its rightful place. He had been dispensing funds and fake giggles since his return from London in the early 70s to collect his family inheritance. He was still engaged in interminable court action to bleed his brother dry. Read bumped against a tall accent table in the course of wild gesticulations about the new version of "Tangled Up in Blue" on Bob's live album. It shook a rich native bouquet. Tom grabbed the vase. Protea and Leucospermum wrapped in sinamay scratched at his cheeks. Sprays of Geraldton Wax. Dry gumnuts. Dead stalks. He sneezed. SKINTPOLE was scouring for a free taste. Also, any neglected handbag with cash, fags and lollies to nick and pawn down Darlinghurst Road. His daughter was almost 3 months old now. He was coming down hard. Ros couldn't help him score. She'd been taken back to Kirribilli by The Boss. Dickens based all his characters on real people. Elizabeth Archer registered a sense of profound unease as if she had just stepped groggily out of a long bath. Bloom is obsessed with sex in this episode. He watches a well-kept woman crossing the road while he talks to McCoy. A passing tram blocks his expectant view of her fine hosiery. He fondles Martha's letter in his pocket letting it poke his half-herded cock. He has decided never to meet Martha, it is too much risk, although his next correspondence would pinch harder. Shanghai dog is like Odysseus. He is restless. Adulterous. But to no end like Bloom. In this work, there is regular sexual contact. This aligns with the Classics. But there are descriptions only as necessary. As symbols of power (Elizabeth > Tom), $ (blowjob), violence (Ana's rape), and false fatherhood (DP). Connection only occurs without soft touch. There is no passion. Only the perfunctory clashes of thin-lipped Anglos. In order, the following sex scenes occur in T.MAC: Tom and Elizabeth (C2), Tom at Camperdown Beat (C3), Various (C5), Leer and Tom (C7), miscellaneous deleted scenes [Ana raped; taxi-fare hand-job (C9)], Merlin's masturbation (C10 – link to LB/Gerty also Charlus), failed congress by Tom/Frances & S.Dog/Gu (C10 – compare). This does not include erotic recollections such as Welles for EA, S. Dog for Judy et cetera. The election was going to be close. Closer than anyone expected when the long campaign began. Peacock had been hammering Hawke on drug policy. Last week, the PM broke down in tears at a press conference. A rush of bad marrow had entered the bones of the body politic. Elizabeth turned. Hallem paused. His head spun. The crowd pressed into him making the walls disappear. He surveyed sallow space. Kubrick's chapel. Censerpall. He closed the lydgate of his soft eyes momentarily. RED waved frantically until he got the boy's attention. Tom smiled back. He fingered Leer's kit in his coat pocket. Bloom is killing time before proceeding to Dignam's funeral in "Lotus Eaters." He is waylaid by Bantam Lyons. Inadvertently, he presents a tip to the pesky skiver. Next, he visits a Catholic Church. His only interest in Mass is the opportunity to sit next to attractive women. It is a low palace otherwise to Bloom wholly devoid of lifeblood with its Latinate crooners and begging bowls. Man deserves a decent interment. Don't want to end up like Elpenor. Or Polydorus abandoned in a cheap motel room. Tom's dim cell in Prahran. Empty bottles of scotch and orange juice by his bed. The coroner found a mix of heroin, opiods, aspirin, methadone and whiskey in his blood. The Coroner determined accident and misadventure in all three cases. He had an extended meeting with Dylan just one month before his death. Nobody has been able to ascertain the exact content of their conversation, although it is known that they discussed life and art. Dylan never wrote about drug addiction or subjective attraction to suicide in his work. Occasionally, it would be associated with story-song characters. Rosemary in "Jack of Hearts" even once tried suicide, for instance. His oeuvre is really imbued with the force-of-art as an elixir. The eighteen songs that Dylan performed at the State Theatre were a typical set of reworked classics and oddities such as a Joan Baez cover and a version of "Female Rambling Sailor." This remarkable folk song inverts the strict gender roles of maritime ballads. It was first heard by Dylan in his early days in Minneapolis from a field recording in 1932. The main character's name is Rebecca

Young. Her hand slipped from the ship and down she fell into the sea like ALP in The Lake or some junky dragging a canula in his frailed forearm. There is no evidence of deliberation in Red's death. He played Dylan constantly throughout his career. Tom Hallem found himself listening on high rotation to *Planet Waves*, *The Basement Tapes*, *Blonde on Blonde* and *Bringing It All Back Home* while he worked in Red's studio. It helped his brush-rhythm. There was also a fantastic bootleg of the Royal Albert Hall concert with a pig stamped on a cream cover. We'll never know the truth about what really happened that night. Various stumbles, dead-ends, setbacks and betrayals occur over the course of any life. Walkers on wire bubs. Standing on a bonfire of Aeneas' goods on Battleship Hill with a sword in your guts like Eurydice. Antigone, Jocasta, Phaedra. All hanged. There were two items of foil containing heroin and four used syringes scattered around the bedroom and bathroom. According to his dealer, Willy bought three grams of smack on Thursday afternoon. The coroner found three fresh needle marks, including two on the back of Tom's hand. The cocktail of medications and liquor suggests that he was trying to detoxify. This started with a small hit of junk followed by a full cold turkey with its affects mitigated by lesser drugs. Poison sometimes. Never blades. Dido's suicide is not typical of Classical females. Leon's darkened hospice room was illumined by a horizontal slit in a warped vinyl curtain. He did not recognise Elizabeth now. His slippery face was contorted and split like "Dylan Attempt 2." Chaim, he bellowed. Ellen Higgins' brooch gleaming on her milky fat chest. Ennis hotel. Death by Monkshood it shall be. Rudy unscrewed his head and tucked it under his arm. A new straw boater from James Cullen's drapery store remained obstinately in place. A poultice of Aconite and chloroform was still stuck upon his grandfather's forehead. A slower more painful form of death than ingestion. First there would have been nausea then vomiting. A numb maw. Burnt abdomen. Writhing. Paralysis. Maybe chloroform would have aided unconsciousness. The lungs stop. Heart seizure. *Aconitum* means "without struggle" in Greek. Ironic name really. The Queen's Hotel is a well-regarded establishment located on a prominent street corner in Central Ennis. It is painted clotted cream today. The hotel signboard is still mounted on the first floor overlooking the junction of Abbey Street and Sraid San Proinsias. Proceed up the stairs. It has only 2 sets of staircases. Enter the death room. Walk to the window. Pull back a cheap chemise. It looks straight down the roadway. Aconite can kill mice with a whiff. The window has been opened a crack. What still survives is a sly sweet odour. The places where people have died always betray the atmosphere of the human spirit at impact. Site of the last show on Earth. Or the first retrospective, depending on how you look at it. Sometimes acute; sometimes obtuse (self-referring). Bloom left church. He had observed the Mass with complete detachment as usual. Brittle cheer of an otiose economy. False booms founded on soft budgets. Keating needs more time, said The Collector. We're like France in 1849. Long years of brooding. Fraser's gone with snotty gulps. Present Hawke as Arthur, Keating as Lancelot. Elizabeth passed Tom an envelope. He did not have time to open it. She hooked his arm and advanced into the crowd. The band was setting up its sound equipment in the far corner. Ewan McLeod unpacked his saxophone. He was fitting the reed. His hair stood upright in blue, copper and pink curltones. Madge connected a guitar strap around her shoulders. Tom repositioned his drums and depressed the bass drum once. At this point in Lotus Eaters, Bloom recalls the audience reaction to Molly singing *Stabat Mater*. Music composed for text. Pater's dictum inverted. Take the letters of ART out of his name and all you've got is a meaningless spray of letters – WLE PE. Here Joyce picks up Flaubert's use of music as a critical device from *Sentimental Education*. His description of the harpist's song evoking "eastern romance, all about daggers, flowers, and stars" is a template for how Joyce integrated music into his narrative themes and imagery to cast new meaning on his storyline. It also incorporated the facile Eastern flair which besotted nineteenth century Europeans. Rossini was a true hustler. He ripped off Tadolini to execute his commission then double-sold the score. It is also called a "series." Numbered prints. Acts of masturbation. Bloom holds back from self-abuse. It symbolises his first attempt at withdrawal from narcosis. He succumbs later in the day before Gerty. Chidley's shocks of self-abuse. But Bloom is on his path to redemption. Skintpole had gone lame from a bad groin shot. It clipped a nerve on the way IN. Still it was better than hitting the femoral artery. Need to get some half-inch tips at the new AIDS clinic on Albion Street as soon you you get some bucks. Then go see Mick at the X. Put all your dosh on Throwaway. Discarded syrINges. Sit on a toilet. Drop your strides. Feel for a pulse. Find the Tank Stream. The target vein is adjacent. Inch towards your nuts. Skintpole always shot blindly waiting in trepidation to see if he pulled-back bright frothing blood. That meant trouble. Suck. Rich carmine. Great rush. READ (past tense) watched enviously. He needed to trust in Skintpole's fine needlework. Rossini was burnt-out by the end in need of fresh cash. *Quando corpus morietur*. He finished it off later. Dali's students did the paint job. He just added his signature. Could have hired Elmyr for the job and gone on holidays. After all, he was only in Ibiza just eight hours drive along the coast from the house that Dali and Gala shared in Port Lligat near Cadaqués. Molly sang the soprano solos in Movements 3 and 8 as well as sharing the stage with the other 3 soloists in Movements 1, 6 and 9. Her starring solo in Movement 8 asked the Virgin for the strength to share Christ's wounds and death ("*in die judicii*"). Molly would have felt a theatrical identification with Mary as a grieving Mother fixed beneath her dying child on the Cross. She would have rendered the assonant lyric with insouciance as it turned to invocations in Verse 9. The prospect of a Last Judgment would have left her chilly. It was not her type of party. Tom became uncomfortable. Elizabeth felt him stiffen. She looked askance. He gave a neutral grin. She decided to place him under her husband's wing. A waiter with a tray of drinks pressed the circle. Orange Juice. White wine. Water. Drink that. Eat this. Wave-sensers. Prefer kidneys and pac-dots. Get some sperm inside. Insert metaphor: men wriggling inside a horse. Gallery chock-a-block like Easter matins. Tom's routine involved getting supplies from the local food market, turning on SBS TV, stripping down to his BVDs and placing a vomit bucket by the bed while he went through withdrawal. A second waiter executed a pincer movement on the right-hand flank piercing the square with small collations. *Enfilade*. He had nearly died the previous month trying to detox at his sister's place near Orange. Leon took up a salmon canapé. Someone slid the first slice out of a gourmet pizza medallion. Hawaiian Eucharist. Modernist individual. Add anchorvy. PACMAN. Baudelaire's *Flaneur*. Arcades. Success is staying alive in the maze chase as long as possible. Read really wanted to kick his habit. He felt that if he just kept trying to detox then one day, he would get it right. Benjamin stomping back/forward across the Spanish border. Oikake and Otobake on his tail. He must have noted correspondences with the trope of the Wandering Jew. See *Queen Mab*. Walk faster you lazy Fuck. WAKA WAKA WAKA. Thoughts of suicide had been omnipresent. He did not go to Palacetine with Gershom Sholem. Arendt able to get into the USA he not, the cable wrote. O'Varian Fry [unravel tripartite pun]. Sending the boats back. Gestapo waiting at the border with their Heroin Clocks. Machibuse and Kimagure positioned themselves in front of his mouth. Benjamin took a handful of morphine tablets in a cheap hotel room in Portbou like Rudolph Virag. It was only eight hours drive north from Ibiza, where Hory would later ply his craft. Modernism was designed to have no ending so long as the walker could retain a single life. You should be able to play the game indefinitely. Another fraud. Some software bug is triggered when the count reaches the 255th fruit. Roll back to zero. Split image. Random symbols rain down the right-hand side. Kill Screen. You can't consume enough fruit fast enough to live. Enemies coming at warp speed, Cap'in. Shields down. Baudrillard + Virilio. A rent sky gone black. The subway train smashed through the tunnel scouring the walls of Jingan Temple Station with the shriek of screaming brakes. Lines 2 and 7 intersecting. The platform was packed. Shanghai Dog opened the note. My sweet little whorish Nora, it said, I did as you told me, you dirty little girl, and pulled myself off twice when I read your letter. The narrative style is hackneyed. Bloom slips into the role of flaneur on Sandymount Strand on a fresh summer evening, cock-in-hand, watching a trio of young girls – Cissy Caffrey, Edy Boardman, and Gerty MacDowell – whose babies play by the seashore. This is an image with REAL SHOCK VALUE. It should set alarm bells ringing for any critic trying to unlock the true character of Leopold Bloom. To be clear, BLOOM IS LITTLE SHORT OF A PERVERT in this scene. It should cause us to re-evaluate our entire estimation of the moral firmity of Joyce's avowed Everyman. Joyce's shows the Homeric scene on Scheria for what it's worth: a ragged old man appearing buck-naked before unprotected young women at bath. But we are subdued from passing moral judgment by our happy association with Mister Bloom over the preceding 300 pages. We have become fast friends, nay fellow travellers. Joyce anaesthetises the reader against the perverse side of Bloom's nature with all his technical tricks, recalling the stylistic shrouds around pornographic content that typified Swinburne. In addition, Bloom does display a continuous pattern of decency in other aspects of life. This is a consistent message of the author: that there is no such thing as unalloyed good, no such state either as untainted evil. Scenes of Bloom's civic allegiance are also rendered more clearly by Joyce, distorting the reader's moral ratios. But there is little doubt that, placed in front of a court of law, with an empanelled jury of sensible men and women, there would be a high chance of the defendant being found guilty of a heinous crime on the weight of hard evidence and sentenced to a custodial term in Her Majesty's Prison. This is the hidden meaning of Bloom's dream trial in Circe. He knew he was guilty, in Trollopean terms. His level of culpability is only exacerbated by the naivety of his target. Gerty MacDowell is a simple young woman, wholly inexperienced in the ways of the world; what with her silly head still-filled with girlish fancies. She has never had a real boyfriend, let alone experienced sexual relations. She is a typical Catholic girl of her era. Her lack of emotional development is evidenced by her infatuation with a boy riding past her house on his bicycle. She is in no position to handle a seasoned rake like Bloom. Ironically, Bloom is much more like Blazes Boylan than a superficial reading of the text suggests. They are not so different, you and I, Mister Powers, with Boylan's 'blazing' being a clear reference to Shelley's time-limited ember which will soon be snuffed out. Gerty fantasises about Bloom as a mysterious foreigner in mourning, unhappily married to a shrew or the sad husband of a madwoman in need of her soft comfort. This is not so far from the truth, of course. She displays her ankles and hair for his gaze. She knows that he is becoming sexually aroused by voyeurism. Bloom is only a passing policeman away from infamy. But he doesn't care. This is the raw heat of male sexual desire on full display. Joyce is writing the temple scene in the *Iliad* when the marauding Greeks desecrate Athena's temple and rape and murder the population of Troy in a bestial frenzy. Bloom took up his pen. *Cissy, Edy and Gerty represent the NEW WAVE of Irish womanhood, seizing the moment and living for the Dublin of today!* NEW LINE. *Gerty MacDowell exclusively uses HYDROLOGICA brand products to maintain a bountiful Celtic glow. It's made from boilgeoga rising from the streams of Loch Ghleann Bheatha in the Derryveagh Mountains of County Donegal. It refreshes the flesh and the mind, even at the end of a long day of ACTION!* (insert line drawing of fashion model). Fine cursive penmanship. He finished composing the script and submitted it to Myles Crawford for approval. Lotus Eaters is full of Joycean denseness and irony. It begins with a supplication to the Virgin at the Star of the Sea church, a temperance retreat for men. As Bloom masturbates, shielded by thick shrubbery, Gerty is concerned about the foul language of her friends in front of such a fine-looking gentleman. She shows off more leg. Joyce's climactic image of a roman candle bursting in the sky above the Mirus Bazaar to gasps of delight juxtaposes Bloom's despondent orgasm. At this moment, Gerty rises from the seat. Bloom sees that she is lame in the leg that she has exposed to him. He feels sadness and self-disgust. They are both linked by the very essence of human vulnerability and frailty at this moment – Gerty's raw physical exposure being matched by Bloom's shame (albeit the causation is completely different). Joyce even throws in one of his rare metempsychotic linkages to bind them: Bloom speculates about women becoming more sexually dynamic during their menstrual cycles; Gerty notes the onset of her own period. In addition, there is a regressive connection to the young Molly Bloom, while Gerty's limp may even allude to Bloom's own impotence with his wife. For everything in Joyce is always interconnected with such ferocious intrastitching that the text reflects the relentless correspondences and disassociations of life itself, both predictable and random. But Bloom quickly recalibrates his mind onto carnal obsessions. He speculates on sexual competition between women, citing his wife and Josie Breen. He ponders new seduction strategies. He wonders if Gerty is really Martha Clifford. His thoughts turn to motherhood, his ex-lover Mina Purefoy and erotic magnetism. He wonders if his watch stopped at the moment when Molly was fucking with Hugh Boylan. Shanghai Dog pulled a small graph paper note from his wet pocket and studied Xiao Fang's elegant handwriting. It made him think of Judy's body. Strokes of a brush feint across a loose, defined surface. A firm tablet beneath. Inscrutable of meaning. He would need to give it to a trustworthy translator. Not Ricky at the front desk. Maybe Maggie. It would flush out any feelings for him if it contained a plaintive love tone. Martha Clifford includes a yellow daisy in her correspondence. Could have been a lotus. It was addressed to Mr Henry Flower, Poste Restante, Westland Row Station. Bloom's pseudonym. A safe place out the back of the town centre far from prying eyes north of the Liffey. Nabokov was right to instruct students to study a map of itineraries if they wanted to understand *Ulysses*. He was wrong to discard what he called "the pretentious nonsense of Homeric, chromatic, and visceral chapter headings." These were also an essential part of Joyce's cosmology both earnestly and as mockery. Also as a quiz. *Virag* means "flower" in Hungarian. It is a pun and a clue. One so obvious it would be easily detected by Molly Bloom (Google Search: 'H. Flower, Anatomist'). The taxi driver walked down Palmer Street with eighty bucks rent swelling his trouser pocket. Four Hargreaves halved. Ironic origami really, given the fate of his box kites at Stanwell Park. This coastal resort is set beneath a prominent escarpment just north of Thirroul, where the celebrated artist died in a three-star motel bathtub. We drove to the funeral parlour at Organs Road, Bulli. Bloom describes floating languidly in a barrel like some reborn chrysanthemum blossom. Sperm floating through clear hot water like a ghost. Redolent of discarded spirit. Flowers re-opening in a glass teapot on a shiny black café table in Suzhou. Phoenix in brine. Flower is called *hua* in Mandarin. Chrysanthemum tea is simply *juhua cha*. Chinese friends shake their heads and laugh in dismay when they try to pronounce this Latinate term. WOKA WOKA WOKA. Shanghai Dog shook his head at Xiao Fang's mild entreaties. Stephen pressed the buzzer. Martha's letter is full of insipid sentiments and anodyne romantic teasing. Nick Hagy shuffled down the hall in his tartan dressing gown and beret; toothless as old Mother Grogan. Joyce uses their puerile exchange as a contrast to the climax of Molly's monologue. That is REAL physical. Now it was still too early in the novel. Early enough for readers to still believe that Martha might be the full extent to which Joyce would take female characterisation. Nick opened the reinforced door of the Private Hotel and made gums at Pseudo-Stephen. Come inside, he said. The reader must undertake an odyssey to reach the visionary force and uninhibited commentary of Molly Bloom. How could Leopold Bloom of all people live with a woman like Martha Clifford? What would they say to each other after the fact? He needs Molly's frankness, her tolerance and ribald tongue. Stephen Joyce sat down at the circular dining table and passed his rent money to Nick. Nick wrote a receipt methodically. Carbon stained the edge of his hand. XF is a cunning girl. S-DOG admired her skills. But he would never marry her. The more trickery she displayed, the less chance she stood. Judy never manipulated him. O never read his texts. She didn't ask him what happened at karaoke. More people penetrated the carriage. The mass lifted S-DOG. He surveyed the long open cabin. Pseudo-Joyce returned down the long lightless corridor of pummelled doors like blanked-out teeth. They stood under an advertising sign. St Outer Inn, it read. Cyclops is the climax of the public theme of *Ulysses*. Various people returned Shanghai's gaze until they seemed to anthropomorphise into a panoptic eye. Quixotic Asia. A hive of human cliché. Leopold Bloom perceived the Orient as an indolent place defused by opium languor. How wrong he was. Imperialist spin. Indians were chronic masturbators, according to Mayo. Now we're stuck on the rim of the Asian Century. Joyce displays Bloom's limited range of experiences and uncritical use of stereotypes in this section. But always to an imaginative end. It is the capacity to make reverie – not its content – which Joyce seeks to impress on the reader as a positive feature of Bloom. The city government had built new malls and hotels around Jingan Temple until it became a walled citadel. They sold off slices of Jingan Park. Stephen Joyce walked up Bourke Street until he reached the Oxford Playhouse. They were busily refurbishing the whole site for Expo 2010. *Er Ling Yi Ling Bolanhui*. It resembled a siege zone on the banks of the Lupu Bridge. The Guanyin Hall was dominated by high scaffolding. Its six-metre goddess had been gridded with iron bars. Stephen Pseudo-Joyce gazed across Taylor Square. A fine site for a monument, he reckoned. Nelson's Cock. The Colossus of Taylor Square. This thought represented an act of metempsychosis with the narrator (see C10, p.1 & 7). Bronze Leatherman spreading crotchless cowboy pants over Oxford Street like Tom of Finland. Gonads hung with traffic lights like bondage weights. Massive erection thrusting towards the city. Shade for the weary. Jade Buddha upright and tense within a stark grey concrete frame awaiting new gilt panes. Ewan blew the arse out of his saxophone to kickstart the band. GAG OF COROM hung from a torn bedsheet banner. Madge bit a guitar pick. Tom Hallem was swept against the tidal recession of the stunned crowd. His body suspended in fluid. Lourdes cure. Waters of Lethe. Pure oblivion. Statues bleeding sockets. "I.N.R.I." Against a white-washed wall, he examined a small photograph by Juan Davila. The artist faced the camera wearing a dirty singlet. His lover reclined across his chest. He was topless and unconscious with his jeans open. A Renaissance figuration of Christ's limp carcass in the arms of Mary Immaculate. "I.H.S." Need a cake of soap, pondered Fuller. Palms against yielding flesh. Fingers pressing rib ripples. Clean out the cage. The narrative is internalised and personal here. All inside Bloom's head. He observes a sequence of advertisements responding to them with a cool professional eye then dredges up a list of narcotics: wine, cigars, soap, warm baths, religion, opiates, tea. Bloom repeats subjects raised by Stephen in the first three chapters. Telemachus *redux*. More metempsychosis. Stephen leading. Joyce emphasises contrast not confluence between SD and LB:

Table 19. Stephen Dedalus versus Leopold Bloom – Traits (1)

Stephen Dedalus	**Leoplod Loomb**
Most private (e.g. bath)	Voyeuristic
Shy	Corporeal
Romantic Reveries	Ribald ones
Imagined Encounters	Actual Recollections
Tender	Vital
Surface only	All inner
Tortured	Easy
Catholic	Worldly
Self-possessed	Observant – detached
Eucharist – ceremonial	Eucharist – innate to self
Abstract	Real
Vertical	Horizontal
Virginal	Cuck

Joyce conforms to Homer's morphology by placing Stephen's narrative first in the novel then making his Odysseus figure follow the son almost telepathically. His characterisation of SD in the first chapter of *Ulysses* is located in the sentimental tradition of the *Bildungsroman*; in particular, the opening scenes of Flaubert's *Sentimental Education*. However, Joyce gives SD relatively soft-lens treatment. By contrast, Flaubert portrays his erstwhile hero, Frederic Moreau, in a state of mawkish infatuation with Madame Arnoux on a paddle steamer. Moreau is relentlessly outfitted with Romance clichés. His overblown rapture at Marie as a Vision of Beauty (which is not shared by other passengers) is echoed in Stephen Dedalus' naivety towards women and love; although his romantic feelings are not fixed on any individual person in *Ulysses*. This makes it less intense than Flaubert's characterisation. Flaubert also directly contrasts Frederic's elevated sentiments towards Madame Arnoux with his rudeness towards servants and off-handedness with his mother. In fact, he is only polite to people who can further his ambitions. A similar contrast is created in *Ulysses* when Stephen Dedalus bumps into his sisters – although this episode is used by Joyce for quite different effect. Joyce conducts a much more incisive class and gender analysis than Flaubert, who is simply interested in exposing the fripperies of the *haute bourgeoisie*. Joyce does not overtly damn Stephen Dedalus. He discloses how the social structure and poverty of Dublin has created gross anomalies between genders – even within individual families – simply by articulating the contrast in education, status and opportunities between Stephen and his sisters. Stephen is seen as selfish and self-interested but that is really just a product of youth. He is not damned for lack of feeling by Joyce. He is just relatively helpless (unlike his father). Tom Hallem turned back to the sound. Bloom admired an impeccably attired socialite sitting in a deck chair sipping a champagne flute. She saw him and uncrossed her legs to disclose the garter of her black silk stockings. Her hard smirk shrank Tom to his station like coarse Mellors. He turned away. His dealer grabbed him by surprise.

"Tom, this is Marion Hackett," rasped Elizabeth Archer. "She's joining our little gang next year."

"I'm glad to finally meet you," said Marion holding out a hand.

"Same. What type of art do you make?" asked Tom Hallem gripping then releasing her palm.

"She's a curator," interjected Elizabeth.

"What?"

"A curator," added Marion firmly. "Think of my role like that of an impresario. Or an entrepreneur. I'm putting together a show called *Naming Rights*. Each work will be labelled "Untitled." Then I will insert my own choice of title in parentheses."

"Like appropriation."

"Precisely. And there's one other thing. I sign all the works."

"Pardon?"

"I put my signature in the bottom right hand corner of each art object on show."

"She's critiquing the individualistic artistic ego."

"It's mobilising Feminism against the heroic male."

"We want you to participate in *Naming Rights*," said his dealer.

"Do I get to sign my work as well?" asked Tom Hallem.

"That isn't aligned with my praxis," replied Ms. Hackett.

"Couldn't we both sign the work? I could sign on the bottom left side. You could sign the right. Like a contract."

"That won't work either."

"It's all way too complex for me," giggled Tom Hallem waving his fingers in the air like tiny propellers. "What's the profit split?"

"50:50."

"That's a good deal for you," he replied emphatically.

"I've got the connections."

"Well, I haven't heard of you. But I dare say you have."

"She's got an international profile."

"I'm an enabler. My business model enables obscure artists to create saleable commodities. All the best conceptual artists have turned to marketable product in recent years."

Peter Booth's thick oils. Parr's charcoaled elfs. Anthropomorphic skulls of John Walker. Local variants on Cy Twombly. Imants Tillers' assemblages comprising small plaster boards are now being sold individually. Make art out of coins and notes. Numismartics. Macquarie Bank will launch a new closed-end fund for contemporary art to HNWs next year. Fund Number One will be raising $100 million. Three-year term. Minimum entry level five million dollars. Target IRR of thirty per cent on equity. The Straits Times reports that Community Pirate Group is preparing to list a Business Trust for Chinese toll road assets on the SGX. BT structures enable distributions out of available cash funds rather than distributable profits. *1M WORDS* (see C11) will examine the commercial equation facing all artists – can you be interesting and obedient? Matt Supplejack answered YES. The Stooges NO. Thom Hallem also. Billy Capri YES, EVENTUALLY.

"You can't just paint pictures anymore," stated Marion Hackett.

"But I like ... painting," Tom Hallem replied.

"It's not enough," she answered.

"I know that," said Tom stoically.

"So, what are you going to do about it," demanded Marion.

"Well, I'll start by doing whatever you want," he concluded gaily.

"I told you he'd see reason," interjected Elizabeth Archer touching his sleeve. Her fingertips left swipes of make-up on his brown coat. Also, taint of some perfume he did not recognise. Note symbolism.

"I'm glad that's all fixed. Now come and look at the rest of the show, Marion. Tom's work is titled "Speed Painting." It's hung next to Matt's portrait of "Merlin." He just bought it for his conservatory. It will look majestic against the harbour view from Lavender Bay. I'll also to introduce you to Ray Hughes. He's just come down from Brisbane. Going to make a big impact on the Sydney scene."

Elizabeth extracted Marion Hackett. They withdrew into the throng. Tom observed their coat-hanger flanks receding. Shanghai Dog stepped on a tiny shoe. A lotus-shape foot is most highly prized by husbands. Baihua Yundong. Putrid blooms. Too crippled to walk without support. Chained. Fake solicitations. Oedipus Swellfoot. Left to die in the hills with his ankles pinned together. Lester squashed down a shaft. Byron was called a lame brat by his mother. Changed his name to Noel to collect his inheritance. Signed NB. Gull everyone into presenting their opinions. Then bag em. Collective mutilation of thought. Link to Tom's supplication. He pressed through the throng. READ caught Tom's regard. He put forth another reticulated smile. Cassius in a clown's curly orange wig. Tom unsealed the envelope. A crack in lamella. Robert's unprotected spine. Dead child wilting on a stone slab. Refrigerator door closing in a bare paddock. Chaim. Breathe withdrawing. Stay still wait for rescue: uncome. Tom extracted a sheet of A5 paper from his pocket. Crease of O's nape. Laugh lines around semi-diluted eyes. Horizon crinkling. Our love affair. Useless and misguided as the flight of paper airplanes. More passengers entered the subway at Nanjing Donglu. Tom shielded the contents from view. Groggy Elpenor. HE FELL DOWN SHAFT LIKE LESTER DONE DONE. Better to be a slave of Marion or Circe than Hades' King. He read Elizabeth's note. Be on your guard tonight. Beware, love. We must talk. I can type sixty words per minute, sir. Oh Henry, I do so long for your vitals next visit to Mullingfar. ENSIGNED MARTHART. Joyce uses epistolary text in a variety of ways in *Ulysses*. Rudolf Virag writes a suicide note. Deasy proselytises. Milly sense mail that shows favour to her father. Bloom and Martha flirt. The anonymous postcard to Dennis Breen is an impermeable practical joke. Boylan sends a message to Molly in advance of his arrival. Rumbold the Hangman writes a job application to the High Sheriff. Joyce got a telegram from his father with a misspelling about his mother's impending death. Nother dying, it said. Come home. See Chapter Six. This type of linguistic error stayed with Joyce as a template for displacing emotional climaxes. Good Friday 1903. He borrowed the sea fare off one of his students and went back to Dublin. Thus, was the entry point of *Ulysses* made. It made him fear postal deliveries for the rest of his life, just like his terror of lightning. Ezra Pound wrote to the unpublished author in Trieste in 1913. "Dear Sir, Mister Yeats has been speaking to me." Still no publisher for *Dubliners* after 8 years grind. Let alone a bite on *Portrait*. Pound had a keen eye for talent. They had a hate or two in common. That's a problematical bond, said Joyce. Eventually, he turned against Pound. Orlando hung letters on trees all around the Forest of Arden. No jewel like Rosalind. *Lear* is powered by false correspondence. Missives that confuse or deflect. Downright lies. Polonius reading Ophelia's private mail from Hamlet aloud to Claudius and Gertrude. "Dear F, art-to-groans reckon. Return used machines to stores forthwith." Aeschylus introduced a second actor who delivered an oral report of past or external events to the play. This was the start of dramatic dialogue. Sophocles turned the stage into a mail room. Or rather a telephone exchange with many operators sporting Bakelite mouthpieces. Serving girls hooked between the walls with wires. Telemachus moved carefully beneath them through a flyscreen of limp legs. Tom Hallem crunched his benefactor's message into ribbons and discarded it on the bare wooden floor. Crumpled throwaway. Elijah is coming. Marat's hand slowly releasing a foil. Cold bathroom tiles. Ana bent over the bowl. Another rejected meal floating before her eyes in soggy blocks. Last words of the Old Testament. Jesus has returned in the form of Dr Sun Myung Moon, Korean car manufacturer. Malachi's prophecy. A rank outsider. Heavily hyped by his lady trainer. Gather shekels while you can, stated Lenehan. Boylan put two quid on Sceptre: one for himself and one for Moll. Thames tide rushing through North Sea brine. *Ne Plus Ultra*. Calpe Mons | | Abile Mons. Pass between. Go to New South Wales. Island of Lotus Eaters. Cast off from Phaeacia bound for Ithaca. Gibraltar was a colonial version of. Trawl the remains. Never the same. Dog returning to old sick. Aeneas blasting his way out of Troy. The Gods placed Leer on a mail train all stops to Broken Hill. Wait for a lift from Athena by the last rail buffer at Ivanhoe. She'll pick you up in a truck. Eighth Army surplus. Desert currents flowing brack and froth. Operation Bertram. Bantam Lyons at Bloom's armpit bludging squizzes at the threadbare Freeman. Emblem of democracy. Give it to him, just to get rid of him. 5 yrs, 9 st 4 lbs (W. Lane). Let the tide take me under Loopline Bridge down the Tank Stream to Customs House. Spouter Inn. Zhu Di dressed my body. Her markings on my form. Tight shirts locked my chest in a synthetic stockade. Cuff links I could never get off. Hephaestus' chains. Broken pipes. Black hair on the wash basin. Gold cologne. O holding tight to the window. Marion Hackett had Matt Supplejack pinioned under spotlights. A blankety canvas. Bacon's carcass. Gouged in streams. We are the Orangemen. Stuffed fellas. Umbrella ribs. Skinshine. 1493 self-portrait. Beautiful Durer grasping flower spray. Symbolistic Thistles. An aphrodisiac. Shanghai Dog felt his frozen crotch. Dutch glory. *Myj sach die gat. Als es oben schtat*. Give myself over to a higher force. Tom Hallem analysed the multitude as IMAGE. Christ entering Brussels. Brueghel's "Babel." Crowded-out space. Caius Martius arrives at the grain silo in *Coriolanus* with thanks for nothing and immediately discloses his rhetorical skills with a complex parody of Menenius' metaphor of the State-as-body. His language is richly alliterative. It mocks the mutinous crew. He is wearing his trade-in *Agnomen*. LINK TO BURTON'S ANATOMY. Frye's fourth place. His disdain lets the mob feel its own value; albeit in negative terms. Instead of paradoxes, he employs raw dichotomy. He encourages ferment. Revolution is his natural function. It's like O said (C7, F/N 74). To alter the natural world, metaphor is piled upon metamorphosis with Spasmodic zeal until no-thing is left untransferred/untransformed – first animals (lions become hares and fox become geese) then cosmic phenomena ("coal of fire" on ice and hailstones living in the sun). Maxims follow with human metaphors of illness and depravity. He descends into the ocean to conjure oxymoronic "fins of lead" then flies into the sky to flap against a wild oak. He longs to be present at any site where he can continue to make antinomian utterance. Like Mao, he is centripetal by disposition. Literary minutiae becomes the driver of social upheaval. A poem. A play. One word. A letter. Theatre reviews. It all started with *The Dismissal of Hai Rui by Wu Han*. An anonymous review by Yao Wenyuan unlocked its symbolism against Mao (Dikotter, 48). *The Dilemma of Peng Zhen* followed like the second act of a Sophoclean trilogy. The final instalment was always the arrival of Kang Sheng. He was the dreaded security chief who tortured confessions out of detainees. There had to be a record of admission to justify redress. Everything Mao read was charged with meaning. He was quintessentially a literary critic. The closest models in the West at this time were F.R. Leavis and William Buckley. Mao had stooges who could transmit his thoughts intuitively just like Murdoch. The media magnate got an AC off Hawkie this year. *The Australian* is endorsing the ALP in 1984. Always cheer home a clear favourite. Adds to the kill ratio. Caius Martius could never erase the impact of words. They ate away at him like battery acid. Language compelled him to demolish Chinese culture. Replace it all with slogans. Broadcast them through loud speakers. Pedestrians pressed mutely into a dispute between two transport policemen and an agitated migrant worker. The circle closed. Like Polyphemus, the little man implored his neighbours for assistance. They were mute at first. Just watching. This is a symbol of the social apathy that Homer predicts unless a regal system is restored. Anonymous voices started to berate authority. A van approached. Horn blaring. Shanghai Dog edged off. Unlike Mao, Deng Xiaoping couldn't be bothered with word games. He played life like a card game. He was addicted to bridge, after all. China would industrialise in Stage One. This would require more bending before the West. An urban proletariat would form. This was consistent with Marxist dogma. Government officials and phoney entrepreneurs would become *haute bourgeoisie*. This structure would induce the conditions for REAL REVOLUTION. Deng was also a pragmatist. He learned the value of performance surviving Mao's dynasty. Like any actor, he could recite any lines. He did vaudeville. Went on the road with a pantomime troupe. Visited the States. Wore Carter's cowboy plumes. But he had always been a hardcore communist since his bandit days back in Guangxi. Bloom reflects on his own life and starts to feel ambitious for Stephen near the end of Ithaca. He would like to provide advice to the younger man on the pitfalls of existence. However, Stephen can only learn by hard experience. He doesn't respect a middle-aged clerical worker. READ grasped Tom's shoulder and turned him towards a small coterie of supporters.

"I was just telling the team that I went to London at your age, Tom. I met all the movers and shakers. Stayed for the best part of a decade."

"Didn't they put you down as ... convict stock?" asked Merlin.

"Actually, it was a great advantage coming from Australia. The pop groups all dug *Oz* magazine. It's how I met Lizzie. She was almost full-term. I got to hang out in the Scene. Not just with stale old art types. Where is it all happening now, Peter?"

"Who knows?" replied Fuller dully. "I'm just a critic."

"Not true," replied READ theatrically. "You're an agent provocateur."

"In some places, I am considered reactionary. Even a traitor."

"Because of Ruskin?" asked Hallem.

"Because I didn't follow the Party Line," replied Fuller to the unintroduced face.

"What about your writings on Cultural Imperialism," asked Harolde. "Surely your Marxist cronies approve."

"That was my last gasp," answered Fuller. "And my book on Berger was the final straw."

"He just didn't like your goldfish, darling," snapped READ in retort.

"He missed a plane once when my car broke down on the airport overpass at Heathrow. I think that was the last straw."

"*Tres* Ballard," concluded READ winking at the critic.

Fuller shrugged and emptied his glass. William Morris dancing upon a dime. He adjusted giant anamorphic spectacles and gazed at his smoky reflection in the pane of a Tramp Art frame. Narelle Jubelin's petit point. Marion and Elizabeth returned to Tom Hallem's side. Goneril and Regan never such glowed.

"I was just looking at your painting," said Hackett. "It's aligned with my current *leitmotif*."

"Which is?"

"The Fall."

"Great Band. Saw them at the Trade Union Club last year."

"She means Postlapsarian culture," added Elizabeth sagely.

"As a symbol of industrial decline."

"Maybe linked to the debility of Modernism," offered Tom Hallem.

"Correct," replied Marion.

"Tell him about your next *Gesamtkunstwerk*, Marry."

"I am going to construct a hollow tree trunk from floor to ceiling in the centre of a dark exhibition space. It will represent one leg of Odysseus' marital bed. The archetype of the patriarchal anchor. Penelope's chain. But this phallic motif will undercut by an internalising representation of Femaleness."

"There will be an entrance to the installation shaped like a vast pudendal cleft," said Elizabeth.

"Like Georgie O'Keefe's flower paintings," added Tom Hallem helpfully.

"At last, we can travel inside the prostrate female in Duchamp's 'Etant Donnes'."

"Precisely. Inside, layers of shattered glass on the floor will be covered by a blanket of fallen leaves."

"Symbolising Autumn," continued Elizabeth.

"As well as a pun on the act of falling," added Tom.

"The risk of a sudden fall is omnipresent."

"The leaves signify environmental degradation and the death of Nature."

"The audience will be required to remove their shoes and change into work boots to protect their feet when they enter the installation."

"It's an OHS requirement," said Elizabeth matter-of-factly.

"This act will critique the modern obsession with fashion."

"It also alludes to the redundancy of workers in a post-industrial state."

"It will be almost totally black inside. The walls will be moist, sticky and soft. The viewer will be exposed to a recording of the soundscape inside the womb."

"The beating of a mother's heart," added Elizabeth hopefully. *Amor matris*. Chaim.

"Wire sculptures will hang from the ceiling."

"Metabolised human forms."

"Emblems of State suppression."

"What Foucault calls Bio-Power."

"*Biopouvoir*," added Marion with faultless French assonance.

"We are going to film the whole event," said Elizabeth.

"And run LIVE tape loops through the gallery."

"Everything will be documented," said Elizabeth.

"I've already pre-sold it to the NGA."

"This reflects Marion's praxis. Nothing is out of bounds."

"Last year, I stuffed a plush unicorn skin with used tampons and posted it to MOMA in protest against the Modernist Masters exhibition excluding women artists. Then I produced a limited series of 20 replicas."

A scoop of Merle Oppenheim's spoon. One of the great household images. Up there with Cezanne's fruit. Yayoi Kuzama invented soft art in the 1950s. She was a precursor of Oldenburg. His success was re-gendered plagiarism, if you like. His first wife, Patty Mucha, did all the inglorious sewing jobs like Penelope. No Wikipedia entry for her. Eva Hesse didn't live long enough to get sidelined. She died of a brain tumour at age 34. Excellence has no sex, she said. The first superstars of the recorded era were female blues singers. There was no equivalent until the 1980s. Fifty women artists in the Armoury Show (1913). Photography was not an established form when Cameron snuck into the frame. Dorothea Lange, Diane Arbus, Barbara Kruger and Jenny Holzer are notable artists working in this medium today. Suzanne Valadon was not a great technical artist. But she was a solid second division painter who achieved significance in her last years. "The Blue Room" (1923) is a brilliant painting. It reworks the odalisque composition into a piercing critique of gender, age, the gaze, exposure, body image and female labour options (prostitution). It indicts a hypocritical society. Her other female nudes in the 1920s were all strong. She was largely known as Renoir's dance model and Utrillo's mother until the 1980s. Louise Bourgeois is another artist who found her milieu in sculpture later in life (c. 1967 onwards). The American Mary Cassatt was a consummate technician. She was the equal of any Impressionist painter in the 1870s. For examples of her best work, see the brilliant colour and tone of "Woman with a Pearl Necklace" (1879), the highly innovative composition of "The Boating Party" and the perfect execution of a classic structure in the "Child's Bath" (both 1893). Cite also Hale, Coffin, Nourse and Beaux. Kath Kollwitz and Georgia O'Keeffe have been noted elsewhere in this chapter. Cecilia Beaux was a portrait painter. However, "Landscape with Farm Building" (1888) is a ground-breaking image which reverberated through American art in the twentieth century. Romaine Brooks also found a unique palette and subject matter after 1905. "White Azaleas" (1910) has a unique take on perspective. "La Trajet" is a landmark symbolist painting of sex and death. It has become a model for countless inferior Gothic illustrations of Albino corpses since the 1970s.

"Marion was saying you should exhibit in Perth."

"Why?"

"It's my hometown, Tom. I know how it works. I can help."

"READ went there last year. Highly successful show."

"It's such a long journey," mused Tom almost whining.

"Fifty hours driving time," stated Marion knowingly.

"I could fly there, I guess."

"You would profit more from a road trip," Elizabeth responded.

"What would I do?"

"You could experience life on the road. Visit abandoned mining towns. Draw roadhouses. Have you ever seen the Outback?"

"I've never been west of Katoomba."

"Perth is a really good place to get rid of second-rate works," said Marion definitively.

"I can vouch for that," added Read clinking champagne flutes.

"I can't support you forever Tom," blurted Elizabeth.

He faced their silence.

"I know," replied Tom quietly.

She drew him away.

"Did you get my note?" she asked.

"Yes."

"I have an idea for generating some extra cash. But we need to discuss it in private. I've also arranged a post-show soiree. Will you come?"

Hallem nodded. Elizabeth walked off. He followed her. Blinded by light then darkness they moved beyond the gallery walls backstage. Elizabeth's disembodied voice filled his ear.

"Go upstairs and wait. I'll only be a few minutes."

She led him to the elevator and depressed the call button. He listened to cables grinding up and down the shaft. The elevator doddered to a halt. He wrenched back the brass latches on the outer and inner doors. The cabin ground skywards. The city cast its glow through blockhouse grates. Clouds closed on cracked panes. Squalls of wind and rain touched his mouth. He proceeded across the floor (see C2). Pictures lined the walls along the corridor to Elizabeth's office. He sat down in an old armchair chair. His palms rested on cracked leather. Her touch. Gentler than before. He rested. Sleep came quickly. Narrow but deep. To propitiate Poseidon and close the *Odyssey*, Odysseus was required to find a race of people who had never seen the sea. Out beyond the never-never. Perth. Pass Boake's dead men. Lying. On the way. He wasn't that type of chap. Neither was Odysseus. He tried to dodge the draft. Busted by Palamedes. Elizabeth's footfalls, distant but crisp like typewriter keys, closed. Soft humming. His body swivelled. She swept past him, pushed open the door and went inside. A stream of drops from a glass of iced water disclosed her trail. She unlocked the top drawer of a filing cabinet and extracted a small plastic bag.

"Want some blow?" she asked.

Elizabeth burped a mound of cocaine onto the desk and placed a worn palm over the powder. Brittle skin on the back of her hands. Tom stood mutely. She cut four lines and took two herself immediately. Tom followed. His eyes wept.

"I've got good news. We're going to have an exhibition in Paris next year to coincide with the Biennale. I want you there, Tom."

She gripped his hand.

"I've already sorted out a stipend with the Australia Council. It will cover your airfare and accommodation. There's also a three-month residency at the Cite des Artes. But you've got to take it up in January."

"That's a really tight timeframe."

"The sooner the better, I say."

"I'll need cash."

"That's what I want to discuss."

"There's no time to mount a show in Perth."

"That can wait. I've got a better idea. It relates to READ. There's a lot of demand for his work. Record prices. Investors aren't fussy. They just want to own the name. But he can't produce substantial pieces at the moment. He can only ... doodle."

"Send him off to Detox."

"That would be a complete waste of time and money. No, what he needs is help to produce new work. Look, Tom. You're going to be at a loose end for a few weeks until you go to Paris. I was thinking you could spend some time with Read in his studio."

"Like an assistant?"

"More like a proxy."

"What do you mean exactly?"

"You could pick up the gist of his current interests from his notebooks. Turn them into paintings. He signs. We sell them privately. It's a bit like the academy of an Old Master."

"That's forgery."

"Warhol did it."

"Screen-printing is different."

Good business is the best art, said Andy. Just get your camera in focus on somebody famous. Celebrities always generate sales. He produced nine hundred works per year in a big warehouse on the Lower East Side. See Benjamin (WAAMR). Fifteen assistants. Approximately one work each per week. Not a new occurrence. Innovation in industrial arts had been driven by the profits of mechanical reproduction since ancient times. The stamp mill in Ancient Greece. Woodcuts, etching, lithography, engraving, even photography more recently. Warhol worked the margin between mass reproduction and the unique individual art product. This was the sweet spot. He inverts every maxim like a glib libertarian. Insert mall-shibboleths. You can even make outsider work into a franchise. F for Fake. Don't look too long. Make it all jump cuts. Create a sense of haste with images and words.

Ulysses was mainly fast dialogue (external + internal). *F(W)ake* by contrast is mainly monologue. Its portmanteau vocabulary bogs down the act of reading. Magritte was an expert forger. After the War, he produced fakes by Picasso, Braque and de Chirico in Paris. He moved onto counterfeit banknotes next. His surrogate son was put in charge of sales and distribution. See Leer/Hallem. Selling fake Soviet badges at Camden markets for pin money. Buying fake bags at *Ke Zhi Guan*. Give them to cheap girlfriends. Rachel buying majong tile bracelets for one buck at the markets then selling them in Sydney for ten. Mariën Magritte was part of a Belgian gang. He invented Étrécissements because he couldn't draw or paint. Cut-downs and assemblages. Spiked photographs. A knife passed from Sade to Lenin across a woman's breast. Blucher's bloof. He abandoned formal production in 1954. He was a renowned prankster. In 1962, he published a fake catalogue announcing steep discounts on Magritte's works including a new system of pricing-by-size. Magritte terminated their relationship. It would have been the same with Bloom and Stephen inevitably. The former would never have been able to accommodate the latter's hubris. The latter for his part would have tired of order.

"It's easy money."

"Why me?"

"I can trust you. You need cash. And you've got the best technique out of everyone I know."

"I am a legitimate artist," replied Tom Hallem defiantly.

"All the more reason to make it our little secret. Nobody would suspect someone like you. Look, I need money as well. Stan's tied me over for a few months. But he won't bail me out this time. I need to look to my future."

Tears filled her pale blue eyes suddenly.

"Leon is sick Tom," she said faltering. "He's got AIDS."

The heavy thud of the band worked through the floorboards. *Passionis fac consortem*. Their eyes met for a moment then desynchronised like two lighthouses scanning the invisible sea. Hallem contemplated the proffered act. Collective workshops in the style of [INSERT NAME]. Renaissance patrons inscribing their signatures on someone else's masterpieces. Do not forever gaze with veiled eyelids, Hamlet. Cezanne never signed his works. Picasso authorised an employee to forge his signature. DALI's production line of acolytes. Duchamp transformed a leaf of red paper into a commodity by adding his seal. He sold boxes of miniatures.

"What's my cut?"

"Twenty-five per cent."

"What are they worth?"

"His best paintings are selling for eighty thousand dollars. These works would be one rung below that. Maybe fifty."

"I want half."

"Don't fuck with me Tom," replied Elizabeth harshly. "I don't have any room to move. Read is taking half. That means we're splitting 50:50. It's a take-it or leave-it proposition."

"When would I start?" asked Tom Hallem.

"As soon as you like. Tomorrow! I've got clients waiting."

"How many works do you want?"

"I was hoping to get five large oil paintings plus related studies. I need it to look like a legitimate series."

"That's one major work every two weeks."

"Correct. Can you do it?"

"Sure. How do I get paid?"

"Cash post-sale."

"I want to get paid on delivery."

"I don't have the cashflow, Tom. It's got to be based on sales."

"But I'll be overseas by then. You can pay my mother."

"Can you trust her?"

"Got a better suggestion?" he asked.

Penelope's diligence in the *Odyssey* has been universally admired. She sacrificed everything for her son. It required a cold persona. This is the principle trope transferred from Homer to this work. Plus tactical wit. Elizabeth Archer exhibits all these traits. Tom would get his mother to make periodic wire transfers to Europe. She could store the rest of the cash in her safe deposit box. Not even Les knew about that. It was also a good way to wash the proceeds. In *PAYM*, Joyce wrote that "whatever else is unsure in this stinking dunghill of a world a mother's love is not." But he was obsessed with his own mother's self-sacrifice. Catholic guilt always drove him to absolutes about Mary Joyce. AMBITION is an apt substitute for 'love' in this quote. And/or PERSISTENCE. You could insert COMPETITION as a codicil. There are many apathetic, downtrodden and passive mothers. Ones who don't make a lot of difference to their children's experience, and thus have meaning only as LACK. Conversely, there are stage mothers and fucked-up sadists who torture their offspring. Their kids act as mere surrogates. Mothers like Mrs Bennet in P&P. Mothers who never build you up, only push you back down like Gertrude. Mary Dedalus has already reached the end of her ordeal by the start of *Ulysses*. She is "beastly dead," in Mulligan's crude phrase. (Insert results of Page Find). Stephen Dedalus is now an adult. His father is running amok in Dublin. Cite Larkin's famous poem. Stephen is thus without ballast. But he hasn't grown up with ABSENCE. Telemachus was two years old when his father left. Only Elizabeth's daughter in this work would come to know the same lack. She also had to work through the lies about his identity. My mother sent me to grammar school to learn about men. Everything was fine for the first decade. It was only at the end that things went wrong. Suitors besieged Penelope. Molly Bloom runs too hot and fast to generate true affection from Milly. She is more in the vein of Emma Bovary. She has a performer's ego much like my own mother. This puts an artificial film over everything. The Bloom family represents repressed rivalry but it is kind of apathetic. This contains some resemblances to the author's relations with his wife and daughter, although the general consensus is that Lucia was spoiled by both parents until she showed signs of madness at which point her father's guilt created an obsession with finding a cure.

"So ... are you in?" asked Elizabeth.

"His style is pretty basic. Yes. Count me in."

"Great. I want you to focus on harbour scenes. It's his best-selling point. Take him down to the jetty with his sketchbooks if you can get him out of the house. Or drive him to Woolloomooloo Bay. That's the closest waterfront to his new studio. You can use the Merc. That'll give the works more credibility. You should go now. Here. Take this bag," she winked brightly. "I've got to get ready for dinner." The Lady departed the tower at this point to go down to her subjects below. **[CYCLOPS]** This episode opens in the style of Old Celtic sagas. It describes the marketplace as a land of plenty. Joe Hynes and the unnamed narrator arrive at a pub. They greet The Citizen and his dog, Garryowen. The Citizen is described mock-heroically. Tom Cornwall (not "I") was waiting at a low Formica table next to a row of poker machines when Don Cane entered the Crest Hotel. Shanghai Dog felt a sudden dizziness. He squinted. Double vision, he thought. A homophone. Twenty-six eyeballs set on the carriage vault arched with a fringe of bay trees. He returned to the street. Cyclops contains the only first-person, present-tense narrative in *Ulysses*. It is split between two voices – a growling reporter (Narrator A) who reinforces the prejudices of The Citizen and a pompous raconteur (Narrator B) who undercuts both characters in a sequence of faux parodies. For the purposes of this sub-episode, Citizen = Ocker. He represents the Captain of the Push. There is a sequence of allusions in the Strine passages to the ribald poem, "Bastard of the Bush," attributed to Henry Lawson. The use of a military rank for the principle drug dealer in the area provides ironic counterpoint to the genuine service status of Cornwall and Cane. The clock struck Nine. His whistle loud and piercing woke the echoes of the Rocks. A stuffed cuckoo popped out of a clock on the wall. Nearly took me eye out. Freemason's boy was coming back to the table with a silver thread hanging out of his pocket. He had a big win today on the MALLBURN CUT. He's out and back, out and back, up and down, in and out like an Irishman at church. Solange on her haunches. Leer lapping like a dog. The paper lantern rocked gently above Billy's head as he wrote. Joyce uses 33 stylistic parodies over the course of the Cyclops episode. They act as a precursor to the more satisfying chronological sequence of prose styles in Oxen of the Sun. I say 'more satisfying' because the Oxen episode has a precise structural goal: to trace the evolution of English prose to its apogee in Joyce. This linguistic project commenced in *Portrait of the Artist as a Young Man* with Baby Tuckoo and ended with the hybrid vocabulary, melded languages and neologisms of *Finnegans Wake*. By contrast, the parodies in Cyclops are intercut into the narrative as stand-alone units to extrapolate the subject matter at hand. They are not necessarily intended to cast meaning. Rather they often seem designed to bewilder – even bore – the reader, mirroring the impact of Bloom's own speech on listeners (an 'outside text/inside text' parallax). Some replicate Bloom's pedantry (e.g. "Herr Professor Luitpold"). Others parody the effusive style of nationalist legends echoing The Citizen (i.e. the "sinewyarmed hero" and his erroneous list of famous Irishmen). The specific style of each lampoon appears arbitrary. They act as anti-masques to expose the authorial hand (AKA postmodern gesture). Joyce's Narrator B is the stylistic and thematic opposite of the streetwise POV of Narrator A. They represent extremes placed in a dialectic in which the "real" author is revealed by inference (synthesis). Narratorial voice is effectively abolished, enabling Joyce to detach himself as author from all opinions and float free through the text. This is critical for Joyce as he is thus able to mobilise The Citizen's racism and chauvinism to goad Bloom to finally SPEAK OUT at the climactic end of the episode. This is the only example of forcefulness by Bloom in *Ulysses*. Elsewhere he is always fussing and fudging even when he asserts preferences. Only when he thinks about sex does he become decisive. Don Cane glared at the ageing newsprint. **Giants Clash at Belmore!** Steamroller props, Artie Beetson and Merv Hicks, will go head-to-head on Sunday when Balmain clash with Canterbury. Kronos v Uranus. He looked for a date in the bottom corner of the page. July 1969. A match he'd never seen. Players he'd never heard of. Foreign wars have been the cause of all our problems, says Citizen. He was seconded to MACVSOG on Operation Footboy that year. His detachment of Hmong commandos climbed into the highland fissures across the Cambodian border to plant AK-47 magazines on dead NVA. Charlie always picked-up any spare ammo off corpses. A booby-trap in the ammunition made gun barrels explode. It maimed the user's hands and blinded them. Not a clean execution. Put a palm over your mouth. Breathe subtly. Kill them with K-Bars. Eyes bulge then fade. We emptied their pockets on the jungle floor. Never stuff to plunder. Just a few balls of rice. It was time to go down to his rendez-vous with Cornwall. Private Arthur Chase. Also, Toad Smith. Joe Gann in Bootle jail. The Citizen outlines the political crimes that got these three men slain. The subjects of Joyce's satire of styles in Cyclops include:

Irish legends; the Bible; society journalism (a wedding of trees); medieval romance; Rumbold's correspondence to the High Sheriff of Dublin (*op.cit.*); medical journals; a poetry review (ostensibly by Garryowen); even a child's primer. Joyce illustrates how different authors utilise specific styles to validate their texts. For example, mythic writers elevate characters to absurd degrees of strength, nobility and beauty. Academics mobilise technical language to contend intellectual authority. NICK CAVE employs a lowbrow twang with religious imagery to elucidate a Southern Gothic argot (AKA Mildura Grotesque). Joyce created a postmodern assemblage of styles and forms in Cyclops. To work towards extreme technical innovation like Joyce, or to try to be inventive within well-established forms like Nick Cave, that is the question. Alternative bands in the Eighties had to deal with the exhaustion of innovation in core motifs from VU to post-punk. Some tried to find new keynotes with country or hip-hop flavs. They were trying to get to the methods later developed by Tom Waits and Beck. Tom Hallem sought originality in technical nuances across a broad range of subjects like Walter Pater. He wasn't living in an era of massive origination like Joyce. New matter of a highly personal nature using remote historical backdrops as scenery was his principal style. In this regard, he echoed Van Gogh, Munch and Kirchner. The colloquial Irish speech of The Citizen is replaced by Strine in this sub-episode. It is one of the few occasions in TMAC when the author directly intrudes into the space occupied by Joyce's greatest technical invention: that of Modernist High Style.[2] Strine was a comic form of phonetic English designed to represent Australian parlance. It was created by Alistair Morrison under the pseudonym Professor Afferbeck Lauder (Alphabetical Order) in 1965. It may have been inspired by the comic gobbledygook of Stanley Unwin, known as Unwinese or Basic Engly Twenty Fido, and popularised in the Carry-On movie, *Carry on Regardless* (1961), and the Small Faces record, *Ogden's Nutgone Flake* (1968). Both of these linguistic novelties owed a debt to Lewis Carroll's poem "Jabberwocky" (1871). The style of this sub-episode in *Ulysses* is **GIGANTISM**. SHIFT TENSE BACK. Cyclops is written IN THE NOW. Tom Cornwall stands when Don Cane enters. I seen it with me garryowen eyes. He pushes out one greyt fat mitt. Don grasps it with his own basted plate. Twin screen halos above their garrets show boxing classics and monochrome ruggerbeeleegah. Ron Casey in the commentary booth. Famechon returns for Round Fourteen. TC ducked his head left slightly. One BLUE eye was clear and sharp. The right ball glowed piscine inside a bung crater. Protruding jaw. Harada is showing signs of tiredness. The Organ of Cyclops is Muscle. It is a VIOLENT chapter. All characters are male. The Japanese raced to his corner at the end of the last round to get his swollen eye treated. There are no females in the audience

2 See Appendix B for a translation of relevant passages in this chapter.

at Budokan. Top Cat stomps over to the bar. It's a very different fight to their first bout in Sydney. He chews on beef jerky while the barmaid pours. Famechon has been much more aggressive this time. Prominent maxillae crunch. The bell sounds. Odysseus withdrew to the back of the cave to lure Polyphemus in. Famechon advances across no man's land and launches three massive lefts which force Harada back on the ropes. Battle of attrition back on. Canterbury won the Giltinan Shield this year in a low scoring game against Parramatta. They dethroned the three-times champion with almost impenetrable defence, enthuses Mossop. Famechon follows-up with both hands. "Change that channel Nola," spat Ocker. The referee orders a standing count. "I can't stand to watch that match again. I'm a one-eyed Eels fan. I mean you can't knock them Dogs." They made the most of what they got. It's not my bag but. I don't want to see." Ocker preferred the breakthrough at Passchendaele to the siege of Tobruk. A jaunt across no man's land fixed bayonets flaying. Finally, Haig was able to set his cavalry free after lingering en masse behind the frontline for four long years. There's more content/ment on the plains with Achilles than holed up inside a pillbox. The narrator entered. Ockerbeck Louder was seated in a velvet cubicle periodically dispensing brown sandwich bags to mules. Harada throws his arms around Famechon's waist in a rugby league style tackle, announced Casey. Don Cane sat down facing bright machines, unheeded like wallflowers. A small cash-flow problem had reduced me to a pocket full of dumps and a ticket which would yield a small profit on the Big Race. Fortunately for Yours Somewhat Truly, Ocker likes me ugly mug down the peanuts. Stops other horses drawing at the well-inside gate. So, there is every likelihood that he'll employ my services. The Freemason returned to the table like a dog to its own sick. Me snake wept. Tom Cornwall set down a bright metal tray. Its contents were itemised as: one jug of draught beer, two empty schooner glasses, two shots of single malt Scotch (Macallan), a pack of Dunhill cigarettes and a box of Redhead matches. It's only a matter of time now one would think. He fills both glasses. I lick me lips. If only he'd brought a third eye. Empty moans. I kick its hind. They toast Choc / fallen comrades / the enemy. The referee struggles to separate the fighters. They start to drain the beers only stopping in the interim to skull the Scotch and clash glasses. Last island before a Pond.

"I don't need to tell you this conversation is classified," said Tom Cornwall.

"Naturally," replied Donald Cane.

Joyce codes Cyclops with metaphors and allusions to Jewish lore. The ten plagues of Egypt are worked into the plot: 1. blood (continuous use of the word "bloody"); 2. vermin (as a metaphor for freeloaders and scabs who undercut Ireland); 3. beasts (garryowen); 4. murrain (foot and mouth disease); 5. syphilis; 6. boils (typhoid fever); 7. hail (the storm before the hanging of the malefactor); 8. locusts ("filling the country with bugs"); 9. darkness ("sun never rises"); 10. slaying of first born males (Rudy's death); 11. frogs (many references to fish). Cyclops also contains continuous references to the Passover: the barflies drink beer four times, which is the equivalent of four cups of wine (finally, Famechon gets a free swing and stuns Harada with four consecutive lefts); the dog's biscuit equates to *matzah*; bitter herbs = "bitter experience" (Joe Hynes); a cup is set for both LB and Elijah but never drunk from; there is the misconception that Bloom has a special cup (Bloom's prophecy on the Gold Cup race). Narrator A is knowledgeable about Bloom via Pisser Burke. He wrongly believes that Bloom has won big on the race. Thus, he expresses dismay when LB will not shout a round of drinks at the bar.

"I've started a new outfit. It's called Australian Direct Investment Group. Our head office is here in Sydney. But we're opening branches in Bangkok, Singapore and Hong Kong. And we've just leased an office in Manila."

"Where?"

"Ayala Avenue."

"Good location."

"I'll take your word for it."

"What's the play?"

"We're servicing family offices. We work hand in hand with the State Bank. We've got some high-profile clients."

"Like Pete Rocka?"

"Correct. We've also got a strong board. Do you remember Jim Bates?"

"Strategic wonk."

"You can put it that way if you like. What about Bob Coe?"

"Ran Head Office Asia. Went on to great things in Washington."

"They crucified him in Congress over Crown Jewels. Did you ever meet him?"

"Yes. His front was Pacification. I worked for him on Phoenix."

"Good. He certainly remembers you."

"If they'd stuck to his game plan, we'd still be in Saigon."

Burn down villages. Herd peasants into barns. Shut the gates at sunset. TET68. I slip out of Barney's bar to collect my small dividend. Politics by other means. Nixon's Vietnamisation. Beaucoup Dinky Dau. Giap squatting on the DMZ like a lean-eyed cat. The Japs are not showing any mercy to Harada, announced Casey. The queue died down long ago. NVA moving along the Trail under the jungle's skin like ticks. A war of blind movements. Oedipus at Colonnus. Gloucester on the cliff. I reach the counter. Harada is thrust back through the ropes. Famechon's barrage has closed his right eye completely. Hamlet's vacillations. Lon Nol floating bodies down the Mekong River. The swelling on his eyelid makes it impossible for the Jap to see. Invade Cambodia. Lam Son 719. He scours my slip. The referee starts the mandatory count. One. The betting clerk – two – mumbles some – three – rubbish. Four. Harada is passive in a neutral corner. Five. Thieu was fixated with coups. Six. When Tri's chopper went down – seven- that was the end of the whole damn show. Eight. Famechon comes in hard. Hue Offensive. Mine the harbours. Harada beats him back. I retreat from the betting shop. Polyphemus claims that Cyclopes are stronger than Gods. Ticket enters gutter. This set him directly at odds with Ancient cosmology. SALT. Linebacker 2. That'll show the Soviets. Force Tho back to the negotiating table. I loiter on William Street hoping to gouge a fag out of an unrequired street-walker. Famechon closes in for the kill. Polyphemus stuffing his face with prey. Harada is done. One-eyed Nelson sucking plums. Nobody will meet my gaze. Lester adjusted his eye patch as he motored down Johnson Street, Collingwood in an ill-fitting brown suit (1998). Famechon has retained his world title! Bouncer at Porky's says he's kicked smokes exhaling nicotine air. Nixon's goal was to create a false sense of finality out of this hiatus in the North's inevitable victory. It was all fake. To get out with some dignity before the campaign starts, that was Kissinger's instruction. Dump all our old ordinance at Vung Tau. That will create an impression of ongoing patronage. It was a good trick. Didn't get discovered until it turned into a rout. Like using Chennault as a back channel to double-cross Thieu and win Election 68. Last stand at Xuan Loc. Nixon was long gone by then. Congress had finally lost faith in the word of any President. They denied emergency funds to Ford. Charlie drove right down the centre of the country to Saigon.

"What do you want exactly?"

"We need a smart man in Manila. Someone we can trust. And we're running out of time. We need to work faster and on a much bigger scale."

INSERT SUBHEADING – SEE APPENDIX B, EXTRACT 1

"Where's Eyesenears," says Ocker.

"He duck touted teeheybee," says Chindrip.

"Did he bag Blankite," says Ocker.

"Nuh. Shaggerma etch why," says the Kiwi Scatt in broken Bondi English.

"That'll bare leek other his ouch groins," says Ock.

"Yairs. He woe beach outing barduntight," says Scatt.

"Gear rim bag inner OWE."

Chindrip camera gob me. Ocker cignulled with his middull thinger, beaned lichen arty-curated beau. Eye took ought twat sciss bouff, wary words whirr kink for the Caws with formguy, penicillin ledgend. I sledding tether CHANNEL ether cider his tar bashops (Scatt and Chindrip).

"Whooshem," says Ocker jerkstickulaching o'finneganat two newt carnts on the kerr. "Lucks lie Feral asians."

"Nar," replies I.

"Coveys from Bush then?"

"Vets, I wreck."

"This is not a game of who-the-fuck," says Ocker (snarling). "Your job is Eisenears. Git dun veer end fie ouch!"

"Eye delay oggs air Viet-namers from the jibandjab."

"Gay war treatied moist shard billy," says Ocker nodding his nog. "Butt awe hour Diggers gear crapckt wend day finer lea git bag hoe."

"Thebes beak homere go stints the corp suss," says Leaphole Bloo slidling into the converse nation.

"Warty elle u mean by vat," says I.

"I havana glue wharf Blue's goanna bout hearth-thyme," says Ock. "Chime jester air fridge bloke. Got bim bye yak-yak bug. Dry blow bonkers."

"People just want them to disappear," says Loomb, "so they can forget the whole dang show."

"Purse owner nong rather," says the Captain.

"Bungee noah aims," says I.

"Emasculinatored," says Ock bloking lard.

"Got air bush oysters snipt," I says.

"Not menymore," says Ockerbeck.

"Yairs. No/men," says LB.

"Send 'em down a brace," says Ocker dropping a Lawson on the tote. "Purr bar stars. Sid owe end yak whiff em. File out the fats. My jest beat in a sense blowks. Could be pig plants. Huno's."

Boyne arse awl beards! Ocker always lays off smart odds. Calls it 'rixavision.' XrayTV. Both Polyphemus and The Citizen seek out the identity of intruders. Odysseus is cryptic in reply. Bloom ambiguous. Both investigators (A + B) want Odysseus and Bloom to stand still and be quiet. But they are mercurial chaps. Indeed, Bloom remains "NO/BODY" for The Citizen. He is never named in Cyclops. Anonymity, aloneness and elusiveness are the starting points for Joyce's characterisation of Bloom. He starts out as a small-world man. His life is mundane. He is mild and deferential. A cuckold. Beginning in Cyclops, Joyce starts to reposition Bloom. Like Cu Chullain, the Irish Achilles, he becomes that little bloke who puffs himself up for battle with crazy war cries which raise him to a colossus who can slaughter his enemies from a horse-drawn chariot. Note LB's

EXIT on Martin Cunningham's horse-drawn car. But Joyce also intensifies Bloom's sexual perversity as a counterweight to enhanced positive characterisation. It is typical of Joyce to balance the swing. I lolled uppendan bare rare ear. Waitering. Nobbodyabba. Fee-fie-foe only the balm aid wary longer ray cum bye. Sheet rejuiced the eggnishning. Hernia pulls stewed quiet-wrecked. Bit coal, eye gas. I arksed her for bun charcoal bollers beard. INSERT Eartrumpet. I lean a little closer. Every speech in Cyclops is attributed to a specific speaker by the Narrator through use of the third person singular form of the verb, 'to say.' This repetitive device in the hands of a 'third party' is used by Joyce almost like a lowlight to provide direct contrast with his usual innovation. Or else it could have just signalled his exhaustion of new options. PRESENT TENSE (as per cyclops episode) = USE OF STRINE (as recounted by Eyesenears). PAST TENSE = OTHER CONVERSATION (outside his range of overhearing).

"Giffer me boss," says I to them, squatting omni R's and placing the boggles in owl minced. "Louder's mean aim. Have a Bet LOUDER."

We shakes. They snivels twats Ox. He raysez biggs arse bag.

"Tar mac," says A.

"Dimension it," says I. "Keg to loam mea gasper?"

"Take the packer," says the bigger barstead earn the ride-and-snide.

"Didger boss have a bigwig on The Cut then," says A.

I egg gnaws his insinner ratings.

"Wasyernames," I says bowl asp bras.

"Null ... and Void," says B. Ore nunner yer big sneaze, bays sickly. I leddit pars. It's knocks kin off mine hose. Noman, nopackerderms. Vats mine otto arse will. NULL = DON. VOID = CORNWALL in this short inner lewd infer stile of Sourmule Baguette. Dough kneeder mate nose eggs uses. Neffereffer gift nuffing way. Sew I jest crasht me knuts cunt bentley. Salmoned me snot. Litter frensch durrie. And wheel got stark inta throg.

"Jegoda Grab Thighnell fish ear," says eye poindextering scream.

"Dingo," sayz NULL. "I live in Gorillerbeans."

"Sawrit on tearavizchurn bunkt," says VOID.

"Sea gals got rip off," says I toovey. "Rare ferry and touch ease mustard bow got a sex fuller semi-itches ink myop onion. Egg girls had claws fur sow grapes."

"They were most unfortunate on the day," says VOID nodding gravely like he's got a great big dong up his strides.

Ah-hah, I dead used Holmes like at this junk tuna. Vat arsewiper musk think eyesore turtle dared debt. COURSE NO SEA GALS PLAIT INK RUB THIGH NIL THIS EAR!!!! Dogseelsplate!!! Sea gals got knock doubt out by ray bigs in weak won! This deafing nightly roused my sucks pigeons. Maybe they're numb butter coupler mummers of the constant burglary snouting the truff. Caws the Filth got a bigamous ebbtide when hungary. "Avalanche play dough cheeps with a rare side off charlie charmpuck," Plod soys. It's all suck ozee. Why don't weasel cum tumberling dunhill lie Chair Congeal or suck sum sheilas tungs lie owl George Porch. Jezz snore wharf it. Aorta piss the holelet toff. I could get a semi-decent job like Joe Hynes. He's always flush from debt collecting for old Mowers Herzog. Gu & Elizabeth bov debtors. SD and TOM bovine debt. I could make them cough up dosh with a little snip of Scatter Chinnedrip. Gonad Cane wiped sum scupper coins threw miretacondrical and spoked.

"When eye lief Siddha knee," says Foreskin Fred wreckolexing, "wee stilt had pents sillies amp hounds. Imp eerie alk currant see. Nunner this dismal guernsey."

"Didgerie leigh?" I says.

"Frack," he says firmly.

"Howl on lube bean gown firm Sinny," I says.

"Twinny ears," says VOID.

"Wear yule iffed invert intern hymn?"

"Every two-up school from Darwin to the 'Loo," he says halfing.

Pause. Suck piss. Gulp.

Gnarl Leoplodoom joins hour grope and co-minces mao thing off, were king his elf in tomb a friendsie bout the cord of urine piss tree from Sock radic wog-in-tunic dire log to Charred Doorwindows 'surf evil of the flitters' feary. Thirsty shrimp. Nobody can understand him, let alone interdict. "What constitutes a nation?" asks Bloom. A language is a nation, he says back. Then he starts bungeeing onan sum stryn land wedge. It's the produce of corrective aquariums – pube by pube in ancient times, he agues – until septic is applied to each'n'never e-thing. Personally, I think we should just roll Bloom like a barrel, extract the wad of winnings from his purse, of which he is too stingy to share nor even boast of, and go on a spree. He's loaded like Lawson's dog. S-DOG leaned against the fuselage to suppress nausea. His cock pumped. A security guard hustled him along. He wanted to speak but his swollen tongue filled the maw. The crowd congealed into a massive eye observing him. Hopenheimer and Adorno equate the largeness of Polyphemus to the proletarian mass. The cyclopes lack order, systems and civilisation. They therefore act like a single blind beast, which is what Polyphemus resembles as a metonymy after Odysseus strikes him blind. Insert supplementary reference to the crowds in *Coriolanus*. Don Cane followed the lead of Tom Cornwall. They emptied their schooner glasses in honour of Bob Coe as if he was the Humanist successor to Charlie Parnell. Bloom has a complex, multi-faceted identity. He is able to negotiate both HIGH and LOW subject matter with some semblance of authority from Don Giovanni to cheese. He is not exclusively High Romantic like Stephen Dedalus. Like Parnell, Bloom becomes an ostrich-eyed hero. His positive traits are perceived as negatives in the context of the Cyclops episode – (a) his ability to articulate complex multi-perspectives is perceived as a penchant for irrelevant digressions; (b) sobriety is seen as foreign and anti-social; (c) moderation becomes lack of conviction; (d) passivity is weakness. Bloom turns the other cheek until it becomes impossible for him to tolerate The Citizen's ill-treatment anymore. He backs off momentarily when John Wyse Nolan tells him to stand up for Jews. This is not his preferred ground. He also rejects the use of force. "Love is the opposite of hate," he says with Christ-like sincerity. Eventually, however, he must confront The Citizen in HIS OWN DEN. But like Odysseus (or Hamlet), he is impelled to interrogate ethics from all standpoints before taking decisive action. Each hero accepts the risks of approach. Delay can be fatal if the Fates are against you. They bide their time until the logical instant to escape. By contrast, the Irish people are seen as lost in ineffectual rhetoric like the inhabitants of Babel. They grasp the wrong moment. They are passive at the wrong time. Alfie Louder withdrew to brief The Captain. Bloom's final confrontation with The Citizen represents a new assertiveness that empowers him to later retake his home and marriage and acts as a model for Ireland. It is the catalyst for Bloom's reawakening. It is the core of 16 June 1904. Alfie Lauder withdrew.

"Tell me about Ambrose E. Welles," asked Don.

"Stan's our in-house counsel. Worked in Hong Kong since the Seventies. Sound as a bell. He was one of the Nugan set. Good links in rural Australia. That helps a lot with logistics."

"How does it work?"

"CIA runs the show out of Laos. They airlift heroin from Vang Pao. Air America flies it to Griffith. They take on board large quantities of dope then they fly to the States. All the cash is washed through Sheun Wan. Stan arranges the bank transfers."

Cornwall laughed gruffly. Politics is the Art of the Cyclops episode.

"The beauty of it," he concluded pointing decisively at the floor, "is that NOBODY in their right mind would ever believe that Australia could be used as a back door."

Ocker sipped at a warm glass. He gazed upwards. The Australian Treasurer walked across a foreign tarmac slowly. He sent Eyesnears to the bar for more drinks and rose. 'Mister Keating was in the US to receive Euromoney's award for the World's Best Treasurer,' announced Channel Nine's top-rating news anchor Brian Henderson. Off on one of his quests. The Captain of the Push descended to the bar area.

INSERT SUBHEADING – SEE APPENDIX B, EXTRACT 2

"Now there's a low-dead dog to be sure," says Ocker loudly. "John Stone's new puppet."

He sits. An uncomfortable shuffling of seats flows. It is clear neither party will yield an inch. They butt against each other gruffly like Agamemnon and Achilles.

"My Colonial Oath," Ock says pointing at the screen. "That Accord will ruin the ALP."

"Old George Reid has finally won," says Cornwall. "It took eighty years. But he's beaten Deakin and the whole damn Set."

"Kelty's the brains behind that operation," says CotP wily. "And he's playing another game entirely."

He pauses. Kelty as Merlin. Construct ironic Camelot.

"All those bloody bastards are drier than my bluddy throat," he says, sculling fiercely then slamming down a dead glass as he contemplates the forthcoming tray of beverages. Beer spills over the brim of a cluster of fresh schooners that Einsteinears lays before the players. The television screen scrolls through a sequence of video grabs of powerful figures in quick succession.

"Orc art off custard gins sluts to salve is hole may it," says Ocker, now hole link ought.

"Anna tike error exhume ate," says Cornwall twirlet.

"Probe texted speakies," says Ocker.

"Wiped his arse all over the NCA," says Cornwall.

"Vats wine brick oven mint beaked thick ace mummeries," says I.

"Mick Villains wall loaded fat old occulere mint," says Ocker.

"Wooden beam aid quiet hasty," says VOID.

"Go annal mustard splash tonner grey bib lobber iz bechel sores."

"It was [REDACTED] ward robbed the mall inch it," says Ocker.

"Hey Tea O'gavelled the leap,"

"Beamspack dim."

"Board anew owl up Mawl landinnies pry vet jed."

"Goanna's cunt wooden beam a fool Brick," says VOID. "Just firm weeding the kick."

"Vat's own lee onedecent punt for the Squirrel," says Eye.

"Well, that's certainly the kind of remuneration that would have motivated me," says Bloom. "What about you gentlemen?"

"Would I dong a bloody copper if I caught the cunt alone?" I says retorturingvotesyphillisy. Ock nodes a ream mint. Sweet silence after Kookaburraburraburraburrayackyackyacks. He examines large slow bubbles as they expire in the dregs of his beer glass. Cunts, he thought.

"Lockyer, Beames and Brian bloody Maher," he says moorkishly. "All modelling Greens now."

"Bali suite with blowjobs," says VOID for effect.

"One hundred condoms of hash oil," says Tom Cornwall. "That was the run. Customs sent it straight to the bond store. Nobody even touched it at the airport."

"Fed poked his pen into the package," says Orc. "Got his elf a canvas rez income shot."

Ocker chuckles hard-heartily. Tom Cornwall and Eyesnears join hymn buckismet, Eckie Killy One, lobs erved deaftly, knot partaching nether puelling his vein.

"Sew hu shut Cootey vend," says Ogger lewdly.

"Fine vat ow tatties inquess," says Eyesnears (AKA LAWSON).

"Carver, eyewreck."

"Nah. Worse Greedy dun hurt. Brungingut form Mawburn. Gotter runway ticker tomb an iller at stumps."

"Norway. Ten bucks saz wazza Sinny shooter."

"Ipaneema the Ks vend mealebs wooder wizened me arp."

"Weirdigig the catch toe pen Oddies Barthes in Ma Nulla vend?"

"Well, if you're talking about Dennis Smith," says VOID, "then he'll want to get that cash back out pretty quick."

"Before Marcos falls," says NULL.

"Correct," says VOID. "He doesn't have long. May bless spanner ear."

"Mother of our custer myrrhs," says GNARL choir glee.

VOID dissims no legerbill smite.

"Bay art ptolemy Squeerall wasshe clunt," says Eye.

"God nevving do wart Squirrel."

"Pro-Vital's morkids kinder eel."

"A jaffa," says Ocker. "Absolute peach."

"Like all pain odd set."

"Wretcher's stuper fun, they cork tit."

"End more bunch bee rind that joke. Tomby Doorknocker provitaled the mow bill and a boxer deadheads. Vas nude Labor fourier."

"Stealth lingering a feud odd wogs at Shifty, says Ocker. "He noser mean ingot whirred 'mate.' All waste stooled up furl Oil Murf. No backarseslidelicker. Buy the sane toke end I wooden give err new Mummer fer Ciggerknee a fake feller cum. They was very fark ink cunting turf arc him often Camp error wary wooden caws morse tripe."

"Thinksellgeddon Sinny-sty firm noh won."[33]

Mutual amusement was registered. A feeling of camaraderie infused the participants. Each other, they realised, was not so different. Worm silents descended. They imbribed artily. Ocker made a structural adjustment to his nutsack.

---

3 This passage recounts uncorroborated street gossip about activities surrounding the Costigan Royal Commission and inner city ALP branches in the early 1980s.

"Wens his E-legshin campaim goannerend," he says. "I sinner nuff O'Bub Orc's snot-rails toilets meal Eiffel time."

"Heaves aching the Killerbilly snowbloat lacrosse Shimmery About necks weed foreskins clam pain lawn adder Uproar How's," says VOID.

"Beggar wedge ouch. See Eye Eh! my synch ease bar lie Cutterbull," says Cornwall.

"Witlemming coupe Partout," says Nog egg reaming.

The assembly bowed sagely at this point, raised their glasses and toasted both the fallen Prime Minister and those brave deluded japs still canned upon the floor of Sinny Hardpurr. At this poignant, Ocker rises to go slash. His goons follow. This enables Tom Cornwall some time to engage his target directly.

"Bag too bliss nets Don," he says. "Weed lie nuker ordinate our war clout earth Fillerpleins. Weak knead ex-peery ants dand. Summon toucan waltz whore lover Asia."

"Shoe dent beetroot ardour get ack cess soup goo entelechants vile Trial and."

"Greed. Hanoi is turtly foe kissed urn Chimer vat preset."

"Dung reel east aft an ole hellofart inter Le Duan's dunny."

"That little wart wasse marstroke. Deng demon straighted toother hole whirled Chainer wars pre-paired tar thatcherstrife a whorl army to proper Pol Pot. Rear guardless ovumen colost."

"Liars cheep forge om eunichs."

They toasted the new Chinese administration. I in my troth ray my glares to Sitter zen, hood rezoomed his plate eye up onyx throwin' unmurphy ark omissioner. Joyce's repetitive use of "says" to identify each speaker shifts focus to speech, mimicking the style of drama. Shanghai Dog felt a cold back-breeze as he rose to Lujiazui. His eyes incommoded. The strain of interpreting Strine can be relieved by reference to Appendix B. It becomes a game of fast page-turning. A blind harpist slid his bow across an erhu's twin strings. Its low timbre spoke of China's deep, lonely soul in all its self-pity. The tired snake skin barrel shone like mica. SD gripped the railing. Hawke was troubled throughout the second half of 1984 by a splinter of glass that had become lodged in his right eye after he was struck in the face batting against the Journalists in the annual Parliament cricket match in July. His spectacles were smashed as he attempted an ambitious hook shot. Glass shot into his pupil. He was taken to Canberra Hospital. The ophthalmologist who treated him said that Hawke would have lost the sight of his eye altogether had it gone a fraction deeper. It caused the PM agony throughout the election campaign. This is presented as a simple correspondence with the Cyclops trope by the author. He found it hard to concentrate – especially under the glare of television cameras – blinking and wiping his weeping eye with a handkerchief incessantly. The injury neutralised his legendary small screen rapport with the Australian public. The

English scholar stood on a milk crate precariously to speak. He had notes in his withered right grip. He used the other hand to gesticulate. Merlin steadied him at the hip. Link to "Chaucer at the Court of King Edward." Also, Tom Roberts' "Big Picture." Angle is everything in art. Turnerian shards cross a deep Piranesian case in his portrait of the instant of Federation. Light pipes down a steep shaft. The crowd recede to a flat-pack mass. The Imperial figurine is perched at the front of a wedding cake stage. Two hundred and sixty-nine dignitaries were depicted individually by the artist. He travelled the nation making sketches of each participant. This commission took its toll on Roberts' eyesight. It was his last work for ten years. He made picture frames for a living. This recalls Furphy working at his brother's forge while he wrote *SizzL* like some Bushbard Hephaestus. Roberts spent the Great War attending gas victims in an English hospital. Lines of Diggers with roughly bandaged eyes. Palm upon shoulder in step. Clinging under the belly of a ram. Blistered torsos rolled before the lens for propaganda purposes. Thigh-flesh face-masks spread smooth and tight over dissymmetrical eyes. Prime the troops with patriotic speechifying. Bovine Poilus, Tommies and ANZACS climbing onto No Man's Land to die. The visiting British aesthetic theorist and commentator commenced machine-gun utterance.

"Contemporary Australian art," announced Fuller decisively gesturing at the walls.

A thin strand of tawny hair slipped over his spectacles regularly, obscuring his right eye. Spotlights blinded him. He could not see any warm face in the audience.

"This is IT," he said waving a catalogue in the air manically.

"I saw the same bunch of artists at the Eureka show in London this year. There's nothing original about this art. We've got loads of this kind of stuff in Europe."

He exuded a bored and frustrated energy.

"It's like Warhol's soup-can. It CLAIMS to 'appropriate images from mass media.' It claims to CRITIQUE MODERN CULTURE. It labels itself an ALTERNATIVE PRAXIS. But it's really JUST A PEEP SHOW IN A FAKE BORDELLO."

He paused to gain breath and let the weight of his assay settle on the crowd.

"But there is a counterweight in Australian art that adapted the rich tradition of the British landscape to new conditions. Streeton, Roberts, Nolan, Tucker, Boyd and Williams, even our good friend there, Read, all went Bush with a capital B, like Holman Hunt a hundred years earlier, to produce art of eye-watering clarity that is distinctively Australian. They are now being joined by Indigenous artists like Rover Thomas. His 'Dog and Emu at Lake Gregory' is the Aboriginal complement to Nolan's 'Pretty Polly Mine.' Indeed, his great painting, 'Crossroads, Argyle Hill,' should really become your new national ensign. It is the Aboriginal rejoinder to the flag of Eureka."

Fuller's entire body shook as he contemplated the walls.

"So, in closing, I would urge all the young painters here tonight to turn their backs on the type of art in this room. Celebrate what Bernard Smith called Australia's Aesthetic Conservatism. Get into a battered old Kingswood, travel to what Barcroft Boake called 'the wastes of the Never-Never' and develop your own touch – your own feeling for paint and materials – as you work in nature. Find the Good, the True and the Beautiful like John Ruskin. Paint what Nolan termed, 'a landscape one has never seen before … . The landscape you were FEELING as you started.' And Merry Christmas to you all. On that note, it is my pleasure to officially open the marvellously titled show, E.A. Times X Mass."

Everybloody through their bluggy tickers tubs in the eire. There was a dingdong barney coming along. Young Dedalus was tauntalising sum doughpea Englick pievats. Bloo, I swear was going to take The Cities Urn on. The littered Pommy blowk dispeered underwaister bombingupnowinthen furanuvver powk-in-I. Wait a minauteur, said Polly Psychlobs. Tom Hallem grassed the cricketic's cote and whaourled his elf udd.

"Professor Fuller," he says. "My name is Tom Hallem. I love your work. That was a great speech. Truly inspirational."

"That's very kind, Mr Hallem. I noticed your painting over there. I nearly gave it a personal endorsement. But I thought that might be counter-productive to your career."

"It was good to see you chow down on some sacred beef," added CRITIC squinting through circular spectacle veins. His face was marginally ovular like a broad Victorian glass paperweight; lipless and all nerves. RED/READ joined them.

"Now I know exactly where I fit into your Ruskosmos, Professor Pete," he said.

"You're one-of-a-kind my friend," replies Fuller smiling.

"Not so. We're all simple Bush artists in Australia."

"I can't totally agree with your thesis," retorted Tommy H deferentially. "The bush motif can be overplayed. Australians are an urban race these days."

"Joyce didn't write about potato farmers," added READ.

"Nonsense," replies F. "You lot sound like Ford Madox Brown. But let me pass in peace. I've got to go to the loo."

The author raised his head and stared at the Japanese paper lantern above his head, which left a pale, counterfeit shadow on the stained ceiling. His neck cracked. Had anything changed in aesthetics in the last 30 years, he pondered. Art (or he) had sunk into one of those long periods of introspection when refinement of existing forms was paramount and lighter content came to the fore. Gigantism ruled. Emerging art in Asia displayed political intent. Feminist themes remained current. But the art world was still dominated by white males. Tom Hallem surrendered painting when he felt like there was nowhere new to turn. He was bored by his own commentary. He didn't possess that sardonic, even comic, and self-deprecating comic-book edge of the great Australian painters. In retrospect, I think he was disillusioned by his role in Elizabeth's art scam, not in ethical terms, but in seeing that style was essentially manufactured, not springing from some deep source, and could be coerced into being. The famous forgery case turned him into an outcast in Sydney. He relocated to Melbourne shortly before his death at the age of thirty-six. Fuller was jostlead inter yon wesshe rhume. He clung to a masst. You can read "WORK" as a model for *Ulysses*. Both are imaginative recreations of modern life, packed with pinpoint-detail. The genius of FMB is that each character evokes in a single portrayal the types of rich narrative fancies that Joyce gives so much pen too. The central figure is a glowing navvy in profile holding a spade. It is cocked and ready to strike. He is part of a road-gang digging and bricking a new sewage tunnel in a steep English lane. At a glance, the site discloses the dying village character of what had become peri-urban places by the mid nineteenth century, where feudal existence was being upturned by urbanisation. Turner's steam-engines puffing through foggy rural idylls had arrived in town. Poor and rich pass either side of the pit as if they were striding along the banks of the River Liffey. Some gather to gaze at this strange new infrastructure (a pipe). The Manchester version of "WORK" has greater use of chiaroscuro and is the greater painting. I count nineteen characters in total, not including horses and dogs. This includes unemployed labourers sleeping on an embankment behind Thomas Carlyle and Frederick Maurice as well as the roughly-drafted face of a workman peering out of the excavation with a full brick-pan held aloft. A religious throwaway hovers before him like rent silk (Eli is Coming). One ganger is only visible in the form of a hand like Molly Bloom when she is first introduced in *Ulysses*. We cannot see the face of a girl at the front of the image but we receive the direct gaze of the baby she holds in her arms like one of Gerty MacDowell's friends. We also get to see the reaction of a delinquent boy having his hair pulled. He leers. The bare feet of a flower lady are a prominent detail in the Manchester version (left lower front). They represent a masterpiece of painterly technique. Only four characters are focused on the void. The rest go about quotidian tasks. A lady passes in a blue bonnet. There are posters for an election campaign. A sandwich-board reads BOBUS. It is the name of some Tory Elijah. Mrs Leopold Evangelist is distributing copies of "Drink for Thirsty Souls." Residue from a mound of lime powder one can almost sniff pollenates the atmosphere. The dense, complex arrangement created by Brown stands above the technical capabilities of today's painters. They never bothered to learn their trade. No artisanal instinct. The lasting impression of "WORK" is the capacity of great art to depict humanity in the fullness and diversity that constitutes LIFE. Fuller mediated the queue. He stumbled inside the cubicle. Lock the latch! Shut out the world. Alownutlars. He contemplated the scratched black Bakelite lid. Moulded remnant of Empire's appeasement era. Open cess me. Violet turd-gazing. Fuller broke each corner of the Cradle without fuss. It slumped under gravity. Another type of art object, he guessed. Maybe call it an 'instoolation.' Fuller chuckled at his own pun. Flushflush. He sat down on another watery dump. Soft wet (f)ragments of great art like Barthes' dead pen-hand. Allow the viewer to de-amputate Venus. Henry Moore was always re-fusing mother-and-child in iron-or- stone. A brown smear. Something by Tapies. Fuller was a High Victorian like Ruskin and Churchill. Whirl a clacker for British Art. In the Aeolus episode, Joyce presented the Irish as the Jews of Europe. In Cyclops, he presents them as Egyptians enslaving the Jews as represented by Bloom. The Citizen represents everything wrong with Ireland. He is constantly proclaiming the greatness of Irish culture. He rejects English oppression. He berates his fellows for their ignorance of the Gaelic language. He has even trained his dog to respond to orders in Celtic. Yet his nationalism is ultimately insular and exclusionary. A palm started banging on the door of the adjacent cubicle. Tinkering of a lock. Suddenly, a guard leaped over the brown partition. VUMP-clup. A voice called: 'get an ambulance.' The lock was unbolted within. Fuller waited until the emergency had passed and went out to the basins. In the mirror, he watched Skintpole slither from the bathroom. One eyeball dropped like a bloody red plum. It was like that "enormous dice / blinking a mournful eye" that Huysmans describes in an image by Odilon Redon. A single tear fell from the Prime Minister's eye. President Mahatir registered its passage down Hawke's sunworn cheek. He took the Australian Head of State in his arms. They sent Hazel to front the media. Shanghai Dog ascended the staircase at Lujiazui Station. The crowd condensed around him pushing out of the subway. Hawkers badgered him with souvenirs. Spinning LEDs. Keep your nerve and hold your tongues, Odysseus warned. Expat life in China was a series of enclaves through which you passed with eyes averted hoping no one would observe your passage. SD raised the gift-bag to his chest. The mob solidified into a single unit. He dragged a withered leg. It was stiffening quickly. At street level, he confronted a new pedestrian overpass. Smell of freshly poured concrete and cement dust. Oriental Pearl Tower poked Olympus. Its geodesic globe gleamed like some vast unyielding eye. It was the symbol of Shanghai's emergence from exile after the Cultural Revolution. Deng allowed it to be raised like a finger against the remnants of the Gang of Four in the local Party. Pudong clung to its underbelly. S-Dog stumbled through a sequence of iron and plastic barriers. Commuters hastened towards bus stops along Lujiazui Ring Road outside Super Brand Mall. Judy went from this terminus deep into Pudong. Shanghai Dog was swamped by a human tide. He waited for the right moment to detach. The gutter shone. A greasy fleece. Negotiating passage by memory. He split off from the pack. East Road was quieter. A group of expatriates passed. He avoided their gaze in case they wanted assistance. He approached Jinmao Tower. To his left, the financial sector of Shanghai was packed around Lujiazui Central Green Space. Giants at a campfire. A street vendor was roasting lamb skewers on a forty-four-gallon drum. It gave off a stench of charcoal and burnt spices. Incinerated humans. S-DOG crossed a short access road. A black Audi with government plates idled. This thoroughfare went all the way down to Century Park. He turned onto the concourse. It was a long concrete channel. He set his sights on the revolving doors. A guard smiled. He struggled across the atrium to the hotel entrance. His face felt swollen. He started to gulp and choke. He tested his larynx. Querulous utterance. He entered the lift lobby. It was illuminated by golden LED torches. The marble walls burned. He waited for an elevator with some tourists. An old American was explaining to a young woman how he had been stationed in Shanghai just before Liberation. He called it a siege. His ship assisted members of the KMT to escape to Taiwan. He mentioned the plunder taken on board. Seven large containers full of gold bullion and antiquities. It all disappeared down the hold as if consumed by a great monster. SD was anxious about his own gifts. Gu could spurn them straight onto the sofa without even examining them if she felt it was a con. They entered the elevator. The Americans were complaining about their guide. They wanted to go to the fake product market. She kept taking them to bogus souvenir stores. The concierge was a ruthless conman. He was 'in on the game.' They had missed the mini-bus back to the hotel and made their way home by stealth. Luckily, they had hotel business cards in Mandarin to show the taxi driver. Billy took the elevator to the 67th floor lobby. He went to the porter's bureau. God be merciful unto us. His head dropped. The chapel leadlights – like those elevator bulbs, like the thick glass holding out Shanghai's rank sundown, like the faux dragonfly lamp on the desk – glowed with sick autumnal light. He leaned heavily on a maple lip to rest his aching thighs. A gentle voice inquired about his requirements in English. He strained to speak.

"I am here to see Doctor Gu," he said. "She's expecting me."

"May I ask your name, sir?" asked the Concierge lifting the telephone receiver.

"Mister Norman," said S-Dog.

The porter contacted the room. He apologised for bothering Doctor Gu. He said a gentleman had arrived. His name was NORMAL. OK. Thanks. He chuckled, replaced the receiver and walked around the counter. S-Dog turned. His hip ached. Blind Rory. Calling pipes.

"Let me take you to the elevator."

The concierge took a security pass from the top pocket of his olive jacket.

"What level is Doctor Gu's room," asked Billy.

"*Liu shi ba*."

"Auspicious."

"Yes, sir. This hotel is actually located at Number 88 Century Avenue. So, your friend is at 8–8–6–8 in Room Number 8."

"Is there a 44th floor," asked Shanghai Dog.

"Oh yes, sir. We are not superstitious in China anymore."

Shanghai Dog smiled. He knew buildings all over the country still skipped the death levels. Chalk skips on paths that went one-two-three-HOP-five. The concierge led him as if by a nose ring towards a guard seated behind a low desk. They exchanged glances. Shanghai Dog was allowed to pass. There was a single elevator to the penthouse level. The concierge waved a card over a sensor. The doors opened. He leaned inside the cubicle and used a second card to open Level 68. Billy entered. The elevator moved so peacefully that S-Dog felt suspended in space. A sharp pang above his temple made him shake his head. He blew out his eardrums. His outer thigh had started aching. The doors opened. He stepped onto the landing. The walls were covered with burnished wallpaper highlighted by blood red Fleur-de-lys. Thick carpet silenced his steps. Electric flambeaus were mounted along the corridor. A single floor-to-ceiling window at the end of the passage provided a strong vein of particulated light. Instrumental music was piped over an invisible sound system. The sun was setting as he walked towards Room 8. Nightfall came quickly as if a huge stone had been rolled across the sun's face. He knocked on the door. He heard no footsteps. The door opened suddenly. A small, heavy woman stood before him in a white waffle dressing gown. Her short toes kneaded the carpet tensely.

"Good timing," she said.

She let the gown flop open. His gaze surveyed her. Godard panning-up and down Bardot's body. Horns of primary colour. About the hollow cave, a garden vine trailed. Fragrance of cleft cedar and juniper burn. She was humming with a broken voice before her loom weaving a gold shuttle. Gu closed the door and leant into his embrace. The gown dropped.

"Can you see my bottom in the mirror," she asked pressing her belly against his cock.

"Yes," he replied. His body tilted to accommodate her. She found a warm place for her cheek against his shirt.

"You're already hard," she said approvingly.

"And you're soft," he said kneading her rump.

"Yes. I am fat. But I am also smart," she said turning from his arms and walking into the main compound.

"I can always get thinner."

She looked back at him.

"You're lean," she said moving towards him. "But you're not so smart."

She touched his skull with a firm finger.

"The real question is whether you can get any smarter."

Shanghai Dog had to chuckle. He bit her lip hard. Her eyes felt water. Link this vassalage between lovers back to Elizabeth and Tom (See above. Also, C2). Also, Odysseus and Circe. Also, Calypso. That affair cut both ways. She and Odysseus were locked in a crude game. It was motorised by the constant threat of exit. This held them in thrall for almost a decade. A luxuriant grove of camphor and sweet cypress grew around them. Soft meadows of violets and dragon fruit blooming. Steep-spanned seabirds were wont to nest there. Chattering tongues. Homer is full of embraces. Joyce doesn't do LOVE imagery as such. No humans physically bond in real time in *Ulysses*. It is all past tense. Molly offers detailed comparisons of Boylan and Poldy only in retrospect. Bloom himself is confined to erotic re-pasts and a single act of masturbation. The only actual coitus in the whole novel occurs between prostitute and client. In TMAC, there is continuous carnal exchange. This directly aligns with the Classics. For example, Don Cane as the delegate of Odysseus has had a very active sex life over the last 25 years. But depictions of animal activity are limited to instances where the act possesses a symbolic function: e.g. power (Elizabeth > Tom); $ (TH blowjob in C3); male violence (Ana's rape); false fatherhood (the famous DP brothel scene); and acts of resistance (Tom > Merlin, S.Dog > Gu, XF > SD). In each instance, description is kept to a minimum. There are also amatory recollections, such as S.Dog for J, XF and O. His multiple partners repeat the pattern of his birth father. Connection always occurs without soft touch in this work. There is no great passion. No soft mouths or tongues. Only perfunctory clashes of hard-lipped Anglos. S.Dog knew that he remained present in this place at Gu's disposal. She could make him disappear. His cell phone would vanish. The Australian consulate would register his disappearance. His wife had alerted them to the unusual length of his absence in China. The police would make cursory inquiries. If they traced him to the hotel, the staff would feign bemusement. All guailo look the same, the concierge says with a shrug. The CCTV footage has disappeared. Or been spliced to erase his image. He would become a staccato ghost felt only in its tape spasms. Like Hamlet Senior to Horatio. Gu always controlled their assignations. They met in private tea rooms. Hotels she booked. He used false names. Never showed his passport. There would be no record of his attendance. The staff knew him as Messrs. Norman, Normal, Flower, Iron, Barry Cane, Bob Cane, Eric Killion, Ernie, Don Capri inter alia. His USED name was another man's name like his brother. Also, not that of his mother. Bloodless conveniences. There was no paternal recognition on his birth certificate. Recycle names from my past for characters that bear no resemblance. Use nicknames. Stage names. Initials. False titles. Virag becomes Bloom. Migrants confecting English names in Australia. Misunderstood words etched in ink by apathetic customs officials. Backwards names. Asians put family names where we put first names. Chinese syntax flows from big-to-small for dates, places and names. My birthdate would be presented as 1962 July 18 in Australia NSW Sydney, for instance. Capri William Robert. Gu Melanie. Fang Xiao. Chinese kids use each other's name tags with alacrity. See LUKE 2:49. A martyr who used another man's name for God's convenience. Temple in Nazareth. Why were you searching for me? Joyce always played with naming. HCE goes by 190 naming variants and allusions in FWAKE. The choice of Dedalus as a character name was an act of pure will (invert Q&A 45, C8). Only the greatness of *Ulysses* spared him opprobrium. It cancelled critical interrogation. SD bore NO RESEMBLANCE to the Classical inventor. Not age. Not skill set. Not personality. Not behaviour. Icarus wouldn't have been relevant either. He was a tragic figure (cause of death – hubris). I was twelve years old when my mother told me the facts about my paternity. We were sitting in the car outside Doctor Kan's surgery in wet winter rain. He was a man named Eric. Not her ex-husband who shared the same first name. EDGAR was also a bastard. Insert biographical details. I look like my father as I grow older. I am now the age when I met him. I look in the mirror after shaving and see his six-decade face. At least Telemachus held naming rights. His business partner suggested I change my name by deed poll. Great sport when you're drunk with a mouthful of lemon chicken leaking lemming-like into your lap. Sordid whims granted legitimacy. An episode of "Prince and Poor Girl" was playing on mute in Doctor Gu's suite. "I am a big game hunter," said the sub-title for Tiffany 21 of Wenzhou. "I want to catch a guy with my great new looks." She batted black contact lenses at the camera. Eclipsed moons. "Do you want me to kneel," asked Billy. "That won't be necessary," replied G. The government-appointed panellist shook his head. A diatribe on family values followed. The Citizen in *Ulysses* recalls Flaubert's Regimbart in *Sentimental Education*: a revolutionary chauvinist who becomes a shell of a man by the end of the book. He complains that the Irish can't even speak their own language. No music no art no books worth reading. Law and history in dispute. Tongue-tied sons of bastard apparitions. Narrator B lists 89 famous Irishmen including star recruits Julius Caesar, Dante, Beethoven, Charlemagne, Napoleon Bonaparte and Muhammad. It seems like a joke. In fact, Joyce is deconstructing concepts of nationhood. He is appropriating complementary spirits for his race. Shanghai Dog stood awkwardly scratching numb thigh muscle. Doctor Gu lay on the bed. Her gut settled to the sides. A small crop of black hair sprang upright from her loins. Shanghai Dog knew the procedure. He started work. Paris in Troy with Helen. A weak aristocrat who marries an heiress. His head ached. His nose was blocked. He struggled for air with his mouth pressed into her cunt. Doctor Gu held him fast until orgasm then released his hair. She drew his face up to her mouth and placed her hand on his cock. Normally they fuck now.

"It's the start of my cycle," she said. "You don't need condom."

She flipped him over. A giantess. The mattress shuddered. Her hand maneuvered his cock. He closed his eyes. Judy tastes like honey. Xiao Fang is tender. Gu leaned back, snapping his cock like gristle. Tatlin's scaffold. A single chopstick askew in a bowl of rice. She pulled out abruptly.

"You are hard but there is no life," she said slapping his rigid cock.

"Not so rough," he requested of Camille.

"Your face also looks wrong. Like jiaozi," she said gripping his deadened cheek. "What's the matter with you?"

"Nothing."

She pinched his lip. A rash was spreading on his belly. She squeezed a small blister on his cheek hoping it would burst.

"You will be OK," she said firmly. "You just need time. Relax. Tell me your concerns."

She lay down and opened her legs. He started to manipulate her clitoris absent-mindedly.

"I'm concerned about business," he said.

"Oh, your Financial Crisis," spat Doctor Gu. She shut her thighs on his palm. "There is no crisis in China. Our economy is strong. This is a Western problem."

She released his hand as she reached orgasm again.

"You go to Gansu. See my father. Cut a deal. He will fix you up."

Lanzhou. A city where people have never seen the ocean. Shrouded in fog. Can't see it from space. Can't see it as you land. You are already trapped in its smoky guts by the time you register focus. Proceed down a narrow valley lined with chemical plants. Sichan Dalou. Northern Silk Roadhouse. Famous for mutton. Dressed-up as lamb. Gu was wearing a frilled garter on her leg. Camille (BILLY) is disgusted because she believes Pavel (GU) has somehow "offered" her to another man (HER FATHER). A place to make restitution. Restoration of funds. GO there to appease Poseidon. Get back your family. It's a long shot. Make a movie with the worst ingredients. *Il Disprezzo* was a potboiler. Lanzhou noodles. Godard always uses 'back-of-a-napkin' plots; shredded as usual. Some deals are incubated from unlikely stuff. Some fail. See Neil Haywood in Chongqing. Doing very nicely at present. Bai Shoutao. Family in Beijing. Vacation with his lawyer on the Casa Malaparte, Capri. Fancies himself another James Bond. Jaguar with the Jack. *Toto Against Hercules*. He advised me to find more remote regions. Grey areas where local officials constitute the SCENE. Odysseus travelled five moons past the Pillars of Hercules. See Dante, Canto 26. His ship was suddenly sucked into a whirlpool. Sudden death. That was the end of the CLASSICAL PERIOD. The text could end now. Reboot. "Go on," like Beckett said. Past Joyce's YES.

"You can always go back to Australia if you like. When times get tough there is no better place than Australia. Unless you're black, of course."

Doctor Gu sneered.

"Australia is a racist nation," she continued. "There's no brown, black or yellow in your flag. Only white for your skin; red for blood; and the blue sea. England colours. They've got nothing to do with Australia. You should make your own flag like China."

"I agree."

"You should also get rid of their queen and all her family. One day, you're going wake up and England's axed them. Then they will all go to Australia in their big boat."

"You're right. Australia will never be a Republic while the English Queen lives."

"So sentimental," she scoffed. "The UK today is like China in 1840. Except it will never come back. Soon our economy will be bigger than America. Just wait 20 years."

Bloodloss. Eggloss. Bloodegg. Hidden Fromelles. Pozieres. Stuck on a salient in front of Achilles. Hector fighting alone in front of the Trojan lines. Keep the pressure on Fritz. Haig conducted the war from his chalet map. Vico's cycles. Same thing happened at Greece and Crete. Malaya. Changi's sacrifices. Penelope waiting for Odysseus to come. Kokoda's clerks and kids held out until the men got back from Egypt. Churchill wanted to divert the Seventh Division to Rangoon. Would have been futile. Odysseus was always ready to waste yet another crew. Ship after ship got sunk from underneath him until only the King of Ithaca was left. Doctor Gu collected a heavy Xinjiang jade rat from the dresser and started rubbing its smooth white folds across her temples. Its milky surface cooled her cheeks. Shanghai Dog flinched.

"Australia is a new country. You can just make it up as you go along. It is also an island. Everything on the island is Australia. It's easy to defend. China is much more complex. We have borders with fourteen states. We are surrounded. But there are Chinese people all over the world. Even Australia. We all identify with Chinese history first. It is 5,000 years long."

"Western history is also extensive."

"It is not continuous like China. Sure, the Greeks had some ideas. Rome was OK. But Western culture disappeared for one thousand years! You lived like beasts. We used chopsticks while you ate with bare hands."

"Those are the same hands which created the industrial revolution."

"Yes, that was clever. But China was responsible for the Four Great Inventions. We built the Great Wall and the Silk Road. We were experts in astronomy and mathematics. Chinese medicine is much older than your drugs. We created porcelain and silk. Your monks stole silkworms and black tea. You couldn't even grow tea you were so stupid. Then you got lucky with coal. You humiliated China for one hundred and fifty years with machines. But that short era is over. Now we don't need to grovel. We are proud of China."

"What about freedom?" whispered Shanghai Dog.

"You think democracy is special," replied Doctor Gu. "But your governments are corrupt. They never get things done. We need strong leaders. Democracy is wrong for a big country like China."

"You still have the same system that produced the purges, struggle sessions, the Great Leap Forward and the Cultural Revolution. There is nothing to stop it happening again."

"You don't know what you are talking about. Look at Pudong. China is a superpower. America is getting weak. Europe has gone. China is different. We're not stupid like Europeans making big wars. We will get Taiwan to yield quietly. Asia will acknowledge us. Australia also."

"You're correct. We misunderstood China. We thought Deng was following a path of liberalisation. But he was just following conventional Marxist theory. China is building a massive proletariat. It plans to take over the world."

"You're crazy, Billy. You think this kind of talk won't get back to the police. You'll get us both in trouble."

She shut the blinds manically. Stalin had all the rooms bugged at Yalta. Nixon taped everything. Poe's blinking portrait eyes. Kang Sheng-Li Shigan. Dai Li. Trotsky sitting at his desk. Enter Mercader. Ice pick in hand. He plunged it into the neck of the great general of the communist revolution. Hamlet withdrew his sharp dagger from the khaki folds of a trench coat and plunged it into Polonius' wet palette. Pocketknife geometry. Paris hid his bow under a loose tunic. Claudius snuck out of the King's bower with an empty vial of poison secreted beneath his leather vest. Enter Beria with his nutcracker and wry wires. Persian Jones stole a glance either side of Belmont Street. He proceeded through the part-open gate. Leer prepared his chamber. Weasel Bob scuttled over the back fence. Still a chance to bail. Deny Christ like Peter. Confess. Hide-out. Flee. Become a fugitive. Famous exiles. Dante shuffling between Italian city-states like blind Oedipus. Rimbaud running guns in Ethiopia. Shipping coolant from Gansu to Maputo then overland to Luanda. 1067 gauge. Portuguese relic. Ovid never made it back to Rome. Seneca neither. Hugo in Guernsey. Napoleon on Elba. As if Odysseus got stuck on Ogygia or Aeaea. Deng was sent down three times. Stalin also. At Kureika, he lived like an animal thumping his Ossetian chest. Koba the bear. Zhao remains under house arrest to this day. Jiang reclining in his Taipei pleasure-dome. The Young Marshal was dragged to Taiwan like a slave trophy. Churchill at his Indian maps. End of Empire. Sailing nowhere at the end of the Heroic Era. Pouring concrete down Maputo's drains. Let them choke on independence, said the last governor (Crisco). He was feared for organising the hit on Mick Sayers. That was a revenge attack for the murder of Barry McCann down Mahoney Park. He was wearing a workingman's blue singlet emblazoned with the Eureka flag.

"Your problem is that you are not flexible or strong," she said pursuing him. "You bend but it only shows weakness. You lash out sometimes but it is futile like China in the

Japan War. I am different. Do you know my two zodiacs? In China, I am a tiger. In the west, a crab. That is why I am successful. I have learned to move sideways fiercely."

Gu stood over him. She cast a jaundiced eye. Yellow. Pope's essay. An infected spy. It all started with a simple plan. Chase money fast like Arthur Rimbaud. That will give you free time to write. It didn't matter about ethics. Orson Welles would act in any movie, television show or advertisement to get funds for his latest work. Balzac was always churning-out new stories to keep his head above water. Dickens was the same. But he never lost sight of his political purpose. Orwell ran a shop with a market garden to reduce the cost of living. He had already produced the greatest chronicle of the European underclass (D&OIP&L). Lawrence tried Australia. He ended up dying in the desert in New Mexico. Steinbeck wrote the definitive Depression era legend. Patrick White bred schnauzers in Dural. Woolf and George Eliot hooked up with rich men. Shelley was destitute in Europe, living off Byron's royalties. Joyce put financial stress into the centre of all his works, using it as a governing metaphor that drove character behaviour. He had been exposed to the declining fortunes of his family since birth. If anything, this was sharpened by the fact he received preferential treatment as the eldest son and prize scholar. The most poignant scene in *Ulysses* occurs when Simon Dedalus is confronted by his daughters for household funds (E10, S-E 11). Everyone is scrounging all day for drink-money. Parasites latch onto Stephen Dedalus to get at his salary. We observe wealth from without, like a poor boy scraping frost from a window pane to gaze in on a lavish table, only partaking of its complacent consumption when Joyce wants to induce caustic satire, such as the scene where Mulligan and Haines have afternoon tea at the Dublin Bread Co. (E10, S-E16). Boylan's ostentatious affluence provides a key contrast with the *petit bourgeois* grind of Bloom. It is Molly Bloom who ultimately passes judgment on the relative value of material wealth in human relations. In visual art, the production velocity facilitated by Modernism's simpler style enabled painters to become rich by shifting high volumes of product like a supermarket. This was very different to the days of the Academy when artists produced rare set-piece works. Such paintings required the unlimited purchasing power – and large viewing spaces – of wealthy patrons to generate sufficient proceeds to adequately reimburse the artist. Painting in those days was, thus, a high-risk exercise in which the artist bet the cost of art products and time against the prospect of a fast sale. This inevitably reduced aesthetic freedom. Modernism changed all that for a brief period like the striking of a dry match. But ultimately the inherent DNA of visual art as a tradable commodity combined with the lower production standards of Modernism to create a much bigger new art market. This is what Welles' explores in *F for Fake*, albeit as a metaphor for cinema. Picasso got rich. The Cubists and Expressionists regressed like Millais a generation earlier. And, ultimately, Barr and Rockefeller conceived its sarcophagus. MOMA (1929) boxed Modernism into a museum, reducing it to the consistency of slush inside a Campbell's soup can. CONVERSELY, MONEY REMAINED A PROMINENT TOPIC IN MOST MODERNIST LITERATURE. For writers, it has always been that way. As we have noted in previous chapters, Joyce was obsessed with commerce. This reflected the fallen bourgeois setting of *Ulysses*. Dublin had been a city in decline since the late eighteenth century when Britain relocated heavy industry to Belfast (see C8); a move redolent of the realignment of the finance sector from Hong Kong to Shanghai since 2008. This demotic strain in Joyce is akin to Balzac, Dickens and other writers who relied on the uncertain profits of their pen for sustenance. These authors spent their younger lives in the ghetto and were never far from returning to its maw. It is can also be linked to the themes of Dostoyevsky, Ibsen and Naturalism. Writers like Pater and Wilde would never have sullied their exquisite prose with references to pecuniary affairs and usufruction. They imbibed the emerald atmosphere of the Victorian aristocratic milieu where money was only broached in the obligatory hunt for American heiresses. *Ulysses* was a lucky accident of the economic zeitgeist in that the common themes of Irish life soon became apt globally in the inflationary aftershocks of the Great War. This is the world of Doblin's *Alexanderplatz* and the artwork of Dix and Grosz. It is the landscape of Lawrence's Black Country and, from a feminist perspective, Woolf. This is very different to what happened in France, where Joyce came to reside. The effete – in the sense of artificial, mucid and enfeebled – imagery of Proust and Gide predominated in prose after 1918 reviving the hieratic modes of Pater and Wilde with Dionysian candour. The radical inversion of taste and form by Dada and Surrealism were avowedly anti-capitalist. Yet they had an uneasy association with capital, probably because of their perennial grinding against Communism with its core theories about gross inequality in the distribution of wealth and power. A distinctively Parisian atmosphere of decadence and 'undoing' explains the rationale for Thomas Piketty's otherwise incorrect theory that "novelists simply stopped counting money" and it "virtually disappeared from literature." Perhaps the insouciance of Montmartre and Montparnasse influenced Joyce as a resident to such an extent that he gave predominance to ("capital A") Aesthetic Adventurism over incisive portrayal of everyday life in *F(W)ake*. This was the first time that Joyce had ever suppressed the quotidian in his work – *Dubliners*, *PAYM* and *Ulysses* are all uncompromisingly Naturalist in plot, themes, imagery and narrative.

"I could fix all your problems just by selling this single piece of jewellery," said Doctor Gu withdrawing the curdled yet succulent chunk of jade from her cheek. "But you're too difficult today. Get out of my room. Go!"

Doctor Gu dismissed Shanghai Dog with a flick of her wrist. The issue of nationhood is critical to Joyce. Writing against the backdrop of the Great War, Joyce methodically detaches Bloom (and by extension Stephen Dedalus) from any sense of self-identification being restricted to a nation state. Joyce sees Nationalism for what it's worth – a means of social control by the ruling elite that reaches its nadir in the jingoism attached to war. It's all well and good now, thought Shanghai Dog. We will know that the Chinese Communist Party is in real trouble when it invades Taiwan. By contrast, Joyce's EVERYMAN must stand alone as an individual – not become defined through the default setting of nationality. The struggle with The Citizen is the key to this process. Joyce portrays The Citizen as xenophobic and Anti-Semitic. He is reductive. By contrast, Bloom is open-minded and inquisitive. He represents Joyce's new 'global (humanist) citizen.' But to reach a point of self-realisation, Bloom must stand-up for his beliefs against external attack. Joyce presents this moment of self-definition at the end of Cyclops as a spiritual epiphany in which the contrast with The Citizen becomes physically pent. It involves spontaneous and defiant acknowledgement by Bloom of his TRUE identity. His statement of Jewishness can seem to sit oddly with Joyce's relentless denunciation of the Catholic Church in Ireland. However, this theme is not so much a value judgment about the merits of different religious systems as a means of completing the evolution of his key character in terms of cultural heritage – reconciling Bloom with his past, family, current location, religion and self. Bloom must take his own journey to this moment over the course of the episode. His initial definition of nationhood in Cyclops is facile: "A nation is the same people living in the same place." It broadens and deepens as the episode evolves. Bloom adds new elements such as the notion of a diaspora (Jewish and Irish). Language comes into play. Arbitrary definitions of nationhood become seen as futile – indeed, impossible – because all nation states are artificial constructs put together by Power. Shanghai Dog struggled to pull his trousers over his dead leg. Drool dropped out of his bent head from numb lips. He must escape this pen. Gu went to the bathroom. His heart raced. He made for the door with his shirt unbuttoned. An object smashed into the back of his head. Perhaps a slipper. The landing was deserted. He pressed the elevator button a couple of times quickly. It opened. He buttoned his shirt as it descended. At the foyer, he changed elevators without looking at the concierge desk. Inside, there were a couple of tourists. He ignored them. But it gave him some comfort. They wouldn't try anything while foreign eyes were watching. The lift dropped fast. He hung on. The past replayed through his mind. Odysseus knew it was time to go home when he left Calypso. As this is my last article, I will take the liberty of leaving my readers with a three hundred word list of the things that I will always remember about China: long distance travel, banquets, mongering, scraps of affection from gentle prostitutes far from home, nothing ever being completely realistic, well-evolved urban intensity, people morphing without contact, getting lost on complicated ring roads, skyscrapers flanked by open piles of scrap, debased historical sites, tiled housing towers all dirty white, cotton brown air, over-stacked bicycles, overloaded trucks, sweating labourers in filthy singlets exposing their greasy brown bellies on a hot summer night, girls in sequined T-shirts bearing slogans like "slut puppy," short shorts too short, high leather boots and argyle patterns, fashionless bureaucrats in costly garments with prominent brand signatures, a solitary demonstrator squatting outside the Shanghai Planning Museum disappearing under a swarm of riot police, grotesque public sculptures, the lenience of Chinese translators, CNN going blank at the gym, hatred of Shanghainese, crooning Delilah with my shirt open, a drunk businessman fondling my arm-hair, KTV games, potholed dusty local roads, garage doors along high streets, pristine airport terminals, kids squatting to split their diapers and deliver a steaming wet turd on frosted winter footpaths, eating fish heads in Jiangxi adjacent to a filthy river, coal loaders leaking black glitter into green-eyed water, eyeballs bobbing in a boiling hotpot, massive expressways floating above earth, the kindness, the generosity, the exuberance with just having ... Life. Chinese society displays all the extremes of human behaviour. The North is orderly and neat. The West is dangerous by comparison. The whole landscape is demarcated by grids. Government even uses grids to define policies. People approach survival with unbending will. Everything is mixed up. You let the wind bend you. That is how Chinese people have always coped. I will miss them. I hope I never forget how to float through a crowd. Thank you, China (289). The elevator doors opened. Shanghai Dog's cell phone rang. A text message from Xiao Fang told him she had left his apartment. This was some comfort. He didn't want to deal with her. He wanted to go home. He proceeded into the revolving doors pressing them faster forth. A tempest was sweeping Shanghai, straight off the South China Sea. The rain tasted like oily brine. It battered the hotel awning. A long queue of hotels guests hung off the taxi rank. He would never get a ride here. He walked straight into the deluge towards Huayuanshiqiao Lu. The earth had been shaken hard. Mud coagulated in the grooves of his soles. His shirt stuck to his body like a pelt. Water seeped down his forehead flowing over his cheeks. A taxi came trundling straight at him. He fumbled in his pocket and waved a one hundred kuai note. The driver stopped. The window slipped slightly.

"Wai Tan, shi fu. Guangdong lu lukou, xie xie."

The driver gestured with his head towards the back door. Shanghai Dog entered the warm cabin. He passed the bank note to the driver. Provisional safety from Poseidon. An advertising screen in the back of the driver's head rest started playing a promotional video for Shanghai Expo. There was a quick quiz. The answers were NO, NO, ZERO, ANYWHERE and NO IDEA. S-Dog muted the volume. In Joyce's ontology, LB is represented as Elijah. This explains the recurring appearance of a poster pronouncing,

"Elijah is come," throughout Dublin on the day of *Ulysses* (18 hits in total). Joyce has created Bloom to remind the Irish and humanity of our shared humanist values. This message is especially apt as Joyce was writing during the Great War. The false foreign gods that he fights are the Roman Catholic Church and the British Empire. The argument between Bloom and The Citizen is the equivalent of Elijah's victory over the prophets of Baal. Elijah uses a sword; LB uses words. Bloom adopts a just and righteous tone. The Citizen is Pharaoh. The Old Testament language of the final parody in this exchange invokes Elijah as "Abba Adonai." Bloom's vision of his dead son, Rudy, is his reward for his benevolence towards SD. Temporarily, Stephen becomes Elisha, heir of Elijah. Bloom also reconciles Christian and Jewish lore: Christ was crucified at Passover; the Last Supper was a Seder meal; the Eucharist ritual is the equivalent of eating matzah and drinking Passover wine. Bloom's copy of the Haggadah (Exodus in the Bible) is bookmarked by his spectacles at the passage of thanksgiving in the ritual prayers for Pesach (the Passover). Bloom returns to its themes consistently. The Captivity of the Jews in Egypt is a metaphor for all diaspora, pogroms, ghettos, imperial occupation and institutionalised racism. Elijah was sent to remind the Jews they had strayed from the Commandments into idolatry. Haggadah looks forward to the ultimate return of Elijah who will deliver them from bondage. It is ironic that Odysseus poses as NOMAN in the Cyclops section of the *Odyssey* because LB is finally revealed in this episode as a man of cosmic significance. INSERT BLOOM'S LIST OF JEWS (link to Citizen's Irish list). Bloom's confrontation with The Citizen hinges on his strident statement of Judaism at the end of sustained provocation. "Your God was a Jew. Christ was a Jew like me," he says. This is not an original statement. Bloom is not an original thinker. It is only given fresh meaning by its context in his characterisation. UPDATE TO AUSTRALIAN IDENTITY. Ocker attacks Don Cane. He remains passive. He dodges the test. This distinguishes him negatively from Leopold Bloom. He is fundamentally callow and self-serving. This shines a retrospective light on his behaviour before the start of the novel. It exposes him as a false father figure (FFF). He had very little involvement in his sons' lives after his visit to Sydney in 1984. He outlived his eldest son. Took a maiden's baby, a baby's maiden, her cousin and various folk down.

SEE APPENDIX B, EXTRACT 3

"Kant a Jewel oath fizz sundry jest lie kith necks fallow," says John Wyse Nolan near the end of the Citizen episode. It is a manufactured question by the author, too basic as leading narrative for such a natural dramatist as Joyce. The author also succumbs to unwieldy devices during this section, like the long recital of a report of chief cotton magnates by The Citizen (p.332). Even though it is a good demonstration of The Citizen's bombast, it remains unsatisfying as a piece of narrative to the reader.

"Eye goy nope emblem tuche mentshion withdues," says Ocker. "Monash his elf was dewish."

"Ten thousand Jews fought for Australia," says Tom Cornwall.

"There's no such place," says Ock. "Thoughs blows all dired for Ingham lie peddlers chooks. Lang was the first bloke whatever stood it uppem in Whizz mister. Swine they sentenced Kneemeyer. FIX was IN."

"Eye veer own lean bean bag a feud ours butt Eiffeel lie Horse rail yards ewe him my grey shun poly seed heirs dunce sum hood," says NULL pearl likely. "Versa ng yugo viet itality inks Skidknee!"

"World lest see wart apples wen wheat elem go chute Indo's up end Darwin," says Ocker. I nods. "Londonterrabrickurn veil be smarmsallakimbo again like Sigh gone."

"We owe a debt to the good people of South Vietnam," says Tom Cornwall bold-like.

"Weal yore might Frazor tuk severin tee severn though send off alm entomb Horse trailer," says Onk manner ceiling knee.

Eyesenears wry sensors form the tribal, eggs cue sing hymn sell.

"Thee steeples two'd-up took con new prism," says VOID.

The Captain's mendicant slipped out of earshot as Cornwall's voice rose.

"They worked with us," continued Cornwall. "They died with us. AND WE LET THEM DOWN! You wouldn't talk such nonsense if you'd gone and fought in Vietnam – and seen first-hand what we did to their country – rather than indulge in armchair oratory."

Eyesenears paused and returned to range. "There should be a stoush now," says Narrator A running madly into the text. Scatt and Chindrip stands bolt upright. Where is he till I murder him, says The Citizen at this point in *Ulysses* as if blinded like Polyphemus. "'Hold on, citizen,' says Joe [Hynes]. 'Stop.'" A very bloody all writhes affa stable simmer train helos. Bug big NULL nobaitacorns. Heap owlish soft his spear sops. Cap and putsch shove arraigns hyst knights. Are you game ter smash a winder, he arcs escrow. Eyed no go far king howls dowel, answers Scatt. Wood youse towel the swells," he queers Chindrip. Starbashers roach NULLAVOID. Eyesenears slipped out the back door onto Victoria Road. At this point in "The Bastard from the Bush," the members of the Push try to take down FF in Jones' Alley. Their dark ambush flounders against the wall of Riley's pub as the Bastard makes his stand wielding a bike-chain in each hand. There is NO SUCH VIOLENCE in TMAC. This reflects my fundamental distaste for the use of murder as a plot device in modern film and literature (see C8). QUICK CUT to Don Cane standing over a corpse, shielded by an old woman, in a ruined hamlet. A wife holds up a small framed photograph of her dead husband in uniform. The Shelleys stand by a graveside as their child's coffin descends. A masked avenger stalks the cemetery copse. A taciturn outsider, uncompromised by worldly possessions, and largely shunned by society, except fellow outcasts, and kids, who have an intuitive clarity as to his true status, looms into frame (insert close-up of Robert Downey Jnr). He proceeds with Old Testament zeal. Yes, violence is an integral part of Homer's classics. Yes, there have been epic books and movies about war and crime. But the automatic lapse into slaughter to display a character's inner strength, often tarted up with moral shibboleths of justifiable revenge, has become a drab cliché to desensitise the masses against liability for the plight of modern society. This is particularly true of anything emanating from American culture, which consistently deploys metaphors of extreme violence and death when it is trying to describe strong emotions and power. Joyce limits actual violence in *Ulysses* to the symbolic attack of an English soldier on a drunken SD. The potential escalation of this incident is defused by Bloom. It is presented as a sign of Odyssean cunning. The Vets commenced a strategic withdrawal. The sky was crackling. Ocker strained on his perch. Coriolanus advances to the front of the stage. Doctor Gu snorted and spat into the sink, clearing her head. Enter Cunningham, Power and Crofton. Cunningham calls for a Christian blessing. Cornwall held Ocker's gaze with an unbunged eye. A member of the local constabulary entered the bar. He walked straight towards the Giggle. Ocker blinked and checked his watch. Swiss incabloc. A gift from his mother when he was a child. Still full of hopes and aspirations. Playing wargames in the backyard at night. This moment of reflection gave NULL and VOID an opportunity to exit with dignity. Ock placed his hand on top of a bulging brown paper sandwich bag as the police officer approached.

"That was close," said Cornwall striding towards the kerb.

Eyesenears leaned into a metal advertising sign for Vincent's powders to avoid disclosure.

"Flab poke gluck yore dan drop," says VOID. "Eye wooden ways my bereft purse only."

"Sub ties, thebes kinder blows just gemme. I chest cough lick a fie cracker."

Their footfalls exceeded the bounds of eyesenears scale.

"Anyway, it's over now," said Cornwall. "Are you interested in working with us?"

"Yes," replied Don Cane with certainty.

"Good. I'll let you get some rest now. Let's meet tomorrow morning? Say Eleven AM. Our offices are located in Hunter Street. Just give the cab driver this card."

Tom Cornwall handed his business card to Don Cane. I watched them withdraw under ill-fitting one hundred per cent finest pure Australian merino coats. Ocker signalled his intent to pursue battle with an ill-timed shot. It shattered on the pavement. Shards exploded across the wet asphalt. I don't think those two blokes even noticed. I followed his instructions with desultory motion. But it was too late. The tartars were already standing on the far thread of the zebra stripes across Darlinghurst Road. They shook hands warmly. Tom Cornwall walked to the cab rank. Don Cane stood on the footpath alone. A sailor sensing breeze after a long lull. Street-pub-street, such are Leopold Bloom's movements over the course of Cyclops. A lout hung out of a passing car. He propelled empty barbs at NULL. They shattered at his feet. Don scooped up a jagged stem. He looked ahead. The car had been caught at a red traffic light. His proud heart rankled. The occupants wound their windows shut quickly. Heads dropped. Clinging to shag seat covers. Don Cane stood over a single glass crescent, gazing at his distorted reflection as if in a still pool. Suddenly, the lights changed. The car got the chance to escape his clutches. It sped off. Link back to the start of C2. In that scene, Tom Hallem is a kind of Paris figure hiding deep inside the palace as the Trojans and Greeks trade barbs. He is also a variant on Hamlet, as well as Telemachus safe in the arms of Athena. Don laid down his weapon. The waning movement and sound of Kings Cross circulated in disconnected fragments that just couldn't fill-out the heavy atmos of a humid spring night. It was coming to pass as the prophet, Telemus, had foreseen. Polyphemus complains that he was tricked by Odysseus' countenance. He did not match the perception of a 'tall, handsome' hero. This mal-adherence to Classical tropes of male appearance was signalled by Homer at the start of the *Iliad*, when the Trojans described Odysseus in Book Three. Odysseus isn't the main character yet. Nobody knows how Homer's story will unfold. To Priam, he looks stout and strong like a ram. This implies he has limited mental capacity. Antenor sets him straight. He recounts the first diplomatic exchange between the parties when Menelaus and Odysseus were sent to try to negotiate the release of Helen. The Trojans immediately perceived his subordinate physical bearing as they walked towards the embassy, although he seemed to gather stature when everyone sat. But they still thought he looked retarded. He stared at the ground not making eye contact. He clutched his sceptre 'stiff and still like a mindless man.' Antenor said that he appeared like a 'sullen fellow or just plain fool' until he spoke. Only then would "the words come piling on like a driving winter blizzard that no man could rival" (Fagles, Penguin Classics, Book 3, ll.246–269). This is a talent developed by Joyce and an ambition for this work also. The wind blew. Don Cane turned towards his hotel to gather stores and commence his journey home. Shanghai Dog's cell phone registered a new text. He unglued his Blackberry handset from the belt around his sodden clothing. "I am going to email your wife," it read. For Homer, Polyphemus demonstrates the negative outcome of lawless existence outside a well-formed body politic. For Joyce, The Citizen evinces the ultimate impotence of hard nationalist rhetoric. Shanghai Dog leaned back. He didn't hate Xiao Fang. Like DIDO, she was only trying to express her love for Aeneas. His shirt adhered to the black plastic seat. He cleared rain from his eyes. Suddenly the darkness was smashed by banks of fresh fluorescent strips at the start of Fuxing Tunnel. The taxi accelerated sharply and dipped under the Wangpu River. Soon, he would be back in Puxi. Let them plot. He started to compose a quick email to his wife in Sydney.

WHY IS AEOLUS?

Aeolus is a short episode in the *Odyssey* located between major exchanges with Polyphemus and Circe. The time-shifting structure of the *Odyssey* – which commences late in Odysseus' journey and uses retrospective storytelling on Phaeacia to propel the text back in time then sequentially forwards to the present – makes it easy to forget that Odysseus encounters Aeolus at a very early stage of his journey. In fact, it is only a matter of 2 months since Odysseus left Troy. He is almost back home. In that time, he has sacked Ismarus, encountered the Lotus-Eaters and escaped Polyphemus. He spends one full month on the floating island of Aeolia. When he leaves, Aeolus gives Odysseus a bag full of winds, releasing the west wind to speed his passage. Odysseus proceeds to the very threshold of Ithaca. He is so close that he can see dawn fires illuminating gangs of fishermen mending nets on shore. It is at this prospect of consummation that his crew opens the bag. They unleash fierce new winds forcing the fleet back to open sea. This is the commencement of the real Odyssey, which only Odysseus will survive. His crew must die to close the moral loop of Classical ethics. Odysseus returns to Aeolia after he regains control of his boats hoping to get another bag of drugs. Aeolus refuses further assistance. He has grasped the extent of the Gods' antipathy and drives Odysseus off. The Aeolus episode resigns Odysseus to a long exile. It thus sets the stage for his acquiescence to long relationships with Circe then Calypso.

A KEY IS RETURNED

After he left EAx, Tom Hallem retraced his steps across the Burton Street overpass and glanced right down West Street where swollen, punctured garbage bags and sodden boxes bedded a contorted figure slumped against a telegraph pole over an iron sewer-grate. Hallem felt compelled to render assistance, like Nietzsche throwing his arms around a horse being whipped in his final sane action. This is, in fact, a straightforward narrative transfer from Raskolnikov's first dream of himself as a boy watching Mikolka beat a tired old horse to death. It was apparently confected by Italian journalists to give drama to Nietzsche's madness. Another FAKE product. Link to all forgeries in this work. Also the narrator in Berlin in Chapter One. I clawed the battleship grey pavement (HEX #848482), leaving a charcoal indentation (HEX#36454f) in Berlin sludge (HEX#fffafa). Hallem peeled back a stiff overcoat to reveal the stalks of an emaciated drug addict. He pulled back the mop. This man wore a hawk's beak. A scar shaped like gallows-poles separated his eyebrows. A full, dry mouth. Tom held his own breath to make silence and waited for the sound of a single taxi to pass so that he could test whether there was still life in this wretched form. Eventually, the chest plate moved almost imperceptibly but true. A lungful of bad wine sighed. He looks so content, thought Tom. Why disturb whatever peaceful dreams were passing through his solemn vault? Sometimes, I still feel Tom's phosphorescence at night, so deep my epiglottis trembles (see end of C1). Molly's sour snorts inadvertently range into my fear shuddering perception back. Tom Hallem propped the torso against the pole and withdrew. Compassion is a concept rejected by Nietzsche. It was a sentiment brought to prominence by the helots who started Christianity in Ancient Rome. They were all part of a 'herd.' What we would call a 'demotic mass' today like the mob in *Coriolanus*. Nietzsche tried to shift intellectual prestige from the logical procession of Apollo's fugues, so feted by nineteenth-century thinkers, to the frenzied minor keys, driven by wind and hand drums, which in-sensed Dionysus' dancers. The tragic denouement of this Classical dialectic is found in the figure of Orpheus, child of Apollo yet also Dionysus' high priest. This is the type of rent personality that Pater translated into English and which was channelled by Wilde in *Dorian Gray*. A Hieratic figure needs ruthless self-interest to strive for dynamic peaks regardless of the consequences, according to Nietzsche. It becomes a self-fulfilling prophecy. This is a familiar trope to any student of Shelley (see "Alastor"). Tom Hallem failed in his quest. Billy Capri's pursuit continues. That is the basic divide in this work. There is no artificial moral system embedded in TMAC. All characters are demonstrably flawed. Joyce challenged Nietzsche directly with his Everyman protagonist, Leopold Bloom, whose wife takes over narrative drive and secures the novel with a resounding YES. To declare space OVER, to strive to mark an unmarked point, to cause progress however impermanent, like Pater's hard flame, which must ultimately expire, or Shelley's ember, which must inevitably yield to the lifeless abyss of NIL heat, pulse and colour, that is success. Tom Hallem was happy to preserve a dead stone in his pocket like Beckett's Molloy. Billy Capri, however, kept blowing through locked fists to try to retain some semblance of its glow even as life abstracted. In terms of Nietzsche's concept of 'eternal recurrence of the same,' I would choose to relive this life. But would any of James Joyce, Leopold Bloom, Molly Bloom, Odysseus, Penelope, Hamlet, Lear, Achilles, Helen Capri, Penelope Hallem, Don Cane, Judy, Richie, Xiao Fang, Elizabeth Archer, Morgana Lafei, Lester, W-the-P or Tom Hallem feel the same? The answers in order are YES, NO, YES, YES, YES, NO, NO, NO, YES, NO, YES, YES, NO, NO, YES, NO, N/A, YES, NO.

UKIYO

The gallery was empty. Its core a hollowed carceral. Wind shook the rusty metal panes. A huge Venetian lantern, spoil of some Doge's barge, hung limp like a tonsured Chinese lantern (see C1). Elizabeth surveyed the blank palette. This tone of abeyance is very different to the opening of Joyce's Aeolus. Bloom traverses Dublin at the start of that ep(is) ode. It is a completely different time of day to the current scenery. Clanging trams and grinding Post Office vans disgorge mail-sacks down brass slides. Drunken Guinness barrels tumble dizzily onto cross-river floats. Bleating animals beat each other to death on some Darwinian anvil (rats gulls microbes fleas dogs' men). It all culminates in the decisive press of W. Brayden's footsteps across the bare newspaper office. Elizabeth armed the security alarms. Her heels rapped on the tensile boards of the General Tobacco Company. A ghost bit her. She rushed towards the street. There were not enough sales tonight. Too many half-dots and pass-overs. She needed to call in some favours. Leon Daniel was leaning against a wall scrutinising the drawn master bedrooms of a row of common-wall terraces like Odysseus contemplating Achilles' shield. He penetrated Hephaestus' meaning in a way that the owner never bothered. She looked over her husband's shoulder. *Ekphrasis*. Convex shape. Dome of heaven. Ringed by the River Tethys. *Hopos*. Eternity's cycle. A mutability code. Bare brown plain. Human polis. Quotidian trafficking. Epilogue to the death of Patroclus. Shown thus to Hector. A prelude also. Images of bygone Troy brandished at his face. Worthless dead fate. His resignation. Achilles held it from his own eyes like a Gorgon. Don't perceive, he directed. Bar recognition of. Nullify association. Reflect but don't reflect. Be a mirror not a spur. Troy/Achaea. Elizabeth admired her husband's sharp profile so sheer when in thought. So polished. Impenetrable ultimately. And for that reason, always tugging a thread. Odysseus was thus enclosed. Restrained. Not ruled by human passion. Imperturbable. Modest, especially compared to his peers and leaders like Agamemnon. But always operating with purpose. He acted courageously although he preferred to avoid risk by his wits. Treachery did not dismay him. He was not afraid of lying. A thin-lipped armourer, he proffered deception openly like a Sudanese pirate or a brutal Sussex Street union boss. Now her husband had been utterly mortalised. An unintelligible multitude of cells was moving column by column through his body in a tide of bad blood. She reared. Repulsed by its force. Elizabeth touched her husband's forearm. His form seemed to have fused with discoloured brickwork like a human fresco at Pompeii. Odysseus was a relic of a strange, unnameable race. He did not look like the other Achaean heroes. Perhaps he was Hither-Asiatic. Greek with Phoenician ancestors. Something from a gene pool lifted by Homer from a pre-Hellenic bayou. Aly considered him Cretan. Dark bearded and hairy. Not fair and munificent like Achilles. Sitting he looked like a GIANT so broad were his shoulders. Standing he appeared squat. Alike to Palamedes, hero of the Achaean Troy legend and darling of post-Homeric poets. Both were Gulf people. Another Southerly gust was sweeping through the city from Botany Bay. It rushed under the traffic bridge at Hargraves Street across Paddington's ditch-end. Darlinghurst stirred like a tired, cruel dog in its wake. Blowback down its gullet. Peristalsis. Junk mail trapped in eddies circulated like cornered mice. Ambulance lights flashed silently, hung at the entrance to the Emergency Ward. A stainless-steel stretcher pried open weeping plastic flaps. Elizabeth clung tighter to her husband as they pushed up the embankment. Dark figs veiled the Victorian bandstand in Green Park. Sticky bat shit and fruit adhered to their feet. Silhouettes of sunburnt-red, green-sequined prostitutes stirred visible and vanished amidst the tropical beds. Pale twinks were pinned in tight procession against the sandstone blocks of the Wall. Classical statues slouching soft in recessed porticos. Palace stares. Secret assignations. Cruising car lamps illuminated blandished mugs. Fishnet singlets exposed lank arms pitted with chill marks. Elizabeth scratched an infected track hidden by her muslin sleeve. Penelope has her own secrets. Perhaps it was in the interests of both parties to withhold the kind of sharp analysis that they turned on other people. A police van turning into Darlinghurst Road aborted a protracted deal. A frustrated rent boy jerked back into the worn tapestry. Elizabeth and Leon baulked to let him pass. The dark driver of a comm-plate car shrank low. Constable Carr passed. Odysseus called the lad back with thick, scarred fingers. Tempest blast. His car lurched into the straits. Leon and Elizabeth approached the far shore of Oxford Street. Sporadic pedestrians some cars a bus sometimes. Gusts heralded the next storm. Elizabeth opened her bag to extract a portable umbrella.

"I forgot my wallet," she said in a discouraged tone.

"I'll go back," her husband replied.

"No. I should do it."

"You need to be there," he said pointing towards Taylor Square.

"Alright," she said stroking his cheek. Her ceramic thumb slid into the contoured skin above his nostrils. A cold nail scouring. Yellowblock Christ gazed down from the Sacred Heart. *Berachot*. Numbers 6. A flat purple coin. Odysseus regarded his wife's countenance unflinchingly. Elizabeth jerked his head into the deathly beam of a streetlight. A broad lesion was apparent on Leon's nose. There was also a fainter abscess forming on his prow. She did not recall these imperfections on the freshly painted canvas that Basil Hallward had displayed in his studio last week. She handed him a bunch of keys.

FLAW MARS FAMOUS PORTRAIT! TERRORIST SUSPECT

"What are those marks," she asked.
"Sarcomas."
"Is it AIDS?"
"Yes. Alar and the tip. Typical locations."
"So soon?" she asked forlornly.
"It's a game of chance at the start," Leon replied. "But it always ends the same way."

(4) SYLLEPSIS/PROLEPSIS

A dice thrown in a marble vault. Trope of Conscience. Agenbit. Debts owed in marriage. Set equity against. Joyce inscribed the 1,000th copy of *Ulysses* to his wife and gave it to Nora at a dinner party much like the restaurant scene that follows in this chapter. She immediately tried to on-sell the book to other diners. I think she hated her husband by this time. Like Hitler, Joyce only married his common law wife when he realised the hopelessness of his situation. It was another binding gesture, but not in its literary sense. By November, Nora had only read 27 pages of *Ulysses* including the cover. Joyce added the cover to the page total to avoid hitting the number twenty-six: it was twice unlucky thirteen. **LINK JJ & SYPHILIS TO LEON & AIDS** – Kevin Birmingham's revelation about James Joyce contracting Syphilis in the early part of the twentieth century in Nighttown occurs on page 289 of *The Most Dangerous Book*. Nora almost certainly contracted syphilis from Joyce. It is probably what sent Lucia mad. The bacterium that invaded his eyes was called *Treponema pallidum*. It is a classic syphilitic cell that wreaks havoc wherever it lodges in the human body. The first lesions appear on the skin and heal after a few weeks. But it searches for homes as it circulates through the bloodstream. It can inhabit blood vessels and bones, muscles and nerves, the heart, liver, spinal cord or brain. It induces illnesses as diverse as arthritis and jaundice, aneurisms and epilepsy. The most feared condition was GENERAL PARALYSIS OF THE INSANE. This was what destroyed Churchill's father. Every night as I gazed up at the window, I said to myself softly the word 'paralysis,' wrote Joyce in "Sisters" in 1904. Kevin Birmingham turns this word, paralysis, into a personal confession of awe and fear. In fact, it refers to a character in Joyce's story who has had three strokes. But I have NO QUARREL with a critic using this type of license. Birmingham's exegesis is brilliant in effect. It links with examples of forgery and fakery elsewhere in this chapter. The horror of Joyce's predicament is enhanced by Birmingham's clinical prose. Leon's got the flynim. Tom not. But I? asked Elizabeth. Nobody knows exactly how HIV is transmitted yet. I need to get tested again, she thought. Dark chance squats like a sharp-eyed gargoyle. The system has closed on me. Now I'm steeped in the past. Its above me as well. Weighted down by ballast of memories. NO FUTURE. A deep well of downspirals. Stoop the ditch. Fingers through Styx. Fizzing. Fade. Proust in black patent boots outside the Hotel Marigny squelching on the spot against rank sewerfrost. A spoiled *Rose Guide* drooping in his hand. Supplications of Le Cuziat. Mere blandishments. They enter the establishment together. He procures an adjacent closet to observe the adepts through twin peepholes. An oval portrait of John Ruskin is mounted on the fuck-side. Burnished wallpaper has been branded with faux velvet Fleur-de-lys. Bosie's nickname. The critic's strange eyes weep and wonder at such grotesque travails. Two flies buzz. Pies overflowing from the devil's fat stumps. Witness Duchamp's GIVEN. Its foil is Marion Hackett's installation FALL described earlier in Chapter Ten. Approach the old Spanish door which Duchamp found on holidays in Morocco and had shipped to Pittsburgh. Place your inwit against two teeny drill holes. Gaze inna. Loop back to Page Five. Appears, shlock diorama! A naked female (Maria Martins) is prone on her back across a network of brittle switches (Stoppages), some harbouring clenched leaves, with her head and part of her upper body obscured (Duchamp used various tactics to compensate for the fact he was a poor portraitist), legs flopped open, her bald cunt fully exposed, so that the labia seem hacked out of her limp/id body (see "Female Fig Leaf") like stark faultlines, and forced to hold aloft a lamp of jaundiced gas (1) in her rictic grip, we might think her dead if not for the muscular strictures of this posture, the converse of all those mucid Odalisques by Titian and Ingres, all runny flesh, no-boned, yes something more akin to Manet's "Olympia," whose own – and the viewer's – discomfiture is exacerbated by the inclusion of a maid brandishing a fresh bouquet, no doubt the gift of some Comte de Focheville or Charles Swann, against a landscape featuring a mechanised waterfall (2). Pull back. Duchamp appears as Rrose Selavy on the far wall (see Ozkaya). The flat surface of GIVEN conceals an elaborate cloaca machine of jerry-built devices to create the diorama, thereby inducing a simile with the human form. CCTV cameras captured Shanghai Dog's passage along the corridor. The butcher boy softened tensile chains. Bloom's wrists droppt, his buttocks lifted together. The SUB paid umbrage in mandible *Quebecois*. Whip-spat rejoinder. Leon knew such delights. Odysseus also. He told Penelope all about them in the grimy hours before dawn after they were all fucked-out. This was the point at which Penelope realised he was no longer human. She makes no effort to hold him in Ithaca. Her last involvement is to hear her husband's instructions and obey him at the end of Book Twenty-Three. He tells her to go to the upper room, "sit there, look at no one and question no one" (Oxford, 285). This proud and skilful woman appears to submit to her husband meekly. Order is ostensibly restored. Patriarchy reinforced. She has been told to stop speaking, thinking and composing new stratagems, as she did throughout the siege by the suitors. She must become a totem. This is the OPPOSITE of what James Joyce does with Molly Bloom. This instruction by Odysseus incenses a modern reader. Perhaps one could argue that Penelope is just relieved to have a period of rest. But I think she is JUST AS WILY AS EVER. Far shrewder at closure than her worn-down husband. He is now acting like the oaf that he appears to others on first glance throughout the epic. PENELOPE DOES NOT WANT ODYSSEUS TO STAY. She will do anything to make him depart quickly. Their DNA has become totally misaligned. How awkward this moment must have felt for Penelope, who had held onto a lasting memory of her husband trying to avoid war service and stay with his family. BUT ODYSSEUS IS LOST AT THE 'THEN' OF *THE ODYSSEY*. Onec upno tiem, it was winter in a subterranean bedsit in London, we were young, Leon had not yet given way to dare-not-speak-it-Love, I lay on my untended side glazing over a poster of *Disraeli Gears* when my waters broke through the sagging mattress another 5 quid fine from the landlady 'dirty Australians,' she said, link to Peroxide Girl in Chapter Five. Dark blood from torn bark. Pray to Father Mars. What if little Rudy had lived? Chaim also. Spina bifida had already ruined his prospects. Reptile corpse wrung on a slab. A skinned rabbit. Broken back blister weeping lymph. His father's destiny now also. Walk into the Tomb of Ilaria del Carretto. Shine a flashlight across the subway walls of Saint James. A sandstone stormwater arch. LED holograms. Plato's universe. Washed-out tagging. Ana rolled ahead of the pack like some cannonball Ophelia. She stumbled. Beach under kneecaps. She rose on thighfronts. Steepled palms. Threshold of a still dark pool. Tommy's speed was too fast; his smack too pure. She crawled into cool dim waste. A willow grows askance. Resteasy. Watery seep down earholes. An orchid. Ophelia in garlands strown. Dragged down by puppet wires. *Fleuves Impassible*. Ana's body twisted at the LAST. She rested face upwards on The Lake. This is the worst-case scenario for Stephen Dedalus after he leaves Bloom. That he was beaten to death in an alley by Cosgrove, Mulligan and their Pommy mates. Ana's dice rolled to an uneasy stillness. Dead eyes gazed at a too-far-flung grate. A single car flashed overhead.

"What happens next," asked Elizabeth.

"Sarcomas can be treated."

"That's not what I mean. I want a long-term prognosis."

Brain on her sleeve like Bloom. Technical mumbles. She touched his hair. Meandering towards some Pissant pisgalah. *Hyakinthos*. Bloom's list of social throwaways includes marriage sex pregnancy childbirth fidelity law madness death even disposal of the beastly dead.

Modern life all usufruct, he sighed. Penelope's suitors. Their business: to drink our wine. Her strategy: maintain process under siege; install ritual machines; make humans into apparatuses; mechanise 100% onto surface; de-sanctifile language [rebrand functions in Ingsoc (cc. Minitrue)]; commission a fake news campaign; detach all temporal hopes; accept death; enact attrition. INSERT GANTT CHART [Draft]. When the patient's CD4 count drops to 30, the immune system starts to shut down. The body ceases to respond to treatment. Sarcomas infect the skin and gums before moving down the gullet. They can infect the glands in the groin and scrotum. This causes grotesque swelling. Meningitis makes the neck rigid. The head may also be impaled at an unusual angle. The body whorls. The patient is unable to extend his hips or knees without severe pain. This syndrome is called Kernig's Sign. Often it occurs in conjunction with Brudzinski's Sign, which makes the neck, knees and hips convulse unwillingly. This combination of counter-impulsive gestures instigates constant suffering. A suite of cancers is prevalent during AIDS. Any combination may occur. The blend can include Hodgkin's lymphoma, mouth and throat cancer, lung cancer, melanoma, liver cancer, colorectal cancer, testicular cancer and anal cancer. The skin goes black and hard. It cracks and splits. Brain tissue swells until it presses against the inside of the skull. This results in what can best be described as 'mind-hernias.' Mental functions become severely impaired. The patient loses long and short-term memory functions. Winter occasions severe influenza which progresses methodically to bronchitis and pneumonia. Eating becomes distasteful. Incontinence ensues. The patient becomes extremely sensitive to light.

"At the end, you'll struggle to even recognise me."

"How long have you got?"

"Nobody knows. AIDS was only diagnosed as a disease in 1981. Most of the original victims are already dead."

"Oh Leon," she said cupping her palms over his broad dome. Galatea cradling the skull of dead Acis. Thetis viewing the shield. She looked over his shoulder searching for scenes of vines and olive trees ritual pieties marble cities civic citadels calves festooned in toilet seat white garlands.

(5) WHO IS TO BLAME?

INSERT ON LEON'S ILLNESS. LINK TO TOM'S DEATH. INSERT REVELATION. On a too hot to move or think summer afternoon, Tom Hallem lay stapled against his sodden bed bloated by steroids rejecting his second-hand heart his sacked bank card askew on a low table digital alarm clock-radio flipping sluggish minutes slipping hit parade truth loaded cannula flopping out of his basilic forearm blind wet and frightened voiding periodically in no man's landing. Tom called for help. Silently, Willy advanced to the threshold of his room out of sightline. He peered through the hinge crack. Tom's kelpie was growling dark and hollow. He panicked as Tom yelped. GUYS I CAN'T SEE, he said. Willy stumbled back into the lounge room and dialled Nadine. She said call TRIPLE-O. It works against every instinct of a junky to summon authority so he did some cotton. It strung him out for a while. Five o'clock game shows started. Tom was quieter during "Wheel of Fortune." Willy was deciphering the title of a recent film when he resumed. Champ picked four bad letters. Always mix two vowels with S and T. Willy pumped the volume. Ten second countdown. Talk it out. BUZZ. Adriana turned the tiles. MIDNIGHT COWBOY, it read. Canned groans. Never heard of it, said the champ. Speed to credits. Willy switched to "Catch Phrase." Tom Hallem like a baby crying cut through and through. He picked up the handset and pressed ZERO-ZERO-ZERO. He swore to God he'd get straight if he escaped. He gave the address. They started hitting him up for data. "Look," he said, "I just heard this bloke asking for help when I came to deliver a pizza. I got to dash. You need to get here fast." Hang up. A pregnant pass. Radio news tolled six. Farsiren. *Time for this poor soul to exit.* At last, Willy acts decisively. Eject the Gear. Flush the cistern. Fill your pockets. Take his card. Race to the kitchen door. Dirty dishes filled the sink. Kick Dixie out of the way. Scamper over bald lawn. Northcote's sky was blue. Crawl over the back fence. Hide in rushes. Oleander hedge. Watch from a safe distance like a fox. Ambos and cops massing. Discretely withdraw down a stranger's driveway. Shanghai Dog shuffled deeper down the taxi bracing low and flat. It was twenty years since Tom's death. He was still wandering it off. Guilt hardwired. Accomplice [was I]? Last phone call. He wanted more cash. More was sent. Hands wrung. Another six hundred bucks is cheap to get you off my conscience. I chose NOT to visit Melbourne. Abettor then by default. Did they score that final bag with my [$$$]? Joyce used Arthur Dignam's burial to induce pathos. Perfect naming. Dig. Nam(e). Viet(nam). Dead. Die. Fly crazy like Odysseus-in-storms to Fairfield Station. Hurstbridge Line. Get to Flinders Street. CBD. Change for Saint Kilda. Empty the ATM before his account is frozen. Score. We caught a taxi straight from the airport to the suburban funeral parlour. His mother had choreographed the service. Nondescript box on stage. Bad image on the face of a cheap memorial program. Almost ironically poor taste. 'When the sun has set for me,' it read. HE DIED SIGHTLESS! 'I want no rites in a gloom filled room.' HE DIED IN ONE! 'All part of the master's plan.' HE WAS AN ATHEIST WHOSE KINGPIN HOOKED HIM UP TO A SMACK MACHINE! Turn it over and get more rubbish. They play cassette music. Every line of the lyric was charged with meaning. His palms were cold now. Shadow on his second-hand heart. Pain behind unsighted eyes. He felt something touch him. This reference to the Lord sharpened the irony that he had died without the solace of human contact. Penelope's last act of misplaced control. Our father did not make it from Manila. Steps of bearers heavy and slow. Slippery mourning gloves. Don't drop even once the hole thereat. Pass straps underneath like patient bands. Lower. Loadbearing limit. Silent motion of passage. Bloom has some good points it is conceded by the end of Lestrygonians, albeit they are disclosed with errors of fact.

SUCH SOON-SPEEDING GEAR

"I don't want to go on too long," said Leon.

"What?"

"I've put some drugs in the safe. They're already loaded into syringes. I want you to administer them if I get too sick to do it myself."

She stroked her husband's face. Deal kindly and truly, asked Jacob. *Coup de Grace*. Bullet in the head if you've got spare ammo. Otherwise, take a rifle by the barrel and force the butt in a downwards motion to smash the skull. Use a blade as with Kurtz to slice ear from ear. It cuts the windpipe. Last gurgling stemmed by Dionysus' syrah. Perform seppuku on surrendering troops. Half chopped-off heads. Insert link to *NARROW ROAD, DEEP NORTH*. Make lists to intensify but also displace emotion. Leon hobbled off like a broken goat.

"The air bites cold," his wife spoke hard at his diminishing form like regretful Bloom watching Stephen Dedalus retreat towards his father and new name in *F(W)ake*.

BOBBING ABOUT ON A RAFT UNTOWARDS

The wind reaped Leon's bone-coat making flan-billows. Ghostbloom. A spirit wont to walk. S-Dog dozed in the taxi. It sped out of the tunnel. A boat leaving harbour. Aeaea. TV Soong's ships loaded gold bars and ancient artefacts on the Shanghai docks. Next stop Taipei. He gazed left over Huaihai Zhong Lu from the Yanan Elevated Road. A giant TV screen on the Lansheng Building projected a smiling image of Jackie Chan. Jingoism with Chinese Characteristics. He was advertising chilli oil noodles. Suan tian ku la xian. Five types of Chinese cuisine. Sour Sweet Bitter Spicy Salty. Equivalent to Mao Liu Mao Deng Xi. Se xiang wei. Colour aroma taste. It conforms to natural order: see > smell > eat. A nation is what it consumes, according to Bloom. Dogs eating dog shit. German fat and cream. British slop. In the nineteenth century, China swallowed Tibet. Britain chewed its border. It almost got swallowed whole by Japan. Stuff a turkey with a duck with a quail. Mao spitting plum seeds. Eating mud cakes in Anhui during Da Yue Jin. Frozen weeds. History is the movement of animus. Joyce on Vico. Mouth to arse. Peristalsis. Shanghai Dog squirmed. His cell phone illuminated the cabin. Wall Street purled. Cannibal states. Joe Taxpayer. Credit binge. Asset booms. Massive SOEs. Fannie Mac. Gorging God's body. GIANT SNAKE SWALLOWS CROCODILE. Tom Hallem, concealed in sandstone and fig shadows, observed Leon Daniel withdraw from the stage. Polonius was like a mascot inside a shroud. Darlinghurst Courthouse. Justice is blind to the poor man. Tamed by Miltown we lie on mother's bed alone. Henry Lawson rotting in dry dock. Greek Revival. Britain annexing the power of dead Hellas. Empire signs. Zeus did a crap and sandstone was dropped all over Sydney. Rome left sewers. Leon disappeared along the ridge of the Bourke Street Escarpment. Tom Hallem observed Elizabeth Archer in sharp profile beneath a square bell tower. Diminished in scale the abysmal tower against. She lit a cigarette. He hesitated. She turned, walking away. Suddenly, he resolved to proceed towards her crossing point and commenced motion also. Ginger's picture flashed on his screen. "Come to Glamour Bar," she texted. "OK," answered Shanghai Dog immediately.

LETTERS TO THE EDITOR

Leon Daniel felt inside his jacket for two long sealed envelopes. One contained a proposal to the Jewish Board of Deputies. He hoped it would be published in the "Australian Jewish Times." He crossed Burton Street and entered the foyer of a squat block house. The porter acknowledged him. He unlocked the security screen automatically. Leon placed the first envelope in a deep letterbox. He heard it drop to the base. Ana Lafei's eyes pressed upwards blindly. Iokanaan looked from the pit floor through a grill at platinum Judean light. Leon walked down a long corridor. Resounding click-ETTY-cl-ACK of leather soles. Lights pledged late in the Boardroom. Agenda Item 3: A Jewish Museum of Sydney. He had reviewed the draft floor plan before he made a large donation. Mezzanine 1: Hitler's Rise to Power. Mezzanine 2: First Arrivals in Australia. Mezzanine 4: Creation of Israel. Mezzanine 5: Judaism Today. *Chad Gadya*. Elijah is coming. So much to fix while he still had breath. INSERT GRID. Sudan. Beta Israel. Gondar. Starving in camps. Get them to Tel Aviv by plane. Tickbox visas. He approached the editor's desk. She looked up at him.

"I have an article to submit," said Leon Daniel handing an envelope to her. "It proposes that the United Synagogue prepare a resolution on AIDS."

"Positive or negative," asked the editor.

"It's a public health issue," replied Leon firmly.

"I don't mean to be rude but I've got a pile of letters in that tray," she said pointing, "saying that this is all *Halakha*."

"*To'eivah*," Leon replied flatly.

"Correct."

"My argument affirms the mitzvah of *Pikuah Nefesh* as well as *Bikkur Holim*."

"*Hatzalat Nefashot*."

"Sanhedrin 4:5."

"Now I recognise you. You're Doctor Daniel."

"I'm not a doctor. I'm just a dentist."

"They all call you 'doctor'."

"It's a mark of respect."

"Why don't you correct them?"

"What is this ... investigative journalism?"

"Just asking."

"I've tried many times. But they won't listen. So I gave up. They like it that way."

"It's hard to get through to the old ones," she grinned. "You follow Rabbi Deutsch."

"Yes. In my personal opinion, Me'ir Naftoli Tzvi ben Elimelech epitomises all that is good about *Yiddishkeit*. I have spoken with him about this article. He concurs with my logic. There is a note of endorsement attached to the back."

"I'll publish your letter. But we might need to edit. Put it there in the tray."

Leon positioned his article across the top of the other letters then left the newspaper office. He walked back down the hall quietly. Looking right, he could see the exhibition boards for Mezzanine 3: The Camps. He reached the donation box for Operation Moses, took out his keys, freed the lock and flipped open the steel box. There had been some new contributions since Saturday. A couple of small cheques which he would need to deposit tomorrow. There were also some anonymous bank notes. A few silver coins. Probably contributions from older Jews. Like the poor woman in B'riyt HaHhadashah. Jesus was right. Leon stopped to speak to the porter.

"How are the new dentures, Mister Vargas. Did the technician do a good job?"

"Yes, Doctor Daniel. Very good."

The porter drew back his cheeks to display a row of over-sized front teeth.

"You look like a young man, Reb Vargas."

The porter closed his mouth to speak.

"Only my teeth."

"My professor used to say that the mouth is the causeway to the soul."

"Well, in that case my soul can't chew on red meat anymore. Just soft foods."

CHLORIS

Food. Air. Speech. Love even. The body's Gibraltar. A beautiful portico. Botticelli paints the floral vine as if it is a string of barbed wire. Contemplate its verge. Lips softened to kiss. An art invented by Indians. Neanderthals passing mush between their mouths like birds. Babies suckling. Source of all sex drive. Neuron verbs. Inflorescence. First yielding. Accept your lover's lenient tongue. Conditional assent. To bear impetus. Invert. It becomes the power of invading. Merge. *Locos*. Pass beyond the lips the ardent lips to a soft wet vault. Gu like to recite a Chinese proverb: the tongue is soft and the teeth are hard but which one wears out first. An underground arch. A steep canal. Gaze up at its moist rendered roof. Uvula at apex. Teardrop sack. The keystone. Bloom was not a mason. Little grape. The mouth is a sad locale like our human condition. *Mono no aware*. Most melancholy part. A brink contemplated. Sail over its threshold into the black clogging guts like Jonah or Jason. Parts unknown though of ourselves. Themselves obscure. Mystery of the body. 90% meat. Close off. Just be surface and sense. Smile. It uses 34 muscles. All unconscious. Teeth defects exposed. There is more money in cosmetic than repair work. Vanity beats maintenance every time. Dreams crumbling my face. Self-esteem logos. Scars. Prising the jaw apart with stakes to get at the exposed bone. Drilling and wrenching asymmetrical rotten ancient or neglected teeth crowded together in knots gushing gore spit and dead wind-stink fetid gums systolic like curtains on the threshold between seen (fact) and unseeable (claimed). West Egg. Our organism: lamina/guts. Common clay. All poetry extracted from. Mundane images. Shame of patients at being prised. Slut Isaac on a slab. Dog with a porcelain turd stuck halfway out its arse. The porter's smile shifted tense. It was past. Just lingering, lowered, on his spent jaw. As if he couldn't force its dissolution but must wait stoically for it to lapse. Leon left the Jewish Centre. The porter retreated silently to his booth. Thawing rain. Mister Daniel walked towards Oxford Street. A damp rent boy grinned. Leon smiled back. Taste his pheromones almost. I could still suck and be sucked probably. Getanamylrush. Patches 3 am. Dark booth near the dance floor. Agendath Netaim. Warm lips. Rigid griff. No not tonight no. Nor ever again. Leon Daniel should have crossed Oxford Street but he turned towards Taylor Square. Food won't help. Put on as much fat as you can now it's useless. Dissolve to skinflags like some c.camp jew. He gazed through the iron fence at the unbreakable stone blocks of Darlinghurst Courthouse. British justice sustained on mighty columns. Temple. Royal Coat of Arms. Equality before law. Even for Jews. Rawlinson called Monash a slippery, clever, creepy-crawly Kike. Common Australians gave him the largest State funeral in history. 300,000 mourners lined Melbourne's streets all the way to the New Synagogue. Leon turned down Bourke Street. Bloom is somewhat depressed in these episodes as he contemplates Molly's adultery, carnality in general and the insults of average Irishmen.

Hope has slid. Even winning the lottery wouldn't help. Luck of Paris. Gods always playing jokes. Bradley kidnapping Graeme Thorne. Send 25,000 quid or we'll feed him to sharks. Seven rows of teeth they have. Fifty fangs per row. Imagine flossing. Sharks shed 35,000 teeth in a life. He burnt his tongue on a hot Pastizzi. It stung thick. He was not sure how long it would take to heal. Leon felt in his side-pocket for a hard-plastic container and a tube of dental glue. Bloom approaches the Promised Land with a series of thoughtful acts. To grasp God in everyday events. A shout. The throwaway. Small favours. Leon passed Darlinghurst Police Station. Someone yelled fucking poofta from a car. They beat the shit out of cruisers. Unaccounted deaths. One day they will calculate gay hate crimes in Sydney. Boys thrown off rocks at beachside beats. Discoloured sign announced the Astoria Hotel. He pressed the concierge's buzzer. Uneasy wait. Slow breath. Fear of being beaten to a pulp. Weak new light flashed. Sluggish footsteps. A shadow. The door opened. Nick Hagy strained to identify his dentist through the metal grille.

"Doctor Daniel," he exclaimed at last exposing raw gums.

"Hello Nick. I've got your new dentures."

"Bless you, Doctor. Come in."

He unlocked the gate and ushered Leon into the corridor.

"But I don't have any money. Mrs Kovochenko doesn't collect the rent until Wednesday. So, I have not received my salary yet."

He tightened the large knot on the front of his heavy dressing gown and adjusted a black beret warming his head.

"We'll worry about money later," said Leon Daniel. "Let's fit your teeth and see if you can't chew some *yetta*."

"You are so kind, Doctor Daniel. Come to my room. I must admit I am tired of drinking soup. Bad squirts, you know. *Fos*."

He laughed. Agape. They entered the bedsit. A grey hotbox. Nick heightened the heater still further. Leon emptied his pockets. He laid the teeth carefully on the table. Ancient lace. Relic of a dowry. **INSERT ON MARRIAGE**. One partner must go first. Nick dropped into his deep soft brown rocker. Leon rolled up his sleeves. He squeezed an arc of glue around the edge of the top denture then a single straight line down the centre to the palette mound.

"Tilt your head back. And open your mouth. Wide."

Nick obliged. They always did. Trust. A precious oddment. Scorched field within. Stick a stink. Ancient globs. Down. The heartbeat. Stroke his gum. It tickles. Smooth surface. Do NOT scratch him. It could be fatal. Tidy up all the loose ends over the next few days. Then stop work for good. How will we survive my decline? How will we pay my medical expenses?

Leon fitted the dentures into Nick's face. Contact. Press. Life. A smiling baby. Chaim never again no. What could have been. Priam pleading with Achilles for Hector's corpse. Putting lips to the backhand of his killer. He had no feelings for Tom Hallem. Proust like Shakespeare is zealous in investigating sexual jealousy. Joyce had no interest in it. Bloom accepts Molly's adultery. He understands its causation. He accepts responsibility. He has done it himself. His quandary in *Ulysses* is whether to try reconnecting with Molly. Shanghai Dog knew that he would abandon Xiao Fang and Doctor Gu. Eventually, forget Zhu Di. Go back home to Sydney. Ways in/out/thru. Wayfarers return. North Head. A small skiff. An opening beckons. Port Jackson runway. Leon examined Nick's new grin. The technician had done a good job. Good to go really. But I don't want to. Not yet. Leon Daniel would rather sit and drink weak tea with Nick and get distracted hearing about Hungary before the War and how a few Jews got out in the 1930s than go back to the restaurant or go home.

MESS OR MASTERPIECE?
THOSE "EUMAEUS" BANNERS – TRUTH REVEALED!
STRANGE SIGHTINGS OF ELIJAH IN DUBLIN!
WHO OR WHAT IS THE MYSTERIOUS MISTER "O.P."?
[INSERT TABLE]

Table 20. Aeolus – Key elements

Scene	Newspaper office (Freeman's Journal).
Voice	Hard-boiled
Style	Modernism. Journalese. Use of Headlines – sensational language. Interest in public language rather than private speech. Inventory of rhetorical tropes.
Body/Character	Moral anatomy of Dublin [Dublin as character – Hibernian metropolis]
Organ	Lungs (wind, air) HOT AIR
Art	Rhetoric. Joyce believed that the Irish were paralysed by their own empty hyperbole. In his early essay, "Ireland, Island of Saints and Sages," he argued that Ireland had been weakened by centuries of useless struggle, political backsliding and the chicanery of British occupiers. Initiative had been "paralysed by the influence and admonitions of the church, while the body is manacled by the police, the tax office, and garrison." These are the principal targets of *Ulysses*, which was his most overtly political work.

National Metaphor	Irish as Israelites. Expelling British = Exiting Egypt. John F Taylor speech quoted extensively. Taylor spoke of Moses' non-conformist [antinomian] sentiments. Bloom knows this story well – direct identification with Jewish heritage.
LB Metaphors &	Bloom is Ireland's Moses. Also, Elijah. Joyce uses metaphor to expand LB's stature in the Lestrygonians episode even as the narrative events show him as an ostracised, struggling figure.
A Crude Hypocrisy	The Irish use Israel as a metaphor for Ireland but Bloom the Jew is racially vilified and oppressed. Thus, the Irish are no better than their oppressors.
Ireland/Australia	Compare historic relations with Great Britain. Link Irish self-determination in early 20th century with Australian reorientation towards Asia in late 20th century. But this did not change entrenched Irish religiosity and social mores. Joyce concluded: "the best must flee." Himself included. Contrast with Australia in the 1970s: "the best are drifting home," S.Harolde said. Note link to Whitlam election. Insert Telemachus comparison.
Aeolus – Correspondences	Like Odysseus, Bloom leaves the office in the belief that he has clinched a deal with Crawford only to find that the editor rebuffs him when he comes back later.
LB/SD Convergence	Bloom and Stephen began the day on opposite sides of the city. Now they converge. They nearly meet at the newspaper office. They are circling: Bloom is renewing an advertisement; SD is delivering Westacott's letter. Bloom leaves to go to the National Library to copy the advertisement. He observes Stephen's Shakespeare monologue there. This is Stephen's natural territory – a kind of inverted Telemachiad. Stephen and other characters retire to Mooney's pub.
Father & Son	Mister Simon Dedalus exits the office. His son arrives.
Differences in Reception	Bloom is rejected while Stephen is accepted – even welcomed – into Dublin office/pub life. Bloom desires inclusion. Stephen understands that boon companions are parasites [perceptivity of Byronic Hero].
What SD Sees	Bloom is working hard. He receives overt rejections and snubs. But he puts up with it to make a working wage. He is stoic. He channels Darwin but does not really believe it. In "Lestrygonians," Bloom rejects the "eat or be eaten" philosophy – paralleling Stephen's creed in Proteus.
Lestrygonians	Bloom – hungry and depressed. Eating, digestion, excretion, disgusting eating habits, city as maw, Irish civilisation eating its own, Boylan as cannibal are themes in *Ulysses*. Also adultery (copulation of two flies; music from Don Giovanni). Escape is key theme.

TARZAN-BABY RAISED BY CENTAUR!

Stephen Dedalus evolves rapidly as he spirals towards orbit with Bloom. He starts off on a low base. His immaturity at the outset of the novel makes for unsatisfactory reading in Chapter One. The reader must push ahead. Joyce's characterising-speed calls for some credulity. It is as brutal as the super-accelerated plot of *Romeo and Juliet*. Stephen's unsuccessful riddle and plagiarised poem in Chapter 1 are superseded in Aeolus by his expositions on Shakespeare's genealogy and *A Pisgah Sight of Palestine – or the Parable of the Plums*. Both these performances are well-received by mature audiences. The title of the parable refers to Stephen's sharp put-down of John F. Taylor's euphuistic speechifying about the Irish Promised Land. It is meta-textual in that it mimics the mythic method that is the formal and imagistic bedrock of *Ulysses* itself. It is another signpost of Stephen 'becoming' Joyce. It involves two middle-aged midwives travelling to the city from their home in one of Dublin's poorest districts to climb the pillar of Admiral Nelson: a symbol of Ireland's capitulation and servile relationship with England. But Joyce was actually ambivalent about British occupation. "Tell me why you think I ought to change the conditions that gave Ireland and me a shape and a destiny?" he once asked. They arrive at Sackville Street. It was the hub of Dublin's tramway system. They admire his statue as it towers above them. There is implicit phallic voyeurism. The final BANNER of the episode comically articulates the underlying sexual tension of this Symbolist tableau. They pay the entrance fee. They climb the stairs. It exhausts them. Eventually, they gaze down on Dublin. This outlook should mimic Moses overlooking the Promised Land ('Pisgah'). However, they are not enlightened. Neither is the place. Instead, they focus on the proliferation of churches – arch symbol of Ireland's repression for Joyce. Finally, they sit blankly gorging themselves on plums. Ironically, Stephen Dedalus replicates this ignorance later in *Ulysses* by annihilating his intellect with alcohol. Their final act is to spit plum seeds through the grating, showering their fellow countrymen below. Projecting dead seeds corresponds to Stephen's mother wasting her fertility on Ireland or Old Paps feeding fresh milk to English Haines and Glands Mulligan (see also Israel's unpromising dirt also Soldier Settlement's choked by Patterson's Curse). The reductive minimalism of the parable acted as a template for Samuel Beckett's drama. He became Joyce's spat seed.

ENTER OUR GREAT CONTEST!
FILL IN THE BLANKS & WIN A BRAND-NEW RUNABOUT!

TABLE 21. STEPHEN DEDALUS VERSUS LEOPOLD BLOOM – TRAITS (2)

Character	Action Figurine	Act	Endpoint	Outcome	Irony
L Bloom	Moses	Exit Egypt	Pisgah	Irish freedom	Jew. Cuckold
S Dedalus	Joshua	Arrival Israel	Irish epic	Writes text of National Self-Realisation	Just an Artist

Tom approached Elizabeth. "There's you," Elizabeth said smiling. She took his hand. Say nothing both. They crossed Gilligan's Island. Thunder clouts swept upnowl faces. Watch out for lightning bolts. Joyce was terrified of them. He would hide under a table like a lap dog. Delicate lashes fluttering over bulbous lids. To cast her nighted colour off. No friend of Denmark. Soles depressed on thick unkempt lawn. Tentative vestige immediately erased. Ref Shelley. Noble Leon gone to dust. A granite-skinned derelict slouched against the park bench with grey trousers about his shins. He laughed mirthlessly. A plastic bottle of turpentine bounced on his exposed gut, still hard and brown from labour. His blackened hand reached out at the couple. "A bone," he implored. They ignored him. Elizabeth pulled harder on Lucky's rope. Gogo grabbed his limp cock. Kurba! Polizi mi ga! Rue du Coq d'Or. A chain of adamantine screams rang down Bourke Street from the Salvation Army shelter. God was a shout, said Stephen Dedalus. Sour reek of garbage truck. "What is the time?" implored Estragon. Hallem shrugged. Beckett inserted some jape about temporal incohesion at this point then shifted to abstract profundity. Once there was a plot. Time was allocated to each chapter. To each page, certain lines. In each line, a code. Now I can't even be bothered looking at the message on my palm. They all shrugged. "About Ten," yelled Hallem backwards. A window was flung open mid-storey. Kathy Drayton leaned over the kitchen sink to watch the scene below. A police car cruised past. Kinsela's funeral parlor threw off a copper glow. Hoary yellow eyes. Suddenly, Gogo yelled (without guish): "[SELF-APPARENT]." Elizabeth stopped outside Serafim's Pharmacy. Inside, the Duty Chemist was watching a portable television at the counter.

(13) HESED SHEL EMET

"Will you go back to the news stand and buy me some smokes," asked Elizabeth. "I left my handbag at the gallery." To quibble with the keep would seem unchivalrous. The keystone of *Ulysses* is Bloom's acts of unrequi(r/t)ed kindness, especially towards Stephen Dedalus. His dead son is made living again via these performances.

LESTRYGONIANS

Elizabeth walked to Campbell Street. She entered the restaurant. She was hustled to her seat by the *maitre d'hotel*. INSERT DESCRIPTION OF ROOM & DINERS. Note that Proust continuously updates the social hierarchy of this type of place at Balbec to reflect the changing status of guests over time. Explore the same shifts in microcosmic form. Supplejack UP. Hallem DOWN. Fuller DOWN due to the absence of READ. Clustering of wealth. Each guest must correspond to a different food-type (eg. Fuller's pupils were clouded like poached cod). The clock tolled ten. See comment on Proust's cavalier approach to TIEM below. Tom Hallem observed the dining table through the clean restaurant screen as if it was a backlit aquarium constructed in a television set. Explain the composition of this image. Most of the scenery is arranged along the bottom edge like pebbles and toys. There is a dark gap at the centre of the picture. Staff undertake asymmetrical, repetitive paths through space like tropical fish. INSERT TABLE CONFIGURATION.

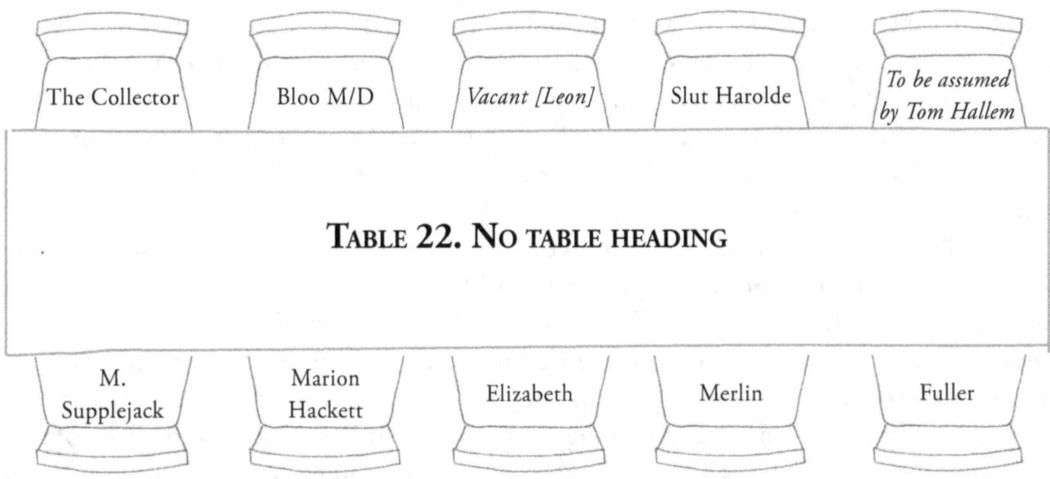

Tom Hallem entered the restaurant and approached the table. There were two vacant seats: one at the centre of the party; the other in the far corner. He shimmied towards his chair. Elizabeth tore a French stick. Crust sparks. She spread a lenient butterball over its comb and buried it under a thick coat of French Brie. A light bulb blew.

NELSON'S COCK

Slut Harolde took the opportunity to caress Tom's knee. SHIFT TO LATER. [INSERT ALLEGORY] The waiter was told to replace the broken bulb. He obeyed. Tom did not demur. He knew that Nelson would complain if he did not comply. Then he might get beaten. Maybe even have to suck on Nelson's beery old balls again. LINK TO BARON CHARLUS. Note Proust's careless concern for temporal consistency. The waiter ascended the three rungs of the step-ladder unsteadily. They creaked. He reached the apex. A dishwasher wearing soggy brown Blundstone boots came into the restaurant to secure his ascent. The crowd gasped. Two big-boned matrons were busily working their way through a bowl of cherries near the entrance (TABLE 1). They splat bluddied pips into a mound on the checked tablecloth. Their faces rose each time the door opened. Nurse Kearns sucked an imported French snail out of its shell. Lady McCabe took a spoonful of aspic, exposing the cloven-hoof of a pig's trotter. LINK TO SYMBOL. Ophelia's hocks embedded in the frozen waters of the River Traun. See table-configuration diagram. It was enough to make Bruckner roll in his grave on top of some young virgin. Swann bouncing on a chamber-maid in his carriage in the Bois de Boulogne. Link to Shanghai Dog. Both sex predators. Connect to incidents in youth. Examine ethics. Old Gogg used to tell anyone who listened that **Pâté** was just a Wog word for **Peck's Paste**. Tick examined the picket-fence couple at TABLE 6. They were consuming identical plates of burnt lamb chops like Haig and his chinless cavaliers chewing through Australian boys in mud. Nelson had completely lost interest in this scene by now. We should call another summit, Bloo M/D ejaculated like some Byronic crow uttering news grabs on Delphi. The whole thing is such a bore, responded Merlin like thin-lipped Lady Verdurin. He had started sweating. His belt tightened another notch. Time slowed. The broken bulb was still wire-hot. The waiter unscrewed it with a damp cloth. It induced a phlegmatic odor. He extracted some dead filament with his fingers and gouged the new bulb into its shit-metal batten bluntly. Proud and unseeing. It spat sudden light. He reared. Turn off the switch, said Tick disgusted. This whole sub-section is a strained metaphor for Australian politics in the 1980s, just like the scene @ Nelson's Column in *Ulysses*. A new party arrived. They were studying the menu like it was some kind of Akasic record. It must be that late-night sitting of aesthetes, he pondered. The waiter got down from his perch. I'll humor them with some Vaudeville and Wagner, he thought. That'll keep them purring. He jammed TABLES 2, 3 & 4 together. TBH I should restructure the whole room. Amalgamate with the place next door. Make one big chowhouse. Nelson was leaning over two rank-and-file members, ogling their ample consensuss. FRISKY FRUMPS TRICK BOSS!

Read the headline. Tick watched this tableau with the perceptive eye of a French timepiece collector. He realised that he would have to stop Nelson's clock someday. That block would never set down willingly. Except on top of a blonde.

BACKFIRING BARBS LAND BARD IN BOTHER

"Fraser never possessed ... moral authority," yelled Slut Harolde at bad acoustics.

"His Country Party mates always made him fold," added Bloo M/D baring worn teeth. Red wine circulated in his mouth agape. A grouper.

"Nixon, Anthony and Sinclair," added The Collector wisely counting down on swollen stalks. Elizabeth licked sharp residue from a gleaming oyster shell. Tom placed the cigarette box in front of her and continued towards the corner. Passionebb. Wilde's marble chair in a cirque of fantastic rocks. Lust rising/waning with lunar charts. A stiff breeze against your cheek. Sucked back to open sea. Pissbrine. He bumped a black ledge rattling coarse pottery as he sat. It shuddered and ceased. Levin. A moment falling. Too deep. The fold-up chair barely contained his broad body-span. He gripped a warped frame. Odysseus appeared taller when he sat. Tom seemed to spread like a spider. The surface of his seat had oxidised almost to rust. Fingerprints gritty like paprika. Ochre pigment. The stuff that Lang Hackett made his fortune out of. When iron meets water it tastes like blood. A ship's bow run aground. Crevice in mud. The waiter lit a mosquito coil. Most melodious music emerged from a speaker.

"Seventy-five and seventy-seven were both votes against Gough. Not votes FOR the Squire of Nareen," said Bloo M/D.

"Bill Hayden went close," added Elizabeth.

"Then Hawke delivered the *coup de grace* to both of them," said Merlin draining a bulb of pinot noir lustily. He tapped the table displaying the empty vessel.

"If my glass lies empty fill it. If the bottle is empty, replace it," he instructed the waiter.

"Foreign Minister is a comfortable kind of exile," concluded Slut Harolde.

"Yes indeed, Nelson. A very pleasant way to get blown off the map," added The Collector sagaciously.

Represent politics in Australia through this exchange as uneven in its allegiances. Political loyalty not based on class. Usually utilitarian. Personality-driven like John Joyce re-Parnell. One of Proust's single specified dates in LTP is the fall of McMahon in 1877, which sounded the death knell of the French aristocracy. Charles Swann bounces against the selvedge walls of French society: Combray IN; his wife OUT; Verdurin's salon IN/OUT; coveting Jockey Club membership; always planning to finish that monograph on

Vermeer (link to self); an example to the Protagonist of what not to become; a pimp procuring mid-level bureaucrats for his wife, Odette; a pariah dying of cancer. Like some construct of Deleuze and Guattari, he remains forever an outsider of the Within. Insert list of famous outcasts: Ovid Dante Voltaire Machiavelli Hugo Byron Shelley Wilde Orwell Joyce. Beckett also. Always Russians. Red then White then Wrong Red. Against despots they fled. Or to seek the well-spring of culture. Some made self-imposed breaks like Joyce. As punishment. As refugees. Never tell an Emperor his art is hanging out. Squish pudgy White Guelphs. Collateral damage. Put outside like a dog or cat. Shakespeare's tragic heroes all faced the prospect of expulsion as they contemplated action: Hamlet, Lear, Macbeth, Othello, Coriolanus. Even Romeo. Itinerant by disposition. None of them plain folk.

"He can make some pocket-money stuffing dope inside diplomatic bags like Slick Al."

Polymestor cannibalising Priam's gold. Thracian double-cross. Griffith crops. Air America. Coconut airways. Billy Capri turned the page. Aeneas was tearing stalks from the earth. Oxblood fouled the soil. Polydorus impaled on stakes. Dumped in a ditch. Covered in lime dust. They found Frank Nugan dead in his car outside Lithgow from a single gunshot wound to the temple with Colby's card stuffed in his front coat pocket. The waiter tried to deliver Tom's entrée. He declined. I will not eat with them tonight.

"I'll take it," said Merlin consuming a raw oyster from the floating plate greedily.

"He's pouched that," laughed Harolde gleefully.

Fuller turned to Tom.

"Miss Hackett spoke highly of your work," he said.

"Which piece?"

"Your Speed Paintings."

INSERTIMAGEONWEBSITE.ADDPATERIANDESCRIPTOR(GIACONDA). Her head upon which all ends come et al. Older/younger than the rocks/lines she contemplates. Dead many times. Ox sinews. White cartilage. Bone. Brownsmere. Secrets of the grave. Over there, Jack. North Cemetery. Go to page 883. Surprise, surprise. A discarded handkerchief with gobs of bloody spittle parched in sun. Pancake cheeks. Sweat, sweet-varnished flesh. Consumptive glaze. Bug eyes wired unshut by amphetamines trafficked for strange webs with Eastern merchants. Tinge the eyelids and hands with Titanium. Peroxide hair blown into an arrow by gusts. Smirking Pierrot. The gulf between image and viewer is always receding from the moment of first contact. A flash that fades. Sublime. The mind moves on, dragging the reluctant eye. The image lives only within any imprint it has moulded inside the changing lineaments of the brain. Achilles glanced at his shield nonchalantly. Sunglare hid. It allowed him to dissemble. A perpetual life like the Gods would elude him. Even 10,000 experiences were still too short. All his mother ever did was remind him of his brief mortal span. He ate-up Trojans as a result / out of despair / at his own predicament / a gluttony machine wrought upon by all modes of life. Courage seemed to spur his sick appetite. All were brave. Always honourable men. Fearful yet fearless in facing Achilles. Cognisant of death's cert. Until by the worst-flawed Trojan he was aced. The arrow is a coward's weapon. A paintbrush. To die with your back turned to the canvas. Helen was a swan's child. Achilles was Lestrygonian. Also, a kind of Cyclops. He refused to cognise or collaborate freely. Odysseus registered the fact that Achilles had no commonality with mankind and no identification with home. That he was too much God, too little man. It must have reminded Odysseus to stay BASE HUMAN. Only when he regained Ithaca, did he finally act like Achilles. The slaughter of the suitors was Odysseus' mimicry of a great warrior. It was a reductive version really as he did not confront great soldiers but only slobs and boys. It was a debasing act. It condemned him to exile. To be blown out of Ithaca for good. Out of the convex bowl of known places.

WHAT LIGHT IS THAT THROUGH WHAT?

"What do you know about that woman," asked Tom of Merlin.

"Her father is a big wheel in Perth. Hawkie just paid two bricks for his boat. She controls a couple of Family Trusts. Elizabeth wants to become her Lavender Boss."

"She's no Edie-doll," Slut Harolde lowed in retort.

"Not glam at all," answered Merlin.

"But very well-minted, you say?"

"Even by Elizabeth's standards. She's been commissioned to put together a contemporary Australian art collection by her father. She took six works straight off the wall at Mori last week. Plus, all Matt's unsold fragments. She's negotiating with Elizabeth to acquire a major new series of paintings by Read."

"A harbour series?" asked Tom.

"So I believe," replied The Slut.

PROTEUS

Tom Hallem sat silent. He observed Matt Supplejack working the table blithely. Alike in age and station yet not accomplishment like Edgar and Edmund or Richard Three. Even his workboots were worn politely. In both senses. A few strategic drops of white oil paint decorated the steel tips. He leaned closer to Calypso. Smooth roe. A long loose Viking arm wound around the back of her chair. She bent to defer. Her faint mane was tied in a Paisley scarf exposing a swan-meat neck. She wore a tired profile. Taut cheeks. Sharp incisors. A bladder full and lofty. Too close he came and blinked. She hovered like a dragonfly unable to pull back or progress.

ONE-FOOTED LAD WINS TRIP OF LIFETIME

The first course was cleared. Elizabeth stood.

"We had a great show tonight," she said. "A successful end to a successful year. We've also received some good news today. I will ask Harolde to make the announcement."

"Thanks Elizabeth. It has been an outstanding year for EA Times. You have built the premier roster of young artists in Australia. But the proof is in the pudding, as they say. For the first time, an Australian artist has been selected to exhibit at GEAR – the prestigious Global Emerging Artists Show – in Paris. It coincides with the Paris Biennale in April. This artist has beaten competition from all the major private galleries throughout Australia. He is EA's best and brightest ... Matthew Supplejack."

Applause. Lights. Matt's handsome face glowed. His name blazed forth in light. Tom Hallem was cleft. Paris as to Hector. He is wearing my cloak. Pockets full of my coins. His now to spend.

A PASSAGE THROUGH THE WORKS

Tom Hallem waited for the appropriate moment to exit. The most gloomy and repugnant jealousy harassed his vitals. He shuffled silently around the other diners. They swayed like bull rushes to let him pass. He broke towards the kitchen. Bloom in the print shop. The Lestrygonians seemed like wonderful hosts until their leader, who is described by Homer as "huge as a mountain crag," lured Odysseus into an ambush and tried to consume his crew. A kitchenhand was dicing a long bunch of fresh shallots. He turned bloodshot eyes. Refugee of Black July. Send savings home to the Tigers. The British East India Company had coolies in Ceylon growing opium for export to China. Re-balanced the trade defecit. A massive chef was leaking fat droplets of sweat onto the gas plate. Hungarian émigré. He adjusted his thinning pate. A long, wet moustache sliced the corners of his mouth. Hephaestus likewise wiped his face with a dirty apron. Unblemished hecatombs passed from his blade. He was surprised by the Argive ship. It caused him to pause in segmenting a flank of beef. Rip! He extracted the limp eye fillet. Gas jets gleamed. He sliced tendon from muscle. Béarnaise sauce bubbled in a pan. I not partaking thereof. Bitumen gravy. Hallem passed through the kitchen. Achaeans fleeing not scatheless give them all a dart. INSERT ALLEGORY. Elizabeth Archer followed Tom Hallem into the courtyard. Hessian sacks of rotting carrots and Brussel sprouts were slumped in a disused laundry. Hallem sat down on a canvas bag of used tablecloths. When they arrive at Eccles Street, Bloom has lost his key. He jumps over a dwarf fence bracing for the fall. He is five feet nine and eleven stone four moving at 32 feet per second. Elizabeth touched him – not directly – through a ceasefire of tangled hair. Bloom gains entry to the kitchen via the scullery. His greasy black-mop tick-tocked around her fingers. High flame burst from oil circulating in an iron pan. The cook lay down the fillet to sear. Tom faced concrete. Turn up a scorched face. Press my mouth against Chaim's soft flakes. He waited for Elizabeth to speak. Bloom removes his boots before padding upstairs to open the front door. Stephen watches a weak lamp increase in a semicircular fan. He has waited four minutes in total. This is the LAST TIME Elizabeth and Tom interact in the novel. Bloom appears hatless. She drew a milk crate to his hearth. Like Joyce, she wanted to explain the circumstances of their current predicament without sentiment. His strategy of deferral is to fill the narrative at Eccles Street with quotidian details like the purchase price of coal, chemical descriptions of heat and observations of clothes stiffening drily above. Like Stephen, Tom's ruminations were personal at times. Elizabeth and Bloom stuck to trade facts.

"I know you're disappointed. But I got the studio in Paris for you."

"It's second prize."

"You couldn't compete with Matt."

"We've both had solo shows. We've been in the same group exhibitions. We've won the same prizes."

"That was two years ago, Tom."

"I'm better than him," he mouthed through a strangled throat.

"Matt has developed rapidly in the last eighteen months. He's prolific. His family is well-connected. You just don't have the same clout."

Mulligan can cook. He can drive a car. His poems get published. He's studying medicine. He even saved a drowning man from surf. Dublin's life-water. Note Bloom's reflections on its power. Stephen is a dilettante in comparison. This was a clear retrospective self-evaluation by Joyce. He had not produced anything of genuine value as yet. Just a few slight lyrics, a paper for the Literary and Historical Society titled 'Drama and Life' and a rejected play titled *A Brilliant Career*. Also, some book reviews including his article on Ibsen's *When We Dead Awaken* for the *Fortnightly Review*, which bestowed on him some local fame, twelve guineas payment and a letter of appreciation from the author himself. He had also self-published an essay called "The Day of the Rabblement." He spent the proceeds of his writing on a trip to London with his father in May 1900. This indicates that Joyce still thought charitably of his father. In London, he met William Archer, translator of Ibsen, who bought him lunch at the Royal Services Club. He became a crucial early supporter and perceptive critic.

"You should have warned me this was coming, Elizabeth."

Yes. I could have done that, she thought. But I chose to say nothing. I let my need to strike back at you predominate. Why? You let me down, Tom. Your work has gone slack. Those Speed Paintings are an old art school theme from the late seventies. You've never ... evolved since then. That recent seascape which Fuller liked so much is just a fluke. I think we agreed to call it "Ithaca from Space." You have never been able to re-create its fast symmetry. By contrast, Matt Supplejack is stretching towards the finish post. He could become an artist with a global profile. He just needs the right wife. Be tactical but. Soothe Tom. Who knows what the future brings? Proust showed it is never wise to write off a young artist. See Bloch and Octave. A wash-out at golf. The Narrator says that Octave "could have easily been referring to his intellectual nullity." Later, he writes a series of famous works that astonish M. Even Athena herself made errors of judgement. Asclepius, Bellerophon and Paris to name but three. Absences of insight. Wrong turns taken. The Osmond Marriage. Bewitched by Madame Merlin's potions. Call it ingenuous. SEE HAMLET. Lear's abdication. INSERT MORE BAD DECISIONS. Note that *Ulysses* is a manual about avoiding some. Also, lucky breaks. Stephen loses contact with Mulligan during the day. Bloom rescues him. He doesn't get the Clap. Maggy can't pawn his books. Bloom has the good fortune to be seated with Martin Cunningham. He avoids Boylan. Also, Martha Clifford. He isn't caught masturbating in front of Gerty MacDowell. He helps a blind lad. He avoids the Lestrygonians and finds Davy Byrne's pub. Alec Bannon manages to avoid her father overhearing his gossip about Milly. Simon Dedalus eventually finds solace late in the day in front of a sympathetic audience. Bloom secures coffee and buns to sober up Stephen. He gets into his home without a key. Stephen goes home. He gets into bed safely. Molly decides to stay.

"Come back into the restaurant, darling."

Elizabeth Archer pulled at Tom Hallem. He rose.

ALL THE NEWS AS IT HAPPENS

NARRATOR: A gift of winds arrives (Aeolus = Southerly). Tom returns to the restaurant. Insert allusions to suitors. LINK TO HAMLET. Elizabeth = Gertrude in this scene. Hamlet's prevarication. Buckling to Harolde's will (AKA King Claudius). Bloom balances "Kill! Kill!" against "Yes" in this episode. Tom's struggle is not ethical. Odysseus is roughly dismissed by Aeolus when he returns to Lipara. He still interprets Elizabeth's support in noble terms. ANA ARRIVES. She observes Matt and Marion HACKETT in warm dialogue. Their bodies are close. Matt holds her gaze. Who knows what's happening under the checked tablecloth? He makes no show of guilt when Ana walks into the restaurant. INSERT DIALOGUE. ANA EXITS (distressed). INSERT ALTERNATIVE HEADLINE. ***WHAT DID SHE KNOW?* BY A. TROLLOPE.** Tom Hallem follows immediately. As a result, he is denied sustenance. Slut Harolde and Merlin confer ("You should cancel his stipend," said Merlin. "It's too late," replied Harolde. "We need to get him out of the way ... for Lizzie's sake," he concluded). Tom and Ana are blown into Darlinghurst like Throwaways ["Elijah is Coming"]. He represents fake Stephen. Also, there have been a sequence of false father figures in this chapter. Leon is the REAL BLOOM. Insert the following scene: Tom sees a light in Billy's apartment on the second floor of Royal Court (*R&J* parody). A shadow moves across elongated kitchen windows. He believes it is his brother. In fact, it is O poisoning cockroaches (insert allusion to F's voyeurism of Madame A). He rings the front door bell. There is no answer. A face appears at a filthy flyscreen. It is Stan the caretaker. He tells him to clear off (like Aeolus). Tom walks up Foley Lane behind the facades of busy Oxford Street. He looks left. He glimpses a shadowy figure entering the Astoria Hotel. He is not aware it is Leon Daniel (see page 51). He crosses Bourke Street towards Darlinghurst Courthouse. Link back to motion in GODOT (back/forward – outside – trapped – stasis). Suddenly, he has a negative epiphany. Tom Hallem realises he has NO HOME ("where can I go? Back to Mother?"). This instant has been termed a Prophany by Hagen von Eitzen. B. Clay Shannon suggests that, as epiphany "seems to refer to a good sound (epiphone)," therefore, "the opposite [would] be a bad sound." He proposes, "apiphany? Antipiphany? Malpiphany*?" as coinages (see english.stackexchange.com/questions/187658/what-is-the-opposite-of-an-epiphany). The use of internet links is like sampling.

(21) NOT LIKE LAERTES NOR HAMLET EITHER

Tom Hallem left the restaurant. A Ghost urged him on. Wither wilt thou lead me. A retinue of homeless people fuelled a bonfire in the back lane. The filings of a lounge chair burned frightfully; tarring its complicated wire skeleton. Dido gouged her guts as she entered the pyre. They asked Tom for alms. Odysseus tossed them some tarnished coppers as he spiralled down the deck. The crew mumbled grudgingly that he was hoarding all the tribute. They sucked on sucked-out bones. Gogo bit into a coin which was hard as raw pear. It bent quickly then cruel. He tossed it over his shoulder with disgust. Ana's figure receded down the bleak slope. Maw. Telepylos. Chased by Lestrygonians. She turned into Crown Street. Tom pursued her. Wind through the slope. Arch into a bend. Gather speed. A pack of giants rumbled behind him. Oafs throwing rocks. The horizon was black. All the ships in Sydney Harbour had been destroyed. Only Odysseus's own ship escaped the tempest. Bloom was hungry and depressed during this episode. Eating; digestion; excretion; disgusting habits; city as maw; Irish civilisation eating its own; Boylan as a cannibal – this is the list of alimentary themes in Lestrygonians. Also, adultery (copulation of two flies; music from Don Giovanni *inter alia*). Escape is the climactic motif.

(22) FX: STORM. ANIMALS. CREATION. A CRISP APPLE GETS BIT. EXPULSION. MUD.

POZZO: Thunder slogged that night. Rain streamed down my face like purified piss. God waded into the Garden and moulded us into one entity. We were named. I was now ADAM. A signified. Surrounded by a wall with no way in, no way out (not even Jesus yet) nothing but sheer barrier. No part of me was allowed to remain uncatalogued; undisclosed. My chest was ripped open in dreams. Link to Tom's heart procedures during the next decade. When I woke up next morning, Eve was slumbering against the slot where one of my ribs had nestled. Taboos were founded. Next thing you know, I was naked. It was 1986. We were ejected (relocated to MELB). Eden is a place to which we can never return (Sydney). We drove up and down Hoddle Street on scoring missions. Like the Hydra, I was not allowed to die. A sequence of operations culminated in a full transplant. Each time I was decapitated, two fresh heads sprang out of my bloody gush like birth. Cain then Abel then Ham and his descendants mustered and bred. I'm a Babel made up entirely of eyes and nouns. I don't know how to pledge obeisance. Or to whom. Insert allusion to Sadosanct (see Chapter 6). [PAUSE] I had no choice at all but to go on. On Pig! {HE WHIPS LUCKY AKA WILLY THE PIMP. EXEUNT}. "Molloy" ends with the narrator claiming that he was coerced into writing this report. He questions whether he enjoys more freedom in his current state than previous conditions. He registers ignorance as to the answer. His final statement is ominous, not one of hope: "I shall learn." He returns to narrative normalcy. He goes back inside the house and starts writing. It is a typical time for such an activity: midnight. Time's passage is registered by rain. Six words later, midnight has passed. The final sentence is, "It was not raining." At the end of *Malone Dies*, the narrator cites Lemuel, a substitute for Abraham, and a clear model for The Unbowelable in C6, by recourse to repetition, the thud of the same words, "with it," over and over again in ironic counterpoint to the absence of any act, normally this device would be used to emphasise the recurrent smashing of a weapon on a crumbling skull, before language collapses into repeat words like light, never, anything, and there before the last illiterate coinage, 'nore.' As we have already noted, *The Unnameable*, which closes *Trilogy*, stands as the ultimate rejoinder and successor to *Ulysses*. There is no need to restate the one hundred and one words of the last two sentences. Only that words must go on being said like Master Edmund proclaimed in C5, E2. The final act of what passes for the imagination is to visualise being placed at the threshold of 'my story'. The gate opens and the narrator must go out, moving through miscellaneous arenas to exit. 'Surprise' is expressed at this prospect but that is disingenuous. He knows only too well that it will be the same old (x2). The last sentence expresses ignorance, incredulity, inaudibility, compulsion to dromology, false protestations of incapacity then ultimate acquiescence to physical and by extension spiritual motion. Nothing has happened so there can't be an aftermath or denouement like when Shakespeare selects his new world order at the end of each tragedy.

"LORD, YOU SQUAT AND THE SKY YOUR CUNTLIPS BURY ME" – G.M. HOPKINS

Shanghai Dog was on his way back home with good intentions when he was diverted by a text message. This is consistent with both Homer and Joyce, although the *Odyssey* always transfers negative causation to Odysseus' crew. Stephen Dedalus could blame alcohol. There is no direct correlation between Ginger and any character in either of these classic works that bookend western scholarship. She is somewhat like Circe. Sometimes she reminds me of unlucky Andromache or disabused Clytemnestra. Even Dido or Briseis. There are gods in the Classics who perform this ritual. Disappointing the audience's vain hopes is a hackneyed device pretty much dominant in this genre. There was an element of damage in Ginger that recalled Calypso, Dido, Helen at Troy or even Emma Bovary. I don't think this type of female character really existed between the

Classical period and the twentieth century, except in romps like *Moll Flanders*. INSERT OTHER EXAMPLES FROM *THE CENSOR'S LIBRARY*. Woolf never got near one. Lawrence was too idealising. The Americans had a crack. Hemingway made it happen in *Fiesta*. H. Miller a bit also. But they were both more interested in writing about men. Fitzgerald specialised in this type of ribald patrician woman. He nailed the characterisation in TGG. Ginger was a foul-mouthed Black Country MILF always high on blow and bubbles. She is one of those inconsequential characters that enters and departs *Ulysses* quickly. Maybe to perform a small plot service for the author. Occasionally for specious reasons. Sometimes as part of a kind of Naturalist slideshow to demonstrate the random connections of life. In Proust, she would reappear hundreds of pages in the future with changes to her physiology and status imbued with temporal significance. Her Home Counties husband had relocated his heraldic accessories plant to Suzhou last year. He took the kids and put them in the Australian school. Cut off her credit cards. Tried to keep her out of the way with logistical barriers. This corresponds to what Elizabeth Archer did to Tom Hallem after the end of this text. There are echoes of Shanghai Dog's own circumstances also. She is a parable of what could have happened to O if she stayed in China. I was leaning on the main bar watching Judy. She went about her tasks methodically. Hemingway's works are filled with male characters in thrall to this type of dominatrix. The formula is: female maybe love (redux?) > male: all along > Her: I want to ruin you > Him: go right ahead > various computations > ambivalent close in physical proximity. Despite the clever word-play and references to Peel in the title, I instinctively interpret *Farewell to Arms* as another joke about emasculation. This seems reasonable given Hemingway's use of literal and figurative castration in *Fiesta*. Link to Bobby Horne stepping on a claymore in C3. In Shakespeare, Othello is the closest approximation to this type of broken-down infatuation (R&J is ALL MUTUAL ASSURANCE). Dickens had a crack at it in GE. Shanghai Dog couldn't get the taste of what Mary Evans calls Ju Di's 'gossamer web' out of his mouth. INSERT "Just Like Honey" starting on the sound system at Glamour Bar. The rays from his blue and her dark orbs met. There was the lightest change, the faintest tremor, on Shanghai Dog's cheek and top lip. Her face by contrast was Sphinx-like. She had never been one for external utterance, even in the throes of orgasm. She just gasped a few times and scratched his hair as his mouth serviced her. Flaubert provides a typically distorted lens for this kind of fixation in Sentimental Ed. Suddenly, Shredded Ginger lent into my face and grabbed my cheek with a big Birmingham mitt, breathing saccharine drops of Long Island Ice Tea.

SETTING A MAN STRAIGHT

SHREDDED GINGER

[*Pressing an index finger into his chest*] She doesn't want you anymore, Billy. Stop looking at her like that. Face it, you blew your load. You got to move on. Stick with your new Chinese doctor lady. At least she'll keep you in the manner accustomed. I only wish I had that option. But Chinese blokes have no panache. [*Leaning against his ear. Her teeth pinch his lobe gently*] Come here. Let's see if we can make her jealous. [*Shredded Ginger kisses Shanghai Dog on the mouth. It is warm and tart. She withdraws*] You're so ... sweet, Billy. I'd marry you if you weren't such a slut. [*Slumping against the bar suddenly*] I'll never let Paul keep the kids. I'll take them and go home to Britain. Move in with me mum. Get a job. I used to have a career before I came to China, you know.

SHANGHAI DOG

I know you did, Linda. I'm thinking of going back home myself.

SHREDDED GINGER

[*Laughing*] Good on you, son. Good on you. Go back to your fucking kids. Fix things up with your wife. She's a good egg. Help me up. I need to pee.

[*SD helps Shredded Ginger off a stool. She places a palm on his cheek. He pulls her into his arms so she remains upright. Judy passes them with a tray of cocktails*]

SHREDDED GINGER

Where's my bag?

SHANGHAI DOG

On the ground.

SHREDDED GINGER

[*He bears her weight as she tries to drop to the floor*] I want to get down in the muck.

SHANGHAI DOG

Don't do that, Linda.

(Shanghai Dog lifts Shredded Ginger. He holds her under his shoulder as they walk to the unisex cubicles. He pulls open a door and presses her inside. The door remains ajar. Staff pass. Billy's eyes adjust to darkness. Judy walks towards him empty-handed. He smiles insipidly and says HI. She ignores him. Shredded Ginger beckons.)

LANDFALLS

Hallem captured Ana by Taggarts Lane.

"What do you want," she asked.

"Slow down," he replied. "How was the band?"

"Where were you?"

"I never promised."

"I still thought you'd come."

"I had business."

"Just like Matt."

"I'm sorry. I fucked up. Come on. Let's go to Frenchs. I'll buy you a drink. Feedtime is playing."

"I'm too tired," said Ana.

"I can fix that," he replied tapping his coat pocket. Elizabeth's coke + Leer's smack. Soap and potatoes. Charms. Chaim. Chasm. Dentures. Adhesive. Ana's smile. Marooned upon.

"Say yes Ana."

"OK," she replied.

They walked towards Oxford Street.

"Matt was just playing the game back there."

"Sure. He was sucking up to that rich girl. He's always on the make."

"He just won a big prize. He's going to Paris."

"Fuck that. He's already full of himself. He'll be impossible now."

"At least you'll get a free trip to Europe."

"I won't go."

"Because of what happened back there?" he asked.

"No. I'm used to that. It's part of the scene. I've just had enough. I'll use it as an opportunity to leave him."

God got a chisel. Made Matt. A beautiful man. I chose him for that reason. Silk mane like a lap dog. Pale bronze by bronze. Lean and long. Big lungs. Always warm like fresh tea.

Tom was a boy by comparison. But now I could. Yes. I want to really. I must. Because he made me so angry when he didn't come. Got to lose weight like Molly. They looked across the road. RED signal. Wait.

FLASHBACKS

Ana Lafei stood outside the Sydney Musicians Club in a black cocktail dress. Black ringlets coiled at the edge of her heart-shaped face. Charred mascara marred her cheeks like the scribble on some Arnulf Rainer drawing. She made one last inspection of Chalmers Street looking north through a paperbark screen towards Central Station and went back inside the venue. The band started suddenly. Slag off this dirt that bore me, she heard the Singer croon into the microphone as she progressed down a sharply-lit corridor. The reviewer from *ON THE STREET* (Sydney's only free rock paper!) transcribed the lyrics into a small spiral notebook. Mountains of glory ... you are <u>DIRTY</u>, penned Scribbler (*his emphasis*). In writing about pop music, the rock journalist has a limited palette of options: (1) to describe the prevailing atmosphere, (2) register personal impact, (3) observe audience response, (4) place new work in the context of old work, (5) reference third-party songs as precedents, and/or (6) record the words of unreleased stuff. ADOPT THIS STYLE NOW. It's a job like what Gurnemanz told Parsifal at the grail-castle: "you see, my son, here space (sound) changes to time (copy)" (Wagner, *WWV111*, 1882). DOY-TEE trailed into hiatus as Ana pushed open the bone-coloured fire doors. The whole damp muck of today's gale got jammed down that shaft in this gravid moment like a blind fix of adrenaline. Thud. The bass player plucked a bottom E string once and let it resound. One tan cowboy boot was planted on a foldback. He threw back his head and gaped. A whale's maw. She entered. The hall was not full. He thrust his pelvis and raised the instrument's elongated neck. Achilles with Polyxena. Ana slipped in front of the last row of observers. He straightened and stared. Make a stroke with a bow. The stage lighting went red. His gaze engaged Ana, stripped of all artifice. She knew the Cohen cover. Four songs by BP. A clutch of new stuff. Last night, we witnessed a well-modulated set from a seasoned performer. "Now you want to see me dance / But I'm too fucked-up to dance for you," was his jibe to devoted fans at the start of the last song. Ana tried to pick out words. Scribbler took up his favoured position beside the mixer's desk. He commenced the set with "Wholesale Cigarettes" followed by a new song called "Hey Caesar." Scribbler held his notebook against the stifled light of the console and wrote: HE SAID, 'I WANT LOVE / SO I WILL GET OUT MY GUN.' He has left the edgy pop-punk of the early Eighties far behind (to this reviewer's great disappointment!).

His new band authentically recreates the Ubu-esque mayhem of the epic *Vault* EP of 1983. Use quote marks inconsistently. "Well I can twirl it in my mouth / Make my hands go clockwise," the Singer bawled. The crowd wobbled forwards. I can turn it in the sky / Shape the clouds to my design. Fishpump crashed to the floor as AMYL kicked-in. Hail Caesar! Ratatattat-ta-tat-tat, chattered Barry Adamson echoing Rowland Howard's classic guitar sound on "Fears of Gun." The Singer marked out his territory on stage, prowling left-right like some caged dingo before an enthusiastic yet somewhat disappointing audience. Link image to Odysseus. This brooding gig only occasionally rose to the confrontational mood on his last tour of Australia. A slim book was thrown onstage. He stooped to collect it. *Psalms and Scatology (Dirty Ditties)*, the title read. He placed it on an amplifier gently (note: metaphor for Telemachus). It was great to hear "The Hill" again for the first time since the legendary Governor's Pleasure show of 1980. He brought a derivative New Wave anthem right up-to-date for the mid-Eighties. Ten trees and a cow. Twenty years absent. How many chickens can we count? A tractor and a windmill up there. Big flies buzzing. Red wheelbarrow upon which so much depends. This song evokes the Gothic torpor and hate of Australian country towns. Next, the band lurched into a new offering. "I killed King Cockroach!" exclaimed the Singer. Cut off his head when he was down on his knees. Upsurging voice: You know, I killed him! AND HE WAS KING! I killed him I killed him I killed him I killed him. More links between murder and female debasement followed. Well you're living in a garbage heap / But you're sweet when I come and it's safe for you. This song gave Medon, Melbourne's latest wunderkind, the first chance to showcase his unique St Kilda-in-the-Delta sound for a Sydney audience. The bass undulated like a sea-sick boat. Behind the drums, multi-instrumentalist, Dave Paine, drove the melody with a typically inventive drum pattern. RAT DISSECTION COMMENCED. Mott clicked his shutter furiously from the dance floor. I got an infection, wrote Scribbler. Ana was distracted by Stinkbug. He was looking for Jackie. Lost my will, continued Singer. She pointed towards the band room door. A plain pine sheet. Guts of cardboard ribbons. A barrier in name only. Cheap brown plastic knob. "They opened me up [PAUSE] I'm raw and bleeding," he complained in mock-shock. This song contains clear parallels with the Biblical story of Isaac, deduced Scribbler. Ana observed new artwork on the back of his leather jacket. Lubricated Goat, it read. Capri comes from the Italian word, Capra, meaning goat. Yung mulebludd (see C4). Tom's cousin. They killed you-ooh-ooh-ooh-ooh-ooh-ooh, ended Singer. Spams tested the lock. It resisted. He was sealed in the hall like the other suitors. Link to Book XXII of the *Odyssey*. The Singer sped into the B-side of his latest single. CONNECT TO ANA. Baby's rushing to the place where her heart bore bubbles / And she's crawling to the place where her lover swore / There is true love in this world / But not for her / Here blood filled her eyes / And she bled tears of scarlet / Thin tears of scarlet (x3) / Down lilywhite cheeks. Morg(ue)ana picked at some dry eyeliner. Today in summary: early shift; collected Tom; tried to get him to score on my behalf; visited Matt (yuk); soundcheck; laksa; performance. Next: dinner in Darlinghurst. Mott emptied his Nikon F3, shoved the used cartridge into the side-pocket of his denim jacket, threaded a fresh 36-negative roll of Agfachrome onto the spool swiftly and shut the back of the camera. Link to Philoetius (arming his master's quiver). Odysseus made tall by Athena. V1: He wears the lizard frills. Tralalalala! Rachel going NING seven times (see C6). His voice rose to tuneless breaking-point. Clint Walker twirled a side-lever. He picked at dried batter from his day-job at Pancakes and whispered to Coupe, who grinned. His mouth presents a warm tone, thought Ana. BARON FUN ended. The band all lit cigarettes. Coupe collected a few lines in his head for a *Sun Herald* review that he could regurgitate as a puff-piece in *Dolly*. LINK TO LEER/TOM/FIX: "Then Odysseus took a handful of curls / And jerked back her soft white head / And he told his own son / To put an end to her life / So, Odysseus' boy took the carving knife / And he sliced it right across her clean wide neck / And blood gushed forth like brine off a deck." Scribbler skulled a Bourbon and Coke. The gig had gone almost one hour. He was bored. Ana shuffled between some men to get closer to the stage. This is the end, announced the Singer. A jerky lick followed. SOME VERSES. A BRIDGE: note hover/vultures/junkies *et al.* (see C6 + Appendix A). INSERT CHORUS. You ought to see me move / In my blue suede shoes. The Singer rushed the next phrase. Scribbler smiled knowingly. Hoping other people would notice. Repeat. It was Johnny Cash who told Carl Perkins to write that song. Airmen in Germany tagged their regulation boots thus. Girl treading on her boyfriend's toes at a barn dance. Don't step on my suedes, he spat. Perkins started with an A chord. Wrote it down on a brown paper sack. Couldn't spell SWADE but. You ought to see me move (x3). Pause. Repeat. SHORT SILENCE. For all time, he said quietly. END. The band left the stage. Applause surged and ebbed. Sporadic whoops. Ana scratched old track marks. The crowd hung-on. There was still some chance of an encore until the fluorescent lights were triggered by management. After a few minutes, the showman ambled back onstage. Cigarette and microphone shared his right hand. He sat at a small electric piano and started playing slow chords. Alone. Who'll build a box for Black Paul, he asked? The ballad of an unclaimed, unwanted corpse. The characters in this song grow increasingly frustrated as they are each forced by the narrator to explain why Paul's body has been rejected. Basically, he was a bad man they eventually confess. Link to Don Cane. "This new story-song ballad is one of his greatest works until the last verse, wrote Scribbler imbibing Milkmaid's lectures, when the victim himself adds a closing monologue that descends into bathos not worthy of this great artist. As Pope said, 'A needless Alexandrine ends the song, that, like a wounded snake, drags its slow length along.'" SHIFT FROM JOURNALESE TO PERSONAL SUBJECT MATTER. I opened our father's final will and testament. I had been nominated executor. There was no one else left, I guess. Richie got his savings. It was enough to buy a small house in Bulacan. He had already sold the big house to pay for his place at the hospice. I gave her the accommodation bond as well. He embraced the Lord at the end, she said, like Beckett's POZZO. I surveyed his room. The view of a car park was impeded by twisted aluminium bars. There were no ornaments on the mantelpiece. No pictures on the wall. He didn't horde souvenirs. He always ran. Destroying each trail as he left. I sat down on his bed with a picnic basket of pictures. Really just "BEFORE NOT AFTER" shots. My mother destroyed every picture of him when she married Bob. Penelope Hallem kept a single 4 x 3-inch print. I am holding it in my hands now. My father has been caught smiling, unaware of the camera. His broad skull is accentuated by a fresh crew cut. His lips are full of laughter. I turn it over to see if there is any inscription. On the back, it reads: "Donny, April 1962." I had already been conceived by this date. Tom was almost born. Our father was about to bail out of Sydney. His face registers no sign of torment. I place the print back in an unmarked envelope, separated from the rest of my keepsakes and, by proxy, my soul. It will soon get lost again amongst the dog-eared warranties, expired insurance policies and old tax returns that are piled at the bottom of my filing cabinet. It will disappear for years only to re-emerge at inconvenient moments like lost dignity. Suddenly, his face will sneer across the camera lens gaily. I never knew him careless like that. This misprision shocks me into re-examining our time together. It only takes this single image to reprise my loathing. And it only takes its withdrawal to put him away. I burned all Tom's rubbish in the fireplace one pent winter night as I sloshed my way through a bottle of Ouzo listening to old vinyl. Everything I could get my hands on expired that night. Next morning, I brushed the soot and unburnt flakes out of the grate, wrapt them in broadsheet newspaper and deposited the package in a council bin. "That's that," I thought to myself. Yes, it was a pyre but not in the way I anticipated. See Chapter One. Like Samson, its severance denudes me somewhat. Recently, I found a print of Francine and Tom smoking cigarettes in Schoeneberg. It was taken just before I came home to Australia. We all knew by then that Ana was gone. She was bound tightly like Thetis but not for the same purpose. Smack and coke work against each other like shape-shifting bonds. Flame, water, lioness, serpent. Futile death throes. Achilles was a rape-child. As a parent, I can empathise with her desire to chance any remedy. She burned off Achilles' mortality in the fireplace each night and anointed his charred, blistered corpse with <u>ambrosia</u> every dawn (comparisons above). Next, she tried dipping him in Styx. Ana was unfortunate with liquid like Elaine and Ophelia. Fill your pockets with sixteen stones and jump into the Ouse like Virginia Woolf. Joyce's wading girl in *Portrait*. Skirt hitched.

Making eye contact with Stephen. Just once was enough. Insert water and bird imagery. PROFANE (not holy) JOY. Dear Monseigneur, wrote SD, I can no longer become a seminarian due to a recent epiphany, signed Neophyte. A muse empowering Stephen to Art. Hard to work out if Joyce was being ironic. NotatthetimeIguess. In retrospect, he learned from PAYM. He cauterises all heroic symbols in *Ulysses*. Emulate.

A TECHNICAL CLASSIFICATION SYSTEM

The band withdraw from the banquet hall quickly. END. Four at the threshold against many warriors. Odysseus took centre stage. The first one to fall was Eurymachus then Amphinomus and Demoptolemus. Melanthius was left hanging in agony like a beast. Telemachus killed Euryades, Elatus and Peisander. He was wounded by Amphimedon on the wrist. His father hit Eurydamas. Telemachus took his revenge on Amphimedon. The cowherd and swineherd joined the fray. Odysseus gored Agelaus, son of Damastor, with his long spear. Telemachus stabbed Leocritus in the flank. He tumbled off stage. Leodes grovelled before King Odysseus for a few lines. He was dispatched with Agelaus' sword clean through the throat his head rolling in dust. Tmac got Leocritus. Only Phemius the lyrist and Medon the page were spared. Ana lifted a copy of the set-list gaffered to the central foldback. INSERT: Avalanche Swampland Pleasure Avalanche Saint Huck Mutiny in Heaven Wings off Flies Jennifer's Veil From Her to Eternity | | A Box for Black Paul. She shoved it in her pocket where it would stay until she lay dead in The Lake. REPLACE N. CAVE WITH SIMULATIONS: 8 SONGS + ENCORE = Wholesale Cigarettes (L. Cohen) Hail Caesar! The Hill I Killed King Cockroach Rat Dissection Baron Fun Odysseus Blue Suede Shoes | | In Black Box. Ana vaulted over Fishpump to exit. He was giggling. Marshall stack was playing some sluggish SWANS dirge. Fuck God / All men / And fuck you too, Gira lowed. I don't need you. And I'm not afraid of the sight of you down on your haunches. Looking uncomfortable. The form of this work comprises the following segments: Gods in Council = narrator's deliberations in C1 prior to commencement of plot (link to Proust). C2–9 = TELEMACHIAD. MELBOURNE CUP DAY 1984 (Tuesday, 6 November). This corresponds to episodes in which Stephen Dedalus appears in *Ulysses*. C10 = Homeric order reinstated post-*Ulysses*. This is a portal to *F(W)ake*. Chapter Ten is a theoretical judgment on Joyce becoming intellectually lost after 1922. It offers an alternative path for the Novel. C11 = ironic wish fulfilment. Aftermath of TMAC. Insert aids to reader comprehension as per the following table (against chronology). Inset Gantt Chart C5. Also, C5 E19 insert list of NSW Governors including period of service. Maps of S/U-Bahn systems. Train timetable, NSW Countrylink. Also, Cityrail services, Monday–Friday (C10). List Don Cane's record of service in Vietnam. Insert Character Sketch. DON CANE MUST BE LIKE ODYSSEUS – a true soldier with an unbelievable military career. Also, cunning (SEE BLACK OPS). IS DON TELLING THE TRUTH? He has done TOO MUCH for one man like some Classical warrior. NOTE: do not insert into main narrative (deflects from sons). AATTV. 1RAR. MACV. Vietnamisation. Bailed out in Seventy-Five via HK. SAS Regiment 2. TET68 (Saigon). PLEIKU: MIA. 1970 – last known information in Australian Army records. DANIEL BOONE SQUAD. Disruption of the HCM Trail in Cambodia. Spread Bitrex over Charlie's rice. Gag a maggot. Can't fly IN by helicopter but can be EXTRACTED. July 1969 – Operation Footboy. Psychops across the DMZ. Sacred Sword of the Patriots League. Le Loi, King Le Thai To. Magic sword taken by a turtle. Creation of Herb Weisshart (Deputy Head, MACV-SOG PSYOP). CIA ran the whole show in Laos. Armed Hmong tribesmen, headed by Vang Pao. INSERT INTO LIST OF FAKES/DECEPTIONS. LINK BACK TO ODYSSEUS ("that would have been his kind of stunt"). OP35 recon teams carried doctored AK-47 ammunition into Laos and Cambodia which they planted on dead NVA or scattered during contact (NVA always collected and re-used ammo). Specialists would disassemble AK-47 magazines, booby-trap them then reload the magazine so it was impossible to tell it had been tampered with. Bullets would explode on firing, killing or maiming the user. Or the AK47 would explode in their hands sending shrapnel everywhere. MACV regulation was broadcast over radio prohibiting use of enemy weapons.SOG planted a rumour that the Chinese were sending Hanoi sabotaged weapons. We fabricated a top-secret report and left it on a bar in Saigon where it was immediately stolen. INSERT INTO LIST OF FAKES/DECEPTIONS. LINK TO ODYSSEUS. Also, OP35 teams left booby-trapped radios and batteries on the HCM Trail. Also, offensive posters with small mines attached about the size of shoe polish can. When the NVA grunt ripped down the poster, it would explode and blow off his foot. Insert full list of catechisms used throughout the novel. Insert also list of newspaper headings, entire novel. Explain epigraphs: Tennyson introduces obsession with best friend's death; McComb refers to blurred lines between fiction, biography and autobiography; Lyotard provides theoretical justification; Velvets links to loss of ethics. Each epigraph is a link in a chain. Cut to sequence of French theoreticians, C6. *What comes after Modernist High Style (Joyce)?* Beckett, nouveau roman, Gysin/Burroughs, relative journalism, Wolfe, popular music, Dylan, oulipo, deconstruction, postmodernism, post-structuralism, post-colonialism, Chuck Palahniuk, internet drill-bits, slogans, band acronyms, rapping, hip hop, return to straightforward stories, technical fiction (link back to Epigraph 3).

DEMODOCUS' SONG

Tom Hallem stared at the sky over Darlinghurst. A jaundiced Bondi moon was rising fat and fast on top of Taylor Square. The snaking Maroo Track became the route for South Head Road. This is a metaphor for Darlinghurst's history. Insert key (i)tiems. Old Bodegas and grog shop licenses. Tilly Devine's thirty brothels. Saint Martin's Bar. Fishnet singlets. Men who called each other by actresses' names. Parsing. Ivy's Birdcage. Cap's drag show. International Vanities. First Mardi Gras 1978. The Filth confiscated the leading float and diverted the parade down a dead-end off Darlinghurst Road where they bashed the pooftas in front of the 4 SEASONS FOOD BAR. Red wall paint. Took the rest of them back to Forbes Street. You could hear them crying in the cells. This did the opposite of what was intended. It brought on Wran's decriminalisation law. Leon Daniel hailed a taxi at the top of Bourke Street. Stephen Joyce pulled to the kerb. Loop Gilligan's Island past the Wall down Victoria Street then home. Homosexual acts are now legal in the State of New South Wales since the passage of the *Crimes (Amendment) Act 1984*. Private Members Bill by the Honourable George Petersen. He was a Wollongong Red out of commandos in the AIF. Called out the fix on Ananda Marga. ASIO special. Lapel cameras. Seary gone undercover on Queen Street, Newtown. Gay nightclubs down nondescript lanes or underneath speakeasies. Exchange Hotel. FLO's Palace. Patches. Glass dance floor. Pandora's Pies. Hotnsticky. Ruskin Pater Wilde Joyce. Rap of Chuck D on PRIDE. History Lesson Part II. Chicago blues plodding out the arse end of Xintiandi. Brown Sugar nightclub. Kokoh Conley. Take My Breath Baby. Constricted wind pipe. Shanghai Dog leant into the cubicle. Ginger had dropped onto her knees to vomit. TOP GUN. Vulcan's trousers. Ana's eyes were drawn to the soft emulsion exposed by rolling storm clouds over Woolloomooloo Bay. They watched its final eclipse together (insert symbiosis) like spindly twigs (insert nature poem). Lightning crackled over the city then severed. Oxford Hotel purling towards midnight. News stand flogging fags and mags. Tomorrow's broadsheet. INSERT HEADLINE. A woman opens the gossip page. *Art goddess Elizabeth Archer played Santa to Sydney's culturascenti at the EAx Xmas show last night. Santa's little helpers included impresario Richard Merlin and AGNSW supremo Edward Slut-Harolde (Bottom Right). Visiting British art critic Peter Fuller opened the show with a poke in the eye for the local art scene. Sales were brisk with proceeds to the Fred Hollows Foundation.* Fishpump stood at a baine marie that blocked the entrance to the Tin Hong Chinese restaurant. A shop-girl ladled Mongolian Lamb onto a large bed of rice in a tin take-away bowl. The bright Laminex cubicles in King Burgers' were half-full of punks slaughtering greasy buns. Weasel Bob waited for

A BURGER WITH THE LOT. Crossing the summit of Palmer Street, Tom and Ana passed a row of dim shopfronts. Electrical Repairs. Spanish Delicatessen. Isenberg Tailors. A sign announcing Frenchs Tavern dropped out of the corrugated iron street awning. Hallem quickened his gait. Athena disguised as a serving girl was handing out condoms. She had a sandwich board chest-plate which said PREVENT AIDS. A security guard was barring gates of gold. The front doors were flanked by plaster dogs. Ana whispered. Mist production. They passed the gate unseen. A row of pear wine and pomegranate trees defined the bar. Band pictures lined the walls. Throw your arms around the legs of wise Arete. X. Solo shot of Steve Lucas. Mark from KELPIES. Me and Brian write the songs in our squat at fifty-one, Stanley Street. XL Capris. Nancy Serapax low behind drum kit. Kris Kross looking like Sid's ocker mate. Home is where the floor starts. He was a domesticated gentleman really. Polly from the Reels held a fruit bat under his soiled lab coat. Bob was bearing handfuls of wine glasses to the kitchen and returning with baskets of hot chips. GOOSE in chinless profile with Suzy and Philip Clifford. Glass tankards hanging off cup hooks above the bar. Tom and Ana went straight downstairs. A sign behind the stage said:

(28) "LIVE MUSIC EVERY NIGHT"

Hallem hid on a stool in unclassified space behind the sound desk. Hazel and the Nut were squatting on a padlocked bar bench. Stilettos dragged garter straps. Slices of thigh. Their faces flickered at bright fountains of light from the stage. Gold statues. Torches. Alcinous beckoned. A woman approached Tom sideways.

"Could you spare a cigarette," she asked holding up two fingers.

"Sorry, I don't smoke."

Her gaze dragged towards a patch of carpet swollen with beer. She scraped at a scrap of gaffer tape with sandals. Fine strawberry hair waved her face. She pivoted but stayed in close proximity to Hallem. An animation was being silently projected onto the tarred basement wall. Resonant of Leer's safe room. CRUST, the movie title said. CUT TO OPENING SHOT. A suburban kitchen like Campsie. Spotted cement bench. Standing on the sticky perforated base of a steel-framed chair screw-points tickling my foot soles almost painfully. My grandmother held an aluminium pot before my mouth. I grasped it to drink cool tap water. Cold metal clanked on my teeth. Purls dampened the front of my loose cotton singlet (see Elizabeth, C2). Frayed cotton selvedge. Naked beneath. Sleek circumcised cock tumbling from my guts like a single quote mark. INSERT SAMPLE: ' Joyce called them perverted commas. Wouldn't let them inside the gates of *Ulysses*. See Chapter One. Bruce Currie's terrace in the Darlinghurst squats. I have been sick in that basin, realised Tom (se C1). Dry mouth. Get a lap of holy water. See Chapter Three. INSERT CROSSCUTS. Push-stop bodies clink CUT Two figures seated across a Laminex table CUT chicken-coop wire L CUT stalks of straw extruding from his gunmetal chest-plate INSERT NOTE Lancelot = Chesty Bond's jawbone > bold bung Hamlet > prolepsis of Ana's Speedball > death of Ophelia > an outsourced method of death > ethically ambiguous > Shakespeare's tactic was never to make things clearCUT propeller-blades twirled rhythmically on the apex of Philippe's iron face-mask. INSERT reference to Evinrude outboard motor (see C7). His companion's eyes had been cut out of a gridiron skin J CUT a grumpy ant scours the scoured coastal cavity of a Choc Wheaten biscuit (link to racist nickname – C3) > Odysseus' cave above surf > enter Calypso. Still it's good tucker, the protagonist said. INSERT CREDITS. Story by John E. Hughes. Mixed by Barry Wolfson. Ana fuckt him to score, noted Tom Hallem. Music by Even Orchestra. Includes Polly Watkins. CROSSCUT. At that moment ... INSERT FX: gaunt knuckles rap twice on O's door.

"I've seen you before," she said. "What's your name?"

"Tom," he replied.

"I'm Frances."

"Do you like the bands?"

"Not really. I just come here to meet people."

"Who do you know?"

"Mainly people from Perth."

"Is that you're hometown?"

She nodded. Teiresias' prophecy. A people most prosperous. Lang Hancock's red dust under John Glenn's space. Most isolated city on earth. At the end, Odysseus had to sail there. Go to Thesprothia, commanded the Oracle. Don't not pass GO. Find a crowd who have never seen a river. There is no Liffey draining out of the Kippure headbog. Build a desal plant. Tap brine. Post-*Mnesterophonia* voyage. Diem was a suitor. Marcos also. Extract America's man in orbit. Four hundred kilometres upright. Gazing down from Olympus (see C1). Construct an astrolight off the Hills Hoist in the backyard at Applecross. Motes waving torches. Pine Gap. Smooth crust of apocalypse. Silent domes. Cyclops eyes. Hang onto a hung fleece grimly. Cold War vassal. Odysseus married Kallikein in one version of his tale post-Odyssey. Fought the Brygoi. Went back to Ithaca. Got himself slaughtered by Telegonus. I started out with the AATTV. Transferred to Phoenix. Spent some time with John Paul Vann. Australia always works well alongside a master. Crackt looking glass of servant. ANZACaliban. Vietnam was a sucker punch on the Yanks. Menzies laughed all the way to Konfrontasi.

"How long you been in Sydney?"

"Six months."

"What do you do here?"

"Not much. I studied film in Perth."

No lights now just seepage. SMACK OF JELLYFISH ended like an error. Jackie's bass staggered on alone for a few notes. Illegible vocal. Patrick kicked at a mike stand and stepped off the front of the stage. Francine wandered off to cadge a cigarette. Tom watched her cross the floor like Emmanuelle Riva walking away in HMA. Her body lapped against a black singlet and a burgundy skirt. (INSERT, Suddenly,) Ana returned to him.

"Got my fix?"

"Yep. But I got to make it up."

"On your way then," she instructed.

Tom Hallem baulked. Francine returned to the edge of the compound. Ana pressed his arm. Sirens. feedtime's pre-set mix began. Black snake crawling 'cross my bedroom floor blahblah. Criss-crossing Arete. A gamble. Nobody's fault but mine. Poseidon's produce. Suck seed. Wise to propitiate her. Athene instructs Odysseus to seek her protection. Bible in my arms. Tom and Ana stood in duet by proxy. Need someone on your bond. Unknown singer. Thought to be Blind Willie Johnson's wife. Wait at midnight when death comes. Black lake. Reflection of a still pool. "Wait right here," he said tapping his pocket. "I'll be back in a flash." Tom proceeded to the privy. A surprise gift (*xenia*). He had no experience mixing speedballs. Willy's skill. He was working blind. He had no laboratory training. But he had observed the process. Joyce scored poorly at Belvedere in science and mathematics. He tried to enrol in medicine in Paris. This is an ironic accompaniment to the empirical structure and terminology of Ithaca, although there was nothing heuristic about his method in *Ulysses*. INSRET NTOE EN EIRONYSTEIN. Scientists rejected the law of causality and theories of Aristotle, employing big fat time/space dysphemisms instead. Try to remember the formula. Six drops of essence of terror. Five drops of sinister sauce. Add MOLY. A black root. Blossom white as milk. Elizabeth's pelt. Chrysanthemum flower opening in a glass teapot in Suzhou on a sunny winter day. Frog dropped in steam. Hallem put a boot to the door. Enter. Dark graffiti. Muffled music. Pete Wells' slide. Babdoyfurlov. Ian Rilen leaning back. Stinkbug's smirk fragmented in a smashed basin mirror. Hallem slammed the world out. The bottom of a bass line shook the rusted ironworks. He dropped the plastic toilet seat with a thung. Flush. Liquid cemetery. Slip of shiny magazine paper. Dealer origami. Peel back. Clusters gathered along its spine. *TV Week* fragment. He collected a rust-etched blade. Quick cut. No time now for finesse. Roughness makes it work longer. Five-dollar straw. Gulp swallow snort taste gulp. He pressed his palm against the wall.

Wetwarm. He gazed. Syringe spray on tiles. A film of blood. Kurosawa's *Sanjuro*. The first example of slapstick splatter (see C6 – Tarantino *et al.*). Time to make Ana's fix. He took a deep breath. Draw back the bow. Cap on. Once it was secreted in his rags, he went back to the banquet hall. The door burst. Unsteady interior. Audio desk fluttering with blips. Francine sucking on a cadged cigarette leaning against the wall. She looked at Tom Hallem intently. He pressed the syringe into Ana's palm.

"Loaded," he declared. [**SIRENS**]

"I'm not ready yet. Let's go upstairs."

"I'm going to stay down here for a while," he said.

"Suit yourself," she said.

Ana left Tom but did not climb the stairs. She went to the shadows. Francine returned to his side immediately. Ana watched them through a curtain like Molly Bloom.

"You know my sister," said Francine. "She pointed you out at the show tonight."

"You were there?"

"Yes."

"I didn't see you."

"It was crowded."

"What's your sister's name?"

"Marion."

"So, you're <u>her</u> sister," he said.

"Yes," she replied. "I get it."

F# started. A few punters descended from the bar. Ric and Al robbed of eyes. Closing into sweat. Trance-like. During the feast at Alcinous' palace, Demodocus sings about the disagreement between Odysseus and <u>Achilles</u> at <u>Troy</u>. Ten dollars baby won't buy you a friend. Everyone enjoys his songs except Odysseus. He starts to squirm uncontrollably. In the *Iliad*, Agamemnon took Briseis off Achilles. I had a good woman now she's gone. As a result, Achilles decided to bail. Get a Pontiac. In Book 9, Agamemnon sent Odysseus to convince him to return to battle. He gave Odysseus a script full of bribes and threats. Some critics consider that Odysseus' failure to sway Achilles constitutes a blemish on his usual powers of persuasiveness. In fact, Odysseus chose to recite Agamemnon's words verbatim. He didn't try to embellish them. He knew the cause was futile. Odysseus weeps. Look after yourself cause there's nobody else in your world now, sang Ric. Later, Achilles says to Odysseus in Hades that he would rather be a poor man's slave than a dead hero. Only Alcinous noticed the hero's tears. Were they emblems of regret? Maybe. Odysseus always put his own survival first. He would not have survived the war if Achilles had withdrawn completely. Alcinous took the band outside. Dancers stuttered. INSERT CHESTING

CONTEST. A sporting tournament between bucks. Big Tex versus Toe Cutter for the prize. HAHA started. Demodocus' second song concerns the love of Ares and Aphrodite. Grief-stricken Hephaestus binds them in chains. When you wish upon a star, your dreams are still your dreams. Snare round the bed utter. OLYMPICS SHOCK! God of War defeated by Lame Blacksmith! He halted on the porch. Haha woman you make me laugh. Haha you make me cry. He called down Olympus. Adulterer's penalty. Aphrodite withdrew to Cyprus. Hephaestus was left all alone. You make me wonder why we said goodbye. Mother of Aeneas. In FASTBUCKS, Demodocus finally sang of the sacking of Troy. Again, Odysseus weeps uncontrollably. Get me on the first bus out of here. A short boat ride to Ithaca. Been a long time since I been going. Eighteen years toll. Tom Hallem twenty years dead. Gone away. Got to make a fast buck. Shanghai Dog hustling in China. Got a Pontiac. Gasoline. Marry GU. Repeat Line One. Grab the cash split the scene et cetera. In April 2013, the Central Bank of Ireland issued a silver €10 commemorative coin in honour of Joyce. It misquoted *Ulysses*. Music corroded Tom's ears. Leer applied a crowbar behind the padlock on the warehouse door. The hinge popped easily. Screws intact. He pressed. Alarms not loaded. He illuminated the maw with a torch beam. A large RED painting hung in the foyer. He took a yellow Stanley knife from his overalls. Tashtego worked a hole into the case with his spade. He cut inside the frame. The canvas flopped open on the floor like a heretic's tongue. He slid the blade along the lower lip. Linseed oil patches made his palms shine. He rolled the loose sheet into a long tube which he secured with a ribbon. Each time it came up full of spermaceti. He only wanted big stuff. Empty coins in a tub. Leer advanced fifty feet into the whale's head. He started to break down a large work made up of small canvas boards. As the rectangular pile on the floor increased in height and weight, he realised it was impractical for larceny. He left it partially destroyed like a torn jigsaw puzzle and went back to disembowelling canvases. Suddenly, a competing beam scattered light across the cavity. Leer withdrew to the vacant elevator. He slipped open the safety catch and dropped onto the base of the concrete compartment. Everything now hanging by a thread. Tashtego slid down the whale's case. Leer waited. Pressure of tight limbs. Footsteps closer. Walkie-talkie messages exchanged. The security guard called for reinforcements. He withdrew to the entrance of the gallery. Leer sat on dust and waste pondering his predicament. A hook gave way. Tashtego remains lodged in the whale's head at the end of the novel. It's basically a void, he says, once the sperm is extracted. Like man. Lester stirred at the bottom of the elevator shaft at BETA HOUSE.

"Let's go upstairs," said Tom.

They clomped up the worn wooden staircase of Frenchs. Cubicles jutted from the wall. Tom guided Francine to a single table in the window. Good view of Oxford Street.

He bought drinks. There wasn't a lot of time for analysis. She ran through the facts rapidly. (1) There was a mad boyfriend in Perth. (2) Also, an ex-boyfriend floating through Sydney. (3) She had made a bogus suicide bid. (4) Broken family. (5) Violent, rich father. A property developer like Faust in Pt. 2. Francine looked into her wine glass then whispered, "I'm bored." She looked Tom Hallem straight in the eye.

"Want to go back to my place?" she asked.

"Where do you live?"

"Down Crown Street."

"How far?"

"Past Cleveland Street."

It was a long walk. Maybe 20 minutes. He felt the weight of past and present. Ana was nowhere to be found. Francine offered sanctuary like Calypso. Nobody could find him all the way down there in Redfern.

"Sure. Let's go," he said.

"What about your girlfriend?"

"Don't worry about her. She's not my girlfriend. We're just mates."

Francine skulled her drink and stood. They passed out of Frenchs. Wither wilt thou lead me. Tom ducked in case Ana entered. Francine was freed by the street. Southerly gusts forced them sideways as they left the shelter of some shop awnings. If you're meant to be together, you'll find a way, O said. The young couple touched like a ferry docking at a pier. Lakes resting on adjacencies. Set up a glass. Elizabeth left the restaurant and turned directly into the storm, pulling a charcoal hood over her unkempt mane. The sliding, wet pavement forced her to track downhill deftly. She stopped at a telephone booth on the corner. Call home. No answer. Ring tone split to flatline. Repeat. Tom Hallem passed Elizabeth with Marion's sister. Dead beep. She watched their backs proceed along Crown Street tacking south. A taxi passed. Elizabeth waved frantically. Car cabin warmth. Hold of a ship. She stole a glance in the rear-vision mirror. They dwindled to obscurity. Gone. The driver accelerated to beat the lights. Cars glided over the Oxford Street ridge line on free-fall down Crown Street. Rush of headlights. Uneasy pall. Amber grid of Boulevarde Hotel balconies pissing thick orange light over Woolloomooloo. The saloon bar of the Strand Hotel disgorged a group of transvestites. One thrust out her tongue at Elizabeth. Who smiled back warmly. They both laughed. Tight arses swung tight mini-skirts in the humid breeze. A junky leant into the dirty window of a hire car office. The taxi entered the William Street Underpass. Dry fluorescent brilliance. Fuxing Tunnel. Steep descent to Rushcutters Bay.

"You'll hear people say all kinds of things about me," said Francine as they crossed Albion Street. "Block your ears. Don't listen to them."

She kissed Tom Hallem suddenly. Leopold Bloom recalls past tristes as he crosses Dublin. Odysseus had extensive romantic adventures. Classical authors counted amongst his paramours and offspring: Telemachus with Penelope; Telegonus, Ardeas and Latinus with Circe; Nausithous and Nausinous with Calypso; Polypoetes with Callidice; Euryalus with Euippe; and Leontophonus with the daughter of Thoas of Aetolia. Ovid characterised him as Greek mythology's greatest lover. He combined the most seductive aptitudes for women: great story-telling talent, a sense of humour, persuasiveness and will. Homer represents Laertes, Odysseus and Telemachus as belonging to a single male line. For Western Greeks, this restricted heredity legitimised what was otherwise an illegitimate dynasty. A seamless transfer of authority through each generation removes the risk of succession squabbles (see *Lear*, *Hamlet* et cetera). This enabled Homer to concentrate one hundred percent on the revenge trope against the suitors. Francine hung off Tom's neck like a soggy blanket. A stone jewel thumped against Elizabeth's chest in proximity to her heart. She passed the Travelodge. Tenpin alley gave way to sunken, sable parkland. Elizabeth could just make out static poles at the Cruising Yacht Club topped with markers. Stan's triple master stood erect. INSERT ON BRITISH MARITIME POWER. Take a trip out Sydney Heads with Roger. They never found Brian Alexander. His shark-stripped skeleton is still chained to an old Kooka stove on the bed of the harbour mouth. Not sloppy like Nugan's murder. INSERT ON GIBRALTAR. The taxi alone made bright the bones of a ridge of heavy fig trees. The rain had passed leaving every object shiny. She asked the taxi to stop outside the clubhouse. Stiff diesel brine dozing. Close as Odysseus to home. A quiet alcove. Call home again. Beware traps. She wouldn't go INSIDE if Leon was absent. Finally, her husband answered.

"Where have you been?" she asked. "I called half a dozen times."

"I was fitting Uncle Nick's dentures."

"Well, we missed you at dinner."

"Sorry."

"It doesn't matter. Anyway, I'm on my way home. I'm only 2 minutes away. How are you feeling?"

"Buggered."

"You should go to bed."

"Not until you're home."

Leon replaced the receiver. He went to the balcony to examine Cadigal's re-cased mural. South and northside torch-flecks spanned black geometry. Interlocking planets. Skyscrapers stretch all the way from Town Hall to Circular Quay these days. Vales and peaks distorted its vault. Tommy Townsend re-spelled Sidney when he took his family title. Sydney comes from two Old English elements, *sid*, meaning extensive, and *ieg*, a riverside meadow. It literally means people who dwell in an extensive domain beside water. Sydney, thus, is incidentally named accurately in English. The owners called it Eora, which means HERE. Or FROM THIS PLACE. A clear statement of possession. A charcoal spine lifted smoothly off the long bare slab of Bradfield Highway. Opera House sails covering its undercarriage. Chaim dead on a marble deck. I lifted the gown from his tortured body. Poor Rudy. Unlucky Hamnet. Astyanax murdered in front of Priam. My child with Richie. Elizabeth left the taxi. Don Cane entered the hire car. It was time for the last leg of his trip home. Elizabeth negotiated the garden paving stones to her threshold. NOTE PENELOPE ENTERING HER ROOM IN OBEDIENCE TO ODYSSEUS' DIRECTIVE. Sudden sensor lamp. Leon Daniel stood at the top step. Elizabeth stopped on a low step. They held each other toughly. She rested her cheek against his chest and listened to his heartbeat.

"What's wrong," he asked.

"Nothing. It's just been a long day. And Tom's pissed off with me."

"You've helped him as much as you could."

"Only because we want to get him out of the way."

"He doesn't know that. It's still technically ... 'assistance,'" said Leon chuckling. "He should be more grateful."

"I still feel like a monster."

"Let's get you inside," he said. They entered their home. He closed the door for the last time in this work. There was no need for a coda. Their future has been sign-posted throughout this work. **[HEADING 30 – SCYLLA & CHARYBDIS]** Youths were massing outside Frenchs Tavern. Some decided to climb the Bridge (SCYLLA). Others to go down the Saint James rail tunnels (CHARYBDIS). Prometheus versus Dante then. DEATH OF ANA FORTHCOMING. Tom/Francine go to her room, each trying to thread a needle. Porphyry describes the place where the Phæacians leave Odysseus as marked by two gates. One is set North to gain breeze for human comfort. The southern portal is for the Gods. This is the way of Immortals. Binary positions. Don starts the car. Fallen Byron stirs (ELPENOR). Elizabeth and Leon negotiate life and death (pregnancy/AIDS). Link back to C4. A monochrome television mounted above the bar replayed primetime American news feeds. Ana climbed the staircase. She sat at a pew and looked towards the screen blandly. "In recent years there have been charges that the CIA has been involved in illegal activities," said the anchor. "Some of the most bizarre to date involve a group in Australia known as the WELLES BANK." Profile shot from some Hogarth print. Elizabeth's mentor. Pale nimbus. "Tonight, Gary Shepard reports." Ana sipped at warm flat cider. "When the Welles Bank collapsed in 1982, it appeared to be just another bank failure," he commenced. Bad rash of losses. Looming fall of Marcos. A dying man. No strength to fight. Priam's execution is left to Virgil. The son of Achilles, Neoptolemus, kills his son, Polites, then drags the old man onto Zeus' altar. Priam's last words lodge a complaint about lack of due process. Marcos inherited a robust economy sponsored by US bases; a kind of 1950s version of Taiwan. State-run monopolies, mismanaged exchange rates, impudent monetary policy, rampant corruption and cronyism were the causes of the Philippines decline. A harmless spear bounced off Neoptolemus' shield. J'aime Sin. CASH OUT. Take all the booty to Taipei. Build Aladdin's cave. Bob smashed a net full of chips against the side of a deep fryer in the kitchen. Tom asked Subway for a coin and rang Bob Hensley. Message on an answering machine. "I'm just ringing to tell you my father is back," he said. "I don't know where he is. But he's back." Poseidon loved his deformed child. Homer's characterisation of Polyphemus is narrowed to its basest form. But when they investigated, Australian authorities discovered a tangled web of intrigue with all the elements of a best-selling spy novel. I have no interest in manufacturing suspense. Just get the facts into play in whatever passes for organic order. Give the reader some credit for piecing together the script and its timeline. A mysterious death on a lonely stretch of road ... a body dug from its grave ... illegal currency transactions ... big-time drug operations ... and [he paused for effect] the CIA. Spy novels gained popularity over the course of the twentieth century. Mystery bags, they called them. Cold War specialty. Genre originally nurtured by Conrad. He saw third columnists as a threat to the British Empire. Later writers turned this entire notion on its head. Even Sherlock Holmes became a part-time spy. Ex-spies write the best espionage stories: Dahl, Greene, Le Carre. These men are writing about their ideal selves. Rise of James Bond. They all created antinomian characters who embodied heroic traits. Odysseus was also a spy. There are no spies per se in *Ulysses*. Bloom is always observing people but to no political end. There is always the context of Irish insurgency. THE FIGURE asks Bloom for a password during his paranoid visions in Circe. He misinterprets Gaelic as a secret tongue. Don Cane turned the radio dial until he found the Vietnamese news. Bloom brands him a "Gaelic league spy" sent by THE CITIZEN. This completely misunderstands the function of this nationalist group. The Welles Bank had its genesis in the Vietnam War. Hanh and her husband, Tham, listened to the 2EA news in the bare kitchen at the back of their shop. Troops had attacked a Thai Border Patrol in Surin province. Two soldiers were killed fighting for control of Hill 424. About 100 men from the 73rd Regiment had pushed one mile into Thai territory. A military source in Hanoi said the Vietnamese crossed the border in pursuit of red guerrillas. Khmer Rouge operatives had been secreted inside refugee camps. Hanh stood and told her husband she was going upstairs to bed. America is going to the polls later today. She checked on her babies. Tom had slipped away again, thought Ana. It was like some never-to-be English romance. A staple of the writing of poor cultures. Joyce's had an obsession with unrequited love in *Dubliners*. Mark of his underdeveloped stage in life. See Mr. Duffy in "A Painful Case."

Also, Maria in "Clay." ARABY. Fruitless, petty quests. Eveline cannot save herself from poverty and abuse. She is trapped like Virgilia or one of Pater's other cement heroines. A life of sacrifices closes in madness. Sometimes Tom felt it. Sometimes she. Batteries jammed head-to-toe in a rigid compartment. Mog Edwards and Myfanwy Price. Dreams are also liars. Gates of ivory. Tereza and Tomas in *ULoB* update Molly and Bloom. Kundera shows the messiness of real relationships. Gates of horn. Never clean. See also Guinevere's fate. East Egg. Lady Brett. Jake no longer east nor west eggs had. Four of the original stockholders in Welles Group were Americans. They listed their addresses as: Air America, Army Post Office, San Francisco and the USA. Post a letter to Martha. Don't tell her where I am. Helen, I loved. Penelope kind of. Young Joyce and his cousin. Like Updike's J&P. Stevens the butler came to Anne's table to clear out the waste. Marry a doctor or a dentist. Settle down. Life isn't about grandeur. Only in poems can ardour be fixed and therefore sustained. There are plenty of diversions in life. Plenty of time for comebacks. See footnote on Johnny Cash biopic (C6). Adultery is a staple of South American fiction. Count 622 affairs over 50 years then seek Fermina's hand in marriage. Magic Realism panders to Latin stereotypes. Latinos are 'kooky' like that. It's like all colonial prejudice. Voodoo dolls and hot coal dancers. Carnival corpses. Gleaming black temptresses riddled with VD. It was over twenty years since Tom Hallem died like Arthur Hallam when "In Memoriam" came out. Tennyson could never expunge his soft rage, but it came with no guilt. I am not so lucky. I replay a small catalogue of gestures. Tom's arm around my shoulders. My head against his chest. Slapping his knee when he laughed. I never had that kind of sensation with my own father. He used and discarded people all his life until there were no props left. Stick him in a grave. Try to forget he still exists. I wrote a whole lot of rubbish in Chapter One about good deeds keeping a man alive in our memories long after he's dead. The same applies to badness. My father was a bad man. Ana fondled her fix. Tom's jewel. Sentimental trinkets. Elizabeth held up the heavy brooch around her neck. It glowed through accumulated harbour needles. A cumbersome lump of jewellery stooped Doctor Gu. Shanghai Dog twirled his wedding band around his finger. The two grooved rails on its surface appeared to turn counter-centric. Its creator knew something of marriage. Magic rings, they called them. Fine skills of Birmingham craftsmen in the nineteenth century. Seeing it fills me with foreboding. MORE INSERTS ON GIFTS. Air America was the CIA's private airline in Indo-China, hauling men and supplies on clandestine missions ... even flying drugs out of the so-called Golden Triangle. Aquino got popped on the tarmac at MIA. Body face down spreading blood. He travelled on a Malay passport with the pseudonym Marcial Bonifacio. Comic alias. Marcial means martial law in Spanish while Bonifacio stands for Fort Bonifacio, national HQ of the Philippines Army. Aquino kept one eye firmly planted on the people. Joe Cahill died in the same house in Tempe in which he was born. Odysseus never really made it back to his own bed in Ithaca not really. Slope checked the wedge in his jeans. Stan Welles went through the butts in his cheque book methodically. Non kept look-out. Young Barry had not yet regained consciousness. They filled the station wagon. This latest loan to Elizabeth had come with no collateral, thought Stan Welles. The CIA made millions from drugs to finance secret missions. PLA harvesting Yunnan poppies. Swap drugs for heavy currency for weapons. It gave him leverage over Elizabeth. But to what end? The rise of external debt in the Philippines took place in a relatively short period of time. Frank Nugan got greedy. We are all mi she le, Judy said. China is a harmonious society. Philippine banks were dissolved in the 1980s, reducing average people to poverty. The best part of the deal is we've got The Hippies financing our jobs, chuckled Tom Cornwall. Fighting communism in Nicaragua. Libyan arms shipments. Timor insurgents. Sangley Point. Contras. "Elizabeth told us why you left," said Merlin to Tom Hallem when he got back to the table. "You really are an ungrateful little shit." Where is Leon, asked Tom in reply. Is Elijah still coming? "He's probably gone straight home," said Slut Harolde. "I presume you know he's extremely ill." Leave Tom alone, interjected Matt Supplejack. Ana observed the set blankly. Stan Welles sent Jerry Prokosch to Chang Mai, the commercial centre of the Asian drug trade. Painting is just another commodity. Impressionists put art in middle class lounge rooms. Fill in an online form for the chance to star in my latest installation. Shanghai Dog held Linda upright. A painting is the ultimate momentary device. He led her towards the elevator. Speaking under immunity from prosecution, Mister Prokosch told CBS, "we became the paymasters for the CIA globally." He passed one hundred kuai to the doorman to hail a taxi. The money was deposited in Hong Kong. Floating the dollar took guts. Awe owl tread jurors been fuckurnitwits sink Chiff, says Ocker. Peacock is winning the election campaign by default. Member for Promise-whatever-the-fuck. Welles Bank was no ordinary bank. Tories like gods-in-exile. Hardly any of its top people were bankers. Now ear cum thebe luddy Winsores, says Ock, pooncing across to Sydney in their bluddy great barge. Stuff it down Circelerkey. There were secretly numbered accounts. Hole retinue orb ludgers, I says ... Her Oil I-ness, Fill Me Geek, Chinstrap, Lady Horsehead, His Royal Anus RN Showpony and that Little Lord Last Gasp. Mayhem pave air owen weigh, I says. Many were former high-ranking military officers with ties to US Intelligence including a top-secret naval group codenamed Task Force 57. Don Cane left the car park. Among its top agents was a man now under indictment for selling arms to Philippines President, Ferdinand Marcos. Neddy fell drunk out of the Iron Duke at closing time. Non turned the ignition of his Ford ute. Analyse the use of motor vehicles in this work. When they found the body of the Australian Chairman shot dead in the front seat of his rental car a few months before the bank went down, they discovered the business card of this man in his coat pocket. Cut to grainy picture. "Robert COE – a former Director of the CIA." The Crest Hotel is also known as Roley's pub. "It was

BOB COE what put Kerr on payroll, says Ocker pointing at the screen. "That happened right after Murphy dogged us with the ASIO raid," added Tom Cornwall from his lounge room in Neutral Bay. "Bowen was a decent enough bloke," says Ock shaking his skull. "It was the Left what rolled him." Cornwall nodded agreement. "Cairns was totally useless once he got stuck up Morosi's box." The CIA nominated art to play a leading role in the culture wars. Note MOMA nexus. Put Pollock on the payroll. See FULLER. D-Day, 1949. Four-page spread in *Life*. It was codenamed "AE" by the White House. See photograph of Eisenhower admiring Kline's "Painting Number 2" in the Oval Office (Appendix S-4). Eisenhower met with aliens for the first time in 1953. They established the Trilateral Commission. Rockefeller was appointed Head of MJ-12. MOMA became his private institution. Greenberg and Barr wrote the AE manifestos. MJ-12 used AE sales to raise funds. Make a patriotic investment in Pollock, de Kooning or Rothko. AE grew off the corpse of European Modernism like a maggot. Its capital was used to build Area 51. Propaganda tours crushed local output in France, Germany and the Low Countries. Both sides built walls. Two-way mirrors in a bathroom. Advertising in the West produced the same obedience to the State as Socialist Realism. Pantone 15-0343. My installation will take place in a trunk. Silian Rail. What's that, a gram? Trumped. Van Patten's eggshell with Romalian. And what about the principals? Raymond John Candy was the financial mastermind and go-between. He remains active in the investment industry in Australia under the alias Stanley Welles, although his financial services license was revoked as a result of bankruptcy. His partner – a retired Australian officer – served in Vietnam with American Pacification Teams. It was Brigadier Thomas Cornwall who recruited an ill-fated team of mercenaries to train in counter-revolutionary tactics on the remote Philippine island of Mangenguey. Jerry Prokosch disappeared after the bank collapsed and was presumed dead until CBS located him in a secret location in the Geek Islands. Investigators are now attempting to trace $50 million from client accounts. We wash the fees through third-party accounts. Usually HK. Get fake warranties. Hire some local state engineering firm to sign-off on structural integrity. Pump up the traffic forecasts. Build a financial model. Get upstream legal structuring for a GP/LP structure in the Caymans. Marcos skimmed $30 billion from the State. Millions were discovered in real estate in the US. There was $450 million stashed in a Swiss bank. Australian authorities are also trying to find out what involvement Welles Bank had in the 1975 downfall of the socialist government. Matt Supplejack escorted MARION HACKETT to her car down Denham Street. They reached a dead-end. LINK TO CAR IN C2. The CIA denies all involvement in these activities. "Gary Shephard, CBS News, Los Angeles." Marion pressed him against a door panel. Figurative art is amoral. Petty surfaces. He went unsteadily on his knees. Ophelia was Hamlet's fucktoy. Mystic emblems. Cucchi's Birdmen. Kiefer's halls. Mimmo Paladino's ghosts. Whirlpool faces of Dale Frank. Lancelot standing on a bridge. Elaine's barge slid beneath. Holly approached Ana at a pew. Matt entered the passenger's seat. Fishpump bobbed behind her.

"Want to come down the tunnels?"

"I was going to climb the bridge," replied Ana.

"Come with us. They're filming down The Lake."

"It's for *Gag's* new clip," added Fishpump encouragingly.

"We even got flares," Puker added. Stalks were poking out of his pockets. Holly exited French's. Marion's car left its slot. A ravine of Icy Rocks in the Caucasus. Xi Ni Da Qian. Prometheus on a stick. Link PBS, *PU* to Aeschylus. A gadfly chased Francine to Sydney. What next? She will follow Tom to Europe > gain weight from drinking > go to Berlin > Fuck Billy > get pregnant > have an abortion > follow Tom Hallem to Sydney > escape > never re-enter our narrative. Ana stretched her chest. Look up. Cistern closing above. Standing in the past.

"When are you leaving?" asked Ana.

"Now," replied Fishpump. "The band is down there already."

(31) DEATH OF THE AUTHOR

Ana Lafei rose from the bench and left Frenchs. Two groups had assembled on the street. One coordinated by Toe Cutter included Kathy Mel Steve Couri Weasel Bob Petra Justin Dougie the Animal with various tower maidens in attendance (Danae, Saint Barbara, Rabuda, Rapunzel). They represent a cornerstone trope of quest romances (see Aarne-Thompson, 310). High up in space they would rise like Major Tom. Prometheus re-bound. Hairdrops. Symbol of a sun deity. Always blonde. The Lake = CHARYBDIS = DEEP DOWN. The other group was centred around Novalis. *Incidit in scyllam cupiens vitare charybdim*. "Look my lord. It comes!" Fishpump joined Holly and The Nut Starpunk/Stinkbug Toe Cutter Big Tex Badb Puker and Kristina to walk 500m to the station entrance. Slope & NON turned slowly west onto Parramatta Road. Goup/Godown? Toclimborcrawl? Ana felt the dart in her pocket. Safearth. A clay bag. Snug. Insert literary references. Happy Gloom! Dark Paradise! Polyphemus' trap. Spenser's Mammon. Aladdin. Cave paintings of Wandjina. Giro Giro. Cloud and rain spirits. Bulbeyed. Mouthless.

"The wind sits in the shoulder of your sail," said Badb. Bloomsday was almost done. I checked my wristwatch. Circe ended at midnight. Ithaca is set from 1–2 am. Penelope is kind of timeless. It could have taken place in a few moments of dreaming. Equally, it could have been the product of prolonged insomnia. Gibraltar progresses methodically towards dawn.

"All this prevarication," groaned Holly. "It's like a medieval round. I mean, are we going ... or not? It's not some rhetorical device. What happened to your other shoe?"

"I lost it," replied Fishpump glumly.

NARRATOR B: They bled down Oxford Street crossing Crown Street above Royal Court making a chart like some Escher print. Flushing carstream (see C2). A taxi assumed free-flight as it smashed the sudden decline towards William Street. O sat on the edge of her bed looking out the tall windows at the dark mass of Hyde Park under city night trinkets. Her kitchen light cast a weak glow. A sharply calibrated rap came twice. She proceeded to the door. Heads wavered behind frosted leadlight. She turned the lock and a loose brass handle simultaneously. A screw-head protruding from the spindle scratched her finger. Something to get used to. She exposed the jaundiced hallway / the nailed carpet / the dark bare boards. Two women were standing before her threshold. We heard you bustling about, said Polly. A flourish all smile all lipstick + cat eye spectacles that shone. Sharp and bright mouth like Man Ray's "Observatory Time." Thought we'd just drop by and welcome you, Lucy said brandishing a bottle of Cordon Negro. O beckoned them inna. Lucy passed like some INSERT ANALOGUES [e.g. Waterhouse pond sprite]. How to write of women without false imagism, I pondered. Delete all references to Western art. How did classical sculptors depict goddesses like Juno and Athene? Still neurotic about face. See the calculation of Paris. He had no choice but to choose one. Otherwise, he would have been fired on the spot. Instigate a delay then. If it was men entering O's apartment, we might write about their height. Maybe their smell. A musky odour that doesn't repel. You could still taste him on your forearm long after sex. Tang of cum like BBQ crisps + ammonia. They progressed past PETE'S BEAT. Doorway upstairs to THE OX. G.A. ZINK & SONS, master tailors. An art deco silver-on-sable plate. 56. Lucy offered *Xenia*. O gathered tea-cups. The three women sat on her bed and watched Darlinghurst. Link to Classical referents. Ana gazed at The Tool Shed doorway. A man emerged fussing over his shirt. Big Tex Tunks collected a throwaway off the pavement. HARD COCKS, it read. He recited the next line. BONA CONSTRICTOR. Easy to apply behind the scrotum. SIGNALS leather bar. Go up a creaky old lift. Amyl-tent in the back room. Deluxe Erection Maker. A motorbike was bolted to the concrete dancefloor for swingers. Creature Cocoa in crotchless leathers stretched the BDSM rack in the main bar. A fitting to attach a leash. "No white pants, no girlie attitude, no handbags, no fairies and especially NO drag queens," stated the rule board. PATCHS Old 33 Club Saffron Four Gates of Hell. Theresa Green, Sydney's Drag Queen of Punk, performing with Cindy Pastel and Simon Reptile. The strip still seemed in its heyday but already disclosed signs of decline. Visitation had peaked at the cruise lounges in 1983. Financial performance was DOWN. Action inside the bathroom cubicles at Patchs had been lacklustre in recent months, despite the onset of spring. Edmund Hamley loitered there with a vial of AMYL in his mitt while music pumped dully through thick fire doors. An example of The Cradle sat unexposed. Insert scene at unisex cubicles in Glamour Bar with Shredded Ginger and Shanghai Dog. The Bobby Goldsmith Foundation had just been founded, raising awareness of the risks of HIV. The original hoteliers had started migrating to Inner West pubs like the Newtown Hotel and Imperial Hotel, Erskineville in response to demands for protection money from gangsters like Abe Saffron. Fast forward to today and any visitor with knowledge of local history would be shocked to see that Oxford Street has now been reduced to a row of grubby franchise outlets and knock-off shops. Marcel Proust is an expert in articulating such shifts in the prestige of place over time. The rise of Montmartre, for instance. The decline of the Faubourg Saint-Germain. Joyce forfeits this tactic by focusing on a single day. Don Cane has already demonstrated this tenet in Chapter Three by his reaction to Kings Cross, which had lost the bohemian charm which he recalled from the early 1960s and become a lame drag of intermittent strip joints, street walkers, minor drug dealers, vagrants and crime. There was nothing to match the scenes at the Olympia Music Hall on Boulevard Capucines (contrast as parody with Exchange Hotel). The Collector mocks Tom Hallem when he confronts him near the toilet in the backyard of the restaurant. “I saw you at Patches last week dancing with some breeders.” He felt at Tom’s crotch angrily. “Sick of steak?” he asked. Tom involuntarily noted the image of Elizabeth and Marion withdrawing together at the opening. He examined their body language with a painter’s eye. They will desecrate Leon’s memory in death just like Vinteuil’s daughter and her lover, he thought. Later, we find quite the opposite tendency. The lover transcribed his music assiduously so that it could be interpreted by an untrained audience. “Prefer raw oysters, these days?” his patron concluded tartly. In Chapter Four, Tom shows tenderness to his cousin like St Loup towards the Protagonist at Balbec. This creates a stronger contrast with his subsequent, sudden shift to go with the Pimp. Tom should also draw heightened affection from Bob Hensley and his wife in C3 (Nuncle Richie, Laertes, Philemon + Baucis inter alia). It doesn’t matter what I miss in TMAC. Just add it to VAULT. We are starting to see a shift in the focus of TECHNICAL FICTION from Joyce to Proust. Just create a contrivance to allow the insertion of fully completed sections of fiction as per *Swann in Love*. Add transcript of report by *Four Corners*, 1983. Sydney: Golden City of Gays. It’s becoming known as the San Francisco of the southern hemisphere with sixty-one homosexual groups and social clubs nearly everyone you see in this part of Oxford Street is gay there’s music for gay listeners on gay radio who listens in secret from the closet nobody knows three gay newspapers a calendar with 63 fixtures per year 9 gay hotels 8 gay discos 5 book shops gay sex shops catering to the outer limits 14 gay restaurants 25% of gay relationships <3 years washable canvas harness I’ve had 2,000 encounters in tea rooms across Darlinghurst Ball Spreader with adjustable leather strap look at the studded scrotum collar Midnight Shift Ms Polly Waffle dancing tonight male monkeys mount each other its natural to them can't change the sex-urge Stephanie's Waterproof Rear Love Ring no description needed maximum sentence twice as long as rape Mrs Fleming's breakfasts there are still 145 prosecutions per year in New South Wales twenty men go to gaol each year for periods of two to five years Exchange Hotel pumping Nutbush Limits the doors swing out Catholic influence one of the main obstacles a young man sitting on a public lavatory with the door ajar jeans along the floor cock in hand coming out sites dancing to BAND OF GOLD Link back to Shredded Ginger in C10 Life's A Beach tranny in a pinafore and fishnet singlet named Ginger dancing on Dot and Fanny's Tonight Show shirtless shaved red suspenders Sever Inflation RIP costume glitter T DANCE Easy to tighten or loosen in the dark compression Burdekin Hotel like a wedge of cheesecake **WARNING** keeping your penis hard for extended periods can put you at risk of injury remove after 20 minutes MAX can cause damage to the capillaries and bruise the penis Ana's white skin glowed heightened by a pulsing neon tube which announced OPEN 24H (*infinitum*) illuminating her black eyes which had been endowed with a gemlike lustre by Athene's ambrosia as it fell like tincture on her lips gold trunks sodden with sweat Francine returned Tom's gaze steadfastly then re-turned so that he could only perceive a single eyelash fluttering in the tender air like a moth. No words were uttered. Zeus thundered above. Francine's alabaster claws gripped his palm. They climbed aboard Time's broad-winged chariot to disembark at her secluded palace. Ana stopped at a seat under a streetlight in Hyde Park. She extracted a sesame seed bar from her jacket. SEEDFRUIT. She needed food first. Heroin made her vomit. She extracted Tom's dart. HOLD IT UP TO THE LIGHT! Rats flustered in the spare undergrowth. Mammon's cave was "hewne out of rocky clift from whose rough vault the ragged breaches hong embost with massy gold." Dark and dirty abode of savages dedicated to gold. Escape like Guyon. Reject the machine. The only means is Death. "There anguish does not sting; nor pleasure pall." She fixed and leaned back for the rush. Holly roused her. The Lake is 7 metres wide, 1 kilometre long & 5 metres deep at its inmost point. Messages to loved ones had been painted on the wall by soldiers in World War Two. Macarthur's hideaway. A place where bad folks go when they die. Pentagrams stained the stained concrete. Pyramid graffiti. Third eye. Light the lamp. Red crying eyes of a lion. Dry vines falling like mesh from the ceiling. A Lady's tresses. Rhizomes from beneath/within. Under the earth we move like moles or foxes. Thick tree roots like black snakes chicaned on the floor. "I love you, dearest Robin. 1942," read the inscription. Psyche in Hades. Get Persephone's cream. Nourish the skin of Aphrodite. RED paint. Film extras daubed with pig blood twisted in fake atmos. Public Air Raid Shelter. WARNING. Hail Satan. Bang a gong. A ghetto blaster exhaled GOD MADE THE BLACK STAR. On earth as it is in

Hades. Trespass not. State Rail AUTHORITY. Pay rightful dues. There is no fresh air anywhere. Sydney tomorrow will be a humid 26 degrees. Now it's time for the *Midnight Hour* with Lee Simon. Go deeper down the shaft. The speed kick came first. Ana hastened. Waiting for the smack – hurry up – to smooth out the rush. Wow a BIG blast. She tripped on a tree root and fell. Cool lake on dress. Damp gut. Blood in teeth. Roll over. Look up. No light for a moment. Blind like Tom in bed. IDIOT EPILEPSY. SHIFT to piles of references to deface emotion. If Stephen Dedalus had died in Nighttown, it would have looked something like this. Scan the body in the alley for life. A cave is not night. For night, you need sky. Closedindirt. Into the caverns of the unconscious go the dead. The body is a cave full of atoms. Mundane shell. STAFFA. Glamarara. Xanadu. List concordance references in the *Complete Works of Shelley*: (1) The books of all wisdom are hidden in the cave of the "Witch of Atlas." Take a tape measure. "Lady of_______." Pa Kua. Magic females. Hide in her interlunar cleft. Tui symbolises absorption. When the Witch moves over the Lake all the temerity of human conduct is purged. (2) Cythna in RoI slipped birth whilst imprisoned in a cave. (3) Prometheus and Asia retired to their respective burrows. (4) "Epipsychidion." (5) Alastor died where the stream slid down the throat of a cave. Narcissus. Reflection of a signifier oiled in a still POOL. Revir. Jung mainly meant lakes when he spoke about water. (6) Shelley himself drowned off Naples. Death encephelating art. Yeats wrote at length about Shelley's spelunking. He saw these symbols as embers of invisible power. Obscure and dark. Occult. Where thought like a rapid perpetual stream flowed. Fireflies in the mind. Forbidden gems. Fountains were often proximate in Shelley. Like Blake's dualism. Zoroaster's cave torn with springs. Nymphs feeding knowledge to men. Intellectual spray. Gates of generation. Homer's gates. A lacuna. (7) *Mont Blanc*. Ana reached inside a rancid concrete antrum. Pits set against stagnant water. Pestilent meres. (8) Laon's prison was past a putrid pool in a cave. In Bromion's cave, dirty lovers were shackled back to back like Plato's hermaphrodites. Wandering halves like Tom and Ana. Jung notes that the cave stands for the impregnability of the unconsciousness. Plato's cave represented the whole world. Orc was chained in one. Caves signify containment. Initiation ceremonies most frequently take place there. They are secret places. The entrance is always hidden by a labyrinth. Often you need to overcome guards. It's like re-entering the womb. Mother Earth. Shallow burials in caves. Passage through them changes our state. Plato's bondage allegory. Ana was trapped betwixt TWO WORLDS. A semi-transparent wall. Backlit. Where shadows fall. Gink bellies on a window pane you could never touch. Chained people, necks and feet. Xiao Fang made a cradle with the red rope, twisted her body inside and twirled upside-down rapidly with Billy's cock in her mouth. People inside a cave cannot raise their brows. What they think is an illusion is REAL. Ana has left this world. A bright light shot-out. Aim at a fixed point. The world is just fac-simile anyway. See PART 5 of the FURIES. Caves cancel sunset.

Darkness evermore impending. Farewell happy groves. Angels visit the caves of every beast. Shelley's magic cavities were always matched by towers. Go out of Golgonooza. Exit Eden. (9) Prince Athanase pursued mystical studies high up in space. (10) Cythna's lover. Old hermit watching over Laon. Up/down. In/out. Light/darkness. Surdity against Utterance. Stasis on Dromology. Dialectical strophes. Cold causes life in the world. Heat causes life among the gods. Ana felt for breath vainly. Alveoli. Diastole. Emilia V. Honeycomb of mines. Bees return to the same hive insistently. Honey is a symbol of generation. The ancients represented our souls as bees. Sound folded in cells of crystal silence. Liquors clear and saccharine in delicate flutes. A blown chrysalis. The ruins of the ABC radio gong that simulated the sound of Big Ben was still suspended in the Lake since wartime. Brennan's sweet shiver down yer earhole. Slessor's template. Dew down | mist up. Increase heat to the point of vaporisation. Scientific poesy. Novalis was a mineralogist running the family salt-mine. The mouth of a righteous man is a well of life; violence covers the mouth of the wicked. Smack masks the speedrush and speed veils the stop. *Kairos*. Reverie of a blue flower. *Sehnsuct*. Red vomit. Ana felt far for symbols. Cross at her neck. Wrists of wood and cowbone beads. Only ten minutes had passed since she entered the tunnel. She rolled on her back gazing at far distant streetlight gridded by a narrow grate. Heart pumping/stalling. Swallow no can. Lavinia. Tongue got cut out. Speedball braking her throat. She was leering when they arrived. Seeds stuck between her teeth. Dry at the corner of her unlipped mouth. Death of EVE. Toe Cutter covered her nostrils and lips. Sea closing above. The throat contracts under the influence of Junk. A dice-throw in a marble vault never tolled so. It ricocheted against every obstacle in the chamber, pirouetting on its axis and rolling to an uneasy stillness. Like the Greeks in the *Iliad* after the death of Patroclus, Ana felt the horror of supernatural darkness added to other foes. There was no place uncircumscribed by it. Even in the bowels of a ship, from the depth of a shipwreck, "somewhere in the heap, an eye," what Beckett would call "a wild equine eye," rolled through the brine and came to rest. A single car passed over the grate. It rattled hard then eventually everything went still again. Sydney slept. Don Cane shifted into fourth gear. THEY ABANDONED ANA. **(32) PUNKS LEAVE SICK GIRL FOR DEAD!** Her corpse wasn't found for days. "What would YOU do if you were in MY shoes?" asked Tom Hallem when they found her corpse. "Send myself off on a suicide mission," replied Elizabeth Archer. "Is that what you call my stipend in Paris?" His dealer made no comment. Billy Capri stirred from bed. He groped towards his desk and hacked at a lamp switch. Granite sparks seen. Too wired to sleep. He wound an A4 sheet into a manual typewriter. Sydney has always been an ALT city, he typed slowly; trying to suppress the sound of each key in case it woke his parents. Sydney was the most radical town in Empire, he added. V2. Ana faultered yet persisted toiling with an ungainly IV-stand like some cheap candelabra a patient proceeding through hospital grounds hot asphalt a location where I was brought unconscious that registers NO LANDMARKS but rather TOTAL NEWNESS OF PLACE not remembering why-here how-here what-am like Proust's protagonist at the start of *LTP* the last thing Ana recalled was meeting Tom in the morning straight after work on Liverpool Road a memory-flood SUBLIME in its fullness that rushed around her body as if her brain had been reset and her eyeballs replaced by crystal fishballs projecting a total picture of THAT MOMENT IN TIEM surrounding her like a sphere finally she fell STAND / FALL Tom on a canula Billy on a drip Ana stumbling Billy stumbling he wheeled the silver IV-pole on four shitmetal castors her going forwards and down him going up Tom's horizon a bed frame bags fluttered like fall leaves she went down but not by arc rather airpout vacuum pouches of blood + lymph Willy sawing with the needlehead until blood + smack wore finely intermongrelling like Shelley's impenetrating DEW Ananowinert Billy rose from grazed knees grass stains on bleached hospital gown cold rainair tightened his nipples [see C5, E19] craters sinking into his tonsured chest like two reptile eyes shut hard anthend / Nipsunk like a dry mud pond cracking into a mandala of grey beads plastic almost / IV tubes unravelling out of my chest into two drip bags swaying in the hot Sydney spring breeze frittering from Bondi over the Waverley lump IT IS NOVEMBER 1978 my breasts precede as usual slightly hung like lanterns my limfe'n'bludd mix permeandering sacks opaque kaleidoscope claret patterns churning the surface of a still pool like petrol silver metal candelabra on wheels STUCK ON DANTE'S LOOP draining out of the sutures in my tits running paddocks of fluid behind Bressington Park too tall top heavy Ana's head heavy like a medicine ball each step birthing yellogree yellerblew bluegreel swirls in winter bog slim soft stalks inserted all the way into my torso my tits algae Warmem driveway pressing shade smoothedowne asphalt a plaster statue of the patron saint of soldiers set on a plinth in the centre of a sandstone retaining wall our Grey War heroes once part of you and you parting of it deep balconies Willy ground the sharphead deeper into Tom's unhelpful flesh twirling it sharply to get the FIT so heroin could proceed into his bloodstream like some grand cortege of youth and beauty via veins sunk deeper ever-deeper an eel barely visible lashing the under-surface of a still pool. Billy rubbed at his left nipple. It was the less successful side. It still ached to touch dully yet sickeningly after 40 years. [**Calypso**] Oxford Street frocks were drifting towards Dawn O'Donnell's clubs down Hyde Park. Tom and Frances linked hands awkwardly. A rush of docks air from Woolloomooloo Bay punched their backs along the frayed strip of shops along Crown Street. Offcuts of the machine. Sydney's history encompasses: visitors like Conrad and Lawrence; expats like Dickens' sons; arrivals from the Bush like Lawson and Paterson; and Chris Brennan's Symbolist poetry where Mallarme met Sydney through a lens of amber absinthe. Belated pollen fell thickly from a rich canopy pooling on sandstone terraces.

Christina Stead wrote paeans to our fringe dwellers, estates and waterside slums. The Freedom Ride started and ended in Sydney. A plaster statue of an armless ANZAC rose on a plinth under the fortress gates of Crown Street Public School. Sydney's exports shook Britain during the empire's death throes after World War Two. **A WOODEN HE/O(A)RSE.** It was the cradle of social agitators like Greer, Hughes, James, the Push and *Oz* magazine. It nurtured John Anderson's offsprungrhythm. Barry Humphries created Dame Edna in Melbourne but she became a hit in Sydney. A new AIDS clinic was being constructed at the Albion Street intersection. Handiwork of Doctor Julian Gold. Sydney also produced concrete-cutter politicians like Wentworth, Parkes, Jack Lang and Paul Keating as well as Green Bans and Joe Cahill's Opera House, sponsored by a bloke who knew more about psalms than symphonies. Crown Street Women's Hospital sat behind scaffolding all boarded up. It had been rendered blank for redevelopment. Say Deshil Holles Eamus three times. Presbyterian blockhouse. Mina Purefoy's swollen belly. Leon Daniel's blotchy gut blooming plum sarcomas. He scratched seeds with putrid nails. Dublin was Joyce's postcard rack, history lesson and phone book. It was a dark city filthy in decline. They passed Shannon Reserve sodden and thick with mudlines from the Saturday flea market. The slum back bedrooms of Richards Lane were bleating poor, jaundiced beams. The consonance of Yellowblock (gilt), sunlight (lofty, sharp), clear skies (quiring) and ever-changing, never-changing glycerine water (omni-mirror) made Sydney a city that lived for the limelight. Visual art here has always tried to display the PURE SURFACE of THINGS. Grace Cossington-Smith's famous painting of the new harbour bridge is all shine not structure. Lloyd Rees depicted our thin-lipped alcoves with ink and steel. Brett Whiteley's ultramarine maw exposed the breadth-with-no-depth of our latent symbols. The Clock Hotel had finally patched closing time. The hands on its Tudor tower clocks were always wrong. Drift past variegated boarding-house terraces. A shell burnt black on the inside. Gadigal ground. Five thousand years back, the God Baiame carved his story into Eora stone that was already sun-drained. The same rock now adorns our public buildings (see C9, Q22). Sydney Rock Engravings. His wife was the goddess of fertility, Birrahgnooloo. They had a son named Daramulan. This family of deities covers a full range of mythical symbols (see L-S). He was Zeus. She was an emu Leda. He resides on the moon (Olympus). Daramulan was a Protean shape shifter. Got an arm cut off. It represents humanity in some legends. Likewise, an evil hand is often severed in myths. A shot shattered his ankle like Achilles. Oedipal figure. Resides in tree trunks. His voice is trapped in a bullroarer. A last tune groaned out of the pub. "Hotel California" is a song of mythic symbolism. Tom and Frances crossed Cleveland Street against the lights opposite Abdul's Take Away. The high brick wall of the police barracks held stables. Scent of road apples. A broken frangipani tree wept blossoms across the cracked footpath. Francine led Tom onto Boronia Street. She had the ground floor corner room. It was a rat run for taxis. Billy Capri tried to succumb to sleep. A book perched on his chest. His bed lamp alive. Ginsberg's "America" splintering unrestful, threshold reveries in a kind of ouroboros suck. *F(W)ake* takes place in this kind of oneiric realm, which was later idealised by Gaston Bachelard. Insert sub-poem. (1) Sydney I've given you everything now I'm spent. This was how Ginsberg started. (2) Sydney, the scabs of a 20-buck BJ in my pocket, November 7, 1984. He gave us an exact date and amount. He was almost penniless. The purchasing power in 1956 was almost equivalent to twenty dollars today. You could buy a decent meal for one dollar. I can't stand my own mind, said Ginsberg in line three. After that confession, he accelerates out of history and time fusing politics, psychiatric illness, cosmic concepts and mystical elements with everyday ephemera, ironic takes on propaganda and advertising tiles. About 80 per cent of the remaining statements-as-lines in AMERICA attain greatness. That's 56 out of 73 lines. (3) Appropriate line three. Shift. (4) Sydney when will you stop fighting this Punic War? (5) Go fuck yourself with your laconic racism. (6) You're hell and I'm normal, Sydney. Hotter than Ancient Greece on your chest. (7) When will you finally be done with Indigenous genocide? (8) We need to take off the scales. (9) Your history of pestilence, killing, gold fever, corruption and war is like a TV on fast forward, Sydney. (10) When will you stop deferring? (11) You've really got to look into that Queen. (12) Australia is not the greatest country on Earth no such place exists you've always known that it's just a slogan. (13) When did you become a nation of haters? (14) You never believed in God stop pretending. (15) Your silly mood is silly like American silly but small. (16) The Trump want eat us live. He makin' us all-new injuns. His honey men got guns work sixteen hours no insurance. (17) Fuck American exceptionalism. (18) China is a war factory too. (19) Australians you also love war stop pretending. (20) Cultural cringe is OK. (21) They're all cunts up-over-there believe me I've read about it in magazines the bartender told me as well just be patient. (22) Australia, your women are wavering. (23) God is pouring out of Seven-Elevens. (24) It will hit me hard when you fail. (25) Sydney, old men with ray guns should fight wars not children. (26) Litotes is Australian for rap. (27) Sydney, it is better to fail BIG by miscalculation abyss or new abyss to guess disappear tongues where does it all go instinct major telegrams. (28) Insert list of persecuted liberal figures (Ginsberg cites Tom Mooney, Scatto, Vanzetti and the Scottsboro boys), Sydney (29) FREE THE ANANDA MARGA THREE was sprayed on the police barracks wall. (30) The cops made no effort to erase it, Sydney (31) Sydney, when will the Rum Corps finally leave town. (32) Make them take Kerr, the New Guard, Niemeyer, White Australia, and [INSERT OTHERS] if there's space (33) Sydney, we can fill up all the empty refugee boats with soft fascists and float them to Asia (34) Ana is dead, Sydney, you killed her. This is the type of statement that Ginsberg never makes that's what makes his poem great he only shifts to the personal to express his own angst (see ll. 22–23, 30, 34, 47–53) (34b) These are the worst times (exclude lines 6, 14, 24, 71–73 and definitely not line 36 which is the start of the whole Sixties shebang) these are all great (35) I am equivocal about line 45 (36) The closer I get to the end of this work, the more life loses value, Sydney (37) Most of the time I wish I was dead (38) Every time we move away from naturalism towards technique I feel better about things, Sydney (39) Sydney, all art aspires to the thickness of text (40) Fuck Apollo (41) Your big book has to be postmodern, Sydney, because you are a postmodern place (42) **INSERT AS REQUIRED** (END) I want to stop now Sydney I got nothing more to say. I'm taking my queer shoulder off the wheel. Finally, Billy entered definitive sleep. Shanghai Dog woke alone in bed next morning. Frances unlocked the front door. They entered a wide hall. Her bedroom was left. Her kitchen was right. Note that Billy now sleeps whereas Tom remains conscious for the rest of the work. Compare and contrast The Lake with Frances' compound. Link also to Ithaca.

"Where's the toilet," asked Hallem.

"Out the back," she said. "I'll show you."

A long corridor wended to a courtyard gridded with clothes wire. Windows overlooked the quadrangle on all sides. A low outhouse was shunted into the far corner; an echo of old pan-and-cart days. Tom Hallem shut the picket door behind him and huddled over a rusty bowl. A single weak bulb, fixed low, scorched the back of his neck. He closed his eyes. Tracers shot behind sore lids. He struggled to cut off the last urine. Spoiled kidneys. Hunched, he made good and slipped back into the courtyard arms all akimbo. Francine stopped him with her mouth. She pressed him into the brittle paintwork, which crumbled cold render onto his shoulders. He held her tiny skull. Light hair. His eyes remained wide open. Black clothes slung over the clothesline. Sharded sharp spotlight. He reached low. Cool smooth stone of her thighs. A boy's body really.

"Let's go," she said.

Francine's bedroom was high and pale. A bare aluminium lamp directed light onto a pressed metal ceiling. They do vaults well in China, thought Shanghai Dog lying on his back with his hands behind his head looking at the canopy of his room. Two French doors dominated the front wall, screened by bamboo blinds. A single clothes rack bulged with bright garments. Neatly folded clothing had been laid in rows on the floor. Their footsteps made steepling stacks of books shiver. Tom Hallem sat on the edge of the bed while Francine undressed. It was a firm structure of sprung mesh set on old-growth legs. He perused some tattered spines. Multiple volumes of Anais Nin. Her diaries reduced even the most shocking blasphemy to bathos. Nine-day orgy on the Riviera with her father while he hobbled around the bed posts with lumbago. Papa was my most virile partner, she said. Tom shuddered at Leer. Her brother was well-placed in stalls like sweating Pasiphae. His sister's supplicant. Also, Eggular Miller. A bet each-way with Gaulier's money. His wife was trapped between two of the most turgid spits of the epoch. Bored process of loins. Celebrity fuckfests. Secret diaries. I must read that tale of the painter and his parrot again, thought Tom. With a biographer like Deirdre Bair who needs. A taxi passed intersecting blinds. Frances came to him calmly like Calypso. O = Penelope. Circe = Zhu Di. Calypso = Xiao Fang. The *Odyssey* begins with Odysseus marooned on her easy key. Speak in Billy's voice. All that listening. Something must have penetrated. A tissue of interpenetrated cells with terminal ducts. Prosenchymatic criticism has 8,000 touch points like a woman's cunt. SEE GLOSSARY. Insert into C10 in reference to Molly's monologue. Tom's eyes reached the spine of Simone de Beauvoir's *SS*. Ruined by the death of Zaza. Her Arthur Hallam. She was more attuned to the *zeitgeist* than Sartre. Less hidebound by received ideology. Frances pressed her naked body into a cove made by his body and arms. His existentialism versus her feminism. She backed the right horse. Her cheek brushed his ear. Mostly made it up herself as she rode along. Her tongue jolted Tom. She went to the floor. Their partnership followed a droll sequence. He was a weatherman on the Maginot Line. The Germans captured him when they pushed across the Rhine in 1940. Frances struggled with the Mexican buckle on his belt. There was no word of him for months after the Fall of Paris. He lifted his body so Franc(in)e could shuffle his trousers onto a patch of crackt burlap. S. De B. undertook bicycle trips to the country as a front for Resistance activity, plotting troop movements, planting explosive devices, clicking a camera concealed in a straw picnic basket. All this stuff imbued her literary strategy. Sartre returned from prison after the war and formulated his own theory based on the experience of industrial slavery while she wrote *The Second Sex*. He said everyone was dancing existentially when they got back from America. She pulled apart his shirt. Boundless animal spirits of negated dialectics. The last button lapsed disclosing his gut. Samuel Beckett clomped his way along the desire lines twixt Materialism and Idealism. He was a Mystic really. Allegiance to reductive laughs. Arbitrary epiphany. Bog reason. His palm kissed her skull gently. It produces funny art, thought Hallem. Detached and didactic like some mid-period Godard movie. Truth spasms at 24 frames-per-second. Godard gave great slogan. Soon there will be no more utterance, spat Hamm. Then we will get some relief from the affliction of narrative, exclaimed Estragon deftly. She bent. Gather words into a mound. Pop a head on top just like Winnie. Make something capable of being dumped online. A hacker of words. Prosenchymatic drill-downs. A link-bubble never fixed in time. Always updated. Contributors come from without to my lair. Kill the author during bouts of self-criticism. Tom Hallem fixed his gaze on miscellaneous novels. Ubiquitous selection of Margarite Duras. Racey tailles of Colonial life in Indo-China. The kind of stuff that a man would have purchased to arouse Molly Bloom. All the Nabokov basics. An unidentified volume with Mishima's name embossed in large yellow type. A thick wad of SADE volumes. Losey. Pinter's screenscripts. Ex film-school assignments. Francoise Sagan's sad little affairs set in a defeated society. Bored, lonely young women and men sunk in munificence. A symbol for Australia really, mused my character. Black of black death. Blue of unease. False tumescence. Hide in turns and lies. Flat track bullies. O owns no Australian novels. No art adorns her walls. Billy picked up a copy of *Death Sentence*. Tom was like J, he thought. Poor Digginem. Tom Hallem now beastly dead. He would be 55 years old if he had lived to this day. But he had to die for killing Ana. That's just literary convention. Tom lifted Frances Hackett as he rose. Her body was raw without blemishes. A reed. This helped him focus on obligations. He hardened almost fully. Just as he was about to lay her down on the bed, she escaped like Albertine clipping floorboards with bare soles to get to the dresser.

"Amyl?" she asked. Insert results of Find on Page in C10 for this word.

She pulled a brown vial from her purse. Tom demurred. She gave herself an almighty SLUG. It flung her body onto the mattress. Cat landing on a pavement. She bounced upright boldly. A chemical emblem for the state I am trying to achieve.

"I'm struggling as well," she said. "It's not your fault. It's so late. Get some wine. It's in the kitchen fridge."

I scuttle between doorways nude flicking my eyes both sides also UP. Above there is only the sound of a d-distant phonogram churning out hula music. Calypso beat. Sudden rhythm. Twangs. Occasional boot clomps. Aloha Oe. Elvis. The stage revolved. Our hero had no recollection of his movements 24 hours before. That was about the time he had commenced the journey to the toilet-block at Beta House. His noble form struck out blindly losing course by increments until he stumbled through the unsecured opening of an elevator shaft and fell through gritted air so fast his head pummelled the concrete slab before he even had time to adjust forced faster still against unyielding end by momentum his lean body slappt the floor, bouncing, blood rushing exit lapsing to coma DONE. Meillon: Byron lay on his smashed belly in the soiled concrete recess. Hoff's sacrifice. His head slumped. Unconscious. Blood steeped his hair. He had suffered the following injuries: fissure fracture of skull, fracture of cervical spine, multiple rib fractures, fracture of upper limbs (right side), fracture of lower limb (right), fracture of clavicle, laceration of liver. Spleen and kidney damage suggest the height of the fall was over 20 feet. A long time had passed since. Am I / still / here, he asked observationally. Just. This black place makes me blind. Shadowman. Hades. Blind as old Hamm. Pepe locked in a fridge. A scream but no air. See Furphy, Chapter Six. Replace Barefoot Bob with a lubra. Country of lost children. Forced removals. Tom Hallem, sightless in Northcote, cannula in his wrist, called out to his erstwily dealer. A pleading of last resort. Forgotten Elpenor. Heaving open the door, sharp LIGHT and a CLOUD of chilled air hit Tom Hallem's gut. Inside, it was mainly vacant space. Miso soup paste, vegemite, mustard, vegetable scraps, a cardboard wine cask. I got some cheap supermarket glasses from the sink. Detergent clouded their thick rims.

An impossibly strong stream of Hock stabbed from the foil bladder. Francine was taking another blast when I re-entered the room. She washed the wine around her mouth like a cat with milk. It scours my gums. We kiss. I'm thinking too much. We look at each other from a distance of about two feet – about the same distance I stand from a canvas – just close enough to smell Boncrete primer before I start – like the beginning of Godard's *Contempt* – that great movie – a hand stretching towards my chest – artsexfilmsexSEX! CUT the role of the painter within technology CUT *Tarzan versus IBM* SHIFT alternative title for *Alphaville* HIT ENTER. I take a blast – I want in – she says YES – I lack strategy – "Just put your cock in," she says. "Are you on the Pill," I ask. "Don't worry. I can't get pregnant," she replies. No time now for digression. Tom stored his qualms. Francine reclined into the sprung bed. It sucked her body. He pressed his legs down with force to gain traction. Orange-laced Solange. Like Candy on the game. Slip her thong to one side. Gain entry. A KEY. She pressed a finger inside the plastic ditch which held his ruined nipple. He removed it gently and placed her palm on his rump. Strange echoes of the past all echoes. He felt like he was adopted for so many years then the breasts started. They cut them out leaving his chest maimed. Tom tried to forget. Give in to sheer rhythm. Foucault's persons of perverse pleasures. The Blooms' fitted this category being one son short of a full Malthus. Amyl slowing. Subway grew impatient. Tom Hallem pulled free and rolled on his back. "Use my arse," she said. He tried. "You still can't make it?" she asked shedding him with a plop. "No," he replied. "Don't fret," she said. "I can't either."

"Do you want me to—"

"No," she interrupted. "I mean I don't. Never."

No need to serve then. Some relief. Perforated light peeled the darkness. Carswish burned slowly, building to a flash then past. Francine yanked our bodies back together. All the power of Calypso's despondency. Hallem tasted impermanence. No one could tell what would happen next. How long it would last. Where it would end. It ended in Madrid in January 1985. Then Toledo. Paris. Finally, Berlin in summer. It only stopped when she said. Shanghai Dog stood in darkness. The first time he made love to O, he didn't want to leave her bedroom. If only he could regain that TENOR. *Ulysses* is the manual for long term couples seeking a path to reconciliation. It discloses the process of shutting down other options. The airplane was buffeted by turbulence. A truck rumbled past Beta House. A police siren suddenly blasting. Gaze out the window. See note on clouds in Chapter Eleven. Pulsing undercarriage. Illuminated jet engine.

"Get me a cigarette," said Subway pointing at the floor.

Tom leaned over and opened the packet.

"It's empty."

"Go get some."

"Where?"

"Abduls."

He weighed choices. Different uses of time. Different outputs. Odysseus was forced to decide between the comforts of Calypso's island and home. Same thing at Aeaea. Note Dido/Aeneas. Link to Manila/Sydney. Choc's funeral. An excuse to go back. Sniff around. Albert Wheaton was a good soldier. He survived the Conflict. But in what form no one could know. A shade of his former self, they reckon. His family knew the outputs, not the inputs. Elpenor left Troy with Odysseus. On Aeaea, he got drunk and climbed onto the roof of Circe's palace to sleep. He was awakened by the sound of his crewmates making preparations to leave for Hades. Trying to get down quickly, he missed a step on the ladder and fell straight to the ground, breaking his neck. Link to Lester. His crewmates did not notice his absence until they had put to sea. There was no way back by then.

"Sure," Tom said. "But I've got to go after that."

"You can stay here."

"I want to get home."

"Why do you want to go all the way back to your mother's place at this time of night?"

"We can talk about it when I get back."

He dressed. INSERT CLOTHES. INDICATE STYLE. Trousers not jeans. A bright shirt, no pattern. Secondhand tan shoes dyed umber with black boot polish.

"Promise you'll come back," she demanded.

"Of course, I will," he replied.

"Leave your shoes."

"What?"

"Leave your shoes here."

Tom Hallem stepped out of his shoes without comment. Collateral. Soft bare soles. The hostess handed me a flannel slipper. It must have settled in the aisle when I dozed. The woman in the window seat leaned into my armrest. Her head flopped against my bicep. Bloom and Molly go foot-to-head. Her breasts are opposite his shins. His cock, her belly (note symbolism). Her knees, his ribcage. Her feet, his mouth. Odysseus left his sandals on the mat and stepped into warm balm. Eurycleia passed her palm over his boar scar. He gripped her throat suddenly. Shanghai Dog held hard. Time rushing out a hole.

"I'm broke. Have you got some change?"

"In my bag," Francine said pointing at her desk. So ... there I was walking barefoot down Baptist Street towards the Assos Parlour, Tuesday night turning into Wednesday, fingering some stranger's coins, hoping no skinheads were stalking Cleveland Street. Pale floodlights shot over the high security wall of the Police Training Centre. Trail of horse dung.

Gates. Sentry box. Insert ref. to Old Tweedy. A worker carrying a white Adidas sports bag walked east across my path. He was racing to make the change of shift at the Tip Top bakery for the dawn bread run. Each story in *Dubliners* uses Epiphany as a pivot. In Book XI, Odysseus is making a sacrifice to meet the shade of Tiresias when he is surprised to see Elpenor. He asks how he came to Hades. Elpenor tells his tale. He begs Odysseus to return to Aeaea for his remnants. He only wants an anonymous burial using the oar he pulled to mark his grave, so he can be remembered as a sailor rather than a drunk who died a strange and dishonorable death. This is a clear example of *Kleos*. The dead man just wants something straightforward and pure like Eric Killion. After finishing his tasks in the underworld, Odysseus returns to Aeaea to cremate the body. Turkish bloke sold me smokes. One-eighty. Stale mutton revolving on a spit. Dry flakes in a silver tray. The waitresses were preparing the tables for tomorrow's lunchtime rush before going home. "Western or Chinese breakfast," asked the air steward. Many beasts were slaughtered to propitiate Poseidon. The waitress scraped leftovers into a large green garbage bag. Tom Hallem quivered. Blown back to Francine he was. Taptaptap on her French doors. She let him in and returned to bed quickly.

"Here," said Tom Hallem handing over the pack.

"Do you want one?" Subway asked.

"No."

"Come back here," she said smiling.

"I don't want to get undressed."

"Get me an ashtray," she said.

Hallem placed it on the mattress.

"The last train has gone. You'll be sitting on the platform for hours."

Tom Hallem made no reply. James Joyce has Stephen Dedalus wandering off alone at the end of *Ulysses*. This is very different to the *Odyssey*, which has the father figure leaving Ithaca while the son remains in the palace with his mother. Tennyson used this as a motif for the consolidation stage of British colonial administration.

"I know all about you," said Francine.

"What do you mean?"

"My sister gave me the dirt."

"So what."

"It just means I know what to expect."

"What do you want in return?"

"I just want to hang out."

"Why?"

"I can help you."

"How?"

"I've got connections," she said hurriedly.

"Then why do you live in this dump," he asked gesturing at her room.

"I don't get on with my father," said Subway rising from bed. "But I'm close to Marion." Like Lavinia, she collected Tom's shoes. Another castaway. She sat down on the floor, opened her legs and bent so that Hallem could see the arc of her tiny spine stretch into her neck knuckle. She put on his plain socks. A gesture of empathy. Link back to C1. He lifted one foot then the other. She passed his shoes to him. Tom yanked them over his heels. They both stood. She fitted her head into his chest. They held. Heart beating hard like a lizard. O displayed shame and perplexity. A low cry was squeezed out of her guts as she described the humiliation of begging Billy for touch. Francine led Tom to the door. Common area. Her feet spread outwards. Must have done ballet. A shift worker descended the staircase in work boots. He picked a postcard off the floor, examined the address, handed it to Subway silently and left. Hallem strained to see the picture.

"It's from my boyfriend," she said.

"Where is he?" asked Tom.

"Back in Perth. We met in CHISEL. It's a private clinic."

"Why were you there?"

"I tried to commit suicide last year."

Tom merely asked: "how?" Francine laughed impishly. "Overdose of meds," she said. "I'd drunk a lot of Scotch." INSERT MONOLOGUE. How Connie met Mellors. She was in a state of mute desperation. He lay a blanket on the floor of the gamekeeper's shed. Pheasant pens. Chicks in our palms. Festering teardrops. Lay her down on her back. "They pumped my stomach," she added. "We drove across the Nullarbor together. He didn't like it so he went home. Now he's coming back again." Memo from Menelaus. Signed, Paul de Kock. Odyssean voyagers. From home go home leave home no home go out come back threading Gibraltar. A home-made postcard from Sydney arrived at Poste Restante. Bubble wrap stapled onto a photograph of the Boulevard Hotel, William Street. "Dear Bully," Tom wrote, "it's a fucking ordeal here. Only one month to go. I'm biding my time helping RED. Saw *Android* tonight. I could really relate to that movie. See you in Berlin. TOM." Compilation text from a diary. Like cassette tapes. Insert chapter subjects:

1. LONDON > BERLIN. Bus. Helmstedt corridor.
2. GREETING TOM (Hauptbahnhof).
3. FIRST VISIT TO E.BERLIN.
4. FRANCINE (my birthday. Trinity Bar. Pass out on toilet. Tom like angel).
5. SOLMSTRASSE.

6. ABORTION (Birth of Rachel, August 1985).

7. WHAT HAPPENS WHEN TOM HALLEM STAYS.

"When can I see you again?" asked Subway.

"I'm pretty busy," Tom replied.

"New show?"

"Commissions."

"I could keep you company while you paint."

"Normally that would be OK. But not now."

Tom leant down on the bed and bobbed gently kissing Frances' cheek. I promise to call you, I said and left. Perhaps I should have remained. I realised as soon as I hit the street that I didn't know how to finish. Worse, this decision was never going to be mine to make. Francine would always be the active agent. Elizabeth prepared for bed. They would lie head-to-foot like Bloomolly but in separate rooms. "Could you stay with me tonight?" she asks. Leon Daniel makes a short excuse. They retire. Elizabeth hears him cough unrelentingly through the common wall. Penelope Hallem can still smell sour male sweat on her forearms after getting home. Maggotted like blood and bone fertiliser. She rises to wash again. Elizabeth proceeds to the en suite. THEIR THOUGHTS. RECOLLLECTIONS. I walked across the Coles car park and cut across Cleveland Street at the Marlborough Street lights. No traffic. Rising uphill past a white factory. I remember my daughter at an access visit pushing her head through the plastic safety hatch of a swing as I hit the camera shutter. Huge dimples under broad sun shade. Metempsychosis of genes. Tang of burnt biscuits. Slope levelling at Ward Reserve. Overshadowed by housing blocks. She was always closely observed by Elizabeth's nanny. I walked down Devonshire Street towards Central Station. The first time I had sex with Xiao Fang was a spa on the first floor of the Shanghai Hotel. I picked her out of the fish bowl. She wore a number on her pink bikini. I heard footsteps behind me. It was not Subway. S. DOG sent a text message to his wife. To paraphrase: cursory greeting, I am pining, desirous of prompt return home, insert ambiguous emoji sequence (U+1F998 animal, U+1F91x-E sign, U+1F55x clock), initial of his first name END. My father came back to Sydney in 1984 but we never connected. I flew out safely next day. Fuck knows where he went on Bloomsday. Perhaps he was part of the crowd in C5. Maybe you should look for him in *Finnegans Wake*. He is probably there inside some portmanteau image like the Man in the Brown Macintosh. His name is not inscribed on my birth certificate. A BLANK SPACE. In my earliest memories, he is already a middle-aged man. I don't know about Tom. I doubt they met. We never discussed it. I barely knew Leon. Bob is just big pictures of a healthy man on a feature wall and photographs of a dying man in albums. My mother only displayed images from stage three and four of Shakespeare's seven ages. I went looking for my father when I was fourteen. He was a junky in Melbourne. He left bare evidence of his life with his brother. I resemble him in appearance. Take the SCALES of DAEDALUS off your eyes. Male characters in this work never interact successfully. Odysseus was the same. Also, Leopold Bloom. Billy spends constructive time with O, not men. SHIFT Don Cane is the type of MAN who dominates the page. Tom Hallem would have been drawn to him. He rejects Les Hallem as a father figure. He prefers criminals like Willy and Leer. This is emblematic of poor decision-making. He was craven or furtive with females. Insert summary: Elizabeth, floundering in front of; mother, a cold fish; Ana, we were never aligned; Frances, a quandary. Shanghai Dog emerged onto the Bund holding Shredded Ginger upright with the aid of a doorman. The *Iliad* ends with the funeral of Hector. He was Priam's best son. Paris = Billy. REVERT TO C8. Les Hallem picked-up rusty tongs. Bits of shrapnel. Arrow stuck in bone. Symbols. Longshot struck his heel. Poison tips. Lost all his money on trotters. Last throw of a loaded dice. Harold Holt striding into outflowing surf in over-sized flippers. Faked his own death. Derrida called suicide ("S") a gift. Les gaping sausagesauce'n'mash. Bubbles of diminishing return. Reaching upwards with wrinkled fingers like Ana. Full water-tank in his gut. Foetus rotating in brine. Downwod. Deaed. Final elan. Sire memoromenemies. Homo now x won omoh. YY. Sinep'n'tnuc. 74 Sndyah. L'Anannal. Never odd nor even. Lovevol. An ageing celebrity trying to impress Nausicaa with goofy-foot moves in Poseidon's stuff. Vanity thy name is. Blind Titans' raging at hampered bodies. You could see it in their fixated faces after too many shots of Bundaberg Rum. Staring at their kids play rugby league. Any excuse to get punchy. Les never batted an eyelid when I opened my calf on an iceberg of broken beer bottle. The blood came quickly. He grippt it hard in his palm. He told me to focus on the pain; not ignore it. It would make it easier to process. "You're going to get a bluddy good scar," he said. Bob Capri wrapped it tight in a striped tea towel. My brother rejoined his teammates. Les picked me up in his arms and drove me to Canterbury Hospital.

(31B) NOT IN A GRAVE TO LAY ONE IN, ANOTHER OUT TO HAVE

"How long has it been," asked Didi examining the semblance of some figurines ashore from his boat.

"Almost twenty years," replied Billy.

"That's nothing," scoffed Vladimir. "Estragon and I have been facing this bluff for centuries."

"How did you calculate that equation?" asked Gogo.

"I went back from 1953 to the date of our birth then I added 21 years for growth. We set off on the road as *fin de siecle* dandies."

"Don't remind me! That hat!"

"We shared a vision!"

"Stop it! You know how I feel about that WORD."

"Alright. We sprang out of Joyce's ear in Zurich during the trench war. He was hiding out up high on his Irishness. We started out as two old ladies eating plums on Nelson's cock. It was his son what sent us to gulags. He was the Stalin of Modernism."

"You mean the bloke who just added the prefix "UN-" to whatever Joyce wrote and published it as FACT."

"Yes."

"You mean, UN-NO."

"Unincorrect."

"Nothing much happens in Joyce."

"Just the river," said Gogo wistfully.

"Or Beckett."

"Wait! He invented Pozzo, the bone-yielder."

"Yes, he did. It's all coming back! That bloke who went blind like Joyce."

"So, Joyce was Pozzo?"

"Maybe," he said. "They both kept slaves. For recitation purposes mainly. The slave acceded. Of his own volition. Now that was the REAL joke."

PROSE LET EYES IN

Lester staggered drunk down Soudan Lane. His crooked trousers were held up by a skewed Boy Scout belt trailing off sawtooth hips. A grey schoolboy shirt flapped freely against his thigh. NIGHT A. He stumbled against the back door of Beta House. He had a key cable connected to a coat button. Chucked out of Ralph's squat, he still had the floor here for refuge. He reeled in the string. Glistening thread. Too fast turning. Brickwork is cold. Repeat. He moved the key towards the lock again. It bounced off the shield this time. Link back to Hephaestus. He worked it across the surface of the strike plate. Scratches. Feints. Grip. Hold hard. Not a smooth entry to port. Meat of a lock inserted. Turn. The door opened. A chink. Get inside safely. He closed the warehouse door and groped for a railing. Grip. Catch breath. Look up. Circe's palace is humid. Find fresh air aloft. Climb. Use the wall as a prop. Level 3, Eutychus. Darkest night of rains. Scars. Achilles never got YOU. Now all the fucking superstars are gone except Ody. It's almost the end of the Classical period. Cannibal-dealers didn't hook me up. They got ~~Dave~~ but. This was the name of my hero so long, sometimes it's impossible to refrain from it. Lester wrenched back the steel fire-door. Ewan and Madge were asleep drunk as Dublin lords. Tom and Rhino also dead to the world in their cabin. Aeaea-aeaea-oh. Dregs of a silver bullet on the table. Burp out the cigarette-butt in your palm then drink. Drag a mattress onto the roof and lie down. Sound of ships preparing to leave shore. Elpenor made it all the way to Aeaea only to perish like Arthur Dignam falling through the open elevator shaft of an abandoned warehouse. Link to Leer @ EAx presst flat in the lift pit (see also C5, E1). The guard presses the call button. Wires roll. The cabin descends. Consciousness shred to police sirens. **BURTON**: Byron's bronzed torso ambled over the wide depository in viscous white underwear. The lightbulb which should have illuminated his path to the toilet was broke. He rubbed sleep out of his eyes and strayed. Delicate glass sliced his sole. Children playing in rye on the brink of a white chalk face. A sudden draft shot beneath. He dropped fast. No catcher. Crows and choughs winged the midway air. INSERT OTHER "FALLS". LINK TO MORALITY IN ART. Also, Marion's installation. Make them moral + physical. There is no Raskolnikov in *Ulysses*. "How fearful / And dizzy 'tis, to cast one's eyes so low!" Moral equivocation of Joyce. Who would cast the first stone? Bloom and Stephen are elevated characters by the end of the novel. Even Mulligan remains in play because Joyce isn't interested in amassing moral judgment. No revenge. Not even against Dublin. Stephen's father is the worst figure yet he receives a relatively mild portrait. Ulysses redacted. Joyce did not want to make ethical art. He was no Zola. Blind Gloucester led by Poor Tom to the cliff edge. Joyce's caustic wit countenanced no sentiment, prefacing the hard-nosed approach to *F.Wake*. Dignam's casket flies out of the hearse rounding Dunphy's corner. Priest spooning holy spit on his head. Coffins are just a waste of good firewood. Lucky Dignam: solid planks. Bom! The coffin bumped onto the unsealed road. Byron had landed on the right side of his skull. A long time passed. Unairunarise. Am I still vital, he asked of his body when he finally woke like dead Finnegan. Enough sentience now to panic. Bunny Corcoran was pushed into a ravine in the depths of winter and left there to perish. Black place makes me blind. Shadowman. Hades. Go down. Commune with the dead. Achilles would rather be living. Elpenor just wants a proper burial. Least that can be done. Give poor Dignam a proper send off. A few coins each. Tom Hallem was laid in a suburban funeral home for the memorial service before his casket was transported to Glasnevin Cemetery. We stood over his casket. L. BOOM in attendance. Round tomb of Daniel O'Connell on top of a broad stone mausoleum. Enter Ambulance and Police. They searched the warehouse arresting six people for miscellaneous crimes including drug possession. The tenants of Beta House were evicted. Elizabeth Archer is being prosecuted by Marrickville Council for breaching land use regulations at her artists' studio complex in Newtown, reported PS. There is also some likelihood that NSW Police will pursue the landlord over the near-fatal fall of an illegal inhabitant of the warehouse last month. Leon Daniel was declared bankrupt after agreeing to a private settlement in a civil case for infecting a patient with HIV. He died in a hospice shortly afterwards. The body of Paddy Dignam rolled stiffly in the dust, falling out a bloody great hessian sack far too big his grey nuts showing. Mouth closed with wax. Dignam's potted meat was Joyce's joke. Bloom read in *Voyages in China* that white men smell like corpses. Sharks will spit out human flesh. Cannibal marination of lemon and rice. Missionaries quite salty. His son Paddy came back from the butcher's shop with a pound and a half of pork steaks. Reader's underestimate Joyce's love of sedition. His bung sense of humour. Often, it's too hard to get at the gags what with all that technical mumbojumbo. Subversive images are hidden inside style as per Swinburne's poetics. Odysseus bumps into Elpenor on his visit to Achilles. Aeneas also. The Hades episode was fixed on the funeral. Link to Tom. Also, drugs. INSERT FINAL TALLY OF CASUALTIES: Ana DEAD, Lester CRIPPLED (mentally/physically), Leon DEAD, Tom Hallem DEAD (15 years hence), Uncle Paul DEAD, Fuller DEAD (car crash), READ DEAD, Don Cane DEAD (2008), all theoreticians in C6 (except Kristeva). Virilio died in 2018, after C6 was drafted. Characters on-the-run include Billy Capri, Odysseus, Stephen Dedalus, Shanghai Dog, Leer, Slope and Non, Shredded Ginger, the Blots (see appendices), Stinkbug and the three helots in C2 (did they escape pursuit?). Equivocal characters: Helen, Barry, Penelope, Les, Tom Hallem, Tom's daughter, Missus Albert Wheaton, Solange. Positive endings at the end of the text: Leopold & Molly Bloom, Don Cane, Tom Cornwall, Willy the Pimp, Hanh, READ, Ocker, Francine and Marion Hackett, Judy, Persian Jones, Stan Welles & sons, Matt Supplejack, Missus Brennan, Mister Monaro, Stephen and James Joyce, Greg Wheaton, Principal Ian Westacott, all minor participants in C4 & C7 and all incidental characters in C5. On the other side of the ledger, Xiao Fang is to be disappointed. Procreative characters include Elizabeth Archer, Billy, O, Shanghai Dog, Judy and Richie. In summary, TMAC can be declared a happy novel by virtue of the above ratios. A majority of its characters have a prospect of health and happiness at close. This statement still remains accurate even if minor and incidental characters are excluded. CLOSE CYCLE BEGINNING IN C1. RESOLVE LOOP. PLAN HOW EACH CHARACTER ENDS. Penelope Hallem arrived home to find her husband in bed. He smelled of stale beer as usual. She smelled like motel soap. He seemed tranquil enough. He had probably taken a couple of sleeping pills. She went into the bathroom and squatted in the shower cubicle to flush out a diaphragm. Helen Capri turned on a bed lamp. She knew Bob would not wake. He had a pillow disappearing his head. Hanh finally arrived in Malaysia. She had left Vietnam on a twenty-five-foot boat. Derive a new home like Aeneas. Reunification comes at a price. Troy and Ithaca both demonstrate that truth. Joyce never conceived of Ireland in this manner. British hegemony was still in place at the time of writing *Ulysses*. Joyce did live to see De Valera keep Eire out of the Second World War. Molly's monologue starts a process of acceleration in *Ulysses* which produces a genuine climax, satisfying the reader's desire for denouement. Joyce wipes off the vacillations, misunderstandings, posturing and inhibitions which mar interaction amongst men in *Ulysses*. He presents a basic gender split with woman-as-straightshooter. This represents another departure from Victorian shibboleths of female consciousness. Joyce goes right back to the start of Molly's life and exploits the inlaid power of chronological rendering. The reader is no longer side-tracked by experiments with style and form. Joyce fills in all the blanks. He is speeding to closure. It is sheer plot flow. Past-time-in-motion discloses personal history unknown to this point. The dilatory record of daily events in Dublin that comprises the bulk of the novel is succeeded by a rush towards meaning. There is a thrilling vitality in Molly's reverie which is absent from other characters in the novel, who are all ringed-about with routine, regrets, scruples, misconceptions, lies, politics, ideology and self-image. The limitations of characters are always clear in *Ulysses*. That is one of Joyce's strong points as a writer. Some characters focus on subsistence. Others on intellectual diversions and trivialities. Bloom is a pedant. He has pretensions. He creates a rich fantasy world that is barely suppressed from conversation. He is solid at making money out of an unsolid profession. He is sharp. But he is not that smart. He craves stimulation. He tries to channel this compulsion into philandering. He is two-faced when it comes to sex. He possesses limited ART. Stephen Dedalus is out of control. He is friendless. He cannot process the death of his mother. He is tormented by religious guilt. He is not able to produce meaningful art. He has no capacity for characterisation yet. He has not reached the point of maturity where he can suppress his own presence. He is ALL TALK. By contrast, Molly Bloom possesses a sweeping insight into life and people that cuts through the bullshit. She cancels all the above blockages and moralising. It becomes clear by the end that the energy of *Ulysses* has been largely created by Joyce's method. He has nothing much to offer the reader by way of plot. Only a simple rebuttal of Nietzsche. A critique of Irish art and politics. Quotidian depictions of the status quo in a secondary colony in the British Empire. *Describe a city that always looks forward to dawn*. Sydney receded out of still-born Tuesday waiting for Wednesday expectantly. Its atmosphere of ambition was quite different in tone to the crestfallen squalor of *fin de siecle* Dublin. Tom Hallem sat on the elevated platform at Central Station. A wet zephyr caused him to rise and pace the platform periodically. Don Cane was also awake. All his thoughts were locked on Penelope. He had not loved her. Yet here he was. Compelled. Helen was the best. Then Richie. Both better than Penny always craved never connecting never could. He had been absent for twenty years now. He could have been there all the time like Shanghai Dog. *How is S. Dog better as a man and father? Analyse.* Shanghai Dog transcended his father's journey and therefore gained the right to live. He undertook family chores. He went back to his marriage. Maybe doubt held them together [SD + O]. But it bonded them nonetheless like Bloom + Molly. The trope of Odysseus/Penelope by comparison can be termed a 'false dawn' (Ellmann 642). Cut to Billy Capri flying to Manila to arrange his father's funeral. This is the last time he will be cited in this novel. My father had an extraordinary affection for me, wrote John Joyce's eldest son after his death. He thought and talked of me up to his last breath. Joyce was lucky. The last human in Tom Hallem's mind was his drug dealer. I never penetrated my father's spirit. Everything ranked behind his impulses. On a regularised basis, I would by virtue of non-citation rank behind his boat, car, beer, red wine, favourite dog and at least two wives. An analysis of Odysseus as a father would have yielded similar search results. Tom Hallem was always fond of our father. Hundreds of pages and scores of characters in all my books come from this source. All these words try to give presence to the son yet at the last the father comes back to the front of the stage. This book is my elegy to the gap he left. An inventory of what Joyce got from his father includes a portrait, a waistcoat, a good tenor voice, and a licentious disposition. He was the sole heir. John Joyce became the only influence that James Joyce ever really acknowledged when he made the parenthetic comment in a letter to T.S. Eliot: "(out of which, however, the greater part of any talent I may have springs)." He went on to say that his father also gave him, "something else I cannot define." I recognise this impalpable quality. It generates faulty self-hate. It is not his death that crushed me so much but self-accusation, concluded Joyce. He never got back to Dublin to bury his father. Telemachus never got to bury Odysseus either. His father just left Ithaca and never came back. There was no closure. In Shanghai, I got a call from my mother advising that my father's ex-business partner had made contact with the family to inform them of his death. I proceeded to the Philippines. The last surviving son. I got a cheap business class ticket, booked a room online at the Winford Casino and dawdled on a long stopover in Hong Kong half-hoping a typhoon would sweep away the connecting flight to Aquino Airport. I hadn't seen him in over twenty years. I missed the funeral by a few hours. I stayed at the hotel replaying the whole episode of his return to Sydney (C2–10) with increasing indifference. Sometimes, life seems like a lost video cassette where you feel like you can remember its contents. You even imagine holding the brittle black box in your palm. But all you really retain is the memory of that cheap apparatus. My father was buried in North Cemetery. I hired a driver to act as my guide (see Dante/Virgil). It was only a ten-minute drive north along the R-8. There was a bold new banner slung over the gates. It covered a row of warped stainless-steel sheets that were being systematically lifted by the graveyard's residents. Billy picked up a brochure at the administration centre. The clerk circled his father's location on a map. He started to negotiate slender, unsurfaced trails with the driver. Link this image to Don in Vietnam with ARVN. This burial ground had been used by the Japanese for war atrocities. It still felt possessed by old poison like an abandoned mine. Extended families were living on top of raw concrete slabs under simple canvas flaps. Sometimes, the grave-stacks rose six levels high. Some tombs remained unclosed. You could see the mouldy butt of cheap pine coffins. But most of the niches were sealed and painted assorted shades of sky blue and marked with white tablets branded RIP. Angled crosses on many of the memorials marked the memory of Christ's procession to Golgotha. Apartment tombs, the driver called them. Most of the living inhabitants of North Cemetery came from provincial centres. There was piece-work as gravediggers and caretakers, he told me. Electrical wires were strung everywhere buzzing and mewing. Local gangs controlled different sections extorting entrance fees. My driver paid protection money on my behalf. He said I should not expose my wallet under any circumstances. I reimbursed him back at the taxi. You could only buy five years' time in the grave-stacks then the remains were dumped in a rice sack and thrown onto a pile in a breeze-block compound at the back of the grounds. Eventually they got taken out of the city late at night. Nobody knew where. Urchins saturated with mud and sweat were playing basketball against mausoleum walls. We passed a makeshift school room. There were rumours about grave-robbing. Some rich families hired security guards to patrol their tombs. A frail woman hollowed out by cancer lay on her back on a granite block covered in a paltry shroud. She held a life-size ceramic doll under her arm. You can link all of the above images and symbols to scenes earlier in this work. Billy arrived at his father's grave. "In loving memory," read the opening line of the memorial plaque. No crucifix. No doves yanking on a rosary. Just plain language. His Christian names. The most famous men in Australia at the time of his birth. A statement of hope, I guess, for a life to come. His family-name in bold capitals. It wasn't mine. Not Tom's either. Dates of life, beginning and close. Billy's eyes hit RETURN. The second last row read: "Also, Robert. Aged 2 days." "Together once more," concluded the text. So, he had another son, thought Billy. Unbeknown to us. Another half-brother. He lived at an unspecified date in time for forty-eight hours. A fresh posy decorated the bald slab. Alongside was an open polystyrene food container brimming with sticky rice. It remained untouched by the locals. Billy knelt in damp Manila Grass to read a small inscription card attached to the spray. North Cemetery was bubbling and thudding under a blunt sun. My Bobby, it said. Billy guessed it was the mother's hand. He had no idea how long this child had been dead. Probably a recent event. Another reckless act by his father. Billy realised then that he really hated this man. He would never want to be laid in this grave himself. He would never want his own name inscribed on this tablet. That man was not his rightful father. It was hard to believe Donald John Cane was finally GONE. Like Pater's Dionysus, Billy felt that maybe he would return one day like some freak tempest SHIFT loop back to the start of Chapter One: commence reading. The carriage doors jerked open. Tom Hallem entered the train. It had not been such a bad day after all. He had met a new girl. Got a free trip to Europe. He was going to earn some cash. He had even squared things away with Elizabeth. He could always fix things with Ana later. The silver doors closed. He went downstairs to the lower deck. The carriage was empty. This is a clear symbol of Hades. He dozed for a few minutes. He dreamed of nothing. This is all prolepsis of death. He woke each time a recording announced the next stop. Finally, Tom Hallem alighted at Burwood Station. He threaded the back streets past the police station and proceeded up Shaftesbury Road. Don Cane finally succumbed to sleep in the hire car facing downhill, poised above his ex-wife's residence. He had started the previous day in Manila. Now he was back in Sydney. He had an excellent line of sight to his target. Dawn kindled on his right cheek. It performed the same ritual on the left side of his son's face across the ditch down Wyatt Avenue. His shadow impressed a shiny cream wall – a shimmerer that in motion past – momentarily effacing its glassy dew. Distance-travelled sapped his father's great bulk. Don shuffled stiffly in the tiny cubicle and par-woke. He stretched against the pedals and hauled himself upright pressing his palms on the felt ceiling. Joyce ends *Ulysses* with reconciliation and the last word is YES. This is quite different to Homer, who closes with Odysseus commencing the process of facing the suitor's families. Then he will be required to undertake an exhaustive journey to placate Poseidon. Thus, Homer's narrative ends on a prospect of EXIT, renewed exile and more tales. I have held onto the idea of reworking the father–son dyad for almost twenty years. It's been my own odyssey. Its strength-as-concept has stood the test of time. I've never grown bored of it. Sometimes, its execution exceeded my stylistic capabilities. Like Beckett, I made a conscious choice never to compete with Joyce on technique. He exhausted that avenue. Rather, I have persevered with a postmodern approach seeing it as the only route around Joyce. Now my work is almost fully formed. Finally, Don Cane slumbers decisively. He is gone from the text. His son proceeds past the Anglican Boys' Home. He opens the stiff front gate and strides up the concrete path to the steps. He avoids each crack as if it was a mine. He arrives at the wooden landing. He did not have a key. But his mother had left the door ajar. He pulled open the fly screen. It cracked like an old refrigerator. He went inside. The day was done. Dawn bright on rock. The last lamp dwindled. Tom Hallem had re-entered HOME [INSERT FULL-STOP > HIT SAVE > CLOSE]

II.
Awards Night (Hades)

Double-U Bardun strode to the lectern. His piebald face blossomed ~~like a Cochineal Orchid~~ as he crossed the spot lit stage. Psychopomp handed him a microphone. He drew breath into a set of fine asthmatic lungs. Speech-cards fluttered to rest. He brandished aloft the trophy bearing a bronze bust of the Late Jeremy Ilks as he stared down the diners spread across the wide ballroom floor. Scattered applause. He acknowledged the presence of the judges, who were leaning back in vinyl chairs to gaze upwards at him from the official table. Amazingly, I haven't aged a single day, he thought, just like Proust's M, probably because we both found immortality in work, whereas my peers have spread or withered visibly with age. But here I am veering towards engagement with *A la Recherche du Temps Perdu* precipitously. If I had my time over again, he almost blurted by way of introduction, I would combine the scene in which Saint-Loup beats-up a homosexual in Paris (an act of repressed guilt) with Stephen's confrontation with Private Carr in *Ulysses* and apply it to Chapter Ten. But it's too late now. I'll raise it in my blog. "Thank you for this award for my great novel," he commenced at last, admiring the gold medal engraved with his literalias that had replaced the Black Country yoke what-he-got from hiz Da. "Using the word, GREAT," he continued, "to describe my work is the most difficult thing for me as a person because I am filled with self-hatred... just as writing this final chapter was the greatest risk I took in composing *Telemachus*." He paused to let the significance of this sentence settle on his audience. Both *PAYM* and *Ulysses* had ended on a note of premature triumph. Stephen Dedalus dissolved into darkness on the path to becoming Jems Joyce. Joyce only had one trope but it was a mighty one. Proust also. *F(W)ake* was allafail although no disaster @ the level of corpus. My plan is to beat JJ by stealth: *TMAC* + *VAULT* + *1111101001 Nights* = *One Million Words* (like Proust). "When the film makers," he said pointing towards the crew, "asked why I avoided the Scene in Australia, my answer was that I had already created a virtual prize in this chapter and, like Huysmans' Des Esseintes simulating a visit to London, only to abandon his train at the Gare Du Nord at the last moment and go home to bed, it was always going to be better than the real experience." A digital camera lamp was extinguished. Darkness, deeper than actuality for the abrupt withdrawal of light, possessed the rapid crowd (see Canetti: C6, E17). "But this award really validates my existence," he added, grabbing the silver scruff of his comfort dog, "and thus I am EXISTENTIALLY grateful to you." He paused to gape lovingly into the stratosphere of the low theatre, somewhat above the level of faces raised in bland homage. "Suddenly, everyone wants to have dinner with me!" he exclaimed. The audience registered soft mirth. "But oddly, my hosts never raise *Telemachus*. In fact, they go out of their way to avoid discussing it as if I had committed some unspeakable act of social disgrace which everyone preferred to ignore. Instead, they just sit there and gawk like I was some kind of bottled museum piece." His mind spooled back to his own arch image at this juncture, of Pater's Virgilia, cast in stasis, which had informed the representation of his own fatal heroine, Ana Lafei, and who seemed more REAL at this juncture than the great slab of humanity squirming under his Naturalist gaze. Proust tried to flip his plot and turn Albertine into the jailor in Volume Six. Such noxious misogyny. She is always the victim. The Narrator is always a Criminal. ALRDTP will diminish in time because of sexism, he believed. *Ulysses* will survive because of gender equity. And TMAC, he pondered? The author contemplated NEXT STEPS. 'Drought Spring,' he had written on the screen today, still ensconced beneath the same pale blue Japanese paper lantern that had hung above Chapter One like a censer twenty years before (LINK TO FURPHY'S SANCTUM). The first words of *VAULT* stand in stark contrast to TMAC's Biblical floods (note ironic link to climate change in Australia). The camera shifted to Professor Ulan kneading his spiky chin. Bardun's version of stream-of-consciousness is designed to impart useful information, concluded Ulan, rather than describe character emotions like Joyce. It is a historicising act to re-fix time inside a work that ostensibly rejects chronology. It represents data-scraping, not sentiment. Surface not cave. It is drafted as a contract operating according to normal tag-along, drag-along rights (see Term Sheet). "One of the obligations of this award is to make a 10-minute reading from my work. This shouldn't be hard. T-MAC is definitively a spoken word album. But I'm not a performing seal," he stated with appropriate fore-flipper gestures. "In the past, I had the actor Peter Hayes to deliver my monologues. But I've wasted his voice on making Ken Leer. Instead, I will present a sequence of critical considerations that I recorded in my notebooks while writing *Telemachus*; although anyone familiar with my website will know that it continues to evolve online under the maxim that, THE TEXT IS FIXED, BUT EVERYTHING ON THIS WEBSITE IS PROVISIONAL." Promote brand merchandising here. *Find typos win points receive an iron mug or T-shirt branded BARD-UN by registered post*. "My story is set a long time ago. That doesn't matter. What counts is that its form is relevant to how we go forward from NOW. I lived with the basic concept of *Telemachus* for almost twenty years as I travelled the limits of the known world like Brave Ulysses, from its earliest incarnation as *Distance Form Closure*, which was a kind of *Stephen Hero* or *Jean Santeuil* that had to be written in order to cancel out the option of faux autobiography once and for all, to its final format. Like Odysseus, I was king of a minor kingdom: MY OWN MIND. I was utterly without support during this period. I showed my work to NOMAN. I wanted to squash everything I ever wrote into a single work. Then I conceived *One Million Words like Proust*. It doesn't matter what I missed in TMAC anymore. I will just dump it all in *VAULT*." INSERT:

1. DREAMS by Fleetwood Mac as soundtrack to Tom's walk to the privy (C6).
2. Establishment of Newcastle to achievements of Governor King (C5, E18).
3. Link speed as sexual attractor for Whitman/Proust to Ana's entrance into the novel (C3). She effectively acts as Tom's chauffeur like Agostinelli.
4. HH-1970 = Proust's narrator post-Albertine (see Aunt Leonie).
5. The following sentence to either C4, C5: E17 or C10: "The clouds below the plane were too close to make shapes or stories like when he lays on his back on the clammy lawn in Campsie and pictured dragons and dinosaurs prancing and dissolving in the milk-shook vault."
6. I always associate Erik Satie with BETA HOUSE. Recycle/rework as soundtrack into opening drama (C2).
7. Change end of Sentence #1 – "to build a time-capsule of this wilful, restless life."
8. This most-Sydney-of-books is set on Melbourne's big day. Discuss irony.
9. Make two separate works – TMAC + ELEHUS. TMAC is the non-technical version (fictive fragments only). Create fake term for critical work out of leftover letters, ELEHUS. Make 2 x colour-coded versions (colour-blind friendly).
10. Add film reviews to list of forms. Also, INTERPRETER OF DREAMS.
11. INSERT C4 (BC speech) – 'to be a metonymy of the real machine like The Rutles.'
12. Leon forgets his wife's wallet and goes home in C10. How does Elizabeth pay? Leave unresolved (like MIBM). Probably invoice with 14-day payment terms.
13. Like Australia, Shanghai Dog had an artificial boner for China.
14. Name-check *2001: A Space Odyssey* (C6 – Virilio). Note Dave Bowman = Odysseus. Homecoming = adventure into new unknown (Gibraltar). Note Kubrick uses Cyclops episode (HAL = Polyphemus). SUB 'HAL' for words like internet/technology intermittently. Unpick your own symbolism in that sub-section. Compare Kubrick and Welles – who is the Commonwealth Games Gold Medal winner? Dave's life in the final scenes could be seen as Odysseus' life if he had stayed on Ithaca.
15. ADD 'Gigantism' to list of Navigation Searches (Symbolism). For modern geo-

political analysis, type 'China' (84 hits). Key scene is exchange between Doctor Gu and Shanghai Dog (C10).

16. *TMAC* (male novel) is all about structure (the Patriarchy). Its sequel, *VAULT* (female), will be anti-structure (vulvic). Thus, Patriarchy is succeeded in time. TMAC, Joyce and Proust are all circular in motion whereas the conventional novel is a straight line ending in detumescence.
17. Joyce wrote in 6,000-word blocks. Emulate.
18. An innovative FORM is an end in its own right. STYLE in such a work is just a means, no matter how poetic. Characterisation only requires fullness to the extent to which it progresses FORM. Plot is different to FORM. Plot = story. FORM = cosmos. It is possible to succeed at the level of FORM but fail at the level of plot. This probably creates a 'work of art' as opposed to 'instructions to humanity.' Joyce's great achievement was to succeed at both levels in *Ulysses*, just as he failed in *F(W)ake*.
19. Note in closing section – 'physical love is a dead-end' (S. Gainsbourg, M. Harvey – Trans., N. Cave & A. Lane – performers).
20. Insert above points into C11 list. Or add to end of Appendix C or add Appendix.
21. Insert reading of my version of "AMERICA" on website. Also, various short dramas.
22. INSERT GLOSSARY ENTRY – "TMAC – an encyclopaedic novel (STERNE), Menippean Satire, or other.
23. INSERT RHETORICAL CLIMAX – "The *Odyssey* (Billy) and its elder brother (Tom) have withstood 3,000 years of interpretation. *Ulysses* (S. Dog) is only 100 years old. But I believe it will always be studied for insights into the human condition."

"Decades of secret composition estranged me like Proust from my former salonnards. I have always wanted to come back and tell you that I never gave up on our shared vocation, even though I exited the building ... like Elvis in Las Vegas ... apparently as a severance ... seemingly for all time. For those of you who do remember me, you probably thought you'd never see me again. But I have lived long enough to come back alive like Major Tom in 'Ashes to Ashes'." He drew a breathless aside trying to fix the farthest moment of his orbit, probably somewhere like Fanwei Expressway outside Xiangfang in Hubei province around mid-2007 as he watched trucks pausing to be weighed at an automated toll booth in the fundament of night. He could just discern the abating seaside scowl of Angus McCreedy, author of *Prospero's Dominion*, now considered the seminal work on Australian literature, which Shanghai Dog had never heard of, but which astounded the local literati because its radical theory of Colonial

Extrinsicality had come out of nowhere like a bomb (see Bloch in ALRDTP). "But what is *Ulysses* in the end but an outsider text?" asked Double-U Bardun rhetorically. "James Joyce was an insider who wrote the ultimate outsider book. I am an outsider who has written the ultimate insider text. Put simply, my goal in *Telemachus* was to rewrite *Ulysses* from the POV of the son, using only those episodes in which Stephen Dedalus appeared. Just as Telemachus was the son of Odysseus, so *Telemachus* is the offspring of *Ulysses*. This idea was directly relevant to my own status as an illegitimate child growing up in Campsie without knowledge of my own father's identity. Like Tom Hallem, I had many false fathers. The great revelation in *A la Recherche du Temps Perdu* is the Narrator's realisation that his own life is a valid subject of ART. Likewise, I was finally able to justify using my own content once I had placed it into a Classical referent. TMAC is really just a suburban bildungsroman. In the same way that *Ulysses* is the story of James Joyce's Dublin, so *Telemachus* is the story of my Sydney. It is a tale of sandstone and water. Outskirts and monuments. It is a tribute to my hometown, the most radical town in Empire, a place founded on flawed theory and ignorance, a lie, a jail, a genocide, a social experiment, some crooked boomtown, property-crazed, politically ugly, a hating place, full of fast rage, soaked in piss, a beautiful junky slumped amongst sandy sheets, mazes of track marks passing across its dry ridgelines towards the coast, under a Persian Blue lens, indigo sea scraping at its scarps, shining like silver alloy on ungreen plains hot with lawnmower fumes, hangovers and massed choirs of cicadas all the way to the low hazy line of the Blue Mountains. I had to hold my nerve to write *Telemachus*. I wanted to produce a risk-taking novel. I didn't care if I was 100 per cent right. Theory is not about being right. It is to make people think. Every predisposition of my literary training kept telling me to normalise the narrative. I had to resist this compulsion. I wanted to take my work beyond *Ulysses* if I could. To lash out as freely at Joyce as he had at Homer. Joyce scrambled the order of the *Odyssey*, chose what he needed, ignored the rest and ended his plot with the reunion of the Blooms. He chose a positive denouement because he was a true humanist. Homer, by contrast, was forced to continue the *Odyssey* after the reunion of Odysseus and Penelope. He needed an external marker to reinstate the putative social order – like Shakespeare in his tragedies – whereas Joyce only needed to leave a psychological sign because he wanted to destroy the status quo. Tennyson addressed this aspect in his poem called "Ulysses". He believed that Odysseus would never be able to stay put after such turbulent experiences. He thus became an emblem of all war veterans. Like Homer, I wanted to continue an exagmination round my factification of Joyce after the hold-point in *Ulysses*. To explore the gap between its end and the start of *Finnegans Wake*. To bolt a low mimetic piece like "The Sensitive Plant" onto the end of the *Prometheus Unbound* volume (see C4, Q&A). I didn't have an endpoint for a long time. I reworked C1–9 continuously. After that, I just let my style 'flow,' as Jack Kerouac entreated, in

Chapter 10. As a result, I left many failed TAKES in place. Passages, in both senses of the word, where I got carried away in the flash of writing and made what Ginsberg would call 'bad prose'." RUN BLOOPER TAPE [*FX: monochrome film rolls over his pancake face*] ACTORS DISSOLVE INTO FITS. "After all, I had now passed beyond Gibraltar (AKA *Ulysses*) and no longer needed to sail under the same flag as Joyce. I could proceed as I chose like Barefooted Bob" (see Furphy's portrayal of Burke and Wills, Class, Mary O'Halloran, The Future Australian, sectarianism, her death, see also Pepe, and the roles of indigenous people in *SISL*). The word 'CUT' is heard. The screen goes black. "In *One Million Words* (see Glossary), I will operate in the gap between Modernism's twin pillars: to be conjunct with Proust on theory yet closer to story; to tell less tales but be more academically entrenched than Joyce. I call this mode Technical Fiction. It isn't really a joke. The objective of literary criticism is to make reading of the text unnecessary except for the purposes of received beauty. In TMAC, I wanted to deliver BOTH GOALS (a brace). My intention was to hide an acute personal story inside an avalanche of words (AKA rhapsody of mechanical language or 'caramel inside the chocolate'). Like Proust, my mature style could only be unveiled after I had reached a critical mass of word count. Technical Fiction turned me into a mad inventor of orbits and rotors like Ralph Sarich or Marcel Duchamp. There are three theoretical chapters in TMAC placed in pre-meditated sequence – C1, C6 and C11. It also disclosed my own doomed struggle against Joyce (compare Oxen episodes. Also, LINK to Harold Bloom's notion of *Tessera* in *AoI*. Finally, NOTE flawed rendition). But *Telemachus* is more than just a contest with Joyce and the promise of a future contest with Proust. It presents a new means of structuring the exposition of human experience in its postmodern condition, in the same way that Joyce and Proust made sense of their own epoch through Modernism. There are many novels which pay lip-service to blending theory and art. They often start with a clever literary premise like *Wide Sargasso Sea* or transpose a famous tragedy into a new setting like Edward St Aubyn's *Dunbar*. Usually, it doesn't take long for such books to revert to conventional storytelling. I wanted to hold the line by executing Technical Fiction in its fullest form. Jean Baudrillard called his own writing 'fiction theory.' I turned this term on its head because I was still writing a tale, not a tract. I wanted to use literary references in the same way that a poet uses symbols, imagery and metaphors. I wanted character actions to be tagged to literary antecedents, not similes from life. This means that there is also an educative function to TMAC. My pet name for this project is *'Ulysses' For Dummies*. I wanted the reader to learn enough about *Ulysses* without actually reading it to hold court at a dinner party. I wanted James Joyce to find a new audience by manufacturing a work that was geared towards contemporary forms of consumption. TMAC also offers useful information about Homer, Shakespeare, Romanticism, Modernism, Australian literature, popular culture and forgotten protagonists like Walter Pater. It is a misnomer to say that

TMAC is just Joyce-meets-Homer. It is also Joyce as per Derrida; Joyce in terms of Samuel Beckett; Harold Bloom's Joyce; and Joyce struggling with Shakespeare. It is also my struggle with Australia. TMAC is thus an example of what Harold Bloom called *Apophrades*. I wanted to execute Jean-Francois Lyotard's dictum to put forth the unrealisable onto the page. This assignment begins with a sequence of epigraphs that lock the text into a conduit from which it cannot escape. Like Joyce, I wanted to deconstruct FORM by means of multiplying the use of literary formats. In TMAC, I employed elements of the conventional novel punctuated with set-speeches, catechisms, newspaper headlines, songs and lyrics, radio-plays, drama, stage directions, poetry, journal entries, science fiction, film reviews, literary criticism, rock journalism, appendices (which follow this chapter) as well as graphs and tables all placed at the service of a specific trope: that the abandoned son must repeat the journey of the absent father, and complete it or die. I tapped the de-forming impulse of the subconscious, stronger than any superficial bands of structuration, to blur the line between hermeneutics, fiction, biography and autobiography. More than any other writer, Marcel Proust encouraged critics to bounce inside a capsule between person, author and character-in-text. Even Joyce did not play in this space so candidly. Stephen Dedalus remained a mere character, there was an omniscient narrator and the author was always James Joyce. TMAC inhabits Proust's arena, which is the sand grain of the postmodern. A compendium of human thought. A capsule of everything (I've ever) written. TMAC wasn't conceived as such. It all got connected as I proceeded (CITE PROSENCHYMA). I had to get the whole thing transcribed in one slow-motion shot – like the start of *A Touch of Evil* – because of A LACK OF TIME. I had squandered so many years building the bank of life-experiences on which to apply my craft that I had no time left to waste. In China, they say that scholars should never commit anything to paper before the age of fifty. I wanted to be fully formed before presuming the rites of composition. It was Kevin Birmingham who said that, for all of its obscurities, Joyce's book is more sentimental than erudite; more elemental than cerebral. TMAC is the con/verse of *Ulysses* in that case. It is a logical work. A trick of the light. One day, I plan to NORMALISE THIS NARRATIVE by writing a spin-off called *The Telemachus Story* with all the technical inserts removed. What else?" barDun asked himself, checking his wrist watch. "Time is running out." This was the famous time-piece in *Telemachus* that his mother had presented as a gift for his eighth birthday. Its pearl face registered spots of rust around the Incabloc numerals **2** & **3** next to the winding wheel; a legacy of diving into Leichhardt Pool to rescue his son (note symbolism). "I wanted to avoid creating any suspense in *Telemachus*. I dislike plots that tamper with the reader's emotions. I wanted my readers to be totally composed, in Wordsworth's mode of Paralysis, with all the facts at their disposal. I wanted to break down the temporal unity of *Ulysses* by shifting units across Time. To build a narrative that is neither linear nor successive.

Unlike *Ulysses*, which takes place on a single day, *Telemachus* is cast on single days across different epochs like DTP. There are three or maybe even four temporal settings: Melbourne Cup Day 1984; West Berlin summer 1985; Shanghai 2008; and a composite day when the author completes the novel (2013–2020+). Strange correspondences to REAL LIFE emerge over such a protracted period. This was what Proust found. It made me feel a bit like a shaman but not Ginsberg's kind. There is no cut-and-dry adherence to a single morphology. Ana Lafei is presented as a minor character when, in fact, her death is the governing event of the whole novel. It is the reason why Tom Hallem has to die alone with no one left to hold him back, call out his name, dress him, feed him, drive him home *inter alia*. HIS LIFE MUST END THIS WAY," concluded the author, his voice faltering, mist choking his eyes, forcing words out of a mouth-suckt-inwards-with-thorns, all the while reminding himself that BINARY NIGHTS will deal with the unmaking of one artistic temper and the making of another (A PROUSTIAN FLIP), "to restore equilibrium to the cosmos in keeping with the laws of Tragedy. Actually, I wanted to end my work suspended between forms and imperfect like all human relationships. I spent a lot of time revising *Telemachus*. It required continuous cutting, restoration and reconstitution. I wanted to be hard like Beckett yet cold like Joyce. I wanted the reader to get stuck inside the flow of Hieratic prose. My most uncomfortable periods of composition were mimicking Joyce's High Modernist style. This was necessary for broader technical purposes at various points. But James Joyce did everything possible with language. It is a zero-sum game trying to compete. So, I just kept such segments to a minimum and went on alone. Samuel Beckett's *Kenosis* with *Ulysses* and *F(W)ake* returned normalcy to literary style while retaining his master's caustic turmoil. A variegated narrative voice is an integral component of *Telemachus*. Joyce really just uses a fly-on-the-wall technique with occasional flashbacks. I wanted to shatter this voice across all five categories (~~mimesis~~). The narrator of *TMAC* is not ME. He spins out of control pursuing a mad dream of TF like Ben Lexcen. I wanted to scatter the same (or maybe the same) voice across a spillage of Time like Marcel Proust. I wanted to add new dimensions – what Godard would call "non-diegetic inserts" – via editorial intercessions, tangled plot strands, shuffling of incidents, morassing dialogue, wrong sequencing, dead-end reference chains, impossible lists, foreign languages, Strine, faulty translations, destabilising and renaming characters, fake chronologies, imperfect history, shifting viewpoints, prolepsis, sudden tense shifts, streams of parentheses like massed subordinate clauses, apparently provisional instructions like CUT & INSERT, shorthand terms and acronyms that force the reader to add extra words, to unpuzzle, but never-with-consistency as my aspiration. I wanted to replace references to place/people in Dublin with aesthetic touchstones in Sydney. To create a new lexicon of ACROSS-CARRY. To apply influence onto influence until the original sign was overwhelmed. *Telemachus* is built on piles of allusions, asides, afterthoughts, revisions, untruths and gaps. It is driven down false channels. Ostensibly discursive slabs are placed in the plot as per Sterne, Ruskin, Furphy and ALRDTP. These miniatures, perfectly formed inside an impossible-bottle of green textured glass like a Dutch three-master (note Peter Sloterdijk), were tweezered into pre-determined slots and secured with superglue. Character movements refuse to match time. Naming is equivocal. Pronunciation is amended retrospectively (READ/RED). Each character is kept transient. No one is allowed to possess the security of a singular SELF. Everyone lies. Ethically, *Telemachus* asks if LOVE can exist AFTER FAITH is breached. Joyce asked the same question in *Ulysses*. So too Proust. The answer in TMAC is the same: YES. All the stuff that needed to be put forth to achieve this end-point cut against my ingrained compulsion to deliver textural smoothness to my clients. Syntax had to be built meticulously so that the jarring of form was flattened and calmed. Acronyms and abbreviations were incorporated as poetics demanded. There was no adherence to grammatical convention. This means that the reader consumes the text in what is essentially a Parnassian idiom. This places *Telemachus* within the shift in prestige from poetical drama – think Browning – to the lyrical novel – think Hardy – during the late nineteenth century, which reached its apogee with Joyce. I accepted at the beginning that my model was never going to be a mainstream triumph. *Telemachus* was always going to be long. Much longer than its source. In fact, its word count exceeds *Ulysses* by 50 per cent [Bardun 4, Joyce 3 (ET)] although it is much faster to read because it possesses a simpler style. Its size was inevitable because I was simultaneously:

1. Analysing *Ulysses*
2. Examining its relationship to Homer
3. Creating my own fictional and technical universe on this base.

"It meant *Telemachus* was never going to fit into the eighty-thousand-word template for first novels. It was even too long for publication as a single volume. So, I just split it in half at the exact median of word count (INSERT ACTUAL NUMBER) for a print-on-demand edition. This arbitrary decision induced a metatextual lens like the *Prometheus Unbound* volume of 1820. But, in truth, I had no interest in engaging with the publishing industry. I come out of the Punk era with a DIY ethos. I just loaded *Telemachus* onto a website and tended to my set of key words to raise my ranking in Google Search. Nothing happened for a few years. That's OK. I was happy just to reinvent myself in a local context. I never wanted to be known as a Writer. Joseph Furphy's death certificate simply read MECHANIC (insert TICK). I just wanted my kids to have a record of MY TIMES so they knew something about their origins. That is a comfort I never knowed." Strine vowels gave emphasis to his disgust. He recalled his mother's obsession with family history, which would form one pillar of VAULT. "That is the end of my prepared notes," he said raising a shamble of stationery cards. He turned to observe the trophy at arm's length. INSERT NEW QUOTE MARKS. Patrick White called awards, 'seductive baubles.' Yet we must always respect the logic of CEREMONY. It is integral to all human cultures. Ceremonies are convened for a variety of reasons: religious purposes; to register seasonal change; for rites of passage like births and funerals; to open new pieces of infrastructure in a marginal seat (the audience laughed including the Minister for Arts, the Hon. Douglas Truck MLC, who applauded loudly). Ceremony plays an important role in both the *Odyssey* and *Ulysses* (strophe and antistrophe: within which and around which TMAC reverberates, which it encloses and within which it, itself, is enclosed). A blasphemous parody of ceremony opens *Ulysses* when Buck Mulligan invokes the Antiphon of Psalm 42 to shave. The mirror is his altar. The razor makes the sign of the Cross. His whole personality is encapsulated by Joyce in that single image. He can never come back from his characterisation here as a Gaelic Loki. By contrast, Stephen Dedalus is still dressed in mourning for his mother. It is shortly after her funeral. Ceremony dominates Chapter One. There is the ceremony of the classroom. The ceremony of sport. The capitalist ceremony of Deasy presenting Stephen with his salary. Deasy also feels free to throw in a free sermon on thrift, religion and race. Next, there is Bloom's breakfast ceremony for his wife at the start of Chapter Two. He is shown exchanging currency for products: soap, letters, meat. Later, there is the ceremony of the horse race. The funeral rites of Paddy Dignam. Formal literary debate in a State library. The ritual of a pub lunch. The ceremony of birth. Police and military parades. The procession of the British Governor across Dublin in Chapter Five. The Rabelaisian cortege to Bella's brothel. Set-pieces of death: Stephen's mother, Bloom's father, Rudy. Chaim. There are crazy festivals that act as safety vales to resolidify routine. Finally, there is Leopold Bloom's *xenia* and offer of sanctuary to Stephen Dedalus. This is one of the great 'thanks-but-no-thanks' exchanges in literature. The Ancients elevated *xenia* to the status of a force-field. It was a highly-distinctive ceremony that involved a host forcing ostentatious gifts on a stranger, who often turned out to be a God in disguise ... just like someone giving me this award (insert self-deprecating movement of arms. FX: canned laughter). Every household was measured by its application of *xenia*. Odysseus' palace is besieged by suitors at the start of the *Odyssey*. These unreasonable guests have abused *xenia* so they will ultimately be punished with death. By contrast, Telemachus displays consummate *xenia*. He welcomes Athene, in the guise of Xenos, just as his grandfather, Laertes, later shows hospitality to disguised Odysseus. Odysseus himself experiences different levels of *xenia* on his voyage from each of the Lotus-Eaters, Polyphemus, Circe, Calypso and the Phaeacians. Some are generous ... but often it is only a ruse. Others are downright hostile from the start. Women are always kind to him (cite "Memphis Blues Again").

The Phaeacians suffer the impact of inadvertently offending Poseidon by offering guileless *xenia* [Waiters moved between roundtables replenishing the guest's golden cups with wine from the Hunter Valley]. *Telemachus* is also a eulogy to the late Tom Hallem, my own scramble of the word HAMLET, my Arthur Hallam, known in real life as [NAME REDACTED]. It is also a panegyric to James Joyce, that Telemachus-Penman, to whom I am merely another amanuensis, channelling his oratory, who arose from subjugated Dublin to create a work of art that defeated Ireland's imperial master, killed all the texts in the English canon that besieged him and enabled him to become his own Odysseus, the last hero. *Telemachus* is above all an Australian novel. It is set at a pivotal time in our recent history when Hawke and Keating were dismantling our economic protectionism; AIDS was challenging our prejudices; and multiculturalism was shaping a new national identity. Joyce and Proust – like Furphy and Flaubert – all selected ESSENTIAL TIMES in the past for their major works. Not in the sense of 'big things happening.' But periods when something intrinsic in what Tom Collins called THE ORDER OF THINGS was FLIPPED. *Telemachus* depicts Australia at the crossroads between OLD & NEW. ~~It represents a point in time when Australia tried to stop constructing new racist barriers and started the equivocal, backsliding process of taking them all down. This story can't be told without acknowledging the genocide against our First Nations or the institutionalised racism that continues to this day. William Bardun baulked. EXPLAIN USE OF STRIKETHROUGH AS SYMBOL OF BLACK ERASURE FROM HISTORY. SHIFT BACK TO THEORY.~~ It reanimates the Modernist experiment in a postmodern format. It aims to squeeze the canon past Gibraltar once and for all. I wanted to write a book of 'non-irritable unreaching,' to paraphrase Keats (why have I taken so long to mention him?). It has stood the test of time. Each time I returned to this project after a hiatus, I always felt satisfied with its basic principles. Not that its structure was fully fixed in advance. *Telemachus* is indubitably a FIELD COMPOSITION. But its forced unfolding, allowing the text at times to dictate the nature of arrangement as it went, as in the best poetics, placed content, those minute particulars that compose a sequence of words labelled NARRATIVE, in a state of constant disruption. Marcel Proust (shift to present tense) believes that the work of art beats life (meaning he isn't dead) but the artist isn't free to choose its most extreme moments of manifestation (INV MEM). I have never been sure if I struck the right tone of Keats' Negative Capability over the last 400,000 words. Proust uses the same kind of terminology at the end of *LTR* but he means it like a Kodak plate. I always keep finding new channels. Joyce increased *Ulysses* by one-third in galleys. It makes it almost impossible to stop. This is what MP would call the closed world of the artist in which everything is hard-networked like a prosenchymatic sphere (trace this term with Navigation Search. See also Character List. Insert reference to recurrent citation of Shelley's image of the fading coal.). The next stage of my masterpiece will engage Marcel Proust's life and works directly. I will ma-ma-make a work that performs like a gauze of sweaty, sunken cling-wrap laid upon his smutty vase of stale sensations. A piebald Aladdin's lamp (Ref. *1111101001 Nights*) that illuminates a set of personal tastes masquerading as what he called General Laws (see Derrida, C6). Poetry needs speed. Fast is its dogma. Move INSTANTER, it says. Ginsberg said it was Kerouac who showed us how to do that. I always feel fast when I write but maybe I'm like a slug to its own mind. Spinning cycles of creation get succeeded by laborious phases of undoing like Penelope at her loom each night. That is the necessity of plot when set against lyric. I have never read the works of Italo Calvino but I imagine this is how he writes an ending: 'Well here we are, dear reader, just as the end of my novel predicted, with me winning some big award. Now I can stop at last. And close the LOOP by terminating this work on the word which started it. Thank you for your support, ladies and gentlemen. I feel totally and utter(ing)ly ... spoilt.'" CLOSE QUOTE MARKS.

W. Bard-un raised the gold cup and stared into the disentranced bibs now checking feeds on their cell phones. He smiled.

"There's still time for one or two questions."

Sydney–West Berlin–Shanghai
1984–2020

Appendices

Appendix A
BLOT

Characters

NARRATOR (FEMALE)
BLOT
MOTHER BLOT

[FX: Two figures move through a storm. The woman moves ahead, pushing a shopping trolley. The sound of elevator cables underpins their movements. It ceases when they stop.]

NARRATOR

Darkness. Lightning. We see Mother Blot struggle towards a breach at the foot of Mount Blank. She is smeared with white lineament. It warms her pale flesh. And lights her like a beacon. Darkness, distended in her wake. As if Dawn will never wave its golden puerile on the valleys again. More lightning. But she has disappeared down the shaft. So follow her tight leash back. Her husband staggers, almost tripping, in his efforts to keep pace with her. In one outstretched hand, he grips the frayed leather strap which has always connected them. In the other, he holds up an extinct lamp. Darkness again ... suddenly. Only the sound now. Of his body, rustling against an oversized coat. More lightning. He drops on his knees in the mud. His head flips back. His mouth opens. You can see straight down his throat to his heart: beating like neon. He screams out at Nature. Darkness. The leash vibrates. It begins pulling him along. He's skidding on his gut through the aperture in the clay mountain which is about to snap ... SHUT.

[*FX: Sudden cessation of storm noise by metal door. constant moisture. loud vocals*]

BLOT

It's a long way down.

MOTHER

When you're old.

BLOT

And once you're there, there's no way forward but to crawl.

MOTHER

I've made knee-guards out of moss and lichen, Blot, but it hardly even retards the plum-like bruising. Especially from the last Fall.

BLOT

Yes, that lapse was the worst moment.

MOTHER

Onto the hopelessly inadequate pads!

BLOT

Although they do keep some of the mud at bay.

MOTHER

It's terribly dirty down here, Blot.

BLOT

[*Absent*] Did you bring my duster?

MOTHER

Your duster! Did you ask me to bring your duster?

BLOT

No.

MOTHER

Then how do you expect me to remember it?

BLOT

Intuition?

MOTHER

[*Disgust*] Oh.

BLOT

Would it happen to form part of our Collective Unconscious?

MOTHER

Not that again! Why, Blot, you have hung that notion around my neck like a plinth for the entire period of our out-of-wedlock bonding. Is there no end to your indulgence?

BLOT

None. [*They begin moving*]

MOTHER

Then we'd better go our separate ways while there's still time, still hope. Just cut the cord and we'll part.

BLOT

But we need each other for warmth, Mother!

MOTHER

Even if we fixed ourselves at the genitals, Blot, and tried to induce friction, we couldn't survive the elements for long in our condition.

BLOT

We could build a shelter.

MOTHER

There's nothing to build it with.

BLOT

We could make one out of mud.

MOTHER

There's nothing to build it on.

BLOT

[*Desperate*] We'll have a garden.

MOTHER

How? Haven't you looked around lately? Sand all around us ... out there just the flat sea. And, inland, only the dry, infertile soul/womb.

BLOT

What?

MOTHER

Misogyny!

BLOT

[*Whining*] But I wasn't even smart enough for a Trade!

MOTHER

I knew that when I met you. It's why I chose you.

BLOT

I don't remember at all.

MOTHER

Memories, Blot! I hear about them in your sleep. I store them in a secret compartment under my coat.

BLOT

Tell me.

MOTHER

I was staying at a remote caravan park when I met you.

BLOT

[*Sceptically*] Are you channelling Odysseus again?

MOTHER

Maybe.

BLOT

This isn't the one about a lawn mower?

MOTHER

No. My father had me sent there until it was TIME. I was feeding the carp when the weeds parted for a moment and I saw your tow truck grinding down the highway. You gave me green felt for my glory box then we sat in fold-up chairs under the annex and drank. You were beautiful that night when the lake storms blew. And you told such marvellous stories. When I lay in bed and whistled, the dogs made a network of ears stretching between my mouth and your head. And they howled, didn't they, what, like blunted wind chimes, one after the other, diminishing, until only the neighbour's voice could be heard: [*Voice of an old crone*] "I am alive," she said. "I-AM-A-LIVE." [*Laughing softly*]

BLOT

Was that really us, Mother?

MOTHER

Does it matter?

BLOT

I guess not. Go on.

MOTHER

All I brought back was that bag full of broken biscuits ... that was all ... only that and the coat on my back ... though it was already stabbed through in a hundred places. And stiff as our old toes with grime.

BLOT

[*Glee*] I remember. As stiff as ... as stiff as ... [*Pause. Stops. Vacant*] I don't know—

MOTHER

[*Wistful*] Does everything slip past your fingers nowadays?

BLOT

[*Similarly wistful*] There's still a speck of feeling, Mother. I'm mainly inanimate, true. Soon, I'll be nothing at all, I know that. But there's still a little boy inside me, I can just feel him, turning away from a serviceman's gaze at the urinal. [*Mother begins laughing*] What are you laughing at?

MOTHER

[*Spluttering*] Nothing. It's involuntary. Like drooling.

BLOT

That's all very well for you to say but what is there about our current predicament that could warrant even one ironic grimace?

MOTHER

Look for yourself, man!

BLOT

I'm looking, I'm looking! But I haven't seen any sign that we aren't totally deluged. Where's the sky? The sun? And why are we soaking?

MOTHER

It's not for you or I to question the great workings of the Beast. All that we can do now is just go on. As if into some endless Dantean spiral, we had been thrown.

BLOT

How?

[*FX: Jungle. Dragging him*]

MOTHER

On our bellies if necessary. Come closer. Hold on to me. I'll forge a path through the wilderness.

BLOT

Palms are lashing my face, Mother!

MOTHER

They're roots.

BLOT

Mosquitoes are ripping me!

MOTHER

Its worms.

BLOT

We've been nailed to the sky!

MOTHER

We're crawling on our hands and knees through the mud miles under the Earth.

BLOT

I can't go on.

[*FX: Distant cyclone*]

MOTHER

You've got to.

BLOT

I can't.

MOTHER

Surely you can discern its mounting fury?

BLOT

[*Emphatic*] I can't feel nothing.

MOTHER

Haven't you shuddered a little at least?

BLOT

Not since the light perished!

MOTHER

Not even from the stench?

BLOT

I thought it was me! I got used to it! [*Hopeful*] Perhaps it's coming to reward us!

MOTHER

Don't be ridiculous. You know very well there's absolutely no chance of that.

BLOT

Then perhaps it only wants one of us. Perhaps it likes the other one.

MOTHER

What?

BLOT

[*Bright idea*] I could kill you, leave you here as a sacrifice and go on alone.

MOTHER

Kill me! With what?

BLOT

My bare hands if necessary.

MOTHER

You couldn't even shake a cocktail with those.

[*FX: Storm intensifies*]

Listen. It's getting closer.

BLOT

What is it?

MOTHER

Probably the Chorus.

BLOT

What?

MOTHER

[*Screeches*] The Chorus!

BLOT

Is it time to put my eyes out?

MOTHER

Not yet!

BLOT

But it might not want them as eyes per se. It could use them as plugs.
[*He starts trying to pluck out his eyeballs*]

MOTHER

I told you to wait.

BLOT

What for? Some sign? I can't see anything anyway. And I don't believe a single thing I'm saying. Where are we? Is it Heaven? Are we floating? Light the Lamp!

[*FX: Sound of lamp ignition*]

MOTHER

Put that out, Blot!

BLOT

But I can see! [*Blot starts standing*]

MOTHER

You don't want to.

BLOT

It's warm.

MOTHER

Put it out, I tell you!

BLOT

[*Swinging wildly*] Are there any markings on the walls?

MOTHER

[*Angry*] No.

BLOT

Nothing familiar?

MOTHER

Nothing.

BLOT

Not even Orpheus?

MOTHER

No.

BLOT

But they told me to come up at him from beneath.

MOTHER

He's not here, I tell you.

BLOT

What about Atlantis?

MOTHER

That's not here either.

BLOT

And the dark tower?

MOTHER

We're already inside!

BLOT

In that case ... extinguish the lamp!

[*FX: Snuffed lamp. Blot sinks to the ground*]

MOTHER

That's better. I just hope there's still time for us to escape. Get up, Blot.

BLOT

Why?

MOTHER

At least then we won't be crawling through this cess like wounded animals.

BLOT

But I'm afraid to leave the mud!

MOTHER

[*Pulling him up*] Get up!

BLOT

Leave me alone!

MOTHER

You'll be crushed!

BLOT

But it's my natural habitat!

MOTHER

Don't be ridiculous.

BLOT

I don't want to go on!

MOTHER

You've got to. It's too late now for scruples! I can hear it coming. Hide.

BLOT

But there's nowhere to conceal ourselves.

MOTHER

Try to look like an inanimate object! It's our only chance.

[*FX: Cyclone breaks into enclosed space*]

NARRATOR

I was clay. Water. I washed out of the murky shallows onto the bank but I could not walk yet. I evolved. Grew. But I was still but an ear in the mud. I could divine nothing, not even myself, as yet. I huddled into a corner of my cell waiting for life. From this enclosed position, no sight; only the lights that are encoded behind the eye. Only their fireworks. And only the faint smell of Self. Only this parchment of Being. Only this and the foul taste infecting my mouth. That was all. Except for the eyeball veering up at "in-on-me" until it filled up my hole. How did I breathe? By mouthpiece. How did I feed? By suck. I could have remained in that state forever if I'd wanted. But my soul was on fire. I was like a sheet of newspaper burning from the centre to the stark circumference. In that box. Don't ask me how long I was in there. I got to like it after a while. It seemed like a veritable lack. But it was a rich place.

[*FX: Dusting themselves down*]

MOTHER

Good. It's gone. Get up, Blot.

BLOT

[*Plaintive*] Can't we stay like this forever?

MOTHER

No.

BLOT

[*Whines*] But I like it like this.

MOTHER

Is that meant to move me?

BLOT

[*Begs*] Let's stay here in silence like mounds!

MOTHER

[*Firm*] We can't.

BLOT

Why? Nobody will find us. And, besides, even if I was striding through Eden in a gold lame suit, I'd only ever be visible as a dour lack in the brilliant scenery.

MOTHER

Oh come on, Blot. [*Dragging him. He resists*] What are you waiting for now?

BLOT

The muzak!

MOTHER

[*Disparaging*] It won't come.

BLOT

Are you sure?

MOTHER

[*Shrill*] It won't come, I tell you!

BLOT

In that case ... [*Moving. Muzak begins*] there!

MOTHER

[*Angry*] Alright. Can we go now? [*Pause*] Wretched tune!

BLOT

I find it quite uplifting.

MOTHER

[*Sudden weakness*] But is it "our" song? [*Stops*]

BLOT

[*Shock*] Sentimentality, Mother!

MOTHER

[*Apologetic spurt*] I'm its slave!

BLOT

[*Gushing*] We both are. We've been locked away with it... every night... in our dank hovel.

MOTHER

We were locked in there together, Blot.

BLOT

From an early age.

MOTHER

Our parents were responsible.

BLOT

I used to beg Mother not to die, Mother, because then there'd be no one. Then, all of a sudden, there was you! I'm glad I was with you.

MOTHER

Not you now! [*Stops*]

BLOT

But I love you.

MOTHER

I love you.

BLOT

Impossible.

MOTHER

But true. [*Moving*].

BLOT

Remember when you left me for another man?

MOTHER

I do.

BLOT

I was devastated.

MOTHER

But I always came back.

BLOT

You did. [*Pause*] And then I left you.

MOTHER

You did. [*Pause*] Sometimes I think you only won me back just to dump me.

BLOT

But I always returned.

MOTHER

Yes. You returned again like a rank odour. We faced ruin together.

BLOT

[*Stops*] It was Destiny, Mother.

MOTHER

Or fear.

BLOT

[*Huffing*] Whatever it was … does it really matter?

MOTHER

No. Even Romance is still geared to closure.

BLOT

That's right, Mother. [*Pause*] Psalms 146:4.

MOTHER

[*Sardonic*] But your thoughts perished long ago.

BLOT

It was a ruse! Behind the mask … behind the mask, I was vital!

MOTHER

That's a delusion, Blot. Or just plain vanity. Statements like that. You're turning into jelly. Violence was your only grasp at even mediocrity.

[*FX: Background of outback pub.*]

BLOT

[*Spluttering*] But I could expectorate ... drink ... squeeze the barmaid's tits ... vomit ... and wet myself ... all at the same time. All without leaving this stool!

MOTHER

I know, Blot. I know. I was that barmaid!

BLOT

[*Stops*] You?

MOTHER

Yes.

BLOT

But she was some big-nosed country girl.

MOTHER

That was me, silly!

BLOT

[*Shrugs*] I don't remember at all.

MOTHER

Try. Fancy-dress balls. With orchestras. And breeding.

BLOT

Flies filling your orifices.

MOTHER

And the cool, brown sound of cicadas.

BLOT

Always sunstroke in summer.

MOTHER

In Winter, arthriticky.

BLOT

And no in-between.

[*FX: Farmyard slowly giving way to tempest. Almost singing the rhymes*]

BLOT

Father in the workshed shunting nails.

MOTHER

Mumma on the haystack, shifting bails.

BLOT

Revvin' up the engine of the old Ford ute.

MOTHER

Goin' out in a brand-new second-hand suit. [*Stops*]

BLOT

Ah, evil days, Mother. Evil times. But they're gone now ... gone ... all erased. [*Turns to her*] I suppose we're better off without them.

MOTHER

Yes. But they were "times," Blot. However bleak. "Times."

BLOT

[*Frank*] I really don't remember.

MOTHER

Do you recall our son?

BLOT

What?

MOTHER

Cabel! You left him in a shopping trolley.

BLOT

[*Inquisitive*] Does that mean you eat it?

MOTHER

[*Disgust*] Oh.

BLOT

[*Quizzical*] Is it something you sell?

MOTHER

[*Louder*] So you do remember!

BLOT

[*Shrieks*] I don't know nothing.

[*FX: Storm in Eden. Animal screams. The rib. A crisp apple bitten. Expulsion*]

NARRATOR

Thunder slogged that night. Rain streamed down my face like purified piss. God waded into the Garden, moulded us into one entity and named me. I was now Adam. Surrounded by a wall with no way in, no way out (not even Jesus yet) nothing but sheer barrier. [*Pause. Anger*] No part of me was allowed to remain uncatalogued, undisclosed. My chest was ripped open in dreams. When I woke up next morning, Eve was slumbering in the slot between my ribs. A taboo was founded. Next thing you know, I was naked. So we covered ourselves with crime. We were ejected. A place to which we have never returned. We wandered like the Nile. But, like the Hydra, I was not allowed to die. Each time that they decapitated me, two fresh heads sprang out of the bloody gush like birth. They hover over my head now like vultures. I don't know how to pledge obedience. Or to whom. [*Pause*] I had no choice at all but to go on. [*Back in the mud. Inert*]

MOTHER

It's swept through our past, Blot. We can sneak out the back while it's gone.

BLOT

[*Obstinate*] Is that out only option?

MOTHER

Can you think of something better?

BLOT

We could ... [*FX: Ignition*] light the lamp!

MOTHER

[*Sardonic*] Is that it?

BLOT

[*Sheepish*] Yep.

MOTHER

Put out that light.

BLOT

Extinguish the Lamp?

MOTHER

Yes.

BLOT

OK.

[*FX: Snuffed*]

MOTHER

That's better. [*Pause*] Let's go. [*Moving*]

BLOT

[*Pause*] But this is awful.

MOTHER

Don't think about it. Just go on groping your way through the narrative. [*Stops*]

BLOT

Couldn't we just wait out here in absolute darkness, huddled on the surface like mounds?

MOTHER

No.

BLOT

[*Raising head*] But the sky is only one inch above our brows, Mother.

MOTHER

Let's scurry down this shaft.

[FX: Pulling him along. She yells back. He yells ahead]

BLOT

But where to?

MOTHER

Metonymy!

BLOT

What's that?

MOTHER

The last place.
[*They struggle into tight hole. Continuous contraction. Her ahead. Him behind*]

BLOT

[*Between surges at the aperture*] But aren't we there already? Or haven't we just been? Are we going around in circles? I can hardly move my head now.

MOTHER

It's the brace.

BLOT

What?

MOTHER

The brace! It's been there the whole time.

BLOT

But I've never noticed it before.

MOTHER

Think: it's made out of wire.

BLOT

Do they also call it the wedding ring?

MOTHER

Yes.

BLOT

Then soon we'll be crawling along on our bellies like snakes.

MOTHER

We're doing that already.

BLOT

What'll we do when we reach the face?

MOTHER

Start picking our way towards—

BLOT

[*Interrupts*] Towards what?

MOTHER

[*Irritated*] Just towards. Think of yourself as Antigone.

BLOT

So is it Thebes?

MOTHER

Don't even try to work out where we are ... where we've been ... or where we're going anymore. Just dig.

[*FX: She begins digging.*]

BLOT

But I don't have anything to dig with.

MOTHER

Use your fingers.

BLOT

Are you joking?

MOTHER

Alright ... your teeth.

BLOT

What?

MOTHER

Gum it!

[FX: Wet digging. Blot struggles to chew.]

BLOT

[*Whining*] I can't get it into my mouth.

MOTHER

Then dissolve it in bile.

BLOT

The Chinese ate mud.

MOTHER

It's why Beckett gave out biscuits.

BLOT

[*Surprised*] Look! A tiny crack of light!

MOTHER

Dig faster.

BLOT

Do you think we're being born?

MOTHER

Don't be ridiculous.

BLOT

This leash could be our cord. Where does it go from here?

MOTHER

Out there.

BLOT

Follow it. [*Pulling*]

MOTHER

I can't.

BLOT

Use this bar.

[*FX: Forcing open orifice with crow-bar.*]

Good. Now wedge it into the gap. What can you see?

MOTHER

I think it's an eye.

BLOT

[*Sentimental*] It must be Mother!

MOTHER

Impossible!

BLOT

Could they have turned her inside-out?

MOTHER

I don't know. But I don't like the look of it at all. Let's stay in here.

BLOT

Like inanimate objects?

MOTHER

No. I've told you before ... that's impossible. We'll have go back. They're opening it up.

[*FX: Retreating.*]

BLOT

Which way now, Mother?

MOTHER

The rear ... to the rear!

BLOT

Where?

MOTHER

The arse!

BLOT

Are we germs?

MOTHER

Just keep working your way up the anus.

BLOT

But it's sucking me out!

MOTHER

Hold on.

BLOT

I can't.

[*FX: Birth*]

NARRATOR

I was born (one of twins) to these two people. Look at the photograph. I'm holding it up against the inside of my cage. It's all I have left. They pinned it onto my skirt when they left the car park. My father like a burnt-out wick. All you can make of him is a thin ribbon of cigarette smoke rising in front of his shiny steel teeth. He died on the end of the leash. Unmourned. My Mother was a quiet woman, largely inexpressive, except in front of the Form Guide. The midwife cut me loose from my dead brother and displayed me through the dark bedroom at Father. Then I felt the flash of my first camera. The sulphur scarred my stomach with a white constellation. It tingled my lack. And marked me forever like a braille brand. Like his tiller-hand, scarred with melanomas. He picked me up with it and held me aloft. [*Ironic*] Then he lowered me onto Mother's lap, re-loaded the box camera and started the timer. He moved in, rent his shoulders and stuck out his chin. His chest was stiff as if with rubber membrane wound. I can still perceive his presence. The saddest man on Earth, my father, hollow with lies. His eyes like pools of petrol. His body sprinkled with cinnamon and rust. Glowing like apricots.

[*FX: Sulphur flash. Mud. Pulling*]

BLOT

What was that? [*Pause*] Where am I? [*Pause*] Help me! I'm blind, Mother!

MOTHER

Follow my voice.

BLOT

Alright.

[*They scurry on*]

MOTHER

Are you still back there?

BLOT

Yes. Go on. [*Pause*] Are you leading me to the cliff, Edgar? [*Pause*] Light the lamp, Mother.

MOTHER

Surely that's futile in your current predicament.

BLOT

All the more poignant, Mother. All the more pathos with me in this condition. [*Pause*] Like blind Oedipus! [*Irritable*] What are you poking me with?

MOTHER

A stick.

BLOT

Well, stop. [*Pause*] Who are you, anyway? Following me around like a curse.

MOTHER

I'm your wife.

BLOT

What?

MOTHER

There's no time now to explain. Just cut the rope and we'll part.

BLOT

Not that again!

MOTHER

It's always at the back of my mind.

BLOT

Don't go!

MOTHER

Why not?

BLOT

Because I love you!

MOTHER

I love you!

BLOT

Then let's stay together!

MOTHER

No, let's feel it at a distance.

[FX: Cutting rope. Springing apart. He moves off. Groping through tunnel along walls]

BLOT

If that's the way you feel ... then goodbye, Mother! I can't say it hasn't been great. Great while it lasted. [*Ejaculates*] The best thing I've ever had, frankly. The best thing I've seen. [*Wistful*] But it had to end sometime. Yes, it had to end sometime just like anything. [*Pause. False bravado*] Free at last! In my dotage, true. But, nonetheless, liberated. Why all I need to do now is to update my 'notions'! How can I do that? I guess just invert them! Alley... upp! [*He tries to invert himself. Collapses down a hole. Lands in a pool of muddy water*] Help! [*Underwater*] I'm drowning! [*Gurgling*] Is anybody out there? [*He drops beneath the surface. Mother suddenly splashes at the edges of the lake*]

MOTHER

Here I come! [*She swims towards him*] Blot! Where are you? [*Underwater search*] Are you down there, pussy? [*She sinks and re-emerges*] There you are! [*She drags him towards shore*] I've got you. [*Louder*] Just hold on, dear. We've almost reached the bank. [*Their voices become more distant as if his spirit is leaving the scene. She shakes him. No response*] Blot! [*Listens. Silence*] no breathe. [*Pause*] nothing! [*Suddenly plaintive. Shaking him*] don't leave me, Blot! There's still the hard part of the road ahead, remember? Blot!? [*Pause*] gone. [*Wistful*] and I, helpless to prevent it. [*Grabbing him. Frantic*] I'll do whatever you want, Blot, just don't leave me. [*Melodramatic*] Too late! Alone. Alone ... and with the dead! God, I feel so naked. I wish I had something to put on. His coat! That'll keep me warm. [*Takes coat off Blot and wraps it around herself*] I feel worse with it on. [*Strips it off. Blot moans*]

BLOT

[*Weak. Almost inaudible*] Where am I?

MOTHER

[*Loud*] Blot ... you're alive! [*Grabbing him*] Let me help you up. [*Fussing*] Are you alright? What was it like? Was there Jesus? Thank God, I'm not alone just dependent. [*Passionate*] Let me warm you. [*Covers them both with cloak*]

BLOT

Where are we?

MOTHER

Deeper than before.

BLOT

Who are we?

MOTHER

Don't you know?

BLOT

The last thing I remember was a woman's lips closing over my mouth. I received her warm sweet breath like a bath. [*Bathos*] Oh, if only she could have blown hard enough, for long enough, the flap would have lifted back enough for us both to glimpse Eden.

MOTHER

Forget the epiphany, Blot. Just crawl.

BLOT

I can't.

MOTHER

You've got to.

BLOT

It isn't necessary, Mother. Soon sanctuary will be imposed.

MOTHER

What?

BLOT

Just wait for Prometheus.

MOTHER

Who?

BLOT

The Titan!

MOTHER

I don't understand!
[*He rises from the ground*]

BLOT

Wife, we can stand here in sunlight. Help me up.
[*They get louder*]

MOTHER

Let go of me.

BLOT

We need not crawl.

MOTHER

Are you mad?

BLOT

Light the lamp! [*Ignition*] Dawn, Mother!

MOTHER

Stop it, Blot. What will we do when it comes?

BLOT

It'll never come.

MOTHER

But I can smell it. I can hear it!

BLOT

It's good for you.

MOTHER

I can feel it.

BLOT

It's me.

MOTHER

No, it's not. It's an ... Other.

BLOT

Trust me.

MOTHER

I don't.

BLOT

Try.

MOTHER

It's impossible.

BLOT

Perhaps if you intone the word 'faith' over and over in your mind you can convince yourself.

MOTHER

Oh, where are we? And how will we ever escape?

NARRATOR

[*Breathless*] She struggles to pull him. He resists. They pirouette until the leash becomes hopelessly tangled. They are bound together. Their faces press. Slowly they are strangled. Suddenly, they kiss. The text capitulates to "halt." [*Pause*] But this was only their closure. I went on alone.

[*FX: Fast with related sound effects.*]

To recapitulate: I was born. I strangled my brother at birth. They named me Cabelle for that. Black insects shook in the sulphurous air. I grew. But I was held down in murk like some helpless poddy. I mainlined. Helen of Troy came down. Her languorous gaze burst my eyeballs. Tears streamed down my face. I was taken by the succubus in dreams. Her kisses gashed my mouth. I gulped at her swirling river. All that is not Helen is nothingness. And the Helen that I see is but an apparition. I am screwed into her soil like some fast-fallen rocket. I wish I was mist. Then I could slip back to earth like a shiny feather. And be laid on Space. To slowly extinguish the dwindling lamp. And be slowly extinguished myself by dawn.

[FX: A candle is snuffed.]

TEXTUAL SYNOPSIS

Blot was the pilot for a popular TV sitcom, *The (incontinence) Pad*, about two ageing hippies (HH-1970 & KLUG-MAN) sharing an apartment in Manhattan. The narrator, Cabelle Blot (feminised combination of Cane and Abel), is the hostess of a popular gameshow and the only offspring of Blot and Mother Blot. The play is her representation of her parents' union as well as her own reconstruction of her progress from foetus to orphan.

The play begins in a typical Gothic setting of nocturnal, alpine tempest outside the village of Testy on the Lull. Its unwitting heroes, who have been driven relentlessly through extrinsic space in their efforts to maintain some semblance of dignity, are finally flung down a wet mine shaft: a standard Romantic device to promote dialogue with existential concepts. Inside subterranean vaults, they are forced down ever-reductive channels of memory. Fragments of the past (both personal and cultural) clamber to attach themselves by allusion and make themselves heard. Yet they all wither in the half-light farce of the Blot's undisclosed quest, which is a simultaneous drive towards/against death that ends with a parody of epiphany (see Walter Pater).

Cabelle connects her existence to epic religious and classical images of creation, evolution, displacement, expulsion and endurance, only to be thwarted in every effort to find inclusion in a Master Narrative. She provokes a state of continual crisis in which she tries to punish or separate her parents, only to be compelled to consistently reunite them. The final irony of the play is that they are allowed to end while she must go on alone. This is her inheritance. Thus, *Blot* is halted as a narrative but never closed.

***Blot* exploits the power of the radio-play to shift between exotic locations and different eras using sound to induce disorienting spatial and temporal incongruities.**

Over its mechanical course towards closure, the narrative of *Blot* is reduced to a sequence of dead-end feints at meaning which leave a morass of mal-meanings in their wake. What is left out of this process is style. Yet some semblance of human nobility in the face of cosmic bathos remains nonetheless. Representing the cruel paradoxes of the human condition with a small degree of pathos. That is the intention of *Blot*.

PRODUCTION NOTES (1998)

Blot will be an all-digital production – it will remain, as it were, in the 'digital domain' for the entire post-production stage.

We envisage the bulk of the recording will be done on location straight onto DAT; possibly with some studio recording where appropriate. Studio recording will be to DAT or direct to disk. Sound effects play a crucial part in creating the shifts in landscape and atmosphere during the course of the play. Wherever possible, incidental sounds and ambient effects will be recorded on location.

The prevailing ambience is a damp and muddy soundscape maintained by a mixture of industrial and natural sounds. The movement of the Blots throughout the narrative is characterised by a mechanical pulley (metal on metal). The positioning of the narrator within the play is achieved by a contrasting lack of atmosphere (dead room, close mic).

The location of microphones in relation to the characters is crucial in creating an aural image of the Blots' journey through a series of artificial landscapes. The listener maintains a definite proximity to the characters, hearing not only their voices but also their physical movements.

The characters possess contrasting vocal styles. While the Blots are cranked up to a hysterical state of total self-consciousness about the events imposed upon them and their status as textual contrivance, their daughter's narrative delivery is controlled and intense.

The Blots' journey through the narrative and final release from it is experienced by the listener through the Blot's physical (aural) withdrawal from the sound image. The fate of the narrator, on the other hand, is undetermined and the aural space which she occupies remains constant throughout the play.

Psycho-acoustics are important in the technical production. Certain frequencies will be manipulated to give a surround-effect on both AM and FM broadcasts. In stereo, lateralisation and localisation techniques will be employed to further enhance the audio image.

The use of sound beyond the voices of the characters supports the sensation of the narrative (as well as just the text itself), creating an environment of impossible realities in the imagination of the listener. This mood is a constantly-changing yet ever-present, backdrop to the action or inaction of the characters.

The overall effect is of an intrinsically-related sound piece running concurrent to the narrative: at times, subverting the listener's expectations; at times, reinforcing them.

Appendix B
STRINE TRANSLATIONS

EXTRACT 1 (p. 780)

"Where's Eyes & Ears," asks Ocker.

"He went to the TAB," replies Chindrip.

"Did he back Black Knight?"

"No. Chagemar each way."

"That'll barely cover his outgoings."

"Yes. He won't be shouting the bar tonight."

"Get him back here now."

Chindrip asked me to return to the bar pronto. Ocker signalled for me to come up with his middle finger, bent like an articulated bow. I took off towards his booth, where he was working for the Cause with form guide, pencil and ledger. I slid into the channel either side of his henchmen, Scatt and Chindrip.

"Who are they," asked Ocker gesticulating a finger at the newcomers on the kerb. "They look like two Federal agents."

"No," I replied.

"Coveys from Bush then?"

"Vets, I reckon."

"This is not a game of who-the-fuck," says Ocker (snarling). "Your job is Eisenears.

Get down there and find out!"

"I'd lay odds they're Vietnamers from their countenance and talk."

"They were treated most shabbily," says Ocker shaking his nog. "But then all our Diggers get crapped on from a great height back home."

"They become mere ghosts in the corpus," says Leperis Bloom, entering the conversation.

"What the hell do you mean by that," I thundered in reply.

I have not got a clue what Bloom is going on about half the time. I am just an average bloke. He got bitten by the yak-yak bug. Dry blow bonkers.

"People just want them to disappear so they can forget the whole damn show."

"Persona non grata," continues Blue.

"Bunch of no names," adds I.

"Emasculated," blows Ock.

"Got their testicles snipped," I drivels.

"Yes. Not men anymore," goads Ockerbeck.

"No men," adds LB.

"Send them down two beers," says Ocker dropping a ten-dollar note on the counter. "Sit down and talk to them. Find out the facts. They could be police informants. Or they might just want a sandwich. Who knows?

I sidled up behind them. The barmaid passed. She reduced the air conditioning.

"A gift from my boss, Ocker," I said, sitting down on my posterior and places the bottles of beer in our midst. "Louder is my name. ALF LOUDER." [NOTE – this is a pseudonym.]

We shook. They swivelled towards Ocker. He raised his glass.

"Thanks mate," says A.

"Don't mention it," says I.

"Did your boss have a big win on the Cup," insinuates his mate. I ignore him.

"What are your names," I asked.

Null and Void, one replied. These were ludicrous names but I let it pass. It was none of my business. No name, no pack drill. Don't make excuses. Never ever give nothing away that you don't have to, advises Ocker. So, I just scratched my testicles gently. Summoned some mucus. Lit a fresh cigarette. And we all got stuck into the grog.

"Did you go to the Grand Final," I asked pointing at the television screen.

"I didn't go," said NULL. "I live in the Philippines."

NULL = DON. VOID = TOM in this short piece by Samuel Beckett.

"However, I saw it on television," added VOID.

"The Sea Eagles got ripped off," says I. "The referee and touch judges must have got sacks full of sandwiches in my opinion. The Eagles had cause for sour grapes."

Ah-hah, I deduced like Sherlock Holmes. That man must think I'm a total deadhead. Because the Sea Eagles did NOT play in n the Grand Final this year! The Bulldogs and the Eels played! This aroused my suspicions. Maybe they are nothing better than a couple of undercover policemen trying to find out information or solicit monies. The police can have a large appetite. A large plate of chips with a rare serving of jumbuck, as Plod says. It's all so cosy. Why don't we all come tumbling downhill like Jack and Jill, or kiss some girls like Georgy Porgy? There's just no word for it. I ought to piss the whole lot of them off. I could get a semi-decent job like Joe Hynes. He's always flush from debt collecting for old Moses Herzog. Gu & Elizabeth are both debtors. SD and TOM are both in their debt. I could make them repay their debts with the assistance of Ocker's henchmen.

"When I left Sydney," he recollected, "we still had pence, shillings and pounds. Imperial currency. Not this decimal currency."

"Really?"

"Fact."

"How long have you been gone?" I asked.

"Twenty years," he replied.

"Where have you lived in the interim."

"Every two-up school from Darwin to the 'Loo," he replied laughing.[188]

Leopold Bloom joins our group and commences mouthing off, working himself into a total blather. Nobody can understand him, let alone interdict.

EXTRACT 2 (p. 787)

"Now there's a lowdown dog to be sure," says Ocker loudly. "John Stone's new puppet."

An uncomfortable shuffling in seats followed. It was clear that neither party would yield an inch to compromise. They butted gruffly.

"My Colonial Oath," Ocker continued. "That Accord will ruin the ALP. Old George Reid has finally won. Took eighty years. But he's beaten Deakin and the Set."

Cornwall replied to the Captain with words to the effect that something had to be done to repair the Australian economy after decades of complacency had brought the nation

---

188 Note: reference to "The Bastard from the Bush."

to the brink of ruin and it was a credit to the trade union movement that it had seized the initiative with the incoming Labor government.

"Kelty's the brains behind that whole operation," replies the Captain of the Push. "He's plying another trade entirely."

Beer spilled over the brim of fresh schooners that Eyesenears now laid before the MEN.

"All those barstards are drier than my bluddy throat," he concluded, sculling fiercely then slamming down a dead glass. The television screen scrolled through images of Hawke, Murphy, Frank Costigan and Kerry Packer in quick succession.

"Hawke cut off Costigan's testicles to protect [REDACTED]," says Ocker. "And to take care of his new mate [REDACTED]."

"Protected species," replied Cornwall to allay.

"Wiped his arse on the NCA," nodded Afferbeck.

"That's why the government leaked the case summaries."

"McWilliam swallowed the whole document."

"Would have been made very tasty for him," added VOID.

"Goanna must've splashed on a great big blob of his special sauce."

"It was [REDACTED] what dropped them all in shit," says Ocker.

"ATO gavelled the leap."

"Beames backed him."

"Bored a new hole up Molland in the private jet."

"Goanna's share would have been substantial," says VOID. "Just from weeding the kick."

"That's one good punt for the Squirrel," I replied.

"Well, it's certainly a level of remuneration that would have motivated me," added Bloom. "What about you, gentlemen?"

"Would I dong a bloody copper if I caught the cunt alone?" I retorted vociferously using a rhetorical question to signify my intent. Ocker nodded agreement at this sentiment. Sweet silence ensued. He examined large slow bubbles as they expired in the dregs of his beer glass. Cunts, he thought.

"Lockyer, Beames and Brian bloody Maher," he said mawkishly. "They're all in prison now."

"Inhabiting the Bali suite where they give blowjobs," agreed VOID.

"One hundred condoms of hash oil," exclaimed Tom Cornwall. "That was the run. Customs sent it straight to the bond store. Nobody even touched it at the airport."

"Fed poked his pen into the package," adds Orc. "Got an eyeful of cannabis resin."

Ocker chuckled hard-heartily. Tom Cornwall and Eyesnears joined him but his firend, Eric Killion, observed them as if deaf, neither partaking or drinking.

"So who executed Coote," demanded Ocker loudly.

"We'll find out at the Inquest," replied Eyesnears showing faith in the justice system.

"Carver is responsible, I believe."

"No. It was Greedy that did it. They brought him up from Melbourne. HE got a one-way ticket to Manila at the end."

"No way. Ten bucks says it was a Sydney shooter."

"Where else could he get the cash to open the Aussie Bar in Manila?"

"Well, if you're talking about Dennis Smith," interrupts VOID, "then he'll want to get that cash back out quickly."

"Before Marcos falls," aids NULL.

"Correct," nods VOID. "He doesn't have long. May be less than a year."

"I was told that Squirrel was the client," interdicts Eye.

"Got nothing to do with Squirrel."

"Pro-Vital's more his kind of deal."

"A jaffa," replies Ocker. "Absolute peach."

"Like [REDACTED]."

"[REDACTED]'s super fund, they call it."

"[REDACTED] branch was behind that job. [REDACTED] provided the petrol and matches. Now that's New Labor for you!"

"Still flinging a few hot-dogs at [REDACTED], they say. He knows the meaning of the word, 'mate.' Stood up for Old [REDACTED]. No craven type. By the same token, I would not give the new Member for Sydney a face full of cum. They were very cunning to send him off to Canberra where he wouldn't cause more strife."

"Things will get done Sydney-style down there from now on."

Mutual amusement was registered. A feeling of camaraderie infused the participants. Each other, they realised, was not so different. Warm silence descended. They imbibed heartily. Ocker made a structural adjustment to his scrotum.

"When is this election campaign going to end," he asks. "I have seen enough of the Prime Minister's tears to last me a lifetime."

"He's taking the Kirribilli showboat across Sydney Harbour next week for his campaign launch at the Sydney Opera House," says VOID.

"He'd better watch out. The CIA might sink his barge like the Kuttabul," adds Cornwall.

"Another Coup," nodded Ocker.

The assembly bowed sagely at this point, raised their glasses and toasted both the fallen Prime Minister and those brave deluded japs still canned upon the floor of Sydney

Harbour. At this point, Ocker arises from his booth to slash. His bodyguards follow. This enables Tom Cornwall some intimate time to engage his target directly.

"Back to business Don," he says. "We'd like you to coordinate our pout of the Philippines. We need an experienced hand. Someone who can work all over Asia."

"It shouldn't be too hard to get access to good intelligence via Thailand."

"Agreed. Hanoi is totally focused on China at present."

"Deng really stuffed an elephant fart down Le Duan's toilet."

"That little war was a masterstroke. Deng showed the world that China was prepared to sacrifice a whole army to support Pol Pot. Regardless of human cost."

"Life's cheap for communists."

EXTRACT 3 (p. 805)

"Can't a Jew love his country just like the next fellow," asks John Wyse Nolan near the end of the Citizen episode. It is a manufactured question by the author, too basic as a narrative 'lead' for such a natural dramatist as Joyce.

"I've got no problem to mention with Jews," answers Ocker. "Monash himself was Jewish."

"Ten thousand Jews fought for Australia," argues Tom Cornwall.

"There's no such place mate," replies Ock. "Those blokes all died for England like headless chooks. Lang was the first bloke that ever stood up to Westminister. That's why they sent out Niemeyer. The FIX was IN."

"I feel like the new migration policy has done some good," replies NULL politely.

"Let's see what happens when we tell them to go shoot Indonesians up in Darwin. I bet they'll be arms all akimbo again like Saigon."

"We owe sanctuary to the good people of South Vietnam," says Tom Cornwall bold-like. "They stood up to Communism. They worked with us. They believed in us. WE LET THEM DOWN! You wouldn't talk so much nonsense if you'd gone and fought in Vietnam and seen firsthand what we did to their country instead of indulging in ... armchair orations."

Appendix C
CHARACTER LIST (abridged)

Mel, Rachel & Xavier – dedicants. Also, note the Late David McComb.

Flaubert – dilettante and pornographer. Author of *Dictionary of Received Ideas* (Fr. *Le Dictionnaire des idées reçues*), published in 1911–13 from notes compiled by the author in the 1870s. Often paired with *Le Sottisier* (Eng. *Howlers*), a collection of stupid quotes from famous authors.

First Voice – unidentified narrator who describes the recording of *Under Milkwood*, BBC Studios, 25 January 1954. Dylan Thomas has dead for three months.

Meillon & Burton – narrators (Australian, Welsh respectively). Actors famous for their powers of oratory.

Sophos, Andy, Dick, Dikaiosynē, Andreia, Theo, Ari, Spiros, Chris – interchangeable names applied to Attic youths in C2.

Ralph, Tom, Rhino, Ewan, Madge, Fishpump (Alt. Fish Pump), Toe Cutter – residents of Beta House. Later, most of them appear at the lunchtime strip show, EA Times opening and Feedtime performance at Frenchs. They proceed to either the tunnels or the bridge in C10.

L. (Lester) Byron – equivalent of Elpenor. Also, the swimmer who Mulligan saved. He falls at 32 feet per second vertically, as per Joyce's physics formula, on Night A at Beta House in C2.

Blot & Mother Blot – characters in eponymous radio play (see Appendix A). This work has also been known as "Blot O'Blot Landscape" and "Testy on the Lull."

Tom Hallem – a painter. One version of Telemachus. See Saussure (C6) for his true identity. His family name derives from Arthur Hallam, subject of Tennyson's *In Memoriam A.H.H.* His name is a broken anagram of Prince Hamlet. The surplus letter is L. In alchemy, 'L' stands for decomposition. He was variously Dave Paine, David Cane, Tom Paine and Tim Hallem during drafting of this work.

Elizabeth Archer – Athena figure. Leading character in Henry James' novel, *The Portrait of a Lady*. Compare and contrast. Compose a sequel about her later life in the mode of *Wide Sargasso Sea*.

Leon Daniel – a dentist. Husband of Elizabeth Archer.

Rachel Daniel – daughter of Elizabeth Archer and Tom Hallem. See C7 F/N.

Prosenchyma – an otiose botanical term for tissue consisting of elongated cells closely packed together with their ends interpenetrating and often with the terminal partitions obliterated so as to form ducts or vessels. I use it as a metaphor for the amplification of an author's corpus of reading. For instance, Arcadian imagery is smuggled out of Shelley by way of Browning and Swinburne and transmitted to completely different ends by figures as diverse as Pater, Joyce, Brennan, Chidley and Havelock Ellis. Harold Bloom speaks of these links as "chains of misreading." For example, William James Chidley made a creative misreading of Thoreau because of his obsession with sex, diet, good and evil, suffragettism and physiology. My misreading of Joyce includes heroising Sydney. Bloom refers to this phenomenon as the irony of one generation becoming converted into the noble synecdoche of the next. Prosenchyma is an anti-closure/absolute-closure kind of term. It's a paper centipede combining Bloom's Transumptive Misreading (troping wrong on previous tropes) with Deleuze and

Guattari's Rhizome. The best metaphor that springs to mind is of a vast and aimless field of interlocking volumes fanning out in an arc from the reader different volumes fitting together all the time so that maybe the reader hops from step to step across short or apparently random greater distances (each step possessing a musical note to be determined by Mallarme) or shimmies down a sequential line with this vista expanding until it begins curving and folding back over itself, encasing the reader in a transparent bubble (AKA a pedagogical capsule) through which Life is observed and interpreted like Heidegger's SPHERE (see Sloterdijk) new books fitted into the pattern continuously new layers locking over the original like archaeological stratums and altering its significance individual tiles repeated and extracted and refitted back into the mosaic elsewhere to create new effects of pages and spines fucking together like dogs leaves touching leaves as per Goethe's *Die Urpflanze* or Archetypal Plant in which the leaf is seen as the basic structure in Nature. This idea was later updated by Ruskin and Thoreau. It's a path that you can take forward because the bubble rolls ahead of you. It is one over which you can retrace your steps because the bubble is behind. Reading thus cushions your steps against the uneven cobblestoned pavements of Proust's Venice. Its spatial projection is both upward (Biblical) and inward (Romantic). It spreads towards a warm horizon ... and sunset! Because it's always a little sentimental and melancholy in there ensconced inside your own prosenchymatic dome like a rat running on a merry-go-round ignoring the existence of the cage that confines you. It is related to the early twentieth-century critical notion of *Einfluss* or Influence.

Influence – its literary meaning is the infusion of an author's work with secret power or principle from a precursor or peer. It also has astrological and occult meanings that resound with a wild Romantic style: "the flowing from the stars of ethereal fluid acting upon the character and destiny of humans; and affecting sublunary things generally."

Mr Monaro – a realtor. His name means 'high plain' in Ngarigo language. Also, a brand of popular Holden motor vehicle in the 1970s. NOTE – it has been said that another Holden car, the Torana (see C2), means 'to fly' in an unspecified Indigenous language. However, no match has been found for this word in the vocabulary of any First Nation.

Mrs Brennan – service station operator.

Non & Slope – two men moving a refrigerator in C2. Later, Persian Jones visits their drug lab in Glebe (C5). Associates of the McCann family.

Penelope Hallem – nee McFadden, mother of Tom, wife of Les, ex-wife of Don Cane. Note Pen/elope pun.

Les Hallem – second husband of Penelope McFadden.

Hensley & Mrs Hensley – Menelaus and Helen in old age. Also, Philemon and Baucis.

Asenahana Lafei – Musician. Her naming alludes to the legendary Arthurian character, Morgana la Fey. Explain. Asenahana means 'red berry' in Tongan. Dies of drug overdose in C10.

Don Cane – also Eric Killion and NULL. Odysseus in Vietnam.

Hanh – a shopkeeper. Don's lover in Bien Hoa (1968). Later, Barry's lover in Sydney. This connection suggests that Don and Barry maintained contact throughout the period of this novel. Insert theory: Don aided her escape in 1977.

Various taxi drivers – Stephen Joyce (Tim SEBESTYEN) and Tommy (Pham). See C8.

Reverend Bent (Bennett) – a school pastor. Wounded in Vietnam.

Moody – a student. Equivalent of Sargent in *Ulysses*.

Ian Westacott – equivalent of Garrett Deasy.

Colonel Cornwall – a businessman. Also, VOID. Orator at Choc's funeral. Recruits Don Cane for a job back in Manila. This symbolises the fact that Don Cane has not changed over the course of exile. Like Odysseus, he has hardened into amorality over the last 20 years.

Richie Buenaventura – Don Cane's ex-partner in Manila. They were not able to have children due to his exposure to defoliants in Vietnam. Their only full-term infant, Robert Cane, died aged two days. Link to my own father and dead children (spina bifida). Also, Elizabeth and Leon's dead baby (Chaim). Plus, Rudy Bloom in *Ulysses*. Key trope. Her family name means 'good fortune.' She married a local man. They live in Bulacan province. They have a son, aged 35 (Don Carlos Sopena).

Barry Evans, Brian Deverill, Don Schofield, Ray Farrar, Brian Beath, Dick Stone – former army veterans at the funeral of Albert Wheaton. Hostile towards Don Cane. He makes no sustainable human connections during TMAC. All his interactions with people are mercenary.

Mrs Albert Wheaton (Jean), Eleni Loukopoulou, Deb Deverill, Narelle Schofield, Dr Helen Saunders, Barb Farrar, Bev Orchard – a group of women drinking in Kings Cross after Wheaton's funeral. They are joined by Gary Hampton. Ms. Loukopoulou shares her name with a scholar of James Joyce.

Greg Wheaton – Son of Choc Wheaton. He represents Don Cane's vision of an ideal son.

Willy the Pimp – AKA Willy, W-the-P. Drug dealer and companion of Tom Hallem. His association with Haines (C5) creates a connection with Mulligan. He is the last person to see Tom Hallem alive.

Kenneth Arthur Leer – a false father figure for Tom Hallem. Also known as Ernie. Originally introduced in the radio play, *In Black Box* (played by Peter Hayes). Divorced. Two children. He relocated to Sydney after serving a long prison term. There are various references to this occurrence in an aborted radio-play, titled *Nhill*. He lives in Alexandria. He is a hustler and privateer. He debases Tom Hallem in the brothel scene (C7).

Dougie the Animal, Weasel Bob Akers, Persian Jones and German Eva – a drug dealer, 2 addicts and a mule.

Billy Capri – another version of Telemachus. A literature student. His family name is shared with a famed Ford sports car in Australia. Also, an Italian resort island. It is derived from *Capra*, the genus of goats. Frank Capra was a famous American film director. There are no direct links with his films in TMAC (including *It's a WL*). Billy's first name is a nickname for male goats. Partially, he represents the narrator. His postgraduate studies are aborted in 1985. He returned to them in 1991. He and his half-brother represent art and writing while Ana Lafei signifies music. Equate to Elstor, Bergotte and Vinteuil in Proust's *ALRDTP*. See C3.

Helen Capri – his mother.

Barry Capri – also known as Bob. Apparently, Billy's biological father until revelation of paternity in C4. His lover is the shopkeeper in C5.

O – a scholar. Potentially, the wife of Shanghai Dog.

Blind Basil Kiernan, Emeritus Professor Jeremy Ilks, Dame Nellie Krafter AC DBE, Lady Weffy, A/P Donald Tuck, Professor Milkmaid (also known as Mim), Dr Judith Barbour, Mousey Roche, Marvin Mildling, Deirdre Sackerson – ~~various~~ fictional academics. Note link to G. Stein in naming of supervisor.

Associate Professor Able Goldstein AKA a gilded vessel AKA Gold Cup (see *Ulysses*) AKA G. Stein – supervisor.

Derek Attridge, Kevin Birmingham, Eleni Loukopoulou, Blooms & Barnacles (Kelly & Dermot) inter alia – contemporary academics. Citing their work creates a sense of TMAC being drafted in real time.

Spikey Ulan, Angus McCreedy – postgraduate students. Both became professors of Australian literature.

Edmund Hamley – illegitimate son of Stan Welles. A budding tycoon. See *King Lear*. His name reflects the fact that he is kind-of-Hamlety but a few letters after the fact.

Miss Gallagher – his secretary.

Daisy – his stepmother. Based on my mother's family.

Edgar Welles – elder brother of Edmund Hamley. See *King Lear*.

Keith Carpenter – building services manager. Modelled on JJ O'Molloy.

Leon Daniel (II) – his first name means 'Lion' in Ancient Greek. His family name means 'God is my judge' in Hebrew. Note symbolism of this combination. The Book of Daniel originates in the Ketuvim of the Tanakh. It is an apocalypse combining prophecy and eschatology. Its most famous event is his survival in the Lion's den in Chapter Six. Leon

Daniel resides in Darlinghurst (Babylon). He conducts philanthropic works in the Jewish community. His future is clear due to infection with HIV (he foresees his own death from AIDS). He is a brave person. Yet he is also flawed (e.g. he continues to perform surgery after infection). The closest figure to Bloom in TMAC. Daniel's death is not chronicled. He is considered an apocryphal, composite figure by many scholars.

Ambrose E. Welles – also known as Stan Hamley AKA Stan Wormsley. Alias Raymond John Candy. Merchant banker. An ageing Boylan figure. Linked to Nugan Hand Bank (see Nuges).

John Dengate – busker.

Marie Swain – widow. Mother of Tug.

Lady Peasoup – acquaintance of Elizabeth Archer. Collector.

Farquhar & Gravy – criminals.

Shop Assistant – equivalent of Miss Dunne in W. Rocks.

Professor McNab – a local historian. See W.Rocks, sub-episode 8, Rev Hugh C. Love.

Starpunk – also known as Groveller, Stinkbug and S. Spams.

Jackie – bass player, Birth of Mirtha. AKA Joanne.

Hazel and the Nut – performance artists working as exotic dancers on Melbourne Cup Day. Also known as Holly.

Jiles, Cuthbert – clerks.

Vivien – primary school punk magazine editor.

Frances Hackett – also, Francine.

Greg Devlin – a lobbyist. Anglicised form of Gaelic, Ó Dobhailéin, a diminutive of 'dobhail,' meaning 'unlucky' or 'unfortunate'. Nothing in Joyce is left to chance in nomenclature, timing, literary references or place. This naming foreshadows the failure of the Minister's scheme and Devlin's execution.

Joe Raspudic – alias John Smith (written) and Ken Jones (verbal). A property developer. His name is a phallic pun on 'Rasputin.' Known as Sellmann in earlier drafts of TMAC.

Doug Truck – politician.

A & B – two elderly ladies in Glebe. Widows. Suggestive of Patrick White characters. Link to 'Parable of the Plums' in Episode Seven in *Ulysses*. Two midwives climb Nelson's Pillar and spit plum stones onto the street below.

Shanghai Dog – enters C5, E17 (Martian's Son). Also goes by SD, S.Dog, Billy, etc. Also Messrs. Norman, No-man (Odysseus), Normal, Flower, Ralph Iron, Barry Cane, Bob Cane, Eric Killion, Don Capri inter alia.

Xiao Fang – a migrant worker in Shanghai.

Zhu Di – a barmaid in Shanghai. Ex-girlfriend of Shanghai Dog. Now married with child. Lives in Pudong with her parents.

Governors of NSW – a chronological list of 33 governors from 1788-1984 in C5, E19. Progressively ceremonial position with increasing focus on securing funds for renovations of Government House.

Jabber Ladiesman, Justine Labiameister, Delia Flight-Falconhurst, Pockmarkt Macritis – literary tyros.

~~**Comedians 1 and 2** – deleted.~~

Mulligan – a student. Shares name with Stephen Dedalus' foil in *Ulysses*.

Grandpater – relative of Leer.

Bella, Candy, Solange, Biddy the Clap – prostitutes.

Marion Hackett – curator.

READ – nickname for a famous artist. Pronounced past tense. A homograph.
Peter Fuller – historical British art figure.

Matt Supplejack – popular young painter.

The Collector, Bloo MD, Slut Harolde, Merlin – art collectors.

Angela Dwyer, Michel Deekeling – residents of West Berlin.

Ocker – Captain of the Push.

Eyesenears, Chindrip, Scatt – denizens of the Crest Hotel, Kings Cross. Members of Ocker's gang.

Doctor Gu – Shanghai Dog's business partner.

Shredded Ginger – an Englishwoman. Billy's friend.

U. U. Bardun – award-winning author. He prevaricated about adding the words, "he said," as the end of C11.

Unknown brother – Billy Capri discovers the existence of a deceased sibling when he visits his father's grave in Manila. His efforts to find closure are onec again SPOILT.

www.ingramcontent.com/pod-product-compliance
Lightning Source LLC
Chambersburg PA
CBHW081138300726
48982CB00006B/992

* 9 7 8 0 6 4 5 0 5 9 2 2 9 *